UHURU

UHURU

A NOVEL

BY

ROBERT RUARK

HAMISH HAMILTON
LONDON

First published in Great Britain, 1962
by Hamish Hamilton Ltd
90 *Great Russell Street London WC*1
Copyright © 1962 *by Robert Ruark*
Reprinted 1978

ISBN 0-241-90671-7

Printed in Great Britain by
Lowe & Brydone Printers Limited, Thetford, Norfolk

This book is for
HAROLD MATSON
with gratitude and love

FOREWORD

THE TITLE of this book is *UHURU*, the one word most frequently heard in East Africa these days. It means, roughly, 'freedom' and is used and abused according to personal inclination. In some instances this can be tragic.

'Uhuru' is a Semitic word used commonly in both Arabic and Hebraic, and it sneaked into Swahili, which is the lingua franca of East and Central Africa, via the slave trade. 'Uhuru' is synonymous to 'l'indépendance' in the Congo, or 'free-dom' in West Africa. It has become in recent months so much a part of daily use that it is employed by black and white alike, in much the same sense that 'liberté, fraternité, égalité' were adopted in the French Revolution.

One can rarely pick up a newspaper in East Africa today without seeing 'Uhuru' glaring a dozen times. One cannot stride a street or ride the roads of even back-country Kenya without being greeted by the old Churchillian 'V' finger sign, or a Nazi-esque flattened palm accompanied by a ringing shout of 'Uhuru!' One cannot eavesdrop a conversation amongst white or black or rich or poor station without hearing the word repeated over and over again.

Each native African has his own concept of 'Uhuru'. For some it is a mythical description of a round-the-corner Utopia of slothful ease, of plentiful booze and an altogether delightfully dreamy state in which money grows on bushes and all human problems are ended. To the nomadic grazier it means endless flocks of lovely useless cattle and gorgeous land-ruining goats —with infinite vistas of lush pasturage, and water galore between two suns' march. To the ivory poacher it is an absence of game wardens and stuffy restrictive game laws. To the meat-eater it is limitless meat and plenitude of free salt; to the drunkard a sea of honey beer; to the womanizer, a harem which stretches to the horizon. To the peasant African farmer, it is the white man's magically rich and loamy land which will certainly be his on the magic day of 'Uhuru', when the white man is driven from the continent and all the carefully nurtured soil reverts to the African. To the wilfully lawless, 'Uhuru' is a licence to rob and steal, to kill without punishment and to flout rules of decent human behaviour with reckless impunity.

'Uhuru' to the white man takes on a slightly different complexion. 'Uhuru' is regarded as a threat—a threat to his white property, a threat to his white women, a threat to his white life of toil and his momentary white life of ease with plenty of black boys to hurry at his bidding and to murmur respectful

'Yes, Bwana' to his every command, no matter how illogical. 'Uhuru' is a threat to his concept of himself as a white master of a suppressed black race, and represents a sudden violent rearrangement of himself in the old Poona '02 concept of 'Bwana Mkubwa' or 'Great White Lord'.

To some whites who love the land, who were born on the land and who cherish the African, the grimmer aspects of 'Uhuru' are an implicit tragedy, for these people are Africans too, and they have nowhere else to go, no other life to lead. 'Uhuru' to them can mean a sacrifice of a lifetime of back-breaking toil and the destruction of a created beauty selflessly performed as a labour of love.

Finally, at the moment 'Uhuru' would seem to be at the disposal of Every-man to use as best he can for good or evil. 'Uhuru' today is literally a 'Shauri ya Mungu'—an 'Act of God'. For this reason it seems obvious that there could be no more fit title than *Uhuru* for this book.

This is a true story. Perhaps the characters are technically fictitious, but there is nothing in this book which has not happened, is not happening or will not happen in the near future. This was always intended to be a book of fiction; unfortunately I have found myself hoist on my own knowledge of the African continent, where I am seeing the fanciful structure of my fictitious effort reproduced every day in the world's press as actual fact.

There was a time in the preparation of this book when I doubted what my own eyes and ears were observing. It was necessary for me to repeat over and over again, 'but I *am* in Kenya and these things *are* happening'. I had to remind myself that it was true that I was sitting in a bongo-trapping camp at the top of the Aberdare Mountains with a Kenya three-generation settler, who once had built a tower in which to confine his wife and children during the Mau Mau Emergency—when, with his face blacked, he was hunting down a Mau Mau general. What made it extremely difficult to believe was that the general at that very moment last year was an employee of the National Parks, which made my friend's rare antelope trapping effort possible. The general also at that moment last year was squatting by the fire outside the tent. He had not changed his politics, although he had temporarily packed up his panga. He was merely resting between engagements.

Times have changed in Kenya since I wrote a book called *Something of Value*. The titular chief of the most important political party in Kenya today is an ex-Mau Mau 'detainee'. Detainee is a polite word for the people they put behind barbed wire for being connected with the massive operation of murder.

You will find the names of real people in this book—actual people such as James Gichuru, Kenyatta, Tom Mboya and other members of the emerging African political scene who are vibrantly alive today. There is no escaping the use of these real people in a book of fiction about Kenya today, just as it would be completely silly to avoid the fact that the New Stanley Hotel in Nairobi is owned by a family named Block. Or that Sir Patrick Renison is the present Governor of Kenya.

The man Peter Poole who figures largely in this book was real, and was hanged last August for cold-bloodedly killing an African. Some of my fictitious people have cold-bloodedly killed other Africans as well, but never more fantastically than the way in which Patrice Lumumba was slain by his own Congolese people as a political expedient.

I have employed a witch doctor to some fictitious effect in this book. He actually was very real. His name *was* Kinyanjui, and he had drawn a magical circle around the most practical farming operation I know—Sasumua, which is owned by my very good friends the Nightingale family, who live in South Kinangop area of Kenya, and who never locked a door during the Mau Mau Emergency because of the potency of the magic charm which old Kinyanjui had placed upon the farm. Kinyanjui is dead now; whether dead by white man's poison or black man's incantation or mere old age is difficult to say. But it is pitifully true that the magic ring no longer exists on Sasumua.

One of the more frightening aspects of fiction these days as a means of livelihood is, with the competition from the daily press being so much more fantastic than any creation of imagination, that the poor novelist finds himself in active argument with history before he gets his imaginative effort on the market.

It was five years after the publication of *Something of Value* until the famous Corfield Report substantiated the bare facts on which my fictitious creations were founded. As I finish the last chapter of this book I find the bones of my fictitious ending already on page two of the *Daily Express*. And on page three is a factual replica of another fictitious device against which I first argued strongly with myself as being much too unlikely a gimmick to make the story go.

If one has lived in Africa as frequently as I have, one gets almost but not quite used to presaging history. It was thus in the Congo last year. I knew the Congo would blow up, and so wrote in a series of articles. Unfortunately my timing was slightly askew. It took them two more weeks to explode in the Congo than I had calculated.

I am also certain that it was not my imagination which supplied the fact that a white acquaintance named Venn Fey sent his wife and children out of Kenya last year because he knew on good authority that his youngest child was earmarked as a human sacrifice in a black oathing ceremony. Subsequent outbursts of oathings and retributive murders for old Mau Mau scores have since caught up with my flights of fancy. Nothing has changed the solid substance that 'Fey's Peak' was named for Venn's grandpa.

I am throwing myself on the reader's indulgence for the usual free play with dates and time as a dramatic necessity. I would assure those who seek to find themselves as real people in my fictitious characters that they will be disappointed, since my creations of fantasy are such an amalgam that they would never fit the chromosomes of any particular living person. Only the people who are specifically named as real *are* real. Geography has been purposely confused and I have even dared to tamper with the seasons.

If you would indulge a selfish line or two purely for the author's own satisfaction, I would like gratefully to remind Aunt Nell and Uncle Max Nightingale, and Barbie and Jim and Venn and Jack and Brian and Tubby and Harry and George and Rene and Mickey and John and Ken and Eric and Helen that they have unwittingly played a tremendously helpful part in the shadowy life I lead with a typewriter. I would specifically like to thank Mr. Bronislaw Sirley for possibly the most fortunate accident that ever befell me, and to express my measureless gratitude and loving thanks to Eva Monley, who made most of this book come true. And, as ever, a special nod to Alan Ritchie, who performed so much of the heavy work of actual physical production of this monster without undue whimpering over endless, killing hours of weary toil. And always, of course, Jo.

My use of the words 'nigger', 'Wog', 'coon', 'Nig', and the vulgar like is not a personal habit of the author, but is a custom of speech regrettably still practised in real life in Kenya and elsewhere, sometimes, surprisingly, by black Africans themselves. They also refer to the *m'zungu* as the 'Goddam White man'.

I should also like to remind the reader that Africa and its problems are very large, and that I have only attempted to treat with a small segment which may be typical of the times. I prescribe no cure, and point no moral, and can only testify that I have endeavoured to write a truth, although its form may be fiction.

ROBERT RUARK

Palamos, Prov. de Gerona, Spain.
Baragoi, Northern Province, Kenya.

BOOK ONE

CHAPTER ONE

BRIAN DERMOTT whistled softly as he drove. From time to time he sang scraps of songs in a tuneless voice and now it was 'Get Me to the Church on Time.' He could see the sweet green island of the District Commissioner's *boma* up ahead, to the left, and in a moment now he would be approaching the sentry box. He could see the hot morning sun heliographing bright meaningless messages off the roofs of the Somali shanty-town, off the crazy-leaning houses built of flat-pounded tin jerry cans, and he had passed a few Somals along the dusty road, the men striding haughtily ahead of their women, who walked fluidly beneath the heavy loads they bore on their heads. Just seeing them walk, exaggerated behinds swaying, slim shoulders squared and breasts jutting firm and arrogant, was like hearing the cool trilling of an Arab flute.

Brian Dermott reached over and lightly punched the sleeping native who slumped in the seat beside him.

'Wake up, *nugu*,' he said. 'We are coming into the town. Time to get dressed. Sit up straight and try to look like a human being, even if it's hard for you.'

The native grinned and reached into the back of the car and brought forth a tattered, much-patched khaki hunting jacket, which he slipped on. Brian Dermott had been speaking in English, with the exception of the affectionate *nugu*—ape—but his meaning was clear. When Kidogo left civilization he took off all his clothes, except the shorts he wore out of deference to the clients. When he came back he put on his one shirt and one pair of town shorts and was so accorded to be formally clad. Now he punched Brian Dermott in the ribs.

'*Wewe nugu vile-vile*,' he said.

'Oh, me too, huh?' Brian smiled. 'I forgot. Hand me my shirt.' The native, Kidogo, reached back once again and produced Brian's safari jacket. Kidogo shook out the folds, pounded out the dust and handed the jacket to his master, who braced the jiggling steering wheel with his knees while he shrugged the faded hunting shirt over his bare brown torso.

'Fighting fit for the mad whirl of the city,' Brian said, and pulled up the car before a sentry box. '*Jambo, baba*.' Brian nodded to the *askari*, who saluted. A zebra-painted barrier pole closed the road in front of the sentry box. Brian reached out a hand, and the *askari* went back into the box for a big flat brown book with a canvas cover. Brian found the 'out' column opposite a line which gave his name, the licence numbers of his vehicles, his business address and post-office box number, plus the names of the white people in his party and the number of natives. The entry showed that the business address was 'Brian Dermott Safaris, Ltd., Box 60019, Nairobi.' Date of entrance had been Wednesday, August 10, 1960. He wrote down the date of exit as August 17, 1960.

He was relieved, he cruelly told himself once more, to be rid of the idea of Valerie, as well as of her physical presence. Strange how little emotion he had felt when he actually put her on the plane—knowing coldly that he was seeing her for the last time, bar the most unforeseen of accidents. There had been no belly-twisting wrench—nothing comparable to the shock of losing her eight years ago when she had still been legally his wife. They had said a nearly dry good-bye this time, and she had kissed him coolly on the cheek, looking beautiful and smelling lovely, as always. Dear Valerie, who never belonged in Kenya, and was finally smart enough to know it. They said you could lay ghosts by facing up to the things that frightened you or bothered you. He was alive again, he told himself.

Brian Dermott felt good. He felt good about the safari. It had started well. Nice people, the new clients. You couldn't always tell right off, but these looked promising. Paul and Kathleen. Brother and sister. No problems with the animals so far. Wild *or* tame. Lion and elephant right out of the box. Clients still firmly in hand.

It was jolly good luck that they did seem nice. It was rather difficult to clap your ex-wife onto one plane and commence a new project with a fresh batch of people from another plane in the next hour or so—difficult unless the new people seemed likely sorts.

It was natural that he had felt a little down. When Valerie had come back to Kenya again, three months ago, they had cherished some extravagant hopes of picking up the old threads. But you just couldn't do it. There was too much old ache and vacant space between them. She was right about chucking it in finally. They had nothing left. Even bed, although certainly no longer tragic in its frustration, was not really very good. The bodies were there but what had first welded them was gone. Vanished in the mists, as the Kikuyu said. Spat out clean and all forgot.

She was still so beautiful too—more than he had remembered, with the great gipsy eyes and the Spanishy hair. And she had come back—back after nearly eight years. And they had been embarrassed, first, and hesitant in talking, and after the first attempt at reviving the physical relationship had killed embarrassment, they still had nothing to talk about. There just wasn't anything there.

She had refused to go back to the Farm, for which he couldn't blame her, considering the wincing memories. They had made a short picnic safari, like the first one, and that had been painful, too. So they had stayed in his bachelor flat, at first, and that depressed her, so they had tried a cottage in the Norfolk, and that had also depressed her. And finally they had moved

4

into a suite at the new New Stanley, so recently face-lifted as to bear no resemblance to the old life in the old Nairobi.

'Quite frankly I was a damned fool to come back, darling,' Valerie had said, sitting with her long legs tucked under her on the divan, while Brian made her a drink from the little icebox-bar in the corner of the room. 'I thought perhaps that time——' she shook her head. 'But time hasn't changed it or you or us. In 'fifty-three I was frightened and bored. Now I think I'm frightened worse of the change that's come over Kenya. And I know I'm bored with all this talk of *uhuru*. Nobody talks of anything else, and I swear I think the settlers are more frightened of the coming freedom than they were of the Mau Mau in the old days when everybody wore a gun.'

Brian turned and handed her the drink, snapping the top off a Coke for himself.

'I rather imagine it's me that's at the bottom of the wrong of it for you,' he said. 'Not the people or the change or even poor old *uhuru*.'

Valerie shrugged slightly and sipped at her drink.

'I think perhaps we had more when you were younger and less certain of yourself,' she said. 'I'm not sure I like the dashing Dermott nearly so much as the shy boy who trembled when he kissed me the first time. In any case it's wrong for us both now. If you'll just fix me a flight to London, darling, I think I'd better wander on back to my own piece of bush.' She smiled at him. 'I'm truly sorry, Brian. I shouldn't have come back at all.'

*

'You look very nattily got up and extremely dashable, darling,' Valerie Dermott said to her former husband as he handed her out of his Land Rover at the airport. Her eyes flicked over him. 'Is that a farewell-to-arms sort of uniform, or what?'

'No.' He looked briefly at the four-buttoned whipcord jacket, with its bellowsed back and flared military skirt; at the narrow-legged cavalry trousers and jodhpur boots. 'It's a client-meeting suit. I'm saving petrol. You're going out—I've clients coming in. Lose a wife and gain a client, all in the same trip. The suit's my client-greeting get-up. Impresses them any amount. Just sporty enough to imbue 'em with faith. Like my moustache.' He smiled. 'Come on. Let's go check you in and then we'll have time for a farewell drink at the bar.'

'We make a handsome couple. Twinsies, almost.' She patted her palms down the front of her severely cut beige travelling suit. 'Pity it's not us just starting again instead of stopping for good—or at least permanently.' She reached then for a handkerchief. 'Damn it! I swore I wouldn't cry!' She blew hard into the handkerchief. 'I wish I'd come out by myself. Kiss me now and then go away somewhere while I get on the plane.'

And that, Brian Dermott thought, was that, as he watched the trim proud back in its slim suit walking out on the field towards the crouching jet, the long beautiful legs mounting the loading platform, the square wide shoulders turning for the last time towards the airport. He had waved once and had gone to the upstairs bar for a Coke. He would have vastly preferred a drink of something stoutly serious to match his mood, but that wasn't allowable any more. And even if it were, he didn't want to be meeting the clients with a reek of booze about him. It didn't go with the musical-comedy costume and the air of masterful confidence with which he would run their lives for the next six weeks.

*

There had been no mistaking the clients when they stepped out of the plane. There never was. Paul Drake's letters described him as a banker. Of the sister Brian Dermott couldn't be sure, except that he knew she would look exactly like a banker's sister should look, invariably gauntly elegant and always fashionably minked. There they were: Bankerish, he. Elegant, she. And minked. 'Desert Ember' mink this year. Next year it would be some other colour favoured by Revlon Frères. By now Brian was an authority on all sorts of animals which did not dwell in Africa.

'Drake,' the new client had said, gripping Brian's hand firmly. 'My sister, Mrs. Crane. Of course you have to be Brian Dermott. Nobody else here looks like you're supposed to. I'm called Paul, and my sister answers to Kate. Let's unmister ourselves. Ah. I hope we can get out of town fast. I'm sick of cities.' He looked sidewise at his sister. 'So is Katie. Paris was a bore.'

'Tomorrow if you like,' Brian had said, thinking: *Well, there goes the hanging.* 'The car's this way.' He spoke to the African porters who waited with the Drake luggage on a trolley. Brian noticed that the bags were *not* of plastic, but were stoutly built of old-fashioned and very expensive pigskin. They seemed to be bags which belonged to the kind of people who wouldn't relish hanging around for a hanging.

The new client—Brian always thought of them as 'clients' until they had done something good or bad to distinguish them from the variously shaped bodies he took hunting for money—was thin and sharp-faced, possibly fifty, with sparse grey hair and acute but tired eyes under the gold-rimmed spectacles. The client's sister was on the lean side and perhaps thirty-five, maybe even forty. Difficult, always, to say with American women. She hadn't shown either fangs or claws as yet, but you never could tell until about the third week. Also there was something just a mite peculiar about her eyes.

He liked the male client for several things, so far, but one in particular. Driving up to the first camp, over the baked, washboard road, skidding occasionally on the soft white dust drifted in the ruts, they had come upon something that appeared in the distance to be a body. Brian drove as quietly as possible until he drew near the black blotch, and they saw then that it *was* a body. It lay as still as death, but when Brian came alongside, they saw it was alive, a native. He was sleeping heavily in the warm, soft dust, smack in the middle of the road. He breathed evenly and did not appear to be drunk, but merely resting quietly in the sunshine as if the middle of the road were his accustomed place to sleep.

'Shall we wake this gentleman up?' Brian whispered.

'No,' the client whispered back. 'Let him alone. His century will rouse him soon enough.'

They had driven on then, and Brian was prepared to like the client, even before he saw him shoot the lion and weep over the elephant. Good clients were hard to come by. Usually they were the one thing or the other; some very bad, rarely very good; mostly varying gradations of the nice in-between ones. This looked to be one of the better versions of in-betweens.

*

'We'll see,' Brian now said half-aloud, as he signed his name and capped his fountain pen. 'In any case, we're not home yet.'

He nodded and handed the flat registry book back to the tall Somali *askari*, and clipped his pen in the breast pocket of his bush jacket. The Somali, stiffly starched in his khaki tunic, flipped another sharp salute from the flat bill of his desert *kepi* with the neck-flap on the back, and touched the lever which allowed the barrier to lift. The pole raised slowly, almost in lazy emulation of the salute, and Brian Dermott eased in the clutch of his Land Rover. The car slipped forward, loose sand spurting from behind its rear wheels, and Brian Dermott was back in Kenya again.

Actually, Brian Dermott had just come from Kenya, but not from the common tourist concept of Kenya. It was actually named the Northern Province, but everyone called it the NFD. The NFD—The Northern Frontier District—was not located spiritually in Kenya any more than it was situated in Somalia or Ethiopia or the Sudan. The Northern Frontier was just what its name described—an arbitrarily bordered wasteland, shared by many and truly belonging to none. It was a vast expanse of sand, of mountain, of jungle and thorn forest, of sluggish lazy river, of roaring torrent, of dry river-bed, of searing cold and smiting heat, of grey volcanic rock and enormous opalescent lake, of blinding sand and of dry, stunted, twisted trees and savage, nearly carnivorous greenery.

It was the almost-private land of the elephant and the rhino, who leased it equally with the migrant graziers, the far-roving Somalis with their huge flocks of camels, evil-tempered wealth that carried itself. It was the land of worse-tempered Boran with their high, wobbly-humped cattle; the land of savage Suk and warlike Rendille and handsome Samburu, fighters and nomads all, fiercely united in hatred for each other and in a common lust for water.

The Northern Frontier also belonged to the pathetic vestigial tribe of the rickets-ridden El Molo, less than a hundred bowlegged remnants of a dead civilization, who scavenged Lake Rudolf for its fish and crocodiles, and who had evolved a long, long time after the nameless tribesmen who were now buried sitting upright in lava-rock-heaped graves with their odd reddish-circled signature stones.

7

The Northern Frontier belonged too, to the raiding Gelubba who slashed across the Abyssinian borders to blood their spears, as they had so recently wiped out the whole Turkana village of Porr, at the northern end of the lake. The Gelubba killed lightheartedly, for sport and not for gain, and only occasionally did they bother to slash the testicles from a victim to take back as a gift to the father of a desired maiden. They did not bother to collect such perishable trophies this far inside the border; there would be plenty more people to kill on the return trip home.

The Northern Frontier was spottily ruled by the tiny, *cafard*-breeding police posts, whose few dozen men spoke for a kind of law and occasional order in a limitless sandy purgatory, which froze you at Maralal and drowned you in the Chalbi desert and parboiled you at Baragoi. The North's signature was a signpost which said 'Archer's Post' to the left and 'Shaffa Dinka—Garba Tulla' to the right. If you followed the Archer's Post road you came to a slow-twisting river called Uaso Nyiro, its muddy banks drift-logged with sleeping crocodile and its wind-creaking palms bright with the flashing wings of darting big blue or green pigeons. And if you followed the road long enough you came to the *lugas*, the dry river-beds which were hillocked with elephant dung in the dry—*lugas* with lovely names like Kinya and Kinna, Serarua and Seralippe, Laisamis and Merille.

And if you went to the right on the sanded winding track you would come to Shaffa Dinka with its one street and its rows of tin-topped shanties, with the sleepy Somals and Turkanas dozing in the steaming shade of the over-hanging roofs, squatting on lumpy hard-pounded clay floors, careless of the flies that crawled in and out of their nostrils and over their eyes and sore-crusted lips. You might pause, perhaps, at a tiny Indian *dukah*, a general store, for a word with the proprietor, an almost black Bengali, and his shape-less wife in her shimmering *sari*, with her long greasy hair heavy-ropy in braids over her shoulders. You could then exchange news from the safari broadcasts and swap gossip with the occasional Sikh lorry-driver.

You might buy petrol and Coca-Cola, whisky and gin, beer and orange squash, spare parts for the motor-cars, sweet biscuits and sardines, pickles and cheese and mosquito spray and razor blades and paregoric. And, if you were so minded and had plenty of penicillin, the services of the hip-swinging Somali whore with the *kohl*-smudgy eyelids who ogled you from a starting point somewhere between the noseless leper and the orange-bearded Hadj who wore the henna in his whiskers as a sign that he had been to Mecca and had kissed the sacred *Kaaba* stone.

The life of the NFD was harshly simple. It was ruled by sun and rain, by heat and cold, by wet and dry. It revolved around the dry-river beds, the *lugas*, the Indian *dukah*, the police post, and the DC's *boma*. The dry-river beds were where the sandgrouse flighted in to take their tiny, delicate sips at precise hours of morning and dusk; where the elephants came to tusk up the sand to expose the deep-buried water which seeped from springs below; where the little dun donkeys with the black stripe on their backs, called

Somali canaries, pawed daintily alongside the elephants; where the rhino kicked their dung into great strawy heaps, and where the Somals brought their camels and the Boran their cattle and goats, seeking; always, seeking the water which gathered pitifully around the lichened rocks and stood stinking in green-scummed copper-tinted pools; water foul and reeking of dung and the urine of animals, but water as precious as your own life, and much more precious than the life of another whose knife was shorter, whose spear was less swift. The enormous boulder-rimmed sands of the dry rivers were blinding in the sun, scarred by a million hoof-marks and footprints, prints of animal, man and bird, and occasionally, at the steep-descending, loose-rocked, steeper-rising fords, by the tracks of Land Rover and lonely lorry.

The Northern Frontier was where the DC—the District Commissioner—and his policemen were The Law. The DC could let you in or keep you out, and he could change the rules that bound you by a measured autocratic decision—or sometimes, in past, a momentary whim that might be sired by a prickling heat rash, a severe case of athlete's foot, a herd of marauding elephant, a band of raiders come down from Somalia, a foray of slave-seekers from Ethiopia, a tribal murder or even a purely personal domestic spat between the DC and his wife.

And of course you fuelled and furnished yourself at the *dukahs*, and you left and received mail and messages, and you regarded the tiny towns which held the lonely *dukah* as a neutral ground where you came in peace, even if you departed for war. The DC's *boma* would be outside the town, neatly enclosed in euphorbia cactus like huge green spikey jars and sometimes surprisingly bright with flowers—except when the elephant smashed the cactus fence and trampled the blooms. Close by the *boma* would be the jail and the post office and perhaps the tiny hospital for knifing casualties and heatstroke and gunshot wounds, and other occupational diseases of the NFD. Civilization was centred in the post office, which contained facilities for telephoning—when the lines were not down—telegraphing—when the power was on—and the handbills describing the sins of wanted Somali murderers and Turkana cattle-raiders.

When you left the Northern Frontier you turned for a sad moment and said good-bye to Ololokwe, the lovely, square-headed old mountain that bulked huge on your left as you headed North from Archer's Post. And you said good-bye to the hammering dry heat of the days and the nipping cold of the nights and the velvety, almost furry sky that canopied so low you could reach up and pluck a star to make a necklace for your love.

Then was when you knew you were back in proper, tourist-folder Kenya, when you said good-bye to Ololokwe; then was when you left the filthy, fierce, treacherous, death-dominated, exasperating, scorching, freezing, mountainous, desert-wasted, forgotten by Allah and avoided by Shaitan, awful, terrifying, enticing, ugly . . . *lovely* Northern Frontier, the land that Brian Dermott loved most of all the places in the world.

When you left Ololokwe you stopped at the sentry box and signed the book and then you drove, as Brian Dermott was driving now, into Isiolo, the one-street border town with the big *boma* and the scattering of sleazy huts and corrugated-iron *dukahs*. And you 'stopped at Gandhi's for a Coke and to fill your tank with petrol and to inquire for messages. It was a good *dukah*, with the Indian woman busily pumping the treadle of the sewing machine, and the little Wahindi husband obsequious behind the counter. But it still was not the same as when old Gandhi was alive—old, joke-making, drink-offering Gandhi, so called because he looked a little like the Mahatma. Good old easy-living Gandhi, so easy with his offers of young and luscious Somali girls—so free and generous until the night one of the fierce-nosed, turban-wearing Somali gentlemen stuck a very sharp knife into old Gandhi and let out the free-and-easy, girl-and-drink-offering life in a long spout of blood.

The Wahindi was saying something now about there being a herd of zebras in the street last night, and the DC still complaining about elephants tearing up the planting in the *boma*, and Brian was scarcely listening because he was thinking that, having said *kwaheri* to Ololokwe, he would very soon be saying *jambo* to Kerinyagga, majestic, snow-wigged, stern-faced, snaggled-toothed Mount Kenya, where God lived when He was home.

'I thought you were on safari,' the Wahindi was saying. 'Where is it? Not finishing already? A very short time, isn't it?'

'No,' Brian said, draining his Coke, 'not finished. It's back there. On the Seralippe. Getting over a big elephant we shot yesterday. You know.' He winked at the Indian.

'What brings you back then? Why are you not celebrating the big elephant with the bwanas? No trouble, no sickness, I hope?'

'No,' Brian replied, and swung down from his perch on the counter. 'No trouble. No sickness. Nothing like that.'

He walked to the door, and saw that the African attendant had finished filling his tank.

'Stick it on the chit,' he said to the Indian shopkeeper. 'I'll be back pretty soon. But right now I'm going to Nairobi to attend a hanging.'

The African attendant gave a last twirl to the gas-tank cap and looked up at Brian.

'Of a white man,' Brian said, and got back in his car. He left his words hanging in the cloud of dust kicked up by his wheels.

VALERIE DUNSTAN DERMOTT settled into her seat and buckled on the lap-strap. She heard the solid chunk of the door slamming and saw with satisfaction that there was practically nobody on the plane. That was good—she'd be able to take out two arm rests and sleep all the way to Rome, with luck. She would have a couple of drinks and then take a pill.

She opened her bag and drew out a compact. Her eyes were still scratchy from the unshed tears, and her nose looked a trifle pink. She was sick at heart but she was honestly relieved to be leaving Kenya again. This time it *was* final, as all her thoughts of Brian were final now. That was finished. They were both finished. But she had never felt really divorced from him before. Now she felt utterly and completely divorced.

She sighed as the huge, nearly empty plane trundled out toward the take-off strip, jouncing slightly over the tarmac. Her instinct about leaving Kenya in 1953 had been right. If she had not left then she would certainly be leaving now—as, she knew, so many people who had bravely stayed on would be leaving now, with the government changing and the country coming inevitably into black hands. It was no longer a white man's country at all—no longer a place to live safely and happily with love and peace. She was glad she would not be here when they hanged that poor fellow Poole in the next week or so. Somehow, as an Englishwoman running away from Kenya and back to the safety of London, she felt terribly guilty about the hanging of Peter Poole. She felt guilty about Poole in the same sense that she felt guilty about the man her former husband Brian Dermott had become—as she felt guilty about Kenya, as she even felt guilty about herself.

The plane was racing down the strip now, its jets blasting, and she gave another sharp aching sigh of relief as the wheels came up with a bump and the jet began its climb. She unsnapped the safety belt, took off her jacket, and laid it folded on the seat beside her for the stewardess to take. She was off, now, off and away—safely out of Kenya. She would never come home again, because home was no longer home, as Brian Dermott was no longer her husband, as Brian Dermott was no longer her man. She relaxed the seat control, crossed her legs and let her mind travel backward as the jet hummed monotonously in the sky.

*

When Valerie Dunstan Dermott left Kenya at the height of Mau Mau emergency and went back to London to live, she had at first tried to explain to the people she met at parties that she had left a small and rather complicated war behind her in East Africa. The people she met at parties were quite sure of it; the most dreadful things were always happening out East, and it served Whitehall exactly right. There was Cyprus and Palestine and of course this dreadful man Nasser in Egypt, and there was 'trouble in Uganda with the Mau Mau tribe'—Uganda naturally being a town in the

East African colony of Nairobi, or else Kenya being a city in the Rhodesias or some dreary place like that. In any case it all served the settlers right for being so beastly to the poor natives, and Valerie had given up trying to explain anything after that day in Knightsbridge when she had come upon some worthy lady shaking a poor-box in aid of the suffering Mau Mau tribe.

After a while Valerie stopped telling people that she had been born and raised in Kenya. She was weary of hearing people say 'Oh, how very interesting,' and then making some polite remark about lions or a dimly recalled cousin who had been sent to the Colonies for his sins, such people the while staring over her shoulder or down her dress, depending on the sex of her partner. So far as most of London was concerned, Africa stopped at Suez and did not recommence until it touched Johannesburg. There was some vague idea that the Congo was flung into the middle, but the Congo was teeming with Belgians and gorillas and was therefore hopeless on both accounts, even if you overlooked the climate, which was said to be shocking.

'Oh, and did you do all sorts of amusing things in Africa?' was another line that she heard frequently and which she finally learned to avoid, since she could never fully explain that Kenya was not entirely populated by dissolute younger sons and fugitives from early Evelyn Waugh fiction. She didn't have to be from Africa any longer—she looked Latin, she had attended school in England for ten years as a girl and young woman, and she was certainly pretty enough to stand on her own as that divine young Mrs. Dunstan Dermott with the unbelievable eyes and hair. Neither the unbelievable eyes—which were slightly uptilted at the corners and an odd gipsy blue-green—or the unbelievable hair, which was sleekly black as a crow's wing in the sun—had become any less divine since Valerie had given up Kenya dust for London grit and rolling yellow fog. As she tended towards her thirties, she was quite frequently mistaken for a film star when she lunched at the Mirabelle or danced late at the Café de Paris.

Valerie Dunstan—she never really thought of herself as Valerie Dermott —was almost symptomatic of her times; typical of many upper-middle-class postwar marriages that had been granted no chance to jell, which had left few showing scars, and which were uncomplicated by either children or severe financial problems. When Valerie divorced Brian for desertion in an uncontested action, he had quite decently settled two thousand pounds a year on her, which was ample money for a woman alone. She had not asked for the money, but he had volunteered it, and she had not been hesitant about accepting it.

With it she was able to live in what her friends called a jewel-box of a small duplex flat in Hill Street, a flat with a very large, high-ceilinged pale-green panelled living-room with two bedrooms upstairs and a commodious modern kitchen off the hall. It had a tiny terrace behind, window boxes in front, and cost her five hundred pounds a year in rent and rates. She furnished it in Chinese modern and had sent out to Kenya for a few exotic touches— a sprinkling of African ebony heads and some leopard and zebra skins which she had sewn into poufs for scattering on the dead-black rug of her living-room. Her fireplace burned wood, and she owned a good TV and an excellent collection of recordings for her hi-fi.

Valerie loved her flat. She was just a stone's throw off Grosvenor and Berkeley Squares—she was no distance at all from the Mirabelle and Les Ambassadeurs, from Siegi's and the White Elephant, from all the amenities of Shepherd's Market and Curzon Street and of course a sound pub like the Red Lion. There was the handiness of the Dorchester Hotel, and the quiet elegance of the little Bon Viveur Club for girl lunches. There was nothing lacking in the Curzon Street area—taxi ranks, newsvendor, bank, cinema theatres, butcher, chemist, vintner, greengrocer, florist, tobacconist—a short stroll took her to everything she needed. Her daily came three hours for six days a week and kept the flat spotless. She knew no neighbours to speak to, passed no porters, and was able to live her life without encouraging any gossip whatsoever. She planted geraniums in her window-boxes and tossed together small chop-and-salad meals when she had no feeding invitations. She went to the pictures and to the theatre, read a great deal, watched the TV and played her records. The flat was just precisely large enough to hold an occasional cocktail party or Sunday brunch or buffet, but never capacious enough to trap her into extensive entertaining. Valerie drank moderately, but she kept her little bar well stocked for the friends who dropped in before the theatre or for a nightcap after an evening out.

She was a strikingly beautiful woman now, tall with lovely long legs and pale petal skin and a figure which let her eat anything. She dressed simply in beige and blues and blacks which did extra things for the opalescent eyes and shining hair, and she looked divine in slacks and shorts, in ski pants and jodhpurs. She received more than ample opportunity to show off her body in these figure-testing costumes, because she swam, skied and rode well, and was forever being asked out to people's houses on country week-ends. She had sufficient money to travel decently abroad when the mood struck her, and so went regularly to the South of France, occasionally to Italy and Spain, and usually to Switzerland, to Gstaad or St. Moritz, at least once during the winter. As often as not she was an all-expense invited guest, because Valerie Dunstan was a cheery handsome person who held her liquor well and so far had kept aloof from being cited in any messy divorce actions. If she slept around she slept around quietly and in good taste, or so everyone said. She had, most people said, fixed up her life a proper treat.

Valerie had hated England when she left it after finishing her schooling —and two reasonably shattering love affairs—to go back to Kenya and marry Brian Dermott in 1952. But a short time in Kenya as the wife of Brian Dermott had healed her of colonialism, in much the same sense that the young American naval type had set her dead against uniforms. She had not been prepared for Kenya in its most modern interpretation—she had gone home in 1952 expecting to resume life in a green and pleasant land; expecting certainly to marry and grow suitably plump among dogs and polo

13

ponies and lively Sunday chatter at The Brown Trout or some other comfortable pub; to rear her children strong and ruddy and handsome on a well-remembered farm in easy view of Mount Kenya; to raise them *not* to be drunks and pansies and useless languid lechers.

She had not gone to Kenya expecting to have her easy prospects shattered by a sudden racial tumult that took her almost from a honeymoon bed to the stewardship of a good portion of her husband's ruined family. She had not been prepared to become mistress of a household where the chatelaine wore a pistol as well as a bunch of keys; where you locked away the servants in a compound every day at sundown for their protection as well as your own; she was not prepared for a life in which every creak of floorboard made you flinch with shrieking nerves and every crunching footfall outside might foretell an enemy.

Valerie had wanted a family of her own, as soon as ever she and Brian could start one. She had found her family sooner than she expected; her husband's old foster mother suddenly widowed of the tough little man she had leaned on; her husband's sister, terribly burned in the raid which killed her foster father horribly—and finally her husband's fatherless younger brother, a quiet shy boy who wore a pistol with as much assurance as did his big brother Brian, her stranger-husband.

Valerie had wanted a tame husband of her own, to love and be loved by in the spanking new wing he had built for her onto the family house. Instead she had lost her husband to the black forests where he had gone to hunt men. He had come home occasionally, bloody-handed and heartsick, filthy dirty and usually very drunk from the things he had been doing which caused him to grind his teeth horribly at night and sweat the bedclothes in his nightmares. It had got worse as time went on and the tension mounted; she and Brian no longer made love, because whatever Brian was doing up the mountain had stolen his demonstrable manhood and sex became a grim pageant of nail-biting frustration on her part until her husband became frighteningly resigned to not touching her any more.

It was a pity, Valerie often thought, that she had not been built of the properly corny pioneer stuff like her sister-in-law Eleanor, who had survived it all—had even taken on the black orphan of one of the very Kikuyu gangsters who had killed her foster father, and who finally had evidently repaired her heart as well as she had fixed her fire-scarred face. Nell Dermott was married now to a British doctor, George Locke, and they had both seemed terribly happy when they came to London and called on her with news of home and Brian during the time that Nell was having her burned face redone by the Harley Street plastic surgeons. It was a pity that there were no Harley Street plastic surgeons to repair the kind of injuries that *she* had received at the hands of Kenya and its people. Valerie sometimes thought, when she was feeling lost and lonely on a dreary fog-palled London Sunday.

It was not her fault that she was not shaped to the Nell Dermott mould,

14

Valerie thought. She was not meant to be heroic; being locked into the bathroom by your husband—before you gave up that sort of thing entirely—while you made sure you wouldn't have any babies, was not her idea of utter connubial bliss. She was not brave; she hated living penned up in a land where limitless space was supposed to be as much a part of your life as the furniture; she hated the endless drudgery of housework in a country which was famed for the number and cheapness of its black servants; she loathed the atmosphere of fear and suspicion, the distrust of everything black, even old servants like Brian's Juma—and above everything else, she had none of the old settler's abidingly stubborn passion for the land. It was true that Valerie Dunstan had been born in Kenya, but her people had come to Africa as young marrieds, and had died before the second war, a long time before the going got sticky.

She had wept, of course, when she and Brian parted after that horrid scene in Nairobi. It had all been innocent to the extreme—she was young and bored blue with being cooped up on that lonely farm with death creeping about in the house as well as outside. She had never really been married, and she was already sick of being married and of having no husband at home to make her know she was married.

The Emergency in Kenya was just like another war, with the husbands all away. The women were desperately nervous and angry at the disruption of their lives, and there were thousands of lonely attractive men among the British troops they kept sending out. She was young and she was healthy and beautiful and she liked men physically and sooner or later she would have been playing the old game that had made Kenya famous for infidelity for fifty years. A great many of them had played the game with eager zest—Nairobi had become suddenly very gay behind the tears.

Well, it hadn't come to that. The lost baby had fixed that. Brian had returned to the forests and she had nipped smartly back to England. Perhaps if she hadn't lost the baby she might have stayed, but . . . well. The baby had never got more than started and that was that. And since that time she had loved England, if only for being so different from Nairobi.

Once lonely as a girl in school she had yearned for the violent beauty of Kenya, the infinite landscapes, the blue, cruel escarpments, the long green hills and the wind-rippled seas of golden grasses. She had mourned the bracing nip of evening air in the White Highlands, the feeling of still-untasted freedom, the frightening grandeur of the great dark forests of the Aberdare and the close-touching communion with the wild things; the zebras grazing alongside cattle and the occasional lion sitting like a big dog by the side of the road. She had remembered nostalgically the shabby spaciousness of the homely Kenya farmhouses, and the kind of roughly expansive living which made no special fuss of driving a hundred miles over vile roads for drinks with a friend—she had romanticized the living that had left all doors unlocked and had been deeply shocked on her return to find that now all doors were closed, all windows barred.

Now she loved England for all the things that Kenya had cheated her of; for the tender sweetness of its gentle countryside, its winding shaded roads fluffed with the dainty white blossoms of haw and the showery yellow exuberance of forsythia. She loved the soft rains and even the pressing fogs that shut one in and made an island of a room; the weathered old grey buildings and the bustling traffic and the great stalls of flowers and fruits; the theatres and the lights of Piccadilly and the Strand and the clubs and restaurants of Mayfair; she adored all the entrancing shops with their solid, comforting clutter of silver and leather and woollens. But most of all she luxuriated in the *security* of London—the bobby standing pink-faced and trustworthy on the corner; the bearskinned sentries changing guard in front of the Palace; the almost never-failing courtesy and humour of the cabbies and liftmen; even the imaginative Cockney curses from the barrow-boys, and the pigeon-droppings coppery green on the old statues, steeped her in a warm feeling of safety and well-being. Perhaps she would marry again some day, if she found someone who wouldn't bore her, and she could risk losing the alimony. She did not think of herself as likely to fall madly in love again —after this last three months, she doubted if she had ever been solidly in love with Brian. He had been very handsome, it was true, and he was very romantic at a time when white hunters had momentarily replaced jet pilots and movie actors as glamorous figures. But *love* him? She didn't even know that they would have worked out well in bed, over the long haul, after the first frenzied attraction of two young and beautiful healthy bodies for each other. Certainly this last three months of bed hadn't been anything shining or special. She didn't know if there was anything actually *in* Brian, under the physical strength and charm and good looks—any more, she was forced to admit in honesty, than she knew if there was anything actually in *her*.

Valerie Dunstan, sitting in the air-cooled loneliness of the jet, told herself cruelly now that she was a vegetable, a healthy, beautiful, reasonably happy vegetable. She had no particular scruples about letting the occasional attractive man into her bed if he seemed to want it badly enough. She enjoyed it, as a rule, and she could always find it by crooking a finger, and dismiss it if it got irksome. What she wanted was no real entanglements with heartbreak and misery and most of all, discomfort and uncertainty, at the end of it. She had left her first real love with the American naval gentleman; she had left her illusions about marital security by a burnt-out barn on a long green hill in the White Highlands of Kenya in British East Africa.

Now the plane's loudspeaker system was informing the passengers that the peak of Mount Kenya could be seen on the left. She decided she did not want to see The Mountain, and buried her face in her hands. What she wanted to see again was the little flat in Hill Street. In London, which, forever more, was home.

GETTING AWAY hadn't been difficult at all with the clients, Brian thought, as he passed the Meru cutoff and started up the long steep pull to Nanyuki and thence more or less downhill to Nairobi. It had been relatively as easy as saying good-bye to Valerie. Once in a while he found it a healthy business practice to leave the clients to themselves. Especially after a heady triumph —one of the Big Five, a lion or leopard or buffalo or rhino, or as in the case of yesterday, a really good elephant. Bit of beginner's luck, that Jumbo, almost too good to be true. Who'd have thought to run so soon onto three fine bulls grazing fat and happy as dammit in a bloody deserted native garden, practically up to their knees in goats? The elephants were so close and the wind so steadily right that it was a real piece of cake. But he'd built the stalk a little more difficult than necessary. At these prices the clients expected it to be tough, wanted it to be tough, so they could brag about it later. So Brian had let his spotting glasses drop snugged to his chest by their thongs, had winked at Kidogo, his Number One gunbearer, and they had fancied it up a tiny bit. There wasn't anything he had to tell Kidogo about either elephant or clients. A glance, a snap of fingers, a minute jut of chin, and Kidogo was already reacting ahead of him. They had made some busy show of the approach; the climbing up of trees and the serious peering with the glasses, stalking dramatically half-crouched from bush to bush and always testing the wind and pretending some difficulty in choosing which elephant to shoot.

Brian snorted at the memory. Actually, of the three bulls there wasn't but one real one, and he stuck out like a hippo in a bathtub. Dirty great teeth on him, a cinch hundred pounds per tusk, maybe a hundred and ten, depending on the thickness, the age, and the size of the nerve. The others were better than so-so, and Brian would have had his client shoot either if the days were running out and there were any danger of going to bed with your licence. But here it was just the first week of safari, already with a good lion down, and you stumble bang onto a hundred-pounder and a couple of decent *askari* no more than a quarter mile off the main road, half a dozen miles away from camp, in the clearest kind of country. Those two stooge-bulls would run an easy eighty and seventy pounds, and even a seventy-pounder was damned good ivory these days. And to find a hundred-pounder *and* two big chums, as well. . . . In the old control days Brian could have downed the big chap with a right, clobbered the second with a left, and bashed the third with the swift reload as he stood, ponderously poised, swaying undecided on the verge of flight, waiting to watch his boy friends shudder, topple and crash.

Well, these weren't the old control days, when sometimes you had to shoot a couple of hundred elephants from the marauding herds. And there was only one licence, and here was this great, big, lovely, eminently shootable Jumbo with the long grey logs sticking out of his face, so there was only the one to shoot and the others would obligingly take off. So Brian, still making his great show of caution, although he could have roared up in a red fire-wagon, the way that wind was blowing straight down his throat, led the client up behind a big pink ant-hill just as the biggest bull decided to wander off and leave his companions belly-rumbling mantalk to each other.

The big bull stood, rocking to and fro, his ears flapping flies with the sound of handclaps, his trunk raised and S-curved as the weaving tip tested the wind; making a tremendous *plop!* as he moved his bowels. There he stood, lonely and huge and the colour of the red ochre in the naked patch of dusty clay, a little hard-baked island in the scraggy grey bush of sanse-vieria and scrub thorn-acacia; there he was standing as completely unaware of Brian and the client and Kidogo as if he had been a tame Indian ele-phant in a zoo instead of a wild African loose in his own terrain with two hundred pounds-plus of trophy ivory poking out of his lip. Brian sighed inwardly, feeling as ever the brief stab of regret over reducing that mighty living monument to seven tons of rapidly bloating meat. It had not seemed so bad when he was doing the shooting himself. But this was a good client, trustworthy so far, and he was paying to shoot an elephant.

'Take a rest on the hill here,' Brian whispered. 'Hold it steady on that line between the ear slot and his eye—just a touch, just a hair above that line. It's a perfect set-up for a brain shot. Okay. Take him. He's yours.'

The big double-barrelled rifle had boomed. The elephant dropped, col-lapsed as quickly as if somebody had let all the air out of him. There he was, fore-knees bent, his hind legs jack-knifed backwards like a man's, kneeling on the ground. The trunk had writhed up violently once, and now was stretched out straight ahead of the bull as he knelt, almost as if in prayer.

'Jolly nice shooting!' Brian yelled, walloping the client on the back. 'Right smack on! But let him have the other half just behind the shoulder. We don't want him to get up and take off, so we'll have to chase him!' Out of the corner of his eye, Brian had seen the other bulls clear off, as he stood up in full view of them. That was good. Sometimes the *askari* hung about the fallen leader, making complications, and sometimes the complications were nasty enough so you had to shoot your way out of them. And that meant trouble with the Game Department. It was very funny how much trouble you could have with the Game Department now you were no longer *in* the Game Department.

The client fired again, and they couldn't hear the bullet smack, because they had been very close, no more than twenty yards away from the big chap, and the gun's blast drowned the meaty whonk of the bullet. But Brian watched the flesh flinch, and he reached over and took the gun from his client, passing it without looking backward to Kidogo, the gunbearer.

Actually the second bullet was unnecessary, but Brian Dermott, as a former game warden and a seasoned professional hunter, made an inviolable practice of always killing the big, dangerous stuff twice. He had been a pro-fessional hunter of animal and man for much too many years.

'Jolly good shooting, Bwana,' Brian repeated to the client, with almost honest heartiness, and patted his shoulder once more. 'I don't recommend that brain shot to most first-timers. Too dicey. I can tell you now we didn't need that second shot. But you . . . ' and then Brian stopped. The client was weeping. His shoulders jerked in harsh sobs, and tears made dirty runnels on his dusty cheeks.

Brian lifted a chin at Kidogo, who followed him a few yards away to the shade of a small, scrofulous-looking palm.

'*Hi ndofu mzuri tu,*' the gunbearer said. He was a lean, very black Ndrobo with skinny, bandy legs, and crinkled steel-wool hair. A few long white hairs straggled from his chin and, with his slits of slanted eyes, made him look like an old, very black Chinaman. Kidogo was in truth a wild man. He was of the Wandrobo, the forest people, the detribalized hunters, bee-chasers, poachers, honey-thieves, elephant-eaters. He was probably a Samburu, mainly, with some infusion of Turkana, although he called himself a Nandi for some reason best known to himself, and he had probably forgotten his true name, he had been called *Kidogo*—meaning 'little'—for so long. He didn't know what he was, but Brian thought Kidogo was the best all-purpose gunbearer alive. He had been Brian's dead father's man, and with his great, out-jutting heel and fingering toes, he could walk up a tree like a baboon. He could track, or claimed he could, a shadow's memory over stark stone, and he knew as much of elephant, leopard and bush as any living man. He knew as much as Brian Dermott of most things, and much more of many. He had been with Brian Dermott all Brian's life, some of which time he had served as nurse to Brian, first, and then to Brian's sister Eleanor and tiny brother Philip. He had, in fact, been all the family remaining to Brian Dermott when his father died—until, of course, the kids went to live on the big farm with their Aunt Charlotte and Uncle Malcolm while Brian took Kidogo and struck off on his own as a bushman at the age of sixteen.

'*Hi mzuri* bloody client *tu,*' Brian Dermott said, answering Kidogo's remark that this was a very good elephant with the flat statement that this was a very good client as well. And so the client was. Only the very good ones wept with the realization that they had just reduced the true king of the world to an untidy mess of bloated meat, fly-buzzing blood, dung, seminal slop and corruption. If he wept he was a very good client and deserved the bull, Brian thought.

'*Mupa tembo yango,*' Brian said and Kidogo dug into his only adornment, a leather pouch, and handed Brian a flat, dented silver flask which contained *tembo*—Scotch whisky. The time for tears was over. Now it was time for a couple of drinks to celebrate, and then they could drive back to camp while Kidogo returned with Katunga and Muema and Chalo to hew the tusks out of that vast skull with the big deep melancholy-looking dents in the temples. It was a long, hot, sweaty, bloody job, calling for great skill and delicate care, since the ivory was paper-thin and very brittle as it joined the skull, because of the great pulpy nerve inside. It was almost like eggshell china for a couple

19

of feet, and could easily be broken or damaged. This was too fine a pair to muck up. Brian hadn't seen such a good pair for a year or more. Whose was it, those last tusks? Oh, yes, the Canadian wood-pulp merchant with the sexy wife.

The client was over his emotional fit now. He scrubbed a wrist over his eyes. The tears had cut little rivulets in the red dust that covered a shamed face. Brian shoved the flask at him without looking at him.

The man looked grateful. One of the things which had made Brian Dermott a tremendous success with clients, both male and female, was an ability to convey strength and toughness and skill coupled with an almost feminine intuitiveness and sympathy. Right now this is the only man in the world who had ever shot an elephant and then felt sorry that he'd shot it. No need to tell him most people wished they hadn't, especially after they have done it well.

'Funny,' the client said, wiping his mouth with the back of his hand and giving the flask back to Brian. 'You look different to me now. You look smaller, more my size. When we first came out you looked ten feet tall and I felt like a midget.' This, too, was part of the safari catharsis. Growing up to the country. It always happened one way or the other. Quite a few grew smaller as the country expanded.

'Same old me,' Brian grinned; a big, white, square-toothed grin that gave his baked brown face a fleeting little-boy look, and gestured mockingly at himself. 'Same old *shenzi* shanty Irish. No change in me. It's you who've changed. The Wakamba say that the whole world changes when a man takes his first woman, hears his first lion roar, and kills his first elephant.' *Oh, mamma mia*, Dermott, Brian sneered at himself. Brian Dermott, the African philosopher, who can make up exotic native proverbs to fit any and all occasions.

But it was a good client, better than most, very rich and quite sensitive for a rich man who was also an American. Had hunted hard, shot well, killed it dead, and didn't want to kill it all. So, after they'd cleaned up in camp and Brian was once again Brian Dermott, the shaggy nature-lover turned smooth society hunter, it was quite easy. Brian looked very manly and trustworthy in the firelight, freshly showered and shaved, his grey-streaked bronze cap of hair wet-combed, his full, upcurving lips giving a boyish look to a face which also owned a high-bridged, harsh-cut Red Indian nose, and strange golden cat's eyes behind impossibly long, almost girlish lashes. Brian was wearing now a pair of long white-bleached twill trousers, a light grey tweed hacking jacket, and a blue polka-dotted muffler tucked inside a white silk shirt from a set some Italian clients had sent him specially from Rome.

'I think another spot won't kill us on such a festive occasion,' Brian said, and got up to take glasses from the client and the sister, who was dark ash blonde with silver lights in her hair; really quite pretty in a hungry, tortured sort of way. The grey eyes were surely hurt eyes, like a buck's. They had that unusual sheen of unshed tears that grey eyes sometimes seemed to have.

Won't do much harm if I clear off for a couple of days and leave them to themselves and the boys, he thought as he mixed one more Scotch, and poured two more Cokes. I can spot the signs: Sis is about to succumb to the old B-movie black magic; African moon, hyenas in the night, the sense of vastness of it all, twinkle-twinkle little star and the white hunter growing prettier by the tick. Best give her a small vacation from my charms. It'll be a long safari, in any case, and there's no point in shooting it all in a week.

'I say,' Brian said, as he gave the blue-blazing logs a kick and turned to face his clients in the firelight, 'would you people mind terribly if I left you on your own for a couple of days and nipped in to Nairobi? I'm rather curious about this hanging which may or may not come off tomorrow night. I thought I might drive in early tomorrow and see how it all turns out and leave you to shoot some sandgrouse and spurfowl—unless, of course, you'd like to crack on with the serious hunting. Or want to drive all the way back to town with me . . . ' He let the last alternative hang without much fear of acceptance. Neither had seemed keen on cities. Maybe something to do with Sister Katie's not drinking? Could be. She looked like she'd been a drinker—the way she watched her brother—and the way she sort of clenched her glass, as if to reassure herself that she was drinking Coke without a stick in it. You couldn't tell about the deep ones. They hadn't volunteered anything yet, and Brian made a strong point of never asking clients anything at all. If they wanted to confide they would—and nearly always did, sooner or later. The sister had a very nice, stylishly husky voice which would aptly fit a confessional.

The client took a sip of his drink before he turned to look at his sister.

'That's this fellow Poole, the one we've been hearing about on the news every night?' the client's sister said, in her throaty voice.

'Yes,' Brian said. 'Peter Poole. It's rather an unusual occurrence. He's supposed to hang tomorrow night for killing an African. If he does it'll be the first time in Kenya history that they ever hanged a man for killing a Wog. Might make quite a stir in Nairobi.'

'How do you mean, stir?' the client asked. 'He's clearly guilty, isn't he? From what I've read.'

'Well, there's a chance he may get off; they've been petitioning the Queen directly and there's also a possible late plea of insanity, according to what we heard last night,' Brian said. 'If he does there might be considerable agitation on the part of the local Wogs—all political, of course. But after all they *did* string up a whole covey of Africans last week for killing one old white farmer, and there's a chance there could be quite a riot unless somebody steps on it.'

'And if they do hang this Peter Poole?' the client's sister asked. 'What happens then?' It was strange how many well-bred American women owned husky voices.

'Well,' Brian said. 'If they *do* stretch him, I shouldn't wonder if the white settlers mightn't act up more than a touch. This is Kenya, you know, white

21

man's country and all that, and there is still quite a hard core of old-time settlers who don't hold a black life very dearly.'

'What do you think, Paul?' The client's sister turned to her brother. 'Do you want to go?'

'Not I.' The brother shook his head. 'What with the lion and the elephant all in a week, and everything being so fresh and new, I'd kind of welcome a couple of days just slopping around camp and recapturing my soul, which is somewhere a long way behind me, like lost baggage. Our friend Brian here has hit us with everything in a lump. It's a little hard to absorb it all in one gulp. Do you want to go?' The question was formally polite. His eyes said *No*, you don't want to go.

'I don't think so,' his sister said. 'I'm with you, Paul, I'd like to collect myself a little, too. It's all been so sudden and so too—so dreadfully different and exciting. I don't think I want to add any extra trouble—other people's troubles—to this safari.'

'Suppose we skip your Mister Poole, then,' the client said smoothly. 'You run on in for a couple of days, Brian, and Katie and I will just kind of mess around. I'll brag and she can listen, and we can both rest up a bit and read some detective stories. Okay?'

'Super,' Brian said. 'If that's how you'd like it. Mwende speaks fair English, and so do Muema and Aly. Muema's a good mechanic. I'll take the Rover and leave you the power wagon. Muema can drive you over to Buffalo Springs for a swim. It's just an hour or so away from here, and the water's lovely. Aly'll fix you a picnic lunch in the chop-box, and you can shoot birds until your shoulder's blue. This *luga* and the Serarua and the Kinna are all alive with vulturine guinea-fowl and those big yellow-necked francolin, and simply filthy with sandgrouse. I think,' he grinned, 'to use an Americanism, you'll have yourself a ball without me. It's dreadfully nice of you not to mind my going, though.'

'Forget it,' the client said. 'But don't you get into any trouble. I'm enjoying this, and I don't want anything to happen to our hunter. Do I smell food?'

'That you do. Mwende!'

'*Ndio* Bwana,' drifted back from the cookfire.

'*Lete chakula upesi sana!*' Brian shouted. Then he said to the clients, 'Hanged or not hanged, riots or no riots, I want to be there to see it. It's really a turning-point in Kenya history, in a country where everything seems to be changing overnight. This thing tomorrow will put a big red circle on the calendar. History'll call it the year they hanged or didn't hang a man named Peter Poole for killing an African. That's how history's made, I suppose. Here comes the grub. Memsaab?' He extended his hand to the pretty, silver-blonde tortured-looking sister and helped her out of her chair. 'Unless I'm wrong, old Aly is giving us grilled gerenuk chops tonight, and they're the best the camp affords in this or any other country.'

'I'm sure they will be,' the client's sister murmured huskily. 'If you say so.' She walked off to the mess tent looking, Brian thought, even more attractive in her well-cut slacks from the rear than she did from the front, which was certainly attractive enough for a long safari. He just hoped that between them, the brother and sister could keep whatever was troubling her contained, and not saddle him with any of it.

CHAPTER FOUR

THE CLIENTS were both still asleep when Brian left camp in the rosy dawn; he had told them, when they said good night, not to get up until they felt like it. If all went well he'd be back late tomorrow night—he wanted to stop and see his people on the way back from Nairobi—or at worst, in time for late breakfast or early lunch day after tomorrow. Somehow he thought the clients seemed a little surprised that he should have his own private people. It was more, with clients, as if he had appeared, full-sprung and man-complete, into their lives, like some genie you summoned from rubbing a verdigrised old Arab lamp.

Well, the day was bright and the air was tangy fresh and the francolin ran along the weeded roadside, their yellow throats like jonquils in the sun. Hornbills flew looping in the bush, and a veritable tornado of weaver-birds rolled and twisted in funnelled mass. Kidogo was seated beside him, drowsing, and Brian's morning tea was still warm in his stomach. The cigarette he was smoking tasted unlike any other cigarette of the day, and the Land Rover's motor sang like a sewing-machine. It was a nice day to be driving heedless in the early dew, even if it was a hanging he was heading for; no doubt about it, a hanging had a certain air of festivity to it.

The client-woman—she would probably turn out like most of the others. She would start out by asking how he came to be a professional hunter, and eventually she would want to know what he had been like as a little boy. Yes, pretty soon he imagined this new lady client would ask him, as so many had demanded: *Tell me what you were like when you were a little boy*. They always asked him that question. It was strange how they always chose one of two times. Just before or just after.

'I wonder what *was* Brian Dermott like as a little boy?' Brian spoke aloud, as he often spoke softly to himself when he was driving. He was thinking of himself in the third person, another trick he had fallen into during his solitary years—possibly in some sort of conscious effort to clarify himself in his own eyes.

'What was our hero like as a little boy? My word, what was he *not* like as a little boy?' Kidogo paid no attention. Kidogo was asleep, curled in the far

23

corner, his glistening hide greedily drinking the early morning sun. 'Before all the horse-shit started, I mean ?'

To know about this fellow Dermott as a boy, Brian thought, you would have to know his father, Kegan Dermott—Robert Joseph Kegan Dermott, if you pleased, and in latter years known rather widely and obviously descriptively as Keg. Not Keeg, with the long *e*, but Keg, as in small barrel. As in keg of spirits.

Keg Dermott was what was known in Chronicles as a sojourner. He came, he tarried, he sojourned, and then he took himself off to the greener fields. He had sojourned as a sailor before the mast, windjamming round the Cape when there were still windjammers that went round the Cape. He and the century arrived in Kenya at about the same time—the century, Keg Dermott, old Colonel Grogan that was still alive, today, and John Boyes that they called the King of the Kikuyu then. Brian's father always said his ship went off and left him stranded in Mombasa, but Brian's father always winked when he said it. Mombasa was just a little Arab port in those days, gleaming plasterwhite and softly pink in the sun, with slim, gracious featherheaded palms swaying and soughing in the breezes, with high-pooped Arab *dhows* tugging at their anchor chains off the breakwater, with the soaring thin notes of the flutes and the twanging of the three-stringed mandolins tiptoeing across the moon-silvered, star-dimpled water to join the flattened heavy thud of drums ashore. Keg Dermott jumped his ship coldly and calmly at the age of fifteen. Kenya already had him by the heart by the time he smelled his first hot Africa dust on his first day ashore.

Brian was never quite sure that his father had done all the things he said he did. The old man had an Irish way of re-writing history to suit his fancy, according to the state of the moon and the level of the bottle. His father was fortyish when Brian was born—a lean, long-nosed slow-talking Irisher, russet-haired, with piercing yellow-grey cat's eyes, a lantern jaw and a quirky mouth that twitched his long sensitive nose when he laughed, which was mostly. That was one of Keg Dermott's chief troubles, people said. He was always laughing at something, if only at himself. Sombreness streaked his gaiety like strips of lean in a side of fat bacon, but only on rare occasion.

Keg Dermott had done two positive things in his life. He had married Brian's mother, much to everyone's surprise that Norah Shevlin the District Commissioner's daughter would be after having such a foot-free rogue. But well before he had met and married Norah Shevlin he had made some mysterious money—and had sent off to Ireland for his sister. He summoned his sister, orphaned by then in Kerry, in 1911. She was twenty years old, an auburn-haired tawny-eyed beauty, when she arrived in Mombasa. The Uganda Railroad, on which Keg Dermott briefly bossed a gang of Indian labourers, was operating on schedule now.

Keg Dermott put his sister Charlotte on the train and then set her up in a small house in the shambling shanty-town of Nairobi. She was married in three months' time to a little blue-eyed Scot surveyor named Malcolm Stuart, who had come out to Kenya from Aberdeenshire in 1906 to map the country. On foot, Charlotte Dermott, now Stuart, packed her belongings in a bullock-cart and struck off in the general north-westerly direction of a tall mountain the natives called Kerinyagga, to help Malcolm Stuart map the country. While they were at it they mapped themselves a likely plot in an area called Nyeri, close to a place called Naro Moru, and legally took up the land. Malcolm Stuart called his acres Glenburnie, from the streams that ran through the green and folding hills which looked so much like Scotland, with the broad belts of heather girdling the high slopes of the Aberdare Mountains. Charlotte Stuart bore four children for Malcolm Stuart. Two girls died in infancy. The eldest, a son named Malcolm after his father, was killed by a buffalo some native hunter had wounded and left sick and hateful in the bush. The pain-maddened animal had burst unsuspected from a patch of thorn and had gored and trodden young Malcolm to bloody tatters before he was quite sixteen years old. The surviving boy, Ian, had lived long enough to be shot down by the Germans and to win the posthumous collection of medals, including the DSC and DFC with bar, which now rested on the piano in an upended velvet box next to the smiling portrait of blond young Ian as a flight lieutenant with his new gold wings, and an enormous RAF moustache.

Brian's memory of his mother was rather shaky, running in jerks like an old-fashioned silent film. He remembered her mostly from her portrait, a badly executed oil daubed by some unshaved vagabond artist who had paid for a week's bread and beer by doing the picture when Brian was a tiny boy. The portrait showed enormous violet eyes and curly chestnut hair, with a Peg o' My Heart Kathleen Mavourneen kind of Irish face that had a gay tipped nose and a smiling sweet mouth, most of which had come to repose in the face of his sister Nell. Norah Dermott had been short and rather plumpish after Brian, but she came from a burly family, judging from the speckled yellowed photographs of her father and her brothers. From his mother Brian got the fleshly compactness of body laid along the length of his father's bone. He had some portion of his father's cat's eyes as well, and the basic russet under the bronze of his hair.

His mother's memory was dim not so much from a standpoint of age, for Brian had been a biggish boy of twelve or so when she died having young Philip. Brian had never been a Mummy's boy; he had tagged his father from toddling days, and bitterly resented the *interruptus* of occasional schooling which separated him from Keg Dermott. Brian gained little from school that he valued—he treasured more what he had learned from Keg Dermott with the wild roan hair and yellow animal's eyes.

There could be no summing of Keg Dermott. He spread quicksilvery from the touch. When he settled in one place he pined for another. Distant purple hills filled his vision. He took up land, and let it fall to bits if he ever got it started at all. He followed the gold to Kakamega and to Tanganyika as well, until East Africa gold more or less petered out for casual collection. He yearned for diamonds in Tanganyika, but he was dead and gone when John Williamson stamped a curious piece of rock into the earth with his heel one day for fear his boys would kill him if they knew what that bit of carbon represented, and so Keg never touched on the depthless diamond pipe that created in Williamson a threat to DeBeers in the 1950s. But like Williamson, Keg financed his moonbeam expeditions with the odd borrowed fiver, the stray pound, the occasional ten-bob note, collected here and there and where he could.

People said Keg Dermott could move into a mansion and have it looking like a shanty in a week. He could do almost anything with his hands except make consistent money with them. He started a sawmill and lost it in a card game. He had early worked on the railroad, and tired of it. When the Kaiser's war touched East Africa, Keg Dermott ignored it. He was hunting elephant.

Keg Dermott was too young to have been on the lion-shooting at Tsavo when the Uganda Railway was thrusting westward from Mombasa, but somehow he had learned to use a gun well enough to have gone with the roaring rush of the freebooters when Leopold's tenure at the Lado was released by his death, and the rich Belgian enclave become a bonanza for the fiddlefooted shag-bearded ruffians who saw the no-man's-land as an El Dorado of loose gold and easy ivory. Keg Dermott owned scars on face and body that he referred to as 'my Lado lace' when he was tracing the ribbed welts and angry red rivulets that coursed his chest and legs—this set of grooves he'd had of a leopard; that lump-healed bone had been broken by a buffalo—that angry pair of identical scars on breast and back were gift of the Masai who had flung a greased spear clean through him. Or so he said.

He was always shadowed by the lean, Chinese-eyed, sharp-faced Ndrobo called Kidogo whose real name was long and garglingly unpronounceable. It was never quite clear how the two men had come together; they never discussed whether Keg Dermott had saved Kidogo's life in the well-rubbed tradition, or whether Kidogo had preserved Keg Dermott's neck—or if they had merely shared a *gariba* of water or a gourd of *pombe* or a strip of *biltong* a long time ago. Kidogo, about the same age as Keg Dermott, had been at his side when Charlotte Dermott arrived in Mombasa in 1911. He was still at Keg Dermott's side when Keg died of an accumulation of Africa, which included black-water fever, pernicious amoebic, ancient malarias and forgotten break-bone fevers, and an assortment of the more exotic stomach parasites, including a harassed and hobnailed liver.

This was not to say that Keg Dermott was a noisy drunkard or a boastful brawler or a blackly broody toper. He loved the grog the way he loved the books, simply and wholeheartedly. He had been afflicted by an insatiable lust for both alcohol and literature at about the same time that the idea of steady employment was rejected as unalluring. A disposition to the drink and aversion to humdrum toil was no novelty in early Kenya—an uncontrollable passion for reading was regarded by the immigrant Scots as daft and by the

26

dislocated Irish as downright quare. Keg Dermott was thought to be an odd fellow by most who knew him, if only because his English was often rotundly elegant, always mellowed by the Irish slurring of syllables, and festooned subjunctively by participial negatives in lieu of straight Anglo-Saxon declaratives.

Keg Dermott drank and he read Shakespeare; he drank more and read Darwin's *The Origin of Species* and Gibbon's *Decline and Fall*; he drank more and quoted Synge and the appreciation of him by Yeats; he drank even more and was apt to intermingle Kipling with Coleridge. His friends were Addison and Swift and Boswell, and he sprinkled his speech with Latin tags in the manner of Charles Lamb. He spoke sometimes in brilliant allegory and he was ever a masterful spinner of fanciful stories to small boys, especially if the stories concerned animals.

Brian was reared, then, trotting behind his father and Kidogo in the bush to his mother's despair; served always with a rich collation of heroes both tangible and legendary, and sometimes hopelessly muddled in his head.

From the cheerless interior of whatever shabby little house the Dermotts happened to be encumbering, Brian followed his father and the black man Kidogo into strange and wondrous golden worlds which were dazzling in their diversity. There was Keg's fey universe of leprechauns and Druids, of flame-bearded Irish kings and fiery-sworded lords who forever led their dauntless bands against the wrong. There were feuds and donjoned castles, good and mischievous elves, evil witches and bright-haired fairy princes— and there were also sombre hangings and futile insurrections and broadly moated forts.

There was Kidogo's world, too, his private secret sphere of dead ancestors aprowl in the night, of human curses and bewitched animals and men; of long-sought vengeances and all manner of horrid misfortune begot by supernatural spells and the righteous wrath of the God who sat high on the Mountain. There were rousing tales of old battles and daring raids, of warrior chieftains and massive human sacrifices. And in other tales the people became animals in fabled plays, and often the animals were punished by becoming people.

But it was as well an open, airy existence of bright sun and sheltering sky, of fire's warmth and starry night, of snow-peaked mountains and long green rolling hills. It was enriched by myth, both Irish and African, woven miraculously into a tapestry of accepted childish fact by the flighting fancies of his elders. It was a world in which there was no fear of man or beast—a world of palpable excitement in every waking moment, whether the excitement derived from living animals and men or the almost tangible people who leaped, at Keg's intimate beckon, vibrantly breathing from his books.

Animals—Brian cuddled lion cubs as bedfellows when he was three. Keg Dermott was always bringing something hungry and useless home, his wife said, to nurse and pet until it grew big enough to eat him. Most of the stuff grew up and wandered away to backslide to the wild, but for years Brian

27

was always running across some occasional lion who seemed tamer to humans than the rest, and who looked vaguely familiar about the eyes.

Heroes? Brian was teethed on tales of Tippoo Tib, the half-Arab son of a black slave who became almost an emperor in slaves and ivory and power. He knew people who had *known* Tippoo Tib. He also knew people who had seen Mahomet, the fabulous ancient elephant whose ivory was so massive that the tusks curved down to disappear in low grass and then swooped up again like the runners of a sled that Brian had never seen except in pictures.

Speke and Selous and Burton and Thomson and Livingstone and Stanley were second-hand intimates, almost. So Count Ludwig Teleki had walked to Lake Rudolf from Mombasa? Well, Brian had not walked from Mombasa to Lake Rudolf on the Abyssinian border, but he had damned well walked *and* hunted with Keg Dermott from Rumuruti to Maralal to Baragoi to Rudolf, and it hadn't taken him two years to make the trip, either.

He read of all the wars, and they stirred him, of course, but somehow lacked reality. When very young he had seen men sprawled ungainly dead from a raid of the Suk against the Karamojong, on the Kenya-Uganda border—had seen dead Masai, rumpled and blood-soiled in their lion head-dresses, after a set-to with the Wakamba. Death was commonplace—the Wogs were always doing each other in with pangas or spears or knobkerries or varieties of poisons and bone-pointing spells. Some amok elephant, gone madly rogue with *musth* or the cankering of an old spear wound or a stream of ants up his trunk, was always trampling some unfortunate native or the occasional white settler.

Death was something to be expected, whether from human or animal, and pain was something to be borne. He had seen a Masai, mauled by a lion, laugh contemptuously as he was being sewed up with a sail-needle. He had himself cut a cross on a snake-bite on his own calf, dumped the spread bleeding lips of the wound full of gunpowder and set it alight to kill the poison. Death was something he was used to: he had watched the natives carry people who were still not yet dead out of their huts and leave them for the hyenas so that the *shamba* might not be defiled by the death, necessitating its burning and desertion.

So much his father taught him, and as much more Kidogo, the lean wild Ndrobo with the swinging pierced earloops and the prehensile heels; taught him of bushcraft and the life and habits of animals and birds, of the nature of flowers and herbs, and of course the nature of the African himself. Brian's first language was Kikuyu, then Swahili. He learned English a little later. As he grew older he accumulated smatterings of Somal and Masai and Turkana and the strange crossbreedings of dialects where the tribes intersected. They sent him to school at Nyeri and later to the Prince of Wales School in Nairobi, but Brian had already covered that reading and more; his feeling for ancient history was as keen and real as his ability to track an animal, and the unconsciously knowing fingers of his father had taught him

28

more of working physics, as regards the innards of a clutter of inexplicably ailing machinery, than he would ever learn from a chalk-dusty professor.

It was a relief from schooling in a way when Keg Dermott quit living. Keg Dermott knew he was dying and so proceeded to die without the last-minute absolution of priests or any late-flowing repentances or heroics.

'Ye're a man, me boy,' he said to Brian Dermott. 'Look to your sister and your brother and remember ye're a gentleman born and better educated than most in the things that count. And keep Kidogo to your side; he's a good man and most uncommon for a Wog. I'll be having another nip now, if there's aught left in the bottle.' He had taken his final nip and died and Brian had buried him under a big kaffirboom that shed its rosy petals in a happy, gay profusion on the grave—the grave which was unmarked by stones except where they were cairned to keep off the hyenas.

Brian would have been quite content to continue on in the shabby small house under the big Cape chestnuts, which occupied a corner of his Aunt Charlotte's vast spread of land—and on which his father had been quite satisfied to squat, while always refusing other aid. His sister Nell was verging on twelve, now more than old enough to run the house; his brother Pip was three and a bit, and was a sturdy toddler who ran bare-butted in a shirt and spoke a fluent Kikuyu, if a trifle limited in vocabulary.

But Aunt Charlotte now dared intervene where her illogically proud but admittedly rootless brother had never before permitted sisterly interference. Aunt Charlotte swooped down on the little Dermott *shamba* like a band of raiding Masai, scooped the baby Pip to her bosom, seized Nell by one grubby paw and announced in bugle tones that from now on they were all *her* children, and were going to receive a proper raising in the big house on the hill at Glenburnie.

Brian had not hung about long enough to become an apt candidate for a proper upbringing. He had seen the baby and his sister settled safely in his aunt's capacious hands, in the rambling old house of Glenburnie, and he had observed that there were enough people around the big house to run the *shamba*, and more.

Brian and his cousin left at about the same time—Ian to have his preparation for his bash at the Boche and Brian to whistle up Kidogo and dive into the bush again. This time he went off as a *mtoto*—an apprentice—to a very crabbed and silent Scots game-warden.

It was no accident, then, a year later, with Brian still too young to join up against the Germans, and hoping desperately that the war would last long enough for him to have a rattle at it as well as his Cousin Ian, whose wings were feathering out with the RAF in England—it was not surprising that Brian became, if still not yet a warden, at least a game-ranger. The Old Warden died of the deadly Kenya combination of solitude, altitude and aggravated high blood pressure. They were more shorthanded than ever in the Game Department, what with the war being on and all the able bods dashing off to be heroes while the country that grew the beef and wheat went to bloody rack. Young Dermott, they said, was already living on the place and had been doing most of the Old Man's work anyhow, he and that fantastic Wog of his, Whatsisname, a tame wild man who could track an illegal idea before a poacher hatched it.

And thus at the age of sixteen, Brian Dermott had become a king, as his father, Keg Dermott, had become a king at roughly the same age when he watched his ship sail away and strand him in Mombasa. Brian Dermott had one thing to fret him, and one only: would the war last long enough for him not to miss it?

For the rest, he had no worries at all. God knew Uncle Mac and Aunt Charlotte had had their touch-and-go times of it, with droughts and floods and locusts and rinderpest, but they had weathered God's wrath long enough to whip the rebellious Kenya soil into a surly submission. And now the war was making anyone rich who had a farm and who was willing to work, if only the weather didn't go bloody well mad and the Forces kept up screaming for beef and wheat. Pip had a mother again, and more than one pair of jeans; young Nell, who'd be a buxom young lady pretty soon, not only had found a mother in Aunt Charlotte, but also the kind of steady, solid home which a young girl needed to grow up secure in—certainly a more stable father in Uncle Mac, who adored her in his terse Scots way. And he, Brian, would surely come home one of these days and help with the farm—that's if Cousin Ian wanted him to—when Uncle Mac grew a little feebler and Aunt Charlotte wearied of yelling at the coons to keep them gingered.

Brian had always loved pets; now he had ten million pets, maybe more. He knew the face of every lion for five hundred square miles; he knew when the old ones moved and new prides came in. He calendared births and deaths and entered them in his own log of personal vital statistics. Most of the lions he named after old Romans—Nero, Tiberius, Claudius. Some would come bounding after him when he clattered over the plain in the old pick-up truck that the dead warden had left as leprous legacy. He shot the painfully old and infirm before they had a chance to sample cattle or even natives as a substitute for the game they were no longer spry enough to catch; he killed the severely crippled or sadly diseased before the hyenas had a chance to pull them down and eat them alive.

He lived off his gun—his shotgun brought him guinea-fowl and sandgrouse and francolin; his rifle provided Thomson's gazelle and impala and occasionally buffalo or eland for his table. He fed his game scouts and their families off the bigger brutes, the topi and kongoni and zebra. There was always plenty of meat in camp; the skins of his scouts and their women glistened in the sun with health—and also with the fresh animal fat with which they smeared themselves. He kept a happy *boma*—you could tell by the way the natives' buttocks bulged with their burden of stored fat that came from eating a steady ten pounds each of fresh meat every day. But he never enjoyed shooting for the sake of it. He disliked to see things die, even of necessity.

They roved much afoot, the young Irishman and the old Ndrobo, Brian

30

carrying a light rifle and a small pack of possibles—tea, sugar, tobacco, a flask of whisky, all wrapped in the waterproof poncho under which they both slept, dry and warm from each other's bodies. Kidogo ranged along with the second rifle, a heavy one, balanced over one shoulder, and his spear serving as a staff in his other hand. He carried a pouch which contained the black dried *biltong*, which looked like broad strips of liquorice, a billycan for making tea, and such extra munition as they needed apart from what Brian wore in the loops of the broad leather brass-buckled belt which had belonged to Keg Dermott. With those few things they were self-sufficient for days, even weeks, as they followed game migrations, destroyed snares, filled game-pits, released trapped animals, and occasionally shot the occasional cattle-or-goat lifting lion or leopard that pestered the native manyattas or frightened the women from the waterholes. These creatures Brian shot sadly, after satisfying himself that they were guilty as charged and needed to be destroyed.

Brian was barely seventeen when he killed his first man. They had routed a nest of poachers, destroying the trip-nooses, confiscating the spears, bows and arrows. Two of the men had broken loose, and one had ambushed Brian and Kidogo. A poisoned arrow had zipped past Brian's ear and thudded into a tree. There was a flash as the archer ran, and Brian snapshot him when a glimmer of hide showed again through a break in the bush. They were far from any hospital facility; the native was shot through the lungs with a soft-pointed bullet which made a tremendous mess as it came out of his back. Before the shocked boy could prevent him, Kidogo had cut the dying man's throat with one swipe of a knife. Brian started to rebuke him, but the old man held up a hand and said gently:

'He was dying anyhow, Little Bwana. It is not good to see something dying suffer. We always finish our animals if they are not quite dead after the *piga*.'

'I suppose I'd best report this,' Brian had mused aloud. 'I wonder how one goes about writing a report that you killed a poacher for winging an arrow at you?'

Kidogo had not understood the English, but the puzzled tone had made its point.

'There is no use in mentioning this, Little Bwana,' he said. 'It will only cause trouble and we will have to go to the *Boma* and explain things to the Bwana DC and the Bwana Police and the Bwana Game. You will have to write many reports and they will possibly have to pay blood money to the man's family. He tried to kill you; you killed him instead. We will leave him. The hyenas will scatter his bones and the ants will have the rest.'

So they had burned the man's bow and arrows and had gone about their business. The next week Brian had to kill three elephant and half a dozen buffalo to disperse marauding herds, and felt very sad because the animals had done no wrong but to attempt to feed.

Brian was serenely happy in the bush, with his ten million pets, for nearly two years. When he was eighteen he went back home to visit his family and to join up with the Army. But they circumvented that: Italian prisoners were being sent down to Kenya from Ethiopia and from the fighting in Libya. The prisoners had to be fed, and there was no cattle to feed them, since the settler-beef was needed for export to feed the Allied fighting forces. The vast plains from Rumuruti south, the Laikipia on which the Masai had once lived, were as thick with zebra, grant, kongoni, and topi as a shenzi *pie*-dog with fleas. Some day the animals would have to go to make room for cattle; in any event, and the bloody Eyties had to be fed something.

Brian was suddenly converted from conservator to certified butcher. On government order with government money and petrol, he slaughtered game —shooting from the American jeeps that were beginning to trickle out to Kenya from the wars; shooting with the gun braced in the crook of his steering arm as he leaned across the wheel of the jouncing jeep that ranged alongside the galloping, stampeding game.

Keg Dermott had showed Brian pictures in books of American plains strewn with carcasses of dead buffalo after a whole tribe of Sioux or Black-feet navigated their painted horses among the bison, loosing their arrows at the range of a few feet into the hearts and lungs. He had heard tales from his Afrikaner neighbours of the old Boer *voortreks*, when the Jappies, on their blooded arch-necked stallions, rode into the herds of fat-sterned zebras and plunging wildebeeste that once darkened the South African plains a hundred years ago and more—riding knee-gripped in the boiling dust, stabbing into the withers of the close-packed animals with long knives. They had killed until they had stamped out all the grazing animals, the buffalo and the elephant and the eland and gemsbok and sable until there was nothing in South Africa any more but vineyards and gold and diamonds and people.

And now they were doing the same thing in Kenya—he, Brian Dermott himself, and hundreds like him, were doing the same thing in Kenya. Look at him now, with the dust settling behind him, as he stopped to smear the sweat out of his eyes with a rag and to light a cigarette. On the plains, as far as he could see behind him, there were black hillocks of carcasses, with some few animals still not killed dead, but trying to raise their necks and pull themselves up after he had shot them too far back because of the plunging motor-car he drove while shooting with one hand—killing indiscriminately like a bloody Boer on a horse. Forty, fifty, sixty, seventy animals a day he was killing to make food for the Dago prisoners and planting-room for the farmers who were sure to flock to Kenya when the war was over, and the war seemed speedily to be turning in the favour of the Allies.

Brian, on his last day as a meat-hunter, walked away from the car and vomited. Then he got back into the car, turned his guns in at the police station, and joined the Army. He walked with the Army over quite a bit of Somalia and Ethiopia without seeing an enemy to shoot at. When the peace came he was a lance-corporal in Addis Ababa.

WHEN BRIAN was demobbed and came home from the Army, many things had changed. All the plains animals around Rumuruti and the Kinangop were shot out—the Laikipia was as bare and brown as an Indian's backside except for cattle. There was nothing to shoot around Nanyuki all the way to the Uaso Nyiro except for the mountain game, the elephants and buff and leopard and bushbuck which lived in the thickest bush of the hills—and, of course, the shy bongo which could only be found in the thickest wild grape of the Aberdare as you came over the top from the Kinangop, and some few of course in the Mau Forest.

And in the Masai and round Kilimanjaro in the Tsavo and all round the great migration corridor in the Serengeti of Tanganyika the poachers had been having a field day, as the elephant-poachers from Sultan Hamud to Mombasa had been finding rich ivory grist for the Indians to mill into billiard balls and carve into bangles. The native poachers and the Wahindi and Arab middlemen as far north as Lamu had been growing wealthy because of lack of vigilance while the white game wardens and white game scouts had mostly all been away to the wars, chasing Germans and Italians and Japanese instead of Waluangulu elephant-and-rhino killers and Waikoma lion-mane fanciers.

Kenya was flocking full of fresh-faced, pink-kneed farmers-in-embryo who had been given land options in return for military service by a grateful king; Kenya was on the boom. Nairobi was by way of becoming a proper city instead of a sprawling shanty-town with a screeching core of Indian commerce. Buildings were shooting up and the airport at Eastleigh was receiving its first heavy traffic via all sorts of airlines. Everybody was getting into the airline business, it seemed. Safaris were starting to come out again, and the first of the movie ventures and the camera-snapping sightseers. The Game Department and the National Parks needed men, as the Locust Control needed men to keep the bugs from flying away with the perishing country, as the Public Health needed men to halt the native tide of circulating syphilis. And certainly the farms needed a shave and a haircut—their bwanas had all been off to the wars, leaving the land to the old people, the harassed wives and mothers, and the nucleus of faithful natives that hadn't run off with the troop or flocked to the towns to learn to be taxi-drivers and spivs.

Brian went home to Glenburnie, still wearing his uniform, and was met with a business proposition almost before he had kissed Aunt Charlotte and his sister, who was well on the way to being a young lady, and a damned pretty one at that. She was blooming, was Nell, with her mother's high-tipped Irish nose and the blue eyes and less red in her hair than either Brian or his young brother Pip, who was already starting to sprout in all directions, but seemed at the moment to be mostly feet and wrists. Cousin Ian had been killed by the Hun; Uncle Mac and Aunt Charlotte were family-firm now about wanting Brian to come home and help whip the farm into shape—shoot the buffalo out of the wheat, shoot the leopards out of the pigsty, shoot the elephants out of the maize. Repair the fences, rebuild the barns, reclaim the land, fence the paddocks, burn the bush, vet the cattle—Brian sighed, shuddered and begged off. He needed some time to think, he said. He thought he'd go to work for the Parks as a warden. He'd already been asked on his way through town. Animals—wild animals—were going to be big tourist business in the post-war, and the Wogs and the meat-shooters, the old Boer settlers who took licences for everybody in the family including Grandmum, had played hell with what the ivory and rhino-horn poachers had left.

No—Brian would come back to the farm if they ever really needed him, but right now he thought he'd be happier roving with old Kidogo on a reserve, living out of a tent or in a cane-thatched *banda*. He had seen a lot of scraggly parched goat-country in Somalia and Ethiopia, and his eyes were hungry for Kilimanjaro in the early morning; thirsty for Kerinyagga with her shining necklace of cloud. He wanted to see some broad golden plains and deep green swamps and some lazy yawning lions and some migrating zebra. The Parks money wasn't much, he knew, but he didn't need much money.

So Brian had kissed his Aunt Charlotte and his lovely sister Nell good-bye. *Kwaheri*, he said, and went off to be a king again, scourging his poachers and living happy with his pets, until one day in Nairobi, at the Norfolk hotel, he collided with a beautiful but vaguely familiar face which turned out to belong to little long-shanked Val Dunstan from the farm next door but one—Miss Valerie Dunstan who had spent all the war and more in England attending school, and who was now back home in Kenya for a long visit.

That was in early 1952, after Brian had been a full-fledged Game Warden with a neat stone house and uniformed *askaris* and flowers in the *boma* and a proper registry book at the barrier gate to his domain for nearly three whole years. It was a nice house, primly painted and achingly neat, but it was sternly and antiseptically a bachelor hut, a *thingira*, and it needed a woman's touch to make it more homelike. Brian didn't have much time for coddling flowers, but they grew like weeds anyhow, because of the plentiful water in the little river that ran past the vast grove of yellow-dappled fever trees and purpling jacaranda in which the house sat.

Brian certainly hoped that Valerie would ride out with him some time—it was only a few hours from Nairobi—to see his house and all the animals, including his pet leopard and a new baby elephant, as well as all the millions of animals on the plain. It must be a very long time since she had seen real bush, with lions as tame as dogs and even the buffalo unsuspicious.

Valerie Dunstan took one long, evaluating look at the robustly healthy young man with the hard-cut nose that saved him from prettiness, and the bronze skin that almost matched his eyes and hair in various tones of tawn—she took one deeper look at the long lashes which the sun had burnt to gold on the tips, and the big even teeth that flashed when he smiled and the light that touched his eyes as he talked of animals as if he owned them all—she took one comprehensive look and said she'd be delighted to go and see his house and meet his animals. It had been so long since she had seen any animals she'd probably not know a lion from a hyena.

They had gone, and had seen the animals, and as naturally as the moon rocked gentle and jolly in a soft-napped, star-frosted sky, Brian Dermott had kissed Valerie Dunstan or Valerie Dunstan had kissed Brian Dermott, with lips as red as the hibiscus bloom she had tucked against her black hair.

They had merged the lengths of their pressed bodies in the night-cooled mimosa-scented air and had heard a hyena howl and a lion roar across the glowing safety of the fire and they had become engaged to be married.

Of course it was marvellous fun out in the bush, and they'd always come back on sort of little picnicky safaris, but really there wasn't any money in the Park Warden business at all, and she knew about the wonderful farm that would be his—or mostly his—some day, when his aunt and uncle died. She wouldn't be lonely on the farm: she would always have him with her if he went back and took over the farm; she adored his little sister and his Aunt Charlotte was a sweetie and Uncle Mac a pet and young Pip a duck and of course they were so close to Nyeri and Nairobi that it would be almost like being in town while having all the advantages of living in the country.

She kissed him again, and Brian Dermott was already one step closer to being a professional hunter of big game, by unwilling way of a farm and a few score dead men, before his head floated down from the umbrellaed tree-tops and his feet touched red Kenya earth again.

CHAPTER SIX

I wonder how many there are left running loose, Brian mused as he drove along well past Meru. There must be some old Mau Mau still hid out in these parts. Gone completely utter bush. I shouldn't wonder. We didn't account for them all when we chased them out of the hills. I suppose there'll always be some living in caves like the old Athi and sneaking down to steal and kill stock. We didn't collar them all in the towns, either. Couldn't smoke them all out. Mau Mau just like the Nazis in Germany. Now they lost the war they never heard of the Party. Odd to remember now that seven years ago ninety per cent of the adult Kikuyu population took some sort of oath.

And so now it's started again, Brian thought. The KKM, or GKM, Land Freedom Army or whatever it's called. Wouldn't be surprised if the odd oathing ceremony isn't being held from time to time on our own farm. Hard to say who was guilty and didn't get caught, and who wasn't and did. But as

Aunt Charlotte says, somebody's got to do the work, even if they took all nine big oaths. Certainly a lot of the smarter graduates are big politicians now.

'Well, there are a few planted around here who won't work any more,' he turned his head and spoke aloud in English to Kidogo, who was sitting beside him with his chin on his chest.

'*Nini?*' Kidogo said. He had been half-asleep.

'I said that there were a few of those bloody Mau Mau around here who won't ever work any more,' he shouted in Swahili over the wind. Kidogo nodded his head and looked pleased at the memory.

'Not even for KANU and KADU and Kaynap. Or any of the other alphabet parties.'

'*Ndio*, Bwana,' Kidogo said, pointing to the left and a little ahead. 'See, Bwana. Do you remember that here is where we had the great luck with the gang leaders? Ho.' Kidogo laughed. 'It was on that far slope over there above the bamboo. I was sitting in a tree. I could see very well when the Bwana Don threw the *bombom* into the huts. They went up like that! People flying through the air like birds.' Kidogo swooped his hands to imitate wings. 'And there was that one woman. She ran out and held her hands to her breast like this.' Kidogo clapped his hands to his chest. 'And then she stopped running with one foot stuck up like this.' Kidogo kicked his bare foot, which was swinging loosely over the Land Rover's door, and then held it stiff in the air.

'She was very funny, too. Like somebody caught her with a noose.'

Brian grunted. 'She was funny all right,' he said in English. 'She was funny because somebody shot her in mid-stride. It might even have been me.'

'*Nini?*' Kidogo asked. 'What did you say?'

'*Hapana*,' Brian said. 'Nothing. Light me a cigarette. Take one for yourself.'

Funny isn't quite the word for it, Brian thought. It seems a hundred years ago. It seems as if it never happened except sometimes at night when I wake up fighting the pillow and find the bed sweated. . . . Then it happened, sure enough. It would be very nice if I could only dream all the dreams on the same night instead of scattering them around. Don says he doesn't dream. I don't believe a word of it. Harry Slater dreamed, all right. He dreamed, and not only at night. He must have had it on his mind when that old cow elephant caught him. Well, he won't dream any more. Day *or* night. She really spattered old Harry around the landscape. Funny about him, too. He really liked the killing until he had to shoot his own gunbearer that day. Then he didn't like the killing any more. Lost his guts entirely. He should have quit professional hunting. Shooting elephants on control calls for more concentration than shooting eight Nigs roped to a log. That was quite a day, too. I'll never forget how dignified they were when Harry turned the gun on them. As if any white man's bestowal of death was beneath that special native scorn.

36

That was just one of the dreams. It began, as the dream always began, at Harry Slater's farm, and it took different turnings on different nights. Sometimes the turning led to a cave. Another time it would lead to the big meadow, where they held the mockgrouse drive. Other times it would lead to the little dell, the place where it might have been so nice to have had a picnic that day. And it always wound up the same way, in a sea of blood, with Brian drowning in it, suffocated by it, like that day at the Cruikshank house. Then blood became Brian, *was* Brian. Everything he touched and tasted was blood, until he awoke sweating and sometimes screaming. Even his wife, when he dreamed of Valerie, sometimes became a headless corpse. He didn't scream so much any more now that he had stopped drinking, because he never slept soundly enough to really let himself plunge back into heavy slumber. The sound of his teeth grinding would always wake him. He drowsed, rather than slept, and mostly he could swim away from the dream before it really overpowered and drowned him.

Harry Slater had a farm, ee-eye, ee-eye-oh. Brian's brain hummed—just like 'Old McDonald had a Farm', in the kids' song. *And on that farm he had some Wogs, ee-eye, ee-eye-oh. With a screech-screech here, and a screech-screech there. Here a scream, there a screech, here a yell, there a scream . . . Harry Slater had a farm . . .*

He had been a rather peculiar chap, old Harry Slater. Most peculiar, old-maidy, even, like some bachelors get to be. He was tall, white-haired, slab-sided, shambling, and the sun and Kenya dust had ruptured veins in his bulging blue eyes, leaving them perpetually bloodshot. He was not a very good example of the romantic ideal of the professional hunter. He was rather a bore with the drinks and lame in the easy chatter around the fireside, but he had been Kenya-raised and he knew game, especially the mountain buffalo and the forest rhino. He always got good trophies for his clients, even if he mostly failed to charm the ladies and flatter the men. He hunted on his own, and farmed half-heartedly in his spare time, like so many Kenya small-holders, who left Africans to tend the farm while they took clients out to kill animals, in order to make money for seed and fertilizer and machinery.

When the Mau Mau terror erupted in the Christmas season of 1952 and the killings extended into the New Year, with almost every night bringing a tale of fresh horror on the wireless, Harry Slater's farm had become a kind of informal headquarters for a hairy band of irregulars, as so many other mountain farms had become communication points for the commandos. They called themselves the *Shenzis*—wild men—and the force was composed of hunters, farmers, policemen, trappers, game wardens, and a few Nairobi businessmen of sporty persuasion. Especially, there were a lot of farmers.

Farming was a poor show in those days, because you needed native man-power to work farms, and your labour lines were either running off to join the Mau Mau or being so terrorized by the Mau Mau that they were worse than useless, or else being collected and penned up by the police as suspects. Farming limped more or less to a standstill, and so, gradually, did professional

37

hunting, because the potential clients were reading the newspapers in London and New York and they were cancelling safaris right and left. You couldn't blame the clients; paying a thousand dollars a week to get your head chopped off seemed a silly way to spend money, even if you could tax-deduct it as a business expense.

Harry Slater's farm wasn't much as farms went, but it stood high in the Aberdare Mountains, and was almost entirely ringed in by Mau Mau activity, so it became a natural gathering-place for farmers who had quit farming and professional hunters who had stopped hunting animals and Game Department blokes like Brian who had quit worrying about native poaching in order to band together and hunt men. Brian Dermott was almost a charter member of the corps. So was Don Bruce, another hunter-farmer and Brian's best friend, and Terry Tolliver, the policeman, and Hal Adams, another game warden, and lots and lots of other ill-assorted people you used to meet around the bars in Nairobi and didn't see so very much of any more.

Before the Mau Mau came Harry Slater's farm was by way of being quite a tidy little place. It had an old ruined settler's shack for the main house, which Harry had converted finically and lovingly into a comfortable semi-hunting lodge, a living-room-dining-room-bedroom of cedar shakes with a big knobby grey-stone fireplace, where Harry often housed his clients when he was hunting buffalo or the big dark leopards that lived on the mountain. And then, as the farm filled with commandos, they took a week-end off from chasing Kikuyu, and using sap-sweating planks rough-cut in Harry's asthmatic little sawmill, threw up a dormitory with double-decker beds, then added a sort of lean-to which became a washroom. It even had a rusted tin tub and a paraffin water heater. There was a small vegetable garden, mostly run to weed, some strayed cattle, and a scraggly flock of chickens and the odd milk-goat or so. But when the weeds bearded the garden finally and the Mau Mau butchered the cattle, and the leopards got the goats and the jackals and serval cats pinched the fowl, Harry Slater stopped pretending to farm and built a barbed-wire enclosure which became a proper prison pen for suspects. It occasionally became over-full of suspects and had to be swamped out, as Brian had thinned rhino to make room for Wakamba *shambas*. It was never very difficult to find a volunteer for the thinning chore, because there was always some new recruit in the Shenzis who had lost a wife or child or near relative or friend to the Mau Mau and so was rendered impatient of the prisoners' space requirements and other housing problems. If nobody volunteered for the pruning job, Harry Slater would do it himself.

Brian was one of the first recruits for this. In twenty-four hours' time in December 1952 he had lost a foster-father, a good portion of his sister, and, it proved shortly, all of a wife. He still had Kidogo to help discharge his legacy of hatred. Brian had no heart for game control any more, when you could not even control the people, nor had he any wish to pursue a settler's life in the brand-new matrimonial wing he had built onto his foster father's house at Glenburnie Farm. Brian's new marriage—and indeed his life—had been interrupted by a Mau Mau raid in which his foster father, Malcolm Stuart, had been abducted and later killed and dismembered to make an oathing sacrifice, and his sister terribly burned when they fired the barn in which she had hidden. It had been a stroke of fortune, really, that Charlotte Stuart had taken Brian's brother and wife into Nairobi to see the doctor that day, and their return had both routed the raiders and saved Brian's sister Nell from burning to death. At first they had not been able to hear Nell's screaming because of the noise the horses were making. As it was, Nell was terribly scarred inside and out by the fire. It seemed in Kenya that Mau Mau attacks always left behind the maimed ones to remind the survivors of the dead. Brian still cursed himself for his absence; he had been off chasing poachers on the Tanganyika border, far from telephones or telegraph. After seeing his sister's face when it came out of the first crude bandages, Brian had not felt much like fretting about rust in the wheat, or even holiday-hunting down Waluangulu elephant poachers as an unpaid favour to the Game Department.

When he kissed his almost-new wife, Valerie, good-bye, Brian had thought that it wouldn't take so very long before everything was straightened out, the guilty punished, and normal life resumed. The hard outline of his game-spotting binoculars had come between him and his wife's soft breast, his pistol intruding between their thighs as they held each other in a brief farewell embrace, with Brian impatient to be off. Symbolically, the essential tools of his trade had remained between him and Val, whether he was hunting the murderers of animals or men. Mau Mau had dragged on and on, and the marriage that never had a chance to start dragged with it a while, and then faltered and finally stopped. Valerie had gone off to England, where she felt safe from the awful little things, such as Brian's drunken impotence in bed, and Brian had gone back to hunting Wogs in the hills.

That was all Brian had of Valerie; that, and then some memories which visited him at the oddest times. You might expect them in the dreams that woke him on the verge of screaming, but they had an insidious way of edging between him and his later waking work; crowding between him and some new girl he was about to kiss, as the man-spotting binoculars and the pistol had come between him and Val, suddenly looming when he should have been concentrating on a wounded leopard in the bush, or looking to the immediate welfare of a client when things took a nasty turn with elephant or buffalo. This troubled him, because he had no desire to die as Harry Slater had eventually died, on a routine chore of herd-thinning up north of the Tana River.

The really-married time with Val had been so short; that was it. That had to be it. Brian could laugh about it now, a short, grating baboon's bark of a laugh. There wasn't any real Valerie Dunstan. She never really existed, and certainly she never existed as Valerie Dermott.

All that remained of Valerie Dunstan now was the alimony cheque the bank sent to London every month. He would think of her idly sometimes, but without much curiosity.

Brian's least frightening dreams were the sportier ones, that everyone had joined in. By God, they had had some sport there after they'd got hardened to regarding men as animals. When Brian had shot grouse later in Scotland, the drives had been just the same, except that on this later occasion Brian had been sitting comfortably on a shooting-stick in a peat-mounded butt, instead of on a naked tree-limb, and what came out of the bush ahead of the beaters actually *were* grouse instead of people.

CHAPTER SEVEN

THE SERE brownness of the north lessened more and more as Brian's Land Rover strained against the steep grade leading to Nanyuki. The trees were taller and greener now—cedar and *podo* and wild fig—the forests deeper now, and blacker and thicker. The vast grazing plains of the Laikipia might be sun-yellowed, but around The Mountain it was always green and lovely, with trout lying still in the pools and bushbuck barking in the little glades and dells, almost in your yard. Brian loved these high green hills around Nanyuki and Naro Moru and Mwega—he had hunted and fished them since he was a tiny boy, running as wild as any Ndrobo youth, hunting buffalo Once he had taken a fleeting shot at a bongo, the rarest, shyest antelope of them all, across the way there in the high hills over the moors this side of the Kinangop. Later he had hunted men in the same hills in which he had almost but not quite killed the bongo. Brian glanced at Kidogo, and the game warden still grained in him brooded about the bongo. All those thousands of hungry Mau Mau forest gangsters had trapped and killed hundreds, maybe thousands, of the big, red white-striped ghostly timid bongo. Maybe the bongo and true wild men, uncurried Ndrobo like Kidogo, were dying off and when the last handful was gone there would never be any more.

No rain here, either, even if the forests were evergreen in the stands of towering fig and aromatic cedar. Nary a patch of cloud in the sky, and they must be screaming for rain on the Laikipia. Brown as your hat and the cattle bawling round the fast-drying boreholes. They won't scream for a while on the Kinangop, but when they do you can hear it all the way across the Aberdare. Passionate farmers, the Kinangop people. Third- and fourth-generation Kenya folk. Rough-handed pioneers, like Brian's people. Never wasted a speck of land, as a rule, and lived close to the Wogs. Everybody surprised eight years ago when the Mickey Mice wiped out the whole Ruck family—

father, mother and child as well. Brian had been camping just about here when he heard *that* on the wireless, oh so long ago.

Brian drove on and presently came on to Nanyuki, the Nanyuki which was one of the social centres of his careless youth, the Nanyuki of the racecourse and the Army barracks and the police post and old Patel's big *dukah*, where all the Patels still called him *Master* Brian. If he drove straight he could go right on down the hill past Thomson's Falls and onto Gil Gil and then stop off for a drink and petrol at Naivasha and make the easy slow crawl up the escarpment with its tremendous long view of the yellow rolling Rift valley, stretching past the old volcano Longonot all the way to Tanganyika and that other mountain where the Masai God lived, Kilimanjaro. *Oh*, his brain sang discordantly, when I was young and a drinking man I used to stop at Naivasha for a quick one and then crawl up the long hill and never stop for a second until I could see Ngong's twin bumps and then a quick dart into the Njogu Inn for another one, and by the time I hit the village I was ready to roar and to roll. The old Njogu Inn, that I never go to any more, like I never use the Thomson's Falls road if I can help it any more. . . .

CHAPTER EIGHT

IT HAD all come finally very clear that day on the hill near the spot the Mau Mau gangsters referred to as Njogu-ini. Brian and Don stopped at the entrance to the thick forest to rest in the shade of a big sacred fig tree the Kikuyu called *mugumo*, where the almost physical presence of Ngai was often felt, and where some of the more devout gang leaders, like Dedan Kimathi, who called himself Field-Marshal, came often to pray and replenish his spirit. It was at the top of the Aberdare, in the formidably meshed bamboo thickets that could turn back an elephant and which sometimes popped like gunshot explosions when the sun first warmed and then caused the expanding gas to burst the bamboo sections. Njogu-ini was on the long ridge of thick-wooded highland, some twelve thousand feet up, which extends to the Aberdare forests from Mount Kenya.

'I must say you're an ugly basket,' Don Bruce said to Brian Dermott as they leaned back against the fig's superterranean, radish-like roots that drooped like fingers to the ground. 'Here, have a cigarette. It may be the last we'll have for quite a spell.'

'No uglier than you, Othello,' Brian Dermott said, and laughed quietly. 'But I must agree we do make a lovely pair of burnt-cork comedians.'

Both white men were wearing tattered jackets of ill-tanned bushbuck hide, with the hair side out. Their trousers were multi-patched and tattered below the knees. Their long hair was false—kinky wigs plaited and wrapped with twine into short pigtails. Their faces were stained mahogany-black, like their arms and legs and entire bodies under the skins. Brian wore an ammunition pouch of leopard skin slung over his shoulder—Don a similar satchel of monkey hide. Under their hairy jackets belts concealed pistols and long, very sharp knives. Also looped under the belts were short wire strangling-cords with carved wooden handles.

'Jolly good thing we've both sort of niggery eyes,' Brian said. 'At least we don't have to wear contact lenses like some of these baby-blue-eyed blokes in this silly bloody minstrel show we're on.'

Don Bruce chuckled. With his red hair wig-covered, his small snub nose and brown-button eyes, he resembled a huge African.

'I'd hate to go home wearing this muck,' he said. 'Old Peggy'd be a cinch to take a shot at me. What year is it?'

'Nineteen fifty-five.'

'Seems later. Nineteen fifty-five and I'm still chasing these bloody Mickey Mice in the wild wet wood. I thought it was nineteen sixty at least. When I took over the tracker school I thought I'd finished with this Boy Scout nonsense. Wonder what feeble-wit nominated me for this one?'

'Me,' Brian said cheerfully. 'I'm the clodpate in person. It's my last shauri, and I wanted you along for auld lang syne. I'm sentimental that way.'

'Thanks very much for nothing. I was happy on the farm. And I thought you were going off safari-ing with the millionaires? What about this new venture of yours?'

'Cancelled,' Brian replied. 'For the moment. Somebody else's taking them out. The cops asked me to play with this particular part of what looks like the start of a last roundup. Nothing much left now except Himself and a few lieutenants.'

'Well,' Don said, prising a tick off his leg and cracking it on his thumbnail. 'I hope I don't have to sleep under any more mildewed skins with any more gamy gangsters in the next week. I stink bad enough on my own without acquiring any more of that extra, delicious *essence du Mau Mau* that these gallant unwashed knights of the forest have accumulated over the years. Last time I came off one of these masquerade jolly-ups, Peggy said I stank like a polecat for a week. She scrubbed me raw but I still stunk.'

'I don't think we'll have to sleep with them tonight. Kidogo ought to be along any hour—or day—with some fresh gen on this last batch we've so kindly been allotted by the Intelligence types. I told him we'd meet him here in a week's time. Certainly from the sign nobody's been near in a week or more. We're alone at last, my love.'

Don Bruce grunted. He made a face at a Colobus monkey that ran down the tree and paused, chattering, at the forest edge.

'*Shhh*,' Brian said. 'Look there at the edge of the clearing. Poor little blighter.' He tilted his chin. 'Yonder.'

A tiny red forest duiker, not much bigger than a fox terrier, had limped out of the tangled mass of rotting undergrowth, towering ferns and fallen bamboo. Its left forefoot dragged and flopped. Something had caught it, and it had broken free.

'Bastards,' Don whispered. 'See. It's still got a bit of wire looped round its leg. Mau Mau snare.'

Brian reached automatically towards the Patchett submachine-gun which rested against one of the gnarled airborne *mugumo* tree-roots, then dropped his hand.

'Can't shoot it, of course. Can't make noise. Forgot for a second,' he muttered. 'Wait a minute. Keep still. Maybe I can put it out of its misery, poor little chap.'

He fumbled under his hairy jacket for his sheath-knife. The little buck was standing alertly, less than twenty yards away, sniffing into the wind away from the men. He had not yet seen them, and the wind took their low voices away. Brian balanced the knife for a second in his palm and then hurled it sidearm. It took the little gazelle behind the shoulder, sinking nearly to the hilt. The animal tottered, fell, kicked with its three good legs, and lay still.

'Nice going, chum,' Don Bruce said admiringly. 'You can still throw that thing, can't you?'

'It's a good knife,' Brian said. 'I was taught by a good teacher. Old Kidogo.' He walked over to the dead animal, pulled out the knife and wiped it clean on the dead creature's dark red coat. 'Poor little fellow,' he murmured.

'Christ,' he said, as he sat down by Don again. 'I hate snares. I hate any kind of trap. If they'd just kill the things they catch, instead of leaving them dangling or choking and always breaking something. Poor little beast. At least the *fisi*'ll eat him dead instead of alive tonight.'

'Poor old unreformed game warden,' Don said. 'Poor old nature boy turned man-hunter.'

'Hell, I don't mind killing the men,' Brian said. 'They've earned it, and more. What I do object to is the animals. You know, I'll bet the Micks've snared thousands of bongo since fifty-two? Not even the old Mwathi were any better with trip nooses and deadfalls.'

'True enough. They—*psssst!*' Don lifted his chin towards the thick forest. A whistle had sounded.

Brian whistled two short, sharp blasts, and was answered by a long one. He nodded with satisfaction.

'That'll be Kidogo and Company,' he said, looking at a wrist-watch. 'Practically on the dot. We've another three or four hours till nightfall.'

'Good man,' Don said. 'I wonder what manner of surprises the old boy's got up his sleeve for us this evening?'

The old Ndrobo was overdressed, for him. He was wearing a bushbuck hide jacket, hairy side out, and a pair of tattered shorts. He had even gone so far as to acquire a cap of serval-cat fur. He carried a sawed-off shotgun and a spear.

Kidogo took off his cap and scratched his white-woolled skull. Two other men, similarly dressed, had come out of the bush ahead of him. They were both former Mau Mau, recent captives who had seen some momentary, expedient light and were temporarily working with the white security forces' pseudo-gang leaders like Brian and Don against their old comrades of the bush. They carried no guns.

Kidogo grinned, and put out his hand for a cigarette.

'Cows,' he said. '*Ngombe, mingi, mingi sana. Watu, mingi, mingi sana.*'

'How many cows, how many men?'

'I don't know exactly. Maybe thirty, forty men. And women too. Maybe fifty, sixty cows. Big raid last night at Mwega. Maybe come thirty-five miles with the *ngombe*.' He grinned again. 'They tied knots in the cows' tails and made the cows haul them up the hills.'

'How do you know this?'

Kidogo coughed, and looked embarrassed.

'Two men of the gang fell behind. One of them told me.'

'Where are the men?'

'They died. They were very badly hurt in the fight when we captured them. They were very stubborn men.'

'Oh, God.' Brian looked helplessly at Don. 'What are you going to do? I keep *telling* him we want captives and somehow they always manage to die resisting arrest. Where is the gang?'

Kidogo turned and pointed in the direction from which he had come.

'Over those hills there,' he said. 'Perhaps seven miles, maybe a little more. Before they died the men said they were headed for a new place in a clearing at the bottom of a little valley. You cannot see it unless you are very high, and then not well. The bamboo is thick right down to the cup of the valley.'

One of the other Africans now was busily replaiting a pigtail of his partner. The plaits made delousing easier. Brian walked over and touched one man with his toe. The hair-braider looked up and grinned. He had an evil, half-healed scar showing angry pink across his dark face.

'Very recent gallant ally,' Brian Dermott grunted. 'Still bears the stigmata of conversion to the true faith. *You*,' he said, to the grinning man. 'Kimathi's people with the cows?'

'Yes,' the man said too swiftly. 'Kimathi's people. His woman is with him, and perhaps his brother.'

'That's a bloody lie,' Brian said. 'Kidogo was dead right to fetch this sportsman along. I happen to know that Kimathi's slapped a ban on cattle rustling. Makes too much noise—makes too many trails, makes the people careless. Kimathi'd raise hell if he knew. Kidogo!'

'Bwana!'

'Put the handcuffs on them. Here! Use mine for one of them. And rope 'em together. At least one's a bloody liar—old Scarface Al Capone here,' he had resumed English as he turned again to Don. 'Keep an eye on 'em as

44

we go. They can't run far but they may call out or try something tricky. If they squawk shut 'em up any way that's quiet.'

He nodded towards Kidogo. 'If they make a sound——' he drew the edge of his index finger across his neck.

'Yes, Bwana,' Kidogo said and smiled happily. 'I hope the one with the scar makes the first sound.'

There was no difficulty in picking up the track. The raiders had kept to the elephant trails as much as possible, driving their cattle ahead of them, scorning the usual practice of covering their track. The elephant and rhino of the mountain had bulldozed well-defined paths through the heavy mass of windfallen bamboo, and the way was clearly marked with splatters of cow-dung and broken fresh shoots of the young bamboo, crushed ferns and snapped stalks of the low bush.

'We will not be able to see the fires until we are very close, Bwana,' Kidogo said. 'But if they are there as the men said before they died we will certainly be able to hear the cattle bawling before the men can hear us. We can walk boldly for a while, then, and use a single torch held downwards when it becomes fully dark. They will not be able to see it from below. Not in this bamboo. It is woven thicker than a sleeping-mat.'

'Where are my other men?'

'They should not be far. I told them to wait close by another *mugumo* I know. They will be there. They are all good men, I think, and Muema is leading them in my absence. What do we do with these porcupines that we have handcuffed? Would it not be simpler to slit their throats?'

'No. None of that. Nairobi doesn't approve of that. When we come to the other men we will tie them securely and put gags in their mouths with bark and leave them at the *mugumo*. I can't help it if they are afraid of the dark.'

'I don't see why you go to all that bother,' Kidogo said. 'They are not people. They are only Kikuyu.'

When they had stumbled a bit farther along, Kidogo held out his hand, palm pressing backward, and suddenly called like a bush baby. The call was answered, and he called twice again.

He nodded to Brian.

'That would be our people,' he said. 'Come. They will know more.'

A finger snapped twice, making a sound like a breaking twig, as they approached the place where Kidogo said the other nine men waited. In a moment there was a scuffing of the bush and Muema, Brian's broken-nosed Wakamba gunbearer, slithered like a snake through the bamboo.

'Forty-five people,' he said swiftly. 'Only twenty cows now. There were more but one band broke away and scattered and the leader would not let the other men follow. It seems that two or three little *shambas* have all merged together to have a feast, or something of that sort. They have brought the women to take away the meat and dry it, I suppose.'

'Who's the leader?'

45

'I do not know. I have seen one man talking much to the rest, but I do not know him. The leader is certainly not Kimathi. I know that mother-defiler. I should; I had him under my sights once and the gun jammed.'

'Well,' Don Bruce said. 'It seems we collect no Field-Marshals tonight. What do we do now, Daddy?'

Brian pulled fretfully at his moustache.

'I don't like it about the women,' he said. 'But there's no way in God's world we can collar forty or fifty people with our ten boys—not unless we sort of reduce the odds a touch first. *Aghhh*——' he made a gagging noise in his throat. 'I don't like this, but we can't do anything else. We'll throw a half-circle round the camp, creep up as close as we can, and wait until they get stoked full of meat and start to sleep off the jag by the fires. You take Muema and four and I'll take Kidogo and the same. Pity about those other blokes. We could use 'em—if we could trust 'em. But losing them does give us a couple of extra weapons.'

'Roger. What time does the party start?'

Brian pulled off his wig and stuffed it into his pouch before he answered.

'We won't need these flea-catchers any more,' he said, and looked at his watch. 'It'll be nine or ten before we come up to them. There's a little moon —not much, but we can see to crawl the last few hundred yards. I'd say that I'll make a wide sweep round to the far side after you're pretty well posed on our near side. Let's say about four-thirty. That should give every man jack of 'em a full gut and pleasant dreams.'

Don Bruce grinned suddenly, his teeth showing white in the night. Only the whites of his eyes and the teeth were visible against the black of his face.

'What's so funny?'

'I dunno. I was just thinking. Here's me, father of two and another a-building, Honest Farmer Don the ratepayer, out here in the black night with my face full of burnt cork, wearing a wig on my head and contemplating the murder of a bunch of strangers as they lie sleeping off the first full meal they've had in months, probably. And it could even be some of your or my cattle they're eating. It seemed a slightly ridiculous game for grown men to be playing at, that's all.'

'I couldn't agree more,' Brian said. 'I'm getting too old to play cowboy and Indians. However. It's dark enough to risk one more smoke before we crawl on. Stick your head in the hollow tree to light us a couple and keep the coal covered with your hand. It'll be the last for sure now until dawn's early nausea.'

THEY WALKED, stooping, skidding on the bamboo windfallen slippery under foot, cursing silently as their ankles caught in the long withes that seized them with the nagging vehemence of snares. From time to time when the forest gave over to a particularly thick bamboo belt, it became simpler to crawl the smaller game runs, each man following the feet of the man ahead of him. Kidogo had taken the point, with Brian behind him. Suddenly Kidogo made a slight popping sound, like a nightbug, with his tongue snapping against the roof of his mouth, and pressed backward with his palm. A long, gurgling bellow had come faintly through the black.

'*Ngombe*,' Kidogo whispered as Brian crawled silently beside him. 'Cows over there. Maybe three quarters of a mile. I know the place. The men were right. They would go there to camp because it is difficult to see a fire from any distance at all—and then only from directly above. And it is very difficult to get directly above because the slope is long and gradual and very thick. That is good for us, Bwana. There are no open glades—just bush and game trails and the bare spot at the bottom by the little stream. There is a salt lick there, I think.'

I hope they haven't chased any nervous rhino off it, for us to stumble on, Brian thought. That was one of the worst aspects of this business. The big animals, the buff and elephant and rhino, were so frantic from the plastering the RAF had been giving the forests for the last couple of years that they'd charge anything.

Brian felt himself, checking the equipment. Pistol. Check. Handcuffs— missing. But they were on one of the men back at the *mugumo* tree. Strangling cord—all right. The piano wire with its wooden toggles was securely looped in his belt. Knife. *Knife? Knife!*

'I've lost my knife, crawling,' he whispered in Kidogo's ear. 'I've lost my *knife*.'

'You won't need it,' Kidogo said. 'Perhaps we had better pass the word back for Bwana Don to come up with us and bring his people.'

'Right.' Brian snapped his fingers in a twig-crack and the man behind him crawled alongside. 'Word back to the Bwana to come with his men.'

He waited until Don Bruce inch-wormed along the ground on his knees and elbows. The two disguised white men and the two blacks, Kidogo the Ndrobo and Muema the Wakamba lay on the ground together in the form of a cross, their four heads almost touching, their lips within inches of each others' faces as they whispered.

After Kidogo had outlined the basics of the terrain, Brian said, talking tightly with no expression, lips barely moving.

'We'll go round the top, Don. You stop when you can hear the cattle plainly—say a quarter of a mile from the noise. Move using the noise when you—why am I telling *you* how to move? Give me a couple of hours to get round with my people. Make it three—it's nine now. That'll be midnight.

Fan out as well as you can and keep Muema in the middle so he can keep tab on his end. I don't really trust any of these other buckos.'

'Close as we can or safe distance and then make a rush for it or what?'

'You can't rush for it. Bush too thick, Kidogo says. They'd all be gone before you got there. Close as you can but for Christ sake nobody getting in front of anybody else. Understand. Muema?'

'*Ndio*, Bwana.'

'I would say four ack emma would be a nice time to start pouring it in.'

'Suppose we can't keep sked? Suppose something happens and one of my boys—or yours—has to tune up or lose the whole contest?'

'That's why I say give me three hours to get round. I can probably do it in half that, but give me the full three before you start drawing in. If I have to light this thing off, chime in, ready or not. I'll do the same for you. But let's try to keep our kiddies silent until Mummy gives the word at four. Mummy will be me, with Mummy's little baby here.' He patted the sub-machine gun in the dark. 'Understand *saa kumi* Muema? *Saa kumi* Kidogo? Not before unless Bwana Don or I shoot? *Hapan apiga paka ya saa kumi?*'

'Understand,' both Africans breathed together.

'Okay,' Brian said. 'Let's get cracking. Don't get too bored, Don, and don't start anything just to keep warm.'

'I won't. I've got my financial worries to keep me warm.'

'I was kidding. Luck, chum. See you at the head-counting.'

'Luck.'

They won't get bored, Brian thought—not at the idea of only three or four hours to wait. These are the boys who can lie silently and never flick an ear for two, three days at a time in the cold and that ever-dripping rain. These are the boys who don't have to ask Teacher's permission to go.

They were able to make most of the long stalk on foot, now, crawling through the meshed bamboo only in spots, for which Brian thanked God, seeing as they'd have to creep that last five or six hundred yards anyhow, and that could easily take two hours of painful wriggling. His hip felt nervously light without his long, haft-weighted knife though. It was like losing an old friend. Maybe one of the tail-end charlies had picked it up. In any case they'd have to retrace the track on the way back to pick up those two gagged johnnies they'd left by the *mugumo* tree. He wanted to find that knife. It was a very old friend and knew his hand.

Suddenly a hunch rippled his spine with light chill fingers. He dug under his bushbuck-hide jacket and took out the strangling cord. This was easier in point of time and expended effort than hands, although he'd used his hands a couple of times. The trouble with hands and stiff-crooked elbows was that you generally needed to get a knee into play, and you also needed space. Wogs were, with grease smeared on them, about as slippery as snakes, and they were difficult to keep a grasp on. Also a man made a lot of noise, arms and legs thrashing about, when you strangled him. This cord was another thing entirely.

48

His fingers traced it knowingly in the darkness. The slim round piano wire never snarled, but kept the fairly stiff shape of its loop. The sandpapered grooved wooden handles were smooth in his grasp. He did not return the strangling cord to his belt, but looped it round his neck and tucked the wooden handles inside his hairy jacket. Now he felt better. He smiled slightly, sardonically in the darkness. Now, as the women said, he had something to do with his hands.

Kidogo was crawling, and he was crawling towards a slight flush of light. The bamboo had thickened until progress was very slow. It was, Brian thought, like trying to force your way through huge wet slick fingers which let you slip a trifle before they dragged you back to squeeze you in the gigantic sopping palm again. Suddenly Kidogo's feet stopped, and Brian crawled abreast of him, waving an arm for the men to circle in.

There was a glow of fire in the sky now, an explosion of showering sparks in the air, but it was impossible to see people or cattle. The slope downhill was gradual; it meant that when they drew in to encircle the camp they would have to crawl very close to the edge of the clearing before they could see anything at all.

'No good trying to watch the elephant through the binoculars when you have to kill him with the spear,' Kidogo grinned at him. 'They are there and there they will stay. We will go all the way round and come down close. It is best not to come very close until late—but we cannot afford to risk being too far away to see to shoot if the Bwana Don and his men shoot first. That is possible: it is clearer on their side than on ours. Someone may see them approach and sound an alarm.'

'You're the boss,' Brian said.

They sweated their way round the top of the ridge in a long, sweeping half-circle, drawing appreciably closer in the downhill direction as they moved, until at midnight they had come to within three or four hundred yards of the enclosure, which they still could not see, but could hear as if it were within touching distance. A sickly moon rode the sky, but its light was too feeble to penetrate the forest. The noise was frightful now, the terrified bawling of the cattle, and certain moans and groans which had not been audible before.

'We go close now,' Kidogo said. 'We go close and wait until you shoot, Bwana. Then we all shoot. *Kwaheri*. Look after yourself.'

'You too, *baba*,' Brian said, touching the old man on the shoulder. *Baba. Father.* Well, Brian thought, out in this stuff he's a pretty handy father to have around. He began to inch forward, crawling towards the sounds, approaching to where the firelight now brightly lit the sky.

CHAPTER TEN

DONALD BRUCE had an easier time of it than he had hoped for. The bush was somewhat thinner on his side of the little valley, which made it easier to crawl but likelier to be discovered. It seemed no time at all—and time dragged when you crawled in the wet sticky compost of a mountain jungle, tearing your hands and barking your knees and being lashed bitterly in the face by whipped-back withes and malevolent thorn-branches. He would welcome the shooting, although he hated the idea. If you had to do it he supposed you had to do it but you didn't have to like it. Some of the boys he knew were getting to like it. But if you didn't like it the faster you did it and got home the better. You could wash most of it off you at home.

He supposed he liked natives, but he couldn't stand it the way they were with animals. They had no conscious feeling of cruelty, evidently. An animal was an animal. He had seen them slowly break each major bone of a goat as they repeated the oath: *If I lie may this oath kill me and my bones be broken as I break the bones of this goat.* He had seen sheep and goats disembowelled while alive, and sewn up again after various things had been taken out and put in. He had seen them tear the eyes out as part of the sacrifice, and skewer them on *kei*-apple thorns. He had seen them catch birds and blind them with thorns spiked through the eyes, laughing as the bird fluttered wildly. They always laughed; it was a big joke to see something hurt or crippled.

They had no feeling for animals—none at all. An animal had no sensibilities. And they carried the same callous cruelty to people if the people were at all outside a circle of friendship or family. He had, then hidden as he soon again would be secreted, once watched a Mau Mau oath-eating ceremony in the earlier days of the Terror—watched it in these same wet cold hills. On that ceremony the brains and heart of a small child had been used. That it was a *black* child, one of their own, had made it all the more horrible. And what made it even more horrible was that the child's father, who would not take the oath, had been forced to watch his son slowly quartered. Then he had taken the oath, eating portions of his own flesh. And then Don Bruce had lifted his Patchett gun lovingly.

He would lift it lovingly again, soon, because what they seemed to be doing to the cattle—he gasped now as he crawled closer and saw the spectacle at the fire clearly for the first time—was as bad or worse as what they did to people. His finger tightened on the trigger-guard—he did not dare trust his hands on the trigger—as he watched.

The gang had driven the cattle into the little bald hollow in the cup of the valley, with the bamboo rising steeply on all sides. There was one high shoulder of rock, with a man sitting on it. He could barely define the man's outline against the blaze of the fire.

A demon's ballet of people and animals was taking place around the fire, which was consuming bamboo stems as thick as your thigh, leaping high and making a tremendous popping crackle, shooting barrelsful of sparks

50

towards the sky. He hoped the fire would die before Brian decided to open the party. It would be difficult to differentiate between the explosions of the bamboo and the explosions of a gun until you saw the bullets kicking dirt and the people dropping. At least they would be shooting downhill and into the ground. After all these years he would hate to have his friend Brian Dermott accidentally on his conscience. He had enough on his conscience already.

Bile rose in his throat. The gangs were very systematized, he thought, biting his lower lip. There was a woman holding the tail of a bellowing cow while laughing ragged men cut its legs off with single sweeps of pangas and simis—or worse, hacked and haggled away until the bone gave and the beast was left to roll like an animated barrel.

Along the line of butchered animals men were moving to wrestle the leg-less cattle's heads around before they sawed into the jugulars and started the blood pumping. Women walked behind the men, catching the spurting blood in bamboo and gourds. Behind the women came the butchers, hacking off shoulders, chopping at rib sections with the heavy saw-edge of the pangas, groping red-handed into the guts for livers and lights, cutting steadily at whole hindquarters. Others were skinning the dead animals, and women were sitting crosslegged on the ground, stripping the large intestines of their dung before they threw the fat whites tubes of gut onto a growing pile—the women cleaning stomachs of digested green fodder to get at the tripes; women scraping great globules of raw fat out of the stomach cavities and cramming the tallow into their mouths with bloody fingers. Their hands and arms were dyed in blood, their faces scarlet-smeared thick and dripping in the leaping firelight.

The living cattle with their amputated legs groaned and bellowed and finally finished with long hoarse rattling sighs as their throats were cut and they bled to death. The killers killed, the skinners skinned, and the butchers butchered. According to some sort of prearrangement, the women of the butchers gathered up the quarters and the sections of ribs and lugged them off inside the edge of the bush. Then they took pangas and started clearing space in the underbush, scything at the young, green bamboos, and now Don saw half-grown children fetching dead firewood of a more substantial nature than the bamboo. No more than twenty yards away from him, a small baby sat cooing and gurgling on the ground as its mother stacked meat into a pile, and another woman began to nurse a fire. The child was playing with the teats of an udder which had been sliced completely off one heifer, bringing the nozzle of one teat to its eager pursed mouth. The growing fire lit the baby's face in the shadows, making it shine.

Don Bruce looked at the radium dials of his watch. Twelve-thirty. Three hours and a half more to lie on his belly in the wet grass and watch an orgy which, painted in its horror by blood and highlit by the leaping fire, looked more like his imaginative picture of The Inferno than anything he had ever conceived. There was one woman below him who had transfixed a calf's

51

whole rib cage on a slashed spear of green bamboo, and the smell was delicious to the nostrils, even if the sight of the still-living cattle with the stumps of legs and the men armpit-deep in butchery was enough to make a vulture vomit. Only twelve-forty now. It was going to be a long, long night. He rested his chin on his crossed arms and watched the devil-dance in the firelight, listening as he watched to the gasping moans of the legless kine.

CHAPTER ELEVEN

THIS IS about as far down as we'd better go for a spell, Brian Dermott thought, and reached ahead of him to touch Kidogo's bare leg. I know what's going on—I don't have to see it. Four little points of light were showing deeper inside the bush, now, which meant that the women would be dragging off their personal chunks of butchered meat and making cookfires. They'd let the big fire die as soon as the butchering was finished. I guess Friend Donald is practically a guest at the feast, he thought. Kidogo said you could see from a longer distance out on that side—bush thinner and patchier. In any case it looks steep enough for us not to shoot into each other. I'd hate to widow Peggy Bruce, her as big as a house with that new *mtoto* she's building in her tummy.

He turned his head slowly towards the old man, who craned his neck until his ear touched Brian's lips. 'We'll spread out now,' he said. 'You keep an eye on three of your blokes, and just get as close to two fires as you can. Don't shoot until I do unless you have to, and don't let those other chaps shoot at all until after you do.' He could feel the old man's earloops move against his mouth. 'I'll leave my bloke here. Tell him. I'll crawl a little lower and over to the left, to where I can take the two top fires. Tell my chap to concentrate on the one nearest him on the left. You take the two bottom ones, right? And pay no attention to the big fire, or to that sentry on the rock. Shoot into the sleepers.' The old man's ear moved again and Brian wriggled off until he found a game trail that twisted towards the little amphitheatre.

This was more like it. Now he could see down into the arena, and what was better, he could command a fair look at the two top small fires. He'd just ooch a touch away from the path and stick his head out from the thick bush for a peek once in a while. Nobody would be leaving those fires permanently in the middle of the night, not once they'd started eating. Eat-sleep-wake-eat-sleep some more. Christ, what a mess they'd made of the cattle. *Agghh.* He choked back a retching sound in his throat. Not the place nor neither the time for queasiness.

It was black as the inside of an elephant here in this bush, Brian thought, which is what makes those doings look so horrible down there in the firelight. I'd like to have some of that Whitehall bunch here in this wet stuff with me, freezing their balls off and watching a gang of future prime ministers capering around those mammocked-up cows, with their self-determinating faces dripping fresh blood and guts. Well, this is a nice snug nest, right here behind this lovely rock, which has probably got a snake under it.

He switched his brain off and lay, cold and brightly awake, staring at the animal trial. He did not want to look at the eating and the carving of the carcasses that was still going on. He could see it through his ears more plainly than he wanted to, in any case. His fingers stroked the action of his short-nosed gun, caressing the safety-catch. He moved slightly and for no particular reason took the strangling-noose from round his neck. He felt the cold wood of the handles, dew-beaded and wet now, and the thin wet wire. It was an old commando silent-warfare trick he'd learned from one of the boys at the *Shenzi* camp. Chap had been in an irregular unit which gave Jerry hell in the old days of the war, when they were shoving those braw Special Force laddybucks ashore in rubber boats, with blackened faces and long knives and various handy little personally improved devices of their own. So simple, really. You just crept up behind your sentry and made sure his head turned away from you. You flipped the loop over his chin and yanked sharply, taughtly tight, twisting with your little wooden handles and *zaz*—just like one of those wire-cutters through a cheese. No muffled yells, no kicking and thrashing and unnecessary noise out of those blokes. Not with this dandy little piano-tuner. No manhunter should ever be without one. Three A.M. now. The time *does* fly when you really know how to wait. Matter of congealing your head in aspic like a potted shrimp.

Hsssst. Brian's brain wriggled out of its aspic. Something was coming along that game trail. Coming up from the fire. Coming his way. He froze inside. It was a man; a man making no attempt to step softly. *Why, out of all the game trails in the Aberdare does he have to choose this game trail as the way to the men's room?* Brian's brain asked: *Why not any other game trail? Why does he have to be so bloody fastidious about a leak?*

The feet kept coming closer. It was a man all right. Scuffling along on the track. Coming closer. Why doesn't he do his business and get it over with? Brian's brain was actively annoyed. I hope that *nugu* I've got with me over there to the right doesn't go jumpy on me and cut loose with his chopper. Don't shoot, Gicheru or Kungo or Percy or whatever your name is. Let the nice man enjoy himself. It'll be his last good one in this life.

Here were the feet now. They were stopping in the game trail directly opposite Brian's face. about a yard away. Lying with his feet uphill, chin downhill, Brian found himself looking at the calves of the man's bare legs. They were bare because the man wore shorts. Brian knew he wore shorts because he was now dropping the shorts. He had come to relieve himself, that was certain—and right by Brian. Too much rich fresh meat eaten too fast on a shrunk stomach. Gone straight through this gentleman, no doubt,

53

which is what fetched him from his sleep of the just by the cozy fireside in the bosom of his dear family. Oh, Lord, please let him be brief in his natural functions and go away. Watching the man's backside lower itself seemed fascinating to Brian. Did the man have no cartilage in his knees at all? Lower, lower, and suddenly the man was startled by some slight noise in the bush, as an animal rolled a rock or perhaps one of Brian's own men moved slightly.

The squatting man, startled, lost his balance briefly, reached out his right hand to steady himself and placed his palm firmly on Brian's fur-capped head. His gasp and Brian's lunge came together. Brian's chest crashed into the man's shoulder as the noose flashed up and leaped like a silver serpent around the man's throat. Smothering the man's body with his own, Brian jerked once with both hands, sharply, then twisting and hauling on the handles. Suddenly there was no more head on the body that pumped and jerked convulsively under his own as he seized the thrashing arms and pinioned the kicking legs.

After a little while only the man's neck pumped and all else was still except for quivering. Brian moved slowly off the headless body, raising himself an inch at the time by stiffening his arms and legs. What was on his chin and neck dripped. He slid himself backward, now, slowly off the body, and when he had got clear of it he took his wig out of the ammunition pouch and wiped his face and throat carefully, then threw the pigtailed wig away. There was nothing he could do about the front of his coat. It would just have to stay wet until it stiffened on the bushbuck hair and it would stiffen very quickly at this altitude. Blood congealed swiftly in the cold.

What a business, Brian thought, actively irritated at the dead man. Business of blood and other people's bowel movements. I can't risk waiting here in case this sportsman's old lady misses Daddy in the night and comes prowling back here to search for him. I better just get myself down there to the camp-fire and find a cosy place to rest my *bunduki* and be ready to open the betting if anybody else seems restless. I would say that a good safe range for elephant is thirty feet. That ought to be enough for a parcel of sleeping Mickey Mice.

Brian cleaned his throttling-noose with a handful of leaves and stuck it in the ammunition pouch. He didn't want it round his neck any more right now.

He made no attempt to wriggle through the thicker stuff now, but went carefully on his hands and knees down the game trail, pushing his gun ahead of him. The trail broadened more and more as it came closer to the opening by the salt lick, and the going was easy. He looked at his watch as he made a frequent pause to listen. It was three-thirty anyhow, and time enough. Everybody'd be set by now and waiting for the first note on the old tuning fork.

Ah. This was fine, right here. Nice little bit of rock. Just about the right height to steady an elbow on. Nice and comfortable for a bloke's knees, as well. Mustn't do to get cramps in my knees. Mercy, no. Cramps very bad for knees. Extra clips, fine. Action—e-a-s-y. Action, fine. Nothing in the muzzle. No sticks, stones, harmful irritants, blonde hairs. lipstick marks?

None. So far so good. Let us see what we have here before us, apart from a low, dying fire and a pile of bloody cowmeat. Awful lot of snoring going on —maybe these blokes had some booze along as well as food. Maybe they're making their own *pombe* up here now. Nothing would surprise me about these chaps. Imagine. A whole herd of cattle forty miles through bush that would discourage a snake in some spots. And killing and slaughtering as casually as if it were the abattoir outside Nairobi. Then eating a gutful and lying down to sleep it off as calm as you please. I'll never understand Wogs all the way. They'll always surprise you.

One-two-three-four-five-six-seven-eight—eleven men and five women at this little hearthside. How about the other? Seven-nine-fourteen and only three women. I bet these women are kept pretty busy on the balmy moonlight nights. *What* a thought. They must have sentries somewhere. Not that it makes a damn if everybody's as close as me. *Oops, watch it there, Jack, you're rolling into the fire. You'll burn yourself.*

A man, lying with his knees drawn up towards his chin, had flung out one hand in his sleep and it come to rest on a core of glowing coal. As he raised, cursing, to rub at his hand, he looked straight at Brian.

Brian lifted his Patchett gun slightly and sliced the man in half, then depressed the muzzle and swung the barrel in a slow sweep along the sleeping figures by the fire. He slapped in another clip and swept the gun again to the second fire, twenty yards away, where people were beginning to sit up in bewilderment as the guns of Brian's people began to chatter on two of four sides of the enclosure. The sentry slid off the rock and Brian saw him fall as somebody, possibly Don, to judge from the succinct burst, cut him down. After a while, when he quit shooting and looked at his watch it said four-zero-two. He nodded in self-commendation, and stood up to yell for a cease-fire. Those that were leaving had left. Those that hadn't left weren't going anywhere.

CHAPTER TWELVE

WHEN DAWN had pushed some reluctant lemon light into the sky, Brian stood up and bellowed for the men to come into the clearing. There had been no casualties on his side. The gangsters, what few had got away, had run off without firing a shot. Which was logical enough, Brian thought. There wasn't anything visible for them to shoot at, even if most of them hadn't taken off without some of those curious handmade zip guns which his people were now collecting. His eye caught one—quite a fancy Mauser arrangement on that one, he thought admiringly, particularly when you considered its owner tooled the action out of a brass door-bolt.

55

A couple of the maimed cattle and some half-dozen of the people, mostly women were still alive. Brian saw Don Bruce walk over to the cattle and heard the jumping *bump-bump* of his weapon as Don put the muzzle close to the cattle's heads to finish them off. One of the wounded Mau Mau men made a flopping effort to get up, a *panga* in his hand, and Don swung the gun-barrel lazily away from the cattle and shot the man in the head.

'*Naughty*,' Don Bruce said to the half-headed man. And then to Brian:

'How'd you like to have *this* for breakfast every morning, along with your *East African Standard*?'

He swept a hand around the black bare circle of burned-off grass, where some of his men were kicking the big fire into a blaze again. It was still very cold in the dew, with the sun not yet high enough to burn the clamminess off the keen mountain air. It was a scene from a butcher's shop in Hell, with the dead cattle and the dead people mingled with half-fleshed carcasses and stacks of fresh bloody raw meat in an arena that was gummy with the blood of both cattle and men. The flies were already heavy-footed, and the vultures swam in slow lazy circles in the sky.

'The only thing I ever saw worse was on elephant control in the Turkana country,' Brian said slowly. 'All the Turks came for miles around with their women and knives and spears. They actually crawled into the dead elephants' backsides looking for titbits. Bloke prowling inside one Jumbo got stabbed dead by his cousin, who was working with his spear on the outside. But at least the elephant were dead before the Turks started cutting them up. Not like these——' his eyes raked the sprawled black bodies on the charred sward, watching the few wounded who sat up now and stared with dumb hurting eyes. They were lean and filthy and stank to the skies. From the healed scars of thorn-wounds and general filth of patch-on-patch clothes and length of beard and hair, some of the men must have been in the hills for two or three years. They seemed, in their reeking hide jerkins and make-shift pants, considerably more animal than human, and were all in miserably thin condition. Life had been hard in the mountains for the last two years—a long desperate cry from the arrogant early days when the Movement was popular and the women in the *shambas* ran a steady courier service of food and clothes and medicines and arms to their heroes hiding in the forests.

'This *is* a sort of elephant control, if you want to think of it that way, and I do want to think of it that way,' Brian continued slowly. 'Everything these bastards do is unnatural and against their own beliefs and their own people —Well,' he broke off briskly. 'Let's count the corpses and cut off the hands for the fingerprint boys and see if any of these wounded are portable. Personally, I see precious little sense in lugging them back through this beastly bamboo just so the law can stretch their necks in Nairobi, What do you think?'

'I'm a lousy witness,' Don Bruce said. 'I arrived at the show early. I saw what they were doing to the cattle.'

'I am going into the bush,' Brian said to Kidogo. 'The Bwana Don is going with me. We have wasted much ammunition. Your men must learn to improve their shooting. Do not waste any more ammunition.' His eyes flicked the wounded briefly. 'If any more cattle are alive, put them out of their misery.'

Kidogo nodded.

'Yes, Bwana. It is not good to see things suffer. But Bwana?'

'What is it?'

Kidogo jerked his head toward the bush.

'By one of the fires. Come with me. There is a dead woman.'

Brian walked into the bush until they came to the place into which he had first shot when the man rolled over and burned his hand. There was small movement in a tangle of bodies.

'*Mtoto*,' Kidogo said simply. 'See. Its mother is dead, but the child is unhurt. Shall I . . .'

A small black round face with terrified eyes peeked from the cold nest of its dead mother's arms. It had huddled close to the body for warmth but was shivering now in the morning chill. Its nose had run and the snot had caked on its lips. But it had not cried, was not crying now. Perhaps it had been taught from infancy *not* to cry, as the Red Indians were said in some books to teach their papooses not to cry.

'Yes,' Brian said. 'You might as well. Poor little chap, no mother, no father, no future—No!' he suddenly shouted. 'No, God damn it. *No!*' He went over and picked up the child, which suddenly opened its mouth and screamed. Brian handed it hastily to Kidogo.

'Wrap it in something and give it to one of the men to carry. We will take it back to the farm and give it to one of the *shamba* women to raise.'

Kidogo smiled.

'That is what I expected, Bwana,' he said. 'I had already named it.'

'What did you name it then, *mzee*? This makes you its foster father.'

'Foster father with *you*, Bwana. I named it Karioki—the one who is restored to life.'

'Well, find something and blow little Restored-to Life's snotty nose and let's get on with searching these people for anything we can find that's useful for the Bwana *Think*.'

Kidogo snatched a *shuka* from the body of the child's mother and wrapped the baby in it. The child, which seemed to be about two years old and reasonably well-fed, quieted when the smell of his mother's body in the clothing wrapped him round. They walked down to the clearing again, where the men were methodically cutting the hands off the corpses and searching the clothes and parcels. There were thirty-nine dead in all—eight women, two young girls, six youths who were little more than boys, and the rest bearded, scarred veterans of flight and raid. There were no wounded—they had obviously died of their wounds.

Some of his men had taken pieces of the fresh meat and were cooking it round the fire. Brian started to say something, and was stopped by Kidogo's hand on his arm.

'No, Bwana,' he said. 'These men were Mau Mau themselves only yesterday. They were Mau Mau and animals and now they are hungry and the cattle are dead anyhow. They cannot bring the cattle back to life and it is a shame to waste good meat if you are hungry. Let them eat.'

'All right,' Brian said. 'But I want to get out of here. Where's Bwana Don?'

'Coming,' Don Bruce's voice bloomed suddenly from the opening of the trail where Brian had hidden. 'I say, Brian, I stumbled over something in that game path. Gave me the fright of my life. Black gentleman with no head. You?'

'Me. Unavoidable. He had to spend considerably more than a penny, and he chose me as his latrine site just before the fun started. There wasn't anything to do but use the old Rachmaninoff approach.' He touched the throttling-wires that looped from Don's belt. 'C-sharp minor.'

'Well, chum, it may interest you to know that I am a thorough type. I scouted round in the bush a little to see if I could locate the rest of our friend, and I did. The expression was rather nasty, but identification is unmistakable. You may not have collared any Field Marshals, but you have just removed the head from the neck of a proper General. The man who came to call on you, my boys tell me, is none other than General Kerogi himself—the jolly old Poisoner. For this I imagine you get another gong. He'd be about second or third to Kimathi now, I shouldn't wonder.'

Brian grunted.

'Teach him to choose his latrines with more care in heaven,' he said. 'Come on, for Christ's sake, let's get out of this slaughterhouse. The flies are getting me down, and it's not fair to keep the deserving vultures waiting.'

'All right. I couldn't agree more. We still have to retrieve those chaps we left at the *mugumo*. I say, what's that Kidogo's got? As I live and breathe, it's a child.'

'Ours,' Brian said. 'Yours, mine and Kidogo's. We're co-fathers. The poor little brute's mother was dead—*she* was one of mine, too—and for all I'll ever know his father was the character I guillotined in the game trail. Least we can do is to take him back to the farm and settle him on one of the *shamba* women. Aunt Charlotte won't mind. She's dotty on kids, black *or* white.'

Don shrugged.

'Maybe it'll buy you a credit in the Hereafter,' he said. 'But not if the brat's papa sees you first.'

They picked up their guns and called to the men, who fanned out ahead, sniffing on the blood spoors of the wounded who had fled into the bush, of the unwounded who had run away. Tonight, tomorrow, the score would fatten as the trackers used their polished skills and savage knowledge of the bush to hunt down the men with whom they had slept and eaten as recently as last week. Brian noticed that Kidogo was carrying the child himself, slung in a sort of packsack as the Kikuyu women carried their children. He had given his double-barrelled shotgun to one of the other men to carry for him. Already the vultures were sliding down from the sky, to perch in a semicircle around the butchered cattle and scattered handless corpses of the stripped people.

They alternately walked and crawled through the bush until they reached the clearing on the edge of the forest where they had left the handcuffed men. The men were not there—only a tattered piece of clothing, a twist of rope, a shred of hat, the handcuffs and some scattered blood-scabbed bones. Two paunch-heavy vultures got up from the ground and flopped heavily away, and from deeper in the bush came the wrangle of hyenas.

'You were pretty psychic about the hyenas,' Brian said, as he looked at the blood-scuffed ground and touched a gristly shinbone with his toe. 'Must have been rather nasty, at that. Poor bastards.' He shuddered slightly, and looked at his hands.

'If I weren't certain before, I'm certain now,' he said. 'The people are finished, the animals are finishing, and I'm finished. This last bit finishes me.' He flexed his fingers and then put his hands behind him, out of sight.

'And if the country's finished, I might as well help it along. How would you like to tie up with a safari company, Don? We'll hunt animals for the rich people and make some money out of the Decline before it Falls, and leave political enlightenment to the younger boys with the stronger stomachs. What do you think?'

Don Bruce looked at the towering *mugumo*, the prayer fig, with its small many-doored cathedral of exposed roots, and then turned unconsciously in the direction of Mount Kenya.

'Anything you say, Boss,' he said. 'When the farm will allow me, I'm your man. Now come on—let's get out of here and clean up before we get drunk.'

'Why do we have to wait until we're clean to get drunk?' Brian said, and started walking down the hill, his gun held by the barrel over his shoulder, with Kidogo and the child following along at his heels. In the distant bush a rhino whuffed and a bushbuck barked, and above the towering trees, the vultures still sailed in the clean blue sky. Don Bruce handed his friend a knife.

'I found it on the trail,' he said. 'You ought to be more careful. You might never come across a fine knife like that again.'

CHAPTER THIRTEEN

BRIAN DECIDED on the just-opened new road that bypassed Nyeri, and pointed the car towards Thika and Nairobi. You overshot everything on these brave new European roads these days. Only ten, twelve years ago—ten minutes, it seemed—and the only decent hardtop you had was what the

Eytie POWs built down the escarpment on the Nairobi-Naivasha track. Pretty soon you'd have the long straight four-lane from Nairobi to Nanyuki, a mere couple of hours sloven driving, when my God, it used to be pulling eye-teeth, the red dust choking you in the dry, the roads grease-slick and murderously sticky in the wet. Before long you wouldn't be seeing the 'wet-weather' and 'dry-weather' alternate road signs any more. Humming on raceway wheels over the new broad black-top outside Nyeri, he felt vaguely regretful that you didn't have to go through the little towns any more. You lost touch with the people that way. Nyeri was such a pretty town, especially when the jacarandas and bougainvillaea and frangipani and kaffirboom were all in bloom at once, the great purple and pink and white and red blossoms quarrelling with each other for attention in the eye, like dressed-up natives at a big *ngoma*. And he missed stopping at Fort Hall for a beer and a sausage roll with his little Wahindi chum at the *dukah* there. Beer . . . even on the tarmac his mouth was dry and the thought of a long cool one came and was put as swiftly out of his head. No more cool beer for you, Dermott me lad, he said. And a bloody Coke isn't worth the trouble of stopping.

'*Hapana simama shamba yako?*' Kidogo had asked as Brian nailed the accelerator to a steady sixty after they'd passed the turn-off to Naro Moru, where Aunt Charlotte's farm was. 'No stop your farm?'

'*Hapana,*' Brian said. 'We'll see the old Memsaab and the rest of the people tomorrow. I want to be in town before lunch and we'll only get held up at home.'

'*Ndio,*' Kidogo said, and went back to sleep. One of the more comfortable things about Kidogo, Brian thought, is that he never argues on my grounds. I wonder what he thinks about, or if he thinks at all, when he's out of the bush? I wonder if there's really anything under that black hide but living machinery when he's out of the bush?

The Nairobi road was thick with traffic, as the half-finished construction job presented the usual road-blocks of old petrol tins, and time-wasting labourers, while the mighty rollers smoothed the hot wet-glistening tarmac. The crinkled hills should have been greener, but it hadn't rained here in a long time, and the native crops looked dusty and sadly sparse. Crops stayed green up high behind him because there was always some cloud around The Mountain and the Aberdare slopes. The settlers had surely known what they were up to when they chose a huge hunk of the Highlands and pro-scribed ownership to the farmer-blacks. Brian had flown over the whole area a few weeks before. You always got the picture much better from the air. When you were up there with the birds, another spot in the sky, you could see the mapping of the glossy deep green coffee *shambas*, the brighter stretches of wheat, and later on the snow-drifted fields of pyrethrum blossoms, the big money crops. You could see the black-green clumps of tended trees that made windbreaks, and the paler shades of the spiky sisal. Sisal was money again, he mused. It fell off terribly after the war, when they were trying to substitute nylon and the other laboratory synthetics for everything.

I guess they found that there were some things you could still do better with the old things. Like a rope for hanging, he thought suddenly. When they string up Peter Poole tonight you can bet it won't be nylon that snugs around his neck. It'll be honest homely hemp, twisted into rope in merrie old England.

It was a big market-day somewhere, he reckoned, as he saw the streams of Kikuyu women walking, bowed under donkey-loads of bananas. Here was one young woman, all fancied up for the market-place in her best *shuka*. She was even wearing a brassière; they'd become very popular in the last year or so. Her *shuka* was gaped open in the front, the better to show the shrieking patchwork pattern of the home-made bra. She forked a baby on her hip, and toted a load of bananas on her back, noosed by the carrying thongs that graved deeply into her forehead. There was another small baby in the crook of her arm, and by all outward signs another *mtoto* well along in her stomach. In the old days you wouldn't have seen that, not even when I was a kid, Brian thought. In the old days before brassières got stylish they needed heaps of wives, because they had tribal laws against sleeping with their women while the women were still nursing babies. If a chap didn't bestir himself and buy himself some extra wives, he went without bed-comfort for about two years after his woman became heavy with child. They weren't so dumb in those days. Even killing the firstborn twins made sense. Too much strain on the mother. Everything they used to do had a reason. A woman couldn't work in the potato fields while she was feeding one baby at the breast and carrying another in her belly.

The men, he noticed, had changed even more than the women and seemed to be changing that much more each year. You had to go really deep into the bush up past the Kinangop, maybe, to see the old-time Kyukes, away up in the hills where the hut consolidation schemes hadn't taken full effect and the Kikuyu still lived in little isolated patches of mud-and-wattle beehives instead of in bloody great villages. There you'd still see the occasional elder in a monkey-skin cloak, and at least the standard male uniform was the old Army overcoat and the rain-melted hat. And still some bare feet. But the men you saw about now, even out from the towns, all seemed damned well dressed.

They look like a new race, he thought—even in ten years they look like a new race. All the smart-alec young bucks in town, with their fancy 'uhuru' uniforms, white shirts and black pants and red neckerchiefs, giving you the V-for-victory sign and the loud '*Uhuru*' hail when you say '*Jambo*'. *Hello* has now turned to *Freedom*. Or death if they don't get it—and maybe Death if they do.

'And *Uhuru* to you too, chum!' Brian yelled, as a straggling line of Kikuyu men gave him the *V* sign and shouted '*Uhuru!*' at the speeding car. Brian reversed the *V* hail to where he was looking at the palm of his hand, and the jabbing upward thrust of his spread fingers was the vulgar sign of the classic insult. '*Uhuru* to you, and see how you like it when it comes! Right up the backside!'

Uhuru, indeed, *L'indépendence* in the Congo. They couldn't spell freedom, let alone define it, much less practise it. Their freedom was a freedom to kick hell out of each other. Brian nudged Kidogo, who blinked his eyes and grinned. His fantastically flexible horny feet almost clasped each other.

'*Uhuru*,' Brian said, watching him out of the corner of his eye. 'And how will you have your *uhuru* when it comes? In a package or in a bottle? Will you eat it on the spot or take it with you to count in quiet? Will you bury it in a cave? Speak up, you grub-eating future prime minister.'

'Huh?' Kidogo was not quite awake. '*Nini?*'

'I said "*Uhuru!*" Freedom, you bloody *nugu*! Don't you know what freedom is?'

'*Hapana*,' Kidogo said. '*Hapana iko uhuru*. I haven't got any. Did you wake me up to ask me that?'

'Sure.' Brian liked to talk to Kidogo in English, of which Kidogo knew possibly six words, all of which were affixed to 'bloody'. 'Everybody's jabbering about *uhuru* now. It's all the rage. What kind of *shenzi*, what sort of wild man are you, you don't know about *uhuru*?'

'I don't know what you're talking about,' Kidogo said with dignity. 'If you want me for anything sensible like a flat tyre, wake me up.' He turned his back, hunched down in the far corner of the front seat, and went back to sleep again. Brian grinned. There weren't many Kidogos left, either, and just one was worth a million of these damned dressed-up spivs you saw these days. He swerved his car to avoid a head-on collision with a Volkswagen full of Africans, which pulled around a big Moslem construction-lorry at the top of a hill. Brian cursed. The Africans in the Volkswagen had laughed at him as he was forced to pull out of their way. The Volkswagen had a *Learner* sticker on it. You saw more and more Africans in motor-cars these days. Used to be that a bike was the limit of affluent aspiration.

He was in thick sisal country now, and the great spears of the rubbery-looking plants were coated with inches of grey dust. There was one thing to be said of sisal. It might take you seven years to make a money crop, but it was a hard plant to discourage once you had it well and truly going. It didn't mind dry weather. Sisal, Brian thought, is one of the many big differences between the African peasant farmer and the white settler. Just show me a Nig who'd wait seven years for a return on a seed he planted—or for that matter, show me a Nig who would really bleed and suffer over coffee and tea the way you have to midwife it before you start to pick the money berries. Maize they'll grow and potatoes and wheat, because you can sling it in after you've burnt off the high grass and something'll poke its head up so you can chop it off and sell it in the market. Cane they'll grow because there's really no way you can keep sugar-cane from growing. *Shauri ya mungu*—that good old God's business. But do you think they'd plant a tree on purpose to fend the wind off the crops? Cut it down, to watch it fall, more likely. Buggers chopped 'em all down, all those lovely cedars and gums and wild hyacinths, and used them for firewood. Let the land blow away. Serve 'em damned well right if it all wound up in the Indian Ocean. *Uhuru.* Everything free to waste —even the land. *Our* land that *we* made. Brian was coming into Nairobi now, into Muthaiga, into proper white man's comfortable country once again.

He turned off the tarmac into a gravelled drive which wound through a neatly clipped lawn, under tall trees of jacaranda and the rosy kaffirboom. Some recently cut-back frangipani, old ones with gnarled boles and thick, rough branches like a working-man's stubby fingers, thrust their waxy pinkish-ivory flowers and faint fragrance at him as he drew the Rover to a halt in front of an open car-port. It was a pretty convenient block of flats at that, far enough out of Nairobi to be quiet, and with the Muthaiga Club just across the road, in case a bloke craved a drink. Well, if not a drink, in case a bloke wanted to shoot a round of golf or chat with somebody at the bar. Trifle stuffy, trifle Poona 1902, the old Muthaiga, very *pukka sahib*, but still the best the town afforded, and there was a time when Muthaiga as a district was *the* place to live. Of course that was before the town went completely mad and started having convulsions all over Ngong and out Hurlingham way. We've got more boulevards than Paris, and more cinemas than London, Brian mused sourly. And we've even got a Drive-In. This one-time buffalo-wallow, this elephant track, is a metropolis now. It has a drive-in theatre. *Uhuru* to the lot. I'm filthy with honest NFD soil and I shall wash and climb into my hanging-clothes. Neat blue, I suppose, for such a solemn occasion.

*

Brian mounted the laddery stairs to a second-floor apartment and unlocked the back door. He noticed automatically that somebody'd left the scrub bucket and mop on the porch. He'd give Kidogo a few bob and drop him off at the safari-stores on the way in. He should have done that before but he hadn't thought of it, woolgathering the way he'd been. Might as well let the blighter keep sleeping in the car right now. He wouldn't know what to do if you let him in the house. He never sat on a chair in his life. Chairs were for later—after *uhuru.*

Brian opened the door and flicked a light-switch. It was a small flat, small for Kenya, which ran to big families, and not a very well-furnished one. He had had it for a long time—since just after Valerie had left for London. This flat was just what it seemed—an adequate convenience for an occasional city-dweller. What was it the American girl, the ardent naturalist-photographer, had called it? A 'fornicatorium'? Valerie had spotted that aspect of it, on this last trip. She wouldn't stay in it.

That's what it was, no doubt about it. A place to keep your city clothes and to bring a woman for a fast impersonal roll if the signs seemed affirmative after a long night on the town. A fornicatorium, with a big divan and a couple of overstuffed easy chairs and a small fireplace and a real, genuine, imitation Kirmanshah rug from Mombasa on the floor. A not-too-expensive record-player and a stack of modern records, some of them now divested of their covers. A small bar with a lock-up liquor cabinet in the corner. An impersonal row of books—detective junk brought back from safari, and a few modern novels in bright jackets. Some hasily purchased hunting prints on the rough plaster wall. Two bedrooms and a bathroom and a small kitchen with an electric icebox and a lockable food cupboard. Nothing to identify it with a home. It looks more like a hotel room than a hotel room, Brian thought, and today I'm not the only occupant.

Brian went into the kitchen and noticed half a dozen used glasses standing on the sink, some coffee cups and a couple of plates, stacked but not washed, beside them. There was new beer and Coke in the refrigerator, and part of a carton of eggs. Butter was in a covered dish, and somebody had opened a jar of jam.

'Pip,' he said. 'Brother Philip, come to town to play house with that girl of his. Sloppy young bastard.'

Brian entered the bedroom and saw that one bed was rumpled, still with a sleeping dent in the pillow. A shirt, a pair of drawers and some socks were tossed into one corner, and a trench-coat was flung across the foot of the bed.

'Pip, all right,' he said aloud. 'I'll leave him a nasty note and ask him to lunch at the Norfolk.'

Brian sang off-key in his shower. Considering that I came to town dead sober for a hanging, he thought, as he soaped the Northern Frontier lava-dust out of his thick, greyed hair, I feel pretty cheerful. A real drink would make me feel cheerfuller, though. After he had showered he ran a tub and lazed in the water for fifteen minutes or more. He could feel the ingrained topsoil of the NFD melting out of his pores. Then he switched on the shower again, cold this time, and yelled as the icy needles pricked him. He shaved very carefully, and walked in his shorts to the living-room to pour himself a Coca-Cola. He pushed once more the thought of beer from his mind.

He opened the door of the clothes-press and flipped a finger over the line of hanging suits. There was quite a selection for a poor white hunter, he thought. Poor white hunter, my foot. I'm the Dermott you read about in the *Saturday Evening Post*. I'm the *Reader's Digest* Dermott. I'm the *Life Goes on Safari* Dermott. I am the dude hunter, the international society pet. My aching ass, he thought, it's all front and I am twice as phony as the movie stars I stand in for from time to time. What I am is a lousy bush-ranging animal nurse, and I'd go back to it like a shot if I thought the country had a chance.

They were nice clothes, though, well and carefully chosen with a keen eye to quiet. Most were English, but some of the evening and sports wear was Italian, and he had a whole closet of American sports clothes which had been more or less forced on him by the American client who'd had him visiting in Palm Beach and Nassau that time. Beautiful stuff in cashmere and light tweeds and fine supple broadcloth and heavy Italian silk. Brian liked clothes, and besides, dressing well was good business. Now he chose a double-breasted blue suit he fancied especially, and took a stoutly treed pair of black calfskin shoes from a neat row in the closet.

After he had dressed, with the exception of his coat, he scribbled a note to his brother and propped it on the bar. Then he slipped into a shoulder-harness that was hanging in the closet, and dipped a hand into the khaki musette bag with which he always travelled. He took a short-barrelled ·38 Smith and Wesson police special revolver out of a scabbard and slipped it into the shoulder holster. Then he put on his coat and snugged it around his body. The bulge under his left arm was barely noticeable. He locked the door and went out to the car. Kidogo was awake.

'You look very *maridadi*, Bwana. You going hunting for a woman or you going to kill somebody?'

'Neither,' Brian said, sliding under the wheel.

'Then why are you wearing a gun under your arm?' Kidogo asked. 'If you don't want to kill anybody?'

'Mind your own business,' Brian said, pressing the starter. 'I'll drop you at the stores, and you can spend the night there. We'll go back to the Farm tomorrow and see the Memsaab Mkubwa and Memsaab Nell for a little while before we go north again to the safari.'

'That's good,' Kidogo said. 'Just like old times in the Mau Mau.'

'How like the old times in the Mau Mau?' Brian asked idly, turning into the road.

'Well,' Kidogo said. 'In the old days, when you left town you took off your necktie and your pistol and threw them both into the back of the *gari*. Then when you came back to town you put the necktie and the pistol back on. That's why I asked you if you were going to kill somebody.'

'Well, I'm not,' Brian said. 'Here. *Ha-yah*. Here's some money. Don't get drunk. I'll see you tomorrow.'

Kidogo looked vaguely disappointed when he got out of the car.

'We haven't killed anybody for a long, long time,' he said, and walked off to the stores where Brian kept his safari supplies and tenting equipment.

Looking at the thin, thorn-scarred black legs under the shabby khaki shorts, seeing the almost frail-appearing set to the lean shoulders under sun-bleached, much-patched jacket, seeing the big splayed toes and the long horny heels kicking up little puffs of dust as Kidogo walked towards the stores-shacks, Brian felt suddenly a wave of tender paternal concern for the savage wearing only his old cast-offs and his knife in the sheath; the savage shorn of his spear, lonely and misplaced away from the desert and mountains. He looked so—so sort of *small* and defenceless and out of his depth in town. He looked neither small nor defenceless when he was naked among elephant, or track-ing men. "Dogo!" Brian called, without knowing why.

Kidogo stopped and turned his head.

'Bwana?' His hand reached round to scratch the small of his back.

'Nothing. Take care of yourself if you go into town. Don't—don't get into trouble.'

Kidogo's shoulders jerked in a short laugh.

'The elephant does not concern himself with hyenas,' he said. 'Why should I bother with these *fisi* in the white men's clothes?'

'Hyenas eat dead elephants,' Brian shouted at his back. Suddenly he felt as all right about Kidogo in town as he always felt good about Kidogo in the bush. All those old memories were making him edgy, he supposed. The more he saw of Nairobi, the city, the less he liked it, the more ill at ease he felt in it. Maybe the reason Kidogo was all right was he didn't think about it.

'I'm getting to be as bad as Pa about the good old days,' he murmured. 'I suppose it's a sign of advancing age. But if I'm nervy, I rather imagine I'm not a patch on poor Mr. Peter Poole about this time of day, his last day on earth. I wonder if they'll give him a drink?'

It had only been five years since Brian had nailed a sable's head on his office wall and tacked a name-plate on the office door. The firm had been an instantaneous success; he advertised the best and brimmingly delivered it. He only slept with his female clients when it could not be avoided without hurting the lady's feelings and wrecking the safari, and then was generally able to manage it in such a fashion that he was still drinking their whisky when the safari finished. Except he wasn't drinking their whisky any more. His liver wouldn't let him.

He had come, he thought, as he drove now towards Nairobi and the expected hanging of a man named Peter Poole, a very long distance in accomplishment, for good or evil, for a simple fellow named Brian Dermott, who might just as easily be awaiting hanging himself this night of August 1960. It was a long road for a game-warden who had lived for the love of animals to the white hunter who lived now for the death of animals. And who had chosen to live for the death of animals only because the animals were going, anyhow, as the country was going, as the people of the country were going, as he himself, Brian Dermott, was going. At least the animals he killed or caused to be killed now would be used and possibly cherished in death, for the remembrance of what they had been like in life, rather than slaughtered anonymously and impersonally in nooses and starved in game-pits and sold for blackmarket meat and ivory for bracelets and aphrodisiacs for impotent old Hindu men. He winced at the word impotent. He did not like to remember the word *impotent* any more than he liked to remember the word *burning*.

I have as much right, he thought, to the animals as some bloody Giriama who chops off a rhino horn to sell to the Mombasa boys to ship off to India in the *dhows* to deliver to some damned teased-out old man to grind up and dump in his tea to create false erections so that he can breed more damned Wahindi brats. But perhaps I could have used some rhino horn once myself, once, he thought, and grinned sourly at the memory. Brian shrugged slightly and turned his car towards the Norfolk Hotel. There was generally someone there he knew. It was almost pre-lunch drink time at the Norfolk Hotel.

HIGH, HIGH above the vulgar new town that sprawled sloven as a slut, the vultures wheeled, turning in space, gliding patiently to nowhere on stiffened wings. Apart from the circling specks, the Kenya sky was a blameless blue, fluffed only slightly by cloud away down towards the Rift; pointless cloud, hanging wistful and listless over Longonot. Dust talcumed the scaling eucalyptus trees that lined Government Road, and squished soapily under the wheels of Brian Dermott's Land Rover as he turned off into the bumpy alley leading to the Norfolk Hotel's back court. Dust lay heavy on the bougainvillaea, fuzzed the drooping flowers in the front patio. It wouldn't rain today, any more than it rained yesterday. All it did was bluster and go away.

'And this is supposed to be the short rains about to be starting,' he said aloud over the gear grind. 'Weather gone bloody well mad, like everything else. One year it pours with it for twelve months. Another year it doesn't rain at all. But I suppose it'll be pissing up north, pretty soon, and dry as my mouth in the Masai. Everything tail-end to.' He shook his head, gazing upward at the sky. The birds still sailed on effortless wings.

The cobbled courtyard was sardined with shiny new autos, but there was one sliver of parking space, and Brian nosed his car into it. There was nobody sitting on the little verandas of the old cottages, and no parrot in the tree to tell Brian he was a clot. The departed parrot, like Moussa in the bar, was parcel to the older, better days, when a bloke could depend on the weather, at least, and—some of the time—on the people.

Brian Dermott swung his body out from under the wheel. A boy and girl, damp-towel-wrapped over their bathing-suits, were coming out of a narrow, steeply stepped path which led from the new swimming-pool. Brian thought, as he walked up to the hotel and turned left on the back veranda, I'll never get used to the old Norfolk having a swimming-pool. Any more than I can get used to the New Stanley having a proper French sidewalk café, and niggers drinking in the Stanley lounge. At least, he thought, they don't seem to have adopted the Norfolk bar as a steady stampers. Not yet, anyhow. Maybe old Delamere's ghost frightens them away. A kind of white scarecrow for black birds. He turned right into the dark, gloomy-oaken bar. A Goanese steward, heavy-set and cheerless, looked up from a column of crabbed figures he was adding with a stub pencil on a piece of lined tablet-paper. An African waiter, wearing a red fez, a white drill jacket, and a white split-tailed sarong, stood spraddled in the door, his bare feet solidly planted on their horned soles. He was staring hopefully at the vacant front veranda, which had not yet begun to swarm with the noontime drinking crowd. Another waiter, similarly clothed, was behind the bar. He was leaning out of the big square serving window, his elbows braced on the sill talking earnestly in Meru to another unseen waiter on the front veranda. Brian's hard town heels clacked on the floor, but neither African reflexively started at the sound of footsteps.

'Good day, Mr. Dermott,' the Goanese steward said, and leaned forward over the bar. 'You are looking very well.'

'Thank you,' Brian said. 'I'll have a Coca-Cola, please.'

I wonder how many gins I've absorbed at this one bar, Brian thought; this one particular bar, not counting all the others, how many whiskies, how many beers? How many laughs, how much fun, how much ragging, at this old bar, before Moussa moved out and took all the gaiety away with him? Moussa's lonely at the Stanley, Brian thought. At that little bar in the Grill he hasn't really got anybody to talk to like he used to in the old days.

Brian Dermott looked about him. There was nobody in the bar—nobody in the booths, nobody perched on the stools. Only he and the Goanese and the two waiters in this room which had known so much laughter, so many fist fights; this room which had seen the *old* Lord Delamere, his long mane shaking like an angry lion's, capering up and down on the bar and suddenly jumping feet first into the milling bodies, laughing and flailing with his fists, screaming a Masai war-cry and kicking with his tiny feet. A long, long time, he thought, since old Delamere and his hairy henchmen got drunk and shot the tiles off the cottages.

He lit a cigarette and tasted his Coke without enthusiasm. That's the story of my new life now, he thought. A Coke without enthusiasm. What is a Coke, Pepsi or the other kind, at the end of a long hard day, with the dust furry on your legs and stiff in your hair, your lashes clotted with dust; dust in your teeth, caked animal blood under your nails, hands filthy, your eyes red from sun and wind, your lips cracked and black from sun and dust and thirst? To hand you a Coke when what you want is just one beer, just two beers, icy cold and the tin drained in one long swallow, to lay the first dust; then the harsh bite of gin strong in the bubble-bursting tonic or sharper in the greenish martini, and then the brandy after the coffee and then the dark, brown Scotch in front of the fire until food and fatigue and grog and satisfaction sent you off to sleep to the hyena symphony. And now, he thought —me, I, *mimi*, Brian Dermott—*now* I drink Coke. I drink Coca-Cola and Pepsi-Cola. I drink lime juice and orange squash. I drink lemonade and iced tea and iced coffee. Anything that's wet but isn't alcoholic. What a fine white hunter I turned out to be. A disgrace to the whole profession. A kick in the pants to the legend of the zinc-lined belly. *Will you have some more tea, Madame?* his brain mimicked, as old Eric used to mimic him when he called Brian the 'Society Hunter'. Will you have a Coca-Cola, for Christ's sake? No, Madame says: no, for Christ's sake, Madame will have a double martini, and easy on the vermouth, and then Madame will tell me how well I'm looking and how much she admires me for sticking to my five-times accursed Cokes and all the wretched squashes and sickly ades. Except this new Madame I just left. She drinks Cokes too and doesn't look any happier about it than I do.

Yet, Dermott, he said to himself, tell me what I'm going to do? Tell me what else I'm going to do, if I want to live? If this is living. Changing all your odd ways and habits, even up to one of the small comforts Ngai grants you in your old age. Grog. Booze. *Pombe*. Call it what you want, if a man drinks enough of it, it's part of his personality, like a moustache or on some people, a gun. Like this gun, which is damned uncomfortable. They're going out of fashion too, he thought. *Guns*. I never thought they would here in Kenya. Maybe everywhere else but not here. At least one chap found out that they were out of fashion. He's finding it out today. The hard way.

'Give me another Coke,' he said to the steward.

'Don't overdo it, chum.' A small, dun-coloured man had walked in the door, blinking from the bright sunlight outside. 'That's two Cokes in a row. You're really knocking them back. Remember what the doctor said. Moderation, he said. In all things. I must say you're looking very fit. The best I've seen you in donkey's years.'

'Go to hell,' Brian said. 'I wish I could say the same for you. You look awful. Wha:'ll you have?'

'Pinkers,' James Bartlett said. 'A double pink 'un, please, Fernandez. I intend to look awfuller. You know, Brian, I admire you tremendously. The stalwart self-discipline, and all that sort of rot. Will-power by the bag. Who'd ever have guessed that the old Brian Dermott was a flaming teetotaller under the skin, eh?'

'It's something nobody'll ever accuse you of, you rum-soaked fact-mangler, not so long as other people pay. I suppose you've scribbled your usual bloody screed for London, wallowed in all the gore, painted the misery starkly so the press can muck it up for the misinformation of millions?'

'Please, Mr. Dermott,' Bartlett said. 'You overestimate my importance. I am only a poor stringer for His Lordship's great daily newspaper. I am not the man to cover the juicy ones. Don't tell me you haven't seen all the types, complete with slouch hats and trench-coats? The New Stanley's loaded with them, all writing for posterity and tomorrow's fish and chips. Ever since His Lordship got the fright of his life with that buffalo or elephant or whatever it was, Africa has assumed *eee*-normous importance in Fleet Street.'

'It was an elephant,' Brian said. 'I know. It happened on one of my safaris. Impressed His Lordship any amount. I shot the beast out of his lap almost as an afterthought. Pity I didn't let him be trampled, but I thought it might have reflected discredit on me as a white hunter, even if it were a boon to the world. It's not done, I suppose, even by today's relaxed standards. Losing clients, I mean. Good thing there's something still sacred out here, even if it's only a bloody client.'

'Don't brood,' Bartlett said. 'At least you've still got a one-piece neck. That's more than you can say for some people right now. I thought you were on safari. Come back specially for the hanging?'

'I suppose so,' Brian replied. 'Have another. If ever a man earned a limp neck he bought it. Fun's fun, but these days, I suppose one doesn't dash about doing Wogs in broad daylight, even if the Wog does chuck a pebble at your dog.'

'He could have beaten it on that insanity plea if they'd offered it earlier. He was proper crackers if anybody was. But it's too late now. I just checked Government House. No change. He'll swing, all right.'

'Maybe he isn't any crazier than a lot of us,' Brian said. 'I imagine that right this minute he reckons it was all a lot of bloody political fuss over just one more dead Wog, and that the cavalry will gallop up and save him before they slip on the old hood.'

'They strung up five coons a week ago for killing just one old farmer,' the newspaperman replied. 'Another three went with them for some trivial sin against the state. You can't hang eight men on one Thursday and *not* hang another man a week later just because he's white and the corpse is black. This was plain lousy timing on Poole's part.'

Brian shook his head.

'I know, I know,' he said. 'But somehow I can't believe they'd hang a white man here just for killing a Wog. Justice or no justice, they never used to hang *white* people. Not even for killing other white people, as a general thing.'

'That's old-fashioned thinking now,' the newspaperman said. 'Do you want another Coke?'

'*No*, I don't,' Brian said. 'I'm sick of the sight of them. Fernandez! Make me a double martini!' He turned to the newspaperman. 'Six months I've been sucking on this confounded pap, and I'm fed up, feeling like somebody else.'

'Well, just don't let me be the cause of your fall from grace,' Bartlett said. 'Certainly you're not mourning the imminent passing of Master Peter Poole?'

'I'm mourning nobody's passing,' Brian snapped. 'I am having a drink to my bloody brother-in-law.' He paused and amended himself. 'My brand spanking new bloody-brother-in-law.' He bowed slightly. 'Here's to my new-bloody-brother-in-law, the noble doctor. Your health, Dr. George Locke, who put me on the wagon for my own good.' His voice minced. 'You'll have one fit too many, Brian. One day you'll black out and when you come back you'll be soft in the head, Brian. Or paralysed, Brian. Or dead, Brian. That liver will stand just so much punishment, Brian!'

He bowed again, and drained his martini in a gulp.

'*Ngine*,' he said. 'Another, steward. You can leave the ice in this time. This time we'll drink to my new liver. Six long months to the day it's gone without sustenance. Poor thing's dying of thirst.'

The newspaperman looked at Brian Dermott curiously. Brian Dermott would be thirty-five, thirty-six, at most, he thought, but even with the clear funny yellow eyes and the tanned face unpuffed, Brian Dermott looked a good forty-five. He remembered the first time he'd seen Brian, skin sick-bleached by many mountain-forest months away from the sun; Brian wearing filthy shorts and tattered tennis shoes and an old hunting jacket so often washed by Africans that its original green was only faintly hinted. That time Brian was masked by a week's dust-streaked tawny beard, his uncut mane of liony hair was falling over his bloodshot animal's eyes, and he kept throwing the hair back with a jerky nervous gesture. This was in the bar in the Mawingo Hotel, outside of Nanyuki, long before the Mawingo was sold to the Americans to make it something ritzy called the Mount Kenya Safari Club—swimming-pool, Swiss manager, Hollywood blondes, $500 entrance fee, complete. Brian Dermott was surrounded by other people no cleaner than he, and they were all very, very drunk indeed. They were celebrating some special event which all the other drunks kept saying deserved a knighthood, or at least the George Cross. Actually it turned out that Brian Dermott did receive the George Medal for whatever it was he had done that made him so drunk that time. That was a long time ago, and when Brian Dermott went to London at the Queen's invitation to receive his gong, he might well have been wearing the same suit he was wearing now. And looking, Bartlett thought, much the same. Except for the close-trimmed moustache that made his face harsh under that Roman-coin cruel nose. Except for the bulge of what could only be a gun was making in his city suit. Except older. And that wasn't *all* moustache. Certainly he was just as thin. But it was a different kind of thinness. Before, the flesh had been dripped off his bones by sweat and other things.

'You look about as much like a white hunter as I look like a newspaperman,' Bartlett said, thinking aloud.

'Both types have been very badly misrepresented in fact as well as fiction,' Brian said. 'What brought on that startling conclusion?'

'Nothing much. I was just remembering the first time I saw you. You wouldn't remember. You were quite tight at the time, and very dirty. You looked as if somebody from Hollywood had cast you to be played by Stewart Granger and the make-up man had gone mad with power. Actually you looked more like Humphrey Bogart in *African Queen*. Now you look like a bloody banker. Except for the hands under those starched cuffs. They haven't changed.' He wouldn't mention the gun, Bartlett thought. That hadn't changed either except that now Brian was wearing it inside his coat instead of flapping on his hip.

Brian looked briefly down at his neat blue double-breasted suit, at his well-shined black shoes. He touched a small-figured blue tie with one thick, square, heavy-fingered brown hand, and smoothed the close-trimmed moustache. He smiled.

'When one comes to town for a hanging one doesn't generally wear one's ordinary working kit,' he said. 'The stretching of young Master Peter Poole is a solemn social occasion for Kenya. Equality has officially arrived, even if it did come tied up in a hangman's knot. Actually, I thought I looked rather sweet in my neat and clerical blues. Pity I can't grow you a new set of hands.'

'The day you look sweet will be a frosty Friday,' the newspaperman said. 'I don't know. You used to look larger than life, somehow. Now you seem to've shrunk a little bit.'

'Hadn't you heard that, too? All white men have shrunken a touch,'

Brian said. 'We loom not so large in Africa as of yore. Clean living and rampant black *free-dom* tends to shrink one. You don't look so large, yourself.'

'I've always been the little man,' Bartlett grinned. 'People started calling me "Boy!" when I was a lad, working as an office slavey in Liverpool, and they never got over the habit.'

At the accented *boy* both Negro waiters looked up automatically, and then pointedly gazed away.

'I shouldn't use that word with an exclamation point after it any more if I were you,' Brian said easily. 'It's an old-hat habit you'll have to cure yourself of. Mr. Mboya and Mr. Macleod don't care much for it. Bad form, in these brave new days, to call a boy *boy!*. The winds of change, you know. Sweeping the African vocabulary clean.'

'I suppose he'll be a hero, now?' The newspaperman raised an eyebrow. 'Saving he's well and truly strung up at eight P.M. this day of our Lord of August nineteen sixty?'

'Poole? No indeed. Not bloody likely. Not Poole. Silly ass to kill that black gentleman in full view of the jury, so to speak. Maybe he'd have gone free on one impulsive bullet, if he'd been wearing a gun.' Brian almost said 'like me' as he smoothed his coat-front. 'Sending for the pistol on purpose, with the boy already running away, is what will stretch Mr. Poole's neck. Orders from Home. After all, a white jury sentenced him, and all his appeals were heard and rejected by whites. His own people gave him the thumbs down. No hero, our Mr. Poole.'

'But,' the newspaperman persisted, 'just after I came here, when the Emergency was only just declared, a white man shot a Negro down in cold blood in front of this very hotel, right over there by the theatre, and finished him off in full view of a whole busload of travellers. They didn't hang *him*.'

'That, my lad, was back when war was war.' Brian said. 'That was when nice old ladies and small children carried side arms and were encouraged to use them. That was when . . .' he paused, and swirled the liquor in his glass. 'Should we change the subject?'

'Right. Care for another tot? My shout this time. Then I really must fly. Witherspoon from the *Clarion* craves the pleasure of my company in his suite.'

'Thanks. Yes. I'm just killing a little time here to see if my brother Philip comes round.'

'That's a nice young chap, this brother of yours. I've seen him round and about the village. Coming on for quite a man now. Big bloke.'

'He's not so very old, but he's beginning to fill out. Well, here's cheers. My God, it tastes nice. Hasn't changed a bit. But I think I'd best not dive too deeply into it. My bloodstream is one hundred per cent pure, and my liver as virgin as the new-mown snow. Hallo, speak of the devil—here's young Pip now. *Jambo*, young fellow. Come and have a tiddly with the ink-stained wretch and me.'

'You're not on . . . You *are*,' Philip Dermott said. 'I thought George said . . . I didn't know you were in town, Brian.'

'Well, I am. Came in for the hanging. Left you a chit at the flat. As for the grog, George *did* say. But Brian said different. And get that wifely tone out of your voice. We're related by blood and I'm still sufficiently senior to take you over my knee. What'll you have?'

'Gin and tonic, please.' Pip Dermott sounded a trifle self-conscious. Brian nodded at the bar steward and rubbed a forefinger lightly on his brother's lapel.

'He's grown up. I gave him his first beer from this bar. He was fifteen then, and it was the same day that . . .' Brian's face darkened. Then he smiled. 'I figured he'd earned a drink that day. Well, good luck, Philip, my lad. Cheers!'

'Been quite a time since I saw you, youngster,' Jim Bartlett said, raising his glass at Philip Dermott. 'Seems you've grown another foot. You're bigger than your brother. How old now?'

'Twenty-two. Almost.'

'That's not quite accurate. He's just turning twenty-one. Pip takes after his father, all bone. Our old man was a beanpole, too.'

Young Philip Dermott did stand a good three inches over his brother's solid six feet. He had his mother's deep-blue, nearly gentian eyes, and an almost girlish mouth. It went oddly with a jaw that contained much of his dead father's lantern. His hair was cropped short in a wiry crew-cut. His body was lean, almost shambling, and would never fill out to Brian's hard, bevelled compactness. Philip Dermott was dressed neatly in a city suit, a grey flannel.

'In town for the hanging, like everybody else?' Jim Bartlett smiled.

'No. Not really. Maybe partly. Some business for Aunt Charlotte. With the bank. And some other things, as well.'

'I think my kid brother has made a cardinal mistake,' Brian said to the newspaperman. 'He's gone and got himself almost but not quite engaged. Cut down in the flower of youth.'

Philip Dermott played with his drink and didn't answer for a moment. Then he said abruptly:

'Brian, Don and Ken gave me a lift down from the Stanley. They were taking about sending you a safari broadcast. I don't know about what. Something to do with the office, I suppose.'

'It's always something to do with the office. Why in the name of God I ever became a Limited instead of just being plain Brian Dermott I will never know. I used to think it was tough enough satisfying one client at a time.' He turned his head to Bartlett. 'Now I'm chief nanny to ten white hunters, two secretaries, two accountants, and a general manager. Come on, Pip. Finish your drink, I'm starved. Nice seeing you, Bartlett.'

James Bartlett watched the brothers leave. *The town is certainly changing,* he thought. *And the people as well.*

BARTLETT THREADED his way through the tables that crowded the side-walk café. No doubt about it, what had once been the *old* New Stanley was as fine a pub as you'd see this side of Suez, and better than most of the London hotels. Bartlett waved at a few people seated drinking and eating sandwiches at the little tables, and walked through the lobby and over to the lift. He was late, but Witherspoon wouldn't mind. Witherspoon would be curing his head and telling his fellow craftsmen about some extraordinary feat of journalism he had performed during the landings at Anywhere during the last large war. Witherspoon was the kind of journalist who had made *all* the landings, even if they happened simultaneously on two sides of the world. And who's to say no, Bartlett thought, in the jet age you can *be* on both sides of the world at the same time if you consider the time changes. He'd liked it better the old way, he thought as he entered the lift and pressed the 'Seven' button. He was remembering the first day he stepped off the South African Airways plane and climbed in the little van for the hotel, after passing the uniformed, very *pukka* beshorted gentlemen in the passport controls, and the immaculate, turbaned, bearded Sikhs in the customs. That was the old airport. The new Embakasi airport now looked like any other—like London, like Paris, like New York. Everything looks like everything else these days.

But it's true you no longer get that impact, that overpowering blow in the face, as he had, Bartlett thought. That day when he first drove wide-eyed down Race Course Road, butting through the native slums, through the howling, reeking bazaars, where every smell known to the East mingled in one magnificent ripe stink of rotting fruit and dust and dung and curry powder and wet plaster and no plumbing and ancient filthy habits.

The noises were as exciting as the sights and smells. Fifty dialects woven into the blare of Indian and Arabic radio broadcasts and the tinny screech of hand-crank phonographs. Women shouting in high shrill voices and dogs barking and children scurrying and crawling between the plodding pink-scabby, white-scaly dark legs of the adults.

Then you could really see the bush native come to town. There an occasional haughty Masai wearing nothing but a spear, wire ornaments, red-ochre make-up and a goatskin cloak . . . here an old-fashioned Kikuyu in a monkey-hide cape, with enormous carved wooden plugs in the distended lobes of his ears; women clad only in a one-piece *shuka*, with the invariable babies slung on their backs, a tiny woolly head peeping from under an armpit. The men mostly wore appalling tatters, with varicoloured patch-on-patch, and all the droopy felt hats seemed to have been left overlong in the rain.

The bazaars reeked of urine and dung and rotting meat and gooey sweets and swarmed with flies, hovering in clouds over offal in the dusty street. The colours of the people ranged from shining plum black of Negroes to the lighter Swahilis from the coast, the ivory-skinned Arabs in *djelabah* and *caftan*, the swarthy Greeks and the sallow East Indians. the fiercely bearded

Sikhs in brilliant turbans, the hawk-faced sun-black Somalis from the northern deserts. Cicatriced dark faces under the bright red *tarbooshes*, and here an Arab woman with a dainty *haik* drawn across her face, showing only a pair of enormous eyes, and tiny slippered feet peeping from a shapeless robe.

It all seemed very romantic, that first time, because in the next few days you might easily be going out in the vast plumy plains of Africa to shoot a lion, and perhaps you didn't really want to shoot a lion. Everything about the town was romantic, the eddying crowds on Delamere Avenue and Government Road, the seething bazaars by the old mosque, the black traffic policemen in neat starched khaki and high blue puttees, the brown-kneed settlers in shorts and floppy double terai hats, the busy drinkers in the bars at the Stanley and the Norfolk, the waiters and room boys in the white nightdresses called *kanzus*, padding silently barefoot across the tiles. Now most of the help wore pants and tennis shoes as a badge of emancipation.

That had been colonial Kenya—White Man's Country, it was called— forty thousand whites and six million blacks. That was the country in which every native, regardless of age, was called 'boy'. And less than ten years ago. My God, a world turns in ten years. Whatever happened to Hitler?

How it all has changed, Bartlett thought. The slums and the old bazaar quarters have been razed—burned down during the Emergency, which is what the Mau Mau terror still is so precisely, so veddy-Britishly euphemistically called. You do not see so many natives clustered in the streets any more, not in the swarming knots of yesterday, because the still remembered bitter history of the Mau Mau conflict has made mobs unpopular with the cops. *And* illegal unless it's an *ngoma*, a dance, or a licenced political do. And now we get Radio Moscow and Radio Peking in Swahili loud and clear on the wireless.

The natives in town looked different, apart from being better dressed today than before. They no longer seemed to stare flatly with the African's masked gaze, but looked more obliquely, perhaps more slyly. And less, considerably, respectfully at the white bwanas and memsaabs.

Mau Mau had come and had been put down, and that new secret order, the KKM, seemed to have been effectively doused for the moment. But the isolated attacks on places and persons still happened, and were increasing, and the paper was always full of local politics bordering on violence. In the older days you heard a low mutter of distant thunder in tomorrow's Africa, thunder which would swell to the relatively brief violent squall that was Mau Mau, and would be followed on some vague tomorrow by a massive, horrible, full-scale eruption as if all the sulking volcanoes in the world had exploded in sudden, simultaneous fury; as if all the sleeping earthquakes had conspired to rive the earth. Bartlett thought with a start as the lift stopped at the seventh floor, and the door slid back: *But tomorrow is today!*

As he rapped on the door of 711, Witherspoon's suite, he wondered idly what the big foreign correspondent wanted to see him about. Certainly not

Peter Poole. That was with the gods. Probably an interview with His Nibs at Lodwar. They all wanted to see Jomo Kenyatta at Lodwar, and the Colonial Office wasn't having any. Not right now, with the Congo aflame and the papers full of the troubles. There was enough trouble in the Kasai and in Katanga without stirring up the animals here at home. Bartlett smiled sheepishly as he pushed open the unlocked door of Witherspoon's suite. Now, after only nine years, he said to himself, I'm thinking of Kenya as 'home'.

*

Witherspoon was not in his suite. A note on the desk proclaimed his presence in the Grill Room. Witherspoon was waiting for Bartlett in the little vestibule in front of the bar at the top of the stairs.

'I got bored and thirsty and came on down.' Witherspoon said. He was a big man, beefy, with a pale skin and a lion's roach of hair. 'Got a table? Sorry I kept you waiting.'

Bartlett made his voice apologetic. 'I got hung up at the Norfolk.'

'That's all right. Yes. Over there by the window. Come on.' He led the way down the stairs and raised an arm. 'Albert!' The blond headwaiter raised his head from a customer and beckoned.

'Look,' Bartlett said as the headwaiter steered them to a table. 'Just look who's come to the party, for to see and to be admired. None other than the self-appointed Premier-elect *and* the loyal opposition. And what seems quite a lot of the Cabinet-to-come, some fine day. Trust Kamau to show himself, though, and to bring Ndegwa with him. Black solidarity; all personal differences buried at the moment, while they hold their own preview-wake for Peter Poole. Much more effective now than after the fact. And wouldn't you know they'd made themselves conspicuous in the most expensive and best restaurant in the best and newest hotel in town?'

Albert seated the men in a far corner, several tables away from the Africans. The bar steward came to take their drink order, and Bartlett reflected, as he ordered a martini, that this was about four before lunch, and he would certainly need a siesta afterward, especially if they had any wine.

'The fish looks good, and I see there're some Mombasa oysters,' Witherspoon said to Bartlett. 'Shall we have a bottle of the white stuff? Might as well go the whole hog. I've written tomorrow's piece and I think I'll sleep the afternoon away. Until hanging time, that is.'

'All right with me,' Bartlett said. 'The sole's very good here.'

'A bottle of the Reisling, very cold.' Witherspoon said to the wine waiter, and to the hovering Albert, 'two dozen each of the oysters and then the sole with a mixed salad.' Then he gazed across the room at the African politicians.

'They all used to look alike when I first came out here,' he said. 'Now they they all look as different as Europeans. But they all still seem a little bit undressed in white man's clothes. Look at your next Prime Minister.'

Matthew Kamau (real name Kamau wa Muthenge, but mission-named for an apostle by the Catholic fathers who had taught him) was thin and the colour of rain-polished asphalt. He was a handsome man and, like most African politicians, young. His hair was tightly kinked, with a shaved part on one side, but his cheekbones were high and his nose flat only at the tip. He had a long jaw, and he smiled as he said something to the man on his right, Stephen Ndegwa (real name Ndegwa wa Muchiri). Matthew Kamau was a handsome man by any standards, and his smile made him charming as it showed square white teeth flashing in the shining soot of his face. Even sitting he gave an impression of height. He was wearing a light grey suit and a blue polka-dotted tie with a soft white shirt. A massive gold ring glinted on the third finger of one sinewy, long-fingered hand, and the polished nails shone bluish-white against the black of his skin. The eyes were huge, the whites sparkling against the reddish black of the irises.

Stephen Ndegwa was a big man; burly-big all over. His face was broad and flat and more of a brownish colour than Kamau's. His nose and cheekbones were flat and broad, too, and the lower jaw thickly fleshed and strong. He had a bulldog look not often seen in a Kikuyu. Stephen Ndegwa looked more like a heavily made-up white man than he looked like a Negro who had run about naked on the slopes of Ol Kalou as a child. His eyes were heavy-lidded and moved slowly in their sockets. The whites were not clear; they were tinged with yellow and webbed by pink veins. Stephen Ndegwa was said to be a heavy drinker in private, while Matthew Kamau was abstemious. Both were, at this moment, president and secretary, respectively, of the new Kenya National Amalgamation Party, KNAP.

Stephen Ndegwa's old party, the Kenya Moja—'One Kenya'—had been called moderate by the whites, and from time to time had been accused by the blacks of too-active Uncle-Tom collusion with white interests. The year 1960 was a time of scrambled loyalties, of frantic chestnut-pulling, with Tom Mboya fleeing his old People's Convention Party to line up with the recently released Mau Mau leader, James Gichuru, in the new Kenya Africa National Union as a stroke of purest political expediency. With splinter parties such as the Kenya Africa Democratic Union and offbeat Ginger Groups and Youth Wings splitting the common front of black national intent, Stephen Ndegwa had arranged a long secret conference with the younger man. Matthew Kamau, a brilliant trade-union leader and already the semi-official voice of Kenya abroad when East African independence was mentioned—a voice more musically tempered than Mboya's, more urgently persuasive than Ndegwa's.

There was no doubt about it, they said in London and in America; Matthew Kamau was The Man of Tomorrow when all of Africa would be free and even, possibly, united in a great brotherhood of states. Kamau was arrogant now; an orphan, mission-raised, he had gone through Kenya's higher-paid schools, had attended Makerere in Uganda, and had studied a year at Oxford and also at the London School of Economics. Harold Laski had taught him political science; on frequent visits to the United States, close observation of American union leaders like Walter Reuther, George Meany, David Dubinsky and, latterly, Jimmy Hoffa, had inadvertently taught him political practicality. Lord Keynes influenced his economic thinking, but as in the case of Tom Mboya, American ebony athletes, brown entertainers and cream-skinned professional Negroes had shaped him from an obscure African politician into a sort of international fad.

In the last days of 1959, with African independence occupying more and more space in public conversation and with the press leaping frantically onto its juggernaut, Matthew Kamau had found himself on the covers of no fewer than three weekly news magazines, topping Mboya by one. The churches loved him for his asceticism and piety; the foreign union leaders drenched him with money; the entertainment world lionized him and the lecture agents wept for speaking engagements. He kept ministers waiting for appointments and was eagerly stalked as celebrity bait for the routs of Mayfair and Manhattan. The advertised or even rumoured presence of Matthew Kamau, polished, handsome, and always impeccably dressed, assured a fanciful success and certain press coverage for any event given by the tireless party-throwers.

White women pawed him with their eyes and their hands and he continued to be vastly charming to everyone, black and white, male and female, while nimbly avoiding the embraces of the women and drinking nothing stronger than coffee with the men. This reticence could not be said to be typical of his associates, who quietly accepted the favours of Kamau's pantingly eager female overflow, which found hopping into bed with African politicians new and chic in a jaded white world that used to leap just as enthusiastically into bed with Harlem orchestra leaders and Senegalese boxers.

Matthew Kamau, who had dexterously avoided going to jail as a Mau Mau even after hopefully trying to inherit at least one of the vacant shoes of Jomo Kenyatta in the old Kenya African Union, had strained aloof from allying himself with any new party until he had seen how the ashes shook. Then he had finally spoken long and seriously with Stephen Ndegwa, who was solidly respected by the whites both as a lawyer and a reasonable man. Kamau had been more than content to control his unions and play the lecture circuits and shine at official functions abroad, since he had observed the sweaty squabbles between such power-grasping politicians as Mboya and Gichuru, Ngala and Odinga, Argwings-Kodhek and Munyua Waiyaki, Arthur Ochwada and Mungai Njoroge. Kamau would rest and happily let them kill each other off. He was as rabidly an advocate of 'undiluted democracy' as Tom Mboya, who had amassed so much mileage from the cry of *One Man— One Vote!* Kamau wanted his *uhuru* just as swiftly and just as completely as the wild-eyed Oginga Odinga, KANU's Russia-loving, costumed and capering vice-president; just as insistently as Mboya, KANU's sex-appealing Secretary, who was also a fashionable pin-up boy of the international labour, entertainment and social world; just as imperiously as Kwame Nkrumah in Ghana. But more important, to Kamau's way of thinking, he wanted his undiluted democracy with the dignity of Julius Nyerere in Tanganyika, without the certain-to-be-fatal Communist complications of Sékou Tourè in Guinea or the tragic clownishness of Lumumba in the Congo. He wanted it all, but he wanted it on his terms, with the world making a loud kissing mouth in his direction.

And so he turned at last to Stephen Ndegwa, the respected moderate, as Doctor Kiano was ostensibly moderate, as Doctor Kiano was generally respected. The upcoming electoral equation for the free common-roll voting was clear—a million black voters to a possible thirty thousand whites, a physical majority of six million blacks over sixty thousand whites and Asians. Matthew Kamau wanted his party to control those black votes, and with them ministries and eventually, the job of Chief Minister; possibly—who knew what might happen?—Prime Minister of a huge Federation in Kenya and Uganda, Tanganyika and the Rhodesias. Some day the Portuguese would lose control of Mozambique as well. Who could tell? Alexander the Great had conquered his world at a younger age than Matthew Kamau.

So they had formed a party—the Kenya National Amalgamation Party, euphonically known as *Kaynap* as against the KANUs and KADUs. So far it had worked well, with Kamau flourishing the torch of independence as he harangued his organized mobs of as many as twenty, thirty thousand screaming people with the rhetorical questions they so loved to answer: 'Whose Kenya is it?' *Roar:* 'Ours!' 'What do we fight for?' *Roar:* '*UHURU!* 'Will you ever stop fighting for freedom?' *Roar:* '*NO!*' from thirty thousand hysteric black throats.

Yes, Kamau could wave the torch, and Ndegwa would silently applaud, for the fruits were ripening, now that Mboya and the rest were fighting like wild dogs after having blackjacked the Colonial Minister last spring at Lancaster House in London—bulldozed Iain Macleod into giving the Kenya Africans a common-roll vote, a clear implicit majority, more ministerial power, and soon—very, very soon—complete independence. Gichuru and Kenyatta and Mboya had built it, had ridden the winds of change, and they would squabble themselves loose from it if they were not careful. And in the meantime, it was good to work with the sardonic, quiet, immensely capable Ndegwa, with whom Matthew Kamau shared so many views. Save one basic:

Kamau wanted his independence now, all on a platter, with himself as immediate Chief Minister and as for Ndegwa, who knows? Certainly not President or Foreign Minister. And in the meantime, Ndegwa was very useful.

Ndegwa knew exactly what Kamau was doing, what Kamau could do, and how much Kamau was to be preferred, so long as it was spell-binders and public-opinion merchants you needed—how much preferred over the Mboyas and Gichurus and the old, battered, imprisoned Kenyatta. He saw eye to eye with Kamau over nearly everything, save one basic:

Ndegwa wanted his independence later, gradually, with the whites and Asians integrated expediently into an African majority, with himself as eventual Chief

Minister. And as for Kamau, who knows? Certainly not President or Foreign Minister. But in the meanwhile Kamau was useful.

And in the same meanwhile, both men chattered pointedly to the other members of their party. Ndegwa, powerful and rumpled in a carelessly tied cravat and a spotted blue suit, scattered crumbs as he talked with the man on his right, a pantherish, almost foppish man named Abraham Matisia. Matisia wa Matuku was the third most important member of the group. He was a Wakamba from Machakos, also missionary-educated at home and then extensively trained abroad, and he had first served admirably as a vice-Kamau in the Kamba country where the Kambas, similar in many respects to the Kikuyu, were elephant-hunters, poachers, wild meat-eaters, and fighters, often contemptuous of their Kikuyu cousins as farmers and city slickers and sea-lawyers. Matisia's grandfather had eaten men, and so, perhaps, had his father, although his low, cultured voice was almost crumbly-sweet and mellifluous. He was a very handsome man as well, with a thin, straight nose, a hairline moustache over full red lips, and his Kikuyu and Swahili were as good as his English, which was perfect. He was a powerful, polished orator, and his hatred of the white man was surprisingly vehement for a Wakamba.

It was surprisingly vehement, that is, until you remembered that he had rather tolerated the white man up to one particular day—the day he had got caught up in the massive Operation Anvil, in which thirty-five thousand natives were arrested in a single violent sweep. Caught up, and clapped into jail like any Kikuyu, despite all his protests that he was a Wakamba of Machakos and innocent of involvement in Mau Mau. Abraham Matisia had been an undercover lieutenant, working directly with Matthew Kamau in the Kikuyu effort to draw their Wakamba cousins into the bloody brotherhood of Mau Mau via the old Kenya African Union, which bred so many politicians before the British killed it and drove its members underground . . . the same old KAU which could be seen on all sides today, but under names like KANU and KADU and KNAP.

Abraham Matisia had not enjoyed being yanked brutally from the old KAU headquarters in a raid, seeing fellow members spattered by gunfire—finding himself manhandled by two grinning Wakamba *askaris* who laughed and cuffed him silly when he protested that he too was Kamba and no Kyuke—that he was merely an innocent bystander. He had been stripped and searched and kicked and clubbed and defiled, the orifices of his body poked into to the accompaniment of many rude jokes and much rough laughter. And he, Matisia, the descendant of kings, had even been held face down into the filth of a public latrine!

Matisia had a long, long time to think behind the wire in the horrible wet heat of the mosquito-buzzing, swampy outskirts of the ancient Arab village of Lamu, where he could see the *dhows* come and go as they plied to Zanzibar on the old slave routes, sailing their illegal ivory back to India, hauling their cargoes of spices from Zanzibar, taking their hides and rugs and coffee and tea to far places which he, Matisia, had seen before the white men's tame niggers shoved him face first into the faecal muck of a public toilet!

He thought and he sweated as he swung his mattock on the clearing projects. He thought as he ate the stinking food and scratched the lice and submitted to the kicks of the guards and listened to the fanciful plots and the interminable plans of the prisoners, already scheming against the day they were released. He forever thought, and out of it grew hatred and more hatred for the white man—hatred double-distilled for the white man and his women, for the white man and his ways, for the white man and his possessions—possessions Matisia wanted not so much for their intrinsic worth as because he would be taking them away from the cursed *mzungu*.

He, Abraham Matisia, with all his education, could never stand for the Legislative Council—not under the current structure of white man's law, because even when he came free he would be permanently branded by his jail sentence and enjoined from office-holding. But he did not want to flaunt the public face of politics, in any case. He would prefer to implement from the sidelines. He knew much of implementing from the sidelines. And he had studied much abroad—studied in London, studied in France, even in Moscow for a short time. Power was seen at the top but it came quietly from the back room. He, Matisia, if he ever got out from behind this bloody wire, away from this bloody prison food, would be the king of the back room.

But before he became king it would be necessary, first, to attach himself to one of the big face-men—a man like Mboya, whom he knew from the Kenya African Union, a man like Matthew Kamau, whom he also knew from the KAU. Of the two he fancied Kamau; he thought there was more solidity to him than Mboya, who was all talk-talk-talk until he was prone to jabber himself right out of eminence and final major consideration. Also Mboya was an uncircumcised Jaluo, which would certainly count against him in the end. The Kikuyu would surely run Kenya, the Kikuyu and their cousins, the Wakamba. He would limpet onto a Kikuyu, like a sucker on a shark. Kamau would be his shark.

In the unpleasant present of those dreadful detention days at Lamu, the guard was turning out the men again for more work on the useless roads that sank into the stinking mud of the historic urine-reeking Arab slaving port of Lamu, which was as old as Zanzibar, older perhaps even than Mombasa. But some day—well, London would have to listen and then they, the political prisoners, would all go free, and take up the sword again. *And* avenge themselves of the abuse they had suffered, the beatings that had scarred them, the cuffs and kicks and insults and indignities. Kamau would be his man, his shark, if he lived, and Abraham Matisia was going to be very careful to see that he lived to graduate from this new university which nobody had ever suggested he might attend.

And he had graduated, finally, when the first of the amnesties were declared, and he had come a long way, a very long way. He still served Kamau, first as undercover agitator, and now as chief lieutenant in charge of things that Kamau's high scruples found either politically impracticable or morally distasteful. Abraham Matisia regarded nothing as distasteful so long as it was practicable; so long as it was feasible morally, politically, or otherwise. He accepted the white women in London that Kamau found it preferable to repulse; he laughed as he bedded and cared no snap for the fact that he played jackal to the lion. He would never understand the Englishman, he supposed, but he understood the Englishwoman very well. Dissatisfied bitches in heat, all of them—or most of the ones he met, at any rate.

Matisia appropriated funds for his 'expense account'—Kamau seemed not to care if Matisia never told him. There was plenty of money in the union kitty, and Matisia was a very important man in the union. It took money to travel to London and to live the life of an important man.

Occasionally, there was a certain amount of organizational violence which Matthew Kamau preferred not to see or even to know about, and Stephen Ndegwa might not have permitted. To this end Matisia had his own lieutenants. They needed few instructions now. Most of them had come from the prison pens of Lamu and Hola and Manyani.

After the straggling skeins of Kamau's groundwork had been gathered into the whole hank that was now called Kaynap, Matisia had openly started organizing political meetings with special attention to the breaking of the right heads, and had taken over the organization of political leadership from the District level right on down to the barefoot messengers. The branch offices of Kaynap in Nyeri and Thomson's Falls and Thika and Rumuruti were his responsibility; the organization of the labour forces on the farms came under his hand; even the recruitment of office workers and government employees was his special province. Matisia had very little trouble with his organizing—he had learned much from the study of labour techniques in America. A broken arm was a warning, a cracked skull was a reprimand, and an occasional lamentable accident, usually fatal, was an ultimatum. After that, violence was seldom necessary—bar of course the occasional refresher *pour encourager les autres*. Matisia liked the suave violence of the French phrase. He thought of it very often.

He admitted the necessity of violence, but was seldom present when it was used any more. He was no longer personally angry at the black people who had mishandled and degraded him when he had been packed off to prison as a Mau Mau terrorist. Accidents of one sort or another had happened to those men and to most of their families, and there was no longer any black malice in Matisia's soul. He saved all his malice for the white man.

Matisia was a busy man, and sometimes he could barely find time to oversee some rather lucrative businesses of his own. He never used either union time or political party time to enforce the little details of protection for weak shop-owners and small beer-hall proprietors, for dance-hall and rooming-house operators—nondescript people who needed organized protection against those cynical opportunists who might trade on changing times to cheat or otherwise despoil them. A quiet interest in a small trucking line, a native taxi-van company, and in the orderly administration of a few gambl-ing-and-woman rooms made Matisia a reasonably and quietly wealthy man, since it was difficult to find the correct tax forms on which to justify most of his income. Like so many other Kenyans, he sent as much money as he could to a Swiss bank account. For many of these smaller banking transactions he found the Asians handy—especially Asians like Mr. Vidhya Mukerjee, who seemed to be monopolizing the attention of his leader, Kamau, as they sat at this solemn lunch in the Stanley Grill. Mr. Vidhya Mukerjee was a canny man—he believed in the separation of business and politics whenever possible, only mingling the two when the former was impossible without the lever of the latter. Also he never confided his private dealings in Kamau, or even in Ndegwa—although you wouldn't think it to see them as chummy together as they were at this moment.

Kamau was speaking, with large gestures and great animation, to this Mr. Vidhya Mukerjee, a slim, bucktoothed Hindu with a pale greenish skin and large, liquid eyes. Like Ndegwa, Mr. Mukerjee was a lawyer, London-finished after initial schooling in Bombay. Mr. Mukerjee was Mr. Ndegwa's partner in the firm of Ndegwa, Alibhai and Mukerjee, which dealt mostly in property transactions and the conversion of other things to cash.

A great deal of Mr. Ndegwa's business among both white and Asian was effected by Mr. Mukerjee, who had gradually assumed a reputation as a sort of buffer state between the African and the white Kenyan. He was trusted to a point by both sides, and exemplified the habitual Asian position of maintaining nearly as possible the middle road. He dressed always in Euro-pean clothes, but his wife, when she appeared publicly, wore the sari and a sapphire stud in one nostril. They had a child a year and were among the acknowledged leaders of the Asian community, being nearly always invited to the larger grab-bag parties at Government House, when the Governor was laying on a 'representative' gathering for visiting dignitaries. Mr. Mukerjee could always be depended on to steer a careful pathway in any discussion which might prove embarrassingly partisan. That he was cordially loathed by both the African and the white colonials bothered Mr. Mukerjee not at all. His balances in the Bank of Baroda in Nairobi, in Bombay and Calcutta and in Switzerland were considerable, and his real-estate holdings, most of them under proxy names, were large.

The men chattered animatedly, fully conscious of the stir their presence created. The conversation was entirely in English, and dealt with such diverse topics as the next race meeting at Ngong and the ridiculous steep-ness of Kenya income taxes. The name of Peter Poole was sedulously avoided.

Bartlett and Witherspoon were halfway through the fish course when the Africans and the one Indian rose and left the dining-room. The native waiters stared after them as they walked slowly across the room and mounted the steps.

'They've shown the flag,' Bartlett said. 'They have made the happy multi-racial appearance. They will now disperse to various rabbit warrens and cut up the basic topic. It is a pitifully short price that Mr. Ndegwa and Mr. Kamau will meet under the rose some time today, and I shouldn't imagine that their appraisal of past events and today's major topic will differ much from ours. Except that emphasis will be placed more on future happenings than the little venture into equality they have just celebrated by appearing, bold as brass and neat as pins, in the stronghold of the enemy. I do not imagine that either Mr. Matisia or Mr. Mukerjee will be included in the chat between the Messrs. Kamau and Ndegwa. To each his own will occur later, and very much in private. I wish I could be a fly on the wall. Is there anything else I can help you with right now, Witherspoon?'

Witherspoon shook his head, picked up his change, and said good-bye to Bartlett at the left entrance. A couple hours' shut-eye wouldn't hurt him before he tackled his story. Must be old age or something, he thought. Used to be six or seven gins and a bottle of wine at lunch didn't bother him at all. Maybe it was the Nairobi altitude after all.

CHAPTER SIXTEEN

THEY STOOD in the doorway of the Norfolk dining-room, waiting for the headwaiter, a slim Goanese named Louie, to beckon them to a table in the large, overcrowded, old-fashioned eating-room. The Norfolk dining-room would never change very much unless Nairobi's passion for modernization ran completely amok. Its heavy wire-netted (for locking) service bar-and-cellar was behind the obvious cash-box, in the corner to the right. Deeper into the room, also to the right, a long white-clothed side table bore the weight of the huge salt hams, the green-mottled cuts of brawn, the purplish rolls of salami and sandwich meat, the pink York hams, the massive joints of cold roast beef, the carcasses of cold fowl, the cold beans and potato salad, the dishes of green peppers, onions, tomatoes and mustard pickles that made up the invariable cold luncheon in every good, clean, simple backwoods hotel in Kenya. The fact that the Norfolk's rustic location had now been gulped by a greedy city had not changed its bucolic character; at bottom it was still a clean, simple, back-country hotel, such as the Pig 'n Whistle at Meru or the White Horse at McKinnon Road, or any of the little, individually run hostels at Rumuruti or Nakuru or Kitale, where Mine Host tended bar and distracted Mum drove the waiters and the sweating cook-boy to fresh, un-African effort. Telephonic communication was still well-nigh impossible at the Norfolk; by the time the boy with the chalk-scribbled blackboard had located the desired party, the frustrated caller had rung off, in disgust.

The Norfolk entertained an international overflow, of course, when its ultra-modern sister, the New Stanley, was splitting its seams, for in recent years Nairobi had become a kind of African crossroads similar to Singapore in the East. But the constant heart of the Norfolk's clients was still old, hard-cured Kenya folk; pre- and post-1914–1918 baked-face red-necked types who had come to the colonies to wrest a life from the cantankerous clay which was rock-lumpy and cement-sticky in the wet, which blew away in clouds of red dust in the dry, and which washed, during the torrential northern rains, down the Tana River as far as fifty or sixty miles out to sea, making a great red stain on the bosom of the Indian Ocean. They said a farmer must hurry his crops in Kenya. The careless Kikuyu had levelled the noble cedar forests from Nairobi to Nanyuki, chopping the stately trees for firewood, and if a man's earth didn't wash away in the rains it would blow away in the long droughts. And like as not if you made a crop you were working mainly for the locusts, which periodically arrived in hordes vast enough to halt trains.

Let the young folk sprawl their sunburned long legs across the sidewalk at the Stanley's Thorn Tree; let them drink in the new lounge upstairs and dance in the fancy Grill; let them dine *à la carte* on foreign foods. The older folk still came to the Norfolk, where the food was as predictable as Louie's gold-toothed smile; good sound food which took a firm clutch o' the gob. This was the food they ate on the farms. Why should they change a half-century of habit when they came to town among the young Kenya cowboys, the tail-switching young gels, the spivs, the uppity blacks and more lately, the bloody refugees one saw all over the place these days?

But they were of a minority now, the old boys, with the sun-faded blue eyes, ragged moustaches and necks as cross-hatched by wrinkles as their ancient tweed coats; the old, stooped, weather-punished men, with Kenya callous on their broken-nailed liver-spotted hands, and Kenya malaria for-ever in their blood. A minority too the old women, leathery, sun-wrinkled sallow women, roughly rouged and powdered for the city, with hands worn fine by work, and bodies sagged shapeless by childbirth; bodies now made even more shapeless by baggy-seated skirts of ancient oatmeal tweed. Man and woman, they wore common-sense heavy-soled shoes and stout stockings, with no pretence at lah-de-dah finery. The flowered fancy silk and cotton dresses and the disgraceful short-shorts and skin-tight toreador pants and even tighter buttocks-squeezing blue jeans were for their daughters and granddaughters. The pipestem cavalry trousers and the *maridadi* sports shirts and loud sweaters and horse-blanket hacking jackets were for their sons and grandsons. The older folk dressed this old plain way at home, and they would dress this same old plain way in the cities, by God. They sniffed when they saw the African servants wearing tennis shoes; it was well known that a Wog couldn't function, much less think, with his shoes on.

Less and less frequently they came to Nairobi and the Norfolk—less even to the Stagshead in Nakuru since it had gone so fancy. Why, in the Stagshead, a man had to prove he was on safari or they wouldn't let him in without a coat and tie! What they liked was what they'd always known; a hotel where the barman-owner occasionally shouted you a drink and talked knowingly of crops and weather and cattle ailments. Space ships were beyond their comprehension or interest. Atomic potential for war held less menace than tomorrow's rinderpest or screw-worm. Let the world fret and fume about Khrushchev and the latest balls-up in the United Nations; lions still stalked their stock, leopards still slunk off with their pigs and dogs, and they still locked up the tea and sugar, the grog and the guns, because the Wogs would would steal anything that wasn't red hot or nailed fast.

When they spoke of 'the war' it was what they called 'the Kaiser's war' or the 'Fourteen-Eighteen war,' and the most serious inconvenience to their lives in recent years had been the Emergency. A confounded nuisance, the Mau Mau, with the troops clumping about all over the place and your best native labour being whipped off to jail by some half-licked cub of a police officer. Damned small wonder the Nigs had their tails on their shoulders today; they'd nothing to do but grow fat in jail and think up fresh deviltries. Like as not your best Wogs got clapped inside and learned new nastinesses from a few bad hats, while the actual, truly sinister types went scot-free and worked for the government, laughing behind their hands. Shocking bad handling all the way, the Emergency. If they'd left it to the settlers they'd've settled it in a flash. As it was it cost a bloody fortune and proved nothing except that the only thing a coon really understood was a boot in the backside.

The older people grumbled, drinking their pink gins and their warm beers on the breezy veranda. Then they went inside and ate swiftly and hungrily, not talking as they ate. Then they would go outside to where they had parked their *garis*—their Land Rovers with lorry bodies, screened with strong wire mesh so you could lock their contents away from black, thieving fingers; their pick-up trucks and their occasional saloon cars. They would wake the drowsing car-boy with a gentle kick or a shake, and they would drive back to Nakuru or Kitale and heave a sigh when the headlights wavered up the crooked road to the accustomed peace and shabby comfort of home.

*

Ten years ago, Brian Dermott thought as he and Philip waited for a table to clear, no more than ten per cent of the people in this room would bear the *Ausländer* stamp; the obvious red-faced Boer *en route* to South Africa; the obvious transient Britisher who looked naked without his rolled umbrella; the occasional fat-necked American businessman or the just-arrived self-conscious big-game hunter in stiff unwashed khaki safari clothes, bedizened in bullet-loops and broad hats with leopard or snakeskin *puggrees* round them; now and again the ill-assorted crew of a foreign cinema company, looking as obviously strange to the terrain as the script of the bad movie they would

86

eventually complete, and finally the occasional fussing flock of missionaries, headed for the darker areas of the continent and looking lost outside of Milwaukee or Manchester.

There were mission-folk here now. You could sort them out from the other Congo refugees, who showed some distant kinship with the Kenya settlers in their old stained shorts, long socks and raw-calf shoes, their flap-tailed sports shirts and floppy hats.

'Look,' Brian said, and nudged his brother. 'The Christers took off, too. When the chips were down they ran, just like everybody else. All the teaching, and the painful pulpit-pounding, all the insistence that there is no God but their own God, and just look at them; they had to git up and gallop, too, like the rest of these poor sods.'

'They didn't forget their fancy cameras,' Philip said. 'Look—the Leicas and Rollies and the little Jap ones. And the boxes with the wide-angle lenses inside.'

'I know it,' Brian said. 'They never stinted themselves much on the sharp equipment—shooting cars and guns and cameras. We used to have a rude song about it: "*Mimi nataka* headskin for the Lord." Last time I was in the Congo they were using their own aircraft to travel from hither to yon. A couple of them had a spot of bother with the Wogs when they were making their rounds in cars, and so they took to the air. I never held them with much as very useful, but I feel sorry for them, all the same.'

'So do I,' Philip said. 'They look so—sort of pathetic. It doesn't seem fair for people to have that much blind impracticable faith, work themselves to death trying to convert the heathen, and then find out that the heathen they converted consider them as just one more damned white man—perhaps a touch kinder than the ordinary *colon*, and so that much more likely to be despised. And certainly the first to be hit. I supposed that's why they've been raping the nuns and burning the missions.'

'Sad bunch,' Brian replied. 'They stick out like sore thumbs. Did you ever notice, Pip, that they're always either too fat or too thin, and that they seem sort of lost, no matter where you find them? I've seen them from one end of this bloody continent to the other, and they always share the same thing; that sense of sublime, pitiful faith that God will provide in the wilderness when they couldn't track a crippled elephant in a snowstorm or live a week away from the supply depot. Look at that chap.' Brian pointed to a lean, stooped man of fifty or sixty, with cavernous cheeks and red-rimmed feverish eyes. 'He looks bewildered even over there by the buffet table. He wants Divine help in choosing between the beef and the ham.'

'They must have done—must do—some good,' Philip said. 'Else they wouldn't keep sending them. People have to put a lot of pennies in the poorbox to keep them out here.'

'Maybe they do, maybe they don't,' Brian said. 'The purely medical ones, like old Schweitzer, yes. Old Schweitzer treats them like Wogs and cures them if he has to kill them to do it. The Come-to-Jesus ones, the reformers and the changers, I'd say *No*. I think that basically the African hates them worse than he hates the old hard-handed *kiboko* colonial who beats him when he's bad and pats him on the head when he's good, and who doesn't care a whoop how many wives he's got so long as his goats don't overgraze the Bwana's cattle land. The African can understand the sundowner settler with the purple face. Can he understand the men and women of God? I think not.'

'There's Louie waving,' Philip said. 'Come on, let's sit down. That lobby is packed with starving refugees.'

They were seated by the Goanese steward in his white *stengah*-shifter, and ordered beers and the Madrasi curry. Brian sat facing the dining-room door, which was still thronged with pressing people held back by the other Goanese steward's outstretched arm.

'The trouble with all these people is that they don't adapt or even try to adapt themselves to the African and the country,' he said, snapping a breadstick. 'The country doesn't rub off onto them, and God knows they haven't changed the country any. Nobody has and nobody ever will. If these missionary types had tried to shape their teachings to the African, instead of trying to force the African to fit the teachings, they'd have a different proposition. It could have been as uncomplicated as circumcision and not eating pork in hot countries.'

'True,' Philip replied. 'Here's the boy with the curry.'

It was true, almost pitifully true, Brian thought, as he spooned the mango chutney, the hot peppers, the bananas and the shredded coconut onto his mound of rice and dark-meated, black-gravied curry. Just look at them, milling around like strayed calves in a strange herd. They have been deserted momentarily by their God. Their clumsy kindnesses have been repaid by death and destruction. The feeding hand has been bitten; the loudest psalm-braying convert was the first to find the whisky and probably led the pack when it came to raping the nuns and firing the mission. But the Christers will come back again, Brian thought, to turn the other cheek, without having learned anything more useful than a little extra humility from the last bitter experience with the African.

They never changed, coming or going, the mission-folks, whether they were Belgian or American or French or British. They rejected factual Africa, spurned its protective coloration, and the day they left they knew as little of the true nature of the place and the people as the day they arrived, even if they'd been out for forty years. They tended the sick and they taught by rote in classrooms; they parrotted the Gospel and they railed against sin and its sister, nakedness; they preached pants and politeness, the true faith and sanitation. And they lost their converts with the same speed that they gained them.

*

Actually, Brian thought as he played with his food, if you wanted to switch things around a little bit, most of everything from Genesis to Exodus could be handily applied to the Wog. For or against. One way or the other. No wonder the poor bugger was confused when the mission-chaps preached heavenly salvation at him and then hurled hell at his head.

'What are you wool-gathering about?' Philip said. 'You've scarcely touched your curry.'

'Nothing very much. I guess I was brooding about the missionaries and trying to remember something from that simplified Bible we've got at the farm. You remember, the one the Catholic father left the old man when he died from blackwater. You ought to remember; Aunt Charlotte's drilled enough of it into your knotty little skull. It was the one with the pretty pictures.'

'Oh, sure. I re—— What's all the commotion out there in the hall?'

'I dunno. Something. Let's go and see.' Brian shoved back his chair. They walked to the door and pushed through the crowd. One of the Belgian refugees, a middle-aged, unshaven, fattish blond man, in a dirty sunburst sports shirt with the tails hanging loose, was weeping, and the hotel manager was trying to calm him. An Indian cashier was waving his arms and noisily trying to explain something to the manager.

The fattish blond man was scooping handfuls of money from a canvas bag and throwing the bills in the air. They eddied in the breeze as they drifted among the packed people in the lobby. The people were bumping each other, falling over each other, as they clutched for the cascading bills. 'Worthless, worthless, worthless!' the man was sobbing. 'All my work, worthless!' The hotel manager was hanging onto the man's arm, and talking rapidly, shouting over the Indian cashier's wail.

'Please, sir, please, sir, don't do that!' He suddenly snatched the bag from the Belgian's hand. 'All of you, now, go out to the veranda and let my boys pick up this money! Out, now, all of you!' He made pushing motions at the crowd with his free hand.

The weeping man's shoulders shook with sobs. The manager reached into the breast-pocket of his jacket, pulled out a carefully folded silk show-handkerchief, and shoved it into the Belgian refugee's hands.

'Control yourself, for Christ's sake, man!' he said. 'Here, come back with me into my office. I'll see that you get your money back!'

'I don't want it back!' The man's voice rose again almost to a scream. 'It's no good, it's worthless! Your cashier told me so! All I wanted was to change enough money to buy some lunch! And he, that Indian, said it was worthless, that he couldn't change it!'

'Get yourself in hand, man,' the manager said. 'I'll be pleased to give you lunch until you can see your consul and arrange to get some money. Calm yourself now, and come along with me. A good stiff drink will do you a world of good, and then a spot of lunch'll make you right as rain.'

'I don't want your charity! I want to change my money! It was good money, the best in the world, less than three months ago! Congolese francs, Congolese gold francs, and now your Indian won't change them, the bank won't change them! Do you think my consul has the money to change them? There is no government in the Congo any more!'

'Come along, man, come along with me,' the manager said. 'Come and have a drink in my office and I'll give you some money. You can sign a chit with me and redeem it when things straighten themselves out. You!' he said sharply to the waiters and the porters. 'Collect that money, every bloody note of it, and bring it along to me in my office. You!' to the Hindu cashier, who now stared slack-mouthed and breathless. 'See that none of that money sticks to their fingers, or you're all sacked! Come with me, sir, please come with me, now!' He shrugged despairingly as he and the still-protesting Belgian pushed through the straggling crowd. Running an orderly hotel was not the easiest job in the world these days. It never was, but it seemed especially complicated now, with refugees about.

'That wasn't very pretty,' Brian said as they returned to the table. 'Rather spoils one's appetite. I suppose it's a blow, at that, to suddenly be kicked out of what you've always regarded as home and to find out what money you could salvage is worthless. At least until they find out who's running the show in the Congo. If they ever do.'

'I suppose it can't be helped, but I can't see that hysteria solves anything,' Philip said. 'I'm for the cold cuts. You want some?'

'No. That money-throwing bloke wrecked me for the cold cuts. I'll just finish the curry and top off with a bit o' cheese,' Brian replied. 'Then let's get out of here. All these moaning refugees make me nervous. There's something shameful about running away just because a few Wogs cut up nasty. I still can't help but think that they're a poor lot, these Belgians. They dropped everything and took off.'

'You may be right,' Philip said. 'It only takes a day or so in Nairobi to make me homesick for the farm, Belgians or no Belgians. Finish your curry; I'll fetch you some cheese. I've a date to take Jill to the films after I run some more errands for Aunt Charlotte.'

Brian looked out towards the door again. The waiters from the veranda were still scratching up vagrant bills of Belgian Congo money; elusive, worthless bills that fluttered like crippled birds along the floor. He turned to his brother.

'To the films? They don't start until six. If you go to the movies you and Jill'll miss the excitement—if there is any.'

'That's why I'm taking Jill to the movies,' Philip Dermott said. 'To miss the excitement, if there is any. Here, have some cheese.'

BOOK TWO

THE BLACK sable bull with the great scimitar horns, and the coarse mane stiffly roached on his arched, swollen neck stared arrogantly out the office window as Brian pushed open the door on which the words 'Brian Dermott Safaris, Ltd.' were cut in gold letters on a mahogany plaque screwed to the blonde oak of the door. It was a good bull; Brian had shot it a dozen years ago on the Ugalla flats outside Tabora in Tanganyika. It was an apt *insigne*, as well, for an expensive safari-outfitting company—proud and elegant, rare but not unobtainable, massive but graceful, fierce but beautiful; sharply black-and-white in its bulked strength and cleanness of line. The sable suggested everything Brian wanted to convey of Africa when he was considering a suitable game animal for his letterheads and advertising; everything for which—he hoped—the new firm of Brian Dermott Safaris, Ltd., would stand in a highly competitive business.

'Hello, Hazel,' he said to one of the succession of assembly-line receptionists who came and toiled briefly at the desk by the door until such time as she wed a white hunter and cursed herself on the second pregnancy for marrying into a profession she knew enough about to know better than to marry into. 'Where's Don?' The salient contents of Hazel's pale blue angora sweater were wasted on him.

'In talking to Ken and Grace. I'll call him.' She picked up the phone and flicked the inter-office switch. 'Welcome back, Boss. You in town for long?'

'Just the day and night.'

'We don't see much of you any more. Hello, Grace? Will you tell Don, Brian's here, please.'

She cradled the receiver and smiled at Brian, showing all the teeth she was paid to display. She had been smiling at Brian for the six months she had worked in the office. She had abandoned any hope for a romantic future there, but she kept smiling anyhow. She was a nice girl, Hazel—freshly out from England within the year, pretty enough, and still vaguely thrilled over the idea of meeting the usually rich and often famous clients who laughed and joked with her; who sometimes took her out dancing, and who occasionally sent her little presents after a successful safari.

Brian walked over to her desk and flipped the pages of a flat morocco-leather book, its pages calendar-stamped and bearing the sunken gold imprint of the big sable bull on the wall. It was the bookings journal.

'Full, I see,' he said. 'Into year after next. Oh, how the money rolls

93

in. And out. Having any fun, Hazel? Going to marry anybody any time soon?'

Hazel managed a small simper and patted her carefully crimped blonde head.

'Some fun. A little. Nobody serious yet. Nobody's asked me.' She peeped at him coyly through the mascaraed palings of her supplementary lashes.

'Don't let it get you down.' Brian reached out and touched a gingerfinger-tip to the lacquered terraces of her head. 'You will. In this buckshee marriage brokerage I run, you will, all right.' He looked around. 'Oh, Big Don, Hi.'

'Quit annoying the help and come along with me,' Don Bruce said. 'I want to talk to you and this place is a madhouse in the afternoon.'

'If you say so.' Brian's eyes flicked over his partner. Don Bruce was wearing his hunting-clothes—bush jacket, slacks, and rough-calf desert boots. And he was also wearing a long-barrelled German Walther automatic pistol in a scarred holster. 'Ta, Hazel. Be a good girl and I may buy you some dinner one of these days.' The receptionist waved as they went out the door. As it closed slowly behind them on its shock-absorber, Brian thumped the holster.

'You look like you're off to the wars,' he said. 'Careful you don't frighten the clients. You *can't* be meeting anybody in that rig. Bloody gun's longer than you. It looks positively indecent.'

'No more than you with that thing inside your coat,' Don Bruce said, and the merry brown eyes were not merry over the button nose. 'At least I'm dressed for the gun.'

'What's all this about, anyhow?' Brian asked, as they climbed in Bruce's car and threaded through the traffic on Delamere Avenue. He swung round in his seat and looked at the hard, weather-gnawed face of his oldest friend, with the sun-mottled, bleached lips and the bones showing strong under the taut chapped skin. There was some strain around the eyes and a distrait look he hadn't noticed for a long, long time. What Don said was true enough; he didn't have the face for tragedy or even seriousness. The bright chipmunk-brown eyes and the snub nose gave him an oddly boyish, carefree expression that understated the toughness of his capabilities. Don was a hard-riding polo-player in the country matches, and had been a slashing footballer and a very fast boxer. As he farmed more and hunted less, he had lost much of the basic blithe spontaneity that had made him a rather strenuous relaxer. Farming clawed and bit at a man; Don only took a safari now when he actively needed the money—new farming equipment or a new baby, depending. He'd even sold his little string of polo ponies. Those personally and schooled nags were about the last thing Brian reckoned old Don would get rid of, with the possible exception of his guns.

'What's chewing on you?' he asked again.

'It'll save until we get to your place. I still don't like to drive and talk. Remember the house rules?' Don Bruce grinned slightly out of one corner of his face at Brian.

94

'I remember. But I guess I've broken them both in recent years, and will again. But they were pretty good rules, at that. Practical. No talk while drive. No booze while hunt.'

Don parked the car with some of his old flair, and they entered Brian's flat. Don flung himself into one of the big horrible overstuffed easy chairs, and arranged his face for an unpleasantness. It was a look Brian had seen before—generally as they dived into thick stuff for something wounded that promised to be ugly.

'You want a drink?' Brian asked, moving to the little bar.

'Yes, by God, I do. Blast the house rules. I can use one and I need one.'

Half-facing Don Bruce as he poured the whisky, Brian noticed that Don's hands trembled as he cupped a flame to cigarette. He tipped a little extra into Don's glass.

'Here, son. Cheers,' he said, and sat down in the other chair. 'Spill it. What's on your mind?'

'First things first,' Don Bruce looked acutely miserable. 'I hate to ask it, but I guess I've got to. Brian, would you buy my farm?'

'Christ, Don, don't jump at me that way! I thought you asked me if I'd buy your farm. What the hell would I do with another farm? I don't even work the one I've—we've got. You can't be serious?'

Brian tasted his drink and looked at his friend. He was pale under the weathered skin and the strain was more evident in the eyes. Don's eyes had a way of retreating into his skull when he was very weary. He was thinner, too, but hard work in the heat would account for that. The change was there in Don's eyes, and it wasn't fatigue.

'I guess you are serious, at that. Don, truly I don't know. It's a difficult position to explain. I don't really *own* anything. Except the safari business of course, and by the time I've parcelled out the shares at the end of the year —well, profit cut six ways isn't much profit after the expenses and overhead and taxes. You'd know that as well as me.'

'I know it. I wasn't referring to the safari business. I don't think that'll last more than another year or so, either, the way things are going. But what I guess I actually meant—hell, Brian, it's hard to say. But I know you and your Aunt must have made a devilish lot of money on Glenburnie. We aren't too far away from each other. I'm not asking the earth. I want just enough to clear my debts and pay off the Land Bank and a little left over to start fresh somewhere. Somewhere out of Africa. *Anywhere* out of Africa.'

Brian's first impulse was to protest, but instead he got up and paced the room. He watched Don finish the drink and then took the glass from his hands and filled it again. He put in the ice carefully and swirled the liquid around before he handed it back to Don. He tossed the non-existent forelock out of his eye and rubbed his moustache.

'I don't know exactly how to answer you, chum. Like I started to say, I don't really own anything. I imagine the old girl'll leave Glenburnie to me and Pip when she dies, because Nell's married now and I suppose they'll be pushing on some day. But then I hadn't really thought of Nell's new husband. Maybe they'll want to stop on. In that case I suppose Nell'll still have a third interest in Glenburnie when Aunt Charlotte pegs out, which she probably never will. Nell being married puts a new complexion on it. George hasn't got anything. We're all sort of squatters, in a way. Excuse me, please, for wondering out loud. I was more or less talking to myself.'

Don Bruce grinned a little.

'Take all the time you need. I'm still drinking your whisky.'

Brian paused to light a cigarette. He spoke flatly.

'If you want to sell your farm and we have the money and the old girl thinks it's a good idea then I—we'll—buy your farm. I don't want the bloody thing but it's a good farm and I know what you've put into making it that way.'

'Only my heart, soul, back, hands, hat, ass and overcoat. Not to forget my last two polo ponies. Excuse the drama, Brian. I don't express my humble gratitude very well. Nobody's buying land—everybody wants to sell. And now I suppose you'll want to know why I come snivelling to you with my troubles?'

'It would be a help,' Brian said quietly. 'If you want to tell me. But I thought you just asked me if I wanted to buy your farm. I'm not buying your bloody memoirs.' His voice hardened.

Don Bruce got up. He put both hands on Brian's shoulders and shook him gently.

'I feel a proper bastard, Brian. I apologize. I never asked anybody—any-*bloody*-body for any-*bloody*-thing in my life before. But in this case I don't think I can kill my own snakes. I came at you tail-end-to. Mind if I start over, after saying first, thanks again, chum?'

'You'll have me in tears, Big Man,' Brian said, and cuffed him lightly on the chin. 'Get on with you. Forget it. Tell me or don't tell me, whatever makes you feel better.'

Don Bruce's face tightened.

'It's hard for me to believe sitting here that I have just asked you to buy what I used to think was my life—would always be my life. Eight years ago we all thought that once we had the Micks put down everything was going to be sweet sailing. Else I wouldn't have married. Else I wouldn't be whining to you now. *Uhuru!* Shit, what a selling we got last spring in London at Lancaster House. Macmillan with his "winds of change". And Macleod threw us right back to the same people we were shooting and hanging and clapping behind bars six years ago. It seems a bloody century. . . . I saw Peggy at lunch. She didn't eat any. She just made a hair-raising dash to town and brought all the kids with her. You know Peggy; does *that* interest you—that she'd suddenly swoop off the farm with all the kids and lug them to Nairobi when we were planning a little beano all on our own, away from brats and calving cows and glandered ewes and sick Wogs and spavined horses? It interested *me*. I can tell you, and that is why I am going to sell the

96

farm and if I can't sell it I'll bloody well flog what sheep and cattle I can on the sneak and let the bloody banks go stuff themselves!' Don struck his knee with his fist.

'What did Peggy have to say, then, that's got you in such a sweat?' Brian looked keenly at his friend. Don was trembling again.

'I didn't put it to you this way before I found out if you'd take the farm—I didn't want it all on my fear and your friendship. I'm frightened, Brian. I'm scared bloody stiff! Not for me—not for me personally. But just damned well frozen with fear for Peggy and the kids, and sick with fear of what the future looks like.'

'Okay, okay,' Brian said. 'Calm down. You're scared stiff. What did Peggy tell that's got you behaving in such an undonly manner?'

'My kids are fourth-generation Kenya, Brian.' Don's voice was level, now, by effort. 'They are Africans just as much as if they were black as Mboya. They have a right to live in their country—a country that their great-grandfather started and that their father helped pull out of a miserable mess. And I don't want my kids slaughtered! And I don't want my Jock being split open for some filthy bloody oathing ceremony because of something I did! I don't want my wife ripped open and her belly stuffed full of stones after the bloody apes have finished with her like they're doing with the women in the Congo! And what's more I don't want us to have to live in fear of it! I don't want to go to bed with it and wake up with it every day! If that's living in Africa then I say the hell with Africa!'

Don Bruce put his face in his hands. He raised his head, after a moment, and shoved out his glass. He smiled in embarrassment.

'You'll probably think I'm hysterical, or over-melodramatic, or at least half-mad, but I'm not. This morning, on the farm, a succession of peculiar things happened to Peggy. . . . First you have to remember that my baby, the last one, little Jock, *is* more or less a Kikuyu. You were away, Brian, you weren't at the christening, but there was a hell of a big do. All the clans from both sides of the ridge came and pitched up on the farm, I killed some sheep and cattle and we had a whacking great *ngoma*. It carried on for days. The Kyukes gave little Jockie the usual mumbo-jumbo—you know the old-fashioned drill.'

'I know it. Go ahead. Remember I was brought up just across the hill from you, and just about the same way.'

'I don't know why they raised all this special christening fuss about little Jock—presents and the money and the spitting and the rest of it. They'd brought a few gifts for the other kids before, the odd sheep or goat, but nothing very special for Ellen, nothing out of the usual for Angus and Lois. But for Jock, the last one—it was like the old days my father used to talk about. They fair showered him with gifts. The kid's really born in the tribe and at the time I thought that it was jolly fine.'

Don Bruce paused to wipe a sweat-beaded forehead.

'You have to remember some of the other things, too. Recall we never had any trouble on the farm during the Emergency? Everything was fine on the farm until Peggy's old man went off to join the KPR and got scragged by some of Kimathi's people and left Peggy alone. Peggy ran the whole shebang most of the time I was off in the bush tracking niggers or teaching the troop how to track them. Maybe she didn't run it well but she kept it together. We had a tame witch doctor on the place. Old Kinyanjui. Very powerful old bloke, or so the other Wogs evidently thought. Drew a magic ring around the farm. Cast a whole flock of spells. We didn't lose any cattle and we didn't have any raids. None of the boys ran off. We were about the only farm that didn't lose labour.

'Kinyanjui told Peggy then that she had nothing to worry about. She believed him, as she's always believed anything they tell her. She's as much Kyuke as me. She didn't lock up everything and barricade the doors like a lot of people did. She reckoned that if she was going to get her throat cut she'd get her throat cut, and a few odd doors more or less wouldn't make any difference, specially if they fired the house.'

'I see they've started that again, all over again, the house-firing, I mean,' Brian said. 'Two inside the last two weeks, according to the paper today. A woman and four kids yesterday. Almost like old times. Sorry. Go ahead, but I want you to know I'm following you.'

'Kinyanjui died about three months ago. I was off on safari way the hell and gone up around Singida. Naturally there was no point in sending me a message, even if somebody'd told the office. They didn't bury Kinyanjui on the place, oddly. They took him down around Naivasha somewhere and left him to the hyenas. I didn't think anything of that when I came home and Peggy told me. What the hell, he was old-time Kyuke, and he was older than God. I reckoned he'd told somebody he didn't want to be planted in strange ground, like the modern Nig, but wanted to go back to his fathers via the place he started. Obviously, even if I'd been curious, it was too late to do any investigation. What little the hyenas left for the vultures already belonged to the white ants. You can't autopsy a memory.

'Upshot is, about two weeks after the old man kicked off, my headman, old Njeroge, came by to talk some business about the sheep. I went along to his *thingira* with him. We were sitting on our heels in front of the fire, smoking and scratching and drinking some of that vile *pombe* his wives make and talking about everything under the sun except whatever was bothering him. He got up and went into the bachelor hut half a dozen times on one pretext or another and finally he came to the point.

' "Bwana," says he, "Kinyanjui didn't die. He was poisoned." '

Don paused and looked at Brian.

'Brian, I know Wogs, or ought to. I made some crack about it being high time, especially if he'd been taking any of his own medicine. I was thinking, what the hell, these chaps are always poisoning somebody either on purpose or by accident and there's always a lot of loose talk about poison when you're playing about with witchcraft. And most everybody hates a witch doctor anyhow, if only from fear. But then I twigged something a little different in Njeroge's face.

' "*Kweli*," he said. "Truly, Bwana. But not from witchcraft or by any other jealous witchdoctor. He was poisoned as one ordinary man would kill another man, as with a spear or gun. And not by one of the old people on the *shamba.* Two of the new men are gone, Bwana. Gathiru and Kaluku. Those men were hired last spring after the forgiveness when they turned the people in the detention camps free. Everybody here knows he was poisoned, Bwana. They whisper of little else. And now some of the older men speak of taking their families and leaving. They never talked that way during the Mau Mau, Bwana. Only since Kinyanjui is dead do they talk this way. The magic ring is no longer round the farm." '

Despite himself Brian felt his nape hairs bristle, the same old down-rushing elevator feeling he always got when he was tracking wounded unseen leopard or buffalo by the blood spoor; the feeling he got just before something charged or leaped.

'You believed him, then?' he said to Don Bruce. It was a foolish, hollow question. Don spread his hands and hunched his shoulders.

'I don't know if I make any sense,' he said, 'but things were going beautifully when I left the farm to take that last safari. Just having that little extra bit of cash was jolly fine, because the taxes had unaccountably come due again, and I was planning to strike the Land Bank for a renewal on the mortgage and didn't want any tax collectors leaning over my shoulder when I made my pitch to the man. So I confess I left in a hurry and forgot the whole thing—put it down to Nig nerves, superstition, *you* know.

'Then while I was gone everything seemed to go wrong at the farm. Peggy'd got pregnant again, and she'd slipped the baby. She never slips babies. A new species of blight hit the pyrethrum. We had a touch, just a touch of fever in the dairy herd, and the milk went useless. One mysterious fire in the barn. Leopard in the sheep. More cattle strayed. Fences broken here and there. And the strangest damned indrawn lethargy among the Africans, Peggy says. All this she tells me now. You know the black man's secret weapon, Brian, the one when they pull down all the shutters in front of their eyes and you can't get anywhere close to what's buzzing in their bonnets?

'Most of it you'd normally put down to *shauri ya mungu,*—God moves in mysterious ways; a farmer's life is hard; never get mixed up in a business involving anything that eats; we didn't need another baby anyhow; accidents will happen—all the other old soul-savers that keep us from going insane. But this one point sticks: All the bad luck happened since old Kinyanjui died, or was poisoned. Yes, by God, I believed him.'

'Coincidence, superstition and all the apt clichés, as you say,' Brian murmured. 'My old man used to be worse than you. He saw an Irish omen in every cloud and an evil portent crouching behind every ant-hill.'

'Okay, I agree. So did my father. But try this one on for size: Eighteen

99

men left the farm *this* morning and took their families with them! and Peggy —well, you know Peggy. Peggy left the farm too, in a hurry. And what she told me at the lunch we didn't eat, before I put her and the kids into a cottage at the Norfolk, is enough to curl your hair. . . .'

CHAPTER TWO

MARGARET ASHCROFT BRUCE stood only half a head shorter than her rangy husband Don. She was a large girl, generously fleshed, with big bones. She had been born big and was slightly more heavied, now, with frequent child-bearing. Not that the kids had caused her much trouble. Her friends said that it was almost vulgar, the way she had them. 'Peggy goes out behind a bush, like a Kikuyu woman,' they teased her. 'One grunt and she's back with a new Bruce in one hand and a lamb in the other.'

It wasn't all that easy, of course, but Peggy Bruce thanked God she didn't make a great fuss over dropping her foals. This, she said with a grin, was just as well, because all Don Bruce had to do was flap a pair of old jodhpur breeches at her and they were well away on another extra mouth to feed. She didn't mind; she loved all children and it was especially nice having her own around when Don was away on safari so much. She raised them wild, and let them run half-naked with the Kikuyu children on the farm. They were good kids; the two boys and two girls; brown and tough and rosy with health, and if they suffered cuts and the occasional broken bone she bandaged or splinted without maternal heroics until the doctor could come, and they never seemed the worse for the homespun splicing. She was, therefore, surprised when, in the casual expectance of a fifth baby, she felt a sudden twinge and a tearing cramp and then a burning stab of pain, and suddenly she was rummaging in the medicine cabinet because this was one baby she seemed definitely destined not to have.

Peggy was what all her husband's lustier male friends called a good wench, and what the older generation used to describe as a fine figger of a woman. Her hair perchance was tumbled, somewhat streakily blonde, and she had round plump pink cheeks, merry bluebell eyes two generations removed from the Highlands, and the strong white teeth that went with the hearty laugh she fetched up from her guts. Her big, high-bosomed figure was handsomely ample and healthily sexy. She looked very much at home in the overalls and gumboots she wore when she was mucking the pigs or moving the sheep to fertilize a patch of momentarily fallow ground. She had looked very much at home during the Emergency when she ran her father's farm with a pistol strapped to her hip. But she could still pull on a sweater and summon a whistle from the Kenya cowboys who ogled the girls from the sidewalk seats at the Thorn Tree. When she swapped her boots for spike heels and squeezed into a girdle and a low-cut black dress to go on the town with Don, they cleared a swath among the dancers at the Equator.

Peggy laughed with her husband and also at him. If he occasionally took a couple over the mark when he came off safari and some of his weaving chums decanted him onto the front porch, she whipped off his boots and slung him into bed and brought him a non-acrimonious beer for his head the next morning. She liked to drink herself, and generally had a gamey story of her own to contribute when the fire warmed the grog and coarsened the conversation.

The men adored her, for she seldom traded on women's frailer assets. No menstrual moods, no acute attack of the lonesome blues transmuted into boredom and its by-product of coy flirtation, no vicious gossip ever blew downwind from Peggy. She made no passes at the men, and the men attempted no serious shots at Peggy, making her reasonably unique in a country which was noted for the comfortable looseness of its connubial accoutrements.

There was no feminine fraud in Peggy, and she remained happy and secure in the knowledge that her husband implicitly trusted and shamelessly adored her. She did not particularly mind a shortage of frippery and the fact that her scabby old Chev was Kenya road-battered and past its prime. Babies cost a packet, and she knew that Don harrowed every spare shilling back into the farm, with a flinty brown eye to future security for her and the kids. Secretly she was stealing from her own tiny personal allowance for the hazy day when she could buy back Don's polo ponies and surprise him at the paddock with his sacrificed pets. In Kenya polo was as much a way of country life as the beer at the pub. She had loved seeing Don play, the rawboned giant's figure merged into the plunging pony, its sweating barrel grafted to his guiding knees, his torso as much portion to the animal as the horse's neck and head. God knows poor old Don didn't have much fun. Between dawn-to-midnight farming, and back-breaking safari he'd earned a bit of sport, and Peggy meant to see he had it again.

CHAPTER THREE

NOW IT was 10 A.M. on Hardscrabble Farm and time for the morning mug of tea. She'd just sit and sip for a second in front of the fire before she cleaned the muck off herself and get tarted up to drive to Nairobi to meet Don for lunch and maybe the pictures, then dinner at the Grill and a spot of dancing later at the Equator, or that new place, Maxim's, possibly with Ken Jenkins and his Marie. Be the first time she'd been off the bloody farm since she lost the baby. Christ, I hate sheep, she thought, as she poured a stiff tot of rum into the steaming black tea. I've been up since bloody dawn with the silly things. Serve them all right if they froze to death with their wool off. I don't really mean that, she amended rapidly. Lovely, sweet, simple, beautiful, glorious little sheepsie-weepsies. Money in the bank, they are, and God knows we can use it.

Peggy kicked off her muddy boots and swung her thick-stockinged feet up on a zebra-skin hassock. She lit a cigarette and took a deep swig of the rum-richened tea. Her mind ticked off a fast inventory of the children—little Jock crowing over there in the basket; Ellen and Angus both outside; they had gone with her to pretend they were helping with the sheep, and she hadn't the heart to chase them for getting in the way. She could hear them shouting outside—shrill voices mingling now with the barking of the big Alsatian that Don had christened Macleod in mock honour of the Colonial Secretary when the Lancaster House disaster had handed Kenya back to the Mau Mau forces. Little Lois would be sleeping in her crib, at least penned safe from harm's way. If she weren't happy she'd be yelling. And Floss, the old collie bitch, was snoring in a corner, pregnant again. It seemed to run in the family.

She looked around the room and sighed. It was a nice room, nothing grand, but *nice*. Nicer for the fact that Don had done it all—all the house, lovingly, painstakingly, room by room, himself and with his own native labour from the farm. Her Don was wonderful with his hands. The room was witness: the double, high-peaked ceiling of finely plaited Kavirondo cane; the halved-bamboo work on the bar and coffee tables; the great deep-rutted red planks of pegged cedar that formed the three panelled walls; the burly masoned great wall with its huge red-and-blackstone fireplace and massive wrought-iron firebasket and hob; the plaited sisal mats on the floor and the various pelts flung helter-skelter, even the stylishly picturesque iron gates and doors of tribal spears—this was all Don's doing. The house had been a shambling ruin when they'd come to live in it; her father had combined drink with indolence after her mother's death, while she was away at school, and had let both the house and the farm go to rack under native operation. Every inch of the new house, every foot of the acreage had felt the weight of her husband's hands and the force of the endless driving interest that lay always under the lightly joking manner. And now, finally, the cruellest work was done, the place was achingly scourged into its promise, the thirstiest dry acres irrigated, the wasted water cherished, the fallow land tamed and tilled, even the denser bush cleared and most of the rhinos in it shot or driven away. It had been a fine life to live and it would become easier as time went on and some of the dividends of their hand-blistering industry began to flow back.

If only . . . Peggy frowned. These elections next year . . . and after that next year, the following—*uhuru*—freedom. But it couldn't turn into a horrid tangle like the Congo. It mustn't, couldn't be allowed. They had too much invested now to let it go back into careless black hands. She had enough disaster out of that every time Don went on safari. Well, worrying about it wouldn't help. They'd just have to wait and see, for there really wasn't anything else to do—or any other place to go, was there?

There was a sibilant sound of bare feet. It was Murungwa, the old houseboy—older, crankier, certainly less competent with each year, but with the insidious subtlety of most ancient servants now the undisputed master of the house. He had been in Don's family since birth, and had never worked in the fields outside the house.

'Memsaab.' The old African's voice was hesitant. His lean greyish-brown fingers twisted in the folds of his white *kanzu*.

'Yes? What is it?' With Murungwa it was always some fresh problem these days. He was as fussy as an old woman.

'When is the Bwana coming home?'

'Maybe tomorrow. Maybe late tonight. I am going into Nairobi in half an hour to meet him.'

'You will take the children with you?'

Peggy laughed.

'Not bloody likely,' she said in English. Then, in Swahili: 'No, of course not. I will leave the children here with you as always when I go to meet the Bwana for a day. What's the matter with you, anyhow? *Shauri gani?*'

'Do not leave the children, Memsaab. Take the children with you. My daughter has come from Nairobi. Wambui—the one you know as Mary. She has dreadful things to tell. You remember Wambui, the daughter of my second wife? She is the one you put in your own bed when she was so sick that time with the fever.'

I remember Wambui, all right, Peggy thought. I thought Don would skin me for my little Florence Nightingale trick. Cure 'em if you must, but not in my bed, said Don.

'Where is she? What's this all about?'

'She is in the kitchen. She is very frightened, Memsaab. She is afraid to speak, but she says she must. They will probably kill her, but she must speak.' Murungwa paused for an African's dramatic effect. 'I believe her, Memsaab. I am frightened too.'

'Who'll kill her? Don't talk a lot of nonsense. Send her in.'

'Yes, Memsaab. But it is not nonsense. Eighteen men have left the *shamba* since last night. They have taken their women and children with them. I have talked to Njeroge. He is in the kitchen too. The men have left everything—they have taken only clothing and even left the cooking stones behind.'

Peggy Bruce felt for the first time now the clutch of fear on her throat as the old man padded off on his bare feet, his *kanzu* flopping. In a moment a Kikuyu woman of about eighteen or nineteen came into the room. Her hair was not scraped clean from her skull, as with most of the country Kikuyu women, but had been carefully nurtured into a fuzzed growth like a cropped lawn, upstanding in a dense round crew-cut on her head. Her lips were painted thickly, and she had great circles of rouge on her cheeks. She was wearing a sleazy green dress which had obviously come off the rack of one of the cheap-jack shops in the bazaar. She was barefoot, now, and the bunions on her twisted toes showed an uncomfortable acquaintance with white women's shoes. She dipped her head and kept her eyes lowered, the eyeballs rolling sidewise in fright.

'Well, what is it?' Peggy omitted the customary *jambos* and *habaris*. So our little Mary-Wambui is just one more Nairobi floozie, she thought.

'Speak! What do you want to tell me?'

The girl was quivering all over, and at first the words would not come freely. Then, staring at the floor and plucking at her frock, she began to speak. It sounded insane, wild, it sounded almost gibberish, with the sun bright and the birds loud and the children screaming at each other and the big dog barking outside. Finally the halting words began to form sentences and some extra weight was given by the fact that the girl Wambui was talking in such a low, mesmerized voice that Peggy had to strain to hear her.

It appeared that she lived now in Nairobi and worked sometimes in what she called 'a place of drinking beer'. Many men came there, and there was a gramophone and rooms for gambling and for going with the women as well as for drinking beer. There were many such places in Nairobi and Nyeri and in all the larger towns. She went there, sometimes, although she was not a . . . she was not a professional woman. She never solicited the streets and sometimes she worked in the homes of the white memsaabs, washing and cleaning but work was hard to come by these days and her last man had left her. She had never been properly married because her father, Murungwa, could not or would not settle for less than the fullest bride price in sheep or goats or its money equivalent, and no young man could afford the price, and so since she had never been properly married and was now too old to command a price of any sort and long ago had allowed the second apron to be lifted—here she abandoned Swahili and fell into Kikuyu—since she had three children without a proper marriage ceremony she was forced to work for her *posho* as best she could.

'Come on, get on with it,' Peggy said, having heard the same story more than once before. 'Here. Sit down by the fire.'

The girl nodded and sank gracefully to the floor, sitting splay-kneed on her heels.

In this place of amusement she met many men, the voice went on, blood-chillingly soft and monotonous, maddeningly slow, and sometimes after they were sated with women, they got drunk and boasted and exchanged secrets, as men will to prove their importance when they have taken too much *pombe*. Yesterday, she was resting on a pallet next to a room where such men were talking, the door was cracked open, young men they were, wearing the uniform of the KNAP, and boasting of a membership in something else called the GKM. . . .

'I did not understand all that the men said, and besides, they were drunk. But they mentioned the name of this Bwana who is supposed to hang this day and they mentioned other names and one of the names they mentioned was the name of Bwana Don and the Bwana Brian, the baby Jock, who they say is true Kikuyu-born, and so is doubly important as a lesson to others about what they are going to do if . . . if. . . .' The girl's voice died away and tears came to her eyes.

'Have some tea,' Peggy said, attempting to keep her own voice under control. 'Here.' She poured a cup and half filled it with sugar. The girl took it and flicked her eyes gratefully under her lowered lids.

'Now. Tell me what else you heard. Nobody is going to hurt you here. Tell me: What else?'

'They said that if they, the Serkiali, did not hang the Bwana Poole for killing the Kikuyu boy when the boy threw stones at his dog—if they did *not* hang him, every Kikuyu would make his mark on a paper to the Governor, the Bwana Mkubwa ya Serikiali. And they would take the *chitti* to Government House and ask permission to buy Bwana Peter Poole a dog—many dogs. They want to buy the Bwana Poole a dog if the dog was so important that he killed a Kikuyu boy for throwing rocks at it. They want to buy one dog for each Kikuyu to give to Bwana Peter Poole.' The girl's voice died again. Then she clenched her hands and seemingly forced herself to continue.

'Yes. They will each buy a dog and give it to Bwana Peter Poole. But Bwana Peter Poole, if he goes free, must give the Kikuyu something in return. He must give them back the soul of Kawame wa Musunge, the boy he killed with his pistol! In an even exchange for many dogs, he must give back the boy's soul!'

The girl stopped and sobbed. Peggy stared at her, her lips parted.

'And the way to get back the soul of the boy Kawame in return for the dog is to take the life of the dogs! But if it is difficult to find that many dogs they will do as Bwana Peter Poole did, substitute the life of a man for the life of a dog! And it will all be done at once, as it was supposed to be done before in the Mau Mau!'

The girl pitched forward and seized Peggy Bruce around her ankles. Peggy bent and pried her fingers loose, tilted up her chin, and patted her on the head. The girl snuffled, her nose running, and Peggy reached into a box of Kleenex and ripped off a handkerchief.

'Blow!' She said. It was all she could think of to say. The outlandish enormity of what the girl was saying was past her comprehension. The girl took the Kleenex, blew her nose with a tremendous snort, and then wiped her eyes.

'When does all this drama take place?' Peggy asked harshly.

'It starts tonight if they do not hang Bwana Peter Poole! There will be a crowd waiting outside the jail to learn if they hang him! They will know—they have men inside the jail to tell them if they hang him or do not hang him and try to take him away in a trick! It starts tonight and will continue on tomorrow until all the dogs and all the white men and women are dead!'

'But how will they get word to the people in Thika and the Kinangop and Rumuruti and Nakuru and all the other places?' Peggy's practicality sounded stupid even to herself. It all sounded so ridiculous, a weeping whore, transference of men's guilt to animals, and animals' symbolic guilt to men—and then Peggy remembered her childhood and all the things she had heard, her young womanhood and all the things she had seen and *knew* about oaths and ritual vileness and murder in these same hills, and all of it less than ten years ago, and with less excuse—a running noose of terror that strangled the country for seven years.

'They will ring up the *dukahs* on the telephone and they will send men in cars to spread the word. It has all been worked out in advance, these men said. And Memsaab. . . .' Her voice trailed again.

'Yes? What?' Peggy made herself speak sharply and authoritatively, as she had always been taught to speak when dealing with Africans. She barely restrained herself from grasping a fistful of the girl's crinkly hair and shaking her violently, as she had seen Don do to jar an African's memory.

'Even if the Bwana Peter Poole *is* hanged, there are other things to come in the future. When *uhuru* comes and the black man is master, there will be a great screening, as the Kikuyu were screened in what they called Operation Anvil. Then the *Mzungu* will be sorted out as the Kikuyu *watu* were separated. There is a "short list" of people to be killed as war criminals, and a "long list" of people to be punished, and only a very short list of people to go unpunished and to be allowed to keep some of what they have. There will be the same kind of screening that the Kikuyu suffered during the Mau Mau—white men and women will be stripped naked and kicked and beaten as the Kikuyu were stripped naked and kicked and beaten!

'And all the Africans who helped the whites in the Emergency will be treated the same as the whites except worse, for they hate the Home Guard Kikuyu more than they hate the *Mzungu*! In the Mau Mau many bad things were done by the blacks to whites, and worse things were done by the whites to blacks, and even worse things were done by the loyal Kikuyu to the Mau Mau Kikuyu. There will be no white soldiers and police to protect them this time! All this bad memory will be washed out in blood when *uhuru* comes!

'Everyone on this farm was a loyal Kikuyu during the troubles,' she said and her voice whispered dully, hopelessly. 'And the Bwana Don stands high, very high on the short list. There have already been many oathings around the farm, outside the ring of Kinyanjui the witch doctor, but now that Kinyanjui is dead the ring is broken, and now they will have oathings here where they were afraid before. And . . . and they need a special sacrifice for the first big oathing for this farm and it has been decided that, that—' her voice faded again, and died altogether. This time Peggy did seize her short hair and shake her head violently from side to side.

'And what? Tell me what!' She gave the girl's head a final jerk.

'The first sacrifice for this area will be the *mtoto*, the baby Jock, the littlest one! He is white but he was made Kikuyu at the baptism, and so, being both white and Kikuyu, he is twice as strong as a sacrifice for the oathing! He can wipe out the wrongs on both sides as they once slew a black goat and a white ram. . . .' Her voice died completely.

Now the barking of the big Alsatian increased. But its timbre had changed. It was lower now, more fiercely guttural, somewhere between snarl and angry alarm. It was leaving the yard—the barking became less frequent and steadily fainter. The dog was running hard.

Something had to be done about the weeping woman on the floor. What she said made little sense but her abject terror was shockingly convincing. Peggy Bruce had lived in Africa all her life.

'Murungwa! Come and bring Njeroge!' she called. The old houseboy and the foreman came running from the kitchen. 'Take her back to the kitchen! Send me your woman, Njeroge, and tell her to dress the little children. Then you come here to me! Murungwa! You get Angus and Ellen in the house and help them dress for town! And see what has happened to that dog!'

As the men lifted Wambui still sobbing from the floor and hustled her to the kitchen, Peggy darted to a cabinet and unlocked it with a key from a cluster she wore on the big ring hooked to her belt. There was a pistol in the cabinet, an enormous Texas-type single-action ·44 revolver that some American client had given Don. She spun the cylinder and checked it for loads, then shoved the pistol back in its holster and buckled the belt so that it made a bandolier. She slung the make-shift bandolier over one shoulder, the big gun bumping her ribs as she moved swiftly about the room. The baby, Jock, was fully awake in his crib now, and was crying; he had undoubtedly wetted himself. She gave his head a pat, and dashed back to the bedroom. The baby Lois, nearly two, had also awakened, and was bouncing unsteadily on her feet in the crib, clutching the bars as she danced. Her hair was moistly tousled into a twisted peak, like a gnome's, and her fat face was rosy with sleep. Peggy bent to kiss the top of her head, then sat on the side of the bed to rip off her overalls and shuck her shirt and underclothes. She dived under the shower long enough to wash off the morning muck, and then, naked, she rummaged for a girdle and bra and a half-slip and frock. She had squirmed into the girdle and was pulling up the petti-skirt when there was a knock and a soft woman's voice said: '*Hodi?*' It was Wangu, the wife of Njeroge the foreman.

'*Karibu, kuja!*' she said. 'Dress the babies in the Churchill suits—the one-piece overalls. And pack my toilet things and some extra underwear in an overnight bag, and the baby things as well. Here'—she flung a couple of frocks and an extra pair of shoes on the bed—'put these in too. Hurry! *Suria!*' She used the most forceful vulgar word for speed.

She pulled a printed silk dress over her head. She zipped up the side with one hand and ran a comb through her damp hair with the other. She slapped on lipstick any old way, dabbed her nose with powder, and picked up the gun belt with its heavy holstered pistol and strapped it around her engirdled waist, then smoothed the frock over her hips and down her front. Even wearing Don's old cowboy pistol it would not have occurred to Peggy Bruce to go into Nairobi sloppy in slacks the way so many of the women did.

She reached for the telephone and stopped. It was no good trying to find Don; he'd be at Shaw and Hunter's checking guns, or he'd be having a talk at the bank, or he could be having a drink with the boys in any of ten places. It was no good calling the police post in Nyeri; what could she say, how could she explain, over a telephone, to some downy-cheeked KPR subaltern or native sergeant anything as shapeless and foolish as what the girl had just told her? They'd put her down as another damned silly hysterical woman with the wind up over nothing. Supposing they sent men and nothing happened, the next time she called, if she really needed somebody, they'd say oh Christ, that Memsaab of Bruce's is twitched and seeing bogeymen again. She'd leave those things to Don. The thing right now was to button up the house a bit and get those children out of here as swiftly as possible.

As swiftly her mind raced back to the Wilson family; dead—Martin Wilson hacked to death, Marion slashed terribly, the two children murdered; the Stuarts, burned and murdered; the Rucks on Kinangop, mother, father and child; old Ferguson and Bingley; the Italian family; the assistant golf professional in Nairobi; Grey Leakey buried alive and his wife killed and Diana hiding in the attic; that little girl riding her tricycle in Nairobi—all that wasn't panic, all that wasn't teapot tempest, all that wasn't silly damned female hysteria. All of it had happened inside the last eight years and it had happened right here—over there and down yonder and across that hill and bang in her lap.

Peggy paused and went over to the table where the rum bottle sat. She needed to collect herself. She poured a tot, drank it neat and lit a cigarette. Murungwa was back; the dog, he said, had run away. Njeroge the headman was fidgetting uneasily in the lounge. It was true, he said, another eighteen men and their families had left. That was twenty men since Kinyanjui the witchdoctor had—died. There was almost but not quite a question mark after *died*.

'What do you make of it, Njeroge?' she asked. 'Why do the *watu* leave? What is wrong on the farm?' She looked keenly at his face. It was a good face; old, wise, strong and kind. It was hewn in sharp lines, with a high-bridged nose and high cheekbones, a broad forehead and a firm chin. The old headman was light in colour even for a Kikuyu, almost coppery like the Masai. He looked, Peggy thought, like pictures she'd seen of the Red Indians in America—and she thought in silly surprise, conscious again of the dragging weight of Don's ridiculous Frontier Special on her body—against whom they used guns like this in all the bad Western films she'd seen at the Drive-In.

Now the face was more Red Indian than ever in its impassivity. It was ordinarily a face that showed quiet love for Don, and which laughed with the children. Now it was African—all African—and the whole man had gone away and hidden behind the outer face. The eyes were completely flat in their sockets, and nothing of the man she knew came through them.

'*Sijui, Memsaab,*' he said, and the voice was as flat as his eyes. 'I don't know, Ma'am.'

The hell you don't know, she thought. You know all right. You always know everything. She gestured at the kitchen.

'Did she, the daughter of Murungwa, tell you anything?'

'*Hapana, Memsaab.*' Again the dead voice. 'Nothing, Ma'am.'

'Why do you think the men left?'

'*Sijui.*'

'Has it anything to do with the *mundumugu*, the *machawi*? Is it connected to the death of the witchdoctor?'

'*Sijui.*'

'Have you heard anything from the towns?'

'*Hapana.*' Nothing.

'Do you know where the dog has gone?'

'*Hapana jua.*' Really don't know. Negative know. Un-know.

'What's gone with everybody? Why is everybody frightened?'

Shake of the head this time.

'*Sijui.*'

'Are *you* frightened?' She fired the question at him. It almost caught him, but he stifled the start, and arrested the motion of his head.

'*Hapan—naaa.*'

Peggy lost her temper.

'Goddammit,' she said in English. 'Don't just stand there saying *sijui* and *hapana!*' Then again, in Swahili:

'Do you want to tell me anything?'

'*Hapana.*'

'Do you want me to tell the Bwana Don anything?'

'*Ndio.* Yes.'

Oho, so I've cracked him after all. This is worse than pulling teeth; like trying to explain thunder and lightning to children.

'What do you want me to tell the Bwana Don?'

'That one of the breeding-herd cows is sick. She walks in circles and she is bloated and her breath comes hard and smells dead. I do not know what is wrong with her. Perhaps the Bwana Don should tell the veterinary to come and see her. Perhaps it is infectious and the rest of the herd may catch it.'

'Is that all?' Peggy almost stamped her foot in exasperation. That woman comes in with a story like this, and he's worried about some damned old cow. It was the same last week—this is just a different cow with a different disease.

'*Hapana.* No. Tell the Bwana Don we need some more spring-leaves for the lorry. It is broken, and sags badly to one side. One of the boys hit a pig-hole with it yesterday and I have tried to fix it but it will not *tenganeza*. We do not have enough leaves. Also there is a *thahu* in the petrol pump of the little tractor. And I do not like the look of the pyrethrum. The flowers are shedding more petals and there is a strange growth like scale on some of the stalks.'

This time Peggy did stamp her foot.

'Oh, for God's sake, get out!' she cried. 'No—wait. Njeroge. Have you heard anything of the hanging of the white man, the Bwana Poole, today in Nairobi? Anything that might affect us here? Anything about dogs—or white babies?'

'*Hapana*. I only know from the Swahili broadcast on the wireless that a white man is to hang today for killing a Kikuyu boy. I know nothing else. Nothing of dogs except that Macleod is gone. Nothing of children except that all our'—he caught himself again, but this time Peggy smiled tinily—'all *your* children are here.' The headman's hand strayed absently and touched the baby Jock's bassinet.

'All right, Njeroge. That'll do. I'm going in to town now with the children. Bring your blankets to the kitchen and stay here in the house until the Bwana Don comes back again. Look after the place; until the Bwana Don gets back you are the *Bwana ya shamba* here. I hold you responsible. Good-bye.'

Strangely, formally, the headman extended his hand.

'*Kwaheri, Memsaab.*' He included the children with one sweeping wave. '*Kwaheri. Watoto.*' He turned then and walked with dignity to the kitchen.

She herded the larger children into the old paint-peeling Chev, putting baby Jock's basket between her and the harness she used to keep young Lois from pitching through the windscreen. The two elder children, Angus and Ellen, were sitting quietly in the back seat. But why did Njeroge shake hands when he left? He never does. And why did he freeze up on me? He's usually pretty outgiving for a Wog. But where *is* that damned dog? Generally he's already in the car when anybody mentions town, and when you kick him out he's always snapping at the wheels and making a confounded nuisance of himself.

Peggy rounded the neat, whitewashed stone-ringed circular drive, with its inner oval of clipped green lawn and its gladioli and fuchsia and roses in the centre bouquet, its overhanging lofty umbrella of tall trees. She looked lovingly at their house. The House Don Built, with its clipped hedges and the big hydrangeas hugging its foundations, the riotous bougainvillaea going mad on the stone walls and running like gipsies all over the roof. She loved her roof. It was made of the heavy Kavirondo cane—papyrus, actually, just like in Egypt—but it was rain-hammered and weather-pounded into a thick, solid tawny mass that swooped and dipped and curved from different levels like pictures she had seen of Japanese and Chinese houses. As always, she said a silent good-bye to the house.

The Chev's wheels bumped on the rutted roads, hard as iron now in the dry; the deep ruts from the last rains carved as into granite. The roads were framed in skinny eucalyptus, planted for windbreaks on each side of the road.

Don had used only imported Hampshire Downs and New Zealand Romneys for his stud stock, crossing them for the fat lamb crop and breeding them onto the native hair sheep for improved wool. The pure-bred Romneys were grazing now in a field of purple vetch to her right, looking naked and obscene from their morning clipping, with great dye-marking-stains like blood smears on their backsides. In another paddock an old child-worn grade Hampshire ewe looked up from cropping a hayfield. Twin lambs delivered just two days before frollicked and kicked like gambolling woolly lambkins on a St. Valentine's card. All through the high, waving oats she could see the white backs of the grazing sheep, like flecks of foam on a tossed green sea.

She looked over her shoulder once more in the direction of the house, which had disappeared in the small forest of jacaranda and kaffirboom and eucalyptus and Norwegian fir that ran off and away into the mountainside which leaned its heavy cedar and *podo* shelter on to the farm—the mountainside down which the stream rushed and chuckled—the mountainside which was sinister with its occasional herd of buffalo that ranged down to lay waste the plumed, heavy-headed wheat and trample the potato patches and wreck the mealie fields. The mountain still held surprises, its leopard which slunk down to steal sheep and attack the calves, the stray rhino which came snorting onto the road, tacking on the bias like a heeling sailboat as he whoofed and charged blindly. All of this was hers—hers and Don's and then, someday, the children's; that day when the neighbours no longer laughed as they had laughed when Don first put in the drainage system which made water run uphill, and invested years of waiting on a pyrethrum crop which he had seeded in a piece of useless land . . . glorious money-making py which now waved silver in the breeze, ever growing the lovely little insect-killing flowers which was giving them finally some real cash money.

The little river sliced the land here, on their property, and Don had made a big silly project of creating a scenic bridge, such as the Japanese fancied, of unpeeled rustic logs and huge bastions of moss-green granite instead of flat ugly grey concrete. There was structural steel girding this bridge, and staunch airfield-metal landing mats on its bed. What Don built he meant to stay; he wrought his home and his life as solidly as he himself was constructed, with no sharp corners or sag points.

Peggy's Chev bumped down and onto and over the bridge. The big pistol was uncomfortable; she had hitched it round so that it lay in the hollow of her skirt in the valley created by her spread thighs. She had hitched up her skirt to prevent wrinkling, and was sitting on her nylon slip. Still thinking in the Wild West vein, she said aloud to nobody: 'I must look like some floozie out of one of those frontier dance halls in America, my skirts hiked up half around my neck and a bloody great gun for a crotch-warmer. Untouchable Lil, that's me.'

'What, Mum?' Ellen said from the back seat.

'Nothing. Mummy was just talking to herself. It won't be long before we're in town having lunch with Daddy. Won't that be fun?'

'Is Daddy expecting us? We left in an awful hurry. And I forgot to bring Princess Margaret, we left so fast.'

'Princess Margaret will be all right in the house with Murungwa.' Princess Margaret was a doll Don had brought home during the Princess' visit. 'And Daddy isn't expecting us. We—he—may have to stay in town for quite a while, and you haven't seen him in a long time. I thought we'd give him a surprise. Isn't that fun?'

God forgive me, Peggy thought. Daddy'll be surprised all right. He's expecting *me*—not an army.

'I wish I'd not forgotten Princess Margaret. She'll be lonesome all on her own.'

'Shush, kitten. She'll be fine. Maybe we can all go to the movies, too. You'd like that, wouldn't you?'

'Sure. But so would Princess Marg—— what's that hanging on the gate, Mummy?'

Oh God, Peggy said silently. I see it too and I know what it is because I've seen it before. Idiotically the silly parody ran into her brain, the parody dating back to the Emergency: 'I've got a strangled cat and I'm very fond of that, but Mummy wouldn't buy me a Mau Mau. Mau Mau. . . .'

She jammed on the brakes, throwing both of the larger children forward in their seats, Ellen bumping her head and setting up a clamour and Angus being half-stunned in advance of weeping over a cut lip where the back of the front seat had struck him in the mouth. She wrenched savagely at the wheel, wrestling the car around, narrowly missing a drainage ditch as she spun the Chev, which coughed hoarsely as she tramped heavily on the accelerator. When she got back to the bridge she looked in the rear-view mirror and saw gratefully that a copse of trees obscured the gate that closed the fence which separated their property from the farm of Hamish Macrae.

Both children were crying now, and Angus' mouth was bleeding. They were demanding in tear-jagged indignation why she had stopped the car so suddenly, why she had hurt them so. . . . Peggy could think of nothing to say that would make any sense at all, so she snapped, sharply, angrily: 'You were jabbering about that silly doll or you would have seen it! Didn't *you* see it, Angus?'

'See what? See what, Mum? That thing on the gate?'

She forced a nervous laugh.

'I didn't see anything on any gate. *I* was looking at the rhino! Why, you must be blind, both of you, not to see that damned great rhino that was bursting out of that little piece of bush! It almost ran bang into us! It would've wrecked the car and Daddy would've been furious and we wouldn't 've been able to get to Nairobi and we couldn't have seen the movies and . . .' Breathless from her lies, Peggy ran out of invention.

'All I saw was somefin' hanging on the gate. I didn't see any wino,' Ellen snuffled, returning to babyhood difficulty with her words. 'Didn't you see anyfing on the gate, Mummy?'

'Well, the only thing I saw was the old *faro*, puffing along, poppet,' Peggy said, dabbing at the child's streaming nose and tear-wet cheeks with her handkerchief. 'Here, Angus, there's Kleenex in the bag. Use that. You're about to bleed all over your siren suit and I don't want to get the hanky all blood.'

'I saw something on the gate, too,' Angus persisted. 'That's why I didn't see the rhino. Oh, Mummy, do *look* at all the blood. I must have just gallons in me to throw away, because I don't feel different a bit.'

Peggy was getting out of the car. She hitched the pistol round to where it rode on her hip again, and took one look at the rutted road before she sat down on the seat and kicked off her high-heeled slippers, unlatched her suspenders and stripped off her stockings. She got out of the car then, and took the pistol out of the holster.

'Why are you taking off your shoes, Mummy?'

'Why are you taking out the pistol, Mummy?' The boy and girl spoke together.

'I'm going to chase off that old rhino, ducks. If you hear me fire a shot, I'll just be shooting in the air to drive him into the hills.'

'But why are you going barefoot, Mummy?'

'I'm going barefoot, sweetie, because I may have to run if he turns nasty and Mummy can't run in these high heels,' she said to Ellen. 'And you can't go with me, Angus, because I want you to stay with your sisters and little Jock. Also if Mummy has to run she doesn't want to have to worry about you. Quiet, now, both of you. I'll be right back.'

Angus was being maddeningly persistent.

'But why don't we chase it off in the car, like Daddy does? That's fun.'

'When Daddy plays with rhino he always does it in the Land Rover, and besides, Daddy is a white hunter and knows how. This isn't a Land Rover and I'm not a white hunter. That's enough, now. Don't you dare step out of that car, do you understand, or I'll wallop you both. *And* no movies. Hear me?'

'Yes, Mum.' Angus was still persistent. 'But supposing he charges? You're not carrying enough gun to slam a *faro*.'

His mother suppressed a smile. Angus' voice was the voice of her husband.

'He won't charge me—not out in the open and with me on foot, he won't. He'd charge the car, though, when I tried to open the gate, and we'd all be in a dreadful mess. I'll just go and shout *boo!* at him and then fire a shot to see him off. I'll be right back. Enough now. *And stay in that car.*'

She walked down the rough hard-rutted road, carrying the pistol pointed straight down. The end of its tall-sighted barrel reached well past her knee.

*

The big Alsatian was still alive. His intestines spilled past his head as he hung twisting, upside down, gaffed on the sharp iron Samburu spearhead which formed the corner bar of the swinging gate of different tribal spears— the gate which bore the neat lettering 'Hardscrabble Farm', and under it, 'D. C. Bruce'. The dog's breast and throat were gumming with the blood which still crawled from his belly. There was a great stiffening smear on his head, where a stone or club had struck him, but his shoulders still writhed and his feet still scratched feebly at the air as he turned and twisted. The point of the spear which impaled him was planted deep in the underpart of his hindquarters. Macleod's golden eyes turned toward her as she came up to him and he tried to whine through the blood which had run from the wound and flowed over his mouth and dripped steadily splattering into a spreading thick-blackening pool on the hard dusty ground.

Peggy Bruce put the gun's barrel close to the dog's ear, thumbed back the hammer, and blew his brains out. She ejected the spent bullet and re-loaded from the looped dozen on the belt before she holstered the pistol. Then she seized the dog's shoulders and tried to lift him off the spear blade, but he was hanged to high and weighed too much and the spear had pierced too deeply into his groin.

The fence was palinged for a couple of hundred yards each way, with a stout four-by-four runner six inches below the pointed pickets. Maintaining her balance with one hand on the dead dog's back, she pulled herself to the top of the runner and, perching unsteadily, managed to lift the animal clear of the point. He dropped the ground with a thud, and Peggy lost her balance and fell off the fence, skinning a knee in the loose shale of the road.

The Samburu spear was wet and stained with blood, and so was a portion of the gate where the dog had struggled and sprayed blood. She had no handkerchief; she had wiped Ellen's runny nose and left the handkerchief in the car. Peggy hiked up her skirt and stepped out of her half-slip. She swabbed the spear and the gate carefully with sand and rubbed them clean with the underclothing. Then she took the dog by the hind legs and dragged him twenty yards away to a low clump of bush, which effectively hid him. Then, in her bare feet, she carefully scuffed sand over the bloody trail the dog's body had made as she dragged it from the gate. She wiped the blood off her feet and off her skinned knee and wadded the bloody pettiskirt into a ball and hid it carefully under another bush. She pushed the damp hair away from her sweaty face and started to walk back to the car, the flinty scattered stones of the hard-panned road cutting into her feet and making her wince. *I won't cry over the dog*, she said to herself, *I mustn't let the children know. We can always say a leopard got it when we come home again— if we come home again.*

114

She forced a bright expression as she approached the car. They were quite good children, really. They were still in the car despite temptation to chase along behind her.

'Hello, you two,' she said to the older children. 'All well in the nursery?' She peered into the car.

'Sure,' young Angus said. 'Only Jock woke up and started to bawl when you shot at the rhino, and I gave him *such* a smack. He shut up, too, didn't he, Ellen?'

'You didn't smack him as hard as I used to smack *you* when nobody was looking,' Ellen said. 'What's the matter with your feet, Mum? And your knee's skinned, too. Don't you want your stockings?' Peggy was half-seated leaning on the fender, one calf crossed over her knee, squeezing her feet into her slippers. The smoke from a cigarette trailed upward into her face, and she had one eye squinted comically shut.

'No,' she said, and attempted a laugh. 'My feet are filthy. My, but that was a big rhino. He gave an awful snort before he decided to run away. Do you hear him snort, Angus?'

'No, I didn't hear him snort. Did he have a big horn?'

'Not so very. Your Daddy wouldn't have said he was trophy size. But it looked awfully big to me.'

'That doesn't look like *all* dirt on your foot,' Ellen said. 'It looks more like blood. Did you hurt yourself when you chased the old rhino away?'

'No,' Peggy said. 'I didn't hurt myself. I must have snagged my foot on a thorn or something. When I slipped and skinned my knee. It doesn't hurt. Does your mouth hurt, Angus?'

'Not any more it doesn't,' Angus bragged. 'But if your knee doesn't hurt why are you crying then, Mum? There're tears in your eyes.'

'Oh, just this damned cigarette. I got smoke in them. Here, my girl, give me that handkerchief I lent you. Thanks.' She scrubbed at her eyes. 'Better now?' She smiled convincingly this time.

'Better,' Ellen replied. Peggy got in the Chev and started the motor. They drove towards the gate.

'Oh,' Ellen said. 'The gate's open. It wasn't open before. And whatever was stuck on it is gone. Why is the gate opened, Mummy?'

'I opened it after the rhino ran off,' Peggy said. 'Thought it would save me getting out twice.' She pulled the car through the gate and opened the door, leaving the motor running. 'Wait 'til I close it.'

'I'll do it for you, Mum—let me,' Angus cried.

'No—no, don't bother,' Peggy got out of the car hurriedly. 'The latch is very stiff. You sort of have to fiddle it just right. I'll do it. Jiffy.'

She hopped out of the car and clanged the spear-spiked gate close and wedged the drop latch firmly in its groove. She got back into the car and drove hurriedly away.

'What was hanging on the gate, Mum?' Angus again.

'My, what a lot of questions,' Peggy replied. 'Nothing, just an old coat.

Some Wog had hung his coat there when he went into the bushes to spend a penny, I guess. He came back and got it just after I scared the rhino away. You would have roared with laughter. He thought I was shooting at *him*.'

'It didn't look like a coat hanging on the gate to *me*,' Angus said. 'It looked more like a dog or maybe a sheep or some other animal that size.'

Peggy turned her head and fixed her son with a glare.

'It was only a *coat*, I said,' she snapped. 'Now go to sleep like I told you to!'

'Yes, Mum,' Angus said, and looked at her steadily for a moment before he dropped his eyes. 'I suppose I was wrong. I suppose it was just a coat that looked like a dog. Sorry, Mum.'

The Chev hit a rock and Peggy turned her attention to the road, and when she looked at the back seat again, Angus had his eyes closed and his lips were pressed close. He looked amazingly like his father on one of the rare occasions when Don was angry.

Tears came again into Peggy's eyes, and she blinked furiously as she increased the speed another notch.

'He's a man, and he knows,' she said to herself. 'Oh, my God, it's too early for him to be a man. It's not *fair*! He's too young to already be a man!'

CHAPTER FOUR

STEPHEN NDEGWA trapped a belch delicately with his palm as he walked through the lobby of the New Stanley Hotel. The creamed pork chops were not sitting well. He raised a finger, as he stood on the sidewalk, and his white Mercedes—parked illegally inside the traffic peninsula designed for loading guests of the hotel—crawled forward to meet him. The chauffeur had evidently been waiting quite a while. *Yallah*, what a boresome lunch that had been, meaningless politenesses, monkey jabber from trained apes, nothing to drink—bad public relations, Matthew Kamau insisted, to get publicly merry on such a serious day; Matthew still thought of any drinking as a sin, but public drinking was a catastrophe—waiting for them to string up that poor silly white man whose finish was certain now.

'Take me to the bus-stop on the edge of town,' he said to his chauffeur. 'I want to go home for a couple of hours.'

'Not go to the town house?' the driver said stupidly.

'I said *home*,' Stephen Ndegwa snapped irritably and illogically. 'And I don't want to go to the Reserve today in a big white German car. Stop thinking; drive.' Bloody Kipsigi idiot, he thought. But the office pays him, as the office pays for this great white elephant I'm riding in. Perhaps a car and chauffeur is good for business in Nairobi, as going to lunch in the Stanley is good for show. But it is not such a car as I want to drive home in when I am going to the Reserve. Not today. Somebody might roll a rock down the hill on me. Might mistake me for a bwana. Might serve me right at that if I reaped some of what we've so heavily sown. He grinned sourly at the idea.

Stephen Ndegwa kept a proper house in one of the Indian-built suburbs out toward the airport. It was a white man's house, with white man's furnishings, even if the front was a gaudy salmon pink. He had wondered sometimes why the Wahindi always built their houses such horrible shapes and painted them such bilious colours.

Ndegwa kept his city wife in his city house. He smiled without amusement at the thought of having separate houses and wives to fit each portion of his personality. Iris was a church-wife, too, married before a proper preacher. Iris had insisted on it. Iris was very proper in all things. Iris was a Jamaican, very light in colour, and considerably more British than the British. She spoke no Kikuyu and her Swahili was execrable. He had met Iris in England on a fund-raising trip, a long, long time ago—actually it had only been five years, but it seemed forever. She still spoke of London as 'home' whenever she chattered brightly at a tea-party or went with him to one of the Governor's convenient catch-alls or occasionally dined at the home of some legislative council-man. He knew she secretly hated Kenya and his position in it, and thought of his own tribesman as 'niggers'—ignorant, dirty, stupid savages.

Today he didn't want to go to his city house or his city wife. He wanted to go *home*—home to the Reserve, where he had other houses, and his other wives. These were proper wives, bargained for correctly and paid for in cattle and sheep as well as shillings. They had cost him a fortune, even twenty-five years ago as a young clerk when he first bought Mumbi wives were expensive; more, even, when he had purchased Wanjiro. Mumbi was old, barren and very skinny now, but he had owned Wanjiro only—how time flew, he checked his fingers rapidly—twelve years it was since he came back from India as a qualified barrister. My God, she was growing old, too. She was twenty-seven. Thank heaven she and the old one got along pretty well. Mumbi had taken over some of the rearing of the boy and girl he had bred from the body of Wanjiro, and was giving them a proper, old-fashioned raising, despite the time that school claimed them. It was a pity about the two handsome boys Mumbi had given him. Esau would have been twenty-four now, and Abel twenty-two. But they had run off to join the gangs at the beginning of the end of the Mau Mau and had never come back from the forests. He had often asked, but had never learned, whether they had been slain by their own people, or killed by the white forces or whether illness or some wild animal had taken them. They merely went in; they never came back.

'Let me off here,' he said to the chauffeur. 'Come back to this place and wait at six o'clock. And you be on time, hear me?'

'*Ndio*, Bwana,' the chauffeur replied.

'And *don't* call me *Bwana*. How many times do I have to tell you?'

'*Ndio*, Bwana,' the chauffeur said. 'I will remember.' The chauffeur was hopeless. He'd fire him someday and get a Sikh or somebody like that, who understood motor-cars. This bloody Kipsigi thought he knew it all and knew nothing, like all of the Kipsigis. He wears white-rimmed glasses and drives a white man's white car, Stephen Ndegwa thought. I suppose he thinks that makes him a white man's servant and me a Bwana. He also shifts his gears as if he were grinding his teeth.

Stephen Ndegwa saw the Limuru bus coming and got out and flagged it. There was a stop a couple miles farther on, just fronting the hill on which his *shamba* sat. He would be glad to be home for a few hours, glad to be completely himself. He liked to sneak away and be himself once in a while—take off his city clothes and slop around in a *kikoi*. He had to be careful, though. Iris didn't like him coming out here to—as she had once screamed in a fit of temper—to 'play nigger'.

But today he wanted to play nigger. Today he had a great deal of thinking to do, and he did not want to do it permeated by the white smell—the smell of the white man, the white man's food and drink and clothing, the greasy stink of the white man's petrol fumes and belching diesel exhausts. He wanted to do his thinking surrounded by the smells with which he had grown up, the comfortable smells of wood smoke and the acrid reek of goats and the old greasy odour of the hut in which food was cooked and children born and goats kept at night for safety against prowling hyenas and marauding leopards.

Perhaps this was why—politics apart, and it was damned good politics, as well—he had stubbornly cherished his roots in the Reserve; kept his huts and his small herds of sheep and goats and few scraggly milk cattle. His country wives each tended their patch of banana and sugar cane, their potatoes and mealies. Each wife had her private hut, still, and in those huts each wife kept her own cooking stones and took her smaller, weaker animals inside at night. Mumbi was old and stringy and her breasts were like shrivelled pods, but she still had her fierce pride as first wife and mother of two strong, if dead, sons. Dead though they be, she had borne them and raised them to circumcision and manhood. Mumbi was of the old days, and she still displayed the *shuka*, scraped her head clean against the lice, and wore her coils of wire bracelets and blue beads with as much pride as she flaunted the huge carved earplugs and great loops of earrings. Mumbi almost never spoke Swahili, she was that unreconstructed. She would always be unreconstructed. A long time ago Stephen Ndegwa had beaten her for repeated insubordination and she had enlisted the aid of a witch doctor and had set out to poison him slowly. It was not until he had stopped beating her and placated her with presents and much male attention that his guts had unscrambled and his full health returned.

Mumbi . . . named for the first Kikuyu woman, the wife of the first

118

Kikuyu man, Gikuyu. Mumbi the mother of a country, mother of the nine daughters who, when Ngai sent them nine young men, had married and formed the principal Kikuyu clans. Perhaps Mumbi more, than Wanjiro, was the real reason he kept this part of him separate from the political *Watu* who ran with white women and ate every day in the white men's hotels and restaurants. It was so easy for a man of education and money and accomplishment to forget his basic origin. He must at all costs remember his bare-assed beginnings—for every Stephen Ndegwa, for every Matthew Kamau, there were a quarter million Kikuyu who had not 'emerged' from the old ways.

Stephen Ndegwa had been oblivious of the occupants of the bus as he mused, and he got out automatically at the bus-stop to walk home. The sun was fierce in the late afternoon heat; the pitiless sky was unleavened by even a hint of cloud that might contain rain.

Mumbi—old, barren, hideous-beautiful.

And the younger one, Wanjiro—pretty in a semi-modern fashion, scornful of old Mumbi, old-hat, old-timy, old-fashioned Mumbi. Scornful of Mumbi, but envious and frustrated and always bad-tempered over Iris, whom she could not approach in either looks or sophistication. Try as she might, torture it with various patent unguents as she would, Wanjiro's hair would never grow more than an inch away from her head, unless she took up wigs like some of the white women.

I have made the full transition, Stephen Ndegwa thought. Or almost. I am married to a black savage, to a semi-modern native, and to what the Americans call a 'high yellow'—and what she herself considers as a British lady of colour. I am indeed multi-racial, with my white friends, my India partners, Moslem and Hindi, my vari-coloured wives and my several houses. And I, Stephen Ndegwa, still cling to my *thingira*—to my bachelor's hut in which, with luck, I shall soon be sitting.

He came to the rise of the hill, and suddenly felt good—keenly alive and very good. The red soil was dusty, and his feet in their white man's shiny loafers itched to feel the earth.

'My castles,' he said aloud, looking upward to where his *shamba* sat on the brow of a hill.

The *shamba*—the farm—tickled his sense of ridiculous proportion. One day he would have the proper white man's farm, the estate, like the great properties along Naivasha, or the broad coffee and sisal acres with the baronial house that overlooked the broad valley and gave directly onto the imposing bulk of Ol Donya Sabuk—Lady Mac's estate, which had changed hands again.

Or he would have a tea farm, high in the slopes, around Kericho, or perhaps he would have vast cattle lands in the Wakamba country, or what was entirely likely, virgin grazing for modern ranching in the lush Masai grant lands—after the Masai had been civilized slightly and the gross wastage of those great areas in Kenya had been shared out to responsible people like

119

himself who would use them well. The Masai would hate it but they could no longer continue to be a drain, a tourist attraction, at the expense of the Kikuyu, who cried for arable land. A Masai was all fuss, feathers, legend and penis. His spear and his sword were just costume jewellery now.

But meanwhile Stephen Ndegwa had his Kikuyu *shamba*, and quite a decent little farm it was on its dozen acres.

Most of the long sweep of hill on which it sat was bare of trees, but he had trees, a few planted more than a hundred years ago, maybe five hundred years ago. There were the two towering cedars, very old, and a gigantic fig which was said to have been *mugumo*, sacred. This he doubted; it was too close to the Ngong to have been sacred to anything but a bloody Masai, and the Masai mostly fancied rocks and cattle as fetishes. But it was a fine, big, gnarled tree, and it cast a lovely shade over his huts. There was a big *boma* of cropped euphorbia thorn around the inner courtyard to keep the chickens and goats inside the *kraal*, and to keep the vermin, in a measure, out. Large-leaved patches of bananas also cast a lusher, more tropical shade, and there was a kaffirboom which stood as red as a gigantic Christmas candle in his yard. The ground inside the *boma* was bare—his women swept it daily with faggots of bamboo strips. There was a wooden gate instead of a movable trellis at the *thome*; he opened it and stepped inside. Two dogs, yellow and fox-faced, with upcurled, backswept tails, rushed barking at him, and he silenced one with a kick. The other sniffed suspiciously at his trousers, its back hair still abristle.

'*Hodi*,' he called. '*Hodi*—may I come in?'

'*Hituka*—come closer,' a voice said from the centre hut.

It was the biggest of the three buildings, and was different in shape. Whereas two were thatched and conical in the old style, the centre building was oblong, made of white man's plaster, like the police and veterinary posts, and was covered with a flat corrugated-iron roof, with an overhang to form a porch. This was the hut for which Wanjiro, his younger wife, had teased until she got it. The other huts differed only in size, both being made of mud with wattle reinforcements. Next one, a granary, stood on stilts. It was conical and thatched as well, but its sides were of interwoven cane to allow the passage of air to prevent mould of the harvested mealie cobs. That was the domain of Mumbi, his senior woman.

Well apart, in a corner of the compound, its entrance facing away from the other huts, fronting on the Ngong Hills, was his *thingira*, his bachelor hut, into which no woman could enter without invitation. This was where he and his men friends could sit and drink beer; this was where the bargains were concluded; this was where arguments were settled and contracts drawn.

'*Hituka*,' the voice said again inside the hut, and then there was a rustle and his junior wife, Wanjiro, stepped out. They pressed hands flatly, palms together, and stood apart.

'How are the children?' he asked.

'They are at the school,' she said.

'And the goats and sheep?'

'Well, save one. Something took it in the night. It was not well and straggled behind when I herded them into the *zeriba*.'

'Where is your sister Mumbi?'

'She has gone to the forest for wood. It is a long way and she will not be back for two hours.'

'Well,' he said. '*Eeeehhh.*' It was the all-purpose African gap-filler, neither dissent nor assent but only acceptance.

'*Eeeehhh,*' she answered.

She was a comely woman, although beginning to show her years now. In her late twenties she had fattened with good eating and not too much work. There was not, actually, very much work to do since he was rich and sent liberal money, as much as five pounds a month, to each wife. She went for water in the mornings and evidently Mumbi had agreed to collect firewood in the afternoon. They both hoed the planted ground and pulled weeds from the small gardens, and the children tended the sheep and goats when they were not at school—driving them to and from pasturage.

'Will you come into my house?' she asked. 'Are you hungry?'

'I will come to your house,' he said. 'But I am not hungry. First I will go to the *thingira* and change my clothes. I am not comfortable in these clothes.'

'They are very handsome clothes,' she said. 'I suppose such a rude hut as mine would spoil them for your *mucii* in the town.'

Ouch, thought Stephen Ndegwa, in English. I get the idea—I get the message. First she uses *house*—then she uses *hut*.

'No,' he said, in Kikuyu. 'It is just that I am tired of being smothered in the garments I wear when I work with the white man in Nairobi. These are my *kazi* clothes, my working uniform. I come home to relax and drink beer. Have you *pombe*?'

'*Eeeehhh.*'

'Bring me a gourd when I return,' he said.

'Yes,' she said, and turned to enter her house, almost stooping, but suddenly remembering that this house, her house, had a proper door, and she did not have to stoop as one must bend to enter a hut.

Stephen Ndegwa sighed as he walked over to his *thingira* and, puffing slightly, himself bent double to enter the fantasy which he stubbornly persisted in maintaining. 'Oof!' he grunted, drawing himself upright once he was inside. It was dark in there, and cool against the sun's rays. He waited a moment for his eyes to become accustomed to the gloom, stumbling over a three-legged stool which comprised half of the furnishings.

Still unable to see well, he kicked off his loafers and dropped his trousers before he removed coat, shirt and tie. He took off his athletic shorts and singlet, and tossed the lot on a low short-legged cot of crisscrossed leather strips. Now he could see; there was a nail driven into the ridge-pole and on it hung a selection of cheap cotton *kikois*—the shabby Manchester-made material which made a comfortable loincloth when tucked correctly around the waist. He chose a *kikoi* with *Uhuru* and the picture of a cookpot on the back, and secured it round his loins. He sat on the stool and peeled off his socks, which he flipped over on the low bed. He scratched the marks the garters left on his legs, and wriggled his toes. They felt wonderfully well and free on the cool hard-packed earth of the floor. He stooped again and came blinking into the blinding sunlight, naked to the waist, barefoot, bulging over the top of the twisted *kikoi*, but able to breathe. The warm earth of the courtyard caressed his feet, and little puffs of the red dust which filmed the hard clay came up between his toes. A long-tailed lori swayed on a branch in the fig, and two brilliant steel-blue starlings took noisy flight. 'Fa-aaaak,' said the lori, waving its tail, bouncing on the breeze-swaying branch.

Stephen Ndegwa walked over to his wife's house, and said '*Hodi*' again before opening the door. He was quite surprised at the interior. He had not been home for some time, and he noticed now that, with the door open, the hut was bright with light which also streamed in from a window glassed into the other side. The house was cut into three parts. He stood in the living-room-kitchen, which contained the three sacred cooking stones in a corner fireplace of piled stone which ended in a proper flue which angled shakily up to the hole in the side of the plaster wall. There was a stack of blankets piled against the wall, and an array of cookpots lined along the fireplace by the other wall. There was a row of jerry-cans for water, and a tin cup hung by its handle from a nail in the wall. A thin partition of rough boards divided the living-quarters from the sleeping-quarters, which contained what he could see of a low bed like his and nothing else. There was another woven-reed partition beyond that room, where his wife and children slept, and in that room he heard rustling and the feeble bleat of a young goat. That was certainly a modern improvement on the *gechego*—the goat pen.

His wife handed him a tin cup full of liquid.

'Here,' she said. '*Pombe.*'

Stephen Ndegwa grunted and hunkered down on his heels before he drank. He arched his eyebrows in surprise.

'What is this stuff?' he asked. He had been expecting real *pombe*, the gruel-like native beer.

'White man's wine—sherry,' she said. 'I bought it at the *dukah*. I thought you would like it better than beer now. Since you are a city man. You must drink much *pombe* like this when you work in the city.'

'Let me see the bottle,' he said.

She reached behind the row of jerry-cans and fished out a bottle by the neck. It was a bottle of cheap South African sherry whose label decoration of a crowing rooster, brightly coloured, was considerably out of focus and more than a little blurred in the printing process.

'I prefer the old beer,' he said. 'Do you have any?'

'No, but Mumbi has some. Wait. I will go to her hut and bring you a gourdful.' She underlined the word *gourd*, using the Kikuyu *kenya* instead of the Swahili *gikombe*.

Stephen Ndegwa looked round the inside of the hut at the visible signs of sophistication.

God, what a grab-bag of junk—scattered *shukas*, a tin box with a lock on it, which presumably contained her spare bangles and bracelets. There were a couple of pairs of cheap sandals, such as one bought from the Indians in the bazaars. What in the name of heaven did she intend to do with the hot-water bottle? And what was kept in the biscuit tins? He was tempted to look but decided against it. In a way it was no worse than the jungle of personal belongings, the sleazy nylon underwear and violent sunburst dresses that always cluttered Iris' room—the mounds of junky jewellery and out-landish hats and soiled spike-heeled shoes with the Italian needle toes that she forced her corned feet into when they went out publicly. Here was a hot-water bottle; in the house in town, a douche bag hung behind the bath-room door, just as he had seen it in white men's houses.

And there is no doubt about it, he thought, as Wanjiro came back with the beer—it was in a real gourd this time, and smelled potently brewed—Wanjiro was still a good-looking woman. She was wearing her *shuka* tucked over the top of her breasts, which were big and still firm and round under the cheap cloth. She had regular features and lively eyes and a good warm brown skin. Her teeth were white behind the thick-lipped, well-marked mouth. When she squatted on the floor beside him, one flap of the *shuka* fell aside and exposed a plump, firm thigh. She sat, arms crossed on top of her knees, watching him as he drank the beer. She was wearing little jewellery, only one long coil of bracelet on either arm—it would not come off unless chiselled—and one anklet. She had grown heavier, he noticed again; the flesh swelled over the wire-coiling.

'This beer is good,' he said. 'The white man does not know how to make good *pombe*. It is thin and weak and sharp and full of gas. It is the colour of urine and has much the same smell. It does not make you feel good—only full of wind. I like this proper Kikuyu *pombe* better than the wine you bought at the *dukah*. That wine is a waste of money and the bottle would be full of headaches.'

'*Eeehhh.*' Wanjiro seemed disinclined to argue. They sat wordless for a moment. I might as well, Stephen Ndegwa thought. I might as well do it now and get it over.

'Come to the bed,' he said.

'*Eeeehhh.*' She got up and went to the other room and pushed a pile of soiled clothing to one side of the bed. She lay down and, reaching to the top tucks of her *shuka*, undid the loose knotting and spread the cloth aside, leaving her naked on the couch. Stephen Ndegwa merely hiked his *kikoi* up, like a skirt, as he mounted his wife.

When he had finished she wrapped her clothing around her again and said, 'Do you want more beer?'

123

'No,' he replied. 'I would like to talk a little. Go to my *thingira* and fetch me the *sigara* I left in my coat. I forgot to bring them.'

His wife got up and went off to fetch his cigarettes. That's over, he thought. I can rest easy about that for another month. I suppose there are other men to keep her warm when I am away. Have I come so far that there is nothing to this for me any more, or is it just that she is an old wife and one tires of all old wives, no matter what colour they are?

'Thank you,' he said, as Wanjiro handed him the cigarettes. He lit one, and watched her as she reached for a snuffbox secreted somewhere under the *shuka* and tucked a fingerful of the *tumbaku* under her lower lip, rubbing well with her finger between gum and lip. She sat on her heels, watching him, chewing on a little *masuaki*-twig paintbrush.

'What do the women say at the market?' he asked.

'The usual things women say.' She shrugged. 'Cackle. Like guinea-fowl.'

'Do they speak of the hanging of the white man today?'

'Yes. They cannot understand it. They do not see why they would hang a white man now and not hang others before for doing the same thing. They think that the other white men must not like this white man very much or they would not hang him just for killing a black man.'

'Is that all they say?'

'*Eeeehhh.*'

'Do they say that the white man was wrong to kill the African?'

'No. They say that if the African had not flung rocks at the white man's dog perhaps the white man might not have killed him.'

'So?'

'So they say that it is perhaps better to be bitten a little bit than to be shot for throwing rocks at a white man's dog when the white man is there to see the deed. Better to throw the rocks at night or when the white man is away at work and only his memsaab is there.'

Stephen Ndegwa scratched his head.

'I agree. But you are not surprised that they are hanging the white man?'

'No. I am not surprised at anything the bwanas do. Perhaps the white man has women or cattle that some other white men want or perhaps the boy he shot owed some money to the white men and they are angry at this other bwana for shooting him so that he cannot pay. It seems a lot of *kelele* to make over the stoning of the dog and the shooting of a man. Does it concern you? Did the shot boy owe you shilingi?'

'No, he didn't owe me any money. But in a way it concerns me—concerns all of us here. It concerns your children. You would not like to see our children shot by a bwana for stoning a dog, would you, and the murderer go free?'

'Migwe and Nduta would never find themselves in a position to do such a thing. If a dog attacked them they would run away, as I have taught them. It is not the fault of the dog if it barks at black people; it has been taught to bark at black people. In any case it is only a dog, and not important. Some of the other white bwanas must be very angry with this man over something more than shooting a Kikuyu, or they would not trouble to hang him.'

Here Wangiro's eyes lighted.

'Perhaps you have heard something else? Perhaps they are hanging the bwana because another bwana wants his memsaab? We hear many stories about how the white men shoot each other over women. I heard on the wireless at the *dukah* one time that a bwana slew another bwana with a panga, as if they were black men instead of bwanas. Or perhaps this bwana's memsaab told him that the Kikuyu boy had attacked her? White women are always imagining that someone is attempting to steal from between her legs that which she should give freely if anybody troubles to ask her politely or give her a present.'

Now Wanjiro was definitely interested at her new idea. Her eyes sparkled with malice.

'No, Wanjiro, that it not it at all,' Stephen Ndegwa said. 'You are talking like an idle silly woman in the market-place. What is happening is a change. The white man will no longer be allowed to kill the African and go free. He will have to pay for his crime, as the black man has been made to pay for breaking the white man's law. It is a thing called "justice"—the thing that I work for when I go to the white man's courts to argue in favour of our people who are charged with doing wrong.'

'But sometimes they hang the people you argue for in the big palavers when you put on your old man's hair. I have seen you in your wig and in your gowns. You looked very funny.' Wanjiro giggled. 'I sneaked into the back of the room and heard you abusing the prisoner and telling the man in the wig with the red *kanzu* all kind of bad things about the prisoner. You must have told some very bad things, because they hanged him later, I heard.'

Stephen Ndegwa was nonplussed for a moment. Then he laughed.

'I wasn't telling the man in the red *kanzu* bad things about the prisoner. I was trying to tell the senior elder that the prisoner was not guilty of what the Serikali charged him with. I was trying to make the tribunal let him go free!'

'Mmmmmm—eeeehhhh,' Wanjiro said. 'I thought you must have been telling the people bad things or else they would not have hanged him. This, this what you call "justice", means that they will only hang white people now and black men will all go free?'

'No.' Stephen Ndegwa gave up. 'It doesn't mean that at all. It means that the colour of a man's skin will not make any difference in the law courts any more. It means that the white man as well as the black must pay a price—with cattle or his freedom or with his life—if he is bad, if he does wicked things. It is all part of *uhuru*.'

'I hear much of this *uhuru*. I say it myself in greeting instead of *jambo* now. Look, see how I do it.' She held her first two fingers in a V and said 'Uhuru! na Kenyatta!'

'Who taught you that? I didn't.' Stephen Ndegwa said.

Nobody taught me. Everybody does it. They say if we do it often enough‘ we will all get *uhuru* and Jomo Kenyatta will come free.’

'Is that so? And what does it mean?'

'I do not really know.' Wanjiro said. 'Some say that we cannot have *uhuru* until they let Jomo Kenyatta come back to Nairobi and to Kiambu from where they have him shut up away in the north among the savages, the naked niggers. I suppose in some manner he will bring *uhuru* with him. In any case, they say when he comes we will take away all the houses and sheep and cattle from the white bwanas, and all the motor-cars and all the goods in the big *dukahs* and they will be divided among the people.

'Oh, indeed, I have heard the same, and not entirely in the market-places,' Stephen Ndegwa murmured. 'Is there more?'

'Oh, yes,' Wanjiro said. 'They say that there will be plenty of shilingi for everybody, that we can have *fundis* to make our own money, and that there will be no more hard work and there will be plenty of beer for everyone. But mostly that we will all be called Bwana and Memsaab and that if the white people wish to remain here in this country they will have to work very hard for us or we will shout at them and beat them. I do not wish to shout at anybody or beat anybody, but that is what they say, anyhow, when they talk at the market.'

'Very interesting,' Stephen Ndegwa said in English. And in Kikuyu: 'Tell me, does anybody say what will happen if the white man does not want to leave or stay here and work hard so that he can call us Bwana and Memsaab?'

'They say we will drive him into the sea or kill him if he stays.'

'Does anybody say just how all this change, this *uhuru*, will be brought about? How it will come to pass?'

'I do not understand it completely. But they say that men like Gichuru and that fish-eating Jaluo, Mboya, and other names like Odinga and Ochwara will get Jomo Kenyatta out of jail and then Jomo will bring *uhuru*, which I suppose he has with him in this place up north where the naked savages live. And they mention the name of Kamau and another name which I have forgotten . . .' She peeped at him coyly under her lids.

'Another name?'

'Yes . . . it is . . . oh, yes, it is a name like yours. Ndegwa. I suppose it is some relation of yours who is very important.' She giggled again. The little bitch is actually giving me a jolly good leg-pull, Stephen Ndegwa said to himself in English. Now he spoke sternly.

'You know of course that most of what you hear is untrue,' he said.

'Most of everything the women speak about in the markets is untrue,' she replied. 'They gabble like magpies on a dead cow. I do not pay attention to most of it. But I do believe there must be something to this *uhuru*—all this freedom talk—or so many people would not discuss it in so many forms. But perhaps you can tell me one thing: If we drive all the British away from Kenya, who will be left here to give us the freedom that Kenyatta is sup-

126

posed to bring us from the north? Who will be at the *baraza* to take the *uhuru* from Kenyatta and give it to us? And why do not they kill Kenyatta and keep the *uhuru* for themselves if it is such a fine thing? There is much of this I do not understand.'

Suddenly the seed of a fantastic idea sprouted in Stephen Ndegwa's skull. He spoke gently, and patted his wife's leg as he spoke.

'Tell me, Wanjiro,' he said. 'All these women—the women you talk to in the market and at the *dukahs* and on the farms. The good women, I mean, the women like you—do they understand any more of these things than you do?'

'I don't think so. There is much talk, but always the talk is ended with a fight over a goat or an argument over a chicken or a man or a jug of *pombe*, and then it is necessary to go home to see to the herds and the larger children and the talk never gets finished. Women have too much to occupy them to talk forever like men, who need only sit in the shade and drink *pombe*. That is when the big palavers are made.'

'Have you been to any of the big palavers where the big leaders like Mboya and Gichuru and Kamau speak?'

'No. No one has told me to go and I am too busy here on the *shamba* to bother. Also, they say that every man tells a different tale about what will happen and what should happen, and especially about how Kenyatta is mixed up in it all. You do not know who to believe. There must be very much of this *uhuru* if so many people are prepared to pass it around to everybody.'

'Would you believe a woman—not one of these young girls who wear the high heels and carry handbags and are always with the loafers and spivs in Nairobi—but a good woman like yourself, a good woman from a good *shamba* with a good man who sends her money and does not beat her very much? A man who gives her a fine new house and money for *tumbaku* and beads and clothes, as well as meat and sugar and tea?'

Wajiro considered. She scratched her head, and rubbed her gums again with the *tumbaku*.

'I suppose so. If she talked straight. And if she were with her man so that all would know he approved of what she said. This way it would not be woman's idle gossip. Yes, I think I would believe her. If her man listened and did not beat her then perhaps she would be speaking truth.'

'Would you make such a talk yourself if you knew the truths of some of the things they say?'

Wanjiro's eyes widened.

'Oh, no! I would be too frightened! To stand in front of many people and talk! Oh, no! I couldn't! My tongue would turn back in my throat and choke me!'

'Of course you could. You certainly could if you believed what you were saying. And you would make many friends. And you would not have to say it all at once. You could practise. And then some day you could talk to the

127

Kikuyu women and they would listen and respect you. Promise me that you will try, and I will take you to Nairobi shopping for anything you want.'

'I will try if you command me,' Wanjiro said. She smiled. 'Perhaps if I had a little *pombe*—or may be some *tembo*, some white man's whisky, first, I would be very brave and speak loudly and you would be proud of me.'

'You will have some *tembo*, I promise you. A little at first and as much as you want later. Now,' Stephen Ndegwa said, 'I will go to my *thingira* because I want to think of many things. If I sleep, wake me before *saa Kumi na mbili*—I must go back to Nairobi tonight. The car is meeting me at six.'

'Why did you not come today in the motor-car?' his wife asked.

'It is slightly broken—it needed fixing,' he said hurriedly. 'I hope I will be here when Mumbi returns. I wish to talk to her as well.'

'You are not going to ask her to talk to the women, too, are you?' A tinge of jealousy crept into her voice, and Stephen Ndegwa spotted it happily.

'Of course not—not so long as you will speak for me. Mumbi is old—old in her years and in her ways. She is not a modern woman, a woman of today who will understand *uhuru* perfectly. She could never understand *uhuru* as well as you. But'—he said firmly—'of course, if you are afraid to speak for me, then I must ask Mumbi. To a man who is thirsty, dirty rain-water caught in the baobab tree is as good as a lake. Mumbi will be better than nothing, and this is important to my business.'

'I will try,' Wanjiro said. 'You go to the *thingira* now and I will go and collect the children as they come from school so that we may drive in the sheep to the big paddock.

CHAPTER FIVE

STEPHEN NDEGWA stretched full length on the springy couch of laced thongs and, in the quiet gloom of the bachelor hut, let his mind rove free. *It could work*, he thought. I wonder why I never thought of it before. There is no hope for us without the women, for it is the women who are so far behind us, and it is the women who raise the warriors and the mothers of warriors. I am thinking like an old-fashioned Kikuyu, he mused, but at least for once I am thinking straight.

In my father's day, even in my own youth, the good things were taught by the mother to the child at foot, and when the time came for the *kahura*-dancing and then the counsel of the *mathanjuki* before the circumcision the child was prepared for the wise words of his sponsor into manhood. It was the preparation by the mother that made the child fit to be circumcised and become a warrior. We are losing—have lost—most of that and we are fast becoming a people of half-white, half-smart, half-civilized spivs and scoundrels and loafers and whores. *And* politicians.

We will all be lost here, Stephen Ndegwa thought, until we can do something about the women. They are cattle now—lost cattle, with not enough sense to bellow. The young ones no longer command a bride price because they are not worth the money, and if they were worth the money there is no way for the man to get it unless he steals it.

The young girl, even my female child Nduta, has no future unless she goes to school and becomes modernized intelligently, and how can she be modernized intelligently if her mother has no more knowledge of today than a cow? She will go to Nairobi and turn into a jitterbug who lies with any man and who knows not the name of the father of the current brat that bulges her belly. And my son, my young Migwe, he will wear his black pants and red neckerchief and drink on the street corners and lie or steal to get petrol for some broken-down motor-bike and I will be lucky if I do not have to defend him in court. Or worse, he will offend some touchy white memsaab with a cheeky remark and some unreconstructed bwana will shoot him. The white man still rules here. It is not *uhuru* yet—not quite yet.

Stephen Ndegwa sighed and closed his eyes. It was very peaceful there in his *thingira*—the quiet broken only by the comforting sounds of his remembered childhood, the lori shouting 'Faaak' in the trees, the twittering of the plantain-eaters, the distant bleat of a goat. Far away the doves were beginning their evening lament, and there was a stroking hum of locusts. It was good to lie there in the cool darkness, soothed by the beer in his belly and the relaxed remembrance of the warm body of his woman. He doubted very much that Wanjiro received any satisfaction from sleeping with him—the circumcision ceremony had been designed to remove the more sensitively responsive portions of the female anatomy—but in a subtle way it was more satisfactory to the man. There was no necessity to please, none of this nonsense about teasing the woman to the moment of high excitement that the white women clamoured for. He drifted pleasantly into semi-slumber, but suddenly the ever-present pierced him and wrecked his potential for sleep.

The land is ours, we say, the internal voice hammered at him. It was my grandfather's land yesterday and so it is mine today—especially since the white man has back-achingly improved and planted and fertilized it. We have forgotten that it was only bush and plain when the red stranger came; wasteland occupied mostly by rhino and elephant and game that ate the crops. We have forgotten that we killed each other needlessly and that disease and war and wild animals cut us down to a pitiful minimum; that famine and plague and superstition have kept us wedged in a hole like warthogs during all our history. No, now they shout, throw out the white man, and give us back the good old days that Grandfather knew, forgetting that Grandfather lived in fear of spirits and dread of man and his belly was seldom full unless he stole or raided. *Oh, Christ, I wonder if I will live to see even a tiny solution*, Stephen Ndegwa thought, and swung his feet over the side of the cot.

He stood under the tall trees of his yard and gazed about him, at the hills of Ngong on the one hand, the forests stretching to the Rift on the other, the patchwork patterns of the thirsty fields. At the foot of the hill, by the road-side, he could see the neat rows of white-painted plaster huts on the native location; some with the old thatched roofs, but a great many glinting silver as the afternoon sun struck sparks off the iron. There was a line of *dukahs* along the road, and not one of them was owned by Indians now. All were owned by Kikuyu. The older people had kicked and screamed at being moved to the consolidations, but consolidation had been the answer to the Mau Mau, and its expansion would be the answer to the economy. The time of clannish isolation was over—they would consolidate or they would starve, and no amount of *uhuru* would fill their bellies. And no amount of *uhuru* would keep the politicians from stealing at the top unless a good man, a man who loved his people, a sophisticated man—a man like himself—could do away with all the petty jealousies and graspings for power and white-man hatred and lust for unearned properties and turn, by *force* if necessary, these poor bloody savages out of their ignorance and into useful consolidation of their industries and talents.

It did not occur to Stephen Ndegwa that he might not be that man—if he had help. And help spelled more help—forced aid, if necessary—from the white man. And to get that help the white man must be kept on the scene—indulged, even in his bwana whimsies. Jungle lianas already were growing over factories and *shambas* and mines in the Congo; the tribes were sense-lessly warring and the witch doctors were coming craftily into eminence again. Cannibalism was creeping more and more into the news. . . . And the whole world was sneering at black misuse of freedom.

'That kind of news is very bad for business,' Stephen Ndegwa said to the long-tailed lori in the fig tree. 'Nobody will lend us money on the strength of that kind of news. It all comes back to the white man; we must quit trying to ape all that is evil of the white man and learn something about how to be more competently black. Or some other white men—some other Red Strangers—will come and take it all away from us again, and this time there will be no paternal red-faced bwanas whose gin-drinking bark is louder than their bite. You saw how the Russians moved into Guinea, bird; how they are moving everywhere there is a fingerhold. Better the red-faced bwanas than the bwanas with the red flag, bird. Those Red Strangers will not leave you freely shouting your head off in that tree.'

Stephen Ndegwa gazed down the hill. A woman, stooped under a load of wattle-faggots, was toiling up the hill. The carrying strap was biting deeply into her forehead, and she was bent nearly double. She kept her balance with a staff in one hand, and her eyes were fixed on the ground ahead of her as she walked.

'My first duchess,' Stephen Ndegwa said sardonically to the bird. 'And it is yet too early in time for me to offer to help her up the hill, because she would be angry and resentful of the interference, and scornful of me as a man. It

130

is a thing I must remember, bird, when I start a wholesale reform of Kenya womanhood. There is still a Mumbi for every Wanjiro, and for every Wanjiro there is a female child who will not be circumcised or sold into a matrimony for cattle and goats.'

The bird suddenly took flight and looped away.

'I wish I could go with you, bird,' Stephen Ndegwa said wistfully.

Stephen Ndegwa slipped quickly down the hill towards the main road, feeling oddly deflated as he avoided his first wife. He was glad that Wanjiro had not returned with the children. There did not seem to be any way to bridge the personal gap between him and his women. If he had remained static as a bush African, he never need bother to talk with them at all except to command. As it was he had no desire to command and very little to discuss.

He would walk all the way to the *dukah* to wait for the bus, since he was early. He had to meet Matthew Kamau after the hanging, but first he would go home and have a couple of gins with Iris. One of the nicer things about Iris was that you did not have to pay much close attention to her chatter, which was certain to be concerned with 'Home' and the freshest fancied snub she had received, whether from the houseboy to the Governor's lady she had met on the street. Dear God, Iris. He must have been mad when he married her, but she was pretty after the white fashion, and her manners were good outside the house. He could at least take her to an occasional function without expecting her to squat on her heels or poke a hole in the soufflé with her thumb in order to make room for a sliver of meat and a spoonful of gravy.

She would be full of the hanging, he supposed, but it would be a curiosity as idle to her as—he groped for an analogy and chuckled wryly as he found it —as idle as if it were happening in Africa. Stephen Ndegwa sighed again, and thought longingly of the quiet calm of his bachelor hut, where no wife might enter and a man could think in peace.

CHAPTER SIX

FULLY AND pleasantly aware of the white men's stares as they paused in front of the hotel, Abraham Matisia made an elaborately polite good-bye to Matthew Kamau and the others and walked rapidly round the corner to where his car was parked in front of the big *dukah*. There were still a few minutes of free parking time left on the meter. Matisia chuckled. Since the town had been deluged with Somali coins, worthless since Independence Day on July 1, nobody had worried much about the parking meters. The valueless Somali shillings fitted the Kenya slots precisely.

It was a good car, Abraham Matisia thought. Perhaps not so grand as the

131

Mercedes-Benz that had just drawn up to collect Stephen Ndegwa, not so flashy as the Cadillac Matthew Kamau drove, but swankier than a Holden, bigger than a Volkswagen, vastly superior to a donkey or a bicycle. It was a 1959 Chevrolet convertible, painted bright green and white, heavy on the chrome, with gaudily lit fintails. He had just bought it from Vidhya Mukerjee, who had bought it from one of the Belgian refugees from the Congo. The car was practically new, its rubber sound, its interior clean. It had a radio, and also a compass perched atop its many-dialled dashboard. It was slip-covered in white plastic made to look like corduroy, and it smelled good.

Abraham Matisia smiled as he slid under the wheel. He had masses of time to kill before the evening's main event at eight o'clock. He could think of no pleasanter way to spend it than in the manner he intended.

Abraham Matisia almost laughed aloud as he slid out of his parking space into the traffic stream of Delamere Avenue, merging expertly with the speeding motor-cars which flashed past Lord Delamere's statue. When he was a small boy he had seen the white men racing past in big cars like this, and had sworn that some day he would have one like it. He had seen many fine cars when he was a boy, because his father's *shamba* was not far off the main road which led to Mombasa. Sometimes when he came to the *dukah* to buy sugar or a little tea for his mother, Abraham Matisia would see the bwanas stopping for *petrol-i* or a cool drink, laughing with their memsaabs. They always seemed happy and carefree when they were going off on safari away from Nairobi to the palmy white beaches of the coast.

In those old days there was fanciful talk around the cookfires that some day new Red Strangers, the wa-Russias, would come to Kenya to set the black man free. And when the wa-Russias came, to drive the white bwanas from the land, every native would share the bwanas' fine land in the Highlands, and then every man would own a wireless and a motor-car. That was fine brave talk.

Matisia laughed silently. Fine brave talk for that time; marvellous talk for children. Nobody had ever seen a wa-Russia, or knew exactly what a wa-Russia was. So much old man's aimless chatter about wa-Russias, when now it was the wa-Belgas that brought the cars—thousands of Belgians, fleeing in dishevelled, unshaven panic from the uprisings in the Congo. More than six thousand of them, homeless and frightened, in Nairobi alone. So very dirty and homeless and hungry; their children fretting, wearily, irritably; their money worthless; themselves so helpless that the white schools had to be closed in order to make shelter for them. Food had to be given them or they would starve. And they would have to sell what poor possessions they had brought for enough money to get out of Kenya, for the Kenya government did not want them to tarry overlong. The Kenya government was briefly kind enough to white people in need, like any poor relatives, so long as they were moved on, but the Kenya government did not want them as a permanent problem. The Kenya government had plenty of problems of its own. There wasn't enough living room in Kenya now. Not for everybody, black and white, and some day soon the white man's big *shambas* must be broken up and parcelled out to the natives. That is when he, Abraham Matisia, with his connections, would have a fancy wood-sided shooting-brake as well as a Chevrolet convertible, and a big *shamba* of tea or maybe sisal or pyrethrum. He would have a big house, and he would have a white man to work for him as overseer. And perhaps a white houseboy to bring him drinks when he clapped his hands? The idea was intriguing. It would erase some of his memories of the barbed-wire behind which he had been so rudely stowed.

So now the Belgians brought the cars. What will the Russians bring for us when they come? An aeroplane for every man? Matisia chuckled again. Czech rifles for everybody? Two grenades for every cookpot? He knew what the Russians would bring, and he didn't want any. They would bring the same impersonal brutality that the Belgians had practised in the Congo, and tomorrow the natives would wind up working for a new kind of bwana—a bwana from the cold countries, a tougher, harsher bwana who would exact toil with a lash; dispassionate strangers who would separate the indentured men from their ailing women as the Afrikaners did in South Africa: cold, light-eyed, humourless men who would kill without the mock formality of a trial before they hanged you. Abraham Matisia knew much about the wa-Russia. He had spent a year studying economics in Moscow. *Ooee*, but it was cold, and the dreary-pasty people had nothing personal, *nothing*, not even laughter.

No, the wa-Russias were not like the unpredictable white Kenya bwanas, who sometimes got roaring drunk and beat you when you least expected it, or gave you presents when you least expected it, and who fought happily with each other and sometimes even killed each other over women. No woman was worth a killing which risked your neck. Better to beat the woman, if you felt strongly about it, but if bedding with another man did not inter-fere with her work, what harm was done? You own the cow; you own the calf. What matter which bull mounts which cow if the increase belongs to the man who owns the herd?

Matisia shook his head. It would not be very long before he saw her. He was impatient, and these thoughts of mating filled him with urgency. Of course it was not the first time, but it was different here, much different from England and Russia and France and Germany, all of which countries he had seen, and in all of which he had slept with their women. There was no danger to it in those countries, where the black man was accepted either as an exciting novelty or just another man with a different-coloured skin. There was not that extra added fillip to it, that delicious nape-prickle of danger which came with lying with a white woman in a white man's country like Kenya, where many a black man had been shot for a fancied insult to a white memsaab; where the fleeting wild idea of touching a white woman was enough to grey a black man's skin with involuntary fear.

Matisia switched on his radio, which obligingly blared back at him. He pressed his automatic cigarette lighter, and smiled as it glowed red against his cigarette-end. Everything worked well on this *gari* even if it was second-hand. A very good buy, a very good buy indeed, especially when you considered it actually hadn't cost him anything at all. After all, decent transport was a necessary expense—and what were the union dues paid in for, if not for necessary expenses? It was certainly more comfortable than the prison lorry which had wrenched his spine on the long hot trip to the detention camp at Lamu.

His mind skipped back again to white women. Even during the Mau Mau they were not violated here in Kenya. Killed, yes, but not violated. Very few black men in East Africa dared to touch a white woman, even if she might be insane enough to desire it.

Now there seemed to be a whole new trend in Africa—so much so that James Gichuru had felt it necessary to make a speech assuring the bwanas that nobody would rape their precious memsaabs, as had happened in the Congo. Certainly the Congolese rebels had gone mad with lust and, very possibly, Indian hemp or the local *bhang*, and had raped wholesale. Nuns, even, they had raped. Matisia shivered a little. That was carrying freedom too far. He had been mission-raised.

I am no different from the rest, I suppose, Abraham Matisia thought, and he pressed his foot more firmly on the accelerator. Admit it, Matisia, he admonished himself. You too like the white women better than the black. You remember the big, creamy blondes of the Rieperbahn, the *Grosse Freiheit*, in Hamburg; huge, soft-dumpling girls with long coiled ropes of flaxen hair; girls who actually seemed to prefer the black men to the white. And the little swift, darting bird-like girls of France, who murmured, '*Je t'aime, mon cœur*,' while practising shockingly different versions of what he had first known as a very young man as a simple uncomplicated act of animal gratification.

And the English women: ah, the slim, willowy, slightly horse-faced, blue-eyed English women, who looked down their noses at you and drawled disdainfully until suddenly they were naked, writhing in bed and speaking an indescribable filth, making unbelievable demands, and then suddenly laughing at you when all was over, until you felt soiled and ashamed, like a small boy caught abusing himself. I should have sacrificed a whole herd of fat rams to absolve me of some of the things that happened to me in England, Matisia thought.

But I must get over feeling like a novelty with my education; with my position and my money, the money I will have, I don't have to be a novelty, a big black *poupée*, a comical black doll, any more. Any more than I must remember some of the things black men did with each other behind the wire at Lamu. The white woman seeks out bodies not because we are black and a novelty, but because we are strong and virile and bigger in those important parts than the white man. The white man is drowned in drink and rotten with decadence. His maleness is bred out of him. His skull is long and his chin is weak and he does not know how to please his woman, which is why she is always searching, always restless, always finding herself in other men's beds, always seeking the unattainable, even if it meant other women—or black men.

And there is no doubt about it, Matisia thought, the white woman, in her utter shamelessness, with her screams of passion, her sharp teeth biting, her long nails scratching, her wish to hurt and to be hurt in return, is a better bargain in bed than our women. Our women are placid cows; stupid cows, because they were born cows, submissive cows because they were trained to obey or be beaten, and unfeeling cows because the circumcision ceremony meant an amputation of the lusting parts. Cattle indeed, trained to work like dumb brutes and come fresh when they drop a calf, and the act of breeding the calf with one of our women is less enjoyable than actually entering a she-ass, as the Masai do.

Matisia swerved from the Thika road to follow a gravelled track leading to a small hotel run by Indians. It was not a very good hotel, since nothing the Wahindi ever did was quite up to the white man's mark. But it was better than an African hotel. There was a bathroom and a shower on each floor, and not too many spiders on the ceilings. It was cheap, and its owner was proud to have such a distinguished man as Abraham Matisia wa Matuku as a permanent guest. He had been given the best room. It contained a wash-basin with running water and reasonably clean sheets. The hotel sat a quarter-mile from the roadside, rambling helter-skelter—yellow and unlovely under a few dusty, scraggy umbrella trees. Only its façade was painted a bilious, scabbing yellow. The backside went unpainted, exposing rough grey concrete-cinder building blocks. Nearly all the Indians built that way; the fronts painted and frescoed with plaster curlicues, the back as bare as a goat-herd's behind. But it had a slovenly bar of sorts and a dirty dining-room. The food—if you cared to eat there—would not poison you unless you tackled the curry, which would ream a man from one end to the other. Matisia didn't eat there.

He parked his car in front of the hotel, blew a rousing *tah-de-tah-tah* on the horn, and slammed the door. It shut with a solid *chunk*, not a tinny clang like his old third-hand Land Rover made. He whistled as he walked up the steps and into the small, dingy, sparse-chaired lobby, and reached for his room key without looking at the Indian behind the tiny reception desk. He stared over the man's shoulder at the pigeon-hole marked *34*. It was empty. It had better be empty. That was a long dusty drive from Nairobi on a hot afternoon to find the Number 34 key in the box and the owner gone.

He continued to whistle as he walked up the stairs. He unlocked his door, left the key in the lock, walked into the room, took off his coat and kicked off his shoes. Then he rapped on the thin plyboard partition which separated his room from Number 34. A similar knock answered him. He smiled, and began to take off his clothes. He had stripped down to his shorts when his door was pushed gently open, and a woman walked in, holding the key in her hand. She was barefoot, and she wore a belted thin tussore dressing-gown.

'Lock the door,' he said, nodding at the key. 'And hurry with your clothes. That goddamned luncheon took hours.' He kicked off his shorts and sat down naked on the bedside and lit a cigarette. 'How are you, Lise? You look sleepy. As if you just woke up.'

'I had a nap after breakfast. I did just wake up. I was tired after last night. I did not get home until nearly four.' She raised a thin painted eyebrow. 'You know how it is, I earn hard my money.' She spoke good English but with an accent, touched by both Flemish and French.

'Yes, I know. I know you earn hard your money. Or perhaps we should say our money. Come to bed. Pretend I am a paying guest and make me very happy indeed. Pretend I am a white—shall we say—client? *Crachez-moi dans la bouche, et dites-moi que tu m'aimes.*' He laughed as he fell into French. His French was almost but not quite as good as his English. 'After all these years I have never been able to tell the difference between true love and the love one buys from whores, even when they spit in my mouth and tell me they love me.' He watched her with slitted eyes as she dropped the robe from her shoulders, and sat down beside him, her torso naked but her lower body still covered by the robe. She was a big woman, almost as tall as he. Her hair was dyed a sort of indeterminate red, but showed dark at the roots. Her eyes were brown, and her face was pretty in a routine way, a little oversized and slightly puffed under the eyes. The naked upper portion of her body was firm and white, the breasts good. Her painted toenails stretched straight out in front of her as she flexed her shaved legs. Matisia reached over and flicked the robe off her thighs. They sat naked, a striking contrast in ebony and ivory.

'We make a pretty picture,' she said. 'Look in the mirror.' She gestured at a stained, flyspecked, crinkled glass over the cheap pine dresser. 'You, so black. Me, so white. You are very beautiful; *j'aime les hommes noirs.* Is that what you want me to say? Or shall I do this?' And she placed her hand on his groin.

'Do that,' he said, and rolled over to the far side of the bed, pulling her with him. Lightly resisting the pull, she stooped with one knee on the bed and with her left hand scooped up the robe which had fallen to the floor, and tossed it with long practice neatly over the arm of a chair. '*Ah, mon roi,*' she said, and began to kiss him slowly on the ears, working down his neck toward the hollow where his throat joined his body. Matisia stretched, placed his hands behind the back of his neck, and arched his body to meet her searching mouth.

*

'You are a bull,' she said later, lighting two cigarettes and placing one in his mouth. 'A great, black bull.' She was perspiring heavily and Matisia's body gleamed with her sweat and his own.

'Thank you. I give you a compliment in return. You are great and you are white, but you are not a cow even if I am a bull. I was thinking of cows as I

136

drove out. You are certainly not a cow, Lise. A whore, yes, but not a cow.'
His hand idly caressed her thigh as she sat sideways on the edge of the bed.
'You are too active to be a cow. A wriggling python, perhaps, but never a
cow.'

Suddenly he pinched her leg. She flinched from the cruel bite of his fingers,
but looked at him without anger. Her voice was calm and almost disinterested.

'Why do you always delight in calling me a whore? I know I am a whore,
but I do not sleep with you as a whore. It is not polite—*ce n'est pas poli*.
There is no need.'

Matisia sat up, and pushed a pillow behind his shoulders, leaning his back
against the bed-head.

'I like to think of you as a whore because that is what you are when you
leave this hotel. When I wait until nightfall and drive you back to Nairobi
after having used you all the afternoon. I like to think of you as a whore
because when you go with the fine white gentlemen who suddenly need and
want a woman in this all-but-womanless Nairobi, you go to them as a whore
for money at the demand of an Indian pimp if you cannot pick them up yourself. And you go to them to do the same things you do to me but with the
mark of my sweat, my black sweat, on you, and my seed, my black seed, in
you. I send you out to the white man with what they call, vulgarly in England,
a wet deck. A black wet deck.' He laughed. 'I like to think of that—when you
are making exciting love talk to the white men.' His voice mimicked her.
'My darleeng, oh my darleeng, but you are a grreat white bool. *Je t'aime,
mon cœur, mon roi, mon amour. Prends-moi, mon chéri; mon plus, plus cher.*'

Matisia laughed loudly and slapped his thigh.

'What is so very funny?'

'I am laughing because I just remembered all the fine things they said of
me when I received my diploma from Makerere, when I passed out of the
black college to win honours in London and later in Moscow. It was like a
very special and complicated oath-giving. They told me I would do many
things, that I would accomplish many fine things in this bright new world,
but they never told me I would be either a jailbird or a pimp.' He roared with
laughter again. 'A pimp. I could have been a pimp without all that study, all
those horrid heavy, dull books. All you need to be a good pimp I have here
between my legs. In effect I have wasted my time and talent until you came
along, *ma chérie.*'

Lise Martelis did not join in the laughter. Her expression was vaguely
worried, her thoughts flying far away from Matisia's calculated derision. Her
face now had become cowlike, the cud-chewing face of a woman who was
working with her nether body but whose mind was stolidly fixed on more
practical details. Matisia had seen this abstracted look on some of the French
tarts he had used when he was a young student in Europe. It always signified
the impersonal ping of the *comptoir*.

'Have you heard any more about the extension of my papers?'

'I told you yesterday that Kamau was interceding for you. You know it is very difficult to get working papers for Kenya for a woman of your—ah—rather limited abilities. Perhaps a job as receptionist in a hotel, but your being Belgian and a refugee, it is difficult. Perhaps you should go home to Belgium.'

The woman made an impatient movement with her hands.

'You know as well as I that there are reasons why I cannot return to Belgium,' she said. 'The same reasons that took me to the Congo; that took me later to Mukerjee and finally to you and this bed. I cannot go back to Belgium. I was hidden in the Congo, but I would not be hidden now after all the troubles. A black man's white woman would be more conspicuous now than before, when the *colons* were tolerant of anything *les grands noirs* wanted so far as it did not interfere with business.'

'Then frankly, my dear, I fail to see why we would either want or need you in Kenya,' Matisia said. 'I expect that your best hope is to nip off to Uganda and marry a black man. They seem more tolerant of mixed marriages there, especially in Buganda. In the meantime you are under my protection, and you are making money. Now, you are talking too much, and too much talking kills desire. Pretend that I am a handsome black fellow who lives on a big farm just outside of Kampala; that I have plenty of money and might consider marrying you if I find you satisfactory in your wifely duties.' Matisia lay down again, stretching his dark body on the rumpled white sheet. 'Come, impress me with your desirability, for I am an impatient man. It is growing dark, and we must go back to Nairobi soon. What a pity I cannot be seen with you by daylight. I might even take you to lunch in the Stanley, but they are rather fish-eyed there about pretty young white whores in the company of black men, however distinguished the black man might be.'

Dutifully, the woman began to caress him, but her eyes were remote. Matisia suddenly struck her sharply in the face.

'Pay attention to your work,' he said harshly. 'You are worse than a nigger, day-dreaming on your job.' He slapped her again, contemptuously, then held out his hand. 'Kiss it,' he said. 'Kiss my hand, like the grateful bitch you are.'

The woman sighed, relaxed, seeming almost pleased at the blows. She kissed his hand, and ran her mouth slowly up his arm until her face nestled once again in the hollow of his shoulder while her tongue flicked his ear.

CHAPTER SEVEN

DON AND PEGGY BRUCE were sitting smoking on the little veranda of their cottage in the Norfolk Hotel's back courtyard when Brian drove in. That they were likely to be in a reasonable state of exuberance was attested by a

Scotch bottle with two-thirds of its contents gone. As he walked across the cobbles towards the porch, Brian noticed in the dim light cast from the living-room that Peggy obviously had visited the hairdresser. Her hair was softly waved and its streaky blondeness undeniably touched up. Her nails had been newly done, and she was strikingly, robustly handsome in a severe black frock which made heavy capital of a dazzling expanse of white bosom. Don Bruce had shed his safari clothes and was dressed in ordinary town-going blue.

'Back from the wars,' Brian said, bending over to kiss Peggy Bruce's glowing cheek. 'One casualty only. Considerably quieter than church. I did *not* stay to see the meat wagon collect the remains of our friend. I was standing next a couple of old-time Kyukes and they reckoned that there was nothing to be gained by hanging about. "One fight leads to another," one old boy said, and when they decamped I shoved off with them. Disappointing show, I must say.' He held out his hand for the drink his friend mixed him. 'Thanks, chum. I'm dry to the kneecaps. Cheers. Hangings make me thirsty. As the Russian said, *everything* makes me thirsty. You look very sexy, Peggy, for a gal who was fleeing for her life a few hours ago.'

'Why, thank you, kind sir,' Peggy said. 'So do you. Except I can see where your gun's bulging your front.'

'I know.' Brian patted his side. 'And I can see where something even more deadly is bulging yours. Where's that vicious-looking weapon you were wearing, Donald?'

Don Bruce looked mildly sheepish.

'It clashes with my deacon's suit,' he said. 'I chucked it into the safe in the manager's office. Peggy and I have been recapping the situation. Things don't look quite as desperate as they did a few hours back. I expect poor Mr. Poole cleared the air a bit for everybody when they dropped him. You want to park your hardware as well?'

'No,' Brian said. 'I'll just let it bulge. I feel more like me when I've got it on, even if it does give the girls a mild touch of cancer when we dance. Where's Ken and Marie? I thought they were feeding with us?'

'They are. Some minor fracas or otherwise at Limuru. They said they might be late, so they'll meet us in the Grill. Marie's got the wind up a bit, too. Ken says she wants to either sell or rent their little plot and move closer into town. She's nervous living in between the two reserves, Ken says. I can't see why. It isn't as though he was ever away at nights for any length of time. And there's always her mother with her and the kids.'

'Everybody's nervous, I expect,' Brian said. 'You still of a mind to sell up your old homestead then? The Dutch courage hasn't changed your mind?' He gestured at the bottle.

'No, I haven't changed my mind,' Don said flatly. 'If I can get any sort of a decent price, I'll sell right anough. Peggy says *no*, now, that she'll stick, but I still feel basically the same way I felt when I talked with you this afternoon. It's not what actually happens—it's the constant living with what might happen, even if it never does.'

'Well, I'm not leaving—and that's that,' Peggy Bruce said. 'Perhaps I panicked this afternoon, but it was mostly because of the suddenness of everything and the kids. I can get used to living with a gun again.'

'So can I, but I'm not going to,' her husband snapped. 'And you'll go if I say so. You can't tell me that when these baboons come to power in the spring elections it'll be very long before they take over all that nice cultivated land and divvy it up among themselves. That talk's around already. Marie Jenkins told Ken today that the garden boy said that because she was a good, kind memsaab, she could live on the place in the gardener's hut after *uhuru* came—he wouldn't throw her out at all, let alone kill her. Jolly decent of him, I must say. And that, among other things, is what's got the wind up Marie.'

'Well, I wouldn't set too much store by *that*, either,' Brian said. 'She's South African, and they're never very easy around the Wogs. They've lived in that old *apartheid* too long—separate 'em first and kill 'em if they scream.'

'Mmmm,' Don Bruce replied. 'Peggy, suppose you just go and do whatever it is girls do before we leave for dinner. You want to wash, Brian?'

'Nope. I wasn't exposed to the prison air long enough to soil me.'

The men waited while Peggy Bruce got up to go to the bathroom. Then Brian raised an eyebrow at Don and nodded after her.

'She seems bright enough now,' Brian ventured. 'For a girl that was as frightened as you said.'

'Yeah,' Don replied glumly. 'I know it. Now the bad dream's over it didn't really happen. I can understand that thing they say about women not remembering how it hurts to have children. The lights are bright and the whisky's poured and Daddy's standing by now and so what frightened her this morning didn't actually happen at all. I'm going to have a power of trouble moving her. She's stubborn as a Masai donkey.'

'Why move her, then?' Brian's voice was light. 'She stuck before. If she wants to stay on now she won't be lonesome. A lot of other wives are stuck, too. We're all stuck, as a matter of fact.'

'Not me. Even if I had a written guarantee that all this business of today was nothing but nonsense and moonbeams I don't think I'll be able to live under these apes. I don't think that violence is going to be the thing that drives the white man out of Africa. Brian, I think it'll be constantly living with this bloody arrogant incompetence that'll send us screaming mad.'

Brian sighed.

'I suppose you're right,' he said. 'Tanganyika's going pretty good under Nyerere, but I was in Arusha the other day and I promise you the bloke in the Game Department hadn't a clue about filling out the forms. I finally had to do it myself. He was ashamed to admit he didn't understand it. That'll be tragic when it spreads to everything.'

Don nodded.

'Well, that sort of thing and a thousand other complications is what we'll all face *if* we don't get our throats cut and they *don't* steal our land and they *don't* tax us out of business and they *don't* have a Congolese kind of civil war between the Masai and the Wakamba and the Kikuyu and the Luo and the trains run and they *don't* put you in clink every time it's a question of your word against the black man's and they *don't* shut down the papers and *don't* shove the political opposition in jail and *don't* banish anybody who uncorks his beak against the government, such as it is for as long as it lasts.'

'And,' Brian said, 'all of these things that you optimistically hope they might *not* do are being done this very moment in that citadel of the enlightened black land, Ghana, with its Imperial Highness, Emperor Kwame Nkrumah the First.'

'I forgot to mention letting in the Russians and the Chinese and printing their own money and declaring all other currency valueless and impounding all private cars and a few other bits and pieces,' Don said. 'Or turning loose the black police to replace the military or re-organizing the law courts. Hell, there are lots of cheerful possibilities I haven't ticked off.'

'Your trouble's simply that you can't face up to not being a Bwana,' Brian said with mock sarcasm. 'You've been an upper-case Bwana too long. Just like the bleeding hearts say in London. You want to sit on a tall horse and oversee your lush acres and drink long drinks on the shady veranda and beat the naked niggers that wrest your mistress-money from the stolen soil. You are the kind of Englishman who has made colonialism what it is today. Kiss the girls and kick the Wogs. Rape the women and waste the soil.'

'You're dead right,' Don Bruce said. 'I'm a Bwana to the bone. Well, perhaps—here comes Peggy, all lit up for a night out. Kids all right, love?'

'All right. Angus and Ellen are reading comic books. The babies are asleep.'

'Good. Brian, you drive Peggy down to the Stanley. I'm waiting for a relative of yours.'

'Relative?'

'Yep. Your kid brother. I was sort of pressed for a baby-sitter and I ran into Pip and his girl friend having tea just before they went off to the movies. They said they'd be delighted to stand sentry-go over the chicks while the Mem and I kick up our heels. Give 'em a quiet place to wrestle.'

'All right, my cautious friend,' Brian said. 'I hope you can dig up another girl for the evening. I've already *got* mine. Come on, wench, let us dash off and leave this dull husband to brood about our conduct.' He put his arm around Peggy's waist. 'I'll be good to her, Don, I promise you.'

'Beat her, for aught I care, but for heaven's sake don't get her pregnant. I've enough on my plate at the moment.'

Don smiled as Brian handed his wife into the Land Rover and waved good-bye. There were a lot of things to be said for old Brian. He wasn't one to heavy it up any more than necessary. He might, for instance, have mentioned something awkward about this being the cottage which used to be tended by the room-boy whose headless body was found in the street outside a few years ago—headless, very possibly, because the boy refused to let some old tribal acquaintances in to chop the head off Brian Dermott. Brian Dermott had been Number Two on the Mau Mau extermination list at that time, just after the Governor. He, Don, had been Number Three.

*

They drove round the island in front of the Stanley's unloading area and Brian reached across Peggy's knees to unlatch the car door.

'You go on into the Grill and get Albert to settle you while I see if I can find a parking place. God, it looks as if everybody in Kenya came to town tonight. See you in a jiff.'

He circled the block twice before he found a slot in the metered area.

Don was already at the table when Brian walked down the steps to the dining-floor. The dark candle-lit room was crowded, save for a table or two, and their table for five was pushed well back into a corner.

Brian slid into a chair and noticed that drinks had already been ordered.

'Sorry I was held up,' he said. 'I had to call Ken. He and Marie can't make it. Family fight, I think, the usual excuses.'

'Oh?' Don Bruce raised both eyebrows.

'Mother-in-law trouble, actually. The old girl's had another attack of intentional flu, or something. Frightened of the night noises. You two'll just have to put up with me alone. All the best.' Brian raised his glass. 'I think I'll get well and truly sloshed tonight,' he said. 'I haven't been clobbered in a long time. Let's have some wine to add to the day's gin and the delicious whisky. God almighty, look at that. Old home week. Should I ask them to join us?'

Stephen Ndegwa and Matthew Kamau had just entered the dining-room and were being led to a table. Brian made no attempt to lower his voice as they passed.

'Shush, Brian,' Peggy whispered. 'They'll hear you.'

'And why not?' Brian asked loudly. 'It being a free country for at least another few months. I've half a mind to ask them. You know, old-fashioned hospitality. Set them at ease and all that. They look a mite nervous.' He half-rose.

'For Christ's sake, sit down,' Don hissed. 'You don't want a rumpus. Poor old Burrows has enough trouble here keeping a leash on the noisier military element. He doesn't need any added headaches from friends.'

'Oh, all right,' Brian said. 'If you want to keep on playing Bwana and disregard Mr. Macmillan's winds of change. Frightfully up-country of you, though, up-staging our next Chief Minister. What'll we have to eat?'

'Lots of everything,' Peggy Bruce said. 'Starting with the smoked salmon. Anything that is not remotely connected with sheep. Then a big fillet and a huge salad with cheese on it and one of those enormous extravagant desserts you set fire to.'

'You, Donald?'

'The same as Peggy.'

'Might as well keep it simple,' Brian said to the waiter. 'Three of everything, and start us with a bottle of Châteauneuf du Pape. And open another so it can be flexing its muscles. But fetch us all another whisky, big ones, before you bring the salmon.'

'Prosperous-looking place,' Don said. 'I haven't seen it empty since they remodelled the hotel. But it's not like it was in the old days. Tell you the truth, I am beginning to feel more and more nervous in public. It's what you might call an inferiority complex about being white—as if I'd committed some sort of sin.'

'Me too,' Peggy said. 'I have an overwhelming desire to whip off me decent little cocktail frock and prance around in a *shuka*, so's the fashions won't pass me by. I think perhaps dirty great earrings made out of—what's *that*?'

That was a huge blond man, with cheeks like slabs of prime beef, being firmly assisted to the door. He was shouting over his shoulder, '. . . be damned if I'll eat in the same place with a flock of bloody coons after they've strung up one of our own to make room for another filthy nigger in a white man's'—his voice ended in a splutter as he was hastened up the stairs and into the little courtyard. Most of the white eyes in the dining-room swung again to Stephen Ndegwa and Matthew Kamau, who were pointedly studying their menus. It was impossible to see their faces behind the large zebra-striped covers of the ornate food list.

'I suppose we all ought to feel the same way,' Brian said. 'Somehow my racial discrimination doesn't extend to the eating. I've squatted around too many campfires with my Wogs—and for that matter, slept under the same blanket too many times with old Kidogo during the Emergency . . .' His voice drifted. 'I wonder if they won't be declaring *that* again pretty soon?'

'Quite probably, I should think,' Don Bruce said. 'Else this big new base at Kahawa doesn't mean anything. You can't really make coppers out of the soldiery unless you have some sort of local legal structure for it. And I can't believe they're sinking all this money into that big installation unless they intend to make some sort of arsenal for a feeble last stand in the East.' His voice was bitter in its mock quotation marks. 'One solid strip of concrete security in the troubled world East of Suez. We've lost everything else, God knows, except this funny little base.'

'Well, it worries the boys over there in the corner with their heads stuck into the soup,' Brian said. 'They're always speechifying that Kahawa must go. I expect they reckon there'll be life in the old Lion yet if the locals cut up too nasty after the elections. Twenty-five hundred disciplined white troops under professional officers would certainly never let this place get out of hand to run wild like it's gone rabid in the Congo.'

'I wouldn't be too sure if I were you,' Peggy said, pouring oil on her salmon, and reaching for the paprika with the other hand. 'From what I read in the paper, the first thing a black majority in Legco will ask for is a recall of the troops and a closing-down of the base. Won't be the first time we've backed down, either.'

'Let me have some of that oil and vinegar, please, Peggy,' Brian said. 'You're right. But I still think it all started sliding the wrong way when the Yanks let us down in Suez when we had Nasser nailed to the mast. Ever since the Yanks stripped us naked in the Suez crisis every tin-pot country with an axe to whet is clamouring to spit in our eye.'

'What a dreary conversation,' Peggy said. 'Can't you chaps think of something more pleasant?'

'No,' Don said. 'And I must say you've contributed your own bit of drear to the general load. You came in today charged with plenty of doleful drama yourself, my lass.'

'Well, there must be something else to talk about,' Peggy replied. 'How are the new clients, Brian? Fun? Or the bloody kind?'

'Neither, so far. He shoots well, and is rather quiet. She—the sister—I haven't been able to figure. One of the deep ones.'

'Nothing doing in the moonlight?' Peggy leered extravagantly.

'Not so far,' Brian said. 'She's a mite stringy for my tastes. A little on the fashion-mannequin side, all mouth and eyes. I like great, big, luscious, curvy girls, with topsides like *that*.' Brian described opulent globes with cupped, lifting hands. 'Girls like you, Peggy. Something a chap can seize onto, get a firm grip on.'

'You *are* a beast. I was just—— My God! Do you see what I see? I cannot, I refuse, to believe my eyes.'

The men turned their heads to follow Peggy's pointing hand.

An African woman, obviously alone and quite as obviously drunk, was invading the room. She was walking affectedly pigeon-toed on heels so high that she teetered dangerously, and her enormous behind swayed like a separate entity under a soiled flounced bottle-green taffeta dress which was bastioned by an enormous bow, wobbling precariously on her vast buttocks. Make-up had been slabbed on her face as if by a trowel, and she was perspiring through the powder, which appeared to bubble in tiny blisters. Runnels of sweat were cutting through the enormous caked island of rouge on her cheeks, and her lips were greasy in lipstick of a peculiarly appalling light pink.

She was arguing loudly in broken English and spitting Swahili with two captains and the covey of waiters which immediately clustered round her. Across the room, from the corner, the manager was hurriedly excusing himself to dart swiftly through the packed tables.

'I have money!' She was protesting loudly, and, opening a beaded handbag, she scattered red hundred-shilling notes onto the rug. 'Plenty of money! *Shilingi mingi!*'

'Everybody's throwing money today,' Brian murmured, fascinated. 'But that stuff's real. I wonder how old Burrows will wiggle out of this one?'

'Are you joining someone, Madame?' Now it was the manager's voice

144

suavely spreading oil on the ruffled wavelets of his pride, the Grill. 'We are completely booked tonight, as you can see.' He swept his arm around him. 'Allow me to escort you up the stairs, Madame,' and the cluster of waiters and captains closed round her.

'Hold on, there!' Brian stood up. 'It's Brigitte! There you are at last! The lady is with me!' he cried in a loud voice. 'Yoo hoo! Here I am, *chérie!*'

'Sit down, you bloody fool!' Don Bruce barked, and yanked at Brian's coat tails. 'Everybody's looking at us!'

'I am only trying to practise multi-racial co-operation,' Brian said, proclaiming the best of malicious intent in a loud voice. 'I am standing in for Michael Blundell and all the other chaps who promise it in their speeches. I am willing to practise it, since those two gentlemen in the corner'—he bowed in the direction of the African politicians—'were obviously not expecting a member of their own constituency here tonight. Please!' He raised his voice again. 'Show the lady over here, Captain! This way, steward! One vote, one table!'

'I say, you *are* an ass, Brian,' Peggy said, barely restraining a giggle. 'Do sit down and stop making a public spectacle of yourself.'

'I am *not* making a public spectacle of myself, my good woman,' Brian said, still speaking loudly and directing his remarks to the politicians. 'You see before you merely an example of racial co-operation truly at work in a racially unco-operative world. Oh well. If you insist.' He sat down again as the gaudily attired lady was swept away in a tidal wave of waiters and captains. 'I did but my tiny best.' He bowed as a scatter of mock applause attended his resumption of his seat. 'You see? Next time they'll give the lady a table. Who knows? In the bright future, possibly even a lonely *white* woman will be admitted to this hall of culture, and everyone will say that it was old Brian Dermott who drove the first wedge into the solid wall of black supremacy.' He hiccuped slightly. 'Could it be that lack of democratic practice is making me drunk?'

'You ought to be ashamed of yourself, Brian,' Peggy said, and giggled openly. 'I was watching the two black gentlemen just as you stood up. I swear they turned pale, physically impossible or not. For one dreadful moment I'm sure they thought she was actually going to try to join them.'

'*Uhuru* to you, my winsome wench,' Brian said cheerfully. 'Never let it be said that a Dermott left a distressed damsel unsuccoured, dirty as that last may sound. Steward! The new bottle of wine, please, and was that lady one of your wives come to see if you actually were at work?'

The wine-waiter murmured something in Kikuyu about women and *pombe* and the Bwana's bad jokes, and hurried off, visibly embarrassed.

'All right, I'm a damned fool, go on and say it,' Brian said. 'But damn me, I like to see a little unscheduled fluster upset the smugness of both sides. This place has been so smarmy self-righteous since it went multi-racial, and if I know the waiters they're twice as embarrassed by the influx of Africans as the white customers are. But the plates hit the ceiling tonight when they bumped into the first of a thousand similar problems they're going to have to cope with if they're lucky enough to remain open and in business under the new regime.'

'Brian's right, you know,' Don said soberly. 'That black trull will turn out to be somebody's cousin, one day, and the chaps that slung her out will be in trouble. And the first time they bounce some boozed-up coon with no necktie it'll develop that they've just given the heave-ho to the new Chief Minister's Uncle Gitau or Cousin Kariuki.'

'More's the bloody pity, but I'm afraid you are painting a sadly accurate picture, my lad,' Brian said. 'Up to now the blacks who've come here have been painfully on their good behaviour, and damned careful of dress and manners, even if they don't know which knife to use and have to restrain themselves from tearing the meat course apart with their hands. But a short two hours after we hang one white man we have a nigger tart trying to crash the swankiest joint in town. Poor sods. I really feel sorry for the innocent ignorants. They've a lot of lumps in store.'

'Poor old girl,' Peggy said. 'All tarted up in her best, and nobody asked her to dance. At all. One more mark against the white man when *her* time comes to get even. She piled on her best finery and they threw her out of the *dukah*. Poor sad little coloured lady.'

'Has it occurred to anyone that the only native women to publicly emerge in this *uhuru* business seem to have been the town women, the unmarried tarts, the real whores?' Brian said. 'I wonder if that doesn't mean something too— and I'm talking on the Wogs' side. Like always, it's the good folk you don't see, and only the tearaways who poke their fingers in the public eye.'

'Surely it's true. And the good black folk in the up-country are just as ashamed of their white-folks-aping relatives who've come to town as your people would be of you if you wore drainpipe trousers, sported a ducktail hair-do and carried a switch knife,' Don said. 'It's the loafers, the lazies, the spivs and the thugs that're acting up in the Congo now. It was the city slickers and their detribalized wenches who spearheaded the surface troubles in the Mau Mau, and it's the same bunch of city-slicker *shenzis* who are your union officials and small politicians now.'

'Well, along those lines, you've got to call that drunken white man they just pitched out a typical Kenya settler, and you a typical white hunter with too much grog aboard,' Peggy said. 'And me sitting here with half my tits hanging out. What do I qualify as? A lady?'

'We'll ignore the last reference to your unfettered charms, but no doubt about it, we have the name of being a shaggy lot,' Brian said. 'Somehow you never read about the chaps who break their backs and their hearts on this bloody country, and very often in behalf of its bloody people. All you get is Happy Valley, the newest fornication, and some chap shooting off his face to the British press about how the settler's misunderstood. It's not all been

146

gin and jests out here, as witness you people and thousands like them that've damned near killed themselves for the country.'

'This is getting heavy again. I think the time has come for a brandy, some coffee, and a trip to the ladies' loo before we invade the Equator,' Peggy said. 'I think I'll just reverse the order and disappear while you tend to the coffee. And, pray, let us attempt to inject a touch more cheer into the evening. A girl never knows when she'll get to the village again.'

She got up and went off in the direction of the ladies' lounge.

'You've got quite a girl there, Donald my lad,' Brian said. 'What's the next step?'

'Back to the farm tomorrow, I suppose. I'll stick around for a few days and sort of snoop the layout while I wait to hear from your people about buying the place. Then I suppose I'll start the painful business of packing them off to Scotland. The place is finished as white man's country, and damned if I'll turn myself into a Wog just to scrape along. Maybe there's a place for me in Australia or Canada or Alaska.'

'I'd try Australia,' Brian said. 'That thin African blood of yours would never stand Alaska. Here's the coffee. In the absence of Peggy, will you pour, or shall I?'

On the way out they saw Matthew Kamau and Stephen Ndegwa waiting in front of the lift, standing well out in front of the elevator in the passageway. Walking closest to the politicians, as they strode along three abreast, Brian made no motion to fall behind or swerve to avoid a collision with Stephen Ndegwa. Brian's shoulder struck Ndegwa's body sharply. The African turned in surprise, and Brian stared at him coldly, his eyes flat and disdainful.

'Perhaps tomorrow, *uhuru*,' Brian said nastily. 'But tonight, get the hell out of my way, Sam.'

Ndegwa stared at him in astonishment, his mouth slightly open. Brian walked on into the fresh air.

'That was pretty,' Peggy said. 'Why did you have to do that, you cute white settler, you? Whatever happened to my boy Brian Dermott?'

Brian looked abashed.

'I don't know,' he said. 'I really don't know. Very possibly I wanted him to say something so I could dot him one. Sorry. Not like me. Let's go on and be merry at the casino.' They walked silently towards the Equator Club.

As they pushed through the clotted humanity in the smoke-choked night club, one of the African bandsmen was singing: 'Itsy Bitsy Teeny Weeny Yellow Polka-dot Bikini', his impossibly ugly face grotesquely contorted in rubbery emulation of the white crooners he had seen on the films.

'Another candidate for Chief Minister,' Brian said, as he fought his way through the leaping crowd which had spilled off the dance floor. 'Watch me closely tonight, people, I am not in the mood for love, and I shouldn't like anyone to be rude to me. All I can spot on this dance floor is the kind of Kenya cowboy that got us into this mess in the first place, and it doesn't do my disposition very much good to reflect that I'm one of them. Bring the bottle and a bucket of ice, steward.'

People waved. People stopped at the table and joined them for drinks. They vacated their own table and visited others. The men swarmed Peggy; she danced nearly every dance. One of the boy friends of an air hostess Brian knew slightly became ill and friends carried him outside. It appeared that the air hostess, one of the prettier Alitalia lassies, had decided to stay on.

Brian looked drunkenly, owlishly at Don Bruce, as he held the pretty hostess's hand under the table.

'This is roughly where we came in, for sure, my boy,' he said, and knocked over a glass.

CHAPTER EIGHT

STEPHEN NDEGWA knew when he entered the suite that it was going to be an oratorical evening. That was the trouble with a pow-wow between politicians. Politicians did not speak in phrases—only in orotund cantos. He sighed and sat down. He'd try to keep it light for a moment, anyhow.

'We can talk now,' Matthew Kamau said to Stephen Ndegwa. 'Will you drink a brandy? It may possibly settle your nerves after that nonsense in the dining-room.' He spoke in Kikuyu, and swept a hand towards the tray of bottles on the small refrigerator.

'Forget it. We came off very nicely, all told. No bones broken—no scene for the newspapers. Forget it. This is a very comfortable suite,' Ndegwa spoke in English. 'You think perhaps we can afford to keep it permanently after *uhuru*? Yes, I would like a brandy very much. I do not like feeding dry but it seemed a very good idea with half of white Kenya staring at us tonight. There doesn't seem to be room for drunken African leaders these days, not with all the evil our cousins in the Congo are doing us. Not with our people making public spectacles of themselves. Not with the world's spotlight flashing in our face, like a bwana searching the barnyard for a chicken thief. How long since you stole from a bwana, Matthew?' Ndegwa chuckled. 'How long since you ran around naked in the *bundu*; how long since you danced and capered in the firelight, and then sneaked off in the bush to lie with the maidens after the elders were drunk and snoring from the feast?'

Ndegwa got up and walked over to the bottles. He picked up a water tumbler and poured it half-full of brandy, threw back his head and drained it in a gulp. Then he refilled the glass.

'What a pity you do not drink, Kamau,' he said, lighting a cigarette and taking a delicate sip of his brandy, then running his tongue slowly over the heavy, out-turned, sharply cut lips. 'I drink. Jomo Kenyatta drinks. All good Kikuyu drink. Life is just one long beer drink. We drink for peace; we drink for war. We drink at the *baraza*; we drink at the weddings; we drink when we cut the canes to celebrate a birth. We drink when the famine comes, from fear, and we drink when the famine is gone, from relief. Always we guzzle honestly. We don't drink out of politeness—we drink to get drunk and sleep and maybe to roll into the cookfire and burn ourselves. The true Kikuyu's soul sleeps inside the *pombe* gourd. Truly, the strong waters are his elixir of life. . . .' He paused and sipped again, smacking his lips. 'As Kerinyagga is the home of his God, who undoubtedly drinks Himself, else why would He have made *pombe* so important in our lives? Speak up, Mahatma. Speak up, my Pandit, my lean high priest of asceticism. Unravel all the riddles. Tell me what makes the world go round, and do not mention love. Speak! I thirst for your words.'

'I haven't had the chance,' Kamau said, pacing back and forth on the soft pile of the blue carpet. 'You babble on like a woman, like a *nugu* in a tree, chattering at nothing, over nothing. This is a very serious day.'

'Each day we live is a serious day, this one as serious as the last, but no more serious than tomorrow. Yesterday and today and tomorrow. Yesterday and today and tomorrow have a way of welding themselves into one long, final, anonymous sleep inside a hyena. Life is only dung, which fertilizes the soil, and I shall live again as a carnation for your buttonhole.'

'Stop talking like an African. And stop making bad sarcasms. I want to speak seriously to you. We are in a very difficult position at this moment. God damn those crazy people in the Congo! God damn that stupid Lumumba, and that stupider Kasavubu, and that white man's pet, Tshombe in Katanga! And thrice accursed be this bloody governor! A month ago I would have sworn on my grandfather that he and his council would have stayed the execution. Renison betrayed us on the matter of Poole.'

Stephen Ndegwa kicked off his loafers and wriggled his toes. Contentment spread over his fleshy, bulldog face. He hooked the leg of a straight chair with one foot, dragged it over the rug, and then placed both feet luxuriously on the cushion. He regarded his flexing toes, and sighed.

'You know, Matthew, I will always be a simple bush African,' he said. 'For all my degrees, for all my vast knowledge, for all the receptions I have attended when the Queen has come, when the Queen Mum has come, even when the Queen's uncle has come, my feet still hurt. Today I enjoyed true luxury—I spent the whole afternoon in a *kikoi* and my bare feet. I have never been comfortable in shoes or clothes without patches and holes, so that the air can blow through and cool my black backside. When you are Master of all Africa, Matthew, your feet will still hurt. Gratified nationalism will not cure you of your niggerism. You may be crowned Emperor of all Africa, but you will still fear the hyena's wail, quail at the broken cookpot, strangle the breech-presented baby, shun the vulture's shadow, and avoid the milk from the breasts of a woman not your mother.'

Ndegwa's eyes slitted. He loved to bait his colleague, this handsome young Kikuyu, this dynamic orator, this dull, dedicated dog, who was so noisily adept at spellbinding. And so bloody crashingly boresome off stage.

'For all your fiery statements to the press, for all your impassioned addresses to the English and the Americans, for all your talk of *One Vote—One Man*, like our friend Mboya, I think you really want to be a white man, Kamau. I have seen you in London, in Washington and New York, being so disgustingly, nauseatingly charming with your teacup balanced to an infinity of correctness, and I would swear that you would scrub that colour from your face if the great Ngai granted you the right recipe for a bleach. First you take the stomach contents of a goat, *et cetera* . . . You're a frustrated bwana, Kamau, not a simple, dirty, lazy, drunken bush nigger like me.'

'That's a filthy li . . .' Matthew Kamau paused, caught himself, and smiled his most charming smile. He waggled a finger at Ndegwa. 'You're always pulling my leg, Stephen; always trying to take the mickey out of me. Stop it. It is you who really always wanted to be a white man; you who takes the white man's part; you who preach moderation and two-way tolerance, even three-way tolerance if one considers that wretched Wahindi, Mukerjee, as representative of a race; you who always says take it slowly, take it easy, we are not yet ready, *pole-pole*, the white man lives here too; it is his country as well as ours. It is Mboya who shouts "scram out of Africa" to the white man and the world, and I who wear out my lungs screaming freedom to our people. You are the King of *pole-pole*—King Take-it-Easy the First. You are the white Africa, Ndegwa, not I.'

Stephen Ndegwa scratched his head and then his ribs. Oh, God, he thought, now the rhetoric has started. Maybe I can still change it to people-talk. It's worth a try, anyhow.

'All right,' he said. 'We'll talk straight. Would you have let it happen?' he tasted the words softly. 'Would you have taken a little trip to Accra or Dar, to be out of the line of fire, and let it happen?'

'Would *you*?' Matthew Kamau protruded his lower lip. 'How about you, Bwana Moderate, who speaks with two tongues?'

'I'm not the firebrand, and you haven't answered my question. Would *you*?'

'Of course not. Three months ago, yes. But not now. You know that as well as I do.'

'The white men were truly afraid our people would have got out of hand if things had gone the other way. There was plenty of talk among the simpler elements of our people too. More cattle to be slashed. More *shambas* to be fired. More strangled cats and gutted dogs. Mau Mau all over again. And three months ago I know you said *yes*. You said a little bit of *yes*. And you said it without my knowledge or permission. Don't bother to deny it. You said a very small *yes*, a tiny little *okay, boys, just a touch of the old stuff. Didn't* you?' Ndegwa flung the question like a spear.

'No.' Kamau's answer was flat. 'But supposing I had? I merely said then that I wouldn't be responsible if Kenyatta weren't freed. Of course I said it out loud. To the press. Other people said it too. Mboya said it.'

'Damn Mboya. I don't care who else said it. Damn Kenyatta—you know I'm not talking about Kenyatta! Kenyatta's useless to us now. He's no good as a symbol any more. Let him rot in Lodwar. Let him die peacefully. He is an old complication from the past. You saw the article in *Time*. Does the fact that a home-circulation magazine mentions a Kenya "cocktail" made of blood, human semen and menstrual fluid, as symbolic of Africa, help us? That's what the great American Bible, *Time*, called one of the oathing mixtures. A "cocktail", with those delightful ingredients, and sanctioned by our great, if slightly impotent, leader, the Burning Spear. Burning Spear . . . Christ.' Ndegwa spat on the carpet. 'Jomo Kenyatta, the spirit of Kenya, the burning spear of independence. My weary, aching ass.'

'But I *didn't* let it happen tonight,' Kamau said. 'That was Kenyatta's trouble in Mau Mau. *He* let it get out of hand and was powerless when the thugs ran wild. All the planning went for nothing. So I didn't let anything happen tonight—although it was there if I needed it. You may be sure it was there.'

Stephen Ndegwa tugged at his chin. He drawled his words.

'And these hired gentlemen of yours, that Matisia, these labour-union types, that the American politicians so aptly call ward-heelers? They wouldn't be thugs? They're still Kenyatta's people, you know, grown just a little older and not very much wiser and still just as stupidly bloodthirsty. You think you control them, any more than Kenyatta could control them? I don't think so. Not by a damned sight. Quit your pacing and pour me some more brandy. I'm too comfortable to move.'

Matthew Kamau stopped his pacing, and his handsome face contorted, his underlip jutting, deep lines cutting from nostril to mouth. He pounded his lean, corded black fist up and down, up and down, on his clean pinky-grey palm.

'Damn and damn and damn again,' he said. 'It would have been so perfect if only they'd come to the hanging point of Peter Poole before this damned nonsense in the Congo. I could have turned it on, then, for all the front pages everywhere and we would have been a righteous sea of black wrath, storming for justice if they refused to hang him, or a quiet, well-controlled country, refusing to rejoice over the sad death of a white man, while quietly applauding simple justice to black and white alike. Quiet, peaceful Kenya, calm after the Mau Mau tempest, showing its progressive face to the world, suing for brotherhood among black and white in our time. Whichever way the bones pointed. God damn Lumumba, that chattering ape from the trees! His headlines steal my fire!'

Kamau smote his hands together, flung wide his arms in the gesture of an orator, hunched his head between his shoulders and began to pace again.

Ndegwa watched Kamau for a moment before he spoke. He swirled the brandy round and round. He crooked an eyebrow.

'Very impressive. You are coming on beautifully as an actor. That bit alone should be worth another hundred scholarships from the Americans. And now you say if they hadn't hanged Peter Poole, you could have stopped the uprising, then? You could have raised your mighty arm and said: "Slay not, loot not, burn not—not yet, my brothers—because just now it is bad business, my brothers"? Or would you have merely quietly been away for a chat with Nyerere in Tanganyika or off to America for a fund-raising tour among your rich ball-players and night-club singers and even richer politicians who figure that a dirty dollar to Africa is a bloc vote in Harlem? You could have stopped a bloody revolt that you yourself, with carefully timed intent, have been fuelling until you were forced to merge your party with mine out of pure political expediency? You could have stopped it cold, eh?'

Ndegwa's tone was elaborately sarcastic. He wiggled his stockinged toes again, and gazed at them as if they held the answer to his questions. His right great toe perked up, as if listening. Kamau's reply was irritable.

'Stop looking at your bloody feet and pay attention to me, Stephen Ndegwa. I could have made it happen when I wanted it, for it was ready. But I took pains to stop it, no matter what they did to Peter Poole. It could not be allowed to happen, *was not* allowed to happen and *cannot* be allowed to happen now.'

'And how did you stop it, no matter what might happen?' Ndegwa's voice minced. 'How did the leader of my emerging nation stop his wicked children from venting their childish anger on their sworn enemies, the nasty white bwanas who stole their lands?'

'I stopped it as you might have stopped it. I sent people to the locations and to the villages and to the forests and to the white *shambas*. It was surprising how little violence was needed. Sometimes I think the Kikuyu have lost their stomach for blood.'

I'd better not mention the steps I took to stop it, Ndegwa thought. *My steps were simpler than his. Maybe he knows I called the Governor. If he doesn't know let him suppose it was me and I'll deny it just as I deny I know we both made deals with London to keep Kenyatta penned up.*

'Treason-talk, but true,' Ndegwa said. 'We never had much stomach, except for sacrificing helpless animals—and, occasionally, helpless people. Craft, guile was always our strong point. What we need is a warrior race, instead of a race of bloody *babus*, taxi-drivers and scheming politicians like us. So you quelled the riots before they started, did you? Jolly good. Especially in view of that carrier-full of helicopter troops that just landed in Mombasa, that transport-load of the Duke of Wellington's foot soldiers as well. Do you suppose they all came roaring out here just to inspect their new military base outside of town?'

'Damn the Kahawa military base. It will go when we say so, and damn the Turkana and the Masai, and all the rest of the bush niggers. Damn them all for a bunch of ignorant savages. They're useless to us, and you know it. All they care about is their sheep and their cattle herds and to be let alone. All they're good for is to pose for tourist cameras. They do not figure in our plans.'

'Yes, my friend, but add them up and they are still a vital part of Africa. Perhaps they pine for *uhuru* too. How can you say such callous, disparaging things about your poor depressed brethren?' Ndegwa's voice lifted in mock amazement, tinged with spurious shock. 'Surely this is no proper talk to come from the most prominent young nationalist in East Africa? Suppose the papers got hold of your true sentiment about our ragged relations?'

'Why will you insist on taunting me?' Kamau's voice was earnest. 'Look, Ndegwa. For Christ's sake be serious. Consider some items. By hanging Peter Poole the British made a great deal of character in the world abroad at a time when the world is beginning to wonder about African responsibility. You saw these press people—those that came into the dining-room, the ones who are always in the lounge drinking, the ones who continually pass through from Rome and Paris and London to go and write about Africa? These people are writing reams on reams. You have read the newspapers, the news magazines. That is where we fight our war these days, Ndegwa, in the papers and in the magazines. *Pangas* are not good enough any more.'

'Yes, I know.' Ndegwa's voice now blunted its sarcastic edge. 'I know it well. And so far we have done well, very well. This year was going to be the bright year of African independence. This year, nineteen-sixty, the golden year of African self-determination. Everybody was behind us. It was all too beautiful. I was sore afraid it couldn't last.'

Nedgwa shook his head, and held out his glass again.

'I am getting drunk maybe and I don't care. How I would like to have a few—a *very* few moments alone with Lumumba and Kasavubu and the rest of those potato-heads in some dark forest of their own Congo. All the years of planning and the hopes, all the slow and then swift progress, even the suppression of most of the truth about Mau Mau until now. They even forgot the blood and the babies' brains. All of Africa, the world thought, lived in Nairobi, where the noble lords forever roger the duchesses and all the settlers are drunk expatriates, kicked out of England for the avowed purpose of milking the land and exploiting the native. Everything piss-pure and perfect, even the conference in London last year, where we sold the Colonial Office a pup, with nobody blinking an eye over Koinange or Gichuru. And now what do we get? That black son of a hyena with the comic beard and the horn-rimmed glasses! That stupid thief, that postal clerk, that mountebank, that liar, that monomaniac, that braying *ass*, with his white woman and his stupidities mounting on stupidity. That f——— *Lumumba*'!

'May the dogs defile his ancestors!' Kamau shouted suddenly, in Kikuyu. 'May he wander in hell forever as a stinking hyena! May his crops rot and his sheep die, may his daughters become whores and his sons fornicate with their mothers!'

'Heah, heah. To continue—responsible Africa.' Ndegwa applauded politely but otherwise ignored the outburst. 'The eyes of the world are on the Congo. And what do they see? Drunken niggers on Saturday night. Drunken rapists, nun-killers, arsonists, guerrillas, insurgents, mutineers, thieves, liars, incompetents, turncoats, squabblers, civil warriors! All Africa is now the Congo. The Congo is all Africa. Africa is a nun with her belly slit and stuffed full of rocks. Africa is a priest with his ears sliced off. Africa is a waste of burnt villages and starved natives. Africa is no longer tomorrow's hope. Africa is——' Ndegwa paused for breath. 'Dammit, Kamau. You've got me talking like a politician haranguing a mob.'

Kamau stopped him with a lifted palm.

'Let me finish what you're saying. Africa is a dirty joke right *now*, and the dirty joke is being told by a man named Lumumba. They give you the torch of freedom and you set yourself alight with it! And then you turn and rend the United Nations, and then you try and pit the Russians against the Americans, and then you accuse everybody of everything, and then the premier sacks the president, and the president sacks the premier, and the whole world laughs. Laughs at the Congo, the dirty joke of the world—and laughs at all Africa with it. And the Belgians snigger behind their hands. They planned it this way, God rot them. They knew when they handed over they handed over to children. They fled before the shriking savages and enlisted the world's sympathy. They will creep back when the shooting and looting has been put down, and they will set up their puppets—quietly, but ever so quietly'—Kamau's voice minced and almost twittered in its sing-song—'and business will resume and mines will operate on schedule and stocks will go up and the Societé Generale Belgique and its Union Minière will rule the Congo again, if the Russians haven't got it, and then there will be a world war, and . . .' Kamau's voice stopped its singsonging and became almost tearful.

'. . . and then we will never get our dirty work done here to our mutual satisfaction,' Ndegwa finished shortly. 'Don't cry, *mtoto*. Spare me the sympathy-seizing quaver in the orator's voice, little boy. You will still chew your sugar-cane some day, and have six big Cadillacs and a white wife, if you want one. Your muddy little brats will all grow up in a most colourful world, predominantly black, brown and yellow, all frightened green of the Reds. But that is tomorrow. Today we are in serious trouble here in Kenya, and I will be the first to admit it and cry some extra curses on the heads of Lumumba and that pack of rock-apes who've turned loose the more dangerous animals.

'I am almost amused,' Ndegwa laughed softly. 'I *am* amused. We damn and blast the Belgians publicly for granting liberty too soon, to a people unfit to practise self-government, or even to keep their own Force Publique in order and the mails going. And then you and I sit here and curse the same Belgians for their complete wiliness in granting that same independence. The bastards *knew* what would happen. They knew it when they shipped out all

154

the gold last January, and started making preparations to leave the country in its own stinking soup. They hadn't counted on Lumumba making such a complete ass of himself, of course, or that the world would stop turning and focus on the Congo.'

'And in the meanwhile, we now have the world press to consider,' Kamau said. 'The vultures have descended, but with a difference. The vultures have now become eagles. They feed on dung and defaecate gold. Now the world is reading, and believing. The world is beginning to be bloody well sick of our shenanigans.'

Ndegwa wriggled his feet into his loafers, and stood up.

'I must go now,' he said. 'Thank you for the brandy and the fine words. You were most eloquent in your summing up of the situation. So, I think, was I. The Churchillian school of declamation is infectious. It is a pity we had to waste the eloquence on each other. But I do not think that our people are quite ready, as the white man might say, for this sort of harsh truth at the moment. We must consider some ways to make independence, and *uhuru*, more popular with the outside masses with the money. And to suppress our own hotheads who are panting to fling more fat into the fire. *Kwaheri*, Younger Brother.'

'Good-bye, Older Brother,' Kamau said. 'I shall be the first to deny that these words passed between us. Have you any suggestion as to where we might start to regain some of our lost ground?'

'Had you thought of starting a welfare fund for poor Peter Poole's widow and children?' Ndegwa turned laughing in the doorway. 'It would tell the world that we are of a forgiving nature. No, I am jesting, Matthew. I think what we'd better do is get out of town for a bit. I want to be fresh for the New Year and the general elections, and also to give our friends in the opposition every chance to keep on slitting each other's throats.'

'I suppose I could always go back to America and raise some more educational funds—make some more speeches,' Kamau murmured. 'What had you in mind?'

'No, let *me* go to America. We'll all take some trips. I'll go to the United States and meddle in their Presidential election, like Krushchev and this idiot with the beard, Castro. I will pretend I am Mboya or at least a United Nations delegate, and stir up the local blackfellows. Why don't you go to England and steal some headlines from old Banda and his everlasting whine about Nyasaland and the Rhodesias?'

'You do put it rather crassly,' Kamau said, and smiled. 'And Matisia?'

'Take him with you. Send him to some bleeding-heart tea-parties. Maybe he can collect some more education-fund money as well as the sympathy of the ladies. He's very, very good at collecting the sympathy of the ladies. But I'm very serious when I say that it is a good time for us to leave and let the other tom cats scratch each other's eyes out. It's due, and overdue, for a showdown in KANU, and I personally think they'll dump Odinga.'

155

'We can radiate confidence in the emergence of Kenya, confidence in a future black government, confidence—after the Congo the world is ready to hear at least a few black men who don't eat raw missionaries for breakfast,' Kamau said.

'Why, Matthew!' Ndegwa professed shocked surprise. 'You actually made a joke! And speaking of jokes, I think it would be a delightful idea if we left the white leaders, the Blundells and Cavendish-Bentincks, severely alone to pelt each other with harsh words and possibly old eggs. Our black demagogues have been raising so much commotion lately that it has been difficult for the world to hear the white settlers hurl their feeble curses at each other. Well . . . I must fly. Good night, and try to keep Matisia out of the Soho strip-tease clubs.'

He ducked his head, and shut the door quietly behind him.

Matthew Kamau looked at its blank surface for a long time before he, too, kicked off his own shoes, took off his tie, and lay down on the divan to think. The divan was not very comfortable. He swung his legs over the cushioned side and slid down to the floor, where he hunkered on his heels. It had been a long time since he had sat that way publicly, but in the privacy of his own *thingira*, he still felt more comfortable squatting, chin resting on the forearms which were crossed over the upraised knees.

CHAPTER NINE

BRIAN DERMOTT flung the pillow from his head and groped his way to the bathroom. He just made it to the bowl before he was violently ill. He pulled himself up from a kneeling position on the floor and retched again, but there was nothing left of last night's lovely dinner. Lovely smoked salmon, lovely turtle soup with the sherry in it, all the lovely wine and the lovely garlicky steak—*kuisha*. All gone, lovely finished. He felt like several exquisite degrees of death.

'The wagon for you again, Dermott,' he mumbled, 'but not right now and not this day.' Reaching for the brandy bottle he knocked over the gin, but he didn't care. A slug of Hennessey might just possibly stave off death for the moment. Brian Dermott had forgotten that hangovers like this existed— that a day's intake of a variety of things like martinis, beer, Scotch and soda, wine, Benedictine, brandy and finally, more Scotch at the Equator, would have a tendency to tumultuous revolt in a body which had been stringently deprived of any alcohol whatsoever for the last six months.

The phone rang, and Brian leaped a foot. As he picked up the phone in flannel fingers he looked at his watch. Ten A.M. And he was the boy who never needed sleep, no matter how much rest he missed or how much he drank? That was the *old* Dermott, he thought. The new model needs to be run in.

'Hello,' he said feebly into the phone. 'It's Brian here, all that's left of him.' Bad news always came by telephone, and always in the morning.

'I thought I'd make your day complete.' The voice was Don Bruce, and sounded disgustingly cheery. 'How's your head, chum? You were, if you'll pardon my saying so, magnificently sloshed last night. But charming,' he added hastily. 'Utterly charming.'

'What do you want, and why couldn't it wait?' Brian said crossly into the receiver. The brandy was establishing a slight foothold in his stomach and he felt strong enough to be cross.

'I've a present for you,' Don said. 'That policeman cobber of yours, Tolliver, just rang up and said he had one of your dependants in the strong box. Your wild man, Kidogo. Wants to know if he's to be kept in jail, shot, or what?'

'Where's he now?'

'Still in the deep-freeze. More or less handcuffed to the bars. Terry said he took on a better part of the native quarter last night, and the carnage was frightful. Nobody dead, but a long limp line of battered bods.'

'The old man all right?' Serious concern tinged Brian's voice. 'Is Kidogo hurt?'

'Bashed about a bit, but nothing serious. The odd lump and gash. You know Wogs. They use such unlikely weapons when they fight among themselves. But I gather that most of his chums are candidates for the National Health, if any.'

'Any charges?'

'No. Tolliver rang through in a hurry. Said he was going out on a riot of some obscure nature, and would I get in touch with you. Said you were welcome to the wrong-doer if you'd come and collect him. Also said he's bloody sorry your Wog didn't kill the lot instead of just carving his armorial bearings on them.'

'For Christ's sake quit being so amusing,' Brian said. 'Look. I'm dying. Go and collect that baboon of mine and bring him to the flat. I'll hold him in hand until we leave.'

Slowly he started to dress. This time he would be wearing safari clothes. Yesterday's blue suit, from the look of it flung across the floor, had earned a graze in the paddock for a spell.

'I must say you were a gaudy one last eve,' Don Bruce said when he climbed out of his car. 'Here's your wild man from Borneo. I don't know who looks the worst, master or man.'

'Likewise, I'm sure,' Brian said. 'Come in and have a hair of the dog. You too, *nugu*. I don't suppose they'll run me for giving an African a beer to ease his pain.'

Kidogo grinned with bruised lips.

'This Nairobi is a very wicked town, Bwana,' he said. 'Full of bad people. Much trouble.'

'I can well believe it,' Brian said. 'Let me look at you. Hmmm.'

Kidogo did indeed present quite a picture. One eye was completely shut. Strips of plaster criss-crossed his cheeks, and the swollen fingers of one hand protruded from a long bracelet of adhesive. When he grinned again, wiping the beer off his mouth, his lips were puffed, and he seemed to have lost teeth. Seen through his now completely tattered shirt, his ribs wore a bellyband of tape. One of the long loops of his pierced ear-lobes had evidently been bitten through and hastily resewn.

'What happened to you?' Brian asked the African. 'What kind of *shauri* did you get yourself into?'

'*Shauri ya shenzi,*' Kidogo said calmly. '*Uhuru kabisa.*'

'And what does that mean, pray tell—business of no-goods on account of too much *uhuru*?'

Kidogo scratched his head with his good hand. He shrugged.

'When I left you I had money. I had enough for beer and food. I was not then hungry. So I drank some beer in a little shop in Kaleleni. Pretty soon some men and women came into the shop and began to drink beer. Then they laughed at my clothes.'

Kidogo started to spit, but looked at the carpet and decided against it.

'They were not very much men. City men—worthless, surely uncircumcised. But old enough to know better than to laugh at a man of the forest. They wore white man's shoes and laughed at me because I wore none.'

'So?'

'So I said nothing. You had told me not to get into any trouble. So I bought more beer and plucked my beard with my knife blade. Then when that beer was gone I bought more beer. Then the men laughed some more and asked me if I had stolen the money; they asked if money grew on trees or was to be found in bees' nests. I said nothing. I do not talk to chattering monkeys.'

'Go on,' Brian said. 'Then what?'

'Nothing very much. They asked me many insulting things—if I carried a *kipande*, like the other tame *white men's niggers*, for one thing. I told them I needed no written proof of who I was, that everyone knew I worked for my Bwana and I was no dog-dung who had to carry a card to prove that he had not stolen or was not recently escaped from jail.'

'Good for you,' Don Bruce said. 'And what else, *mzee*?'

Kidogo looked at his master's friend with one appreciative eye.

'I told them that the kind of white men they would never meet except as *cho*-wallahs—latrine attendants—called me *mzee*, respected elder, or *baba*, as they called their own fathers. Some of the other men laughed as I said this, and made one man angry. But I was still keeping my temper. I ordered more beer and paid for it.'

'So, apart from maintaining your dignity, and drinking beer like a proper elder, what else transpired?' Brian asked.

'Very little. There was a stool in the shop and I was sitting on it. I continued to sit on it. Until they asked me some things about *uhuru*.'

'What did they say?'

'They asked me where a man like me, a Ndrobo from the forests, would be when *uhuru* came and everything changed in Africa.'

'And you said?' Brian narrowed his eyes.

'I said that when *uhuru*, whatever that was, came, I would naturally be with my Bwana. And then they laughed loudly, and one said: "When *uhuru* comes we will kill your Bwana and take his lorries and his Land Rovers and guns and lands and money, and when we kill your Bawna we will kill you and everybody like you who kneel before the Bwanas. And we will take his women and circumcise them all to make them decent before we use them.'

'And what did you say to that?'

'I did not say anything to that. I picked up my stool by two of its legs and I hit the man who had laughed loudest and who said he would kill you. I broke his head with the stool. Then I hit the man who had laughed next loudest, and broke *his* head. One of the women then jumped on my back and another hit me over the head with a bottle and then another man seized my stool so I drew my knife and stuck it in his stomach, but not far enough, I am afraid. And then everyone jumped on me and started to hit me and I was able to bite one woman and stick the knife again into the stomach of someone else and possibly to injure the manhood of another severely with my knee, if he had manhood to injure, and then they got me down and were trying to kill me when the *askaris* came and threw me in the Kingi Georgi Hoteli. I did not care except for my knife, which they took, for I was full of beer and it had been a long time since I had seen man-blood or heard a skull crunch. I went to sleep in the cell until this morning when the Big Bwana Police came, you know the Bwana Police from the mountain, who helped us chase the Mau Mau in the old good days.'

'Nobody dead, I gather?' Brian turned to Don Bruce.

'One's a little dicky, the one with a hole in his tum. Terry said he'd entered nothing on the books, and it might be a good idea if you sort of got your wild man out of town in case the chap did peg out and somebody had to be charged. Decent bloke, Tolliver. Seemed highly amused at the whole thing.'

Brian turned to Kidogo. He frowned.

'I'm terribly ashamed of you, acting up this way in town,' he said. 'You bring disgrace to me, brawling this way. I have told you and told you that these townspeople are not as you and I. They do not understand us. Now, say *kwaheri* to the Bwana Don, who fetched you, and then I will look at your wounds. You're off now, Donald?'

'Soon as I collect Peggy and the kids. *Kwaheri*, Kidogo. So long, Brian. I'll hear from you about the farm?'

'Right. I don't suppose I did anything unduly awful myself last night? I don't have to expect the police, do I?'

Don chuckled.

'Nothing overly drastic. I had to head you off at the draw a couple of times. You were going to eat one inoffensive fellow alive, poor chap. But we managed to get you and the little airlines *bibi* home intact. She was rather a nice girl. You ought to cultivate that. *I* would, if I thought Peggy'd let me get away with it.'

'I wish I remembered her name,' Brian said wistfully. He raised his hand. 'Take care, Don.'

*

'Now,' he said to Kidogo as he inspected the various cuts and contusions, 'there must be a little more in this than the rhino can see. What?'

'Bwana,' the man Kidogo said. 'I do not like the times. There is much bad talk. I was not so drunk when I fought. These are bad people, Bwana. They are lost and being lost they wish to lose everybody. They are like wild dogs with no game to chase and so they eat each other. They will do much harm to people like me—and there are very many people like me—with all this monkey chatter of *uhuru* and white man's things they do not understand. They hate people like me, Bwana. I think they are ashamed of themselves, like monkeys who have put on a man's hat but realize that they are still monkeys.'

'I know it, chum, I know it,' Brian said. 'And it seems to me that town is not for the likes of us right now. I think perhaps you may have one more beer before we set out to find the Bwana Philip and head for home. Then we go back to the safari and the elephants.'

'That will be good,' Kidogo said. 'Then you are not angry at me for fighting these jackals, Bwana? You did not sound very angry, and the Bwana Police was not angry either—not if he laughed and gave me *shilingi*.'

'I'm not angry, *baba*. Except I don't want you to get hurt by these jackals. Hyenas pull down the old lion. Come on, get your beer and my bag and let's *kuenda* the hell out of this bloody village.'

'Yes, Bwana,' Kidogo said. 'And Bwana?'

'Mmmm?'

'When *uhuru* comes, as they say,' Kidogo grinned through his bruised lips. 'If *uhuru* comes, perhaps it would be better if *I* were the white hunter and *you* the gunbearer. Of course, you will have to call me Bwana, but I will not beat you if you do your work well and see that the clients are amused and keep the guns clean and the vehicles in good repair. I will even give you a little *pombe* from time to time if you will promise me not to get drunk and disgrace me when we come to town.'

Kidogo howled with laughter and slapped his thigh.

Brian aimed a cuff at him, and joined in the laughter.

'It's not too bloody bad an idea at that,' he murmured. 'That way I might at least be sure of a job. Come on, *nugu*, in you go. I want to lose the stink of this place and taste some fresh air again.'

THE CAR wheels crunched on the yellow gravel of the drive that left the hard-baked, wheel-eroded clay of the side road and wound effortlessly around the bottoms and up towards the green-forested side of the hill where Glenburnie Farm sat, crouched comfortably as always, like a lazy old man wedged in his favourite easy chair.

The towering rough-boled trees around the old stone house were green, if dusty, the figs and cedar shimmering in the heat and the mottled thorn acacias distantly looking even more golden under the combined effect of sinking sun and pancaked dust. The great purple-weeping jacaranda blooms had fallen and dried their tears on the lawn; they had long since been swept from the yellowing grasses that now stood stiffly gnarled and coarse from the sun. But the blue of the dam still contained its fleet of Muscovy ducks and garrulously profane grey geese, and the Italianate flower garden still made a brave green oasis in the sweep of burnt brown pasture. God knows how much water Aunt Charlotte was wasting on her precious roses and the drooping cannas that fringed the kitchen garden and swept wantonly from lawn to little lake. His aunt would water a bloody flower, Brian thought, even in the older days when the cattle bellowed from thirst and you only shaved every other day to conserve the water in the house.

Philip Dermott drew the car up to the front walk in a whishing flurry of gravel and killed the motor, which continued to throb briefly. On the wide veranda behind the low bougainvillaea-covered plaster walls that circled the house, Charlotte Stuart sat in her favourite rump-sprung cowhide easy chair. The older they got the more the old lady and the house seemed to merge with each other, until they both blended into the side of the hill. They seemed all of a part, Brian thought, The Mountain, the old girl, the house and the hill that hadn't changed and wouldn't change no matter what the Nigs did and whom they hanged of a crisp evening.

Brian climbed out of the car, and walked up the steps of the veranda.

The old girl, as usual, showed no undue enthusiasm over the return of her nephews. Mac Stuart had been fond of saying that if someone announced a successful invasion of the moon, Charlotte would be likely to inquire as to the price of green cheese. She sat there now on the shaded front porch, an empty cigarette-holder clenched in her strong store teeth, her hands folded calmly over her knobbily corseted stomach, her bountiful bosom rising nobly under her heavily fleshed strong jaw. The amber eyes were serene under tangled reddish eyebrows, as she gazed at the snaggled fangs of Mount Kenya. Two grizzled Cairn terriers that vaguely resembled Uncle Mac slept beside her on the floor of the porch, and did not bother to get up as Brian climbed the stairs. A long silver-knobbed stick leaned against her chair, and one bandaged leg rested stiffly on a hassock.

'D'you have any cigarettes?' she asked, without taking the holder out of her mouth. 'I used all of mine and it's been too much trouble to shout for

Juma to bring more. In point of fact,' she grinned, 'I've been napping. You almost caught me. To what do we attribute the honour of your unsuspected presence? I thought you'd be fleshpotting with the tourists.'

Brian grinned back at her. He gave her a cigarette and lit it before he stooped to kiss her.

'Free meal,' he said. 'I was passing by, and . . .'

She puffed the cigarette and made a motion at him with her stick.

'Go on with you,' she said, and leaned back in her chair tilting the profile that had been lovely, and even now was unmistakably handsome. Her late husband had also remarked once that Charlotte reminded him of nothing so much as a racing yacht with all sails set in a stiff breeze on the homing tack. She looked now almost like a Roman emperor—her nose identical to Brian's, proud-bridged and sharp-cut from tip to nostril, the cheekbones high, the well-fleshed chin firm and strong and unsagged.

'Y'know,' she was saying lazily now, 'I was watching you as you came up the steps. If we could adjust the ages back about forty years on my side, we'd be as much alike as two peas. Even your hair's going grey like mine—a sort of tweed effect.' She touched her own hair, which was done in a heavy loose knot on her neck. Her voice, still faintly flecked with Irish lilt, was as deep and mellow as a man's. She looked as well-kept as any duchess—healthy, handsome, still vibrant, this Aunt Charlotte of his, who had ploughed more than a half-century of her life back into the capricious red soil that had made her and her husband rich in their middle years.

The years had not noticeably faded the clear amber of the keen eyes—they still peered brightly from under the tangled reddish brows. Her motions were more deliberate now, because of the bad leg, but the tilt of chin, the swift flash of hand, were still imperious and could be peppery temperish. She was the *Memsaab Mkubwa*—the Big Missus—as the half-thousand natives who worked her land called her to her face and behind her back, as they had called her husband the *Bwana Mkubwa*, even though Mac Stuart had been a small, close-furled man, with indignant bright blue eyes and a nettled Scots tongue to him. The Memsaab Mkubwa and the Bwana Mkubwa had always got along very well until the Big Bwana had—had been taken away that day. It was not until after Mac Stuart was kidnapped to be killed on The Mountain that his wife had admitted the pain in her right leg and had gone to bed with a phlebitis from the collpased veinous structure.

'So you're back in one piece and naught the worse for the *shenzi* life you lead? And did I not hear that your—that Valerie had come back to Kenya?' The old lady squinted at him. She shivered slightly as the evening breeze brought chill to the broad shaded front porch.

'That you did,' Brian said. 'I put her on the plane for Home less than two weeks ago.'

'I should have thought she might have paid us a call,' Charlotte Stuart said. 'This was her home once. After all. If only for a short time, it was still her home.'

'She said she wasn't up to it,' Brian said shortly. 'Or me either. So she's gone back to England. For good, she says.'

'She was never cut to the Kenya life,' his aunt replied. 'Wrong fibre for it. You're well rid of her. Time you took another wife.'

'That'll wait,' Brian replied. 'And how are you keeping, Memsaab me love?'

'Well enough, I suppose, except for the rheumatiz, son,' the old lady smiled over her false teeth. 'I feel like an old lion on a damp night. I want to grunt and grumble. It's this bedevilled leg of mine. You look quite well, for a white hunter. Still sober, I'll be bound, which is gratifying considering the company you keep. How are all the French countesses and the Texas oil millionaires? Up to the mark?'

'About the same,' Brian replied. 'This safari looks to be a pretty successful one. Got a lovely lion—big black-maned fellow—and a good elephant so far. And the people seem nice. But you're wrong when you say I'm sober. I'm not, entirely.'

'I thought you were supposed to be on the water wagon,' the old woman said. 'For the good of your body and soul.'

'I fell off for the same reason yesterday,' Brian said lightly. 'Mostly for the good of my soul. It was going terribly stale on me. Where's my unpaid physician and his wife? I may as well take my scolding now from all of you.'

'You'll be getting no scolding from me,' Charlotte Stuart said. 'I never lectured your dead father, and I'll not start on you. It's your own precious neck you're risking. In any case it's too late for me to advise you; I didn't start soon enough. George and Nell drove into the village. They ought to be back pretty soon. You wouldn't want to stir the old lady a gin and pink, would you? I'm pretty well settled in this chair.'

Brian dropped a hand on his aunt's shoulder, and she looked up and smiled again. The years left her when she smiled. The store teeth had been very well made.

'You know we *do* look like brother and sister. Except you look younger than me. Sure, I'll fix you a drink. Just let me wash some of this Kenya topsoil off my face and I'll join you.'

'They hang that poor fellow?' his aunt asked Brian's back. The question was casual, as if inquiring after the condition of a vetted animal.

Brian stopped in the doorway.

'Yes'm. Bang on schedule.'

'Mphf.' The old lady grunted. 'Poor show all round. Not like the old days. Hurry with that gin, it's getting nippy out here.'

BRIAN HAD been a man grown for a great many years, forever, it sometimes seemed to him, but he never quite conquered the fresh tiny thrill of home-coming when he walked into the old room—the same big room that had changed very little since he was a toddler.

What was it the bloke had said about everything shrinking as you grew older? This was one room that had never shrunk and would never shrink. The rough red-stone fireplace at the library end of the living-room was still big enough for a boy to walk into without bowing his neck. The enormous Cape buffalo horns lowering over the mantel looked a little dustier than usual, but not much.

The tusks were still there too, the enormous tusks that Uncle Mac shot when he was bashing round in the bush as a young surveyor. And there, in one corner, on the raised portion of the two-level floor, was the baby grand piano which Aunt Charlotte had insisted on buying for Sister Nell at the same time Mac Stuart had sent for the finest billard table in all Kenya. This table was a sort of shrine which had a special wing to itself in an additional room, which you entered at one end of the dining-area and went down the extra steps which helped the big house snug itself into the hillside.

The old oil painting of Brian's mother hung on the wall behind the piano —showing to better advantage dim in the shadows, before Juma turned on the lights which were powered by the private dynamo you could hear humming in the back-garden behind Uncle Mac's pool room. Uncle Mac's private billiard-hall was purely *thingira*—men's domain; harshly masculine with its horns of bongo and bushbuck mounted on mahogany shields, and yonder, a very long rhino horn and a couple of ancient poorly cured lion skins stretched upward on the walls. These were not trophies; shot purposely to deck the walls; they were merely reminders of things that had jumped out of the bushes at Uncle Mac when he was mapping the hills in the century's teens, and which he had shot with Scots competence to avoid being trod on or scratched up.

Brian loved his aunt's old house. He had loved coming there as a boy; loved visiting as a guest when his mother was brought to bed with child, or when he and his mother and little sister occasionally came to stay when his father was off on some scatterheaded expedition or other. It was the kind of house that had been built almost room by room as they were needed, sprawling outward and upward on the side of the hill as the situation required. It was a house that looked like, and smelled of, its owners; a house that quietly accepted ownership and personal adjustment in everything from the leather-framed photos of friends and relatives that stood on the side tables to the *sjamboks* and spears that were bracketed on the walls. Aunt Charlotte had changed nothing since Uncle Mac's death eight years ago. Her deep busted-bottomed leather chair faced his vacant shabby throne in front of the fire, and the fireplace area was fenced by a sofa, snugly to contain the evening group which always sat there for coffee. The fireplace and two seats built inside the hearth—Brian had loved to sit *in* the fire when he was a boy. Now the Cairn terriers had usurped the seats for their own, nestling close to his aunt on ragged pads she had placed on the stone seats.

Nothing would ever change in this house; not Aunt Charlotte, not the still-living presence of Uncle Mac—not the hill on which the house leaned comfortably, as Aunt Charlotte rested for support on her long silver-knobbed stick, even though they occasionally did rearrange things briefly to fit the times.

But by God, Brian thought, he would have to take a month off some day soon and shoot some new trophies for the place before the Wogs poached all the decent game. Most of the stuff was pretty mangy—clapped out. The years and sun had faded the leopard skins which stretched along the back of the spotted cowhide divans to where they were almost albino white and very patchy in the hide. The zebra skins, flung helter-skelter over the oiled, cherry-dark cedar floor, were trodden hairless in pathways, like the tracery of a dry river-bed through the north country, by the ceaseless passage of the feet of men and children and dogs and horny-footed African servants.

The few trophy-horns and skulls that were nailed to the red-streaky cedar walls; the kudu, the Tabora roan, the forty-four-inch sable, the record waterbuck, and the tusks of that big warthog had, all been there as long as he could remember. They looked dispirited, tired and dusty. Old Juma was too creaky to climb up and give them a flick with the dust rag any more. He supposed he would have to have a serious word with Nell about training up a successor to Juma—although the touchy old man would scream like a hyena at the idea.

Everything from the beloved past was here in the house; the Benares brassware and hammered silver trays on the walls; the carved teak chests and round brass-studded braziers from Zanzibar; the ebony idols, the colobus monkey-skin capes and the marabou stork war-dresses; the spears and the shields and the *simis* in their red leather scabbards. True enough, the bookcases had expanded from their original sketchy burden of rawhide-bound journals and the set of Burns and Sir Walter Scott, of books by Bell and Speke, Baker and Selous, because over the years Brian had added rather fancifully to his father's library of natural history and the clients were always sending him a batch of new and expensive books with glossy colour plates.

Brian walked back to his room to change out of his dusty clothes and into the comfort of some vintage corduroy pants and a soft old flannel shirt. The old room hadn't changed in any way either since he was a kid, he thought. It had been his Cousin Ian's room, and it still contained the little-boy books —*Tarzan of the Apes* and all of Zane Grey—and a couple of sets of horns; Tommie and bushbuck, and not very good ones; small shield and a mouldy old quiver of arrows, with its boy-sized bow unstrung.

Brian liked the old, little-boy's room. He had moved there after Ian was killed—and had moved back again when Val had left. He supposed that

Nell and his new brother-in-law were very happy in the ultra-modern extension that he had hand-built onto the old house for him and Valerie to be newlyweds in. Some day maybe he'd go to the other side of the house and see what Nell had done to the place, he thought, washing his hands in the basin. But not right now.

Juma, the ancient Number One, was clattering around in front of the gun-case-bar when Brian walked back into the room. A fire was beginning to crawl hesitantly from the small tepee of wattle-logs stacked under the rough slabs of split cedar which would soon release great oily waves of perfume into the room.

'Hello, Jomo,' Brian said, and smacked him on his plump backside under the white *kamzu*. Juma was a coastal Swahili, who was only a little bit Congolese cannibal under his Arab pretensions, and it always annoyed him to be called 'Jomo', after the Kikuyu political leader. Juma looked about nine hundred years old, was as fussy as an old woman, and his face had the appearance of a peevish prune under his red fez.

'Where's my drink?' Charlotte Stuart shouted from the porch.

'Coming, Auntie,' Brian said, and aimed a friendly routine kick at Juma as he passed. 'Watch yourself, Kenyatta,' he said. 'We may have to hang you yet.'

Juma muttered something and began to turn on the lamps. Then he would go out to the kitchen and prepare the hors-d'œuvre that the Little Bwana liked—the anchovies and salted almonds and potato crisps and twisted salt-bacon-rind—Juma's Moslem soul writhed—twisted *pigskin*, Allah forfend, that came in the vacuum-sealed tins from the big *dukah* in Nyeri. It was good to have the Little Bwana home, even if it was never for a very long time and despite what he fancied as food. Maybe some day the Little Bwana would settle down again and make some children. The Little Bwana had promised, long ago, to name a boy-child after him. 'I'll call it Juma, if it's a half-wit,' the Little Bwana had said. That was when the Little Bwana laughed oftener.

'You took your time with my drink, I must say,' Charlotte Stuart said, tapping impatiently with her stick. 'I might as well have gone for it myself.'

'I had to get into some fresh clothes,' Brian said. 'That road's filthy with dust. Cheers, me dashin' girl.' He clinked the old lady's glass. 'Things running well on the farm?'

'Usual. I don't like this drought. It's lasting too long. We're all right here, but I ran into T.B. the other day in Nairobi and he said things were fright-ful in the Masai—that the Loita *laibons* were moving their stocks down into the fly area. I don't like the sound of that. I don't like it a bit, not for us here on the other end.'

Brian sat down on the steps and faced his aunt.

'No. Neither do I. All the years I've been hunting the Masai, I've only seen them move deeply into the fly area half a dozen times. Any time a Masai'll risk his cattle to the *tse-tse* on the hope of saving a few instead of losing them all, we're in for trouble.'

'Not us, in particular,' the old woman replied. 'We're all right for water here if we watch ourselves. But it's burned flat south of Naivasha, and it's as dry as bones from Kitale west. Well, I can't run the weather. It's one of the few things we have to leave for Ngai'—she nodded at The Mountain—'in these times when they've got machinery for everything else including baby-making; God still seems to control the weather.'

They sat and sipped their drinks in silence for a while. Then Charlotte Stuart said abruptly:

'Have you any idea just how much you're worth?'

Brian looked startled.

'Not really. I haven't thought about it. I don't need much money. I live off the clients and the firm's profits go to the bank. I send money to Val, of course. I haven't any head for business.'

'I didn't mean your safari money. I don't count Valerie. I never did. I mean the farm. Over the years the value keeps mounting and mounting. I merely wondered what you intended to do with it when I die. If anything, judging from the family history.' Charotte Stuart's voice was mildly bitter.

'I don't know, Aunt Charlotte. I guess I'm just a drifter. Like Pa. Nothing seems to mean much these days, I agree. Certainly I'm no farmer. As for you dying—fiddle, you'll live as long as The Mountain, Charlotte me love.'

'The Mountain's been there an awful long time. I don't know. The older I get the less I know. Day by day everything seems more confused. Some-times I wonder if there's any future here.'

She took a firm grip on her stick and held out her other hand.

'Well. Here they come. Hoist me up. I've the devil's own time getting out of me chair as it's older I'm getting. And heavier.' She grinned as she reached her feet. 'Thanks be to the good God, I've still got me appetite, and I've not had to fret about me figger for years.'

She stood firm, her feet braced well apart, to greet her niece and her niece's new husband as they mounted the steps.

CHAPTER TWELVE

'WELL, WHAT price the bride and groom—or almost,' Brian said. 'You both look wonderful. George, I swear you're fatter. And Miss Nellie's blooming. Don't tell me I'm uncle-ing so soon?'

'Not to my knowledge,' George Locke said. 'You'll have to consult your sister. You're looking very well yourself, Brian.' His glance dropped to the glass in Brian's hand, as Brian set it down on a table in order to hug his sister. George Locke's eyebrows lifted ever so slightly as they shook hands.

'Yes,' Brian said, feeling suddenly childishly guilty. 'You're right, Doctor dear. I slipped—I backslid. I fell from grace. I got bored with my own nobility. Before you break out in a rash of fresh diagnoses, I assure you I'll be safely back in the fold again when I go north.'

George Locke shrugged. He appeared eloquently disinterested.

'It's *your* health,' he said. 'Drink, Nell?'

'I'll have a gin and tonic, please,' Brian's sister said. 'What brings you back from safari, Brother dear? Run out of animals?'

'Came in for the hanging,' Brian said. 'Waste of time. Might just as well have stayed on hunting. I expect I'll go back in the morning. I say, let me look at you, my girl. Never more beautiful, I should say. And the job they did in London—super.'

'Really.' Eleanor Locke looked pleased. 'I can't notice all that much difference. Of course, with heavy pancake you can't see it so much as you used to.'

Brian looked sharply at his younger sister. She had been a beautiful girl, a flower-faced young woman before the tragedy which had killed her uncle and left her face terribly scarred from the burning. She had aged terribly when it appeared her face would be permanently disfigured and drawn. Her burned hair had grown back white, and there was a scarred bald spot she hadn't even bothered to hide. She'd borne up bravely, and had carried on through the Emergency vastly better than nearly anyone he knew except Peggy Bruce—certainly better than Valerie, who had bolted for England. Even at the time Brian had marvelled at Nell's toughness, when she went about careless of make-up, her face welted in a livid shiny scar that spread upward from her mouth, through her eyebrow and into her hair.

Now the plastic surgeon's corrective skill in London was apparent. A graft of skin had left the right side of her face a little more shiny, a tiny bit more tightly drawn over the bones, but made up, with a shrewd use of eyebrow pencil, you'd never know her face had been burned off like a patch of bush.

'You're becoming much too smooth, Big Brother,' she said, and her gentian eyes were bright against the smooth tan of her face, under the crisp short reddish curls. 'I liked you better as a shy bumpkin. I suppose you'll have something to say about my dyeing my hair back to its old colour, as well? Not to mention a slight toupee of the same shade?'

'Why not?' Brian ruffled his own streaked mop. 'I look enough like a zebra for both of us. The hair looks wonderful, Nell. You look exactly like my kid sister again, as a matter of fact.'

His sister dropped him a tiny curtsy.

'Thank you,' she said. 'That last sounded as if you weren't talking to a client. Oh, thanks, George,' she smiled at her husband, as he handed her a drink.

'What have you been up to lately, George?' Brian turned to his brother-in-law, and deliberately prolonged a sip of his own drink. 'Healing the unworthy sick, and learning the tribal customs?'

George Locke smiled.

'Only in my spare time. Your aunt and I—but I'll expect that Charlotte'll want to tell you herself. Mostly I've been trying to acquire the barest rudiments of farming.' He looked with mock dismay at long, tapering fingers, and held up the palms for display.

Oho, so it's 'Charlotte', is it? First-name business and all, Brian thought. Do tell.

'I must say honest toil agrees with you,' he said bluntly. 'You looked nearly as bad as I did in the Congo. I still wake up screaming when I think of that do-it-yourself hospital by the river. God, I've been in cleaner jails.'

'It wasn't so bad,' George Locke said. 'I learned a lot about practical medicine in three years with Doctor Schweitzer. I admit that the climate and the menus and the infrequency of grog were something less than madly desirable. Still——' He spread his hands. 'Lambaréné was a lucky place to be, if only because I met you there, Brian, and through you I met Nell, and here we all are. So few people are fortunate enough to start life again with a built-in family.'

Young Philip Dermott had come into the room. He kissed his sister, and walked over to touch his brother-in-law on the shoulder. He glanced briefly round the room before he said: 'Hello, George. Everyone here all right for drinks? Nell? Auntie? Brian? Your gear's in your room, by the way.'

'I can use a refill,' Brian said. 'Thanks, and so can Aunt Charlotte.' He stressed the *Aunt*, and he looked at his brother-in-law, who once again flicked his eyebrows.

The brows were extremely mobile in a long, bony, almost horsy face, the kind of face that one automatically associated with doctors and lawyers and any sort of professional man who smelled of old books and smoked a pipe from preference, rather than as a showy attempt to cut down on cigarettes. George Locke's eyes were lightish china blue, set deep over high cheekbones, and his thin pale skin would always freckle. His hair was a palish sandy blond, almost white, and was brushed carelessly in a side-part which left a little sheaf of hair standing up and falling over his ear in a tiny shelf. He had a small, clipped brush of pinkish moustache which was just discernible with the light against it.

He was tall, well over six feet, and very spare, with slightly stooped shoulders, as if he had spent much of his life on a horse or possibly bending over a microscope. His hands and feet were large, the hands beautifully shaped, and his clothes fell loosely, elegantly from his bony frame. He was wearing an ancient chamois-patched tweed coat of a greenish Harris mixture over a tan wool pullover, and his whipcord slacks were creased and baggy at the knees, but somehow he still managed to appear well dressed. Now he was stuffing a straight briar pipe with tobacco, and Brian had a dreadful feeling that Sundays would find him pottering among the petunias. His voice was gentle—the whole man appeared gentle, too gentle. He was, Brian thought, just too bloody perfect in appearance to be true. He looked like the romantic lead in a play about a widowed scientist. He had his two drinks before dinner, was entirely tactful around the house—what little Brian had seen of him—and was quite good with young Pip, according to young Pip. Well, hell, he belongs to Nell and if she likes him I suppose he's all right, Brian thought. And she's certainly got that smugly satisfied-bridified glow. If only George didn't *look* so damned doctorish. *And* languid. He wasn't just leaning on the mantel. He was flowing from it in a kind of tweedy stream.

'What's this you were going to say about you and Aunt Charlotte, George?' Brian asked, turning from his brother-in-law to his aunt, who was puffing at a cigarette and looking into her pink gin.

'I expect we'll discuss it after supper,' the old lady said. 'I don't like to talk much before meals. It's about a plan for the farm. George and I have been brooding it for quite a spell, and it's about to hatch. Seems sound enough to me. Juma!'

'Memsaab!' came a bellow from the hallway.

'Where's the *chakula*?'

'*Tayari*, Memsaab. *Mimi nakuenda upesi sana*.'

The old lady heaved herself half-out of the chair, and held out her hand to George Locke, as if she were used to holding out her hand to George Locke.

The dinner was eaten in near-silence. Brian turned his attention to the food. The drive and the fresh air and the few drinks had sharpened his appetite. The table, covered in its blue-checked tablecloth with the corners clipped down against breezes, was an enormous single slab of what must have been a gigantic cedar. It was just as well; what Juma would bring generally was enough to fetch a creak from anything less sturdy. The menu was nearly invariable, as changeless as the bill of fare at the Norfolk. First there would be soup because there always was soup, and tonight it was mulligatawny from a tin with some of old Kiptanui's hocus-pocus involving extra stock from game or cattle. He raised his head from the bowl and looked at his aunt.

'Kongoni,' the old lady said, reading the question. 'George shot it day before yesterday. There's a big herd comes down to gobble the wheat. Buffalo too, eh, George? I'd fancy a bit of that buff tongue if there's any left, Nellie.'

'So you've become a hunter, George?' Brian said. 'I thought one in the family was too many. Anyhow, didn't you tell me once you disapproved of killing? Or was that Doctor Schweitzer?'

'Still do,' his brother-in-law said. 'But I'm learning it's a necessary part of farming. Philip usually does it but Philip was away and so I went out and loosed off a few rounds with one of your guns. Scared 'em worse than I hurt them, but I did manage two buff and three kongoni. I've never tasted buffalo tongue before. I think it's better than beef tongue.'

'So do I,' Brian said, finishing his soup, and thinking: already he's first-naming my aunt, and now he's using my guns. Juma came and took the plates and brought a dish of tiny grilled trout, glistening in still-bubbling parsley butter.

'These are absolutely beautiful,' Brian said. 'Not you again, George?'

'I'm afraid so,' George grinned a little. 'Fishing I *do* understand. I used to fish a lot in England before the war. These trout are as aggressive as anything at Home.'

'My word,' Brian said. 'Is there no end to the doctor's talents?' Wouldn't you know he'd be a fisherman? he thought. The tweeds, the pipe, straight out of *The Field*. Wicker creels and the salty old deerstalker hat with the hand-tied dry flies stuck in it. I'm being unfair, Brian thought, spitting out a bone. And I don't even know why. He's really a very nice bloke.

Juma came once more, and this time it was a brown-gravied stew of fowl, flanked by green peas and mashed potatoes.

'Hmmmm,' Brian said. 'Partridge. Positively my favourite fruit, these little chaps. Don't tell me you're a wildfowler as well, George? I couldn't stand it, all in one day.'

'Not guilty this time. The natives catch them in a trap. They've a pen full back in the labour lines.'

'Tell 'em to turn 'em loose, Pip,' Brian snapped, turning a flat gaze on his brother. 'You know I won't have anybody trapping on the place. *Anything*. Not even leopards that kill stock. Hear me?'

'Yes, Brian,' Philip said. 'Of course.' He looked briefly at his aunt for affirmation. Charlotte Stuart continued to eat her stew.

Brian pushed his plate aside.

'Pass me some of that cold tongue, please,' he said. Then, rather lamely, 'I'm sorry. It's just that I've a sort of fixation against traps. I can't stand the idea of anything being penned up. I guess I'm like those oryx and the giraffes on the Laikipia. Remember, Auntie, when we fenced that big range and they all died, even though there wasn't any reason for it? Heartbroken, I imagine.'

'I suppose I agree,' Charlotte Stuart said. 'But speaking of leopard, there's a pair been making free with the sheep. They've set traps because I haven't had the patience to sit up for them like a *client* while they gobble my flocks. Haven't caught them yet, though.' She had borne down heavily on the word *client*.

'For God's sake, doesn't anybody here know how to rig a proper blind and bait? Don't you, Pip? It's child's play if you do it right.'

'I'm afraid not, Brian. I guess I'm not much of a hunter.'

'Well, I'll fix a proper set-up in the morning, and you can take a torch and kill them when they come to the bait at night. It isn't sporting, but I suppose the sheep are more important than sport.'

Brian fell silent as he attacked his tongue and the large tomato salad which Juma fetched with the cheese-board. Fancy anybody not knowing how to get a leopard to a tree. George, of course, wouldn't be supposed to have a clue, but you'd think Pip . . .

George. By God, it was strange seeing old George here at his very own table as a member of the family, Brian thought, peering past the House of Parliament sauce and the ketchup bottles and the pepper-vinegar cruet at his brother-in-law. Of course George couldn't know anything about Africa —not about the real Africa. Being stuck in the Congo with old Doc Schweitzer didn't count as really being in Africa. When he'd met George that time he'd come down with the fevers in the Gabon, George was just out from England, rosy-kneed and pith-helmeted, trying to bury himself in good works. Brian didn't like the phrase, but that was the only way to describe it —*good works* constituted trying to persuade the Congo Wogs that syphilis wasn't necessary, and that ophthalmia wasn't normal.

Definitely a queer bloke, George. He and Brian had talked a lot in the old German doctor's crude hospital that was swarming with baby gorillas, crippled gazelles and strange, sometimes exalted, always indrawn nurses and doctors. They'd talked after Brian's fever broke, and even more when Brian got well anough to take the launch to the very comfortable little hotel overlooking the bluff at Lambaréné. Strayed soul, George, like the others who came to old Schweitzer. George had mentioned that he had lost his wife and their only child in a bombing raid, when he was in a Nazi prison camp while England was rocking under the Blitz. He'd spent the war in prison camps, later in France—and just close enough to home to see and hear the Luftwaffe crossing the Channel every day and night. Must have been pretty tough at that, being shut up so close to home and wondering if each plane had a special message for somebody you knew. Through some sort of mix-up George hadn't even learned that his wife was killed until after the war ended. She'd just stopped writing; for all George knew it was because of another man. Brian supposed doctors had it pretty good, even in Nazi prison camps, but it must have been veriest hell to go on for months behind wire without knowing what happened to your people.

Odd that they'd met the second time. This time Brian was really sick, deathly ill, away the hell and gone in Tanganyika. For two or three years he'd been having these little blackouts, nothing very serious, except it was disconcerting to be feeling fine and then suddenly wake up shocked and bewildered in a strange bed. Then one day he'd conked out suddenly—first feeling a little queasy but no worse than usual when he had a hangover, and then he'd collapsed—bang! Like that. He came to in a shabby native dispensary in Tabora, and there, later, his face zooming up bigger and whiter through the wraithing mists, was old George again. And that was only what, six months ago?

Brian had been struck down by a weird assortment of exotic bugs, a fantastically bad liver—and it turned out later, by a truly spectacular new virus nobody knew anything about, glandular fever. This one had everything—it attacked nerves, muscles, bones and guts with no show of favouritism and was incurable as well. The client had sent for a plane, and George had accompanied Brian back to Nairobi. In the long days after, between deep fits of symptomatic depressions, first in the Maia Carberry nursing home and later back on the farm, Brian had learned quite a bit more about George, who had thoughtfully gone home with him.

Brian wasn't likely to forget the day that George had told him the worst after he had his brain back and was well enough to listen. It was also the same day that Nell's fate had been decided. The good doctor was handing out prescriptions right and left to everybody that day. Brian winced as he remembered George's pleasure-amputating directness, as calculatedly cold as a scalpel.

'You've had a lot of things wrong with you, my lad,' he said to Brian. 'One of them was that infectious mono-nucleosis, which certainly put you in a weakened condition. Those old malarias and amoebics haven't helped you any, either. But what you basically suffer from, my boy, is a liver as fat as a football, as hard as a rock; a weary, outraged liver that just can't take any more alcohol. You've burned the candle for too long; it's a mere puddle of grease now. Your bloodstream's full of alcohol, your tissues the same, your nervous system is already impaired, and those blackouts you've been having are nothing more nor less than actual explosions in the brain. The big one you just had was also combined with a rather specialized version of delirium tremens, and it was touch and go whether you'd ever come out of the convulsions alive. You've been bloody lucky that you weren't driving when you've had these attacks, or you'd have broken your neck.

'You've got one choice now, one only: *Don't drink*. If you don't drink you'll live long and be happy. If you do drink you won't live very long and you won't be very happy—and don't delude yourself that you'll just peg out on a glorious toot. You'll probably be totally or partially paralysed or blind and certainly go soft in the head, and one of the more pathetic symptoms of the latter malady is that the patient is the last person to recognize that he's dotty. You'll lose your faculties and the use of your limbs and wind up with several mucky years of being a damned nuisance to yourself and to everybody else. That's of course if you come out of the next attack at all. They never get milder; they're always more severe, because you burn up millions of brain cells every time you have one. That's your dreary, inevitable future if you continue to drink.'

'I can't drink *at all*—not even in moderation?' Brian had asked. 'This stuff is as much a part of my business equipment as guns and clients.'

'In your case there's no such thing as moderation,' George Locke said. 'You can't tell what it'll take to touch off those explosions again, any more than you can explain why you keep spraining the same ankle over and over again. No, Brian—in your case it's clear-cut: drink and die, or don't drink and live.'

'In that event,' Brian said, 'I expect I'd better change all my old pleasant bad habits and cultivate a taste for ginger-ale, although God knows it'll be a wrench.' He tossed the contents of his glass on the grass, and turned the glass upside down on the table. 'There you are, doctor. I quit. Juma! *Lete*

Coca-Cola moja upesi! But not very *upesi*,' he said, attempting a feeble joke. 'Take your own slew-footed African time.'

'Good man,' George Locke had said. 'Stout fella. And now I'll have a severe word with your sister. This is my day for it. Come along, please. I want a witness.'

They had found Nell with her stringy hair screwed up under a scarf. She looked hot and flustered as she scourged Juma to some distasteful chore, and the burn-scar was livid on her sweaty face. George's 'word' with the sister had been equally short and to the point. One was prone to forget that George Locke seldom raised his voice when he made his points.

'You,' he had said to Nell Dermott, pointing a long, knuckly finger, 'are a damned disgrace. You keep flaunting that bloody great red stripe on your face as if it were a medal. Apart from letting what looks you've got left go to pot, you aren't proving anything by going about pretending to be a souvenir programme from an old war. None of your heroics'll bring back your dead uncle, or un-burn your face. You were enough woman to live through that fire *and* the Mau Mau; you can take yourself in hand now. You're not being fair to your aunt and to Philip and Brian and to yourself—and God damn it, it's not fair to me, either!'

'Not fair to you . . .' Nell had faltered, gape-mouthed and shocked out of her usual maddeningly unruffable calm. 'Not fair to you—how dare you'— she squawked like an outraged hen. 'I never heard of such——'

'Shut up!' George Locke bit at her. 'No, it's not fair to me. Perhaps your aunt and the rest of your family will put up with it out of old habit, but I love you, I intend to marry you, and damn me if I'll live the rest of my life with a war memorial!'

'Hear, hear,' Brian had murmured. 'Good show, *Dokitari*! Go get 'em, Tige . . .'

'There are a hundred good men in England—hell's delight, there are two fine chaps right here in Kenya who could fix that scar in a twinkle,' George Locke had continued. 'I'll marry you still scarred, I'll marry you tomorrow, to be sure you don't get off with some bloody plastic surgeon in London, but I don't intend to live with you unless you fix the face. Where do you want to get married, London or here at home, and when?'

And that, apparently, had been the cure both George Locke and Nell Dermott had been seeking. It seemed to be working fine, and Brian wished he could like George Locke just a little more. He wished George Locke had been as positive with his own life as he had been positive with Brian's life and Nell's life. He wished George Locke hadn't been so damned *right*.

Juvenile bravado made him accept a brandy when his sister poured the coffee and got out the decanters after they'd finished Kiptanui's invariable stewed fruits and pudding and were all seated circled round the enormous stone fireplace.

'What's this project you people mentioned before supper, then?' Brian said. 'This thing you and George have hatched, Aunt Char?' He was sitting

174

on the floor, chin on knees, back leaning against the stone of the fireplace, arms wrapped about his legs in the relaxed after-meal position he had used since he was a tiny boy.

'I want to find out once and for all if you intend to work the land or sell it, or what.' The old lady's voice harshened. 'Because if it looks as if you're not going to farm this land, I've come to a decision. I've talked it over with George and Nell and Philip and they agree. I'm going to cut it up!'

'You're going to do what?' Brian's chin snapped up from its comfortable rest on his knees. 'You're going to do *what*?'

'We have more land than we need,' Charlotte Stuart said. 'We have a great deal more land than we ever farmed. It's been a crying shame, in a way, to let it lie in bush—fallow. George and I worked it out recently. In my parcels we can locate between us a thousand Kikuyu families, just on the unworked land. We can give them ten acres apiece on a scheme—consolidate our own holdings without losing too much current yield—and we can make small-property holders out of a thousand families—half here and the other half on the Laikipia land. We'll start here.'

'I don't understand it at all,' Brian said. 'You mean you're willing to give your land—our land—back to the natives?'

'It's not quite that, not exactly a gift,' Charlotte Stuart said. 'Explain it to him, George. It's your idea basically.'

George Locke bent his head gracefully, deferentially, to Charlotte Stuart.

'If you like,' he said. 'I see it this way: The best hope—perhaps the only hope of this country, this Kenya—is speedily to create a middle class, a thriving middle-class with needs and wants and the possibility of fulfilling those needs and wants. Piddling little peasant-farmer schemes aren't good enough. An unsupervised simple bush native is hard put to work more than an acre of land unless he has some extra skills and equipment and finally, marketing facilities at his disposal.

'If you create a middle class of, say, fifteen to twenty thousand families where you can guarantee them a decent cash income of four or five hundred pounds a year plus their livelihood, and offer them a chance to secure the land for themselves, there's chance for long-term co-operation with the white man. And what's more important, your middle-class families suddenly become the salt of the earth, instead of just hand-to-mouth squatters and sharecroppers. And it is these people who will eventually control the politicians. It is this kind of responsible people, as I see it, who will keep the country from going mad in a scramble to take *all* of the white man's lands and share them out among the favoured few. If every big white farmer in Kenya followed our lead, there'd be land enough for twenty thousand families, without hurting the big properties.'

'It sounds beautiful, but I think you're about ten years too late,' Brian said. 'They want it all, tied up in a packet, and they want it today. Right now. But go ahead. Don't let me interrupt this hasheesh dream of black Utopia. How does it work? Or have you got that far yet?'

'Your aunt and I have worked it out this way, Brian,' George Locke said. 'We give each family ten acres, with option to buy in three to seven years. We clear and prepare the land with our heavy machinery, and pay for the seed and necessary fertilizers. Five of the ten acres belong to the man to grow whatever he wishes—his own kitchen garden, enough room to graze his cattle if he has some, and enough space to grow maize and potatoes and any other small cash crop he can.

'The other five is to be planted in coffee and, in some instances, sisal and pyrethrum, and in the higher lands, tea. As you know it takes three years to get a yield from your coffee or tea, and seven for the sisal. Those are the crops we're interested in—the long-term crops, so that in the meantime he can tame some of the rougher, poorer land and grade it up.

'So here is what we do. We keep him and his family on exactly as before. We pay them the going two pounds a month, we supply the *posho* ration, the salt, sugar, tea ration. We provide the improved huts, and we already have the school. So he works for us as usual. Nothing changes from his present estate. But his family—the wives and daughters and various relatives —keep the long-term crops tended, watered, weeded and the like until they make their first cash crop on our half of the land which——'

'Which they will then hand over to us,' Charlotte Stuart said. 'We get the first cash crop, and in return for it, we make over the land in fee simple. From that point on, he owns all that land, and anything he can grow on it. And he will have had from three to seven years of experience watching scientific farming. He will have had our help for advice and mechanical assistance, and —George thinks—he will have learned some pride of ownership.'

'I don't want to throw any cold water on this gorgeous love-thy-neighbour pantomime you've cooked up,' Brian said. 'Excuse me, Auntie, if I sound rude. But what about all the bums and the drunks and the chronic hookworm lazies? You've got to admit that the Kyuke isn't over-fond of work: he has always abused his own land. How're you going to turn a nation of lazy beer-drinkers into a model community of scientific farmers with thousands of shiftless years arguing against it? Or has the leopard changed all its spots while my back was turned? Did Mr. Macmillan do it with one speech?'

Charlotte Stuart puffed fiercely at her cigarette. Her old tawny eyes were very clear and serene under the tangled red brows.

'We don't have any guarantee,' she said softly. 'But we don't have any choice, either. If we don't create our own strength through at least attempting something like this we have only two other choices—maintain the land under force of arms, which is impossible today, or get out, and I am *not* going to get out. The white man's chance here is to give more and keep less or be faced with one thing—*bloody nothing*. Maybe we'll get damn-all in the end, anyhow. But we will have tried!'

She rapped her stick sharply on the hob in the fireplace. 'At least, we will have tried!' She leaned back again in the deep chair and sunk her chin on her breast.

'Oh, my sainted Aunt Fanny,' Brian exploded. 'You can't be serious, Aunt Char. What about Kikuyu politics? Clan loyalty? Old enmities? Witchcraft? Blood feuds? Curses? Ex-Mau Mau cracking down on loyal Kikuyu? Former detainees working out on the home guards? God's displeasure? *Thahus?* And you, who know more about natives than the natives do themselves? Charlotte Stuart, I'm surprised at you. You sound like a female missionary.'

'Say what you want, it's a chance we have to take,' his aunt said stubbornly. 'Missionary or not, and I'll remind you of that later, my lad. If you're drowning, do you complain about the kind of log you grasp?'

'You've forgotten the women,' Nell Locke entered the conversation. 'And you've forgotten the young people—like Pip. We're adaptable. We'll adapt. We have to.'

'Granted again, Sister, that you'll adapt. You were born adapted. But a few people like yourself can't suddenly change the habits of a whole tribe, a whole people, by keeping on with the same softness that got you burned up. These people take—they don't give. They don't understand kindness— they don't appreciate help.'

'I wasn't speaking so much of the white women,' Nell said. 'I was speaking of the native women.'

Brian whooped with false laughter.

'I have now heard it all,' he said. 'The women? The females—the *Wanawaki*, the she-things—human clods, that have no soul, and know no rights, beasts of burden, the wood-fetchers and baby-bearers? The dumb brutes that are useful only to work and breed? My God!' Brian passed his hand over his eyes.

Nell's face was stubborn, as it had always become stubborn when she closed her mind to argument.

'Not so fast, my lad,' she said. 'Just you think back to what you know of the African woman. Who does all the work? Who really rules the *shamba*? Who was it that kept the Mau Mau alive by sneaking food to the gangs, and who literally taunted and kicked their men into joining the gangs? And then kicked and taunted them out of the idea when they saw it wasn't working? Who in Kikuyu history was always basically behind the wars and the cattle raids? And who has almost sole control of the children until their middle teens?'

Brian yawned. 'The women,' he said. 'And who dashes off to town now to become sluts and slatterns? And who isn't circumcised any more, and so has no status in the tribe? And who isn't worth anything in sheep and goats any more? Who's out of business since they're on the way to stopping multiple marriages? Who's hanging round the fringes with nothing to do except turn into a city tramp? And who wouldn't have it any other way?'

'The women,' his sister snapped. 'And the reason behind everything you say is the chief strength of Aunt Charlotte's and George's scheme. The woman is stateless, or almost, at the moment. She hasn't come out of the tree nearly as much as the man, but one thing that changing times and living close to the towns has brought her is the faint beginnings of a mind of her own. Give her something to do with a purpose and she'll do it—and what's more she'll nag the man into going along with her.'

'Or drive him mad,' Brian said. 'I couldn't agree with you more. And how, I wonder, do you propose to work all these marvels with semi-dumb brutes who used to reckon their worth in how many goats they cost, and how much copper wire they owned, and how many blue beads they could string around their neck? The missionaries have been batting off this wicket for years and got nowhere.'

'*Possessions*,' his sister said grimly. 'In one essential women are all alike— possessions. How many Kikuyu *bibis* have you seen wearing goatskins in the last two years, the last five years, the last ten years? Not a one of them but hasn't got a *shuka* made out of merikani or zanzibari. And shoes of a sort. And head kerchiefs. And houses with tin tops. And hitching rides when they can—or managing money to ride the buses—instead of walking. You can't tell me they love to spend all their lives fetching and carrying just because they never did anything else.'

'That was part of it,' George Locke said mildly. 'We had thought of starting a kind of model housing settlement here on the farm; three-room cottages with metal roofs; central boreholes to solve the water-carrying; some new wrinkles on irrigation to catch the waste water, and finally some organized work forces to clear some of the bush land and create a fuel stockpile, at the same time getting some help from the government on better, quicker re-forestation schemes along the New Zealand lines.'

'*And* some co-operative *dukahs* and our own dispensary hospital,' Nell said. 'And some personal plots of land for the unmarried women to plant for their own. And more schools of course for the kids. And some simple instruction in home economics. And a beer hall, like at Njabini—that might keep them on the farm, prevent 'em from always running off to town.'

'I hear it,' Brian shook his head sadly. 'But I don't believe it. This is Africa. This is Kenya. You're talking about *Africans*—superstition-riddled, ghost-fearing, spell-casting, blood-drinking, sacrifice-making, neighbour-killing, baby-strangling, ancestor-worshipping, lying, thieving, dirty, lazy, drunken goat-loving *Africans*!'

'Wait a minute, Son, whoa!' Charlotte Stuart said. 'If you'll spill me a little more brandy in that glass and indulge an old woman for a moment's garrulous rambling, I would like to refresh you just a little bit on the short history of Glenburnie Farm. It's worth a half-million pounds today if it's worth a farthing, saying I could find a buyer.'

'. . . find a buyer is right,' Brian muttered. 'Excuse me, Auntie.'

'This farm was made with and by Africans,' his aunt ignored the interruption. 'In my life I've seen Kenya change from a blank space on the map to one of the richest countries in the world. We mostly started out like a Wog with a hoe and a bent back. I worked as hard as your uncle. I had my babies like a Kikuyu woman. I delivered Ian myself and helped two cows calve in the same day.

'All of this was done with the help of wild men—people who thought all white people were bewitched, who didn't understand money or weapons or the simplest rules of agriculture beyond scratching a hole in the ground and praying to Ngai for rain. In my adult years I have seen black men come to responsibility and rule.'

'And to Mau Mau and worse,' her nephew said. 'Just yesterday. And the Congo today. Right this minute. Twice as bloody and twice as useless and twice as savage and twice as wasteful as they were when you found them. All their old vices compounded with what the white man taught them laid on. I've seen this in *my* time—cows with their teats hacked off and strangled cats and disembowelled women, and menstrual fluid mixed with human sperm and animal dung and stewed brains for the oathing. *Yesterday*. And burnt-up sisters and murdered uncles. I've seen all that in *my* time. Just yesterday I saw it.'

'I blame the white man for most of it,' his aunt said calmly. 'We destroyed a way of life and didn't give them anything to replace the old ways. We forgot we were dealing with people. Now we've got to recognize that we've failed —and that this *is* their land, and they'll control it for good or evil—and a few white throats more or less won't make any difference. They'll have it, to wreck on their own or to lose it again to whoever wants it that's got a strong stomach and doesn't care about even surface morality.'

Brian got up from the floor and paced. He locked his hands behind his back.

'This is beginning to sound like a bad lecture in the social sciences. Now I crave *your* indulgence to make a harsh truth, Auntie of mine. You may get furious but you can't deny it. The simple truth is that none of you—*us*— white settlers gave a good goddamn about the plight of the poor native, or cared a snap for his future. Not until we got scared. Not until we saw our pretty, easy, lazy life about to crumble. Not until the Congo showed us how fast the bush could grow over white progress.

'Mau Mau scared the hell out of everybody. Up until then you hadn't even been conscious of faithful old Gathiru or Mumbi as a person. Mau Mau gave you a nasty turn, all right—but only a few of you, of us, actually got hurt. We were hit pretty hard in this family, but they killed more white people in traffic accidents in Nairobi this year than they did in the whole damned Emergency. We could handle the Mau Mau—we simply killed them scatter-fashion and shut up the ones we didn't kill.'

Brian stopped for breath and lit a cigarette. His sister and aunt kept their eyes on his face. Young Philip looked embarrassedly at the floor. George Locke held his eyes on his wife's newly repaired face. Brian pointed at Nell.

'Even she weathered it! She finally got her nightmares quieted down and her face fixed and found herself a husband and what looked like a new life.

But what you're in now can't be fixed with a man for your bed, a strip of new skin for your face!

'The lot of you, good settlers and bad, are not conscience-stricken a bloody bit! You're plain scared, shit-scared! When they actually hanged Peter Poole you finally realized it! You can't shoot your way out of it any more so now you want to smarm your way out of it with a lot of wild agriculture schemes and plots and plans to uplift the poor bloody savage, after kicking him in the arse for the last fifty years! Well, I tell you, it's too late! The Wog has got our own dear government and the whole wide world behind him now, and he doesn't want your sympathy or your help! All he wants is your land and your houses and your women! He wants your booze and your motor-cars and your fine clothes and most of all, he wants to be a bwana and shout "*Boy!*" at the top of his lungs! And you benevolent old-world nigger-loving bwanas will be driven into the sea or legislated out of your lands and the country will chew at itself until it's in such a foul mess not even the bloody Russians'll want it!'

Brian paused, and drew a long breath.

'The trouble with all you late-blooming do-gooders and social planners,' he said nastily, 'is that you're about twenty-five years too late, and you're not changing your ways for love of the country or the native. You're just scared witless now it looks like the Nigs'll get their own back and you won't be bwanas any more. You won't even damned well be *fundis* or clerks. If you stay on at all you'll come running when some up jumped nigger claps his hands and screeches "Boy!" '

Brian turned and went to the bar and very deliberately poured three fingers of whisky into a glass and downed it in two gulps. Then he walked back to the fireplace, touched a log into sputtering life with his toe, and sank back on the floor again, his face brooding on his knees, arms locked round his legs.

'Well,' his aunt said dryly, 'that was quite an oration. Including the emphatic profanity. Certainly loud. George?' She turned to her niece's husband.

'I'd be curious to hear more of why Brian thinks it won't work,' George Locke said. '*I* think it will, if it gets any sort of a fair chance.'

Brian glanced sideways at his brother-in-law, the mixture of pity and scorn curdled by sour amusement.

'*Why*, George?' he asked purringly, making the proper name insulting. 'Why? Because you're dealing with niggers first, George, and politics second, George. Between you and me, I've more respect for the poor bloody confused blacks trying to play human than I have for the white politicians who sent us down the drain.'

Brian rubbed his shin and looked up at George again. He spoke precisely, as if explaining something to a child.

'*Why*, George? Because the politicians, black and white, won't let you, George. The Wog politicians don't want co-operation with the white man, with the black still occupying an inferior position. They don't want multi-racialism, George. They've got a tremendous inferiority complex, George—

one you wouldn't know about from your short spate of practising sanitation and brotherhood of man for old Father Schweitzer in Lambaréné. The Wog doesn't want to get along *with* the white man, George. He literally wants God to wave a wand and turn him white. He wants to be a bwana, George. He wants to prove to himself that he can do all the things the white man can do and do them better. And he refuses to admit that ninety-nine per cent of his people can't even make a reasonably decent job of being niggers, let alone competing with white men in the involved world of the white man, George. And that ninety-nine per cent ignoramus is still so stupid he thinks that *uhuru* —that freedom will give him in five minutes all the things the white man has made over the centuries—give it to him in one stroke of magic, and all in one packet, with bows on, George.

'*Why*, George?' Brian smiled lazily. 'The first thing is that even if you could get it going, George, the black politicos would sabotage it at every turn. It would be a step backward for them in this mad dash for *uhuru*. It would shout to the world that they're still dependent on the white man, George. And it would spike their guns on their dearest aim, which is to humiliate the white man, take his lands, kick him out, reduce him to a snivelling whiner for crumbs. Just as they've been all their lives. Aunt Charlotte's scheme— or yours, George, it sounds more like you than it sounds like Auntie—is only a cut better than the *ahoi* system they practise themselves. You haven't been here long enough to know about *ahoi*, George. It's a Kikuyu word meaning "squatter", and the Kyukes hate it. The poor Kyukes are always chiselling off rich Kyukes. They don't want to encourage the habit when they finally come into the really lush acres. Your scheme would be a step up, but the bwana would still be boss, the bwana would still supervise the farms, the bwana would still control planting and harvest and sale and all the important details.

'The *uhuru* screamers—your Mr. Kamau, Mr. Ndegwa, Mr. Mboya, Mr. Gichuru—they wouldn't like to see you people start a black-white co-opera-tive that would do what you hope—create a bloc of independent middle-class African agriculturists. It's the last thing they'd want to see, George, because it would rob them of their own power as leaders, virtual lords over the stupid flocks of people. They don't want a mass of people gradually civilized to where they can stand up on their hind legs and speak decently for themselves. They want stupid, tractable sheep, as Nkrumah wanted sheep in Ghana— as he's got sheep now, no opposition, no rival party, no free press, nothing but Nkrumah, George.'

Brian sighed.

'And if that one particular reason wasn't more than enough, George, you've got the individual Wog himself to worry about. *He* hasn't changed with the winds of change Macmillan yaps about. He's still the same old lazy Wog, who'd rather sleep than fight, rather fight than work, rather argue and drink beer than either fight *or* work. He can't concentrate on tomorrow—you'd never get him to invest seven years, or seven months, of planning on anything that might pay him in the hazy future. Somebody might curse him in the meantime, George.

'He's a Wog, George,' Brian said. 'And you aren't going to turn him into a white man, or even a brown man, with a white man's values as long as they make drums and beer and sunshine and a handy God for him to blame his own shiftlessness on. He's greedy, and thoughtlessly cruel, and he'll do you a nastiness out of his own childish anger, George, but he's not greedy enough to work to satisfy his own greed, no matter what Nell says. Not unless you bloody well stand over him with a whip and kick his black backside when he decides to sleep the day away instead of working. That's *why*, George.'

Brian looked at his brother. Young Philip had been sitting silently through the conversation.

'How about you, youngster?' Brian smiled at him. 'What's your view? Are you with these wide-eyed idealists or against them?'

'I don't see we have any choice,' he replied. 'I agree with Aunt Charlotte. It's either this or get out eventually, whether or not the government pay us. It certainly can't possibly go on as it's been going once they get their independence. No matter what guarantees they make now. They break their word to each other every day as a matter of course. But I can't see that we can do anything else but try and salvage something. I'll do whatever Nell and Aunt Charlotte say we should do with our land.'

Brian scratched his head, then sighed.

'I seem to be outvoted all round,' he said. 'I wish you luck. Just where do I figure in this, Auntie? Do I have any say at all? I mean, wayward boy and the rest, I'm still part of the picture—I might even be defined as an heir.'

Charlotte Stuart looked deeply into her nephew's eyes. 'After I'm gone you and Nell and Philip can work it out to suit yourselves,' the old woman said. 'At the moment I'm *not* dead. Glenburnie's mine. You never really worked a serious day on it, not even after you married. If you had, I'd see it differently. I can't see that you have a voice in what I shall do or not do with *my* land now.'

Brian shrugged. His smile twisted at his sister.

'I guess that deals me out,' he said. 'You wouldn't want to dig down into the old reticule and pay me my whack now, would you, Sister dear? Just on the wild assumption that there'll be anything left to divide after Aunt Charlotte's gone?'

Nell pressed her lips tightly together. Her husband started to say something, thought better of it, and snapped his mouth shut.

'Thank you, George,' Brian said, quirking his lips. 'For a moment I thought that I was about to receive the benefit of your extensive African knowledge. Well,' he said briskly, springing to his feet. 'I guess that's that. I know when I've been disinherited.' He pointedly dusted off his trouser knees.

'I don't suppose,' he looked at his aunt, 'that there's any use my asking if you want to buy Don Bruce's farm and add it to your noble experiment?

It's going cheap, I happen to know. Don wanted you to have first whack at it. It's a jolly good farm.'

Charlotte Stuart looked a trifle puzzled.

'I know it's a good farm,' she said. 'Don's a good steady lad. He's been over to see me several times on one project and another. I sold him some breeding stock last year. He's only just coming into the clear with it.'

Brian smiled, but only with his teeth.

'Don hasn't your sublime faith in the noble savage pulling himself up by his bootstraps,' he said. 'He's had rather a spot of bother I'd not time to mention so far. You'll remember the sort of thing well, the old type of native displeasure, Aunt Char. Dog gutted and upended on the gatepost. The old medicine man poisoned. Twenty of the labourers sugared off to the bush with their women. The odd threat about the baby being nominated for the next really juicy oath-eating ceremony. Himself rather highly placed on the short list—the usual gratitude one's come to expect from the beloved black brethren.'

His sister's eyes widened, and her hand went to her mouth, and then slowly dropped to her lap.

'Sorry, Nellie,' Brian said coldly. 'I know this hurts, but there's an awful lot of getting-even talk going round amongst the Kyukes. You see, George,' he said with elaborate politeness to his brother-in-law, 'there was a touch of nastiness here a while back, called Mau Mau, and all of the club members weren't hanged or shot. Quite a few thousand were clapped behind wire for several years. Since they've—ah—graduated, they've become substantial citizens. Leaders, you know. Politicians with the British seal of approval on them. Union officials. Teachers. Lawyers. Unfortunately some of today's socially acceptable pillars remember rather keenly, and with some long-cherished displeasure, that they had quite a rough time of it—some from the whites, some at the hands of some of their relatives, whom we used to refer to, jokingly, as "loyal Kikuyu" and "home guard". Obviously there were gross injustices on all sides. It's made for quite a lot of bad blood. Most of it still unsatisfied by the usual price of more blood.'

'What about Don Bruce?' his aunt said roughly. 'Stop babbling nonsense. What actually happened?'

'Nothing very much, Auntie, bar the disembowelled dog and the life frightened out of Peggy. They hadn't got round to stock-slashing or baby-killing when I last saw Don. But you see, George,' Brian again spoke elaborately to George Locke, 'some of us, in a doubtless misguided sense of patriotism, killed and otherwise discommoded quite a few thousand black gentlemen in that long, mussy business. And so for some time now, the suddenly respectable survivors have been preparing long lists and short lists of people to be screened. But unfortunately the Wog has a way of becoming over-enthusiastic with the taste of authority and is likely to lose his head and scramble up his instructions. They might even get so addled with blood and grog after *uhuru* that they'd mistake you for an old wicked white settler instead of recognizing you as a leading exponent of land reform. Or,' Brian said brutally, 'they might just need some fresh brains or a spare pair of balls for a ceremony and chop off the first white head they run onto. Even if it's yours, George. They weren't known to be terribly picky in the past.' He looked directly now at his sister, who turned her face away.

'In any case, Aunt Charlotte,' Brian continued. 'To answer your question: Nothing's happened seriously to Don or his family yet. But as he's four kids and a wife he loves, he's thinking that perhaps he doesn't want the kids to grow up in the same old dreary atmosphere. He's tired of wearing guns to the table. He doesn't want to spend the rest of his days counting his kids to see if they're all there!'

'I'd say that's about enough, Brian,' young Philip said sharply. 'You don't have to talk that way.'

Brian whirled. His face paled, contorted.

'Shut your mouth or I'll close it for you!' he snapped. 'You were saying only a few hours ago that the trouble with Kenya was that nobody wanted to face any facts. We'll face some facts now, thank you very much!'

He turned back to his sister.

'You ought to understand how Don feels—you, of all people! You were locked in that burning barn when they dragged your uncle off to butcher him! You got burned to bits and left for dead! Maybe Don Bruce doesn't want to lose a couple of kids to a filthy oathing! Maybe he wants a wife with all of her face!'

George Locke was on his feet protesting, his face flushed with anger.

'Brian! You're not to talk to Nell like that! I don't care if you're her brother, I don't care if it's true, I don't——' His words ended in a choked splutter. Brian Dermott's right hand had shot out and taken him by the throat. The hand pulled George Locke slightly towards him, and then propelled him crashing backward into his chair. Only the weight of the vast oaken chair prevented its overturning from the impact of George Locke's hurtling body. George Locke bent forward gasping, the breath choked and slammed out of him.

'Stay down and shut up, George,' Brian said, without bothering to look at him. His voice was very quiet now and icy cold. 'You're comparatively new to the family. I shouldn't like to see you hurt in a family fuss.' He turned to face his aunt.

'I don't seem to be accomplishing very much here. Do you want Bruce's farm or don't you, I told him we'd—*you'd*—let him know.'

His aunt reached out and rapped Brian sharply on the head with her stick. She jerked her head at a chair.

'*You* sit down and shut up,' she said. 'It's been twenty-five years since I took you over my knee and walloped you. I'm willing to take a chance on trying it again.'

Brian grinned weakly and rubbed his head. His face was regaining colour.

'Sorry, Aunt Char. Sorry, Nell. Pip, George. Everybody. I apologize.

Lost my temper a bit. Don't seem to have as firm hold on it as I used to. Sorry, all. I say, Pip, you wouldn't fix me a Scotch and soda to say I'm forgiven?'

'Sure, Brian,' the boy got up. 'Anybody else?'

'No, thanks,' they all said, together.

Brian took the glass from his brother and drank thirstily.

'Right,' he said. 'I'm a solitary drinker. Right.' He took another gulp. 'I think I'll be leaving pretty soon. I enjoy driving at night.'

George Locke, his face flushed, still coughing, again started to say something, but Brian shut him off with a wave.

'It's all right, George,' he said. 'Save your breath. I'm not drunk, but I always drive better at night when I'm a little tiddled. I drive like the Americans—always on the right side of the road. You were going to say something about buying Don's farm, Aunt Char?'

'I was that. I won't buy it. I'll not contribute to anyone's running off now. That's half of what's wrong with the country—everyone ready to cut and run. I've lived on the land, and with the land I'll stay. I'll not spend a penny to help Donald Bruce evade his responsibility. His grandfather was here when I came, an old man. His father was born here. He's no right to be after leaving his land.' A tiny touch of Irish had crept back into his aunt's voice.

'Very well, I'll tell him he's no right to leave his land, and inform him of your proposed noble experiment with upgrading the scrub native into proper breeding stock. Perhaps, who knows, he'll want to join the club, and you can all take turns baby-sitting each other, as in the old days.'

He looked slowly round the room, as if memorizing it. His eyes rested a long time on the badly executed oil-painting of his mother.

'Nice place you have here,' he said, coolly and impersonally. Then, 'Pip, will you tell Juma to whistle up Kidogo and put my box in the car? I'm afraid to yell for him. He might file a complaint to the steering committee.'

'So ye'll be leaving us this way, with harsh words,' his aunt said. 'Ye'll go away in the middle of the night, like ye used to when there was some excuse for your temper and haste? Like the wild spoiled brat that ye still are?'

'I fancy your anger more than your broad Irish, Auntie,' Brian said, his voice falsely light again. 'Yes, I'll go away in the middle of the night as I used to when the war was on. The only difference today is that it's still on, and worse, but you people don't realize it. George'—he turned to his brother-in-law—'if you find the dairy herd with all their teats chopped off, it's only a symptom of a new disease called *uhuru*. I suggest you kill the cattle immediately and throw a barbecue for the co-operative. Pay no attention to dead dogs on the gateposts. The dogs, like the people, have become careless with good times.'

Juma had come into the room now. The old man was plainly disturbed, the old hands folding the hem of his *kanzu* nervously.

'Your box is ready, Bwana,' he said. 'We had no chance to wash the clothes. Must you leave us now?'

'Yes, you old thief,' Brian said, and hugged him briefly. 'Did you steal the nice new blue sweater?'

'Of course, Little Bwana,' the old man said. 'It is much too fine to ruin in the bush.'

'That's good,' Brian said. 'Wear it against evil. I fetched it to you with that in mind. *Kwaheri, baba.*'

He turned to his aunt.

'*Kwaheri*, Auntie dear,' he said to Charlotte Stuart. He nodded at George. 'This time you've really struck it lucky, Aunt Char. You've lost a *shenzi* and really gained a son. A dedicated farmer with a doctor's degree. He ought to make a wonderful vet.'

He chucked Nell under the chin, punched Philip lightly on the shoulder, and threw a loose salute at George Locke.

'Bye-bye all,' he said. 'One of you might ring up Don Bruce tomorrow and tell him no dice on the farm. I don't think he expected much anyhow.'

At the door he paused, and looked round the room again.

'And George,' he said, his voice mocking. 'Don't fret about me and my drinking. I don't want you to distract yourself from your housing project and all your little agricultural schemes. I'll stay sober. I'll be all right back in the bush where I belong. I find it remarkably easy to stay sober when I'm not subject to civilization.'

'Brian, please,' George Locke started to say, 'it's serious that you shouldn't . . .'

'Forget it. I'll be a good boy. And George?'

'What?' George Locke's voice made every effort towards warmth and concern, sadly and sincerely felt.

'It'll be quite all right, so long as you're running things here, to have the tenants in to dine with your brother-in-law when next I call. I'll be frightfully proper, and even check my pistol at the door. If I'm welcome at all under the New Deal. They might proscribe me. *Kwaheri*, all.' Brian Dermott chuckled harshly and was gone.

His family heard the clang of door, a short curse, and the rasp of brutalized gears.

Charlotte Stuart moved her shoulders in a shrug.

'Poor chap,' she said. 'Poor little chap.' Her voice sounded as if she were describing a strange hurt child. 'And so very little of it any of his fault at all.' She shook her head angrily.

'I think it's time we all went to bed,' Charlotte Stuart said. 'Philip, turn out the lights. Good night, everybody.' She turned and limped off down the hall, her stick clacking harshly on the floor. The others stared at her straight back. Philip Dermott went round the room methodically switching off the lights. The sound of the motor faded, and the house was dark and still.

*

186

Kidogo, only a quarter awake, sulked and shivered in the other seat. He was crumpled in a small ball, feet drawn under him.

'Why do we leave in the middle of the night, Bwana?' he asked. 'I was sleeping dead. I had much meat and they have been making new *pombe* back in the *shamba* of Wareru the herdboy. They gave me some and the fire was warm and I was sleeping very well in front of it. It is cold in this night air. What is so important it could not wait until morning?'

'Nothing. There is a bottle of whisky in my box. Get it for me. Have a drink if you want. It is cold in this night air as you say. Hand me the *tembo* and go to sleep.'

Kidogo sighed. He had driven with the Bwana on many occasions when the spirits lay heavily on the Bwana and he went off in the middle of the night when there was no necessity for it. He hoped the Bwana would pay attention to his driving. Sometimes when he was like this his attention wandered and they ran off the road. Kidogo looked at the side of the road and saw a steep drop. He hoped the Bwana would be very careful; that was a long fall down that hill.

'Bwana,' he said.

'Yes,' Brian said, coughing as the neat whisky bit at his throat. 'What do you want?'

'Sometimes it is better to buy a new cookpot than to try to mend an old one which has been broken many times. It is not worth the trouble and will only want mending again.'

Brian reached out and ruffled the old Ndrobo's head without taking his eyes off the twisting ribbon of road.

'Thanks, *mzee*,' he said. 'I'll keep that in mind. Go back to sleep now.'

'Yes, Bwana. But Bwana?'

'What now?'

'Once I saw a hyena fighting with some wild dogs over a piece of zebra stomach. The dogs were chasing the hyena, who had the meat in his mouth. The hyena looked back over his shoulder to see how close the wild dogs were, and he ran into a tree and knocked himself unconscious. The wild dogs killed the hyena and then they ate the hyena *and* the zebra stomach.'

'Very funny,' Brian said. 'Have you anything else to offer in the way of wisdom?'

'Yes,' the old man said. 'Once before we came away from the farm like this—a long time ago—and for a long time it was very unpleasant. I am too old for unpleasantness. Be careful, Bwana—do not be a hyena and run into a tree. It is not pleasant to be eaten by wild dogs, or by the worms that sometimes feed in a sick man's stomach.'

Brian took another short swig from the bottle that lay on the seat between them. He cocked his head, and increased his speed.

'I feel better now, *baba*,' he said. 'We are not for the *shambas*, you and I, nor for the towns. What do you suppose we are for, *baba*?'

'If I knew I would tell you,' Kidogo said. 'Be careful with the car, and remember, we left the camp on the Seralippe. The last time we left in a hurry like this we overran the camp by twenty miles.'

'I was younger then and had more steam,' Brian said. 'For the last time, go to sleep.'

He began to sing tunelessly, and presently he fumbled a cigarette into his mouth and lit it with the dash-lighter. The night was clear, the stars were crisp in the sky, and he was going north. His mind could see the campfire wink, although he was many miles away from where he had left the safari. The campfire was warm in his heart, and what he had left was no longer home. Home was north, home was with the elephants and the rootless savage nomads, with the dry and the wet and the hot and the searing cold. The tobacco smoke tasted delicious through the whisky-moisture of his mouth. If he drove steadily he could be in camp by midnight, if they hadn't moved it. And if they had moved it, he could find it. There was nothing in the north that Brian Dermott could not find except possibly himself, and he would think about that some other time. He reached for the bottle again. Drinking this way, in little sips, a bloke never got drunk, and it kept his mouth wet and the cigarettes moist. The motor ran well in the night. Everything went better in the night except when you slept. I am happy, Brian Dermott told himself wordlessly. It is good to be going home.

BOOK THREE

CHAPTER ONE

KATHLEEN CRANE was a magnificently filthy woman. Her face was caked in grey dust, and sweat-wet dust had silted blackly into the creases of her palms. Great ochre smudges of Kenya's careless earth rouged her khaki slacks and jacket. Her lips were cracked under the salve which seemed more purposefully designed to accumulate soil than to keep her skin supple. Her nose and cheekbones glowed neon from the sun, and were debating their third peeling. There was nothing she would ever be able to do about her hair again, except possibly shave it; it was lost beyond all hope of hairdresser's reclamation, and she was resigned now to let it fly wild over the bandeau which fended some of its maniac ends from her eyes. Her nails, long scoured clean of polish, showed white against the tan of her fingers. A great splotch of perspiration spread over the seat of her pants, sweated from hours of sitting on the heat-cherishing plastic cushion of the Land Rover. Bug dope had seeped from a bottle and isolated one pocket of her jacket into a large greasy island. Every bone ached with fatigue, her knees shouted cramp, her damp backside was numb, ankles and forearms bore unattractive memories of old thorn wounds, there was a lump the size of an olive on her forehead where a camel-fly had stabbed her, and her right shoulder was bruised yellow from the recurring kick of a malevolent shotgun. She was completely dehydrated, mummified from the dusty drive and the flat smiting sun. She also suspected she smelled bad.

Katie Crane had been in Africa exactly one month, and she thought she had never been so happy.

She sat in the front seat of the Rover, between the two men, her khaki-trousered legs opened immodestly to allow Brian Dermott's brown left hand a free play with the gear shift between her knees. The merging days had melted and run into four weeks now, and she felt that she had been born and reared in this uncomfortable, unladylike, undignified position. She was even able to sleep sitting straight up between Brian Dermott and her brother, Paul. Pretty soon now she and Brian and her brother would raise the new camp site in the new country, and she would be almost sorry to leave the car. She felt welded to it. She felt as though she had never been out of it. The Land Rover had become her home. She took an inventory, now, and smiled. Nothing seemed to be missing, or else she'd have noticed it.

In the long compartment formed by the dashboard in front of her was a box of Kleenex, a roll of toilet paper, three dishevelled paperback books, a tin of peppermint Scotch humbugs, a glass jar of hard mixed candies she had learned to call *peramente*, a bottle of '*Off*', the anti-bug mixture, a carton of cigarettes, a small pair of binoculars, a broken carton of matches, a plastic bottle of sunburn lotion, a small leather-covered half-flask of whisky, an air-mail copy of last month's *Time*, a dirty roll of adhesive, a bottle-opener-corkscrew, a tin box of aspirin and red Swiss knife with a dozen varying blades of assorted exotic function. You didn't really need the bottle opener or the *maridadi* knife. You could easily snap the cap off a bottle under the curl of the Rover's dashboard.

Behind her she knew there would be a spare tyre, a long tool box, and a picket fence of guns standing upright, clamped into foam-rubber cushions. The extra artillery, mostly of the big-mouthed variety, slept well-greased in its jewel-cases against a declaration of war.

Also well-greased and permanently dark-fixtured in the back seat, always standing clinging to the crossbar onto which the upright gun racks were bolted, was the team of Kidogo and Muema, the gunbearers, who seemed to have the vision of vultures and who constantly descried specks which meant nothing to her, but occasionally warranted a tiny tap on Brian's shoulder causing him to stop the Rover and reach for the little binoculars. Mostly he would say quietly: 'I say, that's rather a jolly lion over there, just left of that little hill,' and pass her the glasses; or, less frequently, 'it's another Jumbo, nothing like so good as the one we've got, but decent enough for most people'; or, rarely, 'that's a damned fine oryx; I don't think we're likely to see a better'. And swiftly over his shoulder to the gunbearers, '*Toa three hundred kwa bwana*,' and then commence a devious approach at which she never ceased to marvel. Then, suddenly, he would say to her brother: 'Right, Paul, just when we pass that ant-hill . . .' or thornbush, or acacia, and her brother would stretch his right hand backward to the gunbearers and she would hear the soft mack of the weapon as it was slapped like a big surgical instrument into a doctor's palm.

Paul would plunge out of the car as it passed the ant-hill, or thornbush, and usually Muema, the gap-toothed, grizzled, broken-nozed Wakamba gunbearer, would fall out with him. Then Brian would rapidly drive the car away to some small pimpling hill a thousand yards distant, and tell Kidogo to hand Katie the big binoculars from the back seat. They would stop, then, to get out and limber their legs and view the unfolding tableau through the glasses —to watch her brother and Muema, stalking from ant-hill to ant-hill, from low bush to tree, dwindling tiny black figures printed against vast yellow carpet, until finally she could see Muema touch her brother's arm. The gun would ride easily to his shoulder, he would brace his legs and lean against the side of the hill or bush, or else squat flat on his backside with upraised knees forming a steady, locked rest, as Brian had taught him. Then, usually, there would come the solid *tunk!* as the bullet struck before the sound of the gun's explosion reached them. Mostly the animal collapsed, or staggered in a shrinking circle before falling. Occasionally it raced dementedly away in a death gallop as the tiny bullet touched its heart without breaking bone.

Brian, standing beside her, always knew immediately from the sound. '*Kufa*,' he'd say, if it was a solid whomp—dead. Sometimes he'd say 'Dead, but it doesn't know it yet,' when the animal lurched and then sped away. Once in a while he would say '*Piga*, but too far back,' or shake his head and mutter, '*Tumbo tu*'—'belly only'. Then they would begin to track, tracing sometimes the sprayed pink frothy lung blood or the yellow-bily stomach blood in little clots and ropy slashes. She was allowed to tag along when they tracked, and was invariably awestruck. Kidogo and Muema ranged ahead of Brian like circling dogs, each man pointing rhythmically with a stick or weed and nodding sagely at things she could not see—a scuffed bit of earth, a minute scrape on a stone, a back-bent blade of grass. She tried and she tried, but she could never track, although one day they had followed a wounded kongoni for nearly two hours and she never saw a sign of its passage after the first few bright berries of blood dried away under the hot sun. Brian was usually articulate about nearly everything that he did as a reflex, but he had tried to explain tracking to her and had failed, because tracking was neither a skill nor a science. As far as she could make out it was nine-tenths intuition, if not sheerest magic, and she noticed that neither Brian nor the natives ever really looked at the ground. They seemed to stare out in front of them, on a waist level—what Brian called 'bringing the ground up to you', and followed in the general direction of where it seemed likely an animal might go if you were that particular animal.

After a time, generally short but sometimes unaccountably long, covering sweaty miles, they would come upon the animal, suddenly dead or occasionally down but with its head raised, its eyes hurtful with dumb, baffled anger. Then was when Brian would say quietly to her brother, 'Best slip another behind the shoulder,' or 'Give him the other half in the back of the neck, please, Paul'—or, occasionally, the part she hated most, when one of the gun-bearers would unsheathe his knife, and, warily approaching, seize a horn in one hand and sever the vertebra with a quick, short stab at the base of the brain. Only occasionally did he miss, and then the sight of twisting blade, probing for the spinal cord, made her actively ill.

But that was only the tiniest part, and Katie was no milksop. If you were there to kill, some unpleasantness was necessary and she could understand the necessity. She had long since realized that minks were not born sewed into coats and that sirloin steaks were not spun in test-tubes, and that shoe leather invariably came ripped untimely off a cow. It had taken her a few days to conquer the first aversion to all the blood and slop that attended the death of a zebra which would some day be converted into a frightfully chic strip of upholstery for a modern sun room in Palm Beach.

She had watched, fascinated by the final awfulness of it; the automatic voiding of the bowels, the pumping seminal ejaculation, then the great spilling of hot stinking white shiny-bulging intestine as one of the boys '*toa hi tumbo*'

—split the belly and plunged into the abdominal cavity with both hands to haul out the slippery stomach and scrape off the glistening globules of yellow fat which lined the great gut.

The hot sweet sickish smell of blood, the spilled green-spinachy contents of the paunch, the hordes of fat buzzing flies that came from nowhere, then the vultures circling and finally volplaning down from the sky to light with a bump of their undercarriage; birds looking like horrid sextons sitting in an evil, crooked-necked circle, hopping and flapping with irritable impatience, or waiting lasciviously eager, like nasty unbuttoned old men, waiting atop an ant-hill or on a dead bough of thorn tree for the hunters to be done with their skinning and dismembering. Then, as the bloody-handed gunbearers wiped their dripping fingers on a tuft of grass after loading the severed hams and sections of ribs, and bundling the heart and liver and strips of intestine into the blood-soggy package of the heavy fresh hide, she could see the drooling vultures tense and hop closer even before the people had all crawled back in the Land Rover. By the time the car was in gear and crawling away, the birds were already quarrelling and flapping over the carcass, their bloodied heads stuck obscenely into the dismembered mess. She knew the buzzards were necessary to the scene—knew they were protected and even cherished as scavengers, but she consciously hated the dreadful end of it; the sleek, sun-glistening animal, alert and vibrant with life small minutes past, suddenly reduced to a pile of brownish lumps and picked red-scabbed bones, the yellow teeth ugly in the eyeless skull. She had never really considered the mechanics of death before, but had to admit that she was more fascinated than shocked by the completeness of dissolution.

It developed that Brian was heavily in love with nearly all the animals he knew, and it seemed to her that he deliberately postponed the killing of any of them—until, at last, he sighed and suggested almost apologetically to her brother that the dimensions of whatever it was they were seeking did not figure to improve with further search, and so Paul had best get out and wallop it.

She believed she understood a little better now that she knew more. She had been more interested in photography than in shooting—indeed, she had refused to kill anything with more personality than birds, which seemed, like fish, to lie weightless on one's conscience—and she and Brian had gone alone except for the gunbearers on several camera expeditions when her brother took an occasional day off in camp to ease his blistered feet and skim through the coded batches of money correspondence that overtook them fitfully when Brian sent the lorry into the *dukah* at Isiolo or Garba Tulla for petrol. She was fascinated by everything, but especially by the elephants, particularly the relatively 'tame' ones on the National Park side of the road, where shooting was forbidden unless something was about to bite you.

It was with the elephants that she had first experienced shattering physical fear—the first time when an old dry herd-mistress had broken away from the straggling group and charged them, screaming, trunk-stabbing, ears pinned tightly back, and Brian had performed some new miracles of manoeuvre with the Land Rover. She should have caught tremendous moving pictures of that screeching charge—except that in her fear she had forgotten to take the protective covering from the lens and so had buzzed out several score unfertilized feet of nothing.

On another occasion, they had stalked close to an old one-tusker bull who had been rocking, snoozing, dreaming old-man's nostalgic dreams under a palm along the bank of the dry river-bed. The wind had changed unaccountably, a stick had cracked under her foot, and the ancient bull had suddenly received their scent and blasted a trombone bellow. Perhaps he wasn't charging, but he was bowling full steam in their direction, and Brian had nearly jerked her arm out of the socket dragging her crosswind, her toes scraping only against the higher points of ground. They had come very close to elephant several times after, and always she felt the almost joyful flooding of fear that the great, rumpled, wrinkled relicts of the Pleistocene Age created in her. They were never quite real, those plastic tons of grey wraith that melted in and out of elephant-coloured bush with never a sound, or that occasionally played like happy huge pigs or naughty little boys when they came in the evening to drink and bathe.

She loved the being alone with Brian and the native boys, when Paul stayed on in camp, and they packed a picnic lunch in the chopbox and went off 'perusing', as Brian called it, with no planned objective. They usually stopped under some broad acacias or next a tiny stream to have their lunch, eating unbelievable amounts of clammy canned beans and cold fowl and pickles and tinned sardines. Brian had partaken only mildly since he had rolled in during the middle of the night, drunk as a fiddler's bitch and gravely, ludicrously formal in the exaggerated politeness with which he begged their pardon for his unlikely arrival. Things had evidently not gone well with Brian on his hurried trip to town—later, little by little, as he came to know her better he had confided bits and pieces of himself and his family until, after a month, she felt she knew part of him very well, and knew the other part of him not at all.

She was usually a grave, quiet woman, Kathleen Crane, her grey eyes huge and ready to be wounded in a small serious child's face, her dark blonde hair pulled back tightly when she washed and combed it at night; hair flying wild now in a riot of loose ends in the wind that streamed over the topless Land Rover. She was the kind of woman who looked smaller, slimmer than she really was, and Brian had been surprised at the sight of her body when they had stopped for a swim one day at Buffalo Springs. In the scrap of bikini she had astounding breasts, moulded seemingly larger by the extreme slimness of her waist and generous spread of hip, and long, beautifully shaped well-fleshed legs. It was in clothes that she looked small; she was actually only half a head shorter than Brian; as tall as her brother, and quite unbelievably strong and tireless for a girl. She warmed into occasional brittle irreverence as Brian got to know her better. Her speech intrigued him: it often combined vulgarity with clipped good grammar and always she seemed to see herself with cool composure, as one might discuss a stranger. Sometimes Brian thought she practised mockery to avoid the tears which seemed always to glisten ready in her grey eyes.

They talked a lot when they picnicked, both shy at first, until once the subject of alcohol came into play, Brian mentioning how rare it was for an American that she didn't drink anything at all, and she commenting that she had heard *all* professional hunters were demons with the bottle. Both seemed surprised, as if encountering unsuspected virtue in each other.

'I don't drink now because I'm a drunk,' Katie Crane said very frankly. 'I tried being a drunk and didn't particularly like me in the part. So I decided to quit doing it. This was after the marriage had gone the way most marriages go when one side is steadily sozzled and the other nastily and pointedly sober.'

'I suppose I'm a drunk, too,' Brian smiled at her. 'At any rate I'm not supposed to touch the stuff. Some sort of queer complex of diseases makes me allergic to my oldest and dearest friend, the good Bwana *pombe*. They say it'll kill me if I do it to any degree any more. But I never considered myself a problem drunk. I don't suppose most people do. I was just a chap that liked his grog—booze fit me as naturally as a gun or a good pair of hunting shorts. It fit me too damned well. My brother-in-law, the quack, says my problem is that I could walk off under too much of it. Very few hangovers and always functioned pretty well with it, I thought—as well with it as without it'—he frowned—'until . . .'

'Until what?' Kate Crane asked him.

'Combination of things,' Brian said. 'War and peace. Wife trouble. Family tragedy. The usual. Concerted clobberation. What made a drunk out of you, if a drunk you really were, which I'm inclined to doubt?'

'I don't really know,' Kate Crane said. 'I swear I really don't know. You've seen how very little Paul drinks. It's not a family failing. Charles—my husband—didn't drink any more than the polite usual. Two martinis and a-couple-of-Scotches-at-a-party sort of pinch-faced drinker. And I didn't fiddle with it at all until I was quite a grown woman—twenty-three or -four. Just after I married Charles. But all of a sudden it sneaked up and bit me where I could feel it, and it hurt.'

Brian was lying on his stomach, on a skimpy stretch of clover green that rimmed a tiny stream's sandy, print-scarred edge. He was digging aimlessly at the springy turf with a knife blade, his chin pillowed on one hand. His hair was tousled, falling over his forehead, and he had his knees bent, brown ankles crossed one over the other and gently waving in the slow, breeze-stirring air. It was very cool and quiet under the fringe of palms that guarded the *luga* in cool, striking contrast to the solidly tangible heat of the scorched brown plain on all sides. Katie sat facing him, chewing on a blade of grass, leaning backward with her palms flat on the ground, her legs sprawled apart in a wide V.

196

'You know,' she said lazily, 'I doubt if I'll ever be able to wear a skirt again. A hundred miles a day straddling that rude gearshift, and forever flinging myself around in breeches, I seem to have forgotten that nice girls always keep their knees primly together, and are careful not to show too much leg when they climb in and out of cabs. New York's in for the shock of its tiny life when they trap me back into a girdle and skirt.'

'I rather like you in trousers,' Brian said. 'So few girls can wear them with any sort of dash. I guess most of them aren't made for slacks, which is just as well if you fancy function over fashion. But you look—well, trim, and sort of . . . sort of antiseptically sexy.'

'Well, mercy me,' Katie Crane said. 'Cross-eyed compliments and me all alone and defenceless in the bush. Speaking of being defenceless in the bush, do you suppose there are any snakes in that clump of bedraggled begonia over yonder?' She pushed herself to her feet and picked up her handbag. 'If you hear girlish screams, come fetch me,' she said.

Brian rolled over and braced his hands behind his neck.

'Careful not to get bitten where we can't put the tourniquet,' he said. 'Remember your brother's joke.'

Katie Crane swished her handbag at him as she headed towards the bush. It was very strange, she thought, how soon you became unshy about such things as disappearing behind bushes; shy no longer, even boldly suggesting that it would be a good idea if Brian stopped the car while she sought the ladies' loo. The roll of TP no longer seemed to glare whitely brazen in the catch-all compartment of the Rover, and she, who had always been very shy of natural functions, even when married, had no hesitancy about trotting away to the bush with the roll of toilet tissue frankly in her hand.

Brian turned her open admission of drunkenness over in his head. This was quite a woman, he thought. Thank God for the controlled ones. Behaved herself all the way through; no womanish grizzling, and no obvious itch for the white hunter. Shows how wrong you could be though. When he'd first left camp, after the first week, he reckoned she'd be quoting Hemingway at him pretty soon and complaining bitterly because he didn't have a sleeping-bag for her to crawl into. All told, this was a jolly good safari, the brother still holding up very well as a sportsman and as quiet company, and really a damned keen shot. Here she came back, now, swinging along small-footed and sort of little-girl lanky-pretty in her tailored slacks and jacket. Wonder how a nice woman like that got really dug into the grog?

'If I'm not being rude,' Brian said, 'how *did* you get pulled down by the demon rum? Must be a sad story in it. I've nothing to do but listen until four P.M., except maybe take a nap. There won't be any game stirring until then.'

'I wish I could spin you a soap opera full of dark frustrations and sharply defined tragedy,' Katie said lightly. 'But there isn't any, really. There was, perhaps, a little constant nastiness with Charles—who, with some reason, no one ever called Charlie or Chuck. There was a fellow ahead of Charles who

197

got killed in the war, but nearly everybody my age had somebody ahead of her Charles who got killed in the war. No, I'd say it was mostly boredom.'

'Boredom? That's an odd way for a smart girl to get to be a drunk. I don't believe you were a drunk at all, anyhow. I just think you don't know liquor for all the fine brave things it'll do for you if you encourage it.'

Kate reached over and tickled Brian's nose with a grass stem.

'You know you've got a funny face,' she said. 'Your nose turns down and your mouth turns up. Half of it's a cruel man's face, and the other half little boy. But I'd give my all, including retroactive virtue, if I owned your eyelashes. It's positively criminal of God to waste such lashes on a man and make women like me run around having to glue the damned things on. And it was, too, endemic boredom that made a drunk out of me. I doubt if you could understand, living out here, in all this excitement, what a steady diet of that particular kind of boredom can be like.'

'Maybe not. I could try. The only time I'm really bored is when I'm plodding through paces with people who shouldn't be allowed to come out here and see all this.' He swept one hand around him, encompassing the tall creaking palms and the flashing pigeons, the small meandering stream with its pale evergreen fringe of reeds. 'And I'm stifled in town, I expect—unless I'm pleasantly squiffled. But here—no, ma'am. Never.'

'You've hit it precisely, professor,' Kate said. 'And I'm not unique in my world, either. You ought to try it some time—living in that particular vacuum, with lashings of money since you were knee-high to a grasshopper, a sort of house pet for indulgent, rather unimaginatively selfish parents, with unlimited silly aunts and red-nosed, fruity old uncles dying and leaving you more money—and then finding that there was nothing you really wanted to do with it because you already had it all. And didn't like what you had. It's a most peculiar poverty.'

'Sounds a delicious predicament to me,' Brian said. 'We never suffered much from yacht-poisoning in my family. Pray continue with the tale of woe.'

'Don't you dare laugh, or I won't tell you,' Kate said. 'I'm thirty-five years old and I can't remember ever really wanting anything—or anybody—very badly. Well, when I was very small I wanted to run away and be poor, but that didn't last very long. I was always sort of ewe-necked and gawky as a girl, but I still automatically got to be Queen of the May. And of the Junior Prom. And of the Senior Prom. And the leading deb. And all that jazz.' She made the last sentence sound worse than profanity. Brian shuddered.

'What a barbarous language, Ameddican,' he said. '*All that jazz.* My sacred oath!'

'Everyone else was going madly to bed with boys the year I came out so I went madly to bed with a boy. Everybody else was falling deeply in love so I fell deeply in love with my now defunct hero; whose name was Wentworth Wellborn Copeland the Fourth——'

'—nobody was ever named Wentworth Wellborn Copeland the Fourth,' Brian muttered.

'Was too. One of our very best dehydrated families. Copey was kind of cute if you like the Princeton type and that was the year for everybody liking Princeton types. Dartmouth had fallen out of favour because the Navy swiped it from the students to train naval officers in and they didn't have the big Winter Carnival doings at Hanover any more. Copey was big and blond and very stupid and he looked gorgeous in his blue midshipman's suit. When he got his commission he kissed me true and took up with the F-4Fs, which he could just manage to squeeze into, and managed to get himself shot down and posthumously Navy-Crossed at Kwajalein or some other unlikely atoll. This made very little difference to me because I was playing The Game—which everybody else, married and single, was playing then. The Game was something patriotic ex-debutantes, and I believe shopgirls as well, thought up to see how many service men they could Make Happy Before They Went Off To Die. I made quite a few happy in the friendliest, most intimate sort of way until I met Charles, who didn't want to Go Off To Die without Making an Honest Woman of Me. Pardon me if I speak in capitals. Charles Wanted Something to Fight For. That was lovely little me. And I must say he fought a pretty good fight. He got stationed in Miami, and we had a dreadful war, since it was necessary to commute every morning from the house in Palm Beach that Grammaw Drake left me. Murder.'

'Sounds dreadful,' Brian said. 'I've been to Palm Beach. And Bimini. And —what's the name—Cat Cay? Guest of clients. I had a wonderful time. Drank all night and fished all day, sweating it out. Caught a hellish big tuna in the tournament. Nearly worked me to death. Haven't had a tuna sandwich since. So when the Japs didn't bomb Florida, what did you do?'

'Well, now. We had cocktail parties. Then when the war was over we moved to the Park Avenue flat, the first co-operative, I believe, and had cocktail parties. In the summer we went to the house in Easthampton, and had cocktail parties. In the winter we came back to Palm Beach and had more cocktail parties. We went to Europe and to Japan and South America and had cocktail parties. The family crest was a sad sausage couchant on a toothpick. After a while it was too much trouble to get up in time to get drunk at girl lunches at the Colony and Twenty-One. I never used to count the Cuba libres the really serious drunks start the day with—or the screwdrivers, either.'

'What's a screwdriver, apart from the kind I'm familiar with?' Brian asked. 'This Ameddican. Really.'

'Orange juice and vodka for your health before you summon sufficient strength to go to the bathroom and clean your teeth. Very health-making at first. Much less self-accusing than bloody Marys—much less violently aggressive than martinis, much less debilitating than Scotch. When I got really onto the vodka kick I knew I was hooked. There's some sort of fallacious legend that vodka doesn't make your breath smell, and so you can't possibly be loaded. Believe me, vodka smells, and so, eventually, do you.'

Katie Crane stopped talking. A tiny breeze whispered lightly in the palms, brushing the barest kissing sound against the harsh fronds. A rainbird delivered his three-note metallic *tonk* somewhere, and a kingfisher screamed. Away down the *luga* there was a momentary brief chattering of Sykes monkeys, and the snarling grunt of a baboon.

'It seems so strange,' she said. 'It seems so very strange now to me that I went to Montecatini and got myself dried out; that I tried psychiatry and hypnosis and even, God forgive us all, had a small riffle at Alcoholics Anonymous, which drove me back to drink faster than drink ever drove me to AA. All those dismal people standing up and proudly—arrogantly, even—boasting about what sublime stinkers they'd been, how much booze they'd soaked, how many jobs they'd lost, how many wives they'd beat and how much money they'd embezzled—it turned my stomach.'

Brian's brow wrinkled.

'But I don't understand,' he said. 'Exactly what kind of terrible things did you *do*?'

'Nothing very much. Everything. I expect you've read most of it in those alcoholic confessions they print so many of these days. Sort of Diana Barrymoreish doings, except I was never proud of it, not being an actress or a real extrovert. I wound up too often too late at night in too many stylish Third Avenue gin mills. I wound up crocked in too many oddball places—even too many far-out beds—I'd no intention of falling into. I wrapped myself in a kind of cosy fur rug of alcohol where nothing ever quite touched me. I was insulated. I don't know why I'm telling you all this on such a lovely day. Look at the cute monkey peeking out of the dôm-palm.'

'Never mind the cute monkey peeking out of the bloody dôm-palm. I'm very interested. How did you finally crawl out of this thing? And where was your husband when all this was going on?'

'Oh, Charles was around. Charles was at the Racquet Club and also the Brook. Charles was very busy for a man who didn't do anything at all. He had more unearned money than I did. His people made soap flakes. Charles was actually a most harmless detergent. He regarded me with a certain understandable distaste, and connubial bliss had ceased to be for lo, these many years. Bed, I believe, was actually a tiny touch too sweaty a process for Charles. The peasants shared it so Charles didn't like it. He rose above it. In complete fairness to Charles, he wasn't all that bad. It's just that I didn't exactly choose to regard myself in my true repulsive light at the time, and Charles looked pretty awful through the gin haze, like a shrimp embalmed in aspic. It was only later, when I woke up one morning in a hotel on the West Side with some strange blue-jowled gentleman of whom I had no previous memory, I decided that I was a complete mess. Perhaps if it had been a suite in the Carlyle or the Plaza I shouldn't have recognized the bag-eyed babe in the Wicked-Queen mirror as me. But it was me all right. I threw up when I slid into focus.'

'And?'

'I left. I went home and scrubbed myself inside and out. I still tasted bad and felt bad, but the scrubbing helped. You learn something from marrying into a soap-flakes fortune. Then I felt myself moving to the bar—and stopped with the newest drink in my hand. I was a wreck but not too much of one to call a doctor. In those days you could actually *get* doctors on the phone. This one packed me off to the place in Connecticut which was very strict. No matter how much money you had, you couldn't buy any liquor with it. And when I got sprung I went to Alabama and divorced Charles. I didn't want to waste even six weeks in Reno with the slot machines, getting clean of Charles —and me. And my prim, if not prissy, big bachelor brother Paul, who as you gather is quite a dear old duck, lugged me off on safari as a combination reward-for-valour cum preventive-measure. Big vistas, clean African air, no city temptations. . . . And do you know,' she reached out and covered Brian's hand with hers. 'He was dead right. Bless him. *Bless* him. I think I'm cured.'

'Bless him,' Brian said. 'I'm glad he brought you, too. And if you need curing, I think you're cured. Now, what about a spot of lunch?'

CHAPTER TWO

THIS MAN Dermott fascinated Kathleen Crane—and, she thought wryly, I would not go so far as to say that I am the first gal to discover this. God, what a sensation he must have been in America with all the man-eating harpies he'd be bound to meet with those people who had him over to show off like a tame cheetah on a leash. He seems to feel some things so deeply—so sensitively— and is so completely nineteenth-century callous on the other side. He seems rough-shaped, like clay moulded by a genius child who got bored before the finish and barely bothered to smooth out the less interesting lumps. His love for Africa seems more wrapped up in the scenery and the animals and the few wild natives than in the people, especially his own race—and certainly he's more impatient than not about the existent fact of the country's dive into new ways. Brian Dermott seemed to live in completely separate worlds of the immediate present which he could master, and also in a future over which he had no control and hence regarded with apathy. Now, for instance, this thing of the leopard.

'We've been quite lucky up here,' Brian had said, one night after dinner in the last camp. 'It's been a wonderful month—especially the week we had at Rudolf with the big fish. But we've another two weeks to go, and all we actually want is a really fine leopard. We can hunt The Mountain here, around Nanyuki, and collect a leopard, but it'll be cold and wettish now and sort of dreary in the bamboo. If you don't mind a tough day's drive, I'd say we might nip on back, spend the night at Mawingo in the lush plush joint, and then drive on down to an area called Loitokitok. I think you'd like it.'

'Where's this Loitokitok or however you call it?' Kate's brother Paul asked. 'I'm sort of attached to this Northern Frontier of yours. I still think I'll go back to Maralal and buy those two little Samburu maidens and take them home with me. I like all your wild people up here—especially those fierce-looking Turkana. What've you got that's better in this Loitok-something?'

'Heaps. You'd like it,' Brian said. 'We go down deep into the Masai area right round Kilimanjaro, but on the Kenya side. There's a big swamp there called the Kimani, which is rotten with elephant and buffalo. And leopard. And lion, even though you won't be shooting another. And of course the mountain—old Kili and her twin sister, Mawenzi—comes up bright every morning in your tent. You've had Mount Kenya for a spell. We ought to go and see how the other half lives. How's it sound?'

'I think it sounds delightful,' Kate said. 'I've read so much about the Masai I'd hate to leave without seeing them. You say they're related to our Samburu here?'

'Kind of cousins—Nilotic, Hamitic. Beautiful people, and utterly useless for anything at all in this world except what they do beautifully, which is nothing. Maybe that's why I like them. They're a kind of special luxury—like your Red Indian,' Brian said. 'I don't suppose we'll have them with us in a perfect unspoiled state much longer. The political Nigs are a dead cinch to wallop them as soon as Kenya goes all the way black in the next year or so.'

'I don't quite understand,' Paul Drake said. 'I suppose I've tried to absorb too much folklore in a month. *Why* will the political Africans wallop them?'

'Land, for one thing—thousands of lovely square miles of beautiful grazing country we settled on the Masai in the early nineteen-hundreds. Greedy mouths have been watering for many a year over that treaty land. And then the political Nigs think that the Masai are a shame to the country—an impediment to progress—like the game. They're simple, naked savages who haven't changed a custom since the white man came, except they aren't allowed to raid much any more. And they have to go—just as the animals are going and will continue to go. It's a very sore point with me.' Brian's voice harshened. 'I'd change it if I could—exterminate the townies and keep the real savages properly savage.'

'I can see that,' Paul Drake said, 'but you'll have to indulge a tenderfoot. *Why* does it have to go? Why must the elephants and the Masai go? Certainly people like you and I don't shoot enough of the elephants to make a dent in the population, and we are more than happy to pay to come to the country. Seems to me that both the elephant and Masai would be an asset to national wealth—to tourism, if nothing else, under any sort of government—black or white.'

Brian's voice sharpened.

'You've a great argument, Paul,' he said. 'Try it some time on one of these damned black politicians. For that matter, try it on the impassioned white settler who must have the land for his bloody cattle at the expense of both the wildlife and the wild native. You really want to know why they'll go?'

'That's what I asked,' Paul Drake said. 'Why?'

'The so-called advanced, the "emerged" African is ashamed of his naked brother at the same time he's greedy for the land. He sees progress only in terms of everybody wearing a frock-coat and patent-leather shoes. And for some reason they're literally on record with this idiocy—they think that a backward country can't show progress until after all the animals are dead and the land turned to agriculture. I've actually heard politicians say in the Legco —the Legislative Council—that America didn't become great until you killed all your bison, and that England didn't become powerful until they had eliminated the wolves. Black logic!' Brian spat in the fire. 'All *this*'—he swept his arm around in its characteristic possessive gesture—'all this to go, to make room for bloody shanty-towns and piddling agricultural projects for a bunch of black no-hopers who'll breed themselves right off the land after they've killed everything in it, including their own people, that makes the place worth living in! I'd like to arm the Masai and the Turks and Samburu and turn 'em loose to clobber the whole miserable, sneaking, conniving lot!'

'Here, here, chum,' Kate said soothingly. 'You'll burst a blood vessel. Have another cup of coffee and simmer down . . .'

*

'Strange and rather violent young man from time to time,' Paul Drake said after Brian had excused himself to go to bed. 'Full of contradictions. He has been telling me some little stuff about the Emergency here. He doesn't give himself much the best of it, but I gather our boy was quite functional in these parts.'

'He was decorated twice for some of the things he did,' his sister said. 'Muema told me in his best English. I asked Brian and he admitted it, grudgingly. Seems the Queen hung the medal on him personally.'

Her brother yawned. He tossed his cigarette in the fire, looked up at the clear purple sky above him and stretched.

'I think I'll seek my couch, too. He nearly walked my legs off after that kudu. It was worth it, but I must say I feel it now the excitement's worn off. You coming?' He got up and stood in front of the fire, warming his seat.

Kate smiled up at him.

'No,' she said. 'I think I'll sit and commune with the hyenas a little longer. I may not like the ones we meet in that Loitoki-something. These have been beautifully friendly. Haven't snapped my face off yet, no matter what tall tales our gallant white hunter tells us. Good night, Bro.'

'You know, it's been a long time since you called me "Bro"?' her brother said.

'It's been a long time since I felt like we were kids again,' Kate said. 'Go on to bed, or you'll have me in tears. 'Night.'

She sat and looked at the fire for a very long time, watching the logs crumble and fall into rosy-hearted ash. She caught herself finally in a chain explosion of tremendous yawns, and got up to go to the little green toilet tent before she pulled off her robe and fell into bed in the woolly pyjamas she always put on after her pre-dinner bath. It had been several days, now, she thought, walking down the twisty path with her torch flicking its yellow tongue ahead of her, since she had thought of having a drink of anything more vehement than a Coke.

CHAPTER THREE

So now they had left Mawingo, left the stern portrait of Mr. Ray Ryan staring in the reception hall, left the huge drums, left the big suites with the oily-smelling cedar fires, left the hot baths, the view of The Mountain through the enormous glass windows of the big lounge. Katie Crane was driving alone with Brian. They had left Paul and the power wagon behind in a flurry of dust, and had headed swiftly right round Nairobi.

'You're sure you don't want to stop at the hotel and have lunch?' Brian said, as they approached the town. 'I know we told Paul we'd picnic on the other side, but he's just behind us and we can always flag him.'

'Unless there's something you want to do, no,' Katie said. 'Not for me. I personally don't care if I never see another town as long as I live. Not,' she added, 'that any decent dive would allow me entry in my current state of gorgeous disarray. How can you bear the sight of me?'

'I manage. Actually, I think you're rather fetching with that dirt on your nose and your hair sort of steel-woolly with the dust. However, I may be prejudiced because you behave so unwomanly well on safari. Let's press on then and make the Sultan in a hurry.'

So they had driven on and were waiting now in the tiny, dusty, child-littered one-street town of Sultan Hamud, on the Kenya-Tanganyika border, watching the life of the town stroll by. It seemed a lively place.

'Basin Street,' Brian laughed, speaking rapidly, like a carnival barker. 'De place where de dark and de white folks meet. Crossroads of the world.'

Katie Crane gazed round her, fascinated. Two rather bleary-looking de-tribalized Masai were sprawled on the ground, their backs against the plaster wall of an Indian general store. They wore undented sombrero-like hats, ragged white men's clothes, and were drinking turn-about from a bottle of cheap South African wine. A sweating, shining black Kamba woman wearing a multi-patched brassière was moving slowly through the dusty street, a large basket of yams on her head. She seemed surrounded equally by flies and children. The naked children, pot-bellied and jabbering shrilly, were in turn beset by flocks of chickens and occasional stray goats and pigs. Empty racks with fragments of rotting vegetables still attracting flies bespoke a market-place. Two bare-breasted Masai women, heavily beaded and braceleted, strolled hip-swinging through the centre of the single street, followed by a line of children, completely naked. A barefoot Sikh in dirty baggy pyjamas and soiled turban, his fierce black beard caught in a hair-net, walked into a slab-sided iron-roofed shack which housed the telegraph equipment for the little town.

'Historic country we're in,' Brian said. 'It's not so far from here that the Masai and the Wakamba had a dandy little dust-up not so long ago. *Shauri ya ngombe*—bit of misunderstanding about who was rustling whose steers. Good and bad Injuns left for dead on both sides—Masais bristling with Wakamba arrows and the Kambas nicely aerated with those nasty long-grooved spears.'

They entered the biggest *dukah*, which proclaimed Jafferali on its sign-board, and Katie looked round her. Flyspecked pictures of the old Aga Khan, the Begum, and the new Aga Khan were tacked to the plyboard walls. Garish calendars exhorted no-kink hair-oil, godawful cosmetics for coloured ladies, various nostrums for the purification of the blood, and the undoubtedly benign necessity of cola drinks. She noticed that the coloured ladies and gentlemen on the smeary posters seemed considerably lighter and more selfconsciously European than the coloured ladies and gentlemen outside.

'I am particularly intrigued by this lofty moral legend,' she said, pointing to a violent lithograph which extolled the virtues of cash as opposed to credit. 'Remind me never to lend you any money.'

'I suppose they tack these things up for the poorer natives' benefit,' Brian said. 'Because God knows the country's run on credit—or was. That chap in the *dukah* at Isiolo told me that things were getting tighter all the time. The Indians ship a great deal of their money out of the country—always have—and now the whites are starting to do the same thing as *uhuru* approaches. What with people sneaking out money and nobody investing, with everybody scared stiff about what'll happen next, the country's damned near in a state of paralysis.'

'Stop it,' Katie said. 'No dreary economics, please. I buy my fiscal doom from brother dear. I don't want to hear about commercial sordidness. I'm a Masai belle, and you have to woo me with copper wire and blue beads or you can't come courting to my wigwam, or whatever it is I live in.'

'*Manyatta*,' Brian corrected her, as they walked out into the bright sunlight. 'It's a sort of little flat-topped wickiup, you people call it, made out of limber branches and cow dung and mud and sometimes hides. When Mum decides to move to new quarters, she collects her framework and the skins and piles the whole caboodle on top of a Somali canary—like that little chap over there.' He pointed to a dun-coloured Masai donkey with tiny feet and a stripe running down its back and across its shoulders. It was not much bigger than a large dog. 'Then they set fire to the old camp-ground, to appease the gods and keep down disease. Then they move on to where the grass is greener, or at least existent. Poor old girls never get a chance to settle down.'

He smiled at a Masai warrior.

'*Sobaj*,' he said, and held up his hand, palm outward to the warrior.

'*Sobaj*,' the Masai grunted without much enthusiasm, and stalked on.

'That's Masai for "hello", like *jambo*,' Brian said. 'I don't know much Masai. It's a very difficult language.'

'He's gorgeous,' Katie said. 'If Paul is thinking of buying those twin Samburu chicks, I don't see why I can't have me a Masai to take home. He's really lovely to look at. I bet he smells real ripe, too, in all that goose-grease make-up.'

The Masai stood well over six feet in the dull-red toga which was gathered over the left shoulder, leaving his right shoulder and most of the left side of his body bare. His hair had been fancifully roached and clubbed, and then brought forward to make a high ridge atop his head and fall onto his forehead in a thick, brass-ornamented pigtail with a wire ferrule on its end. The remainder of his locks had been carefully plaited and clay-anointed. They hung to shoulder length in a long page-boy bob of twisted braids. He had been freshly smeared with red clay and grease, and long designs of lime crossed his cheeks and split his forehead between the eyes, disappearing into his hair. His face was partially covered in the brighter vermilion—it had been laid on as if by a giant powder-puff, in one great daub. He wore a tight choker-collar of blue and red beads, with shiny mock-pearl buttons worked in as studs. His vastly pierced ears contained three separate sets of earrings, the largest circlets of copper wire as big as saucers, the smallest thick, polished bone with ebon outsides and china-white insides. His shoulders and chest were dotted with clan tattooing in tiny welts.

Bracelets circled his wrists and ankles. In his right hand he carried the spear of a full *moran*, one grade behind senior, its long bright deep-guttered blade over five feet long. Tucked under the other arm was the inevitable polished baton without which the bush African considers himself naked.

The narrow eyes under the long, low lids were studiedly insolent, and so was the entire mould of feature—thin, aquiline nose, high cheekbones and sensuous lips back-turned over dazzlingly white teeth. The figure, the head, the entire man was straight out of Roman history—a bronze copy of Trajan. His greased sweating body glittered in the sun, and his carriage seemed at once languidly fluid and unbelievably erect. His whole bearing shouted arrogance. He stopped in the middle of the dusty street to talk to a brother *moran* who might have been his twin. Standing, stork-like, leaning on their spears with one foot braced inside the hollow below their knees, they were completely oblivious of the honking of Brian's lorry as it rolled into the village. The lorry stopped dead; the men continued to talk. Their togas fell away from their cocked legs, showing them completely nude. They seemed sublimely unconscious, but were perhaps even more smugly conscious, of the casual display of their genitalia.

'Whoo-ee!' Katie Crane whistled. 'Daddy, buy me that!'

'Why not?' Brian laughed. 'We've plenty of penicillin in the medical kit. And I'll warrant you'd need some instanter. I must tell you and Paul some

Masai lore. Shocking morals, these people have. They pass infection around like it was a horn of beer. I believe the average count puts them at about ninety-seven per cent venereal.'

'We could always boil him a few days and shoot him full of chloromycetin or something,' Katie said. 'I just hate to waste all that gorgeous raw material because of a little detail like rampant VD. Tell me, are the younger ladies as pretty as the men?'

'Catch 'em really young enough, yes. There have been some times, on a full moon, after a longish spell in the bush, well——' Brian rolled his eyes upward. 'But crasser things kept crowding in front of me and my ethereal thoughts. Visions of long spears and very sharp *simis* and angry male relatives danced before my eyes, and remembrances of standing down wind from the local belles came fragrantly to mind. I might overcome everything else, including mutual racial prejudice and a kind of persistent, double-barrelled gonorrhoea, but I don't think I could lick the smell of rancid grease and goat-flavoured *manyatta*. Perhaps, as you say, if you boiled one long enough.'

A sort of rumbling clank, comparable to the noise a large bale of bolts might make if someone pushed it over a cliff, jangled to a snorting halt behind the lorry. Paul Drake climbed stiffly down from the high running-board and made a joke out of exaggeratedly turning his ankles.

'I've been used to American submarine automobiles so long I keep forgetting you need a parachute to bail out of this cement-mixer,' he said. 'Where would a stranger get a drink around this fleabit metropolis?'

'Over thar, stranger,' Brian said. 'Belly up to the bar and name your pizen. I'll guarantee you'll get it—poison, that is. Wait a minute and I'll dig out a bottle of actual non-blinding gin. Let's go inside and let you drink it in the shade. Our Hindu friend has new tonic. Commander Whitehead's colonial emissary just pulled away.'

'You're in rather a bubbly mood today, my friend,' Paul Drake said. 'Good trip, Kate? My God, you *are* filthy, and Brian looks like a chimney-sweep. I thought this was supposed to be the start of the rainy season. Even the black-top was dusty, what there was of it, and that Thika area—— Whew!' He wiped his forehead with the back of a hand leaving a lewd-looking space of eroded brow behind. 'That's a Masai, huh? The fellows with the long sharp sticks?'

'That's a suburban sample,' Brian said. 'They get woollier and wilder the farther out you go. Where we're landing later this afternoon they're complete nature boys. Just blood and milk and lion you-know-whats for breakfast. Like 'em?'

'Certainly are gaudy. Any real man hidden under the do-it-yourself permanents and the home-cooked cosmetics or is it all Elizabeth Arden?'

'Lot of man under that skimpy red shift,' his sister said. 'The wind flirted up one corner and I can vouch for the fact. Yessir. I'm going to buy me a brace of these to keep me company on the long cold winter nights in Palm Beach.' Paul Drake's sister suddenly leaned over and kissed his cheek. Paul Drake looked startled.

'What's that for? Why this sudden burst of unwarranted affection?'

'Because I love you,' Katie said. 'Because I love you and I'm having a marvellous time and you make jokes now and sound like a human being instead of a stockbroker and you don't looked frightened about me any more, as if I were sneaking gin on the side or was about to whip off into the bushes with Brian.'

'Well,' Paul Drake said. 'Try to restrain yourself. You'll be giving the natives ideas. What about that gin and tonic?'

'Coming up,' Brian said. 'I rang the office before we left Nanyuki, Paul. Newspapers and your mail to be delivered here. I'll send the lorry in a couple of times a week. We're only seventy-odd miles away. All right?' They walked into the *dukah* and sat down at a shaky table in the corner.

'Sure. But you could have skipped the papers. That nightly news is gloomy enough. Looks like my man Nixon has slipped; Kennedy's got him on the run. Well, the hell with it. For the next two weeks they can elect the Abominable Snowman and I don't care. Damn, that's good. There's something to be said for this drinking business. Gin seems to taste better out here than it does in New York.'

Brian leaned back and tilted his front chair-legs off the floor of the little Indian general store. He looked at his client, Mr. Paul Drake, member of the Stock Exchange, banker, Social Register, multi-millionaire. Drake was wearing a dun-coloured oil-smeared low-peaked British squire cap which, pulled back on his sparse-haired skull, now revealed a naked expanse of startling white above the dirt-caked sunburned face. He had removed his sunglasses from his nose, which bore a white ring over the bridge. The glasses were hanging, dangling rakishly from one ear. Drake had one insect-chewed ankle crossed over a dirty knee, and his sockless calves were criss-crossed with thorn scratches above the filthy rawhide desert boots. He was fattening up his drink with another stout hooker of gin when Brian started to laugh.

'What the hell are you laughing at?' Drake asked.

'I'm laughing at you—at you and your sister and me, too, I suppose,' Brian said. 'I guess I'm laughing because I'm happy and you people seem to be happy as well. This country vaccinates everybody, but on some it doesn't take. It's bitten the pair of you as badly as I ever saw it. I guess that's why I laughed. I'm happy to see it.'

Paul Drake smiled.

'I suppose you're right,' he said, a little sheepishly. 'I keep telling myself I'm a damned fool, but I think this may be the only fun I ever really had in my life. It isn't just the shooting . . . it's the . . . all this. All of it. Katie's sunburnt nose and my BO and both of us filthy as tramps. Masai warriors peeking into the Land Rover's rear-view mirror. That broken-nosed cannibal Muema. I never knew you could have so much fun being miserable before. Ridiculous. If you're bookable for next year consider yourself booked. It's nice I'm so rich. You have to be very rich to enjoy being this uncomfortable.'

'You're booked,' Brian said. 'But right now I think you'd better gulp that

208

gin and we'll take off. Road's not too good for the last thirty miles or so. The innkeeper says there was quite a lot of rain down thataway, although you'd never know it from here. I hope it did rain, some. It'll green things up a bit and make it pleasanter all round. This can be awfully dusty country. You come pile in the Rover with Kate and me now, Paul. I'll send the other two vehicles ahead again. We'll have some lunch when we find a nice spot and they can be pitching camp while we meander in. I like to get the tents up before night, when I can. Easier on the boys after a long day on the road.'

They had driven through broad green fields that looked like Italian rye but which Brian said was true wild grass just popping through, lightly fuzzing the red earth. The dust had subsided somewhat, and the Land Rover sang smoothly on a hard clay road occasionally rutted deeply by baked gullies where oversized tyres on big vehicles had fought the mud during the short rains of the past week. They had stopped briefly under a spreading yellow-dappled acacia to eat hard-boiled eggs and tongue sandwiches from the chop-box, and Brian produced a thermos full of hot bouillon. As they ate, large herds of zebra and wildebeest grazed tamely in the near distance, showing like chessmen against the gently rolling wave of tender new grass. Apart from the zebra and the crazy-bucking, head-twisting wildebeest, who looked mane-heavy like American bison as they ran senselessly about, smaller herds of caramel-coloured kongoni grazed, staring stupidly and benignly, and here and there small white blurs of horn-heavy Grant gazelles seemed over-balanced as they walked mincingly tilted forward.

'It's a zoo, that's what it is,' Katie said. 'Just one damned huge wonderful zoo. And Brian says it'll all be gone some day—some day soon. It makes me want to cry. Everything seems so happy here—so sort of Garden of Edenish.'

'It is—when you're away from the bloody people,' Brian said. 'Out here everything feels right—in place. I can see it on my face—even more clearly on yours.'

They repacked the chopbox and drove again through country that swelled in hills and rose sharply in heavy stands of forest against the soft-blue distant mountain. The sky was tumbled with fleeced cumulus, as the long rains continued to build. They passed only one stake-palisaded village as they ran on the major road, which showed the fresh scrape of bulldozing. Some scattered herds of Masai cattle fed black and white and red on the green slopes, and occasionally they met thin-shanked Masai men, their spears carried over their shoulders, their laden women trudging behind them, short thick legs sturdy beneath huge pots balanced on their heads. Occasionally the skeleton or stinking half-eaten carcass of a cow exhibited a guardian vulture.

'Been a long drought,' Brian said. 'I suppose these critters died on their way to fresh grazing. No epidemic, but I've noticed that most of the stock is very thin. Of course they'll move out of the swamps and up in the hills pretty soon. Where we'll camp, you can see the progress daily. By following the flies, if nothing else.'

'I'd love to be a lady Masai,' Katie said. 'I really would. Nothing to do but

209

have orgies with the boys, if what I've heard is true, and coax a little fluid out of a cow for the daily meal. You ever taste that stuff they carry in these big gourds, Brian?'

'Once or twice,' Brian shuddered. 'I got suckered into a senior *laibon*'s— that's a kind of chief medicine man and civic-leader type—*manyatta* and they pressed hospitality upon me. You know what that stuff is, of course—a mixture of blood and milk, curdled in cow urine and wood ash. It certainly sustains life. Masai mostly look in peak condition. But my God, it tastes exactly like what you'd expect of a mixture of blood and milk and cow pee and ashes.'

'Gah,' Katie said. 'No thank you. I'll add that to my wagon list. Vodka, gin and Masai clabber. Now, drool, what about the orgies?'

Brian scratched his head.

'I don't suppose you could call them orgies, exactly. You see, the Masai is basically a sun-worshipper. Everything comes from the sun. They are the original fertilization-rite patent-holders. Maybe summat like your old Aztecs. I don't think they consider sex as S-E-X. It's mainly a thing people do, as people like to have lots of cattle to look at and reflect how rich they are——'

'Bankers,' Paul Drake muttered. 'Cutting the coupons.'

'And travel all the time. And not thinking about much but the old traditional wars the white man won't let them play at any more and the lions the white man doesn't want them to kill. Everything that's good comes from the sun and earth, and everything good is cattle and donkeys and goats and sheep. But mostly cattle. They will do anything for cattle. They—this could be a touch gamy, Katie. . . .'

'I'm game for the gamy bits,' Katie said. 'I know about *vive la différence*. Continue and I shall hide my blushes under this six-inch coat of mobile earth I'm wearing.'

'Well, in the circumcision ceremonies, which only come in special years, sometimes as much as seven apart, the young candidate sits on a cowhide and after the medicine man crops a sliver out of the foreskin, the young man then has to ignore the pain and blood and demonstrate his manhood by having successful intercourse with a hole in the earth. And in other fertility ceremonies some of the proven warriors have to do the decent thing by she-asses——'

Brian's voice was embarrassed.

'I suppose they do sound shocking types, but they really aren't. They're— they're just Masai. You see, the young men have to put in about fifteen years of three-stage warriorhood before they cut their hair and get married and start to raise a family. They work hard under the drillmasters and the old *laibons*—a forty-mile march in a day under this sun is nothing, *and* without food or water. So the tribe figures that nothing's too good for the fighting man in his spare time. Soldier's pay.

'So they have free access to all the maidens—and for all I know, young matrons as well, because there doesn't seem to be any real sexual jealousy among them. Apart from a lot of giggling, there's nothing very shy about their approach to each other. All the gals ask is that the boys deliver the potatoes, so to speak.'

'A hard man is good to find,' her brother volunteered brightly.

'Paul! Really! I think we do have a sex maniac on our hands, Brian,' Katie said. 'I promise you he was *never* like this at home.'

'The girls never seem to have any babies until they're ready to settle down with a husband,' Brian continued. 'And a man may establish his right to dally with the maiden by striking his spear into the earth in front of her hut, or merely dragging her off to the bush. Nobody dares intrude if that spear's stuck in front of the hut or on a path leading to a cosy nook in the bush. No mystery, no pretence, very little covering of the body, no shame—and still no licence outside the tribe. They're tremendously race-conscious.

'They look down on all other peoples, as if all the world was a single slave —and yet they've never been much of a slave-taking tribe. Nor were they any use as slaves. The old Arab slavers tried it. They wouldn't eat—died of home-sickness like penned animals. But when they used to fight, they killed *everybody*—old, young, male, female, the lot. Mostly, all they ever stole was cattle.

'They were a dying tribe for a while—as little as ten or a dozen years ago they were dwindling every year. Nobody really knew why—except syphilis and changing times. The reason the ones we'll see are such hearty physical specimens is that natural selection and child-killing as well weeds out the scrubs and the monsters. But lately they've been breeding up, not so perfect, probably due to more medical posts scattered around, and I don't like it.'

'You don't like it? I thought you loved the Masai,' Paul Drake said.

'I do, and that's why I don't like it. In the last two or three years I've noticed for the first time that you see permanent Masai *shambas* with perma-nent stands of crops growing. They're slowly settling down and becoming agriculturists. They can't fight—they've lost their fire. They're drinking more. Around here there are two or three *manyattas* now that are not only permanent, but can only be called towns, with an Indian *dukah*, cheap brandy, tribal police, and an elder with a bloody great brass badge hung round his neck. They're beginning to wear pants—you saw a couple at Sultan Hamud—and old overcoats and hats. They're even getting political. And pretty soon they'll get more and more political and more and more de-tribalized and town-loving and booze-fancying and then they'll crossbreed with the Bantu black gentry and you'll have just another mixed-up bastard population. Farmers!' Brian made a spitting sound. 'Bloody agriculturists, when they used to terrify the whole of East Africa from Mombasa to the Congo—when they used to kill lions single-handed with spears to prove the right to wear the headdress of a man, and when they left a trail of blood behind them thousands of miles long when they made their great trek from wherever it was they were hatched.'

'This Dermott lad really hates progress,' Katie said. 'So do I, unless it's

211

leading me towards a hot bath. Much longer, Bwana? My posterior is one long solid ache.'

'Not much,' Brian said. 'A few miles only. That lovely swatch of green under the knobby hills on your left is part of this Kimani swamp.'

'I really don't care about shooting much of anything any more except maybe some birds and—of course—the leopard,' Paul Drake said. 'You've thrown so much leopard talk at me that I'm about to get a fixation. You've got me thinking they're bewitched, and only come to special magic.'

Brian laughed. 'Just wait until you see your first one,' he said. 'You won't joke. Leopards have a most profound and frightening effect on people. Known to sunder old friendships and break up solid marriages. Well, just round this bend and over that hill and across a stream and up another hill and down and right and there we'll be. It's a lovely spot—and stiff with friendly lions and inquisitive rhino.'

As they came to the top of the last hill, he pointed down. The lorry and the power wagons were long black slugs against a carpet of tender green. Standing also green and cool to the eyes, the mess tent peaked light against a black bulk of trees. A long line of deeper green, lacily friezed against the sky by towering, flat-topped acacias, hedged the outer edges of what could only be a low, wet, vividly verdant swampland which spread flatly until it ran up a yellowed hill which turned darker and darker green as its rounded summit stopped brusquely, clearly superimposed on a higher hill of soft purplish blue. A cotton-roll of clouds tumbled over the plateau of the long blue range, and behind it one corner of Kilimanjaro showed a strip of snow. Its top, however, was lost in a solid cloud bank of dazzling whiteness over the clear azure of sky.

'Home,' Brian said, grinding to a halt. 'Everybody out. Ladies' room going up, I see. Mess tent pitched, tables out, chairs out, booze-box unlocked, fire in arf a mo', other tents a-raising. Dermott organization triumphs again. You'll have your bath as soon as your tents're up, chaps. Have a drink and take it easy while I just go *chunga* up the boys.'

He ran at a lope over to where they were unloading the lorry, leaped nimbly over the cab to the top of the load and standing, fists on hips, began to give orders like a ship's first mate supervising cargo discharge. Paul Drake wandered down a game path to a little bluff below which he could hear the gurgling exciting scurry of a river.

Katie Crane sank into a camp-chair and sighed. This was another close-held portion of it, the little-girl-playing-house part that she loved. This was the night-before-Christmas part and for her it was possibly the culmination of the components of safari which she had, womanlike, sorted into parcels and packets. Once again she was struck by the calculated efficiency which could transform a strip of dung-pebbled sward in a howling wilderness into a thriving village with most of, if not all, the comforts of a good hotel.

Mwende, the old Wakamba-Swahili Number One, was busy with his provision boxes in the green mess tent. She thought idly that some insight to

Brian Dermott was provided by the fact that most of his 'boys' were old. Most of them had been inherited as a smoothly functioning team from the old days of game control. None ever left Brian; some died, some were pastured, an occasional replacement was sacked, but the dependable corps of old sweats remained with the Bwana.

There was a strict caste system in camp, she noted; stiff protocol rigidly adhered to. Mwende, old, snuff-coloured and horse-faced under his little white Muslim *kafiyeh*, was the undoubted headmaster of the crew, although the even older, prune-wrinkled cook Aly, a coastal Swahili and of course Mohammedan, was almost co-equal and rode with Mwende in the cab of the big Diesel lorry with the driver, a burly Luo they called Machoini, 'Four Eyes', because of his glittering spectacles.

The driver Machoini came under the head of technician, since he was expert on Diesel engines and understood every girlish caprice of the massive, lumbering truck. As a technician he associated chiefly with other technicians —with Muema the gunbearer, who also was responsible for the maintenance of the power wagon and the Land Rover. These two usually ate together, and occasionally invited a local expert, tracker or game scout, to feed with them. As gunbearer, Muema divided the choicest bits with old Kidogo; pre-empting the fat, livers and ribs, since they had first whack at the prime portions of the game when it was butchered on the killing scene.

Kidogo, the old Ndrobo, occupied a position all to himself. He ate alone —except when Brian occasionally excused himself and went back to Kidogo's private cookfire to squat on his heels and gossip with the old man. Kidogo was a strange sort of shadow to Brian—combining some multiple aspects of father, teacher, bodyguard, business consultant, last authority on game and country, trusting child, and finally, involuntary conscience. Katie had seen Kidogo rebuke Brian sharply, and Brian had heeded. She had heard them disagree, and watched Brian cede to the old man's word.

Kidogo, then, was different even from Muema, although they shared nearly equal status in the hunting car. Another fraternity apart were the two skinners, who also doubled, grumbling, as porters during the heavy loading and unloading. Finally came the personal boys; one each for her brother and herself, the senior one of whom, Matia, helped Mwende serve at table. Mwende himself was jealously personal nurse to Brian.

The carboy didn't do much of anything but remain leeched to the car to see that nobody stole the guns and equipment when they all left the vehicle to follow an animal. He wrestled out the chopbox and helped to change tyres and generally made himself handy with the thermos and the spare sweaters and the loose ends of back-seat tackle. There were finally four lumpy-muscled porters, who seemed perpetually questing dry dead wood for the several fires that always burned in the camp, and who tugged at the big steamed-out petrol tins when the lorry went on its water-seeking expeditions. One of the porters, member of some tribe which was not defiled by association with the toilet tents, was also called the '*cho*-boy', and his task was to supervise the canvas structure which Brian described as the 'sanit'ry cubicle'. The *cho*-boy dug latrine holes and filled them again, and it was his responsibility to see that the rather primitive throne accumulated no splinters. The *cho*-boy and the kitchen *mtoto*—the cook's scullery boy—rounded out the compact little crew.

Now they were all scurrying industriously to make her new home grow, while she sat and watched the sun squeezing itself to sleep behind the long blue hills. The carboy, the skinners, and the *cho*-boy were busy snaking great snaggled segments of fallen thorn logs from the bush at the edges of the meadow which formed the camp site. Soon there would be a massive heap of logs in front of the mess tent, and already Aly had started pampering a small blaze on the cookfire fifty yards away, close to where the vehicles were parked. Nearly the whole camp burst miraculously from the seemingly bottomless back of the Diesel. The tents came out rolled tight and secured in canvas jackets; the chairs and beds folded onto themselves; the table silver was cushioned in a velvet-lined box, and the plates, cups and glasses were not plastic, as she first had feared, but decent, if thick, china and glassware. The long line of stout, very heavy wooden boxes over which old Mwende was now fussing held all the staples, ranging from tinned goods to cigarettes to whisky —salt, sugar, toilet paper, ketchup, mixed pickles and condiments. Mwende kept a key to all the boxes—only the ready box stood open. It contained odds and ends—books and binoculars and such-like that people forgot at the last moment of moving. The wooden cases of Coke and beer and tonic and wine stood stacked neatly one on the other. The wooden flaps of the heavy box that housed the kerosene-driven refrigerator were gaped open, and a steady reassuring hum promised fresh ice-cubes in a couple of hours. Mwende was already stowing eggs, butter and green vegetables into the icebox, and she saw him slide a bottle of white wine very gently onto one of the wire trays.

Her tent was nearly up; she could hear the splintery smash of the mauls as they sunk the pegs diagonally deep into the stiff earth, and the straining grunts as the boys hauled the tent-ropes taut. Her room-boy Matia was unfolding the bed, and his partner, Chalo, was blowing up the mattress with a bicycle pump. Already the canvas basin-holder was standing, and from where she sat she could see the porters carrying her long black tin safari box from the Land Rover to the tent. One of the men was swishing a *panga* to cut a pathway that led from the cleared space where her sleeping-tent stood to where the 'untouchable' porter was calling for his mate to help him erect the lavatory tent. The four-legged stool with the anti-splinter seat stood primly to one side, and leaning against it was the spade with which the Untouchable had just dug the latrine.

They had lit the big fire, now, and the cook's assistant was staggering balanced between two wooden-handled debbie tins of water, which he placed almost in the blaze. Mwende was bringing the Cokes and whisky and gin and the syphon and the tall insulated ice-bucket now. He opened a Coke for her and unsprung the vacuum top from the ice-bucket. She fished out a couple of cubes and dropped them in the tall glass. The old headboy poured her drink and handed her a fresh packet of cigarettes and a box of matches and slapped down the two books she had been carrying in the glove compartment of the Land Rover.

Her brother's tent was lurching up now, and so was Brian's. The gun-bearers were taking out the cased guns and the put-together guns, the medicine kit and the chopbox, from the back of the Land Rover, carrying them over to a canvas groundsheet under the big acacia close to where they were erecting Brian's tent. Over by the kitchen, the cook-shack tent was already up, and a jumbled mound of canvas even farther away would eventually unfold and blossom into a small village of the boys' shelter halves.

'This is going to be a very happy camp, I think.' Brian had come back now from his overseeing chores. 'Boys like it. Plenty of water in the river for washing and cooking. Won't have the water chore to bother them. Plenty of dead wood, too. Always a help when those two commodities are easy to hand.'

He poured himself a small Scotch and added water.

'What do you think, Memsaab? Bwana?' he asked. 'How about these fever trees?' He waved a hand at the towering canopies of the dappled umbrella thorns, barely visible now against the sky as suddenly darkness plunged on the camp. 'Just like the movies.'

'Wonderful,' Katie said. 'We were just saying.'

'You suppose there're any leopards along this river?' her brother asked. 'I thought I saw tracks down there.'

'Oho. Leopard fever already, like I said, eh?' Brian grinned and sipped his drink. 'Yep. Bags of 'em here. I just had a word with Muema, who's been down casing the joint. One big male and a largish female, fresh today. Not surprising. They'll always stick close to the water and the larder. Masses of impala—I guess you saw that one herd—and plenty of pig, Paul. No trouble.'

One of the room-boys came up from the sleeping-tent area and said something to Brian.

'He says your tent's ready and the *bafu*'ll be hot in ten minutes if you want to lose some topsoil, Katie. I told him okay. You too, Paul?'

'Fine,' Paul Drake said. 'I'll sleep tonight. I'll die. Me for bed as soon as we've eaten.'

Katie saw the boys lugging the tins of hot water down to the tents. One of them was lifting the hind skirts of the tent and sliding in the brown canvas tub, which was shaped like a long, slim coffin and seemed invariably and magically to locate itself over a thornbush or a sharp rock in exactly the precise position to make contact with her behind. The other room-boy was pouring water in the shower tin, which had its own separate tent, about the same size as the latrine tent. It had a tiny boardwalk already laid in front of it, and its raised draining platform was inside. Katie Crane sighed. Brian looked at her inquiringly.

'What?'

'Nothing. I was just thinking that pretty soon I'll have to leave it, and there may never be a next time. It's like building a home you know you'll have to tear down, and maybe never see again.'

Brian nodded.

'I know. It hits me the same way. You always feel a little sad when you make a good camp, because it *is* home while you're in it. And then you strike it and police the bits of paper and bury the tins and suddenly it's just bush again. In a way I feel the same about the whole country as it stands—beautiful but impermanent, and for how long, O Lord, how long?'

The personal boy was back now, to filch two lanterns from a circle of pressure lamps that old Mwende was pumping and lighting.

'*Bafu tayari*, Memsaab,' he said in his soft Wakamba voice.

'See you when I'm clean and sweet and kissable,' Katie said, getting stiffly out of her chair, and pressing down on her knees to straighten the joints. 'Don't drink up all the whisky tonight, gentlemen. Save some for when you've shot the leopard.'

'Anything I do loathe is reformed drunks,' her brother said loudly to her back, as she followed the boy down the fresh-chopped path to her tent. 'They're all the same—awful. Moralizers. Bluenoses.'

His sister turned and stuck out her tongue at him.

'Bluenose yourself.' She hurried down the pathway. 'Drink yourselves to death, for all I care.'

'You know,' Paul Drake said quietly to Brian. 'I really do think she's all right. But I don't think she could have done it in New York. Now, if she could only locate herself a good man . . .'

'She's all right. She'll do fine,' Brian said. 'Katie doesn't need any help from anybody. She's a big girl. The other half before you wash?'

'Thanks.' Paul Drake held out his glass.

CHAPTER FOUR

THE BOY placed one lantern carefully on the little table at the front of the tent and took the other to the rear next the canvas compartment which divided the living-quarters from the washroom. Then he disappeared, and Katie could hear the comforting smooth gush of water as he filled the tub from the debbie cans, nicely balancing the boiling water with the icy cold.

She began to unbutton her jacket, and looked critically, like a good house-wife, around her home. The bed, just so; pale green sheets turned quartering down from the crisp plump pillow over the neat beige blankets. Woolly pyjamas sharply folded atop her dressing-gown. Fresh socks and handker-chiefs, fresh brief pants, fresh bra folded on top of her tin safari box. Clean starched jacket and slacks hanging behind her bed on a wooden hanger. Clean boots dubbined glossy and placed under the canvas-seated chair: for tonight, Russian-topped mosquito boots of soft leather, into which she would tuck her pyjama pants. Clean sweater also on top of the safari box—every-thing ready for tomorrow's use, except of course the nightclothes.

She dropped her jacket on the floor, and automatically checked her table top. Thermos jug full of cold water. Make-up kit, comb and brush laid out. Toothbrush upended in the tooth-mug. Flashlight. Kleenex. Toothpaste. Cigarettes. Cold cream. Matches. The lot. God bless Matia. He never forgot anything—not even the shotty-gun *kidogo*. The little twenty-gauge, oiled, was fitted together and lay, together with an opened box of buckshot shells, just under her bed, ready to hand in case of—what? Probably shoot my own foot off if anything did come in the night, she muttered, kicking herself free of her trousers and letting them fall. She unsnapped her brassière and peeled off her sweaty underpants, and threw them onto the pile of soiled clothing. Bracing herself against the centre ridge-pole, she stripped off her wool socks and kicked them onto the heap. God bless Matia again. The soiled clothes'd be gone by bedtime—returned clean and sweet, washed, starched and pressed when she came into camp tomorrow night.

She walked naked to the tub, the lumpy canvas groundsheet feeling cool and bristly-springy over the cropped grass underfoot. A soapdish sat primly on a folded big towel by the tubside. The water in the tub was steaming gently in the night air, which had suddenly grown nippy cold and was making goosebumps on her bare skin. She touched the water with her toe, then slid into its steamy depth, easing her bottom gingerly to the canvas, remembering old thorns and rocks. She'd have to let the hair go—wash it tomorrow when she could dry it in the sun after lunch. Tonight she didn't care if it got wet—she'd just swaddle it in a scarf and the menfolk could go to blast if they didn't like it.

The bliss of the hot tub was almost insupportable. She lay quietly for a full minute, feeling the ache drain out of her bones and the Kenya topsoil melt away from her skin. She closed her eyes, and felt her mind go as slack as her body. For a long moment she floated outside her body as it lay motion-less in the brownish water. She lay quietly unthinking until she felt the water go from warm to lukewarm and finally to almost cool.

Katie got up, dried herself harshly with the big rough terry towel and reached for her warm wool pyjamas. She stuck her feet into the mosquito boots, tucked in the pants, and then got swiftly into her pyjama jacket and robe. The soft flannel of the PJs felt deliciously cool on her bath-hot body, but the robe managed to wrap the freshly acquired warmth around her.

She twisted her hair into a loose knot and bound her head with a bright kerchief, like the coloured lady in the Aunt Jemina pancake picture, with rabbit-ears standing up from the chignon's knot. Then she looked at her small face, suede-brown, with the cheeks and nose burnt pink, and relieved the whole drab plain with a vivid slash of lipstick. She looked at her nails regretfully; might as well keep them short and unpainted for the rest of the trip. *If they love me at all they'll have to love me ugly.* She smiled at the small face with the great grey eyes, and it was a scrubbed, I-am-a-good-little-girl smile. *At least,* she thought, *I look wholesome. I certainly look healthy.*

There was nobody sitting at the drink-table outside the mess tent, which looked a real dining-room now, with its clean green cloth and napkins and its sparkling china and silver all neatly arrayed. Two big Coleman lamps hissed merrily, one at either end of the tent, purring almost as homely comforting as a teapot going. Black shadows moved quietly across the ground between her fire and the other fires—one, two, three, four fires, now—and the very low sugary rumble of African voices underlaid the night noises.

Brian was obviously having a bath, too. She could see a silhouette move inside his lighted tent, fifty yards away on a little jutland overlooking the river. Brian was truly a creature of habit. He always pitched his tent that way —a decent distance from the clients and their baths and various toiletries; a decent distance away from the mess tent, so the clients might talk normally without considering him if they wished; a decent distance from the boys' tents and the vehicles. Always a too decent distance away from everything and everybody, that was the trouble with Brian. Twice she'd wakened and seen him quietly stalking the night—and once, very late, sitting all alone in front of the fire, lost in the tiny-gleaming embers. That night he had taken his head in his hands and twisted at it savagely, as if trying to shake it loose from some memory that pained him. She had almost joined him that night, but had thought better of it.

The fire was shooting a truly jubilant Roman candle of sparks skyward now, and here was Mwende coming with the salted macadamia nuts and olives and pickles, the tomato juice and the Worcester sauce. He'd bring the hot hors-d'œuvre only when the men arrived, shiny from soap, tooth-marks of the comb fresh in their shower-damp hair. Both of them looked better then than at any other time. Her brother seemed larger, less proper, with his collar open and the fire lighting his new ruddy tan. And Brian, burned as toasted brown as a waffle, could be positively gorgeous with the sun-gold hair tamed and his big teeth showing white against the night-shadowed tan. *Positively gorgeous—what are you thinking, my girl? Could it be you've been in the bush too long, and are about to make the usual shipboard mistake? Well, don't, girl,* she thought; *it'll get you nowhere, neither now nor later. Have an olive, instead. Go take a cold shower.*

She was looking dreamily into the fire and listening to a bush baby cry when Brian walked quietly up and dropped into a chair beside her.

'Look who's all beautiful and clean,' he said. 'Surely not the same filthy female I decanted from the Rover an hour ago?'

'It is indeed I,' she said. 'Tess of the Storm Country. I am maybe the cleanest girl in East Africa. You run a nice motel, Bwana. The service is excellent here. I have an idea: you need a cruise director. Sign me on and I'll never leave you.'

Brian got hurriedly up and stood with his hands behind him, legs spraddled in front of the fire. Katie noticed with some amusement that the country-week-end clothes he had first worn—the too-much hacking jacket, the silk sports shirt—had dived deeper and deeper towards the bottom of his box, in direct ratio to the speed with which they had all become homefolks. Now he was wearing a light wool jersey and an old pair of corduroy trousers, washed creamy from some darker colour.

'I don't think I'd better,' he said. 'People would say we're in love.' He stopped. He hadn't intended the flip line from the old song in *Oklahoma!* He covered it by lighting a cigarette. 'There's the first hyena of our new home,' he said, gesturing backwards past the boys' tent. 'Welcoming committee. Sounds affable enough. Well.'

He moved to the drink table, and reached for the gin.

'I think I will make myself a very small martini. You're all right with your tomato juice?'

'Yes,' Katie said, still amused. 'I'm all right. With my tomato juice. I'm fine.'

'Do you miss it very much—the not drinking?'

'No. Not really. Once in a while. It would have been nice tonight, though. Round off the day, sort of. But then there's Paul. We wouldn't want to worry Paul.'

'No,' Brian said woodenly. 'We wouldn't want to worry Paul.'

'But then Paul is a grown man,' Katie said. 'He wouldn't worry about me if what I did was something he approved of me doing.'

'That was a hell of a sentence,' Brian replied. 'You can get there faster than that.'

'I could get there faster than that if I were encouraged to try.'

'What you need is an end that's worth the means,' Brian said. 'I don't know what the hell we're talking about—do you?'

'Yes,' Katie said. 'I know what we're talking about. But relax. You're saved by the bell. Here comes Paul up the path, panting for his martini.'

'I was just thinking,' Brian addressed Paul, 'that we'd better turn in early after dinner. We have to start thinking leopard tomorrow. It will be a busy day. We don't want to play it too close to the rains.'

'Yes, Paul,' Katie said. 'We have to start thinking leopard tomorrow. Do rains make any difference to leopards?'

'Yes,' Brian said. 'They very seldom come in the rain. I don't know why, except nothing in Africa moves about very much during the rains.'

'Suppose you just settle down in your chair and tell us all about leopards so we'll know what not to do wrong,' Katie said. Her voice sounded jarringly unpleasant, sarcastically edged, even to herself.

'What's biting her?' Paul Drake asked the trees. 'She sounds like a woman for the first time in a month.' He pulled down the corners of his mouth.

'It's been a long, hard drive,' Brian said. He was looking past them towards the river.

'It's the prospect of rain,' Katie said. 'It makes the natives nervous. I'm tired all of a sudden. I think I won't bother with food tonight, fellows.' She got up and suddenly hurried down the path to her tent.

'What *is* chewing on her?' her brother said. 'Did I do something? Did you?'

Brian shook his head.

'No. She was fine two minutes ago. I don't understand women. Best left alone when they're edgy. Come on, let's make a pass at the *chakula* and turn in.'

'She's been splendid so far.'

'She's still splendid. She'll be right in the morning. Mwende! *Chakula!*'

In her tent, Katie Crane swallowed two of the red-green-and-brown sleeping pills. This was a night she didn't plan on walking off her insomnia and no matter what you said, a safari cot wasn't the most comfortable bed in the world to toss on; the mosquito netting interfered. She was only tired. It had been a long hard day, and they had to think about leopard tomorrow. She wouldn't want to do or say or even dream anything tonight that might interfere with thinking about leopard tomorrow. The frosty-looking stars, distinct against the night sky, winked almost into her tent, and down the little river something had set the baboons to swearing again. Perhaps they were thinking about the leopard too.

CHAPTER FIVE

VALERIE DUNSTAN DERMOTT had just let herself into the little flat in Hill Street when the phone rang. She flung off her coat, dumped her parcels on a table, threw herself into a chair and picked up the phone, swinging one stockingless gold-sandalled foot over the chair-arm. She made a fetching figure in white silk blouse and high-waisted narrow black velveteen slacks, her mass of straight black hair caught simply behind with a velvet ribbon. You didn't have to wear a skirt when you shopped if you lived in Hill Street —it wasn't Chelsea, but nobody gave it a second thought if you went to the market in trousers.

'It's Val here,' she said into the phone, a little breathlessly. 'Who is it?'

'It's Dawn, darling,' the stylishly hoarse voice at the other end said. 'You sound as if you've just been chased round the room by some delicious man.'

'No such luck,' Valerie said. 'I've been doing me morning chores in the market. It's such a glorious day after all this foul weather that I've gone quite mad with domesticity. What stirs you so early? You always sleep 'til noon.'

'It's a calculated imposition on friendship, darling. I wouldn't think of doing such a dreadful thing to just anybody. I couldn't be so unbelievably lucky as to find you unclaimed for cocktails and dinner tonight, could I?'

'As a matter of dismal fact, you could,' Valerie said, stretching out one foot to drag a side table closer, and reaching for a cigarette from a silver-and-tortoise-shell box.

'Who's let you down this time?' she mumbled, speaking through the cigarette as she tried to strike a match with one hand against a maddeningly mobile box. 'Who am I substituting for tonight?'

'Nobody. That bloody husband of mine has just rung up and landed me with a hurry-up dinner, some last-minute rescue operation for the Secretary who's gone and fallen sick, damn his eyes. I'm trying to sling something together that won't be too gauche and horrible. It's quite important to Logan, actually. We'll have cocktails at the house and go on to the Savoy for dinner, I thought. They're booked in there. Feed 'em and sleep 'em where they fall. Cocktails would ordinarily be easy but the thing is we're stuck with these two visiting muck-mucks all evening. Do be a darling and say you *will* come.'

'Of course,' Valerie Dermott said cheerfully. 'And who, pray, are these gentlemen that poor dear Logan is stuck with that demand such tender care from the Colonial Office? And why me? I'm just a poor colonial myself, and no very great catch of one.'

'That's just it. These people are from out your way—Kenya. And I have to have at least one person who can make a little African sense with them. Logan says they're terribly important out there right now and the Office is doing everything about them it can.'

Valerie frowned.

'I don't know anybody important in Kenya, really, except some white settlers and pieces of my ex's family. It wouldn't——' A horrid thought struck her. 'You wouldn't be playing a ghastly joke and it's Brian——'

'No, no, *no*!' the voice said, hurriedly. 'Nothing like that at all. They *are* sort of settlers, but not exactly white. In point of fact, Val, they're as black as your hat.'

Valerie Dermott was silent for a second, and then she began to laugh.

'*You* want *me* to come to drinks and dinner with a couple of Kenya coons? You want Valerie Dermott from Kenya to amuse a couple of former black houseboys gone political? Oh, Dawn, sweetie, you must be joking. You couldn't be serious.'

'I'm very serious. I couldn't be *more* serious. And I'm not joking about its importance to Logan, either. I don't know if you know their names—Kamau and Matisia——'

'Every third Kikuyu and every second Wakamba in Kenya is named Kamau or Matisia,' Valerie said. 'But there's only one big Kamau—the politician. If it's this Kamau, I'm fascinated.'

'—it's important because there's some bloody great conference or other involving your country starting this week. These chaps are very very important politically, Logan says, and this conference'—her voice dropped on the other end of the wire—'this conference is supposed to be very very vital to the country, a whole new policy change, or something. Some more of this new independence nonsense. I don't know the ins and outs of all this black-face business in the papers. All I know is that sheer desperation was strangling poor dear Log's voice when he rang me. Seems these chaps just got off the plane and they *can't* let them bash around loose all night. Supersensitivity due to being brunettes, or something. Tag, I'm it, and so are you, plum.'

'But why me—of all the white women in London with clean necks you could dig up—why *me*? I should think I'd be the last, with my case history in Kenya. You and Logan both know the circumstances of my departure— you both know my Kenya background. And couldn't you feed them at home? Give them an egg and turn on the telly?'

'No. That's just it,' Dawn said hurriedly. 'Logan said that was the whole point of asking you. Some sort of public-relations hairshirt the Office has just adopted. *Don't* hide them at home—flaunt them in public. You know, black brotherhood, all jolly chums together, new day a-dawning, lion and the lamb, all that sort of rot. Macmillan's winds of change blowing away old colour clashes in the Savoy dining-room. We're evidently making a strong thing of not being pointedly beastly to the Wog any more. And Logan thinks that you, at least, might be depended on to scrape through the evening without impregnating the visiting baboons—pardon, dear, the distinguished guests of the Colonial Office—with a fierce fresh urge to go home and hack off the heads of all those dreadful leathery colonial women.'

'Well, really,' Valerie Dermott said. 'I can just fancy Brian Dermott's face. He'd go mad and bite himself at the idea. Really.' She giggled despite herself. 'I've had no extensive practice at the social graces with blackamoors, darling. And as for *dining* with one . . . really! Even such a prominent one as this Kamau. I don't think I possibly *could*, Dawn. I'd be completely stuck for anything at all to say.'

Her friend's voice on the other end of the phone grew hoarser with desperate urgency.

'You don't have to *do* anything, or even say much, for Christ sake! I'm not asking you to marry them! Wear a low-cut dress and let them peer down your cleavage and smile with all your teeth and just be A Pretty *White* Woman! This is not a social evening, it's sheer emergency diplomacy— another name for pimping! I'm the madame in this thing, and I need girls for the house!'

'Dearie me. I hope you're not wired for sound in your house, Madame,' Valerie giggled again. 'I shouldn't like that last to get back to His Nibs. He'd get himself even sicker than he is now. It's just that I wouldn't know how to act with blacks——'

'Oh, come off it. I saw you cutting up in Switzerland with that Egyptian last winter, and you couldn't call him a roaring Swede in coloration. I was in Haiti with you myself two years ago. How about that charming *café-au-lait* Pierre military type that you were always doing the slow rumba with at that night-club place in Petionville?'

'Oh, very well. It's not the *colour* that bars me. It's just the Kenya thing that sticks in my craw. But I'll come. I won't let you down. It might be rather fun, at that. My, how the world's changing. What exactly are we wearing?'

'I told you—half your front naked and . . .'

*

Valerie Dunstan Dermott smiled as she rang off. Fancy. Just fancy. Half a dozen years ago we were shooting these people. And now I'm going publicly off to dinner with a couple of them. Things had certainly changed. Everywhere you went now you saw the black faces, not just the Jamaicans with their white popsies, but you saw frightfully well-dressed Africans with frightfully proper whites all over Mayfair. Even Kenya had lowered the colour bars, and they were crawling over the Stanley and the Norfolk as big as you pleased.

Here in London it wasn't just the Paul Robeson-Bricktop-Sammy Davis sort of pro-Negro fad any more. Mayfair'd never really given a hoot about colour. Dawn was right. The chic bored ones saw nothing wrong with a fling with an Egyptian or a Haitian or a Jamaican of *any* shade, particularly on the black man's home ground. And this of course didn't count all the little Pearls and Mavises and Violets in the East End and Chelsea and Notting Hill Gate and St. John's Wood, these days. Piccadilly was teeming with black men and their girl friends. *Reelly*, Myrtle, they're ever so nice, *reelly*. You wouldn't believe it, *reelly* !

It was getting to be the day of the black man, *reelly*, all right. There was probably some vitality there that the white man had lost. They *were* decadent, so many of the young whites. You'd only to look at the negligible chins and the slack mouths and the frilly waistcoats and the long hair dos on the bright young men, the angry young men. But then the brightest young men and the angriest young men always had been pansified. It had been one of the reasons she'd gone back to Kenya in the first place—looking for something bright and young and possibly angry that wasn't a screaming queen. One of the reasons—not *all* of the reasons.

Valerie Dermott couldn't imagine herself in bed with a really black man, although Dawn had struck closer to the mark than she knew when she mentioned the Haitian gentleman. A lot of slow *meringe* music and a cheesy-yellow Haitian moon and the very, very handsome tawny fellow—Dawn was nastily right, as usual; his name had been Pierre—this very handsome unblond Haitian had been batting on practically sure wicket if canny old Mother Nature hadn't intervened and made the whole basic business impossible for the last three days of her short stay in Port-au-Prince. Curse apart, she

223

couldn't imagine herself in bed with an *African* black man at all, although by now she had no particular illusions about bed.

But you did see more and more of it—open marriages, open socializing, between different colours of very nice people indeed, and nobody was very surprised on a tweedy tally-ho week-end when one of the honoured guests turned out to be some charming stovepipe-coloured diplomat from Ghana or the Cameroons or some other unlikely suburb of the world. Especially in France now. The French had always cultivated the coons—now they seemed more than ever deferential as the mess in Algeria got stickier, with the white *colons* cutting up even nastier than her own high-tempered white settlers in Kenya.

There was actually no getting away from it, Valerie thought, as she strolled over to her little bar to pour herself a bitter lemon and paused on the way to switch on her record player. The Africans were permanently with us, and this phone call of Dawn's proved it. Imagine! Valerie Dunstan Dermott, daughter of an old-fashioned empire-builder, former wife of a Mau Mau fighter, actually going out to dinner with a savage from her own bailiwick! Brian would drop dead of shock if he ever even suspected it, married or not married. Even after this latest departure, it would still shake him rigid. The evening, she thought, should be interesting, and then she did a slow pirouette in the middle of the room.

CHAPTER SIX

DAWN ETHRIDGE'S cocktail party was going full blast when Valerie arrived at the slim white Georgian house in Chester Square. She looked spectacular as she gave her modest mink to the maid and walked into the drawing-room, which was full of the usual Whitehall types—Foreign Office, Colonial Office, Home Office upper-echelon secretariat, with a sprinkling of medium-range diplomats from foreign embassies and the occasional spicing of journalist or fashionable industrialist. Valerie, standing in the door in a slim black dress that left her bosom nearly bare under a twisted gold chain with a jade pendant, her shining hair pulled tight behind her ears in defiance of the current beehive-sheepdog vogue, knew most of them from attendance at half a thousand things like this.

She tendered her cheek to be pecked by her hostess, a tall, handsome, wicked-black-eyed woman of forty with bluish-white dyed hair, and by her host, a comfortable twinkly career public servant with a rare-sirloin complexion and a clipped pepper-and-salt moustache. They were among her favourite people; Logan Ethridge had money of his own and was hoping for a major cabinet post on the next shuffle; there was a knighthood just round the corner and meantime he was lying doggo in the Colonial Office waiting for Macleod to slip. Dawn Ethridge was quite Valerie's best female friend; she was alarmingly frank, amusingly earthy, seemed sincerely devoted to her older husband and only wandered therapeutically off the leash when she went away on the yearly holiday her husband allowed her. She and Valerie had travelled more than once together; they stayed remarkably unentangled in each other's hair and shared no deep confessionals.

'What do I do now, love?' Valerie whispered to her hostess. 'Mingle or skulk in a corner?'

'Skulk in a corner,' Dawn Ethridge said. 'Skulk until summoned. Keep your powder dry. Our little black brethren are doing beautifully at the moment. Lucy Maxim's about to climb the leg of the shorter one, and they both seem well bulwarked by the flower of the corps. I shouldn't imagine you'll have to start your heavy work until we depart for dinner. I've managed to collar a suitably titled blonde sixth for the feeding chore. Nice mixed bag.'

'How are they?' Valerie asked, accepting a martini from a footman. 'Smarmy, or straight out of the tree?'

'Neither,' Dawn replied. 'Quite charming, actually. They've both been extremely well educated, I learn, and the shorter one—the Matisia, with the little hairline moustache—is very attractive. He's been everywhere. Even studied in Russia. And the tall one, the Kamau, really has something. I imagine he's magnificent when he starts to bind a spell. Also he knows hell's own number of American actors and actresses and politicians and writers. This won't be difficult, pet. Might even be instructive, if not amusing.'

'Right,' Valerie said. 'I see Ronnie Elliott looking sulky in a corner. I'll go and try to prevent his bursting into tears. It's all definitely off between him and Louisa?'

'I believe so. Haven't dug into that yet. Suppose you find out all the dirt and tell me later. Meanwhile, I shall go and pull Mistress Maxim off the Matisia before she gets all-over lampblack.'

Valerie drifted into the swirling cocktail crowd, and here they were, now, at the Savoy dining-room. She had only met her dinner companions when the cocktail party had come apart and they were ready to leave for dinner. She had gone in one car with Logan Ethridge and the Matisia one. Dawn had taken the Kamau and the other dinner partner, a pretty young blonde-widow type named Marcia Something-Hadley, whose full name had escaped Valerie in the mumbled introductions. The Marcia Something-Hadley was very, very blonde, and did not seem overafflicted by intelligence, but Dawn had muttered out of the corner of her mouth that an impromptu procuress had to do the best she could on short notice, and that Marcia's blondeness must be completely natural, since it seemed to extend to her brains.

*

'I believe you come from Kenya, Mrs. Dermott,' Mr. Matisia said as they leaned back in the Colonial Office's Daimler, with Valerie sitting between the

225

African and her host. 'I know the name well—it's quite common in Kenya. Almost as common as Matisia in the Machakos area, which I am sure you know.' He laughed, showing very white teeth. 'They're my own—the teeth,' he said. 'They're not filed like my father's. I'm the first of the unfiled Matisias. I'm afraid I disappointed everyone terribly in Russia.'

He was really quite handsome, Valerie thought—as black as your boot, of course, but with very straight good features and the most wonderful creamy voice, like so many Wakambas had. It reminded her of the texture of good chocolate fudge. He was wearing a dinner jacket and his black tie was tucked under the laydown collar in the newest London-Hollywood style. His pleated silk shirt, she was glad to see, was unfrilled.

'I seem to know one particular Dermott,' he was saying. 'Isn't there quite a famous white hunter by that name?'

'My former husband,' Valerie said quietly. 'We are no longer married.'

'I'm sorry,' Mr. Matisia said. 'I hadn't meant to be awkward. Please forgive me. Tell me, do you get back to Kenya often?'

'Not for the last eight years—until very recently,' Valerie said. 'My family —my own family—no longer live there. They left before the war, I left during the Emergency. This last trip was just a short visit. Circumstances prevented my making it a long one.'

'Really. A pity. It is such a wonderful country, don't you agree? I know of no lovelier place to live. The Emergency was a most regrettable thing if only because it caused fine people to leave. However, I can assure you that there'll be no more of that. Tell me, do you know my country, the Kamba country, very well?'

'Only through going down to Mombasa on holiday with my people when I was quite a young girl,' Valerie said, and so they had talked comfortably enough, playing African do-you-know all the way into the Savoy and into dinner.

The table was small enough to make conversation easy, once they were in the dining-room. Dawn Ethridge took the opposite end of the table and seated Kamau, as senior, on her right, with Valerie between him and Logan Ethridge. This placed the blonde widow Marcia, who turned out to be a Lady Bostwick-Hadley, across the table between Ethridge and Matisia.

There were big doings at the Savoy that night, some lavish premarital affair of new-riches, and one long table was congested with white-tied people who were subjected to much popping of hotel-sanctioned flashbulbs.

'There won't be any pictures of us, I hope,' Valerie whispered to her host, during one lull in the conversation. 'People wouldn't understand, I'm sure.'

'No fear,' Logan Ethridge said. 'All the formal pictures get taken tomorrow if the Old Man's up and about. The press had their photographic fill when our friends came in at the airport.'

It had been a most pleasant dinner. Both Mr. Kamau and Mr. Matisia proved to have excellent table manners, and they seemed to know and appreciate the fish and the white wine, the grouse and the red, although Mr.

226

Kamau didn't really drink any of the wine. They contrived not to eat with their fingers, and they largely kept the conversation general. Lady Marcia was invaluable. She spent most of the evening trying to locate Kenya exactly, and Mr. Matisia spent a good deal of his evening trying to explain that Nairobi was a city, that Kenya was a colony, and that East Africa was altogether separate from the Congo. Lady Marcia was most informative about the twilight of blood sports and the latest Riviera doings of Lady Docker, and suggested that if Mr. Matisia and Mr. Kamau found time away from state affairs, they might enjoy coming out to her country home for a real English week-end. Mr. Matisia said he would be delighted to come if time allowed, and Mr. Kamau said that he doubted very much if time would allow, since they both had several speaking engagements which would take them to several other English cities, but it was very kind of Lady Bostwick-Hadley.

Valerie kept her conversation mainly to animals and the lack of progress against poaching on the Serengeti, as well as in the Tsavo National Park, which God knows she knew by heart from Brian, and Mr. Matisia said that he hoped to take drastic steps to educate his tribe, the Wakamba, in game preservation, with special emphasis on maintaining the elephant herds and the dwindling rhino as tourist attractions.

'I am afraid that this is going to be difficult,' Mr. Matisia smiled charmingly. 'My people stand firm on two God-given privileges—the right to poach elephants and to steal the Masai's cattle. It keeps them gingered,' said Mr. Matisia. 'They've been terribly bored otherwise since we stopped eating each other.' Lady Marcia thought this was dreadfully amusing, and everyone laughed.

As they sat over the coffee, Mr. Kamau, who had been rather mono-syllabically affable all evening, asked his hostess to dance, whereupon Mr. Matisia asked if Mrs. Dermott would favour him, leaving Lady Bostwick-Hadley to talk to Logan Ethridge. Valerie found it very odd, dancing with a really black Negro from her own country, but failed to notice any odour whatsoever except an excessively clean scent of recent Old Spice shaving soap.

'You dance very well,' she said to Matisia. 'So few Englishmen do.'

'I should,' he said. 'I'm a Kamba. Surely you've seen our famous dances? I can leap into the air and turn over twice under the impetus of enough *pombe*,' he said, and laughed. 'But I don't think the Savoy is quite the place for it. Actually, as I grow older I find I prefer the cha-cha.'

'I don't think the Savoy is quite the place for the cha-cha, either,' Valerie said, laughing herself. 'The cha-cha wants a tiny touch darker, more intimate atmosphere. More suitable in the River Club or the Milroy, I should imagine.'

'I don't suppose you'd care to go on somewhere after our hosts have done their decent best by us,' Matisia said. 'It has been a very long time since I danced with such a pretty girl, and that champagne is making me feel too festive to listen to Kamau talking politics in the suite for the next two hours.

227

Do you suppose we might press on and investigate London when we terminate here?'

Valerie thought for a moment. Why not? It might be fun—might be interesting to see what he's actually like under that undoubtedly Roman-cut dinner coat and the white man's urbane manner.

'Why not?' Valerie said. 'Why not indeed? We'll have to ask the others, of course.'

'Perhaps the others will be too tired,' Mr. Matisia said, drifting easily into a slow rumba. 'It's to be hoped so, in any case.'

They returned to the table, and in a moment, Mr. Kamau asked Valerie to dance. He did not dance so—so assertively—as Mr. Matisia, and Valerie liked him better.

'I seem to remember seeing you once or twice in Nairobi,' Mr. Kamau was saying during an undecided fox-trot that needed no special attention to footwork. 'I remember seeing you go into the White Rhino for lunch once, in Nyeri, and I recall thinking what a pity it was I was no longer the right age to go and seek farm work somewhere round the Nyeri area. I thought perhaps that if I were younger I might get a job holding your horse.'

Valerie threw her head back and laughed, leaning slightly away from Mr. Kamau and looking up into his face.

'You must forgive me,' she said. 'But I said something more or less along the same lines when Dawn asked me to join you at dinner—that I'd never really met any Africans except as horse-holders, even though I'm African myself.'

Mr. Kamau smiled.

'Why did you come tonight, then? It must have been quite a momentous decision for a lady whose family has suffered as much as yours at our hands. Oh, yes——' he said, as she started to speak. 'I know which Dermott you are. Was it sheer curiosity about meeting a Kikuyu as a man for the first time, or was it some obscure method of paying us back for your tragedy? Or possibly, paying back your own people for your tragedy by going out publicly in London with a black man?'

Valerie retreated into a well-tested camouflage of surface *naïveté*—what she called her 'la, sir' pose. This Kamau was a keen one. He had put his long black finger precisely on her shallow motivations—curiosity mingled with some slight schoolgirlish idea of getting even with both the Kenya blacks *and* whites. Still dancing closely with Kamau she leaned even farther back and now was looking almost trancedly up into his eyes, her chin and white throat making a charming flowing line against the blackness of his coat and the polished soot of his face. She turned her head slightly, smiling quizzically, and half-closed her eyes as another barrage of flashbulbs attended some toast or other at the festive prenuptial table.

'Why,' she said, 'Mr. Kamau, nothing of the sort. Mrs. Ethridge is possibly my best friend in London. She has often asked me to dinner with strangers, usually something to do with her husband's position, and I have never failed

228

to find them charming.' That'll steady the black son-of-a-bitch, she thought. Him and his horse-holding compliments.

'Oh, very well,' Mr. Kamau smiled charmingly as per order. 'I shall certainly make every effort not to prove an exception. You dance beautifully, Mrs. Dermott.'

'Thank you, Mr. Kamau,' she said and returned to silent dancing. The music finished, and he took her back to the table.

'—really wouldn't recognize Kenya now,' Matisia stood up and bowed as Kamau handed her into her chair. 'I was saying how things have changed, even in the past six months. Didn't you find it greatly changed, Mrs. Dermott? There is almost frantic building. They have lifted the face of the old New Stanley, until now I'd say it's as fine a pub as you'd be likely to see in Europe. New buildings everywhere—new theatres, new radio centre, and at Mawingo, these American film people have done marvels with the old hotel—swimming-pool, cottages, steam baths, the complete Hollywood-Palm Springs lot.'

'I noticed that Mount Kenya is still there,' Valerie said, deadpan. 'I had hoped they wouldn't move the mountain,' and was greeted with rather more laughter than she thought the line deserved.

'No—they're waiting for the likes of Matisia and me to move mountains,' Kamau said smoothly. 'We've decided to baffle everyone and shift the mountains only a very tiny bit at a time. I think the Congo may have taught the hastier hearts a bitter lesson in too precipitate independence, wouldn't you agree, Mr. Ethridge?'

'I would most wholeheartedly agree,' said Mr. Ethridge, his neck bulging slightly over his hard collar. 'Well, Dawn, my dear, things seem to be shutting down here, and I'm certain our guests must be weary. That's a long flight from Nairobi, even with the jets. Do you think . . . ?'

'I think,' Dawn Ethridge said firmly. She rose, and nodded inquisitively to Valerie and Lady Marcia. 'I'm all right,' Lady Marcia said. Valerie got up and followed Dawn Ethridge out to the ladies' lounge.

'Well?' Dawn Ethridge said as they repaired their faces.

'The Matisia wants to take me out on the town. He wants to go dancing—*without* you people. What do you think? Is this part of multi-racial-aid programme for Logan, or may I play headache and not go cha-chaing with Little Black Sambo?'

'You have discharged your duties tonight like a proper duck,' Dawn said. 'You never looked lovelier, and I'm sure you've filled the Matisia's tiny woolly head with all manner of Oriental dreams of delight involving houris—else,' here she mimicked Matisia's syrupy voice with surprising accuracy—'why would the white bitch come out with me at all?'

'Something of the sort, I'm sure. Surface slick as they are, they're still unsure—and I can't say I blame them. The best tailor in the world can't fix that complexion. I think I won't tempt Mr. Matisia any further. You and Logan can drop me off, please?'

'Surely. The Marcia is staying here. I wouldn't be surprised if there were something doing there if our Mr. Matisia wanted to change his luck. Do you suppose *they* think that way too—changing their luck, I mean?' The idea struck Dawn as very funny, and she laughed aloud.

'I don't know,' Valerie said, putting away her compact. 'I suppose that's the only way one would *really* ever get to know them. Certainly not in the Savoy ballroom. It would be almost worth the experiment to find out if they really *were* people.'

'My dear, you must know by now that *all* men are the same with their pants off,' Dawn Ethridge said coarsely. 'I should watch that Matisia, if I were you. I don't think you'd be the *first* time he ever changed his luck.'

'Well, I'll never know,' Valerie said. 'Perhaps if he came from Algeria or Guinea or some place like that, it might be different. I didn't mind the dancing; I don't mind keeping public company. But the idea of anything else gives me the creeps. Imagine kissing those purple slabs of liver they use for lips. *Ugh!*' She made a *moue* of distaste, and picked up her bag.

'You'll tuck me in, then,' she said. 'You and Logan may come in for a nightcap after we've marooned our friends in the lobby. I don't imagine that even Brian Dermott would find anything to quarrel with in my behaviour this evening.'

CHAPTER SEVEN

DONALD BRUCE was by nature a happy man. He looked a happy man even when he was angry or occasionally heartsick. He was big in the raw-boned Scots fashion—bleak-boned, bleach-hided, splotch-freckled, sorrel-headed —with that ridiculous blob of comic nose lonely isleted in the middle of the tight-skinned chapped face. Donald Bruce had the kind of pink-fuzzed hands that always appeared red and harsh-scrubbed, the kind of knobby knuckles that always looked barked. His best friend Brian Dermott had once said that Don's skin clothed him like an old pair of dungarees—washed a little too light; fitting a touch too tight.

Shaving that morning after he and Peggy and the kids had returned to Hardscrabble Farm from town, Donald Bruce thought through a drift of lather that his face was finally learning how to look pinched without half-trying. It had started even before they left town, just after he had delivered Brian's native boy Kidogo to Brian at the flat. Ken Jenkins had flagged him at the office with the news that Reg Matthews had pulled up lame in hospital with appendicitis just as Reg's clients had arrived at the airport. Ken had offered him a two-months' safari subbing for Reg, and Donald had been forced to refuse because of this bloody nonsense on the farm. That was five hundred pounds sterling well and truly down the drain—and even after

230

taxes, five hundred nicker bought a muckle o' baby bran. But he was only just back off one safari; things were all roiled up on the farm, what with Peggy's do, imagination or not—and there was also the entirely unimaginative reality of the twenty men departing, the old witchdoctor Kinyanjui dead and possibly poisoned, the damned dog gutted on the gatepost, and all the Nigs in a flap. Don proceeded to cut himself then on one particularly susceptible raised capillary just under his nose, and cursed ringingly.

No old-fashioned bush Kyuke would have poisoned Kinyanjui, or even attempted to hire a poisoner, for fear of all sorts of horrid retaliations if by some chance the plot were discovered and the attempted assassination aborted. There was some deeper, more practically sophisticated reason, then, for the poisoning—and here Don grinned sheepishly as he wiped the lather off his face, for he noted he had already accepted in himself as fact that the old man had been murdered instead of pegging out from old age. There had to be a deeper reason, and the reason could only involve himself, Donald Colin Bruce, as parcel to a larger project.

Don Bruce could not remember rightly how many people he had killed, directly or indirectly, during the Emergency—even when they came to sit on his chest at night. But he had certainly killed people he knew—boys from his dead father's own *shamba* and from the adjoining farms. And he had of course been present when rather unusual methods of exacting confessions had been used against the captured Terrorists—or what was worse, possibly against men who had only their word to offer that they were *not* Terrorists. There was no way of knowing how many innocent had died in the hills—merely being black and without alibi was more than enough to toss what was left of the man after the 'interrogation' into the bush for the hyenas to finish.

Don had been younger then. Younger and tougher. A half-dozen dead Wogs more or less made very little difference—everybody was doing it. But now—married, father of four, things took a different aspect.

And certainly, *thahus* apart, there were a great many details to be seen to on the farm. According to Peggy too many things had gone to pot while he was away on the last safari—not exactly to pot, perhaps, but all the things that were apt to creep out of kilter if you left the running of any project to Africans for very long. Peggy used to be more useful as an overseer and she still did a tremendous job with her sheep. But between the sheep and the kids and the house and most of the book-keeping Peggy had her arms full and her lap brimming; it was too much to ask her to stand watch on all the larger aspects of five hundred acres as well. Farms and machinery needed a man, a white man, alertly atop the job all the time, whether it was repairing broken fences, fixing a faulty motor or improvising the compensations one always had to make for weather.

And, Don thought, walking now towards the living-room and the blaze he could already hear crackling, it looks as if we're in for a smacking great drought. Thank Christ for that counter-contour drainage system everybody sneered at. At least we managed to catch some water at the Nought Points in the last long rains. It's soaked well into the ground by now and is still bubbling up in little springs. It didn't all go merrily roaring down into the hill to wind up in the Sagana, which has got sufficient water in it already.

His wife looked cheery enough as she poured the coffee in the cheerful living-room. That was another thing about Peggy Bruce—none of this lady-farmer slopping away half the day in pyjamas and robe; she was already up, dressed, and had obviously been much about. Her normally pink cheeks were polished pippin by the early-morning breeze; her hands were wrinkled-red as if they had just been washed in strong soap, and she smelled of sheep. She was wearing her usual morning costume of man's wool shirt and denim overalls. She had kicked off her rubber boots, and was sitting in her sock feet on the big zebra pouffe in front of the fire. Steam came from the hammered silver coffee-pot, wedding gift of Brian Dermott.

'I heard—I *felt*—you getting up in the black night,' Don said. 'The bed was so warm and lovely I thought it wiser not to ask *why*. So I just slid over into the sweet little nest you'd left and dropped back off to sleep again. What was it this time?'

'Sheep. Bloody sheep. What else? Mother and children doing well, of course. *Why* is it that dumb things always get born when people are dying?'

'Blowed if I know,' Don said. 'Glad to get home after your brief and—I must say—rather excessive night on the town?'

'It's nice to be back home and feel you in the same bed with me,' Peggy said. 'I'm not sure how nice it would be to have come back if you'd dashed off on safari again. Pity about the money, though. I'm sorry about that, sweetie. I suppose you *could* have taken the safari and I'd have made out all right. I always have.'

'Well, I didn't,' Don said rather shortly. 'I didn't, and there is nothing to be done about it. I'd have gone mad worrying about you and the kids—seeing all sorts of bogymen and dreaming all manner of strange dreams. In any case there will be one thousand three hundred and seventy-nine things to be repaired, demolished, replenished and rejiggered. You know that old Kikuyu purification rite—man can't sleep with his wife when he returns from a journey until they've slaughtered a goat and appeased the household gods?'

'Sure. Why? And who needs sleeping with? I thought you took care of that rather neatly in town, my boy.'

'Well, I was just thinking that we don't need to slaughter any goats for *my* purification rites on this *shamba*. By the time I get all the African oversights, avoidances and omissions of memory put right, I will be sufficiently dead to be construed as a sacrifice. I will have appeased the household gods, all right. And mind you, I haven't even talked to Njeroge yet. I just know this is going to be one of those *days*.'

Peggy poured herself another cup of coffee, and her voice turned sober.

'Back home, with the sun shining, and the usual problems that you know you love, are you still of a mind to sell up? I *don't* want to sell the farm, Don.'

'I don't know; I can't say. Of course I don't want to sell the farm. It's part of me and part of you. But I'm firm on one thing; if everything that happened here day before yesterday is a part of a pattern—not just an accident— we're leaving. Where're the children?'

'Babies still mercifully abed. Angus and Ellen out rampaging round the farm somewhere. They got up when I did, and went along to help me birth the ewe.'

'You want to keep an eye on them for the next few days,' Don said. 'And look: I think it might be a very sound move to lock a door on little Jock when you leave the house. For the moment I don't trust anybody very much. And perhaps the other kids ought to be kept a touch closer to foot, as well—at least within earshot.'

'But my darling husband, we never locked up anything in this house in our lives—well, except the sugar and guns and whisky—and the kids have always run wild. We can't just change them to city-nursie-nanny sort of brats over-night. As for locking up the baby, it's just like in the other houses when the Mau——'

'Exactly,' Don Bruce said. 'Turning a key won't hurt. Get one of Njeroge's daughters in to sit with the baby and lock her in too.'

'I suppose the youngest, that bobby-soxer Kamore, could always sit there and brood over her boy-friend in Nairobi,' Peggy said. 'Did you know that the old boy's actually intercepting her love letters now?'

'Well, I suppose he wants to keep her home,' Don said. 'Most of the others have taken off for the towns. Bloody tragedy that—five wives, twenty or thirty children, and not one damned daughter of the last lot worth a bride price.'

'A bride costs from a thousand to two thousand shillings these days, my lad,' Peggy said. 'What Wog in the world has *got* two thousand shillings to spend on a woman? Even at fifty shillings a month they'd never be able to pay off the debt to the old man.'

'Well, it's turning them all into unmarried mothers and whores,' her husband said, getting up and reaching for his hat. 'And speaking of the old man, I hear him giving one of the *watoto* what-for now. I'd better go and see what the ruckus is about—what new tool they've managed to ruin. Round up those kids and keep 'em a little bit closer to heel, will you, wife? I'll be back for lunch at about eleven.'

Don Bruce kissed his wife's round cheek and went out the door, nearly filling it as he passed under the beam.

DON WAS right about the place going to rack when your back was turned. It wasn't until he returned home from safari and started plugging the holes in the daily doings of the farm that he realized bitterly what a literal one-man farm he was running. His was not the biggest property in the world—he kept no more than two hundred head of cattle, counting calves at foot, five hundred sheep and a couple of hundred pigs. But he still used nearly half an African per arable acre—one hundred and fifty natives worked and lived on Hard-scrabble. You couldn't do it for less—the Widow Jensen next door was as good as any man; she was a Dane, and worked as hard as a man, and she still employed thirty Africans on forty acres. And Don worked nearly all his land, apart from the half-acre he allotted each African family to grow their own pigs and potatoes and mealies on. Nearly half of that land had been bush and wasteland—bone-hard dry for eight months a year and a swamp for the other four—before Don had reclaimed it from the strangling bush and roving tentacled Kikuyu twist-grass that starved and soured the soil.

He couldn't have done it at all without Peggy, of course—he'd be the first to admit that. Peggy and great luck with the Land Bank—*and* good weather and a steady firm market for mutton and milk and the luxury money-maker, pyrethrum. The good lord Ngai had spared a smile or two for Donald Bruce, and Don's Presbyterian upbringing did not prevent him from offering a silent nod of thanks towards The Mountain from time to time—or from contributing the annual brace of beeves to his people's festive *ngomas*.

And he certainly couldn't have done it without old Njeroge and the rest of the key people. Njeroge was particularly good for an African; straight as a die and uncommonly adaptable to some rather whimsical innovations in farming that Don had bullied him into accepting against all his ingrained teaching and judgment.

Ploughing and burning were two such things. Don wouldn't allow a plough to be used on the place, except to cut drainage ditches, and he profanely forbade burning as a brush-clearer, even when other people's burning dark-ened the skies and flamed the horizon in great artificial sunsets from dawn to dark. The Kikuyu hands could never understand why they should forgo the joy of touching matches to the grasses in order to shave the earth of its dry, useless mane of coarse stiff stalks.

Don had thought that possibly overgrazing, scandalous overgrazing, might be the answer to clearing the land of the coarse matted grass that jungled it. First he built stout fences and ignored agriculture. He turned what few animals he owned at the time into the paddocked areas and went over to the farm of Miss Charlotte Stuart and begged the loan of a hundred hungry Boran beef cattle, ravenous from their southward trek. He had starved the cattle into cropping the grass to a workable level, thoroughly mowing the vast stretching field of harsh yellow stalks. And they had splattered the dry earth with their dung before the rains.

He had then turned the cattle out and had set his field hands to work with hoes. The greedy-fingering Kikuyu grass was chopped and killed on the surface, to make mulch; the admixture of dead roots and cattle dung was worked into the top two inches of soil; the bed clay was not cut by ploughs, and the great lumps of hoed earth were left to aerate, unbroken and un-crumbled by the razored hooves of animals. They were simply turned raw-side up and left for bacterial action and the melting rains before they were sowed in things like purple vetch to hoard humus in the acid soils. Barley he planted as well; the grain disappeared first into the pigs as food; the straw stacked clean as bedding for the swine; the pig dung soaked into the sty mud as manure and the pigs were trucked off the land, squealing, to have their throats slit for the hard cash which Don deep-tined back into his fat-tening acres.

There were so many things to do on a really hungry farm like old Hard-scrabble. Bit by bit, piece by piece, he had set out to drain a bog here, to irrigate vast rinks of cracked, granite-hard wasteland yonder. He gnawed and worried at the land exactly as a puppy might try to chew his way through a cabin by starting at the corner log; he cleared and filled and graded, always strengthening the poor land by grazing animals on it. He brought the sheep in for three or four days a month into his new pallid clover and just-hearten-ing indigenous grasses—even that much sheep manure would nourish the land.

He alternated cattle with sheep, and found that for some reason the parasites they evacuated were eaten and destroyed by each other—the sheep eating the cattle's worm-eggs as they clung to the vegetation, the cattle con-suming the sheep's larvae. Don used the word *shit* almost reverently, because he lived by it. Old Njeroge and the rest of the Wogs thought he was mad when he made the herdboys graze the sheep and cattle along the public roads, robbing the shoulders of their fertile forage, then penning the beasts overnight in hungry paddocks which stood in special need of manuring. They evacuated much of their day's intake of fodder during the dark hours, enriching the land—and money for store-bought fertilizer was always very short in those days. But just riding now over Don's fortified acres, you could see the difference between what he called 'tamed' land and the land he was still punishing into obedience. On the tamed land the same crop of barley or rye or oats stood a foot higher and waved a deeper richer green than the less lusty life which was striving upward from the land he had not yet completely brought to its potential loamy peak.

The terracing of the drainage system had really been the clincher in earning Don Bruce a name as a complete madman among the Kikuyu. This crazy bwana, they said, had some wild idea about making water run uphill when any idiot knew that Ngai intended water to flow downhill to raise His rivers. No one could farm land on which water stood—a man could not sow a *swamp* in anything but snakes and mosquitoes. Of course some land was lost when the rains came and washed the soil downhill; that is why the valleys were always rich, and why a man erected his house on the hilltop where little grew, planting his millet and maize and potatoes and bananas in the creases between the hills where the rich silt collected. And now this mad bwana thought he could go against the will of God and build terraces and dams against God's intention, to make the water run uphill—not only to force it uphill, but to collect it on the hilltops and command it to sink into the ground, to emerge again at his bidding as springs! He had interfered with God in the making of trees—now he intended to infringe Divine copyright on springs!

This, the Kikuyu thought, was crowding the hand of God too much, but then they saw Don drain swamplands and divert the surplus water to barren wastelands of concrete clay; they saw him grow potatoes on formerly useless lands in order to make a cash crop before his fertilizer had a chance to disintegrate properly and wed with the soil; they saw him put the nourished soil into pyrethrum after the sheep had dunged it to richness as they used the land for a sleeping paddock. And they saw, now, that he had kept the native women busy picking the silvery pyrethrum, once every three weeks for the last two years—pyrethrum, the white man's luxury crop, thriving riotously on land that in their short memory would not have provided nourishment for a sick Kikuyu goat!

The Bwana, Njeroge the headman knew, had literally gone without grog one whole year to buy some stud stock—on credit, certainly everything the Bwana bought he got on credit—from his friend, Memsaab Shalotu, whom the white people called Miss Charlotte, at the big *shamba* Glenburnie. He bought some strange big-barrelled heavy-woolled short-legged foreign sheep that came from across the sea and were not so well suited to the Kenya climate as the lean long-legged indigenous sheep. But the Bwana had turned the stranger rams into close boxes during breeding season with ewes from the native hair sheep and then got even stranger-looking foreign sheep and bred them in turn to the crossbred domestic-foreign stock until now he had bigger sheep that grew heavy wool and thick mutton but still withstood the heat well. He had four different stud stocks now, and never lacked markets for wool and for lambs.

If the Bwana had only been more reasonable about goats, Njeroge thought, you would have to admit that the Bwana knew what he was about. But the Bwana hated goats. He said the goats wasted the soil, jerking the grass out by the roots and ring-barking the trees, eating up forage that was better intended for cattle and sheep. The Bwana forbade any goats on his land, which displeased the women greatly, for what was a true home without goats nuzzling softly and making sweet, nose-itching ammonia smells as they stirred comfortingly in the back partition of the living-hut, the part that was even named *goat-place* in Kikuyu? And how could a man feel truly wealthy if he could not count his lovely spotted goats that the small children drove to pasture daily?

The thing of the goats was irksome in many ways, and Njeroge wished that he could make the Bwana see reason. For a good Kikuyu there were a minimum of fifty-seven daily possibilities demanding the slaughter of a goat to appease the spirits—such simple minor domestic calamities as water spilling while potatoes were being cooked, a child tumbling from its mother's back, a man cutting himself while carving meat, fermenting grain or honey beer foaming out of the gourd—these and similar things demanded the slaughter of goats. This of course did not take into consideration any of the special oaths for purification or reversal of curses or even simply precautionary payment to the *mundumugus* for sage advice and long-distance charms against evil.

But the Bwana repaid that unreasoning blind spot on goats by being very good and understanding about other things: he never went tattling to the Bwana District Commissioner when useless, burdensome old people were helped along to ancestorhood by being left alone a good distance away from the hut, for the hyenas. The Bwana knew that everyone had to die some time, and there was no point in destroying the dead man's seed-hoard, burning down his huts, and moving his *shamba* if all this sinful waste could be avoided by anticipating death a few days or hours and leaving the ailing alone in the bush. What difference did a day or week make to a hyena?

The Bwana never questioned Njeroge too closely when one of the pregnant women failed to appear at work in the fields with a clean-licked sucking child at her breast. The Bwana would assume that something had gone wrong at birth—that the child had been born wrong-end-to, or there were firstborn twins, or the child had been a misshapen monster—or, more frequently in these modern times, was born female in a large family when girl children no longer commanded bride prices and constituted nothing more than extra mouths to feed in a *shamba* already filled with squalling mouths and clamouring bellies. The Bwana would know without asking that the child had been prevented from birth by necessity—the Bwana knew that a child was not really a person until it was a year old.

It was by aid of things like this that Njeroge was able to defend his Bwana against criticism. These things, and a strict indulgence of many of the old good customs which made the Watu forget about the goats.

Kweli, the Bwana was a strange man. He had started by rotating his crops; he said that repeated planting of the same crops burned out the soil, whereas if you continually changed crops, and even left some standing to rot at the roots and fatten the earth as one might grain-finish a penned animal, the land would renew itself and come as fresh for crops as a cow came fresh for milking after she dropped her calf.

But the Bwana took this rotation business a step further. He rotated the *people* as well as the crops! He would not let one man live too long on the same personal *shamba*. He made the man and his family raise different crops, and work on different jobs. He made the men come to know cattle as well as they knew the land that grew what the cattle ate; he made the field labourers work with the Memsaab Peggy with the sheep; he even made some of the younger men like fat Kungo, who had been a little bit to school, learn the behaviour of the tractors and the lorry. He started the young boys as *watoto* to tend the fires and provide scalding water that was always present at the milking, and soon they learned to strip an udder with clean fingers so that no *thahu* would curse the milk with sickness.

The Bwana sent the Memsaab to worm the children as regularly as he wormed his stock, and he hauled them in the lorry to the Bwana Dokitari to be jabbed with long needles against all sorts of *thahus* that might make them ill or even kill them. And he was always harsh about cleanliness. When the Bwana was angry he got angry all over, and cursed everyone, and nothing made him quite so angry as litter around the huts, a mucky barn or unclean clothing on the Watu. Water was cheap, the Bwana said, and so was *sabuni*—soap was nothing more than a simple matter of fat and lye for the women to mix—there was no excuse for anyone going dirty.

And now the Bwana was answering a growing clamour from the women for houses such as they had seen in the new land consolidation settlements.

The women always presented some new problem. They no longer tended goats so they no longer had skins for clothes, and in any case in these modern times a woman would think it shameful, a reflection on her man as well as herself, to be seen publicly at the market-place in skins. They wanted mericani and zanzibari in bright colours—and, God strike him!—they saved the best patches they used to keep to sew on men's pants to make breast-hives now, cloth contraptions that squeezed their breasts upward in unnatural positions. These artificial things that looked ridiculous were copied from the white memsaabs who called them *braziru*. A woman who went bare-breasted was shamed, now, and the brighter the *braziru* the more status the woman had with the other women.

Yes, now the women had their wells or else their water-points; they had their *braziru* to hold their teats up; now they were going to get their new houses with two partitions inside—one room for cooking, one for sleeping and one for either goats or children or both if the Bwana ever changed his mind about goats.

And they would get their permanent plots of land; the Bwana was allocating half an acre to each family, and oh, how sly the Bwana had been about this one! The Bwana had measured out the plots according to the *kitabu*—the long work-book—and he had given the best land to the families that showed the most markings in the *kitabu* for work done! Even the ones who drew the worst land had to admit the justice of that.

Surely the Bwana was giving everyone equal help with seeds and manure and even the use of some machinery—in the man's spare time, of course, and he'd damned well better not break anything—but he was warning that the men who misused the land would find themselves kicked off the *shamba* and a fresh family recruited. The Bwana said he worked too hard himself to waste his honest manure and expensive potent seeds and nurtured plant slips on useless lazy *pumbavus* who were undeserving of help; who spent their time telling lies and talking politics and drinking beer after they took their women's wages.

238

So many of the things the Bwana did that looked foolish at first were turning out to be intelligent—although Njeroge had to keep constantly on the tails of the stupid African farmers, just as the Bwana had stayed on his tail, nipping as viciously as a *tsetse* fly, when they first started doing the foolish things that run against the teachings of the elders and hence were likely to affront both ancestors and God. If you let the workers alone they slipped right back in the old slovenly ways—and it would be as the Bwana said when he ranted and pounded his fist against his hand—they would go back to keeping goats and ravaging the land and would soon be as poor and miserable as always if they did not heed his counsel.

This the Bwana had said, and to Njeroge it made sense now. Perhaps things were not as they were—not so free as they used to be when he was a boy, shooting francolin with knob-ended arrows and climbing to a high platform to wave banana fronds and frighten birds from the millet. But there were not the Masai to kill you now, nor the Nandi; there were not the Samburu to come down across the Laikipia from the sere north; there were not even the Meru to quarrel with, nor the Kambas to contend with. A man could usually sleep soundly of nights in his own house. There were no real famines—if this drought lasted the bwanas would distribute *posho* to the needy, even if the needy were lazy drunkards who should have husbanded their grain during the last good harvest. Plagues and epidemics no longer ravished the land; the *dokitaris* and their white-coated assistants in the medical huts, in the travelling lorries with the big red crosses on the sides, they cast great spells with their long needles against the scarring pox and the death that the rats carried. Even the lepers had homes now—whole villages of noseless people with twisted hands and toeless feet.

When you came down to it, Njeroge thought, this was not the worst life in the world, unless you were a Ndrobo, who died unless he roamed the forests, or a Kamba or Waluangulu or Waikoma, whose life was hunting and poaching.

And so what did this man of the Farmers' Union have to offer that the Bwana was not already providing? He would ask the Bwana now, now that the Bwana was back from safari and already prepared to look displeased about the broken springs of the lorry, the curse that had fallen on the insides of the tractor and made it sick, the *thahu* that had curdled the milk of the cows, and finally, the blight that some enemy had sent to attack the pyrethrum that grew the pretty flowers which killed the bugs in far-off lands. Njeroge knew his Bwana; if he made the Bwana angry enough over the man from the new Union, perhaps the Bwana would stay angry all day, and by the end of the day when the Bwana went for his *pombe* on the veranda, the lorry's springs would be attended to; the stomach of the tractor would be well again; the milk of the cows would no longer curdle and the pyrethrum would no longer be scaly and lacking in the petals. Njeroge had found that time, in all things, was a tremendous healer. And Njeroge had plenty of time—as much time as his Bwana had firm ideas about using it.

KILIMANJARO AND her sister Mawenzi got out of bed a little later than Katie. It was still dark when the boy came with the familiar tea—'*nataka chai memsaab*'—and shook Katie gently. She lay curled in the warm nest of blanket, knees drawn to breast, hating to get up, and despising herself for her sudden fit of femaleness last night. Perhaps I'm not used to bathing, she thought drowsily; it goes to my mouth. Then she forced herself out of bed. It was cold as ice, in the grey pre-dawn, and her underclothing was freezing and night-damp on her sleep-flushed skin. She pulled a turtle-neck cashmere sweater over her bare hide before she reached for the light drill safari jacket. She could still see the last stars forlorn as she dipped her face into the mercifully hot water in the basin. She was foamily brushing the sleeping-pill taste out of her mouth when the snowy head of the mountain first showed pinkly against the fast-lightening sky.

Brian and her brother were both dressed and standing warming themselves in front of the revived fire when she reached the mess tent.

'My God, it's cold,' she said. 'Stand aside, men, and let a lady at that fire.' She backed up against it until her brother warned her with unseemly morning humour that he didn't want his sister coming down with an attack of hot pants at this stage of the game. And that, she thought, whether Paul means it or not, was exactly what I was coming down with last night.

'I'm sorry about my little birth of the blues last eve, gents,' she said, as they entered the tent for breakfast. 'Some sort of unlikely girlish reaction to too much in one day, I expect. Apologies, all. Sent myself to bed without supper, though. I could eat a crocodile cutlet right now.'

She assaulted the cold tinned fruit and then, picking up her plate, drained off the thick sweet juice.

'I suspected you'd be a mite peckish,' Brian said. 'Hotcakes coming up. You look positively rude with health this morning. Sleep tight?'

'Died. Took a couple of bombs. I was still kinked up from the trip.' I was kinked up all right, and not from the trip, Katie thought. 'Did you people say anything interesting behind my back?'

'Two dirty stories, one brandy and straight off to beddy-bye,' her brother said. 'I don't remember getting undressed. Don't eat *all* the pancakes, please, Kathleen. It's partly my safari, too.'

They drank four cups of coffee apiece and smoked the day's first cigarette —which is more than ample justification for lung cancer, Katie thought—and straggled off on various errands before they piled into the Land Rover. Kilimanjaro was fully out of bed now, and bulked unbelievably blue and white in the clear keen morning air.

'Now *there*,' Paul Drake said admiringly, 'there is what I would call a mountain and a half. Served correctly with the coffee. But isn't that an awful lot of snow?'

'I never saw it that far down before,' Brian said. 'Rains coming now for sure. That snow was rain last night over yonder. Nice, friendly old mountain, Kili. Not so austere as her cousin up north. Well, let us ride forth and collect a pig if we can find one big enough.'

They slipped into luxurious, coffee-warmed silence now, as they always did when they actually hunted. Brian drove effortlessly, as always, leaving the clay track as soon as they turned out from camp, following game or cattle trails, Katie couldn't tell which, as he gentled the Land Rover smoothly around rocks and fallen logs.

It was the kind of morning which always seems improbable even to the most calloused Africa hand. It was still cold enough for their breaths to hang smokily before them, and Katie's skin still felt gratefully receptive as the cashmere hugged her stomach and contained the warmth that the big break-fast had built inside her. But the sun had crawled up over the snow-capped round head of Kilimanjaro, chipping the first diamonds off the mountain, and causing the tall yellow thorn trees to glow waxily like enormous painted candles under their green visors of branch.

They drove tilted along the sloping side of the hill that reached down towards the river, and every hundred yards a group of spurfowl scratched and scurried, occasionally to lift and fly squawking, sailing on stiffened wings a hundred yards before they put down indignantly again. Doves looped lazily up in front of the car, settling again a few score feet ahead. Starlings and bee-eaters were flung jewels in the lower trees and clumps of bush, flashing burnished purple and brilliant blue and red. Black ground hornbills walked grumpily, their enormous red faces and beaks making them look like W. C. Fields leaving a bar-room. A brace of Kavirondo crested cranes danced, their gilt filigree of head-plumes nodding; secretary birds used a lot of runway before they took off, only to settle again with a bump and almost a spoken curse, and the majestic greater bustards, as big as overstuffed Christmas turkeys, paced like trotting horses. A honey guide rose and flitted enticingly ahead, blandishing; metallic-blue-feathered, yellow-helmeted guinea-fowl ran by the hundreds in the bright new grass, which carried its night dew still gleaming in diamond droplets on its short stiff ends.

An inexplicable tameness afflicts wild animals in early morning and late evening, Brian had told them, and so it was with a herd of impala that was performing a delicate minuet on the fresh sparkling sweep of green dell which stretched from the cobbled hillside into pasture and led up to the reedy edges of the river, with its dark thick stand of big trees and tangled underbrush. The impala were the colour of new-minted gold, with gleaming white bellies, and they kicked and leaped out of sheer frosty-morning exuberance, butting at each other. This was a large herd of ewes and slim-necked young ones, feeding and caracoling apart from a smaller herd of rams, whose lyre-shaped horns bespoke youth and whose play was more bumptiously boyish.

'The old gentlemen are over there,' Brian pointed to the thicker rushes, under the shadows cast by the radish-rooted wild figs and massive rough-boled gums that strode the river. 'See.'

241

Three sets of horns, backswept, almost square in the classic brandy-snifter shape of mature ram impalas, sailed along the wind-bending grass like ship masts seen across a levee. The impalas never seemed to walk—they glided, when they were not springing into the air or nearly turning somersaults. The horns of these gazelles slid through the green like a barge on the Nile, Katie thought, showing only occasional glints of gold where the sun burnished their skins.

'Leave these in peace,' Brian said. 'Although about here seems a likely place to hang one kill. We'll shoot the bait elsewhere and bring it back to the scene of the eventual crime.'

It was funny how much alike all the animals looked when you first came, Katie thought, as the Land Rover lurched on, wallowing slightly and only occasionally shaking her with a rattling bump. Now, after just a month, even I can tell the difference just from the way they walk. The little Tommies run like hell—except the babies, who pronk up and down on stiff legs like springs. The big white Grants all have hurty feet and too much horn. They walk with their heads hanging as if the weight of the horns was more than they could bear. The zebra gallops and wheels with cutting-horse purpose and trots with dignity, exactly like a horse. The female ostriches fluster and lift their skirts when they run, like a group of old maids heading for the john. And the giraffe moves on two dimensions in slow motion.

Two grey-blue shapes flashed out of a bush and dived across their path. Brian stopped the car. One of the blurs had stopped, solidified, and turned to look over his shoulder. His horns were double-curled and the colour of nut-meats in the sun. Streaks of white ran down from his *kohl*-rimmed eyes, and white Vs formed two sparkling chevrons on his swollen throat. The blue-grey body was streaked in vertical slashes of white, and when he turned to run, he flicked a big white-fluffy tail.

'Lesser kudu,' Brian said. 'Not many of them here. Not so good as yours, Paul.'

'Why, he's painted exactly like a Masai,' Katie said. 'I hadn't thought of it before—the white strips coming from the eyes and the design making the Vs on his neck.'

'I think they're the most beautiful of all,' Brian said. 'They're protected here. Not for long, I imagine.'

He put the car in gear again. They were running parallel with the swamp, and in a moment Brian stopped the car and pointed.

'There's your rhino from yesterday, Paul,' he said. 'Mama and young son —but sonny's damned near as big as the old lady. He'll have a shootable horn on him some day; not bad now. And oh, I say, away over to the left—about a thousand yards. Jumbo.'

Brian called for the extra glasses and Katie swept the yellow ripple of tall grass which grew up and away from the poison green of the rushes. The grey-mud-coloured rhino were quite close, mother and son standing staring with irritated weak-eyed intensity at something they could hear and smell but could not see. The unalarmed flocks of tick birds were easily visible on their backs and heads. Through the glasses Katie could see one bird upended, picking dedicatedly at the female rhino's ear.

The elephants looked like flat brown grubs, or old ant-hills, or shifting formations of sand as they stood eye-deep in the tall grass. Through the glasses she could barely make out a glimmer of ivory, but there was a snorted 'hapana ndoumi' from Kidogo in the back, and a disgusted-sounding 'mwana-muke mtoto tu' from Muema.

'Cows and calves,' Brian said. 'Old bulls still back in the hills, likely.'

They drove again, this time turning up stilted knock-kneed giraffes, long disembodied necks craning stiffly above the short thorn bushes on which they were feeding, and two black-plumed ostriches poised like huge puffballs on a hillside.

'Male ostriches about to breed,' Brian said. 'See how their legs are turning bright red. Necks, too. Make your own moral. Up north the legs turn blue.'

There were impala everywhere, and pale illusions of the ghost-like Grants, with occasional pairs of the fantastically long-necked gerenuk, rearing as they browsed. An occasional wistful-looking hyena sat staring hopefully at healthy animals he would always be too crippled in the hips to catch until some day they became sick or wounded or weakened from childbirth.

They kept to the river, still seeking a warthog, and several times Brian halted the car by bare patches of ground to get out and scan the earth for tracks. Twice they saw leopard signs, three times lion, and always the great broad platter-dents of elephant. Brian grunted at the elephant sign at precisely the same time and in the same way the Africans grunted. Katie had reached the point now where she could almost translate the grunts. This particular grunt was a disgusted grunt, meaning women and children only.

They had driven perhaps five miles when Brian jammed on the brakes swiftly, sending Katie forward against the dashboard. Muema was already twisting the thumbscrews that kept the guns wedged in their padded brackets.

'There's your pig, Bwana,' Brian said. 'Quite a nice old boy. Get out and clout him. He's over there by that fallen log about one-fifty, no more. See?'

Her brother scrambled out of the Land Rover, accepting the loaded gun in one motion as he almost fell to the ground.

Kate wondered briefly at the transformation that came over men at the prospect of killing; her brother's eagerness to get out of the car achieved a sort of graceful ballet scramble, and he did not even look too silly as he threw himself violently to the ground, bringing up the gun to shooting position, his elbows braced on his upcocked knees. Katie found that her breath quickened, too, and she searched for the pig against the dark background of bush—searched and had just found him, standing three-quarters on, big, roach-maned reddish head turned towards the car, abnormally big ears perked and outflanging, white curves of ivory reaching upward to the bumps in his impossibly ugly politician's face.

The report of the gun and the smack of the bullet merged in her ears, and the pig had disappeared from view.

'Jolly nice shooting, Bwana,' Brian said as always, lighting a cigarette. 'That's one more we won't have to chase. Right over. You got him smack on the point of the shoulder. Look, see him kick?'

They drove slowly over the mossy excrescences of rock to where the dead warthog lay thin-haired, tick-ridden and hideous in a spreading pool of blood. He looked ludicrously ugly at close range, with the great knobs like leper-lumps on his hog face, the tusks long and yellowed, a little worn down from rooting, and smoothly grooved underneath from being constantly used as a whetstone for the razored lower ripping teeth.

Brian jerked his head at the boys. '*Tia ndani gari,*' he said. 'We'll stick him in the car for the moment, and hunt on. We'll go up on the high plain and pick up a kongoni for the boys' camp meat, and if we see a likely impala with lousy horns and a general look of being tired of life, we'll add him to the bag. Another pig if we see one. Sorry, Katie. But it *is* shopping day.'

'I'm all right, Bwana,' Katie said. 'Having seen this warthog at close range, I don't feel so badly about the tribe. I'm afraid I'm fascinated only by the piglets. We do *have* to shoot one of those lovely impala?'

' 'Fraid so. There's still a couple on the licence, and they're in long supply here, anyhow. The pig's in,' he said, as the gunbearers jammed the back latches of the Rover's drop-apron. 'Let's go.'

Brian turned the Land Rover in a wide circle and drove in a meandering fashion up towards the top of the hill, where, he said, they'd find a road and follow that until they got up to the high open plains where they'd see topi and kongoni and very probably a few Thomson gazelles—plus, with luck, some sandgrouse for their own private menu. They located the road and had gone no more than another mile when Brian stopped the car again.

'Might as well do that poor blighter as any,' he said to her brother. 'See him?'

Katie looked and saw flecks of gold dappling through the woven green of the thorn scrub.

'That last one,' Brian whispered, 'it's a small bachelor committee of old rams. The chap we want is old as Kidogo and has only one horn.' He grinned. 'Unlike Kidogo, who has many antlers due to being away from his women all the time.' The old gunbearer grinned back at him as Brian touched his head.

Katie watched her brother get out of the car and disappear into the thorn, following just to the right and behind Muema. They were both walking in a half-crouch and picking their way from bush to bush. In a moment she heard the too-familiar *tunk* and then the blast of the rifle.

'Unless he hit a tree he got his impala,' Brian said. 'I must say it's nice to hunt with these one-shot blokes. Saves me a power of walking.' He turned the car off the road and drove twisting, with mighty wrenches of his arms, between tree and rock until he bumped the Land Rover to the top of a cobbly knoll, where Paul and Muema were standing over a red-splashed old-gold body which carried only one horn.

'Time we collect the other *nyama* we'll be a proper meat wagon,' Brian said as they drove on, crossing two streams of swift-rushing black waters, the Rover going in the water up to the floorboards and clawing on the next bank to gain a foothold. It was cool, cool and frightening, there in the heavy shade as they wallowed in the pebbled stream, with monkeys jabbering the length of the dark, tree-thatched watercourse, the birds screaming and the eye unable to penetrate more than a few feet into the black depths of the thick laced undergrowth.

'All this is leopard country, gorgeous leopard country,' Brian said. 'A really smart *chui* need never leave this swamp, because the water never dries, and there's an unending source of pigs and impala always coming to drink. Like living in a free supermarket. But I'd hate to go after a wounded one in that stuff. Thick, very thick stuff, and I have thin, very thin blood.'

The car struggled up and out of the water onto the loose-shaled road of the steeply rising hill, and Katie could have sworn that the vehicle paused to shake itself like an old retriever emerging triumphantly with a fetched duck.

Once they'd cleared the summit of the long hill, the track straightened into a reasonably navigable thoroughfare, rutted by the hooves of cattle and worn smooth by the pads of elephant coming miles to drink. Katie had made a quick-peel job of the sweater while the men were hoisting the dead impala into the car, and now the sun, slanting strongly down, was burning benignly through the light drill and warming the bare skin of her stomach underneath. The air was still sparkling and fresh, and the dust had not yet risen, and she felt a languorous, almost sexually excited sense of well-being.

'We'll just stop here and have a little look round,' Brian said, taking the glasses and leaping out to stand on the hood of the car and sweep the plateau and the valley below with his long binoculars. Kate got out with him, and climbed up on the other fender.

She stood with the breeze brisk in her face, perched atop the metal skin of a Land Rover that was already sun-hot through her crêpe soles, seeing the country's sweep of endless miles of undulant wheaty plain, with its capriciously strewn granite knobs and turreted hills of careless boulder, its huge stern sentinel rocks and in the arroyos, the *dongas*, long stands of trees. The plain was not treeless, it was clumped like an old, run-down orchard with the scrub thorns and *masuaki* bushes and strange cacti—rounded bushes that made little mock apple trees of grey-green against the yellow grass.

The building-size boulders never ceased to fascinate her; some were blue and some red or black in certain lights, and they blurted from the earth with no reason, scattered spendthriftly by the volcanic upheavals that had made the great rift which cracked East Africa apart, which had formed new mountains and extinguished volcanoes and made sere plains of what had been enormous lakes. Then there were always the long green hills; deceptively

245

swelling as gently as breasts until you tried to climb one and suddenly found it full of ankle-twisting loose cobbles and vindictive thornbushes, and what seemed at first so enticing a stroll suddenly steeped to rise straight up as any wall.

Across the plumed grass, at the bottom of the valley, before the valley tilted like a lifted bowl into a really vast grassed swamp which was nearly dry now—and which should be maggoty with elephant and buffalo, according to Brian—there were some moving spots which showed white and red among the black; these had to be Masai cattle.

'God damn it, Paul,' she heard Brian saying. 'I was afraid so. The Masai are in the swamp. And they're beginning to move up to our hills. There's a *manyatta* over there; I'll just see how long they've been on the rove. Rains certainly coming now, if they're trekking out of the swamps and heading up high. Probably march right through our camp.'

He jumped down.

'That finishes any elephant or buffalo in bulk in this swamp,' he said. 'By my reckoning, the Masai must have been grazing down there a couple of weeks, with anything that's wild scared back up the mountain and into the park. Oh, well. We didn't really need anything else. It's just that we might have picked up a really spectacular buffalo, and buff hunting is always good fun. Full of surprises and sudden frights.'

They drove to where Brian said he had seen the Masai *manyatta*. Its *boma* of thornbush had been burned, and scorched twigs still showed in the black scarring of fire and loose grey smear of ashes. The little flat-topped huts still smouldered slightly, but most of the walls stood. A smell of goats and cow manure still hung over the tiny deserted village.

'A proper *manyatta* burns like peat, for a long time,' Brian said. 'This was a kind of hit-or-miss one. More mud than cow dung. Shoddy job of construction.' He kicked a hut wall and a piece of the smoked plaster broke off. 'They've been gone about two days. I expect we'll run into a lot of the migrators as we hunt this country. Tracks I saw back there were all heading up in our direction.'

He started the car again. The sun was pounding down now, and the dust was beginning to lift off the plain as the animals moved. As they bumped along over the rocky track, Katie could almost feel the earth hardening under the steady soaking of the sun. It would be really bumpy on the way home, she thought. The tyres swelled and the earth got like rock, and driving was no fun any more until just before dark when the sun dropped and the dew started to cool things in preparation for the savage swift plunge of nightfall.

BRIAN HAD saved the dead pig for last. He had settled on a site for the hanging in the first glade they had seen and admired in the early morning—the unbelievably lovely Fragonard dell by the rush-bordered little river, no more than a few thousand yards from the camp. It was latish evening when they arrived, tired and very dusty, having hung two others baits—Paul had added another seedy old impala ram to the general bag—after a slapdash lunch out of the chopbox. The whole day, it seemed to Katie, had been devoted to finicky care in choosing just the right tree, with just the right branches, in just the right relationship to prevailing wind, water, cover and even the position of the setting sun. Brian had explained that all this was vitally necessary or there'd be no leopard coming to the blind.

The greening glade was occupied again by the same bouncing herd of impala they'd spotted that morning, and also by a mother warthog and a small fleet of antenna-tailed progeny. The guinea-fowl hordes had increased, and the big yellow-necked spurfowl, the francolin, scratched and clucked and stood on tiptoe to flap their wings. They seemed almost as tame as barn-yard fowl.

'There's your perfect leopard tree over there,' Brian said, pointing, as he stopped the jeep and motioned to the boys to see to the pig, which had bloated horribly from the heat, was abuzz with flies, was setting up an awful stink, and was considerably battle-worn from having been towed behind the car for the last mile. 'I spotted it this morning. We'll shoot a leopard out of this tree, I think.'

'It looks just like any other old tree to me,' Katie said. 'What makes it so special? I've seen thousands of fever trees today that look just like this one.'

'Well, it's got a nice slanting trunk, for one thing,' Brian said. 'You have to remember that the leopard's lazy. He can streak up a greased pole, if he wants to, but he'd rather have a tree he can saunter up instead of climb. And then the first fork is a very nice one—he can sit there and scan the scene before he nips upstairs to tackle the pig. You don't shoot him in the first fork—you wait until he gets to the feeding fork.'

'*I'd* shoot him in the first fork,' Katie said. 'Why don't you shoot him in the first fork?'

'Because it's not done. It's a difficult shot, with not much target area except his head, and you'd ruin the mask if you hit him at all. But apart from that you don't put your gun up until he's in the tree, and if you move while he's casing the countryside there'd be just one flirt of tail and that's the last you'll see of that particular *chui* on that particular day.'

'And so?' Katie didn't know why she persisted in being flip, since both her brother and Brian seemed to take all this very seriously. 'Why didn't we shoot him on the ground, then, before he jumped into the tree?'

'You won't see him on the ground.' Brian was patient, a teacher who'd been through this drill several hundred times. 'That's one of the reasons I chose this tree. It's got plenty of thick cover under it, behind it, and both sides of it. Leopards don't like to cross open spaces. The best leopard tree is generally in a hellish position for following him up if you don't kill him dead. This is in a dreadful piece of bush, so I'm depending on Paul to kill him dead.'

'Thanks,' her brother said, rather feebly.

Brian continued the lecture doggedly.

'I've selected a tree with the right kind of second fork. There's a branch we can tie the pig to by the hind feet, and a lovely branch below and just behind it so the cat can sit comfortably and gnaw his way into the pig's backside and belly—they always like to go in hind-end to, into the soft stuff.'

Kate made a mouth.

'But the important thing is to put the branch he *must* sit on close to the pig but to leave the pig hanging clear so he can't actually hide himself from you by feeding from behind the pig on another branch. And you have to see daylight behind the pig or you won't be able to spot the leopard when he comes, which is generally very late in the afternoon. So your tree has to be located with clear space behind that feeding branch, and also in a position where you'll get the setting sun behind you, or to one side, which will give you shooting light but not glare in your eyes, and which *will* get in the leopard's eyes. And your blind has to be fixed so that there's dark stuff behind *you*, so the leopard can't see you move against the daylight, for the reverse reason that you want light behind *him*.'

'You mentioned wind before. Why do you pay any attention to wind if the leopard can't smell? And if he can't smell, why did we bother dragging these dead animals around in circles?' Paul asked.

'The leopard can't smell much, if at all, but he can hear, and there are other animals who *can* smell,' Brian said. 'Hyenas will follow the trail I made with the pig. Leopard hears them and gets curious and comes to investigate. Now that's enough; I have work to do.' He nodded curtly to the gunbearers. Kidogo went over to the big tree and almost walked up the slanting bole, his prehensile heels gripping the rough bark.

Muema picked up the rope which had been passed through the reeking pig's slit hind legs when they towed him bumping behind the Rover. Muema took the coil in his right hand and, walking over to the bole of the tree, tossed the coiled rope upward like a lasso. Kidogo caught it, and passed it over a branch, paying off the free end until it snaked back to the ground again, whereupon Muema seized it and made it fast to the front bumper of the Land Rover. Brian crawled into the front seat and reversed the engine until the line tautened, then dragged the pig over to the foot of the tree. Then he accelerated, still in reverse, and the pig shot upward to the lofty branch on which Kidogo stood like a black angel awaiting the arrival of Little Eva in an amateur dramatic show.

They began to build the blind, now, using a fallen log and one standing dead acacia as a base, and the structure grew rapidly. In perhaps half an hour's time, the dead branches and one small green tree had been tugged into position so that they formed a kind of bower, the daylight-showing spots being plugged with the long grasses. The bower was open behind, but the rear was protected on both sides by curving arms of brush, and the front was a solid wall of branches and leaves.

Brian took the machete and went into the blind. He carefully chopped the underbrush and roots from the enclosure, and then scraped the earth level with the blunt blade of the *panga*, patting it smooth, with his palms. Then he used his hands to part the thorny front foliage, facing the leopard tree, to make apertures from which the dead pig would be visible. Then he shouted at Muema, who trotted up carrying a branch which he had chopped into a rude fork. Brian dug a hole in the ground in front of the largest aperture, and planted the sharpened end of the stick until its crotch was level with the peephole. Squatting, he sighted through the fork out towards the hanging bait, and then ran over to the base of the tree, where he stared critically at the blind. While he was looking a dove fluttered down from a neighbouring tree and perched atop the blind, teetering up and down on one of the topmost branches of the bower.

'It'll do,' Brian said, walking back over to the blind and fussing with a few stray branches in the front. 'It's fooled the bird.' The leafy structure now seemed to Katie's eyes to be exactly like any of the hundred old brush heaps she could see within a few hundred yards—one green tree surrounded by grass and blown-over dead thornbush.

'There's no halfway on this blind business,' Brian said. 'It's either perfect or useless. Paul, crawl in with your rifle and see if you can line your scope on the bait and the feeding branch comfortably. And move around—I want to see if I can detect any movement. You comfortable in shooting position? Not cramped or anything? It's important.'

'Sure. That pig is so close through the scope you can see the maggots already starting to work on him.'

'It's a little early for the mags,' Brian said. 'Tomorrow or next day. We'll sight your rifle tomorrow so it'll be dead on for fifty yards. Let's shove off, now.'

'It's a lot of trouble to go to for just one leopard,' Katie said, as they climbed back in the car and headed home. 'I hope it's worth it.'

'It's worth it,' Brian said. 'I say, this has been a day. Tomorrow we'll just rattle around and shoot some birds, maybe—I spotted the water where the sandgrouse drink—and check the kills to see if any of the leopards are feeding. Well, children, there's the prettiest sight in the world for my sore eyes. Campfire going and everything neat and shipshape by now. It takes them about a day to really get sorted out after a move, but everything ought to be perfection now.'

He pulled up in front of the mess tent. The cocktail doings had already been arranged on the table in front of the blaze, and the camp, as he said, was truly sorted out into a city. Freshly washed clothes hung on thornbushes, lanterns had already been taken to the sleeping-tents, and the debbie tins of water were spitting steam.

'I'm for a bath before grog,' Brian said. 'And after we get cleaned up, Paul, I'll give you the rest of this leopard business in one gulp, if Katie can stand it.'

'I can stand anything,' Katie said. 'I'm bathing too—and right now.' She hurried down the path to her tent, where her personal boy was already filling her tub.

*

'You realize,' Brian said as they sat before the blaze and sipped their drinks, watching a slim horn of moon cocking over the mountain and smelling something delicious being wafted from the cook-tent. 'Of course you realize that this is about moving time for the average leopard. He's a nocturnal animal, by habit, and the trick is to rebuild those habits and seduce him into being a daytime boy. This frequently takes a bit of doing.'

'You make it all sound so simple, Brian,' Paul Drake said.

'I was thinking the same thing,' his sister said. 'And I was thinking something else, too. I was thinking this: I have seen today all of the careful plotting and planning that goes into the collection of one lousy little speck of spotted fur. I have seen the way you run your safari—every tiny detail thought out and tested before. I see the way you understand wild animals, and the way you get along with Africans. On safari, that is.'

'All right,' Paul Drake said. 'So what's your point?'

'My point is rude and I think apt. If Kenya white people had devoted a fraction of the time and effort you spend trying to convince a lousy leopard to come to a tree so you can shoot him; if you invested a quarter of the attention to detail you spend on the workings of your safari—if you worked a tenth as hard trying to make *people* out of savages as you do to make gun-bearers and personal boys out of savages, you wouldn't have all these troubles in Africa today.'

'Perhaps there hasn't been time,' Brian said mildly. 'Perhaps the mass African doesn't want to learn. Perhaps he isn't capable of absorbing.'

'Rot. Purest poppycock to all of what you've said. He wants to learn. He can learn. And he's plenty capable of absorbing—just as capable of absorption as you've been capable of learning all the ins and outs of animal habit. You know more about leopards than the leopards themselves. You weren't born with spots and a tail. You took the trouble to learn.'

'But . . .'

'But nothing. Don't tell me it's more difficult for a white man to find out what makes a black man tick than it is for any kind of man to get inside a leopard's thinking apparatus. I tell you what I think——'

'. . . what else?' her brother murmured. 'Katie the capsule-thinker.'

'I think that you Kenya settlers really *like* your self-adopted self-pitying role of coping with the white man's burden. You're like doting mothers who lavish

250

all their attention on some half-idiot child and let the healthy part of the family go to pot. You concentrate on the individual rascal or special pet and forget the other ninety-nine per cent of ordinary black people. What the hell would you talk about out here if you didn't have the "African problem" to fill in the gaps in your conversation, such as it is?'

'You'll have to pardon my sister's rudeness,' Paul said. 'She went to one of those advanced schools and took a course in the social sciences. Actually, she was sore at us last night, but she didn't have anything to fix it on. To-night's little outburst is actually retroactive, since she doesn't want to waste a good mad.'

'At least she doesn't throw things,' Brian said, cheerfully, as if Kate were not present. 'One client's wife crowned me with a jug once because she was sore at her husband. Not that I'm not agreeing with Katie more than a little. She's put her finger on one thing—if we'd spent half the time trying sincerely to upgrade the Nig out here that we've spent fighting with each other over him, we'd all be better off.'

'Oh, damn,' Katie said. 'The diplomacy boy is back again. Soft answers making me look rude and sounding off out of turn, as usual. But I'm not backing down. If Brian can teach Muema to be a good chauffeur and mechanic and gunsmith, then Brian's people could certainly have taught Muema's people to stop eating each other and buckle down to the business of living in the present.'

'She hasn't missed a cliché yet,' Paul Drake said, admiringly. 'And we haven't even got to the mistakes the Belgians made in the Congo. Mistakes? It was simply standard banking practice. They kept 'em down on purpose and turned 'em loose on purpose and hoped they'd come trooping back like scared children, ripe for parental chastening and forgiveness. Instead they blew up in Papa's face and kicked Mama right in the crotch.'

'You sound like a white settler,' his sister said.

'I sound like an international banker who knows when the Belgian govern-ment sent the gold out of the Congo to Switzerland so the Congolese would be broke and dependent when they got the freedom they weren't reared to handle. That's what I sound like. I have shares in the Union Minière du Haut Katanga, my dear sister, and I have done business for a lot of years with that elusive octopus, the Société Générale Belgique.'

'I only know about leopards and elephant,' Brian said. 'Thank God.'

'Thank God,' Katie Crane said. 'Not women?'

'Never women,' Brian said. 'Thank God twice.'

'Amen,' Paul Drake said. 'I suggest we eat. I want, for once, to hear the news.'

'You won't like it,' his sister said. 'You never do.'

THEY SAT sat outside the mess tent, listening to the transistor radio and drinking their coffee. Reception was good from the BBC relay from London to Nairobi, and the coffee was better. The moon was still waxing, and the lightness of the air magnified the moonlight and hung spiked halos round the stars. There were no clouds on Kilimanjaro now; her snowy head was clearly visible. They had brought the radio out to the table by the fire. The announcer was saying:

'And now, for the summary of the night's news: In London, African leaders announced firm stand on Congo partition while battle for Kasai rages; in the Congo, new warfare between Baluba tribesmen breaks out in Katanga as Tshombe stands firm against Lumumba troops; in New York, Congolese President Joseph Kasavubu reasserts position before United Nations; in Washington, crisis feared in Laos as troops mass outside Vientiane; in London, Princess Alexandra prepares to visit Lagos for Nigerian independence celebrations; in New York, Presidential candidate John Kennedy says U.S. loses prestige in world affairs; in Cuba, Premier Castro today accused United States of aggression in sugar crisis; in Moscow, Cuban Finance Minister Ernesto Guevara announces new Russian loan; in Leopoldville—Soviet ambassador withdrawn as Congo cancels diplomatic relations with Mbotu interim government; from Augusta, Georgia, President Eisenhower announced today that Cuban sugar purchases may be further curtailed. . . .'

Brian snapped off the machine as the announcer said 'and now, here is the home news from Britain'.

'We'll wait five minutes for the Kenya round-up,' he said. 'That BBC home news is really useless. Mostly about new species of tufted titmouses being seen in Surrey. Dreary picture everywhere, isn't it? I've got to where about all I listen for is the safari broadcasts and the weather reports.'

They sat in silence for a moment until Paul said:

'What will they do in the Congo, Brian? Every day it seems worse and worse. The United Nations is fouling it up, it seems to me, after a pretty fair start. I think they made a mistake, actually, in sending black troops to police the place.'

'I couldn't agree more,' Brian said. 'You just don't send a bunch of crap-shooters to break up a dice game. I can't follow it any more, and I doubt anybody else can. The Nigs have just gone back to playing Nig, with a vengeance, and devil take the unlucky losers.'

'Seems strange to sit here in this peace and beauty and hear all the turmoil,' Katie said. 'Sort of like going to heaven and then getting all the reports from the nasty old world short-waved over the Celestial Broadcasting System. I must say I prefer our kind of hyena to the Russian variety, if that last business in the UN was any sample.'

They sat again in silence, listening to one of Katie's personal hyenas, until Brian fiddled with the knobs on the radio again. '. . . was killed today by a trained lion near Arusha where the motion picture *Hatari* is being made. Diana Hartley, animal trainer for the Paramount picture, was seized by a lion which had been imported from Ethiopia and was said to be . . . *scree-eee-awk* . . .'

'Di Hartley!' Brian said, 'I've known her ever since the war. She . . .' The radio interrupted him with a *scree-eee-awkkk-scree* . . . 'of Carr-Hartley, also well known in animal circles. The trial continued today at Athi River in the Masai-Wakamba cattle-raiding battle in which . . . *scree-eeeak-awww-eek—* KANU Secretary Tom Mboya announced a general strike today in protest against the continued incarcer-incarceration of nationalist leader Jomo Kenyatta. Kikuyu houseboy held in *panga* murder of Asian housewife in Nairobi. More oathings and cattle butchery announced in Thika-Fort Hall area where police said *scree-eee-awwk*. President James Gichuru of the Kenya Africa National Union arrived in London today to attend the meeting of the Pan-African Conclave together with President Matthew Kamau and Abraham Matisia of KNAP. In Nairobi, KANU headquarters was robbed and wrecked as Tom Mboya charges KADU sabotage resulting from Youth Wing riots at Nyeri; Secretary Stephen Ndegwa of Kaynap left today for a speech-making tour of North America; President Matthew Kamau of Kaynap quoted in London as——'

Brian snapped off the news again.

'That's a pretty fair representative bag,' he said. 'Wog politicians, world troubles, the odd flood and famine, the Russians, the UN, the Congo, and your Presidential election. There's nothing I can do about it; I don't think there's anything anyone could do about it. Pity about poor Di Hartley, though. She was raised among animals. Must have done something very wrong with this one.'

He got up and kicked a shower of sparks off a dying log.

'A very hard-luck family,' he said. 'Some families seem to run to hard luck out here.'

'I can't imagine you ever being chewed up by any animal,' Katie Crane said. 'Not after watching you work with them for a month; not after that liberal education on leopards today.'

'I can,' Brian replied. 'There's always the one animal you can't figure. There's always the one you can't gamble on. That's why so many good men I know wear scars. I have one friend, a hunter, who looks like a relief map of Europe from a little do where a leopard out-thought him and chewed chunks out of him. I had another friend who got permanently squashed by an old lady elephant. In just the last month one chum got tossed by a buffalo and broke his back and another got shot in the foot and another lost most of his face in a hunting-car accident.'

'Sounds as if they might have been pretty careless,' Paul said.

Brian shook his head.

'None of them was careless. They got ganged by mathematical probabilities. You know, when Katie was chewing on me about the Africans before

253

dinner, I started to say that mostly we could figure the animals, but because they usually react reasonably and you can play to their strength and turn it sometimes into the thing that trips them. With Africans its different. They play to your weakness and trip *you*. I don't think they understand kindness and gratitude. And certainly no white man can really crawl inside their skulls to find out how they tick.'

'How many have tried? Precious few, I'd bet,' Katie said.

'My people tried. You know what happened to them. And now—wait a minute. Hold on. I've a couple of clippings in my brief-case that I carry around to prove a point with the clients once in a while. I'll see if I can dig them up.'

Brian strode off to his tent, and was back in a few moments with a tattered yellowed *Time* magazine and a creased clipping from the *Daily Express* in his hand.

'Poor Diana on the wireless brought this to mind. It *is* a hard-luck family, and this is very much in point, Katie. I keep these cuttings to show the sceptical clients. Would one of you read these, in that order—the *Time* story first?'

'I left my specs in the tent,' Paul said. 'Katie, move over under the lights and do the honours—if they taught you to read in that school of yours.'

'I don't see the necessity—why don't you just tell us?' She turned to Brian.

'No. I'd really prefer you see it. If you see it for yourself it's not just a lot of white-hunter conversation lugged in by the ears to plug up a hole in an argument. It isn't an argument, anyhow. It's a sermon. Read it, please.'

Katie Crane walked over into a puddle of light and began to read the crumpled, much-handled stories.

KENYA—BLOOD BROTHER *Time Magazine, November* 1, 1954

The Mau Mau rebellion in Kenya was two years old last week. In that bloody stretch of time the Mau Mau have killed or wounded 2,000 loyal Kikuyu natives, 999 African or European soldiers and 27 innocent European civilians. The expensive war against them (present cost: $2,800,000 a month) has resulted in the slaying of 6,741 Mau Mau and the capture of 12,000.

Through the two years of terror, probably no Englishman in Kenya was more sympathetic to the problems and irritations besetting the Kikuyu than sixtyish Arundel Gray Leakey, a resident of Kenya for close to half a century. Like his better-known cousin, L. S. B. Leakey, the world's topmost authority on Kikuyu manners and morals and official interpreter at the trial of Mau Mau Chieftain Jomo Kenyatta, Gray Leakey had been accepted into the Kikuyu tribe as a 'blood brother' and spoke the native language as readily as he did English. Refusing to believe that Mau Mau would harm either himself or his family, he never carried a gun as he made the rounds of his lonely farm 100 miles north of Nairobi.

One night a month ago, Gray Leakey was challenged by prowling armed terrorists. In their own dialect, he told them that he was unarmed, turned his back and strolled away. True to his expectations, they let him go unharmed. One evening last fortnight, however, as Leakey, his wife and his stepdaughter Diana Hartley were having supper at the farm, a band of 30 Mau Mau swarmed out of the woods. Mrs. Leakey rushed to the bathroom with her daughter and helped her escape through a trap-door into an attic above. Mrs. Leakey herself was too weak to follow. When Diana emerged an hour later, her mother was lying dead on the lawn, cruelly slashed with Mau Mau knives. Gray Leakey was nowhere to be found.

For days after, native and European police by the hundreds combed the jungle searching for Gray Leakey, a diabetic who could scarcely survive four days anywhere without proper medical care. Last week the search was given up. Cousin Leakey took to the air to warn other Kenya whites against such kindness and complacency as that of Arundel Gray Leakey.

Katie stopped reading.

'But what happened to him?' she asked.

'That's what the other cutting's for,' Brian said. 'Read on. They never found him, but they found out what happened to him.'

Katie handed him the *Time* clip and picked up the *Express* cutting. She read:

MAU THUGS BURY BRITON ALIVE

Informers reported tonight that Mr. Arundel Gray Leakey, a blood-brother of the Kikuyu, who was kidnapped 11 days ago by Mau Mau, was buried alive as a sacrifice to Kikuyu gods.

This became known after the capture of the Mau Mau leader, Field-Marshal Kaleba, as he slept in a cave a mile from the Queen's Royal Lodge, on the Sagana River.

The informers added that the sacrifice was ordered by a witch doctor who said the gods demanded a white man's blood to bring victory to the Mau Mau.

Mr. Leakey, aged 63, was first forced to take part in an oath ceremony. Kaleba is said to have organized the raid on the Leakeys.

A girl captured with Kaleba had jewellery which belonged to Mrs. Leakey, who was strangled by the raiders.

'Buried him alive?' Katie said, as she finished reading and came back to her chair in front of the fire. 'My God! I can't believe it. How horrible! And he was the father of the girl that the lion killed, that we heard about on the radio tonight?'

'That's right,' Brian said. 'Stepfather, actually. That's why I said that about a hard-luck family.'

'But I don't understand why they'd choose a *friend* for such a terrible thing. Truly, it says here, a blood-member of the tribe,' Paul said.

'It's a little thing we can't seem to make clear about the way an African's

255

mind works. In the Mau Mau, quite frequently the cooks and houseboys were called on to chop the very people who treated them most kindly. In a couple of instances some Kikuyu committed suicide rather than go through with their assignments, because they were damned if they did and damned if they didn't.

'But you see,' Brian said. 'Killing a person closest to you shows how deeply oath-bound you are. And the sacrificial death of one of your own people, who just also happens to be white, becomes twice as potent as an oath when you really need your luck to change. Same as the old Biblical business about sacrificing your own flesh and blood at the Lord's command.'

'I don't understand it,' Katie said. 'I just can't understand it. Why would they bury him alive? Why not kill him first? I see also that he was made to take an oath before they—buried him.' She shuddered. 'They bind him even more tightly as a brother and then they still sacrifice him.'

'What *Time* didn't tell you—couldn't know,' Brian said, 'is one of the deeper-rooted pieces of Kikuyu folklore, of sacrificial ritual. Practically nothing these people do is binding unless a ram or a goat or even a person is slain —that's how the Mau Mau oaths evolved, you know. They were actually reversing the old Abraham-Isaac burning bush-cum-scapegoat business.

'Everything these people do is tied to spirits and curses—even those fine gentlemen who make speeches now in London and wear dinner jackets and eat in the Stanley Grill. They aren't above placating the ghosts with a sheep or paying a visit to the old witch doctor to ensure success in the next elections.

'There is a blood ceremony for everything—weddings, circumcisions, cattle trades, house-building, lawsuits, sickness, bad luck, departure, homecoming, planting, harvesting—name it and they've got a ceremony for it. It always involves some nauseating businesses to do with breaking the bones of live animals and skinning things alive, eating stomach contents and cutting off sexual organs and plucking out eyes to make mumbo-jumbo stew.

'When big trouble, really big disaster, like a smallpox epidemic or tremendous famine or any big killer hits the tribe, one of the most potent of all the rituals is burial alive. The trouble is then buried deep in the earth, to be washed away by the springs. In Leakey's case the big trouble was the white man.'

Paul Drake nodded his head. 'They really had it all worked out for themselves before we twisted up their thought processes, didn't they?'

'They did,' Brian said. 'And of course you see why they'd want to bury Gray Leakey alive?'

'Almost—not quite,' Katie Crane said.

'Luck was running against the Mau Mau, which was really quite religious in reverse concept, even though it was cynically inspired and viciously degraded in practice. They *had* to change their luck; poor old Leakey had the misfortune to be both white villain and respected Kikuyu elder—the perfect scapegoat. So they planted him in the lone prairee.'

Brian hunched his shoulders and spread his hands. 'And the exact date of that was what, Katie?'

'November the first, 1954.'

'Six years ago, almost. So you see. You perhaps also see why my friend Don Bruce is so upset about his latest baby being baptized a Kikuyu—being chosen for a sacrifice when *uhuru* comes? I told you Don wants to sell his farm. It's the same thing all over again, except now the Kyukes will want new blood sacrifices to celebrate a fresh start, with the white man on the run and the Kikuyu on the ascendant. And this time they will not choose a man for their scapegoat, but a white child, also Kikuyu, who will express their thanks to God for their new golden age. It is really quite simple.'

'I suppose it's true enough,' Paul Drake said. 'You keep reading about witchcraft being on the upsurge in the Congo again. I expect you do owe Brian a small apology, Katie. Perhaps—without excusing the settlers for being shortsighted—it's not all quite so simple as it meets the eye. Perhaps we are dealing with a different sort of raw material from the white man, perhaps.'

'Perhaps they're still not out of the trees yet, is what we say,' Brian's voice was smoothly pleasant. 'And damn me if I think they ever will be, not as a mass. How much progress have you shown with your true, solid blacks in two hundred years? How much progress have you seen in Haiti, which has been black and free for over a hundred and sixty years? How much progress have you noticed in Ethiopia, which has been black and free for *three thousand years*, for God's sake?'

'All right,' Katie said. 'I give in on the shades of the mentality thing. Maybe it is basically different and will stay different for a long time. Maybe they'll be like the Chinese and Japanese and never see things quite the Western way. But it still doesn't disprove my argument that the place to start is at the bottom and teach 'em white man's responsibility, if they have to live in a white man's world—not keep them static forever as stupid brute labour and as sort of amusing house pets or else wild, woolly picture-book savages like your precious blood-drinking Masai.'

'Yes, Sister Nell. Yes, Aunt Charlotte. Yes, Brother George. *Yes*, Katie. I agree completely with you,' Brian said. 'All I want to know is how. All I want to know is *how* to find out what the African really wants so we can give it to him. And all I want is just a little outside appreciation of the fact that the white man literally just got to Kenya, himself, and has done one hell of a job in half a century of turning the jungle into something its own people now want to steal and ruin, like baboons loose in a granary.'

'Perhaps the secret's in the women.' Katie's voice was hesitant. 'Perhaps if the women ever . . .'

'Yes, Nell. Yes, George,' Brian said again, mockingly. 'Look, Katie Crane. I don't know of any happy native women, emancipated or otherwise. I don't think they—I don't think they understand happiness, as we understand it. I don't even know that they *do* think. And certainly the men don't want them any way but the way they are—circumcised and pregnant, hard-working and

257

stupid. And even the circumcision's falling off now, with the new ways. I suppose'—he grinned sardonically—'I suppose the missionaries have been telling them that sex can be fun for a woman if it's sanctified by the right God.'

'And isn't sex supposed to be fun for a native woman?' Katie asked sharply. 'I thought you said the Masai——'

'I did say the Masai. But I think it's only supposed to be fun for the man there, too. Certainly the whole purpose of female circumcision among most tribes was based in a desire to dull the sex urge, so they'd stay home and work and not go running off with every randy buck that pleased them in the bushes.'

'I'm a little short on my knowledge of this female-circumcision business,' Paul Drake said. 'Without sparing Katie's blushes, expand it a little bit, please, Brian.'

'It isn't a circumcision, as a man is properly circumcised,' Brian said. 'It is more precisely what is medically defined as a clitoridectomy. Just after puberty they remove the clitoris and a good portion of the—labiae majorae, I believe they're called. Big celebration do for all the girls—sort of coming out, like a ball.'

'Apart from the unbelievably joyous pain of social togetherness with one's classmates,' Katie said, 'what other purpose does this barbarous practice serve?'

'It started out hundreds, maybe thousands of years ago, as a simple device to keep the young girls home—keep 'em from cheapening their bride price by sleeping around and getting irresponsibly pregnant before they were of marriageable age. But as time passed it also took on great social importance. No decent man would marry an uncircumcised woman; no woman could hold up her head in tribal society unless she'd been through the whole course of parties and dancing and feasting in honour of the ceremony. It was the biggest thing in her life, because after the operation she was on the marriage block for true.'

'They still do this, then?' Paul Drake asked. 'Even today?'

'It's falling off—disappearing except back in the hills. The missionaries were always against it. And now the more modern, lipsticked little fuzz-headed tramps you see around town are products of no-circumcision. They ain't married, either. The Kikuyu man still wants his gal properly tended to, or she's not the marrying kind.'

Katie shook her head sadly.

'My God, everywhere you go, woman's lot is miserable. I don't think I'd like being a lady if it entailed that sort of debutante ceremony—although it couldn't hurt much worse than prep-school field hockey.'

Brian smiled.

'Rather a sad thing happened out here during the war, when the good missionaries took up the no-circumcision cudgels. One dry old white disciple was particularly violent against it. So some of the well-meaning native elders figured the old gal had a *thahu*—curse—on her which came from *not* having been properly circumcised as a maiden. So one night a bunch of dedicated public servants, functioning for her own good, whipped her into the bush and rectified the oversight with a knife.'

'I'm certain they meant well,' Katie said tartly. 'And I supposed the operation fixed her up just dandy, and she lived happily ever after?'

'Well, no,' Brian's voice was sober now. 'Not precisely. As a matter of fact the missionary lady was just a touch old for the ceremony. She bled to death.'

They sat silent for a moment.

'I'm sorry,' Brian said, presently. 'I didn't mean to be flip. But you must admit it *is* just one more example of the blank wall you're up against out here.'

'It is indeed,' Paul said. 'It is indeed.' He paused. 'You mustn't mind my saying this, Brian. But you've mentioned that your friend Bruce wants to sell his farm and leave. What would be wrong with my buying it—get somebody to run it for me, hang onto it until we see how things turn out? Bruce could always buy it back if he liked——'

Brian stood up and walked over to the drink table.

'Nightcap, Paul?' he asked, and waited until he had fixed the two drinks before he answered the question.

'You're very kind, you know, and very sincere, I'm sure,' he said. 'But desperate as Don is I don't think he'd want to sell to an outsider who bought it purely out of pity. I wouldn't, in the same set of circumstances.'

'But you've said he's desperate,' Katie said. 'I don't see anything wrong with what Paul's offering. . . . After all, it wouldn't make any real difference to Paul. He's filthy rich, and . . .'

Brian's voice was very gentle now.

'Katie, Katie,' he said. 'Can't you see there's a curious kind of morality mixed up in this thing? Don wouldn't want to do the very thing the Nigs scream about—sell off his farm to some absentee landlord and really cheat some more Nigs out of some more land. Paul doesn't belong here. Don and I and Aunt Charlotte and the rest of the family do. It's our country and our responsibility, not Paul's or yours.'

'He wants money enough to leave,' Paul said stubbornly. 'He wants to leave his responsibility. I'd pay him what it's worth. Money's money.'

'Maybe Don would see it your way,' Brian answered. 'I don't know. Ask him if you'd like when we get back. But I think he'd rather be like Aunt Charlotte and give it away to his own niggers than to sell it to a foreigner, because . . .' his voice fumbled '. . . because then, you see, he'd be admitting everything the blacks accuse us of is *true*. We don't want their accusations to be true. We still like to think that we've built the land and helped the people, too, and are entitled to what we've earned in a country that nobody really owns.'

'I suppose I understand,' Paul Drake said unwillingly. 'No absentee landlords, even if it means getting your throat cut, eh?'

259

'More or less.' Brian yawned, and looked at his watch. 'Do you people realize it's midnight?'

'*I* do,' Katie said. 'God, this has been a day. If you gentlemen don't mind, I think I'll sleep in tomorrow and sort of let you manage without me until after lunch. I want to do my hair, or at least wash some of the sticks and lizards out of it. And between leopards, female circumcision, burials alive and yesterday's trek, I am a real weary woman. Good night, you two stinking colonial imperialists.'

She got up and walked slowly down the pathway to her tent.

'I think I'll do the switch and sit here for a while and listen to Katie's hyenas,' Paul said. 'Thanks for a very informative day, Brian. See you in the morning.'

Brian nodded and walked down to stand in the shadows on the point by the river. Paul Drake spilled another inch of Scotch into his glass and settled down to smoke and stare into the fire. The moon rode very high in the sky now, and Kilimanjaro was brilliant in its icy light. The hyenas hooted, and in the bush something—a leopard or a baboon, he judged—grunted. Paul Drake nodded with his feet in the fire. He was thinking that it was a pity you had to live so long in a country before you knew anything about the country or its peoples at all—and by the time you did, it was generally too late to do much about it. He nodded, dropped his glass, slept, and woke shivering much later, with the fire dead and the moon beginning to fade.

CHAPTER TWELVE

THEY SLEPT late. Paul Drake was just rising with the sun high when he heard his sister whistling outside her tent next door. She was drying her hair with exaggerated vigour as she whistled.

Brian was sitting in the mess tent with what appeared to be his fourth or fifth cup of coffee, judging from the cigarette butts in the ashtray. He looked enormously pleased with himself.

'Hello, you two,' he said, and called Mwende to bring fresh coffee. He smiled his small-boy happy smile at Paul and said: 'I've wonderful news for you. Early unsuspected action. Kidogo and Muema skipped down to the pig-tree, that last bait we hung yesterday, and guess what?'

'I know,' Katie said. 'The leopard ate Muema and Kidogo.'

'Hardly. But the big fellow came last night, and gobbled all of the stomach and most of one hind quarter off the bait. They don't usually feed the first day.'

'How do you know it's the big one?' Paul Drake asked.

'Couldn't be anything else. His tracks all over the foot of the tree, and the trunk fresh claw-scarred, Kidogo says. No female tracks at all. The old gent's keeping his womenfolk out of the commissary until he's had his fill. I think with luck, him being so bold and all, we might collect him today, Paul. If they feed that soon they usually get confident fast.'

'I'm beginning to feel excited in spite of myself,' Katie said. 'I hope he's enormous, Bro, and I hope you wallop him right through a ragged rosette, so's you won't spoil his hide.'

'I hope I hit him at all,' Paul Drake said. 'Let's have that coffee again, please, Brian. We sight the rifle?'

'After you've finished the coffee. I thought we'd take a little reccy and check the other baits. Ordinarily we could sight the rifle here in camp, but we're awful close to the kill. Best drive off a mile or so.'

They had sighted the rifle to Brian's satisfaction, the scope adjusted to zero at fifty yards, and had gone to inspect the other two kills. Brian glassed the first from several hundred yards away, and shook his head.

'Nothing so far,' he shrugged. 'However, sometimes they don't come for five or six days, until you can smell the bait for five miles. Oddly, they seem to be overbold when they wait a long time, too. It's the in-between ones that practise the most caution.'

They drove on four or five miles to the other tree, which was almost a replica of the blind arrangement of the feeding bait near the camp. It too was pitched near the river's edge, but in much thicker country. The kill-tree was surrounded by bush, and was set more deeply back into the jungled trees and tangled dense underbrush of the river than the other two.

Brian stopped the Land Rover on top of a high rise.

'We made an awful lot of noise clanging and banging this jeep going down through those rocks and trying to navigate those Grand Canyon gullies yesterday. If we try a car-approach to this blind we'd scare any leopard that might be hanging around clean back to Tanganyika. And if we stay in the blind until nightfall, Muema'll never get this car down over all those boulders in the dark. I guess we'll just have to walk about a half mile, very, very softly. But maybe we'll be lucky with our camp blind, where the big chap's feeding.' He trained his glasses on the tree.

'No . . . no . . .' he murmured. 'Hey! There's your Bateleur eagle!' he said, as a smallish eagle sailed out of the tree and circled on stiff wings, looking almost like a vulture in the blue sky. 'And . . . oh, Christ! Muema! *Darubini ingine!*'

He took the long binoculars and handed them to Paul, then gave his own short glasses to Katie.

'He's in the tree!' he whispered. 'Look, count up from the bait—one, two, three branches, just to the left of the kill. See him? He's lying full length on that branch. You can see one paw and his tail hanging down! He's a beauty, Paul, really a beauty!'

'Jesus,' Paul breathed, as he looked.

'Christ,' his sister added reverently.

The big cat was sound asleep above the kill, his golden, black paw-printed hide gleaming through the delicate dark fretting of the acacia's leaves. Blue sky showed behind him, and the tail swung curved at the end like a thick question mark. One big paw hung indolently, and the big cat was obviously sleeping off a large morning meal.

'I'll try to slip us away from here without waking him,' Brian said, starting the car. But as the engine came alive Katie could see the leopard stand, yawn, stretch, turn towards the noise of the motor, then streak down the bole of the fever tree like a big lizard. He paused a semi-second at the fork, and then leaped to the ground in a graceful limpid blur of yellow and was gone from sight in the thick bush at the foot of the tree.

'Well, we don't have to be cautious any more,' Brian said, raising his voice to normal as he turned the car. 'He'll lie up in the bush again before he comes to the tree to work on that meat some more. By God, Paul!' His voice held honest excitement. 'Isn't that something to see? Katie?'

'I'm shaking all over, and I'm not even in the blind,' her brother said. 'But, tell me, isn't this rather unusual? Actually catching him in the tree in broad daylight?'

'Yes,' Katie said. 'It seems to me we're fair swarming in leopards. I thought they were awfully rare and you never saw them by day unless you went through all that business you told us about yesterday.'

Brian gave his attention to bumping the car along the hillside, weaving around the bigger boulders and lifting the car gently over some of the smoother, flatter stones, before he spoke.

'I've only seen half a dozen asleep in a tree by high day in my life,' he said. 'Mostly all you ever see is a flash when they jump down, if you see them at all. Our girl Katie's brought us luck.'

'That's awfully thick stuff in there,' Paul said. 'Awfully thick.'

'Too thick, as a matter of fact,' Brian replied. 'And so's the non-feeding one we just looked at. But I'm hoping we won't have to sit for this gentleman or bother with that last blind at all. The other feeder's as big, judging from his paw-prints, maybe even bigger. We're just plain lucky. I expect we'd better go now and collect a few more guinea-fowl at a decent distance away from these kills, Paul, and then let's head for the barn. I'm thirsty, and it feels like a long gin-and-tonic morning.'

*

They were shaken gently awake from their post-lunch siesta by the room-boys. Brian was waiting with the afternoon tea when they washed their sleep-damp faces and came to the mess tent.

'Leopard time,' he said cheerfully. 'Hot, ain't it?' The flat pound of the afternoon sun on the mess tent's canvas was almost audible. The air was very close, and now cloud masses had piled, obscuring the mountain, baling up on the horizon. The rainbird's three-note call was clear in the still heat.

'It's sticky, all right,' Katie said. 'My neck hair is sopping. I sweated a real good stain on the pillow—first time since the north.'

'Feels like what we used to call a weather-breeder,' her brother said. 'Is it?'

'Wouldn't be surprised. That's solid rain tucked away in all those black puffballs, right enough. It'll wool up a little more each day now, and then, wallop! Time to pack up and go. I assume we'll have the old *chui* down and dead and scraped and salted by then, with his wishbone sandpapered nice and shiny to make Katie a lucky brooch. Well, shall us up and away?'

They drove leaning sideways along the slope of the hill. The same green meadowland, as they worked downhill and then flat along the river's edge, was empty now of game. No dainty-footed golden impala fed; no birds scratched or ran. Silence hung tangibly, oppressively, and in the distance, past the purple hills, the sky had darkened from its clear wash almost to sulky violet.

'Yep, she's a-building, all right,' Brian said again. 'Look over there.' He pointed to a low collar of black cloud around the throat of a small mountain. A bluish vertical haze seemed slanted beneath the cloud, almost like a slightly leaning tower of striated stone. 'That's the rains, chums. And every day they'll march closer.'

He stopped the car and walked around to the side. Muema handed him a double-barrelled shotgun. Brian broke it, squinted through the barrels, and then looked closely at the two fat black cartridges Muema handed him.

'Buckshot,' he explained, inserting the shells. 'Wanted to be sure that they weren't fives or sixes. I'm betting you don't wound him, Paul, but if you do and I have to go pull him out by the tail, I don't want to discover in the hospital that we used birdshot instead of buckshot in this blunderbuss.'

Brian climbed in the back, and Muema moved up front to take the wheel. As the car started to move, Brian said: 'Jump out into the blind when I tap your shoulder, Paul, and Katie, you scramble in behind him. Sit on Paul's right. Don't forget your cushions. That ground gets awful hard about an hour from now. And if you want one last smoke, have it now.'

The Land Rover jounced along, Muema driving as carefully and quietly as possible in second gear, following the track that they had made when they first sighted the area and then, later, when they had hung the kill in the tree. They turned right and went slightly more steeply downhill and now Katie could see the brown beehive of the blind, already looking comfortably weathered after only a day, already almost indistinguishable from the other rubbish-hummocked fallen trees and dead-grass-rimmed rocks.

Muema was slowing now, shifting to low gear, and she could feel her brother stir beside her, then spring out of the doorless Rover—almost like the paratroops; she thought *Geronimo!* as she plunged blindly out of the car behind him. She landed harshly on her hands and knees and scurried crawling into the blind. Paul passed her a pillow, which she slid under her backside and then arranged her legs spraddled wide, tucked in and crossed Indian-fashion at the ankles. She stole a quick peek through the little porthole in the leafy barrier of the blind, and found that she could clearly see the dead pig hanging, his hide whitened by the afternoon sun that struck sideways into the deep-shadowed tree.

She turned her head very slowly—Brian had warned her to make no abrupt motions in the blind—and saw that Paul had leaned his rifle against the front of the blind, next the forked stick which would hold the gun when—and if—he fired it. He was sitting, looking intently through his peephole over the crotched rest, his knees drawn up and his arms clasped round his legs. Every muscle in his body seemed tense, and his eyes strained to the opening in the thatched branches.

Brian was not tense. He was lounging well back behind them both, leaning on one elbow, one knee drawn back to rest his other arm. Presently he eased himself a little farther to the rear, turned comfortably on his side, and straightened both legs in front of him. He saw her looking at him and winked.

Katie swung her chin back slowly and stared through her peephole. There was nothing in front of her but a patch of meadow-smooth green ground and a rim of trees lining a rushy river and a tall big-boled yellow-black-mottled thorn tree with a dead pig slung into its rigging. She could hear birds, though—away behind her came the goosed-girl *oohoo-oohoo—oohoo—OOO!* of a dove, and a silvery tinkling bell-bird she'd never heard before.

There was a slight, comforting chittering of monkeys in the bush ahead, where the leopard must come, and the lazy *fa-aak* of the long-tailed bird she could now identify as the lori. And away down the river-bed she heard a harsh castanet clatter of guinea-fowl. There was nothing more of any real interest except the lazy hum of locusts. It was hot though, hot as blazes in that little leafy oven they sat in, hot except for the cool feel of the shaded ground coming up through the fibre sweat-pillow they used in the front seats of the Rover.

A drop of sweat ran down Katie's nose and fell with a frighteningly loud plop. She cut her eyes sideways to see if either man had noticed this un-planned disturbance, but her brother was still pinned to his peephole, and Brian, leaning backwards on his brown bare arm, resting his chin on the heel of his hand, had locked the impossibly long fringes of his lashes, and seemed to be asleep. Katie noticed for the first time that the scarred twelve-bore shotgun was resting with its trigger guard on an old grey turtlenecked sweater which she remembered seeing Brian wear one cold morning. My God, but silence was noisy when you listened to it objectively.

Already one of her feet was going numb. She looked at her watch—five to five. Brian said the leopard probably wouldn't come before six, usually some time between six and seven. That meant an hour, two hours more, before the crash of her brother's rifle or the climbing shaky beam of Muema's headlamps would rescue her from the enforced silence and the maddening little itches that were now beginning to crawl like thistles from one portion of her body to another.

Ah, some action finally. Brian must really be a ring-tailed marvel at building leopard blinds, she thought, for here comes a whole fleet of unsuspecting guinea-fowl. They were feeding straight into the blind, working up from the rushes at the rim of the river where they'd undoubtedly been resting out of the heat. Strange, obscene, naked-headed brutes they were, although the way old Aly boiled them and then served them cold in thick coarse-cut slices, with tomatoes and sliced sweet onions and crisp lettuce from the icebox, was wonderful, and they were wonderful too in soups and stews, and when you shot them young enough, broiled on the grill after being hung a couple of days.

Her dietary habits had certainly changed, Katie thought, in the last month. She had never enjoyed game of any sort, but game was the only fresh meat you got out here, and somehow now it didn't taste full of old gunpowder. Also it didn't conjure up vivid ideas of shot and blood-draggled feathers and limp dead necks. But it was just as well they didn't serve the guineas head and all, as they served pheasant in England sometimes, she thought, as one old yellow-helmeted cock minced up to the blind and fixed her wickedly with a rheumy red eye, twisting his scaly naked neck. They were pretty at a distance but as filthily horrid face to face as a turkey or a buzzard. Her lips formed the word 'shoo' soundlessly, and after scratching industriously for a moment, her friend fed off with the rest of the flock, which was making big oval purple splashes on the billiard-table baize of the pasture.

In a moment the guineas were replaced by the grousy-looking yellow-necked francolin, almost as large as hen pheasants, pleasantly plumed in decent brown and yellow and black, and miraculously, lovingly built entirely of white meat by some epicurean Almighty. Katie had shot a lot of francolin; in fact, guinea and francolin and sandgrouse were the only things she *would* shoot. Her conscience pricked her not at all when she saw Muema scoop up a fluttering, wounded bird and twist its neck. They looked slow in the air, but were quite sporty when the boys chased them up and made them fly high, like driven pheasant, and they certainly made a delicious cold lunch or a fine chunky chicken à la king.

It was the pairing season for francolin now, and also for the guineas. Each day you saw more and more birds leaving the flocks and running by twos. It could be the pairing season for me too if only somebody'd ask me, Katie thought, but perhaps I'd better not dwell on thoughts like that in a leopard blind. Might frighten the leopard if I suddenly leaped on Brian and bore him to the earth—saying, of course, that Paul had to go somewhere and leave us alone.

Alone. I wonder, Katie thought, watching the birds scratch, seeing a hen partridge pecking annoyedly under one wing for some mite or louse, I wonder how much of your life you *do* spend waiting for something to happen—something that's over almost before it's started, and maybe isn't much good after it gets there? I would say that all of my life has been spent alone, until just about now, when I really feel I've shared something with these two Boy Scouts here in the blind with me. It's been a new thing to wake up every day with a sense of urgent expectancy—the thought of seeing something new and possibly exciting, and always beautiful.

Here I sit in a leopard blind, Katie thought, virginal of belonging at the age of thirty-five, going on thirty-six, and I'm tired of it. I want to belong to somebody and do something, anything, before the menopause and the moustache set in. I wonder if I ever will do anything about it, can do anything about it? Maybe I was born allergic to being happy. The thought depressed her.

Now Katie felt a sneeze mounting. Oh God, don't let me sneeze, don't let me sneeze, don't let me sneeze. Don't let me wreck Bro's leopard, don't let me sneeze and make Brian think of me as one more nuisance like all the other women that come on safari and wave their hips and flutter their lashes at him. I will not sneeze, will not sneeze, will *not* sneeze, and I didn't either. It's gone away and will stay away because I willed it that way. I am very proud of me for not sneezing.

Wonder what Brian thinks of when he's sitting in a leopard blind for the thousandth time? He can't be thinking about the leopard. It will come and when it does come he'll make Paul do whatever Paul has to do and then we will all go home and they will have drinks and talk all night about the leopard. But Brian must be thinking something.

Maybe he doesn't mind waiting. Maybe he likes to wait. Maybe he just lets his mind go blank and his spirit roves free all over the world, getting into delicious trouble that doesn't bother Brian at all. Maybe Brian's spirit doesn't even tell Brian what it's been up to while Brian sits in a thorn haystack waiting for a spotted cat to show up to chew on a dead pig.

I wonder what would happen if I did sneeze? I wonder what would happen if I coughed? I wonder what would happen if I did what ladies never do and let go an enormous blast of wind?

Katie grinned inwardly. A nice girl certainly had peculiar thoughts sitting in leopard blinds on hot African afternoons listening to birds go *clang-tonk* and *ooo-hooo—ooooh-hoooo—HOOO!* and watching that little *ghekko* lizard running along the grass just behind the blind and the big black ants in that tiny hill that Brian forgot to scrape over with the *panga* when he made the blind and those guinea-fowl feeding outside as if there was no human within hundreds of miles.

'*Oh, God damn it!*' The oath rolled thunderously.

There was Brian, breaking the rules. Katie was appalled. The curse burst out of him loud and shockingly, shatteringly angry. It wouldn't be an accident, because he was saying it again. Her brother flinched as if a snake had struck him.

'God damn it to hell! Come on, we might as well go on out! I might have known!' Brian's voice blasted the silence apart as if someone had fired a gun in a cathedral.

Now Brian was scrambling out of the blind, offering cigarettes as they stood up and rubbed the cramps out of their legs. He pointed with a toss of head and angry lift of chin over his shoulder. A black-and-white cow was just poking her wall-eyed head from behind a scrubby copse of low creeping thorn at the rise of the gentle hill down which they always drove. A couple of mournful lowings came behind her, and the *clang-tonk* was a cowbell. Both Katie and her brother stared, bewildered.

'Fire the gun,' Brian said to Paul Drake. 'See if you can hit your bloody pig! Go on, shoot!'

Tranced, Paul Drake raised his rifle and they could hear the *tunk* as the bullet struck the hanging warthog.

'That'll fetch Muema with the car,' Brian said disgustedly. 'You might as well have sneezed, Katie, the way things turned out. I saw you—you made a very noble effort to no point. All's wrecked; the thrice-bloody ever-blasted Masai have come to call, with a couple of hundred head of cattle. I might have known this new grass was too short and green and lovely for the bastards to resist—too handy to water and the big swamp. Oh, well,' he shrugged. '*Kwaheri chui. Jambo Masai.* Maybe next year. That's a gone cat, for all our purposes.'

The cattle were cropping out now, muzzling eagerly at the tender grass. They were skinny, rack-hipped, white and black and red and piebald. Most had high, wobbly humps, and their horns had been docked or broken when they were calves to allow unusual regrowth to establish the owner's brand. A few had the enormous, trophy-sized long horns she had seen in pictures of old Egyptian cattle, the kind of horns Brian had told her were common to the Ankole herds in Uganda.

They watched the encroaching Masai. This was a family project—one grey old man with a shortened spear-blade, three women of varying ages, and two small boys. The youngest woman carried a sucking child. They paid no attention to the white people—and little attention to the Land Rover when it came clanking up with Muema disgusted at the sight of cattle. Kidogo was sitting in the front seat with him. Without stopping to say anything to Brian they drove through the cattle herd, bumping curious heifers aside with the car, and occasionally blowing the horn to move a calf which stood braced obstinately in the vehicle's pathway. Muema stopped the Land Rover directly under the tree and Kidogo jumped out to run up the trunk. Muema stood watching as the old Ndrobo hacked at the ropes which bound the pig, and in a moment it fell to the ground with a squishy thump. Its quarter-eaten, stinking carcass was immediately sweatered by the persistent little flies that clouded over the cattle and the tiny mousy donkeys which carried the mountainous packs of Masai household effects.

'Well,' Brian said. 'We might as well go back to camp. It's too late to sit in the other blind—be near dark when we got there and straggled down the hill. We're lucky to know where's another big leopard. We'll just kiss this shap here goodbye. Why the hell these people couldn't have gone somewhere else with their bloody *ngombe*—well . . .' He shrugged again. 'Their country, I suppose. Nothing to be done about it. Where the cattle come, the game ain't.'

Katie found herself suddenly feeling terribly sorry for Brian—sorrier for Brian who had probably seen five hundred leopard shot than she was disappointed for her brother, who had been whetted to a wire edge for his first leopard. Poor little Brian, she thought; made all his plans and plots and showed off all his knowledges and skills and then a bunch of flyblown dairy farmers tore down his playhouse.

Impulsively she kissed Brian's cheek.

'There, there, little boy,' she said. 'There'll be lots more leopards for you to play with. Let's go on back to camp and Mama'll make some nice martinis and we can start all over again playing pussy cat tomorrow.'

Paul Drake smiled appreciatively at his sister.

'I felt like I was going to miss this one, anyhow,' he said.

CHAPTER THIRTEEN

THEY WENT next day to the other blind, where they had seen the big leopard in the tree. The bait had not been touched, so far as Brian could determine with his glasses. They stumbled half a mile down the hill and carefully stalked the last three hundred yards to the blind, painfully bent over, awkwardly trying to melt from rock to brush-heap to tree to ant-hill, Katie striving desperately to avoid stepping on dry twigs or kicking loose stones. She was red-faced and puffing when they finally crawled the last fifty yards, stone-bruising her hands and skinning her knees, until they flopped sweating in the blind. There had been no bugs in the last blind; this one, close-hugging the thick bush of the watercourse, had no cheerful green expanse of grassland between blind and bait to firebreak the insects. The partially chewed, bedraggled impala hung sadly in the tree. The frayed edges of his gnawed-out stomach were oxidized black against the tarnishing old-gold of his hide. Katie sat as sadly in the blind, and the mosquitoes fed eagerly on her hands and face and ankles. She had been encouraged to bravado by the buglessness of the other blind, and had neglected to smear herself with insect repellent.

They sat for two and a half hours until black dark, listening to the swamp noises. At seven it was beginning to turn cold and she had never dreamed of such cramps as seized her legs, or such a bruising ache as centred in her seat. She could have cried with relief as Brian said, sighing:

'Well, that's that, chaps. *Hapana chui*,' and offered her a cigarette. 'No leopard in this tree today—no sign of him along the river. We'd better give him one more day and if he doesn't come we'll see what's doing with the Number Three. But that was a damned big leopard we saw here yesterday.'

They were all cold and tired and bone-sore when they got to camp, and they bathed swiftly and picked at their food. Brian stayed up to listen to the safari broadcast; she and her brother went silently off to bed.

The next day was a repetition, except that this time Katie doused herself with greasy lotion and while the bugs buzzed annoyingly, veiling round her head, they didn't bite her afresh. Only her wounds of yesterday itched and smarted, and she drew a glare from her brother as she fidgeted. She no longer let her thoughts roam; they centred fiercely on her bored discomfort while sitting in a blind full of bugs with two dedicated hunters waiting for something that wouldn't come out to be killed. At least you could *see* elephant; even lion were not so hard to come by.

As they left the blind that night a great swollen drop of rain hit her almost painfully in the right eye. It was followed by a brief but violent shower, and they were all soaked by the time they reached the clear ground where the Rover waited to take them back to camp and a fire. This night was the first night of safari on which Katie thought she would give an arm for just one big, fat snort of anything that was a hundred proof.

'I don't like the feel of this second leopard,' Brian said, as they had their drinks round the fire, Katie nibbling without enthusiasm at her tomato juice. 'I think this gentleman's upstaked and hightailed it. One night away from the kill, yes—maybe he found something nice and succulent a couple miles away, or got mixed up in love-making, or something. But it's not leopard-like for him to desert that kill after he was so cocky about it first day we saw him. He was happy in that tree if I ever saw a well-adjusted leopard.'

'I think we're bewitched,' Katie said. 'You better have one of your witch-doctors tailor-make us a curse.'

'That's been taken care of,' Brian said, and Katie looked up in surprise.

'You're not serious?'

Brian nodded.

'Certainly I'm serious. Kidogo is a *mundumugu* of sorts, especially where it concerns animals. He's already done something with the magic bag.'

'And what did the magic bag say?'

'I don't know. I never ask him,' Brian said. 'I wouldn't want to know in advance if it was dead negative.'

CHAPTER FOURTEEN

BRIAN LET his binoculars fall and reached for a cigarette. It was another bright clear morning, but the clouds were already beginning to mass low and ugly along the hills. Katie and Paul looked at him expectantly.

'Aha,' Brian nodded his head with satisfaction. 'We're in luck. It's been fed on, and fed on well. Too well, I should say. It could be a lioness if the tree weren't so straight up and down—either a lioness or a simply *ee*-normous leopard. But I think there's too much meat gone for just *one* leopard. Very probably a pair.'

'I thought they didn't let other leopards into their trees much?' Paul said. He was beginning to look a little pinched around the nostrils.

'Sometimes. Not very often. Once in a while the old boy goes soft on his girl friend and let's her have an early whack—or sometimes a late one. Where there's a bitch you'll usually find the dog. If the lady spots the kill first, she uses it quite often as a sort of clip joint to pick up her men friends. I swear, I know one old gal in Tanganyika that I've personally widowed half a dozen times, but it hasn't shaken her faith in that one particular tree. She always shows up with a new boy friend—generally large. She likes big men.'

'I think all your shootable leopards live in Tanganyika,' Katie said. 'I don't think there are any more leopards in Kenya now that the first one's gone. He started a vogue. Exodus.'

The sky was much darker, the clouds sagging much lower on the horizon, when the boys roused them from siesta at four. The sun shone eerily from time to time, peeping bloodily round the edges of the blackening clouds, casting strange purple lights on the hills, slanting obliquely on the pillars of far-distant rains. Each day now it darkened earlier in the afternoon, and always the solid shafts of rain seemed closer.

They had been in the blind only half an hour, staring intently at the evil wall of black-green brush. This thorn-armoured rampart was backed by towering trees roped heavy with lianas and with accumulated windrows of brush which eventually became so tightly packed as to be nearly impassable except through the slick-worn game trails.

This last was not a happy blind. It might have been cheerful enough in the sunshine; in the gloom of the cloudy afternoon the bush looked sinisterly black and very, very forbidding. It was located near where they forded the stream, where the leaf-dyed waters hurried dark over the smooth white rock rushing noisily past the slick-lichened boulders, and where the tangled under-brush came right down to the edge of the river and hung, stream-tugged, whiskering over the banks. It was absolutely black to the eye a few feet away from the water's edge—no needle of sunlight pricked through the mat of leaves and twisted vines and broken fallen boles of creeper-strangled trees. There was a strong stench of baboons and mouldy wet leaves about the place. The bait-branch on which the leopard would feed was much lower than the others, and the tree a different kind, considerably more oak-looking. It stood in the midst of a positive jungle of tangled thorn, and was embraced jealously on both sides by arms of the swamp.

A tremendous crack of thunder ripped the clouds and a jagged streak of lightning tore the sky. Purple clouds tumbled over each other and, colliding, clashed like enormous cymbals. The sky blackened almost to twilight, although it was only five o'clock, and a blinding shutter-sheet of grey, warm rain crashed down with such force that the drops bounced in the dust. There was no top to the blind; in two minutes' time Katie was drenched. Moving her soaked head slightly, she could see that both her brother and Brian were equally drowned. Paul was wiping slowly and prayerfully at the scope of his rifle with a soggy handkerchief; too late, he took off his soft cap and placed it round the rear lens of the telescope. Rain ran down his eyeglasses as if they were windscreens; his thin hair clung to his white skull in skinny fingers. She looked at Brian, whose tumbled thick hair was hammered into a thick mop by the rain. He jerked his chin at the leopard-tree and formed with his lips: *Do you want to leave?* She saw her brother nod slightly but emphatically, *No*. Brian moved his shoulders slightly in the familiar shrug, and, raising his hand slowly, wiped water out of his eyes.

The rain slackened then, and stopped. But the sun stayed behind the enormous banks of clouds, and the forest ahead looked even more dismal, as Katie could heard the steady thudding drumbeats of the rain from the leaves and branches of the trees. She squinted through the peephole. The chewed-up bait seemed sadder than ever in its rain-blackened mussy package of tattered hide. A light wind rose, and now Katie began to shiver as the clammy shirt clung to her shrinking skin and the wet wool of her socks bristled cold against her ankles.

Now the rain was starting again, not slashing, not pounding down like the other, striking so hard it actually hurt the skin, but seeping, sliding, sneaking down, lying along and actively pressing on the skin instead of bounding off it. It ran constantly, annoyingly into her eyes. Remembering to move slowly, she raised her wrist to her forehead and when she did she saw it first.

It was slim and beautiful in the first fork, slim and blurred and smoky in the rain. It was yellow no more, only a grey wraith, blending so perfectly against the dark background that she might never have seen it come but for the white flick of its tail-tip, a tail which drooped now with most of the curl gone. Like my hair now, Katie thought wildly, and slowly reached over to squeeze her brother's thigh. She lifted her chin slowly in the direction of the tree and as her brother's hand went towards the rifle the leopard disappeared, appearing again like a drift of sulphuric fog on the feeding branch. It was almost exactly the colour of the dead impala, and the rain had darkened its hide so her naked eye couldn't distinctly pick out the spots. The two animals merged, one dead, one living, and with the wind in their direction Katie could clearly hear the sound of teeth crunching at flesh. The living thing had come soundless; no raucous shout of baboon, no hysteric scream of monkey, no squawk of bird had heralded the coming.

Her brother never fired. Brian Dermott's hand had come over slowly and moved across her brother's vision to his trigger hand. She saw Brian's mouth make the silent words: *No*. With a tiny negative shake of head, his lips moved again. F-E-M-A-L-E they spelled slowly. *Wait*.

In a moment, off to their right, there was a fantastic sudden explosion of savage sound. Baboons abruptly convened a chorus of profanely guttural

271

barking. Small monkeys screamed as if being tortured, and the branches of trees whipped violently, crashingly, as bodies hurled themselves from limb to limb. Birds detonated from tree-tops and fled shrieking, screaming alarm. A steady *huh-huh-huh* was heard now, and then an indescribable spitting snarl ending in a growl that was followed by a different fleshy bubbling scream from a baboon, as if the sound had been torn from his throat.

At the interruption, the feeding female lifted her head from the belly cavity of the dead animal, turned it with a lofty elegance towards the noise and disappeared once more, like a plume of smoke, to vanish from the tree. Katie turned her head towards Brian, who was smiling happily, and forming the word: *Now*, with his soundless smiling lips.

There was another roar and a crash in the bush almost at the foot of the tree, another explosion of monkeys in the treetops and another long giant firecracker trail of angry shouting as the baboons, still cursing, plunged through the thick bush. Then there was another asthmatic, throat-caught *huh-huh-huh* under the tree, followed by a rasping scrutching sound, and suddenly the most evil yellow eyes she had ever dreamed of stared straight into Katie's face. The leopard was huge; he filled the fork; his eyes were everywhere at once.

Her brother moved involuntarily, but Brian's restraining hand clasped his arm. The leopard turned his head slowly, his topaz gaze appearing to strike into Katie's soul, and then the devil disappeared. He did not move: he vanished. As he disappeared there was a slight motion in the blind as Brian released her brother's arm and she heard a tiny noise as Paul slid his rifle up into the crotch of the forked stick and bent to the eyepiece of the telescope. For a second now Katie could see the leopard again; he was standing tall and straight and proud, broad on, head raised slightly by the angle of the branch as he tore hungrily into the rain-sogged meat of the dead impala.

She heard one micro-second of grinding fang on bone before the rifle went off like the explosion of an ammunition dump, rocking the walls of the thorn-thatched blind. The cordite smell hung acridly pleasant in the air, but Katie was stunned and almost blinded for a second by the concussion.

When she could see again, Brian was leaping out of the blind and charging towards the foot of the tree with his shotgun; she saw her brother still sitting stupidly, stunned, his face dead white, his mouth hanging foolishly open. There was a gash over one eye where the scope had reared back and kicked him. The rain was washing the blood down his face and diluting it into little pink trickles.

He scrambled awkwardly out of the blind and stood foolishly, still pale, still gape-mouthed, still holding the gun as if he had never seen a gun before.

'I—I shot too quick,' he said to himself. 'I got excited and I shot too quick. All the waiting and the rain and the other leopard and I shot too *quick*! I was getting the gun on him when it just went off. I suppose I pulled the trigger but I shot too *quick*.'

'Maybe you hit it,' Katie said falsely. She reached in her soaking pocket for cigarettes and managed to find some dry ones in the back of the packet. She lit two with a Zippo and handed one to her brother. 'You probably hit it. Brian took off with that shotgun and disappeared in the bush there. He'll be back in a minute. Maybe it's dead under the tree.'

'No,' her brother said, appearing about to weep, 'Brian won't find it dead under any tree. I shot too quick. I got excited and I did everything I swore I wouldn't do. I just threw the gun up and jerked. After all this—this perfection and to spoil it like a damned amateur, like some damned schoolgirl frightened by a rabbit.'

'Well, just don't commit a hara-kiri until you know,' Katie said. 'You've done everything else very well. It's probably dead there in the bush. You'll find you've shot it very well.'

'No,' her brother said miserably. 'I won't find I've shot it very well. This is one thing I haven't done very well at all.'

They stood lonely in the rain, smoking wet cigarettes, waiting for the hunting car to breast through the grey surf of thorn behind them. Brian and the car arrived at about the same time.

Kidogo and Muema leaped out of the car, and Kidogo was already snapping another shotgun together. Brian said something in Swahili, and Katie could see a wave wash swiftly over the faces of the Africans, wiping out the prints of their eager expressions and almost changing the arrangement of their features. Now they looked greyer, sadder and much, much older.

'*Hakuna damu*,' Brian was saying to the boys. He held up a thin strip of something white and wiggly-looking like a big tapeworm. '*Mafuta tu*.' He turned to Paul, and his face was older, too; he was very serious now.

'You gutshot it,' he said flatly. 'I'm sorry. I hoped you'd missed it entirely. I thought you had, because it wasn't knocked from the tree. It jumped. But I found this.' He held up the white wormy-looking strip.

'Gut. Belly lining. And there's no blood.' He shook his head, and looked at his watch. 'Almost five-thirty. That gives us maybe forty-five minutes of light, in this weather, to dig it out of there.'

He went over to the blind and got his rain-soaked old grey sweater, and knotted it round his neck like a thick muffler. He forestalled Katie's question.

'For giving the leopard something to chew on instead of throat until Muema can scrape him off me—or with luck, shoot him off me before he digs in for the long rains.' His voice was coldly business-like, with no hint of levity. 'Muema's very good at shooting leopards off me. Had any amount of practice.'

Paul was stammering. His face was gradually regaining colour.

'I'm dreadfully sorry, Brian. I really don't know what happened. The gun just seemed to go off as if somebody else pulled the trigger. I wouldn't have shot if I hadn't been sure of killing it—not with all this . . .' He waved helplessly at the dripping gloom of the thick swamp ahead.

Brian smiled slightly now, tightly.

'Don't take it too much to heart. You're not the first to blow his stack over a leopard. I told you a little of how it would be. Well, this sort of talk doesn't produce any sick leopards. Come on, you chaps!' He spoke sharply to the Africans. 'Muema! Kidogo! *Ha-yah! Upesi!*'

'You two stay with the Rover,' he told Paul and Katie. 'I'll be out of *that* in a little while.' He gestured towards the broading tangle of wet bush.

'Couldn't you—couldn't you just leave it and come back in the morning when it's lighter? Bring some more boys?' Katie knew she was saying the wrong thing, but all this seemed so . . . seemed so shockingly abrupt and coldly final.

'It's sick and hurt and angry in there,' Brian said. 'It'll suffer until it's eaten alive by hyenas. And there's always the off-chance it's not hurt so very bad and will recover enough to either collect the first Wog that bumbles along or, worse, be crippled enough to turn permanent man-killer. And apart from any humanitarian aspects, the Game Department take a very poor view of our leaving wounded dangerous animals strewn about. Well,' Brian said sharply to his gunbearers, 'what are you waiting for? Let's get cracking!'

'I want to go too, Brian,' Paul Drake said. 'I wounded it. It was my fault. It's only right I go along and help you with it. I won't be in the way, I promise.'

Brian shook his head irritably.

'If you don't mind, I'd rather you didn't, Paul. I've enough on my plate, trying to watch for the leopard and keep an eye on the boys tracking in front of me. Leopards are tricky. They double back, like as not, and then light on your neck when you've passed. Or wait until you're quite on top of them before they spring. They come so fast they're just a blur. It's why I use the shotgun.' He held up the weapon in one hand. 'Rifle's not fast enough—not enough shock. No, you stay with Katie.'

'But can't you *see* . . . All right. I'll do what you say.' Paul turned away. 'I'll stay with Katie safely in the car.' His voice was bitter. 'Women and children first.'

'It's not that. It's just that——' Brian stopped when he saw Katie Crane's eyes pleading with him. *Take him with you, please, Brian. It's the only chance he's got to be happy for the rest of his life. Don't take it away from him, Brian. Please.*

'Muema!' Brian's voice halted the gunbearer as he entered the bush. 'Give the Bwana your shotgun!' He turned to Paul. He spoke crisply, all friendship gone. 'Now look here. Stay off to my left and well behind me. Don't shoot me and don't shoot the boys. Don't shoot unless it's directly in front of you, and if it knocks me over, for Christ's sake leave the close-separation work to Muema and Kidogo. I don't want my head blown off out of any hurry-up helpfulness with that bloody shotgun. Understood?'

'Understood.' Paul Drake's voice was firm again as he broke the shotgun and checked the loads. He clicked the breech shut. 'You won't have to worry about me. And Brian?'

'Yes?' Brian turned as he started walking towards the leopard tree. His face was irritable and drawn, wet-shining in the rain.

'Thanks,' Paul Drake said. 'Thanks very much.'

'Nothing,' Brian said curtly. 'One more thing. If it jumps you and is on you, throw your gun crosswise in front of your throat and let him chew on the barrel until we peel him off you.'

Katie had been forgotten. She printed their pictures on her mind as they left her without good-bye and plunged into the dripping bush. The two Africans had fanned out, spooring in front of Brian, and her brother walked two steps behind Brian and well to his left. He held the shotgun diagonally across his chest, ready to jump it to his shoulder, and his back looked straight and his head was held proudly.

'Thank God Brian took him,' Katie breathed, as the soaked grey bush closed behind them and silence fell like an enormous sopping blanket on the black forest ahead. She got into the Rover and sat on the wet seat and let the rain hit her in the face. They might at least have put the top on again, she said irritably to herself, rummaging in the dash compartment for a dry pack of cigarettes.

CHAPTER FIFTEEN

AN INSANE desire to scream for joy filled Paul Drake. He had read, a long time ago, Hemingway's 'The Short Happy Life of Francis Macomber', and had not believed the sea-change that faced danger could bring to a coward. He had been moved only by expected awe and then regret when he killed the elephant; he had been only vaguely excited by the lion, and that largely because it was all so new and strange.

But never, never had he thought himself capable of feeling as he felt now, as they inched through spiked bush like dirty-nailed fingers, grey, dripping, hateful bush that clutched at your ankles and cut viciously at your face, bush that dragged spitefully at your clothes and looped around your legs. Trees, living and dead, were woven together in combat nets by the tough ropy lianas and the accumulated mass of thorn. If you took your eyes off the man ahead of you he disappeared, even though you could hear him floundering no more than half a dozen yards ahead of you. Once, some animal jumped from its bed snorting, and Paul Drake's shotgun was up to his face before the beast's frantic plunge took it crashing away with a clack of horn on bush.

The gunbearers ranged, tracking carefully on each side and just ahead of Brian. Paul could not imagine what they saw to follow: there was no blood. The animal was lying somewhere behind or ahead, sick, furious, hurting horribly now from the fiery blast that had torn its guts away and left them

275

dripping tangled from the wound that would not bleed. The boys carried only the long bush *pangas*, with which they occasionally chopped away a barrier branch or used to point at some slight disarrangement of terrain that only they—and Brian—could recognize and diagnose.

Their circles meshed, and Brian seemed always to act as the communications cross-check; each time the circles locked they would form three intersecting rings with Brian in the middle like one of those Chineze puzzles the magicians slipped on and off. Three times they disputed the possible course of the leopard, and each time Kidogo's opinion held. Each time the opinion was verified as either Brian or Muema came on fresh spoor, if nothing more than a tiny smeared absence of raindrop from an otherwise rain-pimpled leaf. Paul Drake's mouth was dry but he felt a soaring happiness; he hoped, he prayed that when the leopard leaped it would leap straight at him and he would blast it as it sprang with its claws widespread and hooked to seize him.

Once, in his eagerness, he pressed a step too far forward, and Brian warned him back with a curt jerk of the gun and a glare. There were no more society hunter's tricks here; no gratuitous posturing and peeking round bushes and climbing up of trees, saying that you could have climbed one of the creeper-strangled giants of which only the gnarled roots were visible. Brian was a man fully concentrated on a job of killing something that threatened to kill them —kill him, Paul, kill Brian himself, and those unbelievably brave black men tracking half-crouched ahead, half-naked and defenceless except for a bush knife and an implicit trust in Brian Dermott.

Paul hoped he would be able to explain all this to Katie some day: he felt he had learned more about the interdependence of black man and white man from this twenty minutes in a baboon-stinking morass of trees and thorns and fronds and great hummocks of interwoven dead branches and grass than he would ever learn if all the African experts combined to explain it to him in the full light of dry day.

It was appalling, this gloom, darker than twilight as they plunged more and more deeply into the Kali-armed embrace of the bush. Light showed through the laced canopy of trees only in minute splashes and holes. Sodden leaves squished underfoot, slippery, and twice he fell with a tooth-jarring defence-less jolt into hidden pigholes—pitching on his face in the wet underbush, once losing his grasp on the clammy wet shotgun. The rain did not fall inside this leafy cavern; it struck the tree-tops and oozed through in maddening big gouts that had accumulated on branch tips, or else gushed in sudden harsh cascades as a released branch flung a shower or a fleeing monkey sluiced a bucketful through the lower branches of his tree.

They came finally to the end. The end was an enormous hummock, a city block long and infinitely wide, looming as high as a house. Brian stopped in a little cleared place in front of this monstrous long house of the melted-down and moulded, laced and weather-hammered, impenetrable mass of vegetation, rocks, fallen trees and possibly ancient ant-hills, compacted as hard as stone.

Brian kicked at the outer edges of the mound, and his foot made a solid sound, as if he had kicked granite. He grimaced, and lit a cigarette. Then he looked at his gunbearers, sodden, thorn-torn, deadly serious. Simultaneously they all shrugged.

'*Eeeeh*,' Brian said.

'*Eeee—eeeh*,' they answered.

'He's in *there*,' Brian said. 'In *that*.'

Paul groped for a cigarette and lit it before he spoke. He was panting, and his mouth was still very dry. A back-whipped branch had struck him on the cut that the kicking scope had opened when he fired at the leopard, and it was oozing blood again.

'What do we do now, Bwana?' he asked, and grinned, relaxed and still curiously happy. 'Crawl in and insult him into action or what?'

'I believe you're actually enjoying the idea of having a hundred and fifty pounds of disenchanted leopard in your lap,' Brian said, and smiled unenthusiastically back. 'This is really a terrible business. There's no possibility of going in after him, even if we had a bulldozer. Too thick, much too thick.'

He turned and spoke rapidly to the Africans.

'All we can do is chuck sticks and stones in there and hope to goose him into a charge. It works—sometimes. You stand over there, and *only* shoot if he comes straight at you or on your left. *Only* to your left, mind. I'll handle the other side here. Okay, *ha-yah*!' he turned again to the boys. 'Let's see some work with the rocks!' He stooped and picked up a chunk of stone which he flung into the bulk of clotted bush. The Africans followed, hurling sticks and stones and screaming at the top of their lungs.

Suddenly the old Kidogo held up his hand.

'*Ngruma*,' he said. 'Growl.'

From the bush, alarmingly close, to the left and just ahead of Paul, there came an unmistakable, throaty growl which ended in a long harsh purr and a sudden rattling, sobbing sigh.

'*Kufa*,' Kidogo said. '*Hi chui nakufa kabisa*.'

'He says that's the leopard's last gasp,' Brian said. 'The dying growl. This I want to see personally before I take his word for it. It could be—it could be any other variation on sick-leopard sounds. What now, *mzee*?' he asked the old man.

'*Ngoja kidogo*,' Kidogo said. '*Mupa mimi sigara moja*.'

'He says we'd better wait a minute and smoke a cigarette,' Brian said, offering Paul the pack and then handing it to the Africans. He picked up another stone and heaved it in the direction of the last roar. Silence followed the clump of the rock.

They threw more rocks, and finished their cigarettes.

'He's either dead, as the old man says, or he's pushed off with a sigh of relief, and in any case we've had him. There'll be no more than another ten minutes of light, and this is one leopard who's not going to catch me prowling

277

around on my hands and knees with a Coleman lamp as I've been known to do in my silly youth,' Brian said. 'What else, old man?'

Kidogo aimed a rapid stream of something in Brian's direction. Brian grinned, but rather weakly.

'He says it's a very good.leopard, a big leopard, and he wouldn't rest easy tonight if he thought the hyenas were tearing it to shreds. He's going to find it for you and drag it out by the tail.'

'Can't you stop him?' Paul Drake asked. 'I don't want the damned thing that bad. I don't want the old boy hurt.'

'I wouldn't try to stop him,' Brian said. 'Reflection on his reputation, judgment, bushcraft—the lot. Professional standing at stake here. I bow to superior knowledge.'

The old man took his *panga* and started to chop his way into the bush. He suddenly stooped and plunged into a hitherto-unseen animal tunnel. Brian got down on his hands and knees and started to crawl after him.

'You actually going in there, in that, with him?' Paul Drake said to Brian's disappearing rump.

'Of course.' A mirthless chuckle came back from the game path. 'Won't be the first time. Can't let him do it alone. Care to come along for the ride? Mind, don't shoot me in the pants with that bloody shotgun if something jumps at you.'

Cursing under his breath, Paul Drake, banker, stockbroker, Harvard '30, Racquet and River clubs, found himself in a greasy animal-smelly, mud-mucky game trail, pushing a shotgun ahead of him in what was almost complete darkness. Thorn bit at his hands and tore at his face. Invisible sharp rocks chewed at his knees. All he could see ahead of him was Brian Dermott's crêpe shoe-soles. Behind him he could hear the breathing of the man Muema who crawled behind him. They crawled for what seemed hours, and for a distance which possibly covered a hundred yards, when Brian's heels suddenly stopped moving. Kidogo was calling back over his shoulder.

'*Iko hapa Bwana chui akufa kabisa,*' he was saying. '*Hi chui Naguisha kufa chini.*'

Brian's heels darted like animals.

'He's found the cat dead,' he said. 'It's got into some sort of hole.'

Paul Drake's knees fairly skimmed along the game trail until he saw Brian's heels turn down and the back of Brian's legs, standing now, in front of him. He scrambled to his feet, and saw that they were in a little clearing which looked familiar. They had come full circle in the bush and there, to his right now, was the leopard. Its fur was soaked.

It was dead in the stumphole where it had crawled, hauling itself along with its belly shot clean out by the ·300 magnum bullet which had taken it low and unzipped the stomach. It had dragged itself until *it* had been stalking *them*. The spread, extended claws were sunk deep in the dirt on the side of the stumphole. It had been bracing itself to spring when it died.

Brian stood at the edge of the little crater, looking at the wet dead leopard with suddenly disinterested eyes.

He half-nodded and waved his hand casually.

'There's your leopard,' he said. 'Jolly good effort on the old man's part. He knew it was dead, all right. Only one error. It wasn't all the way dead. Hate to think of the action in that game path if he'd been too much wrong. Well, Paul, Katie's got her spotted rug for the long winter nights. Come on, lend a hand, we'll each take a paw. Even without his gut in him he's a damned big cat to be dead in a hole.'

Two men stood on each side of the hole, stooping, and seized one of the thick-muscled wet-furred legs. They heaved and the leopard surged out of the hole. Brian knelt and tugged at his head, nodding at Muema to straighten out his hindquarters and tail. He measured him swiftly in handspans, leap-frogging his fingers from nose to tail-tip.

'Reasonable *chui*,' Brian said, looking up. 'Just on eight feet.'

'*Hi mzuri tu*,' both of the Africans said, working up a little obviously spurious cheer. Muema fingered the emptied stomach. He said something, and Brian laughed shortly.

Paul stood silent for a moment, looking at the thick yellow fur, the tremendously long curved sharp teeth still bared in a death-snarl, noticing the unbelievable strength in the broad, talon-shod paws. He looked at the white belly-fur where his bullet had ripped, spilling the guts and finally the life out of the cat which had not bled.

'I wish to Christ I'd never shot it at all,' he said bitterly. 'Anyhow, thanks for letting me come along for the ride, Brian. It was quite an experience, I must say. I don't think I'd want to do it again.'

Brian laid a hand on Paul's shoulder.

'I imagine you feel cheated because it didn't charge and let you prove something,' he said quietly. '*Don't*. Don't let it bother you. You came along for whatever it was going to do, and what counts really is the fact that you wanted to. That's good enough, Paul. I don't take many people into bush with me after wounded leopards, believe me. You're only the second, if that makes you feel any better.'

'Thanks,' Paul said. 'Let's lug this thing out of here. Katie'll be thinking it ate us all.' Each man picked up a leg, and the four men fought their way back out of the bush, the leopard's spine curving down as it sagged between the porters, its tail dragging along the underbrush. Its head had sagged to one side, but its dead yellow eyes were startlingly open, and the long needle teeth were still bared under the stiff whiskers.

KATIE WATCHED the men disappear into the bush with a belly-griping feeling of loneliness. All the world was grey, shading to black—the sky, the hills, the bush, the solid wall of trees which had swallowed her brother and Brian. She was cold and wet and she would get no warmer, even if she tried to wrestle the stiff wet canvas top-covering of the Land Rover over her to make a semblance of shelter.

She tried to visualize what it would be like inside the wall of dripping bush, lost in the threatening silence of the huge-bulking stand of Grimm's-fairy-tale trees, and could not. She wished desperately that they had taken her along, but realized the hollow stupidity of the wish as she knew it had been a concession on Brian's part to allow her brother to accompany him. She would never in her life see a leopard boil snarling from a bush, its fangs bright and paws outstretched with filthy talons hooked and flexed; she would never be close to the shotgun blast that shot it out of your face and ruined its own face if the shooter were lucky.

But she felt something deeply for her brother now, a tenderness and even love she had never suspected in herself. They had missed each other in the city traffic a long, long time ago. He was a good man, she thought, her brother, and she was only sorry she hadn't known him earlier. Known him as he was now, almost boyish with his defences down, playing whole man possibly for the first time in his life, and so ashamed and hurt about balling up the silly leopard business; wounded to the point of tears when Brian so brusquely dismissed his pitiful offer to make amends on Brian's private ground.

She glanced at her watch. They had been gone only ten minutes. It seemed a year. It seemed an eternity. These last few days of silent sitting in the leopard blinds had not been pleasant. She had raked up the dead leaves of her life pretty thoroughly, and was not terribly happy with the beetles and reptiles she had discovered underneath.

Something was moving in the tree. She caught a flick of light out of the corner of her eye, and reached for the binoculars. She braced them on the side of the windscreen, and saw that the female leopard had leaped up into the tree again, seemingly oblivious of the recent shot, the loud talking, and the fact that she, Katie, was sitting alongside the blind in an open Land Rover. The leopard sat on its haunches on the branch, and was licking a paw, exactly like a big house cat. Suddenly it stopped its licking, and disappeared from sight in the top of the tree. Katie waited, and in a moment it was back. Now it reached out one paw and drew the impala carcass in towards itself, and started to eat in earnest. Katie watched in fascination for nearly five minutes, until finally the leopard heard or sensed something else. It withdrew its head from the carcass of the kill, turned it, listened intently, and then sailed as lightly as a flying squirrel towards the ground.

I wonder if she cares if she's a widow so long as she's provided for, Katie thought with sudden disgust. I wonder if I'm like that, as cold and calculating and as selfishly hungry as all that? The war came and I was at a cocktail party. The war ended and I was at a cocktail party. Practically the only time I wasn't ever at a cocktail party when anything happened was when I got my decree from Charles. Useless bitch, feeding on somebody else's kill all your life, she thought, and made a grimace of distaste.

It was getting very dark now, and the rain had settled into a steady light drizzle, almost a mist. It would probably slacken; Brian said it never rained very steadily, but just pounded down in patches and then cleared up again. Very probably tomorrow would be sunny. Most tomorrows were supposed to be sunny.

She lit a cigarette and stared fixedly at the point where they had entered the bush. There was no wind now. The smoke from her cigarette drifted straight up and hung in the rain-soft air above the car in a tiny cloud. It was sad to be so alone—it wasn't *fair* of them to be gone so long on a man's errand she couldn't share. Suddenly she wanted to go to the bathroom, but the idea of going alone into the sopping bush, even a few feet away, was repellent to her. She had camel kidneys; she would wait until they got back to camp, to warm, wonderful camp with its cheery fire and the personals sweating the tin cans of steaming water down the hill to her own private canvas bathtub.

The doves began again, and the rain suddenly stopped. Noises started once more in the deep line of trees along the black swift-rushing river. She could hear the different pops and crackles and grunts, and suddenly a monkey's scream and the squawk of a bird. Certainly she heard more leopards coughing, and half-reached for her brother's rifle on the seat beside her before she realized she didn't know how to make it work. The world was very large and Hell was forever. Nobody loves me and my hands are cold.

Quite suddenly Katie Crane started to weep.

Almost as suddenly she stopped weeping and blew her nose in her wet rag of handkerchief, without stopping to think that there was a perfectly good box of Kleenex in the catch-all under the dashboard. She had heard voices and the sound of crashing bush. In a moment the men came into view, carrying the dead leopard sagged between them. She leaped out of the car, rushed at the men, and for no known reason, threw her arms around the little old gunbearer, Kidogo. She held the skinny wet body tightly before she turned to the other men.

'I'm so glad to see you! I didn't know if you were dead or lost or if I'd be here alone for ever! When you didn't come and didn't come and I didn't hear the guns shoot again, I . . .' Foolishly, Katie Crane realized that she was weeping again.

She went over then and nuzzled her head into her brother's shoulder.

'It's just that I'm so glad to see you,' she babbled. 'So very glad to see you and I'm so glad you got your leopard he's beautiful isn't he really beautiful you'll have to tell me all about him but not please not until we're home and dry again.' She knew she was babbling and stopped.

'Couldn't agree more,' her brother grunted. 'Kidogo found him. He was already dead. Sort of an anti-climax. I was all revved up to be a hero and save Brian's life, I suppose—if I didn't blow the back of his neck off.'

'No fear,' Brian said. 'Were you all right, Katie?' He nodded at the boys. '*Tia chui ndani ya gari.*' Muema jumped up into the back of the trailer, and took the leopard by the two front paws and heaved, with Kidogo and the car-boy lifting the heavy hindquarters clear of the ground.

'I was fine. Very lonely and sort of frightened, though. Oh, and Brian?'

'Yes?' A match lighted Brian's eyes as it flared in the hands cupped around a cigarette. 'What?'

'She came back. The female, I mean. She came back and fed off the kill, exactly as if nothing had happened. Isn't that rather unusual?'

Brian blew out a mouthful of smoke and tossed the match away into the soaked grass.

'I wouldn't say so. There's precious little room for sentiment in this country.'

He got into the car and started the motor. Nobody said anything all the way back to camp.

CHAPTER SEVENTEEN

'MAYBE THIS was just another spasm,' Brian said after dinner. 'It's clear enough now. Maybe that was just some more of this scattergun weather that everybody says the atomic bomb can't possibly be responsible for. Did I ever tell you about the time I saw the flying saucers up in the Northern Frontier?'

'No,' Katie said. 'And please don't, Brian. You don't have to earn your pay tonight. Nothing's going to make Paul feel any better about his leopard. Not even private flying saucers.'

'All right. No personal histories, no folklore. Paul, you're being a bloody fool brooding about this silly leopard. *I* don't care. Katie doesn't care. It's dead and in camp and nobody got hurt.'

'I care,' Paul said gloomily. 'It seems to me that the botch on the leopard rubbed out all the rest of the good things. What was it Muema said to you when we found the thing dead? Whatever it was, it made you laugh.'

'Muema? Nothing much. He was relieved that we collected it without trouble. He has plenty of tribal scars; he doesn't need any more scratches. What he actually said was that it was nice you took the stomach out of it so neatly, it would save the skinner a lot of trouble.'

'I wanted Muema to be proud of me,' Paul said. 'Not making jokes about me.'

'Oh, for Christ's sake! Come off it, Paul,' Katie said. 'It's only a cat—a dead cat. If you want another I'm sure Brian'll be able to arrange it.'

'Sure,' Brian said. 'We don't have to tell the Game Department, they frown on it, but I've a leopard on my licence and it's yours if you want, Paul. We can hang some more baits in the morning.'

'No, thanks. Trip's over for me. I'd just as lief start thinking about breaking camp and getting back to Wall Street. It's been wonderful but I know when the party's over. The party's over. I think I'll turn in, now. Good night, Katie. Good night, Brian.'

He got up abruptly and walked towards his tent.

'Poor old Bro,' Katie said. 'This business really shook him. I don't think he'll ever be the same. As a matter of fact it shook me, too. Too much waiting is always dangerous for a woman.'

'I suppose so. One's been known to come to grips with oneself, and not like it. I don't think much any more. Doesn't seem to be any point to it.'

They sat and looked at the fire for a while before Katie suddenly said:

'Do you still love your—do you still love Valerie?'

Brian looked at her coldly.

'I'm sure I don't know. I don't suppose so. Else I'd have gone after her and dragged her back by the hair, when she left the first time, wouldn't I? If I'd allowed her to leave at all. And certainly I'd not have let her go again, without any big fuss.'

'Perhaps she didn't really want to leave. Perhaps she was just waiting to be wanted—to be needed. Perhaps she waited a long time in London for you to come and get her, and you never did. So she came out again, and you let her go again. What the hell's the matter with you that you let her go again?'

Brian turned to face her squarely.

'Nothing's the hell the matter with me. Everything out here is larger than life, Katie. One of the commonest mistakes the first-time hunter makes is in the judgment of distance. The light seems to make everything very close. In the right haze on the Mombasa road I've seen what I thought was an elephant turn out to be a hare.'

'And that means what?'

'It means that I was young and quite inexperienced emotionally except superficially and Valerie was very beautiful and we had been raised in the almost-expectancy of marrying each other. We did, and too many things crept between us and everything got dirtied up. After, trying to make things come right, it seemed too much like a troop movement. Or perhaps I have known all along that there is no hope for the likes of me, of Valerie, out here. For a long time it's been as if I'd never known her and I'm losing my country fast. Losing Valerie again seemed most horribly unimportant in face of that.'

'I suppose that answers me,' Katie said, getting up. 'Do you ever intend to marry anyone ever again?'

'I doubt it,' Brian said. 'I doubt it very much. Good night, Katie. I think I'll toddle off to bed. It's woolling up again for more rain.'

*

Katie Crane lay in her bed and listened to the thud of the rain on the canvas. The brief clearing after dinner hadn't lasted long. Normally she slept beautifully in the rain. After a while she reached down and found a pack of cigarettes and lay for a while in the dark, smoking. Suddenly she felt she couldn't stand it in the tent any longer. She wanted something to touch, someone to hold.

She got up and found her torch, opened the safari box, and found what she was looking for. She took off her pyjamas and put on the one nightgown she'd brought along, and flashing the light into the little mirror, did something hurriedly to her hair. Then she slipped into her robe and pushed her feet into her mosquito boots with the high flared Russian tops. She leaned over and picked up the little shotgun which lay just under her bed. Her flashlight beam was fuzzy in the grey slanting rain as she made her way through the wet grass towards Brian Dermott's tent. The hem of her nightgown was soggy from the wet grass.

As she walked onto the lumpy canvas flooring of the little veranda made by the double-fly of Brian's tent, she heard him stir and his voice said sleepily.

'*Nini?* Who is it?'

'It's me,' she said softly. 'Katie. I couldn't sleep. I'm dreadfully sorry I'm not a Masai maiden and couldn't find a spear to stick in front of your *manyatta*, but I've brought the shotgun and its resting on your camp chair and I'm wearing a nightgown instead of pyjamas. Do you think that might serve to establish my intentions? The nightgown is a little wet in the hem. I hope you won't mind.'

'You're quite sure?' Brian's voice came thick from the black interior of the tent. 'You're quite sure.' The second time was a statement.

'Quite, quite sure,' she said, and felt him beside her in the blackness. She thought she heard the wet thump of his tent-flaps falling before he took her in his arms. Suddenly Katie Crane did not mind that she was coming back in the rain to feed on someone else's kill.

BOOK FOUR

CHAPTER ONE

DON BRUCE sat in the shade of the Provincial Commissioner's broad veranda and accepted a second cool beer from the red-fezzed houseboy who glided silently out onto the porch on broad splayed feet. The Bwana PC was a Scot like Don—a grizzled lean man who smoked a crook-stemmed pipe and who wore his bush jacket with the air of a tartan, his shorts like a kilt. He spoke still with a pronounced burr, when he spoke at all, for he was a silent man as a rule. And he had lived in Africa for forty years.

'If you took it all separately, Nigel,' Don Bruce was saying, 'if you looked at everything in its place, you'd be forced to say that I was in for a run of ordinary bad luck. But my old grandmither used to say that "mony a mickle maks a muckle", and this muckle was beginning to sort of get my dauber down. And then something happened yesterday . . . an oathing and a suicide. Suppose I go at it methodically, from the beginning.'

'And ye've been home four weeks now since the dirty business of the dog and the warning?' the Bwana PC plucked at his scrubby moustache. 'Aye, start it at the beginning. The suicide will make sense in its proper place.'

'It seems more like four *years*,' Don said. 'Things have not been very bright these days around Hardscrabble, Nigel. Peggy's as twitchy as a pregnant fox, and I haven't told her about the suicide yet. She's fashed at me half the time, and is doing something she's never done in her life—yelling at the children and losing her temper constantly with the blacks. It was as if somebody was working on a well-planned schedule—so much time for so many disasters. At first I got nothing out of my Wogs at all except the usual blank wall. It started with the goats.'

*

It was the second morning after Don and Peggy's return to the farm. They were roused by the unmistakable blatting of goats—and goats at very close hand.

Don pushed his feet into slippers and pulled on an old camel-hair robe. He scuffed towards the front door and flung it open. Still half-asleep, he scrubbed at his eyes. The yard—the gardens—for an acre or more the yard was seething with goats. Brown goats, black goats, white goats, piebald goats; they frisked and butted and bleated and made flatulent noises. They were chewing at the flowers and shrubs, rearing up to get at the taller blooms,

287

pulling at the bougainvillaea, snatching mouthfuls out of the lawn. Three jumped down off the porch as Don came to the door—they had been chewing at the canvas of a glider that the children swung on. Insolently, they had left heaps of pebbled dung as calling cards on the floor of the veranda.

Don turned blindly, angrily, and ran into the house. He fumbled the key to the lockroom from his trouser pockets and, flapping ludicrously in his bathrobe, he grabbed a buckshot-loaded pumpgun from a rack and tore back to the door. Peggy, fully roused, was reaching for her robe and slippers as she heard the shotgun's rattling blast, one, two, three, four, five times. She heard the bleating of goats and an anguished pathetic baaing and her husband's cursing as he reloaded the gun. When she reached the front of her house she was treated to the sight of her husband running full power, shouting, bathrobe streaming behind him, discharging a twelve-bore shotgun at the heels of a fleeing band of what seemed to be at least two hundred goats. Dying goats kicked and struggled half-upright in the yard.

Peggy had wept when she saw the devastation of her cherished flowers. Don had dressed and stormed down to the labour lines and had screamed and cursed at Njeroge. The old headboy knew nothing, he said: there were no goats on the farm and he had no idea how they had got there, or who had brought them. The gate that closed Don's private driveway from the public road was not open. It had been opened and closed again by someone. It took no expert tracker to see that men had driven the goats in from the road at night, and latched the gate again behind the goats so they could not wander away. Njeroge was desolate; he knew how the Bwana felt about goats, and he knew the great store the Memsaab set by her flowers. He would talk to the *watu*, he said. He did not expect the men to know anything about how the goats got into the garden. There was no point in tracking the common road— a hundred human footprints and passing lorries and driven herds would obliterate all sign within a few hundred yards. Whoever had come had come and gone before dawn.

*

'Malice, certainly,' the Bwana PC said. 'More evil mischief than a prank. What then?'

'These letters,' Don said. 'Three, so far. Left in different places. One on the front seat of the Chev when it was parked at the petrol station. One stuck in the mailbox. And another—the worst of the lot—young Angus said a man, a strange Kikuyu, had given him to hand to me. This was just after Angus was let out of school. He said the man looked like any other Kyuke—patched pants, dirty shirt, old hat with a hole in it. You know . . .'

'Let me see,' the Bwana PC said, reaching for the three soiled, creased pieces of paper. One was a lined sheet torn from a tablet; one was written on a piece of mottled brown butcher-paper, and the other was written on an envelope obviously stolen from the White Rhino Hotel in Nyeri. The Bwana PC allowed his pipe to go out as he read the papers, slowly, one after the other.

'Dirty, very dirty,' he said. 'Filthy. But I've seen more o' the same. They're gettin' to be quite common now.'

'Well, common or not, it's hardly a nice thing to receive and scarcely conducive to tranquillity in the home to be informed by some half-educated African or Africans that your wife would be raped and stuffed full of stones, that you'll be left with a mouthful of your own balls, and that your little girl . . . You read the notes,' Don said. 'If I could get my hands on the black——'

'Ye'll not be able to and ye know it fu' well,' the Bwana PC said. 'I suppose ye might as well keep them and see if any more match in the handwritin', but this I doubt. I doubt it very much.'

He handed the dirty papers back to Don.

'Ye mentioned something as well about fire and broken fences? And some of your labour being beaten up?'

'I did indeed,' Don said, 'I did indeed.'

CHAPTER TWO

IT SOUNDED almost like one long whine, Don thought, sitting drinking beer with the Bwana PC and ticking off the happenings on his fingers. Fences— wire fences—had been snipped with heavy-duty wire cutters, in various parts of the farm. Cattle had got loose and strayed along the roads. Carefully separated sheep had been freed from their paddocks. Hogs had been turned out to wreck a yam-field. One whole stand of ripened wheat had been fired; it had been started with petrol and set ablaze and had burned itself out. They had found two petrol tins at the edge of the field. As usual, nobody had been seen coming or going. The blaze had been started somewhere around three o'clock in the morning, and there had been a driving wind to speed the flame along. It had been stopped from further spreading only by a road and a windbreak. Much of the wheat had already been harvested and was standing in ricks, waiting for the thresher. That field was a total, dead loss.

The beaten-up labour was another matter. That could have been a personal vengeance, exacted by old enemies as payment of ancient scores involving anything. An unsatisfactory trade, a beer-hall quarrel, a fight over a woman or a sheep—anything at all. But two men, one of them Wayaiki the pig-tender, had been called from their huts at night, knocked senseless, and dragged off to the bush and thoroughly worked over. No broken bones, but each man had had his face laid open from eye to chin with a careful slash of a very sharp knife. Don had taken them to the dispensary to be sewn up; they would recover all right, but neither of the men knew who attacked them. Or if they knew they would not tell.

'I couldn't get anything out of them,' Don told the Bwana PC. 'I couldn't get anything out of their wives, either. Neither could Peggy, and she's pretty damned good with the women. Solid clam-up. Takes me back to the old days up The Mountain with the Shenzis. Some of them died without speaking then.'

'It sounds a wee bit more subtle now,' the Bwana PC said. 'It has the sound of canny direction more than simple native malice. It's a calculated harassment, like, it seems to me.'

'Well, if they intend to drive me up the wall, they're off to a jolly fine start. Apart from actual money losses, I'm getting so I hate to wake up in the morning knowing I'm going to find something new gone wrong. There was also the matter of the trees.'

The Bwana PC smiled carefully over his false teeth and relit his pipe.

'Aye, I know about your trees fu' well,' he said. 'I've heard people say ye were a wee drap daft on the subject o' trees.'

'Daft or not,' Don said. 'It's not nice to see a couple hundred yards of thriving saplings you've pampered into a very necessary windbreak suddenly hacked as if a lot of bad children with sharp hatchets had been turned loose on a dull rainy Sunday with nothing better to do. The whole damned thing, Nigel, is exactly as if somebody knew all my fondest hobby-horses in this farming business, and was deliberately spitting in my eye—working in exact ratio *against* what I'm *for*. I'm known for paddocking and tree-planting and goat-forbidding and anti-burning, so what do they do?'

'They turn loose a plague o' goats and hack your trees and burn your wheat and cut your fences and muddle up your stocks and loose your pigs to wreck your crops. I'd not be surprised if they didn't fire your pyrethrum next and do something to your drainage.'

Don lit a cigarette and sighed.

'They've not burnt the py as yet, but they've already had a whack at my water. I've found a dead donkey—whose donkey I haven't a clue—in one of my little dams, and a couple of dead goats in one well. And for once, as I tell you, I got nothing helpful out of Njeroge or any of the other Nigs. Njeroge got so he hid when he saw me coming. A Wog can only stand so much bad news before it gets too heavy for him and he throws up his hands. Water in the petrol and slashed tyres on the tractor yesterday would have been about the last straw for Njeroge. I actually believe a suicide in the family was anti-climax.'

'They've done that to ye as well, then? Cut the tyres and watered your petrol?'

'They have. And quite frankly I don't know what to do. We learned last trip with the Micks that you can't live always under arms—that if you post a guard here they slip in and do something else to you over there. You guard the house; they burn the barn. You watch the barn; they fire the house. I've set night watches with some of the men, but I'm short-handed already. I think I told you that twenty took off at the time of the dog business, and I frankly haven't been able to replace all of them. The first luck I've had was last week, when I hired a half-dozen new blokes I didn't much like the looks of.'

'The employment office is swamped,' the Bwana PC said. 'People are fair crying for work. Ye shouldna have trouble wi' help.'

'So you say.' Don finished his beer in a long gulp and wiped off the foam with the back of his hand. 'So you say. But the word is out that there's a *thahu* on the place now the old man—the old witch doctor Kinyanjui—is dead, and the place is no longer protected by his magic ring. Call it poppycock if you want—I was able to prise at least a little something out of my headboy on this one. Such as some new oathing activity and this suicide. You still want the details of that in the order of happening?'

'Aye. Wait, ye'll want to wet your whustle again. *Selim! Lete beer-i ingine kwa Bwana! Na mimi nataka* whusky *moja!*'

CHAPTER THREE

THE SUN was rising over the hill, and Don Bruce was sitting, squatting on his heels, in front of the *thingira* of his headman, Njeroge. It was cool on the clean-swept dirt yard of Njeroge, there in front of the bachelor hut, and the little fire before which they squatted felt comfortable. They were drinking native beer out of gourds brought by the youngest of Njeroge's wives. Donald Bruce did not usually drink beer with his headman so early in the day, but the old man seemed to need it.

'I do not like any of it, Bwana,' Njeroge said eventually, after he had drawn several interlocking circles on the hard earth with the point of a stick. 'I like it less as it goes along.'

'Well, if you think I'm wild about it myself, you're insane,' Don said in English, and then, in Kikuyu: 'Speak, old man. You are old and know much. I am young and know little. What is truly sick here on the *shamba*?'

'First,' Njeroge said, turning his hawk profile on his master, 'I will tell you a story I heard from my father, who had it from the Njeroge my grandfather whose name I bear, who had it from *his* father, who . . .'

'Yes, I know. It goes all the way back to Gikuyu the first man and Mumbi his wife,' Don said. 'Get on with it.'

Njeroge finished his parable. Don lit a cigarette and yawned. It had been a long story about a cowbird and the elephant and it doubtless owned a telling point of duplicity.

'This is all very fine, especially the beer. It was a very good parable,' Don Bruce said. 'What else have you to tell me, *mzee*? What does this lead to? What droppings has the cowbird left behind?'

'These other men that have come to this *shamba*, Bwana. The six men were hired the other day. Not the union people or the political people. These new men speak of something called the Land Freedom Army. It is, they say, a secret thing. It will bring us the land back again. All land—*all*—will come back to the Kikuyu if an oath is eaten and the oath is followed. Perhaps these are the cowbird's droppings.'

'And where do you follow this oath? Do the men say?'

'They do not say. But it is to kill you, Bwana—you and the Memsaab and the children.'

Don looked at Njeroge. The old Kikuyu's voice was as flat as his eyes. He stared past Don, looking at nothing. He seemed uninterested in his own voice. Don again yawned elaborately, patting his mouth with his hand.

'That is very old stuff, my friend,' he said. 'People have been killing me off and on since nineteen fifty-two. Who's going to kill me this time—you?'

'Not I, Bwana. Do not joke. You know that I would die before I would kill you, Bwana.' Njeroge's voice was sadly reproachful. 'But there are others on the *shamba*, Bwana. We have these new people here, Bwana. They are frightened. Some of them are frightened enough to kill you, or at least to stand aside while others kill you. There have been oathings in the last few months—in the hills around here—here, and in Thika and Kiambu and once again outside Thomson's Falls. They are the same oathings that Mau Mau held in the forests. I know this to be true.'

'How can you know this to be true?' Don frowned. This was coming closer to the knuckle now. It always took time—parables, generalities, and then suddenly you hit bone.

'Kamore.' Only a word deep in his muscle-sagged chest.

'Kamore? Not Kamore, your——?' This was unexpected. It was the last thing Don would have expected.

'Yes, Bwana. My youngest daughter. The one who has been sitting with the baby Jock, looking after him when his mother is not in the house. *My* daughter, my seed.' The old man's voice was bitter. His hand shook as he reached for the *pombe* gourd. 'Kamore.'

Don reached out and dropped his hand on the old man's shoulder. He remembered Kamore. She was pert and plump and wore Peggy's cast-offs with an air. She was perhaps fifteen years old.

'All right, *mzee*,' he said gently as if speaking to a child. 'Let's go at this slowly. Easy does it. It is easy to hide from the fast tracker who sees only his own old footprints. Tell me: how did Kamore come to tell you this?'

Njeroge sighed, his carven mahogany face set in sadness.

'She did not tell me, Bwana. I have been intercepting her letters from a young man of the towns. I have not wanted her to become a city slut. This young man is a bad man, not of this *shamba*. He is a stupid man as well. He was one of the wild young men who joined the Mau Mau at about the time it was being broken. That was stupid—he had nothing to gain. He was taken and sent to the detention camp at Hola or perhaps to Manyani, I do not remember. He learned much evil in camp. Now he is very politically minded, Bwana, and he works for a political brotherhood called Kaynap. You know of this Kaynap? Its men have been coming to the *shamba* spending much money on beer trying to buy votes for when the elections will come.'

'I know Kaynap,' Don said grimly. 'Indeed I do. And I know most of the types who run it all the way down to bush level. Yes? So, the letter. A love letter?'

'It was not much of a letter, Bwana. Of course I cannot read, so I took it to the little *dukah* on the road and asked the Wahindi to read it for me. It came as usual from this man—his name is Abel Gakungu—asking my girl Kamore to meet him . . . to meet him at a place called Karinga-*mbile* about five miles from here, between our *shamba* and the *shamba* of the Memsaab Shalotu where you got the breeding stock.'

'Yes,' Don Bruce said, and handed the old man a cigarette. 'Glenburnie. Go on, *baba*.'

'It was a peculiar place to ask a woman to come, Bwana. There is a *mugumo* tree there. That is no kind of a place to ask a woman to come. It is a man's place for the worshipping of Ngai. There was something evil or he would not ask an unbetrothed woman to come to such a place. My daughter is neither married nor betrothed nor is she likely to be.' Again the old man's voice turned bitter. 'None of my young daughters is married or betrothed. Some are sluts of the town. I have tried to keep this one, my youngest, virtuous, but . . . times have changed. No matter. So I sealed the letter and allowed my daughter to receive it. And then I followed——' The old man shook his head. 'I do not want to say more. Must I?'

'You must,' Don said gently. 'Yes. Of course you must. Tell me, *mzee*.'

'I know some small trails, Bwana. I was very cautious as I approached. I slipped through the bush as silently as a snake, and it was not long before I heard the sound of voices. They came from a little clearing at the foot of the tall *mugumo* fig tree. I drew as close as I dared, Bwana, scarcely breathing, but I made no noise.' Now the old man's voice was proud again. 'You can tell from my face that I am of the old ones, of the Athi, Bwana. I am not a late-comer to the forest.'

'Yes,' Don Bruce breathed, with a sudden horrible feeling that he knew what was coming. He wouldn't like it when it came.

'There were a dozen young men gathered under the tree, perhaps, and only three women beside my daughter. There were no other people from this *shamba*. And Bwana, there was no Abel Gakungu there, either. My daughter was very much frightened when she saw that the man who had sent her the message to meet him was not there. She started to dart away, but the men had seen her. They ran after her and caught her and flung her to the ground. She screamed and they covered her mouth until she choked.'

The old man was momentarily overcome. Don reached for the *pombe* gourd and spilled some of its contents in the drinking-horn and handed it to Njeroge, who smiled at him feebly.

'That was good,' he said gratefully, and wiped his mouth with the back of his hand, flicking the foam to the ground with his fingertips.

'Go on, old man,' Don Bruce said. 'Tell me what happened then.'

'In my life I have seen a thousand oathings,' the old Kikuyu said, lifting his eyes to the sky. 'Most of them have been good oathings—reasonable oathings, held by day, with an object of lifting a curse or pleasing Ngai or bringing a bad man to justice. I did not see any of the oathings of the Mau Mau, but of course I have heard much, including the ones when they used women and animals. I did not believe them to be true, Bwana. Also I do not hold with oathings by night.'

Don Bruce said nothing. He believed Mau Mau oathings to be true, all right. He had seen one once—only briefly, because he had been armed at the time and he had other armed men with him. The body of the oath was that if certain things were or were not done, the oath would kill the eaters of the oath. In this instance the oath had been eminently correct. Don brushed his hand across his eyes. Yesterday had crept suddenly back into today. The old man was speaking again.

'It was almost dark when I got there. They sat and drank *pombe* until it was quite dark. It was very cold as I lay in the bush. I could not move, and my bones were cold. Then the women started to gather firewood.'

'Your daughter Kamore?'

'Two of the women and some of the men talked to her, shaking her violently by the hair, and after a while she agreed to do whatever it was they asked her to do. Then they did not hold her any more, but gave her *pombe* to drink. It was white man's *tembo*—gin, I think, out of a square bottle. She made a great face as she swallowed it. Then she appeared to become braver. Once or twice she laughed.

'When it was dark they started the fire. Then Bwana——' the old man's voice was horrified. 'Bwana, they took off all their clothes! They were naked as the Suk and Karamojong! They were as naked as the Agumbu who lived in holes in the ground before even the Mwathi came!'

'Yes, yes,' Don said. 'Go on. They took off their clothes. The fire was very hot, I judge.'

Njeroge's voice was primly moralizing.

'There is nothing wrong about nakedness, although a man should turn his eyes away if he comes upon women bathing in a stream, and no woman should go without her kirtle in front of any man but her husband. But Bwana, these people were vulgar in their nakedness, as white women and men would be if they mingled naked together! They looked—they looked *naked*—as a Kikuyu woman with long hair and a *braziru* and high-heeled shoes and a handbag looks naked, like a harlot!'

'Civilization . . .' Don murmured. 'And?'

Njeroge shuddered.

'I cannot tell you all that I saw, Bwana. Ngai would stop my tongue. My teeth would fall out. They had a white ram and a white ewe. Tethered. The men—some held the ewe and the other men used the ewe as you would use a woman if you were alone with her in a hut. Then Bwana . . .' his voice trailed again.

Don shook him gently by the shoulder, and when he did not reply, shook him harder.

'Yes! Tell me!'

'They tried to make the white ram rear upon and enter the *women*, but the ram would not—he only tried to get away. So they slew the white ram very slowly, breaking its bones and taking out its eyes and its stomach and finally its heart, and then cutting off its genitals which they roasted slowly over the fire until the penis swelled and then they made the women sit and place the penis inside them as part of an oath . . .'

This is really where we came in, Don thought. The last report that even the British press couldn't run, that went on for pages and pages. And that was the year nineteen and fifty-five of grace. Kimathi's old order that we got when we shot up that last gang. *Improve on the various Batuni oaths and pass them around to the other gang leaders.* Dead animals and . . .

Njeroge was speaking again.

'. . . and then they slew the white ewe and emptied the contents of her *chakuma* into the blood and stomach contents that they were collecting in a palm-leaf-bottomed hole in the ground. And then they—the men, some of the men—went with all the women in the same way that they had gone with the ewe—they went with my *daughter*, Bwana!—the same way they had gone with an animal! And the women were made to collect *that* sperm such as they could and put it into the liquid with the other from the dead sheep!'

The old man stopped. The horror of it all was too much for him to shape into words. Don lit two cigarettes and gave one to Njeroge. He shook his shoulder gently.

'Finish it,' he said softly. 'There must be more or you would not have started. Finish it and then you will have vomited it out. All the evil will go into the mists.'

The old headman sighed.

'They pricked the hearts of the animals seven times with an iron nail and added the heart's blood. They scooped the brains from the animals' skulls and each man and woman ate some. They were made to crawl seven times through an arch of banana leaves, where they had stuck the beasts' eyes on *kei*-apple thorns, as is customary in oathing. They drank seven swallows of the fluid they had collected, and were made to swear.'

'Who made them swear? And what did they swear?'

'It was the old Mau Mau oath, of which I have heard, but some things were added. No one man was *mundumugu*. They took turns as leader. All seemed equal in this oath. They swore to release Jomo Kenyatta. They swore to kill all white bwanas and memsaabs when commanded. They swore to turn the other way if they saw a man or woman stealing from the bwanas or the Wahindis. They swore to take back the land, all of it, in the name of the

295

Land Freedom Army. Each man swore to take back the land he was bound closest to. And they were each made to swear one extra thing. My daughter Kamore——'

'Kamore! What was she made to swear?'

'Kamore—Kamore was made to swear to—to——' the old man bowed his neck and for a moment his shoulders shook. Then he raised his head and said swiftly as if ridding himself of the words before they contaminated him:

'My daughter was made to swear that when so ordered she would steal the baby, your son Jock, and fetch him to a place where he would be sacrificed as the white ram was sacrificed! She would bring him to any place they ordered or the oath could kill her!'

Now the old man babbled.

'And each man was made to swear that he would take the white woman he knew best as the white ewe was ravished, and kill her and eat of her flesh later, or the oath would kill him! And the Memsaab Peggy and the female children were mentioned by name! And you were named, Bwana, as a man to be killed, and so was the Bwana Brian, your friend, and many more of the other bwanas who went against the Mau Mau in the hills!'

Now the old man stopped, and his head drooped between his upcocked knees. His arms hung over his kneecaps, hands dangling spread-fingered, nervelessly.

Well, there we have it, Don thought. *So the first story from the other woman was garbled, but this one isn't. This isn't garbled a bloody bit. This one spells it out. We have an eyewitness, if there's only somebody to find and try. I hope nobody saw him or suspected he was there. Better find that out before I leap into action. Christ. They certainly didn't forget any of the old filth while we had them so neatly penned up in the best interests of peace and prosperity for the Commonwealth.*

'Was there more, *mzee*?' he asked gently after a few moments. The old man raised his head once again. He sighed.

'There was more. Much more. They cut up the meat of the sheep and roasted it and they all ate the oath again and laughed a great deal and discussed the best ways of killing the bwanas and taking the memsaabs as they took the white ewe. Then some of the men drew the women to one side and took them again for all to watch. There were many men, you see, and only a few women.'

'And your daughter—Kamore took part in all this?'

He nodded.

'Yes, Bwana. Kamore took part in all this.'

'She ate the oath.'

'Yes, Bwana. She ate the oath.' He nodded.

'And she said—she said she would steal little Jock and bring him to be sacrificed or the oath would kill her?'

'Yes, Bwana. She did not want to take this part of the oath because she is fond of little Jock but they held a *simi* to her throat and cut her just a little

296

and so she swore. She ate some more of the oath and drank again seven times of that *liquid* and swore again that she would steal little Jock as ordered.' The old man nodded, rocking back and forth.

'And all this time you lay there and watched?'

'I could do nothing else, Bwana. I am old man—old and weak and I had only my *panga*. There were twelve, fifteen of the others, and all but the women had *pangas* or *simis*. They were all young men, and strong. I could do nothing but lie there shivering in the bush, Bwana, until they went away. This was about midnight.'

Don scratched his head. His brain was seething, but he kept his voice calm.

'And what did you do after they left?'

'I ran swiftly as I could to the *shamba* and waited up for Kamore to come home, Bwana. It was very late at night, Bwana, when I got home to my *shamba*, but Kamore had not come in. There was no use rousing you, Bwana, until I could seize Kamore to take her to you, trusting then to your advice and your knowledge that she is a good girl and was forced to do what she had to do. This is not a new thing, Bwana.' The old man's voice was gently reproachful now.

'I know it's not a new thing, Njeroge,' Don Bruce said. 'That's the pity of it.'

The terrible pity of it, he thought. It happened over and over again in the last mess. The good ones scared and forced to take the oath and then . . . we collected them, too—as well as, and possibly easier than, those who really liked it.

'When did Kamore come back to the *shamba*?' A sudden thought had struck him . . . a coldly logical, awful thought had struck him.

'She did not come back, Bwana. I did not sleep, I waited up for her, but she did not come back. I was frightened—perhaps some animal had taken her or the men had killed her after all. But then I thought that perhaps she had gone into Nyeri with the other *watu* to drink more *pombe*. She will be back today, I am sure, Bwana. Then we will seize her and make her talk and perhaps she can identify some of the men and the other women in front of the Bwana Police. I did rightly, Bwana?' The old man's voice pleaded. 'I did the best I could. But I was frightened, Bwana—frightened and sick at stomach and sicker at heart.'

'You did absolutely right,' Don Bruce said. 'You're a fine brave man, Njeroge. I'm proud to know you. Now tell me, do you think we could go now and back-track you to where you saw the oathing? Are you not too tired?'

'I am tired but not that tired, Bwana,' Njeroge said. 'We will go now. Do you think that perhaps we may find Kamore if we go back there now? Be sure to take your gun, Bwana.'

'I'll take my gun,' Don Bruce said. 'Never fear, I'll take my gun. But I don't think I'll need it. Not this trip, anyhow.'

'But do you think we will find Kamore?' the old man quavered.

'Yes, old man,' Don Bruce said in a soft and very sad voice. 'I think we'll find your daughter, all right. Yes, I think we'll find Kamore.'

*

'And so, Nigel,' Don Bruce said to the Bwana PC, 'of course we found Kamore. It was one of the easier pieces of tracking I ever did. She was hanging from a tree. She had ripped up her *shuka* and twisted it into a noose and had jumped off a rock.'

'Poor lass,' the Bwana PC said. 'Poor, sad savage lass. They *will* strangle themselves. Ah, weel. We'll just make a jolly guid look for this Muster Whatsisname——'

'Abel Gakungu.'

'——this Muster Abel Gakungu, although there'll be about a thousand Abel Gakungus runnin' loose, and perhaps your guid headboy will be able to identify some of the others if we comb the rogues' galleries. But frankly I have very little in the way o' hope we'll accomplish much. Well, ye ken, Bruce, it's middlin' hopeless. Six million black faces, one as much alike another as the twa peas . . .' He shook his frosty head.

'And what'll ye do now, laddie? Apart fra' keepin' your weather-eye sharp and peeled?'

'I think I'm convinced, Nigel,' Don Bruce said, getting up. 'I think I'll just stop off now and pay a call on Miss Charlotte over at Glenburnie. I've had words with Brian before about possibly selling up my farm to his people. I hate it——' he shook his head. 'But this is really too close to the knuckle now. The other stuff, maybe moonbeams. But this is serious. I can't afford to risk the family for a principle.'

'Will ye tell Charlotte about these doings? All of it?'

'Not unless you want me to. Not unless you plan to broadcast it yourself. It'll do no good and'll likely stir up another panic that'll get distorted in the press. Stop any real chances of coming onto these blokes. Apart from that it'll do my sales talk no good at all.'

'I'd not care to see ye sell your farm to Charlotte under false pretence, Bruce,' the Bwana PC spoke slowly. 'Perhaps ye'd best mention that there's been a fresh outbreak o' oathings, and ask her if she's heard aught on her ain farm. Ye needn't delve too deeply into the detail.'

'Right.' Don Bruce clapped his hat on his head and got into the battered Chev. 'Thanks for the drinks and the listening, Nigel. I'll let you know how I come out with the old girl at Glenburnie.'

'Right. And the best o' guid luck to ye, laddie.'

Nigel Bruce fired his pipe, shook his grizzled head sadly, and clapped his hands sharply for Selim, the houseboy.

'*Lete mimi* whusky *ingine*,' he said. '*Lete mimi* whusky *mkubwa*, double!'

THERE WAS only a small round-faced black boy and a large Rhodesian red ridgeback hound in the flowered front yard of Glenburnie farm as Don Bruce drove up in the cool of the evening.

'*Jambo, mtoto,*' he said to the little boy, a bright-looking lad of about seven. 'Where's the Memsaab?'

'Aunt Charlotte is inside the house by the fire,' the little boy said in an excellent precise English. Don raised his eyebrows.

'Oh. Well, you just run in and tell the Memsaab that the Bwana Bruce would like to see her. Hurry now, there's a good lad.'

'Yes, Mr. Bruce,' the little boy said. 'I will tell her right away.'

He turned to go, neat and very clean in his khaki shorts and jumper.

'Wait a minute,' Don Bruce called. The little boy turned at the steps.

'Yes, sir?'

Don walked over more closely to him.

'What's your name, laddie?'

'Karioki Stuart,' the little boy said proudly. 'I have Aunt Charlotte's name because I have no family of my own.'

'Where are your mother and your father?'

'They died when I was a very little baby. I do not remember them. Aunt Charlotte Stuart has brought me up here in the *big* house, and has given me her name.'

Don patted him on the head, and gave him a little push.

'That's fine, Master Stuart,' he said. 'I've a boy about your age. Maybe I'll send him over to play with you some day.'

'That would be very nice,' the little boy said, and bounded into the house, calling: 'Aunt Charlotte! There's a Mr. Bruce outside who wants to see you!'

Don grinned rather ruefully. What do you know, he thought. It's my god-son, as I live and breathe—the one Brian and I lugged home from the last do. Odd, I never saw him about before. And it's 'Aunt Charlotte', now, and she's raised him in the big house, and he speaks better English than my brats. What do you ever know?

The little boy was back now, smiling.

'Aunt Charlotte says please come on in,' he announced, and skipped off round the corner of the house, calling to the dog.

Charlotte Stuart was sitting in front of a feeble fire with a stack of what looked like architectural plans piled in a heap on the floor beside her. Her bad leg, as usual, was propped on its footstool, and her stick leaned against the old high-armed leather easy chair. Her face brightened in the firelight as Don Bruce entered the room.

'Come over here and give us a kiss,' the old lady said, reaching up her face. 'Since when did you stop making free of Glenburnie—sending messages now, glory be to God, that Mister Bruce would like the pleasure of an audience with Her Worship? I thought for a moment 'twas the Governor at least come to call, for all the seriousness little Karioki invested in the message. Tea? Gin? What?'

'Gin, I expect,' Don said. 'Thank you, Miss Charlotte.'

'It's in the corner, same as always,' the old lady said. 'While you're at it, slosh a little pink in the glass and bring me a gin as well. I've been browsing on this tea until I fair reek of tannin. You're looking very well, Donald. I never see you any more. How's Peggy and all the brats?'

'Fit,' Don Bruce said from across the room, where he was pouring the drinks. 'Couldn't be fitter.'

'That's good,' Charlotte Stuart said. 'Someone—Nell, I think it was—said she'd lost a baby. Terribly sorry to hear it. But I'm glad she's all right again now.'

'Yes, she's fine. She slipped the kid several weeks ago—when I was still on safari. Have you heard anything from Brian lately? I've been so busy over at Hardscrabble that I've not had time to whip into Nairobi to check with the office.'

The old lady frowned, knitting the tangled red eyebrows, a furrow cutting deeply between the eyes over the hawk-bridged nose.

'Nothing for the last three or four weeks, I forget how long. He stopped by on his way north after the hanging. I'm afraid it wasn't too pleasant a visit, Donald. We had a bit of a family dust-up.'

Don Bruce sat down, facing her from her dead husband's chair. He took a sip of his drink and set the glass down on the rough stone of the hearth.

'I suppose we all wrangle a bit at times,' he said. 'People seem nervier these days than they used to.' He twisted his big white-haired chapped hands for a moment before he spoke again.

'Did he mention me?'

The old lady fitted a cigarette into her holder and accepted a light from her guest.

'He did, that he did,' she said. 'But 'twas at the end of the argument and it's slipped my mind until now. We've been so busy here lately . . . Yes. He said you'd been having a spot o' Wog bother on the farm and were considering selling up. That couldn't be right, could it, you wanting to pack it in and leave Kenya?'

She gazed at him shrewdly, her head cocked, and puffed a cloud of cigarette smoke.

Don's voice came hesitantly.

'Well, yes, as a matter of fact it *is* right, Miss Charlotte,' he said. 'I suppose it was why I was sort of—sort of formal when I came to your house today. It was a business call, I suppose, and I really don't know much about talking business with old friends. I might as well come straight out and say it: Would you like to buy my farm, for the price of the mortgage and the improvements? I don't have to tell you it's a good farm or what I've done with it in the last half-dozen years. You'd know that anyhow.'

He picked up his drink, sipped it again, and leaned back in Malcolm Stuart's old chair, looking miserably at the floor.

'I've never been known as a woman to beat about the bush,' Charlotte Stuart said. 'I'll tell it to you straight two ways, so's there'll be no mistaking my meaning. One, I couldn't buy your farm right now if I wanted to. I haven't the money *or* the credit. And two, even if I could buy it *and* wanted to, I *wouldn't*. That clear enough?'

'That's clear enough.' Don Bruce got up from the chair. 'That's certainly clear enough. Thank you, anyhow, Miss Charlotte. I'm sorry to have bothered you. I'll just be running along now if you don't mind.'

The old lady glared at him. She banged her stick on an andiron.

'Sit back down in that chair and listen to me, young man! You used to call me *Aunt* Charlotte when you were a shirt-tail boy, getting into all manner of mischief with my Ian and Brian. It seems to me, as I told Brian when last he was here, I've spared my rod of recent years and spoiled a lot of children, even some I've no excuse for neglecting. Sit down and finish your drink, Donald Bruce, or I'll take this stick to you here and now!'

Don grinned weakly at her and sat down again.

'Yes'm,' he said. '*Aunt* Charlotte.'

The old lady's voice softened now.

'In the last four months,' she said, 'ever since there's been talk of freeing some of the White Highlands to Kikuyu landowners, no less than seven hundred—*seven hundred*—white farmers from this area have offered their properties for sale at sacrifice prices—*seven hundred* since the Land Development Board started talking about opening up the White Highlands to Africans. Seven hundred!' Her voice hardened again and she spat the figure like a curse.

'Rats leaving a sinking ship, all of them. Spineless hand-wringers. They've talked high and proud of all the hardships they've faced, of how many bones they've buried, of how bloody noble they've all been to chop this country out of a wasteland of nothing but useless scenery and wild beasts. And the first time they bump into an obstacle that's been on the cards ever since I landed in Mombasa in 1911, they want to cut and run!'

'But there are other considerations,' Don protested. In my case——'

'Everybody's got his own case, just as the whiners and the runners always make a case,' Charlotte Stuart said cuttingly. She snapped her head erect and glared at him.

'But I won't leave nor will I encourage by word or deed the leaving of anybody else! Not even you for the sake of your wife and children, because if one leaves, all leave—and if they can frighten Collie Bruce's boy Donald, then there's no hope for our Philip or Nell and her new husband or your children, or even that poor little orphan chap that I've tried to bring up in a new world. *Your* contribution to the future, Don Bruce—yours and my nephew Brian Dermott's! That very little boy Karioli playing in the yard.'

'It was a little shock to see him grown so big. Karioki—'Restored to Life", old Kidogo named him when we retrieved him from that slaughterhouse. Seems a thousand years ago . . .' Don's voice trailed, then came alert again.

'Tell me, Memsaab,' he said. 'The countryside is full of talk about this whacking great scheme you've got here—sharing the wealth with the Nigs, and so on. What sort of troubles *are* you running into? They must be thousands of problems if I know anything about farming the hard way.' He inspected the broad calloused palms of his anvil hands. 'And I think I do.'

'Troubles aplenty. Not so many from the Wogs as you'd think. The Land and Settlement Board mainly. The Land Development Board's got a bill struggling in Legco to make a certain amount of land up here in the Highlands available to black purchase, but it's all bogged down in committee or something while the Wog politicians cut each other's throats and screech freedom for Kenyatta, and the white politicians act up worse than the Wogs. I like Cavendish-Bentinck better than Blundell, personally. And I hate to say it, as one of the older settlers, but Blundell's right in playing up his three-faced multi-racial stand. We've got to get along with these people sooner or later and we might as well start being multi-racial now. Else we'll be single-racial in the end, and it won't be white superiority, either.'

Don scratched his rough thatch of carrot hair.

'How can you settle your land legally on these tenants of yours, then, until they straighten out the legal muddles?'

'Blast the legal mummery. It's *my* bloody land and they're *my* bloody niggers. I'd like to see any committee come stomping in here and tell me what to do with *my* land. I've deeded the land to my various families in simple gift.'

'It's not legal, though,' Don ventured. 'Any heir could break it. A committee of white farmers could enjoin you . . .'

'None of my heirs'll try to break it even if I die tomorrow,' the old lady said. 'And I'm too damned mean to die tomorrow. Furthermore, if the good Ngai lets me see spring, that land bill will be ratified in Legco—well before those elections, believe you me, when the *white* politicians start battling each other for the common-roll vote. It's just a matter of months before the country's technically free, with an automatic black majority in Legco. And,' the old lady showed all her false teeth in a smile, 'my Wogs trust me. I've showed 'em the paper, had Philip read 'em the words, and told 'em that the land's theirs—when they've earned it. That's good enough for them. They're working like no Wogs ever worked before, believe you me. And we're not having to stand over them with a whip once they're started.'

'Must be keeping you all terribly busy. If Hardscrabble's any example, you've a lot on your plate, getting five hundred Wog families started on a scheme like this.'

'Five hundred here and another five hundred on the Laikipia place next. It's not so bad as you'd imagine with everyone turning a hand. I could use another good white man or so—you needn't tell him if you see him, but Brian would be terribly helpful, particularly with the mechanical end of it. George

Locke is working harder than any two white men I ever saw, but he's hopeless with machinery. Odd, him being a doctor, that the simple workings of a differential system in a motor-car would send him into a panic.'

Don grinned.

'Some can and some can't. It's simpler on my farm. Anything that goes wrong with the machinery is a simple *thahu* and can be fixed by killing a goat.' His face darkened in a frown. 'You probably heard about my visitation of goats?'

The old lady laughed.

'I did. Excuse me for laughing, but in a sad sort of way I thought it was jolly funny. The only person I know who hated goats on the place worse than you was Mac Stuart. I gave him a pair of goats as a birthday present once, long ago, and he didn't speak to me for a week. Couldn't see the humour in it.'

'I don't blame him,' Don said. 'I suppose it was sort of funny at that. But tell me: what about the division of white labour here? How are you splitting up the chores?'

'Not so difficult. Everyone's pitched in. Young Philip cut short his honey-moon—you knew he'd married that little Gillian Dennis, a lovely child, smart as a whip, make the boy a jolly fine wife, I should think—to come back and work. And you'd never believe what I do.'

'What do you do?'

The old lady grinned broadly again, and made a caricature of crossing herself.

'The good Lord forgive and save me. Poor Malcolm Stuart. Wherever the poor rascal is, I hope he doesn't know. I'—she spaced her words for effect—'*I run a* dukah!'

'No! Not Miss Charlotte Stuart running a bloody store like a Wahindi woman!'

'I see nothing wrong with it.' She straightened her shoulders, and tilted her chin in a mock-heroic pose. 'I am a captain of industry, by God, six mornings a week for three hours. And,' she sniggered, 'I'm having the time of my life. I hear all the juiciest gossip; I'm undercutting the bloody Indians right and left; I'm buying everything in tremendous bulk and saving money for the Wogs in the process, and I'm making a tidy profit on the side. Which, of course, we're ploughing back into the project. What do you think of that, eh?'

Don shook his head in admiration.

'By the Lord Harry, Aunt Charlotte, I have to say I admire you. The idea of the mistress of Glenburnie running a country store to sell snuff and pain-killer to the local niggery is about the last thing I ever thought to see in this world.'

'It's damned interesting work. You know something, Don Bruce? I think I've learned more about the Wog in the last couple of weeks of running a shop than I ever learned in all my fifty years of living here on the hill. Women are the same the wide world over; they jibber-jabber when they get loose from the menfolk and come to the shop. I hear things I never heard as the Memsaab Mkubwa who lived in the big house on the hill. Comes in jolly helpful, too, when the council sits.'

'Council?'

'Yes, indeed. We're to all intents an incorporated city here. Town council; land board; sanitation board; grievance board—the lot. I'm the chairman, or chairlady or whatever. Anyhow, I run it.' Charlotte Stuart grinned again, wolfishly this time. 'With an iron hand I run it. Come multi-racial equality or not, I still run the *shauri* here at Glenburnie. The old Kyuke elders listen to me, I'll have you know, when I pound this stick and yell.'

'I must say it all sounds pretty wonderful, the way you tell it,' Don said. 'How about the girls—Nell and young Jill? And Pip? What do they do exactly?'

'Philip's the general overseer—general manager. We've hired Sikh *fundis* to supervise the Africans in the building, and that really doesn't need a white man's eye, once the plans are drawn. Young Jill is sort of vice-president in charge of housing as well as keeping an eye on the schoolhouse. But it's Nell who's the whiz. She always had more energy than was good for her; she's a ball of fire now.'

'*Whiz. Ball of fire!* Wherever do you pick up expressions like that?'

'Young folks' talk. I get it from Jill. She gets it from the American films, I suppose. If I had two good legs I'll bet I could learn the rock and roll. But to go on about Nellie: she has done some unbelievable things in a very short time with the young native women—the uncircumcised girls and the overdue-to-be-marrieds. You wouldn't believe it, Don. Some of these young Kikuyu girls learn like a streak as soon as anyone takes time to explain things to them.'

'How exactly do you mean?' Don's face was sombre. He was thinking of the young Kamore whom he had seen, this early morning, hanging from a tree in the forest.

'Well, for a start, they catch onto things like simple sanitation and first aid. George and Nell—I must say George is *very* good with the native women, he must have got on very well working with old Schweitzer—have had some classes at night on various topics, everything from personal hygiene to home economics. You can argue your head off about sanitation and get nowhere with a Wog, but if you show them through a microscope the kind of worms they get in their bellies if they don't pay attention to keeping a latrine a decent distance from their drinking water, it assumes an aspect of witchcraft and as Jill would say'—the old lady chuckled again—'if you'll pardon the pun, they dig it the most.'

Don nodded.

'I suppose so. I've been trying for ages, in my own small way, to hammer home some of the basic ideas of common sense to my people, but I guess I haven't been going at it the right way. If Nell's beginning to get the women organized I'd say you might be halfway home.'

'She thinks she's making a dent in them, anyhow. And Don,' the old lady

304

dropped her voice, 'this is purely political, and is supposed to be kept quiet. But there's a big African politician—you know him, Stephen Ndegwa—who heard something of what we intended here. He's in America, or maybe England just now, but he came up to see me a couple of weeks ago just before he left. Now, listen to this.' Charlotte Stuart paused and waved a finger on Don Bruce's nose.

'Listen to this,' she repeated. 'He wants to help. Particularly from the aspect of the woman-family thing. It's been a half-formed idea of his all along. And now he says he can see the practical way of making it work for the first time. D'you know him, Don?'

'I've only just seen him around town—in the New Stanley. He was there with Matthew Kamau the day they hanged Peter Poole. Big, burly bloke. Not so wogified to look at as some of these other rock apes.'

Charlotte Stuart spoke seriously.

'I liked him. I liked him very much. I think he's one of the very few new-crop politicians—maybe he's the only one—who really wants something good and permanent for his people—and who also realizes that you can't do it all in a moment.'

'I'm very interested in this,' Don said. 'Do we have time for one more drink before your people come in from building the Pyramids—and before I dash off to avoid being skinned alive by Mrs. Margaret Bruce?'

'Of course. Make mine a stiff one. I'm enjoying this, Donald, my lad. It's nice to talk to another farmer. I'm surrounded'—she winked—'I'm surrounded by high idealists and the dedicated doers of good, and it's nice to smell a little honest manure, if you know what I mean. The scent of the rose-covered future around here gets to be a little overpowering at times. I'm all for ideals, but ideals never ploughed a furrow or built a dam. It wants sweat to kill crabgrass.'

Don came back with the fresh drinks. He handed one to the old lady, stirred up the smouldering fire with his foot, and sat down again.

'What exactly did this coon have to say? As near as you can remember?'

'We got off with the usual Kyuke platitudes about wind, crops, weather and Ngai's will, first, and then he asked me if he could take off his shoes, his feet hurt. He said that if he lived to be a hundred and became the Chief Minister of all of Africa, his feet would still hurt. We swapped symptoms for a bit, and then he said . . .'

CHAPTER FIVE

FOR SOME reason Don Bruce was not unduly depressed by Charlotte Stuart's refusal to buy his farm. Like everyone else in Kenya she was short of cash, and real estate was a lousy risk at this time. He had never traded in pity, and he had never been indebted for anything without a sound basis of value exchanged. He would not have liked to have been in the debt of Charlotte Stuart. He would scrape the eating money together somehow. He always had.

It has been a horrible day, and I'm glad to see it finished, he thought, as night suddenly fell, and he switched on his lights to probe the darkness. A fire and another drink and some *chakula* and bed. I don't think I'll burden Peggy with all of the details of today. Tell her tomorrow, maybe, when the sun's bright and we can face up to what we have to do, and face it without the night sounds.

He turned off the main road and bumped along the narrow track which led to his farm. His lights tongued ahead of him on the rutted road, rising and falling as the old Chevrolet dipped and lifted on the hills.

As he slowed the car preparatory to stopping to open his gate, the lights shone upward and he saw that something, once again, was hanging on his fence post. It gleamed white in the night, heavy, bulky, and he did not have to walk up to it to know that it was one of his pure-bred Romney rams. Nor, as he lifted the still-living carcass off the spearhead of his gate and cut its throat with his pocket knife, did he have any doubts about the remainder of his breeding herd. He remembered vividly the night of the cattle slaughter in the hills, the hacked and dismembered cattle bawling in their agony, and for the first time in his life when he closed the gate and drove along his own road, across the little Japanese bridge he had built with love because it led to light and love, Donald Bruce wished he were going any other place in the world at that moment but home.

*

The herdboys poked and prodded at the flanks of the sheep, the expensive blooded Romneys and Hampshire Downs that were Donald Bruce's pride and pet project—the imported rams he used to breed up the native hair sheep, the imported ewes for back-crossing against the hybrids. It was growing late. The sun had already settled for its final bloody plunge over the earth's rim.

'*Hayah!* the herdboys yelled, as they hustled the sheep along. 'Hayah! *Upesi!*' The sheep snatched at the grass along the roadside, but the boys would not allow them to loiter. The sheep were being taken to the top paddock near the main gate, a long distance from the big house and from the native living lines, for night paddocking to fertilize sick lands that Don Bruce was in process of reclaiming. The herdboys grazed the sheep along the road by day, and Don Bruce sternly expected each sheep to do its duty by emptying its bowels nightly on the land that hungered for fertilization.

'Hayah! *Upesi!*' The boys yelled, because the top paddocks stood close to the extending dark arms of forest which reached down from the sinister black hills. There would be just time, if the sheep hurried, to turn them into the dung-starved paddocks, rams in one, ewes in another. Then the boys would trot swiftly home before night fell and the demons stirred or the leopards prowled. The herdboys were young, picanins in shirt-tails. They

306

were frightened of the dark, and they were very hungry. They had eaten nothing all day, and their mothers now would be roasting yams and bananas and boiling *posho* by the cookfires. Their stomachs growled and whimpered at the thought of food. But they were good, responsible boys—they counted the sheep on a long stick of wood, cutting notches for each ewe on one stick and notches for each ram on another. There—the last of the sheep was in. The headboy dropped the latch on the gates, and without a word, the herd-boys fled shouting down the road towards home and the delicious savouring smell of the cookfires. If they ran fast and called out loudly they would avoid spooks and ghosties—if they ran swiftly they would soon be safely eating just as the slim sickly moon rode into the sky.

The breeding herd loomed eerily white in the night, now, as the rams moved irritably in the new paddock—still hungry despite a full day of grazing, still muzzling at the poor vegetation of the tired land that would soon be fruity-rich and eager for planting from the incessant dung-pebbling which formed the basis of Don Bruce's organic-fertilizer land-reclamation scheme. Then the little moon lifted higher into the sky, and the square bulks of the heavy-woolled Romneys and Hampshires became more distinctly visible against the black of the weeds, the lowering backdrop of forest.

The new moon ducked in and around the clouds, and long black shadows lay upon the fields. Suddenly the shadows split and subdivided into tiny, independent blobs of darkness. Some of the ewes *baa*ed in fear. These new shadows did not carry the familiar scent of the herdboys.

Ten men slipped into the paddocks. One spoke.

'Cut only the balls from the rams, and rip their bellies as you cut!' the voice barked harshly. 'Cut the bags and the teats from the ewes! Do not kill them! Leave them to die! And Djuguna, Munvua—take a ram and hang him on the gate, where we hung the dog! See that the spear holds him securely! Hurry! The Bwana will soon be returning, and we must be back in our *shambas* before he discovers the sheep! *Upesi! Suria!*'

The slim black shadows slipped swiftly among the sheep, and the moon silvered the blades of *pangas* and *simis* as the men chopped and slashed at the sheep. The animals stood terrified, short-legged and heavy with wool and feed—stood, *baa*ing and bleating in terror, their nostrils crowded now with the hot scent of spurting blood as the men chopped at testicles and sawed the udders from the ewes. The sheep bled blackly on the white of their heavy coats as they fell and writhed in agony on the ground, tripping and tangling in their own looped intestines. In minutes the job was done, and the men fled back into the shadows. From the spear-gate of the entrance of Hardscrabble Farm, the moon shone white on a bulky mass of writhing animal that hung, twisting and turning and blatting in agony, from the spearhead of the Samburu spear which had been embedded in its bowels.

IT WAS strange, passing strange, Don Bruce thought, as he shot the last of the pathetically kicking, blatting sheep in the glare of the torch that old Njeroge held for him—it was strange how unforeseen events could befoul an idea, or perhaps *ideal* was the better word, to a point where everything was filthied and spoiled. He did not care about leaving the farm any more—he would be overjoyed to leave it. He had already left it emotionally; he would start leaving it physically in the morning when he took Peggy and the children into town. He would have to come back, of course, but so far as he and Hard-scrabble Farm were concerned, the backbreaking love affair was over. It had become too much trouble, he thought dully—as troublesome as some woman who had exacted so much from a man that all the loveliness he had sought in her was warped and sullied and misshapen into rather bored dislike.

'Right, I suppose that's the lot.' Don Bruce touched a dead ewe with his foot. 'I suppose you might as well get some men and collect the carcasses. No need leaving them for the hyenas. Tell the men to butcher them tonight and have a feast tomorrow. Compliments of the Bwana. Tell 'em I hope nobody gets the bellyache from cursed meat. Tell them to—skip it.' Don Bruce turned away.

'I am sorry, Bwana,' the old man said. 'I would have prevented it if I could. Perhaps I was careless. Perhaps if we had not found Kamore this morning—perhaps if I had not seen the oathing last night . . .'

'I'm sorry, *mzee*,' Don Bruce said. 'I meant to tell you. I have spoken with the Bwana PC, who now is talking to the police. We will try to find the oath-giver and the oath-takers and punish them. Unfortunately we cannot kill them. The law no longer provides the death penalty. It has been changed.'

The men began to walk out of the field towards the parked car which loomed black in the night.

'What will we do about a breeding herd, Bwana?' the old man asked, presently. 'Will we buy another? What will be put to our mixed-blood ewes in the meantime?'

'We'll buy some more bloodstock some day,' Don said listlessly. 'Mean-time, don't worry about it. Look, Njeroge.' He turned and grasped the old man by the shoulder. 'Listen to me carefully. We are going out of the grade sheep business for the time being. I want you to sell the rest of the sheep as soon as they are old and fat enough to bring a good price. Turn any of the mixed-blood rams in with any of the ewes.'

'But, Bwana, you have threatened to beat any of the boys who allowed the ewes to be bred by the——'

'I know it. Shut up!' Don Bruce's voice was harsh and hurting. 'It doesn't make any difference now. The strain is good enough. Let it breed as it wills. It'll be good enough to sell to Indians.'

'I don't understand,' the old man said. 'You never . . .'

'Listen carefully to me, Njeroge. The Memsaab and the children and I—

for a time, only—must go away. We will need money. Much money. We do not have much money, Njeroge. The last weeks have cost dearly. We will have to sell the sheep—not many at a time, but steadily. I cannot sell them to the Co-operative. I cannot give them to the bank to sell to the abattoir. We must sell them in the dark, Njeroge. Do you understand?'

'I understand what you say, but I do not understand why you said it. You have always told me that things of this sort were not honest, even though other people did them.'

'I know I did.' Don Bruce's freckled face showed pale in the moonlight. 'I did, Njeroge. But those were other circumstances. If we sell stock now through the old sources the bank will take the money. All my creditors will go to the bank with their *chittis* and the bank will write another *chitti* which will take all the money to pay to the creditors. If this happens there will be no money to pay the labour; no *posho* for you and your wives and children. And there will be no money for me to give to the Memsaab and the children.'

'I had thought you had best send them away, Bwana. You will send them away before it is too late?'

'I will send them away across the sea. I will send them tomorrow morning. I will take them personally to a place where they will be safe, Njeroge. But I will need money, that the banks will not let me have, that my creditors will not let me keep. The only way to get this money is for you to sell the sheep quietly, a few at the time, and say if anyone asks that they have been stolen or taken by hyenas and leopards. I will report this'—he waved behind him to where the dead sheep lay—'I will report *this* to the police, and so if we lose more they will blame the gangs. When we have sold some sheep we will then sell some cattle. If necessary'—Don Bruce spoke through his teeth—'if necessary, maim a few yourself, and then say that others have been driven off. Understand me?'

'I understand, Bwana. But it is not honest. I do not like to do a thing like this. And anyhow, who would I sell to that will not go gabbling to the banks and to the creditors and even to the police?'

Don Bruce turned and looked at the old man again, holding him by both shoulders, and speaking fiercely.

'You know why I am doing this, Njeroge! You know why I have to do this! Sell to the Indians! They don't ask questions. There are rich Kikuyu and Nandi! They will not ask questions in Molo about sheep that were sold by moonlight in Naro Moru. Sell cheap, sell for cash, and get the money and keep it until you have sufficient to make a trip to Nairobi worthwhile!'

'And what will I do with it then, in Nairobi? Will you be in Nairobi?'

'No,' Don said. 'I won't be in Nairobi. But I have a friend in Nairobi. You do not know him, but you will be able to find him with no difficulty. His name is Bwana Jenkins—Bwana Ken Jenkins. He is the chief *babu* in the office of the Bwana Brian. He will understand everything. He will take the money from you quietly, leaving you some, and he will send the rest to me. Nobody but you and the Bwana Ken must know. If the people to whom you sell the sheep ask why you want to sell them, tell them that I am a drunken Bwana who has gone off to England and who will never miss a few sheep when he comes back. They will laugh, and slap you on the back, and give you money, because the price will be very cheap and a sheep does not have to put his hoofprint on a *kipande*. Is it all clear? Sell only a few at a time, as if you were stealing, and sell to different people. Do you understand me completely, Njeroge?'

The old man looked at his feet.

'I understand you, Bwana. I understand you and I am sorry that you have to do such a thing. Of course I will do what you ask if you wish it that way. Will you be gone long, Bwana?'

'I don't know, old man. I really can't say. But while I am gone you are the Bwana here. Remember that. You will live in the house and look after things as best you can. I will tell you about the planting tomorrow. We will be planting the easy fast crops; the crops you can raise and sell without too much trouble, even if it ruins the land. This will satisfy the bank and some of the creditors. We will discuss all that tomorrow after breakfast when the sun is shining and we both are not so sad. Thank you, *baba*. You are a good friend, and a father to me as well.'

'I will do the best I can, father,' Njeroge said. Don had turned to walk half a dozen steps before he remembered that in Kikuyu a father often addressed his son as 'father'.

*

As Donald Bruce walked slowly to the house to tell Peggy to start packing everything that she'd likely need for herself and the children for Scotland, he mused wryly that all he would need to make this day a miracle of bitter perfection would be for Peggy to tell him that she thought she was pregnant again. That would really sew the button on it, and even that would be anticlimax. Peggy wouldn't argue now; they had been through all that. There would be tears, of course, but women cried easily and as easily ceased weeping. And Peggy was tougher than he. The children were still young enough for what the American politician Kennedy was so fond of calling 'new frontiers'. They were all young enough for new frontiers.

Don Bruce sighed and opened the door, and a warm light poured from the living-room to make a bright pool in the dark of the yard. Young Angus hurtled through the door to seize his legs as he stood on the threshold, blinking at the strong light with night-accustomed eyes.

'Guess what, guess what, guess what, Daddy!' young Angus' voice was ecstatic.

'What, laddie? What're you so excited about?' Don Bruce bent to extricate his legs from his son's tackling embrace.

'Floss! She's had her puppies! Eight of them, this afternoon! Please, Daddy, may we keep them all, may we?'

'We'll see, Son. Where's Mum?'

'She's in the bath, washing up. She just finished helping Floss with the puppies. But may we keep them all, Daddy? May we?'

Don Bruce sighed.

'We'll have to ask your mother,' he said, and moved over to the little bar to pour himself a very large gin. Maybe Peggy could think of some way to tell the kids that England's quarantine laws did not welcome large families of dogs, or any dogs at all. Peggy was very good at that sort of thing. It seemed a pity that he would have to destroy them all, because you couldn't leave well-bred young animals with Wogs in your absence. And there was certainly no market for day-old collie puppies in the Kenya of today. There didn't seem to be much market for anything young in Kenya today.

He walked to the hall and raised his voice.

'I'm home from the chores,' he said. 'Do you want a martini before we talk?'

Peggy's voice came over the gurgle of water from the bathroom.

'Yes,' she said distinctly. 'I can use a martini before we talk. I can use several of them.'

Don sank into a chair and waited for his wife to come out of the bathroom to join him. In times past this first drink together had always been the peak point of a weary, satisfying day. In a way it was the celebration of their joint effort on the farm. There was really nothing else to be done now but to crate up their life and ship it to Mombasa to wait for the boat.

CHAPTER SEVEN

'I WANT a cigarette,' Katie Crane said. 'I want two cigarettes in the dark, just like the old song said.'

'There's a pack and matches on the groundsheet on your side. Find them?' Brian was lying closely along her flanks. She could feel the length of him as she turned and dropped one bare arm over the bedside.

'Mmmmmm. Yes. Here they are. No matches, though. I must have kicked them under the bed in my precipitous rush into your arms. Do all your women kick your matches under the bed in their precipitous rushes into your arms?' Her nails scratched like chickens on the canvas as she groped along the floor of the tent.

'Now, now. Leave it. Wait a minute. I'll get up and find some.' She felt the cot sag as Brian's body swung itself lightly over her own. There was a pat of his bare feet on the floor, and a sudden spurt of flame. For a second she saw him in the match's flare, starkly brown and heavy-muscled in his nakedness, then the glare left her momentarily blinded when he blew out the flame. Now the two red eyes of the cigarettes glowed as they came towards her in his mouth. He removed one of the glowing eyes from his unseen face and covered the coal with his curved hand before the cigarette's moist end found her lips.

She heard a rustle of clothing as he reached for the wrap-around *kikoi* she sometimes saw him wearing on the way to the shower, and she could hear the whisper of the fabric as he knotted the cloth round his loins. Then he dropped cross-legged to the canvas groundsheet, sitting beside her as she lay on the bed, his chin resting on the crook of her arm. With one hand he hauled up her pillow and doubled it so that it made a rest for her neck. He lifted her slightly upward and guided her head backwards against the pillow.

'There,' he said. 'Nice and comfy?' He moved his face to kiss her inner elbow.

'Lovely,' she said. 'I must say these cots were not designed for multiple languor. Only one to a customer, or better, only one customer to cot, really, unless you're sharing them in that delightful fashion in which we just christened your couch. *Christened?* Perhaps that was a wrong choice of words. Perpetuated, perhaps.'

Brian ignored the last remark but sat, smoking, one hand casually, almost companionably, resting on the smooth cool curve of her hip as she lay facing him on her side. Her cigarette-eye winked at him in the dark of the tent.

'Perhaps you didn't know how badly I needed that,' Katie Crane said presently. 'Would you know how badly I needed that?'

'I think so. I'm not sure.' Brian's voice was slow. 'I'm not sure I understand need in a woman. I'm not sure I know anything at all about women.'

'Surely you know everything about women. Surely in your life with them you must have found some degrees of difference?' Katie kept her voice light. 'Certainly we can't fall back on that old thing about the relative greyness of cats in the dark.'

'I would say no.' His voice was grave. 'It's just that I'm no good at talking about it after. It always seemed to me to be a kind of female self-jealousy which spoiled what you'd just had, talking it over, I mean. Almost as if people were bragging to prove something or reassure themselves, like men boasting about their experiences to other men. Only more vulgar, in a way. And not very intelligent, to tug at it so.'

'Excuse me. I'm smartly reproved,' Katie said. 'I most profoundly beg your pardon. I didn't intend to trample your delicate sensibilities.'

'No delicate sensibilities. Except that for some time I think we have consciously been over-concentrating on the possibility of our falling in love. I'm frightened of women, Katie. They've given me a dreadful inferiority complex. I have never really been able to separate Dermott the surface man, who is really nothing much more than a paid servant, from the exaggerated picture that one's apt to form of a chap who can shoot and track and speak Swahili and who fits the African landscape, including personal stewardship of the African moon. I'm never sure whether anybody's in bed with me or just with the idea, like making a point of sitting at the captain's table or flirting with the pilot of the aircraft.'

'You've never really been in love? Not even with Valerie?'

She could feel his head shake in the dark.

'I don't *know*.' Now the voice held a touch of irritation. 'Perhaps I thought I was, with Valerie. But now I don't know. Particularly after this last visit of Valerie's. I'd never really seen another woman at close range before Val. I was a baboon who was tasting his first banana. If you had called the banana a pawpaw or an ice-cream cone or a sirloin steak it would still have tasted the same. A baboon's got no point of reference.'

'It's not a very flattering analogy,' Katie said. 'But I think you get your point across. How would I qualify as a banana? Over-ripe? Green? Tough? Tender?'

'You're a very lovely banana.' Katie now could sense him smiling in the dark. 'But I was a very hungry baboon. We would have to wait and see perhaps how much of us is due to mutual hunger—hunger by the banana for the baboon, or the baboon for the banana. So often we mis-label hunger and frustration as all sorts of things, including love.'

'I am in love with you,' she said flatly. 'I have never been in love with anybody before. And what experiences I have had with sex have never been anything remotely like this. Never.'

Again she could sense the head-shake of almost irritation.

'Katie, *Katie*. To be in love you have to have something to offer. I haven't anything to offer anybody. Body—yes. But that's a gift that wears out with satisfaction. You can get a bellyful of bananas. I'm afraid of you. You're different from the other women I've known. Maybe it's your money. Maybe it's your frankness. Maybe it's that I just don't trust safari romances.'

'If it weren't for the money would you consider marrying me? If I were just the little girl from the next farm?' Silly female question, Katie.

'I don't know. If I were another one of your Charleses and Whatsisnames, Copey, that got killed, would you want to ask me the same question? I'm a freak for you. You never met a real live bush baby before. I'm a novelty. How much of your life do you want to spend with a novelty? I don't know, and I don't think you do.'

Now Katie shook her head in exasperation.

'You don't give a girl a chance. You've got your fists up because you've formed the idea that everybody wants to sleep with the hunter as part of the safari programme. Maybe most of them do. I didn't. I fought this from the first day I clapped eyes on you at the airport. I know that women are sentimental, and they always like to make believe that this time it's different. Well, this time it *is* different. I don't just want to get laid every night under the African moon with a flower in my hair and the lions roaring in the background. I'd like to have a man to love and to be his wife and work my hands red and rough if I had to. If that would make him happy and make him love me.'

313

Now she could feel him getting up. He was scuffing around looking for slippers.

'I want a drink,' he said abruptly. 'Can I bring you something?'

'A Coke,' she said. 'Don't be too long. It will be lonely here in this life without you.'

I guess I meant *tent* instead of *life*, she thought. The *life* just slipped. Oh, God, I don't want to start anything at my age that I can't finish. God damn all biology. What do I want with a white hunter for people to laugh at me, as they've always laughed at rich bitches who've come home with the Wop count, the Russian prince, the polo player, the bob-sledder, the ski instructor, the cowpoke, the white hunter? What do I want slumming out here, playing pioneer woman in the wilds?

'Tell me something. Tell me honestly,' she said when he returned with the drinks. 'If I had come creeping into your tent three weeks, a month ago, would you have let me stay? Would you have serviced me as part of the guided tour, as you've serviced the others?'

He grunted. *Why* did they always have to talk it to death?

'I suppose so. Yes. If it had come to the flat point of demand. You're a grown woman; what you want to do is your own damned business, and that includes me.'

'But you wouldn't have liked me after? We wouldn't have been as close and friends and confiding? You wouldn't have told me about your father and the early days; you wouldn't have told me about your marriage and the Mau Mau doings and all that? I'd have cheated myself of that part we've had by simply demanding the early service of your body?'

'That's right. I set no great store by the body. You could have had it from the first night, and I would have played obedient stallion to the end. But I would have volunteered very little, and would have cared no bloody whit for you then or ever.'

'And you do care some bloody whit for me now? With a possibility of ever?'

'I think so. You're a touch mad and more than quite a little strayed and I think you're looking for anyone, anybody, who mightn't jump off your lap and bite you, so to speak, just for being kind. I fit the prescription at the moment. How it would be when you're cured of what ails you I can't say. People are always changing doctors if what they order doesn't do the trick.'

Katie sighed in exasperation.

'You build such a strong wall. You try to make yourself sound empty when you're not. You don't offer a chance. You won't *help*.'

Brian laughed shortly.

'I *am* empty. I'm as empty as a whistling thorn. The little bug inside me has gnawed me clean, and all you can hear is noise when the wind blows through the tiny little holes in the shell.'

Katie's sigh was even more exasperated.

'Don't you want anything, then? Don't you want anything permanent?

Would you want to think about permanency with me, if we could make it work?'

'If we could make it work, I could think of nothing lovelier. But I don't see how we could make it work—I don't see how anybody can make anything work. Nothing is simple enough to *work* any more. Christ, this is a dismal conversation. May I come back to bed?'

'Yes,' Katie said. 'You may come back to bed. But I would like to tell Paul about us if you don't mind. Do you mind?'

'No,' Brian said, crawling back under the sheet and drawing her body close to him. 'Tell him if you want. He's very unlikely to shoot me, I should think.'

CHAPTER EIGHT

THE SUN was bright now as she went out of the tent, and as he searched for his shorts and slippers again, he could hear her voice ringing abrasively loud in the cold morning air.

'Good morning, Brother dear,' she was saying, with appalling cheerfulness. 'It would appear you've discovered our guilty secret. It must be *my* conscience that got *you* out of bed at such an ungodly hour, when all the indecent folk are just going back to their own tents. It's all right, dear; Brian and I were going to tell you today, anyhow.'

He heard her brother mumble something, and then Brian yelled for Mwende to fetch his tea and shaving water. As he shaved Brian thought that he had stepped into this one for fair, and didn't very much care if he had. He thought he was in love with the girl; he thought so but he didn't really know. He doubted very much if anything would come of it, and then suddenly he was frightened that nothing *would* come of it.

'I think,' the brother said—and Brian noticed that now he was thinking of Paul as *the brother*, just as he always thought of his people as *the clients* at first—'I think, if you don't mind, we won't chew this over too much. I'd like to be sent into town today, if you don't mind. The safari's over. You can come in or stay on as you like, Katie. If Brian has nothing pressing I'd suggest you stay on for a few days. Muema or somebody can drive me into Nairobi easily. You can probably decide what you want better without me.'

Paul Drake's voice was dry and toneless, almost disinterested. He poured himself another cup of coffee and trailed his cigarette tip aimlessly around the perimeter of the ashtray.

'I don't know quite what to say, Paul,' Brian's voice was wooden. 'I really don't know what to say, except I promise you I—we—I promise you I'd intended nothing of this sort to happen. I——'

315

Paul Drake's voice became drier, like a banker considering an interesting loan.

'I shouldn't apologize if I were you, Brian,' he said. 'Katie's a grown woman. I don't imagine'—he permitted himself the thinnest slice of smile—'I don't imagine you mounted any great campaign to seduce her. I'm mildly curious, only, to know if either of you has any future serious intent concerning each other, or if this was just part of the safari. If the latter's the case, it'd save everyone a great deal of trouble if Katie and you came on into town with me and we had a few drinks and settled the accounts and said good-bye.'

Katie shot a swift glance at Brian. He too spoke without animation.

'Katie and I haven't had much of a chance to talk seriously about anything. This has been—has been pretty new and sudden. We don't know very much about each other—don't know very much about each other that way. Nothing much about each other except what we've all done and said together.' Brian's voice pulled up lamely.

'I think we'll stay on a few days, Bro,' Katie said. 'I'm in no hurry to get back, and neither is Brian. Are you, Brian.' There was no query in her voice.

'No. No hurry. Unless Paul needs me in town.'

'Or unless you think your reputation might be tarnished if we stay on alone? Boys talking and all that?' Katie's voice lilted bitingly.

'Stop it, Katie.' Brian turned his head slowly and looked at her coldly.

'Sorry.' She dipped her head in mock contrition. 'No spades being called spades today.'

Paul's voice was bankerish-brisk, now. He almost rubbed his hands together.

'That's settled, then. I go as soon as I can. You people work out whatever it is you have to work out. You don't need any brotherly advice, Katie. I suppose'—and now his tone edged—'you might have had some experience in these things before, Brian.'

That was the chief trouble with sleeping with clients, Brian thought. All the niceness nearly wiped out now. The niceness leaving and the bitchery remaining. The nastiness always lingering when the niceness is gone.

'I have no intention of marrying your sister for her—for *your* money, Paul,' Brian said levelly. 'I also may have no intention of marrying your sister. And I *have* had some experience in these things. It is not the first time a lady client has been seen leaving a hunter's tent. Sometimes it's regarded as par for the course.'

'Stop it, both of you!' Katie said. 'Go and get packed, Paul. Both of you shut up before either of you says anything I won't want to remember. I don't belong to either one of you. I belong to me. Go and tell the boys my brother wants to go to Nairobi, Brian.'

They had shaken hands cordially enough, Paul saying that it had been the greatest experience of his life, and hoping that Brian would come and visit him in the States some time, coolly excluding Katie from the invitation. Brian had said that he'd never had a nicer safari, that he would take exceptionally good care of Paul's sister for the next few days, and please not to forget to stop off at Sultan Hamud's on the way in for the mail and papers that had been accruing. If Paul would ring up the office from the *dukah* at Sultan Hamud's, Ken Jenkins or Grace would fix him with a hotel and look after his aeroplane tickets and such. If he didn't mind, would he remind Machoini, the driver, to be sure and bring back any personal mail from the office, and the latest papers as well, please. He'd tell Machoini, but Wogs had a way of getting overcome by the town and forgetting the simplest errands. Paul had asked what about tips to the boys, and Brian said he'd handle it, and would put it all on the bill. Katie told her brother to never mind the bill, she'd settle it when she got back to Nairobi.

They felt both guilty and depressed as they watched Paul Drake climb into the lorry with the big eye-glassed driver, Machoini. Paul looked frail, as most people always seem to look frail on departure—small and dry-spinsterish again, as he had looked on his arrival. The whiskery Paul of the occasional, unsuspected coarse joke was gone; so was the Paul of the ill-fitting slang; so forever gone was the Paul of the filthy khaki and the inflamed insect bites. And most of all, gone the Paul who had walked happily into thick bush after a wounded leopard in the rain, who had forever asked eager questions, who had wept over an elephant and even appeared to enjoy discomfort equally with warm gin.

'Do you know, I do miss him,' Brian said, as they walked back into the mess tent, out of the sun. 'I liked him very much. He was a terribly nice chap, your brother.' He clapped his hands for Mwende to bring fresh coffee.

'So do I,' Katie said. 'It's funny. He did turn out to be a very nice guy, my brother. He was so—so little boy about the whole thing. I don't think he was angry at us, at all. I think he was a mite hurt, perhaps, that we had done something which excluded him. Perhaps if we'd asked his permission. It was almost as if it had something to do with that damned leopard.'

'Well, didn't it?' Brian asked gently. 'Are you sure the leopard didn't have a great deal to do with it? If Paul had shot that thing dead and we hadn't had to go after it, do you think you would have come into my tent that night? I don't.'

'I don't know.' Katie shook her head. 'But I'm glad I did and I'm glad we're alone and for a whole day I don't want to talk any more about futures or pasts or problems. The rains'll be here in a few days and we've only those few days to keep seeing the country and each other. Could we please have Mwende pack us a lunch and go picnicking down to that big grove at the bottom, in the big cool swamp, and maybe watch the elephants bathe if we're lucky?'

Brian leaned over and kissed her on the cheek.

'It'll be nice to know that for the moment it still belongs to us,' he said, and got up to see about the lunch.

317

They lay in the shade of an enormous fever tree in the cathedral cool of the big swamp. The two gunbearers and the carboy had withdrawn to some distance way, and were screened by a low-bulking bush, but the crumbly hum of *eeeeh*-punctuated Wakamba voices came lazily in the cool. Katie was lying on her back, her head in Brian's lap. The chopbox gaped open, but they had not yet attacked the hard-boiled eggs and cold fowl which Mwende had packed in clean waxed paper. Brian was playing half-heartedly with a gin and tonic. A constraint had been upon them since Paul had left camp that morning.

'What are you thinking?' Katie asked, and hated herself for asking. All women ask men what they are thinking, she thought, and drive another spike into the heart of love. It's called invasion of masculine privacy, I believe.

'Nothing very much. Everything, I suppose,' Brian said. 'Seems to be the day for it. Us, I expect. Mostly about us.'

'What about us? I thought we were going to give ourselves a day's holiday from us. Pretend we aren't us at all.'

'Can't. I'm a serious-minded fellow.' He smiled down at her upturned face. 'Not one to trifle over-long with a lady's affections. I assume there still *are* affections?'

Katie pulled herself up and swivelled round until she faced him, knees drawn to chin, arms wrapped round her legs. She sighed.

'Okay,' she said. 'We might as well. You tasted all puzzled and frowny last night in the dark. What are we up to?'

'I can't see any hole in the cloud for us,' Brian said seriously. He shook his head. 'No hole at all. I do a recce-run on us and there isn't that kind of a starting-point at all. It's more as if we've already *been*, and just sort of met each other on the way back. Like we'd begun in bed at the seashore and some day I might start out carrying your books. It's back-tracking.'

'I know it, darling,' Katie said. 'I know it too well. Do you know, it sounds very funny, my calling you darling? It's how I've thought of you for a month, but now it sounds very funny to hear when I say it out loud. As if I were hearing somebody else saying it. And you haven't called me anything at all yet.'

Brian rolled over now on his stomach in the grass, and lay with his chin cupped in the heels of his palms. His knees were crooked and his ankles, interlocked in one of his favourite positions, swayed gently in the air. He spoke looking down at the grass.

'I told you once that I wasn't a whole man, Katie. Nothing is simple for me. Everything that I started out to do—to do *firmly*—fell to bits one way or the other. I depended on one way of life—a peculiar security of country, call it. It was a security that embraced work, marriage, future, some measure of honesty and decency and health and happiness and *future*—and now all that

318

has gone away. And so I wonder if I'm any good to you or for you when I can't even decide whether I'm allowed to love you.'

'You're assuming then that *I* love *you*, that this wasn't just another rich spoiled bitch getting her money's worth of safari by adding the hunter to the trophy list?' Katie's voice was hard. 'As you said to Paul, it wouldn't be the first time a client was seen leaving the hunter's tent. I haven't been any rose geranium in the past.'

'Please don't go brittle New York on me. You haven't so far. You said last night you loved me. I can't believe that you were just talking in bed. Don't play with me, Katie!'

'I won't, Brian. I really didn't mean to. And I'm not. I am in love with you and I want to be with you, in some sort of fashion. Suppose you tell me what to do and I'll try to do it.'

Brian scrubbed savagely at his face.

'There's no future here in Africa. We're marking time. That's all. There's no life to be had for the likes of me for more than a year—two years, maybe five. There's no—no *home* to be made. There's nothing to build on. I can carry on hunting for a while longer. But the game's going—unless some miracle intervenes, it'll be gone as soon as this part of Africa's black. There's no future in farming. That's going, too, for white men, and will soon be gone. I'm not fit for anything else but game and agriculture.'

'There is this one fact,' Katie said levelly. 'I have a lot of money. *My* money. You wouldn't have to do anything at all. Or we could buy a ranch. Or we could just play. Or you could get some sort of management job with Paul. Or you could start a safari firm of your own in Canada or Mexico or Alaska. We could have fun running a fishing camp in the Florida Keys or down in Baja California . . . Yucatan, maybe?' Her voice was bright and false.

Brian sat up abruptly.

'You're talking the purest cock, and you know it. Saying there was some avenue we could find with an exit at the end of it, the only way I'd consider it for both of us would be for me to be the giver on the financial side. I couldn't take your money to be a play-acting gigolo-husband any more than I'd accept money from a fleet of whores. There is no basic difference in pimping—it's merely a matter of degree. No thank you very much.'

'I was hoping to hear you say that. But let's consider my end of this for a second. Patently I can't—and wouldn't—marry you, or even live with you, if you were gone out of my life for ten months a year as a safari guide.' She used the word *guide* hurtingly. 'And as patently, no *client*, especially female, wants or would permit the *guide's* wife to traipse along on safari. So this method of making a living's out, since I didn't start off in it from scratch, and won't break in at what could be called the top. Give me a cigarette, please.'

She accepted the cigarette and puffed a cloud of smoke into the trees before she said:

'I presume you noted my tone when I demanded a cigarette. I wouldn't care to marry a man who was subject to that tone seven days a week for ten months of the year. It's only a small example of what I'm trying to say. But I'll do this, and do it with love: I'll buy your friend Don Bruce's farm, give it to you to run, and let *you* meet the payments, pay me back as if I were a bank. Or I'll give my money to Paul, or to charity, or to whomever you say, and take a chance with you shooting vermin in New Zealand or nursing sheep in Australia. Or I'll go home to your aunt's farm with you and work with you and take a chance on the country.' She sighed. 'And love you and help you and work for you and with you. And, God willing, have babies by you.'

For the first time in a great many years, tears blurred in Brian Dermott's eyes. He got up in one swift motion and walked out of sight into the bush. 'Excuse me,' he said over his shoulder. 'Little boy's room. Be right back.' His voice was thick.

'I love you for saying what you said.' He had returned suddenly, and sprawled down beside her. 'But it's not for us. The only kind of life I could give you, you'd hate, eventually—and with it, me. I haven't any faith, Katie. I've been living on the outer edges of reality too long. There's no solution. I'm the sort of bloke who'll probably wind up in Katanga or some place as a mercenary for Tshombe—or for that matter, with the Lumumba-Gizenga forces against Tshombe. Or maybe there'll be a proper war somewhere. A very good, tough, legitimate war would be a godsend for the likes of me; a decently defined war where you could kill or get killed with purpose and even some degree of honour.'

Katie's voice was exasperated.

'That's weak and defeatist! You—a man like you—could do anything you wanted to do if you wanted to do it badly enough!' Again her voice sounded false to herself.

'That's the whole problem, my darling.' It was the first time he had called her *darling*. 'There is really nothing that I want to do that badly. I'm a displaced person in my own time. A lot of those burnt-out people came from the wars. I was never really even in a war to justify the burning. I'm a civilian casualty who merely has heroics without heroism.'

'I expect, then,' Katie said, 'that there is nothing more to be said. I'm not willing to beat my brains and heart out for something that's not worth fighting for. I thought I loved you, and perhaps I do—perhaps I would—if I had a decent opportunity to find out. But I can't do anything about self-pity and weak resignation, which is what you seem to enjoy. Right. Fine. Let's call it a happy roll in the hay, and no harm done. One more shipboard romance. One more trophy on the licence.'

She scrambled to her feet, and she was weeping.

'God,' she said through the tears. 'What a short romance. And don't bother touching me. I'll be finished with this in a minute. I'm only crying because I hate to see small things killed before they've had a chance to grow.'

After a moment she blew her nose.

'Sorry for the display, darling,' she drawled, now. 'Could we go into town this afternoon? There's no point to staying on. I'd just feel apologetic for having gotten myself into this schoolgirlish, red-nosed predicament. I don't know if I'd like to try it another night.' She smiled. 'You know, what the tourist brochures say about the African moon and the smell of mimosa in the air.'

Brian called the Africans.

'*Tia sunduku ndani ya gari*,' he was saying. 'Put the box back in the car. And clean up the *taka-taka* here.'

'No,' he said, 'but there's no point to leaving before tomorrow morning. You'll just have to grin and bear me, Katie. I have to strike the camp, and the lorry's gone, and we'd miss it in the night, and nobody around here to neat up the expedition. It'll be fivish, in any case, before we get back to camp. Sorry. Tomorrow morning it'll have to be.'

'All right,' Katie said, climbing into the Land Rover. 'What does *taka-taka* mean?'

'*Taka-taka* means "junk",' Brian said.

CHAPTER TEN

THEY WERE sitting companionably enough by the fire, although their conversation was forced, when they first heard the rumble of the lorry in the distance. Brian was sipping a brandy with his coffee, and the night sky had cleared, to be moonlit now and lovely fresh. This, Katie thought, is some more of what I shall miss when I get back to the penthouse-and-cocktail set; this glorious peace around the dying fire. Corny or not, it has more point than anything I've ever experienced, the fire hissing low and the hyenas tuning up and the bush baby's eye burning red in the firelight, with the occasional nightjar screeching and ghostily swooping. Here is peace and if there were some way to keep it, I'd sure as hell hang onto it. I'd be a game-warden's wife or a trapper's squaw in Alaska. But I don't think the young man here would be likely to listen to any more suggestions involving me and the simple life. He seems to relish gloom.

They could see the lorry's lights dipping and tilting now, and before long it waddled into camp. The driver, the burly Machoini, got out, yawned, stretched, and reached into the cab for a bulky packet of mail. He said something rapidly to Brian in Swahili.

Brian came back to the fire, in a moment, with the packet.

'Masses of mail and lots of papers,' he said. 'Machoini had a good trip. They made it into town by lunch-time, so he picked up the fresh vegetables and the mail and papers and decided to ram on back. Damned good effort, I'd say. Fourteen hours for the round trip. He reports your brother's settled at the Norfolk. They were full up at the Stanley. Here's your letters. I'll just pump up the lamps a bit and we can move back into the mess tent where the light's better.'

Katie got up and went into the brightness of the tent. She clipped a bit of twine that bound her letters into a packet, and there seemed to be nothing but some Lord and Taylor's and Abercrombie and Fitch bills.

'Let me have one of those papers, please, Brian,' she said. 'I don't seem to have any communication except old bills that have faithfully followed me. Not that I was expecting anything monumental. What have we?'

'About all of a week's worth of London airmail editions and the latest Nairobis. Nothing much but politics in the Nairobis. I'm just starting on the British effort. I love the *Express* and the *Mail* and the dear old *Clarion*. Here —take a few.'

Katie accepted a sheaf of the British papers, and was immersed in a headline which said FISH IN THE CHOCOLATE STIRS SCHOOL RIOT and was reflecting that in no country on earth did people perform so perfectly for the penny press as in England when she heard a small gasp from Brian at the other end of the table.

'What's up, chum?' she asked pleasantly, thanking God for the arrival of the papers. 'Somebody die and leave you a fortune?'

Brian slapped a paper into her hand, and stabbed at three-quarters of a page with one brown forefinger.

'You've asked me about my wife,' he said. 'I never had any pictures of her to show you. I now have a picture of her to show you. Here. She'll be the lovely white lady dancing with the nigger.'

He got up and strode out of the tent to the drink table, which still sat by the fire. She could hear the gurgle of liquid rushing out of a bottle to meet a glass.

There was no denying that Valerie Dermott was lovely. She was lovely as she swung, intimately, in what seemed more of an embrace than mere dancing linkage of hands and arms with an extremely black man in an extremely well-cut dinner jacket. Her chin was tilted; the long white line of her neck was lovely. Her eyes were half-lowered, and she smiled a secret, intimate smile of complete happiness at her partner. The whole pose spoke intimacy—one black hand cradled her hipbone and drew her pelvis in towards his groin; her shoulders were flung back and her breasts tilted in abandonment as she rested lightly in the black man's arms. He was smiling down at her; the smile spoke possession as her smile responded in happy acceptance.

The thick black print leaped at her: *Valerie Dermott—Matthew Kamau— Kenya—Brian Dermott—White Hunter—Mau Mau—Kenya National Amalgamation Party—Conference—Nairobi—Decorated twice* . . . She shook the paper to make the blur disappear and read distinctly now:

PREMATURE CELEBRATION OF INDEPENDENCE, said the headline. And in

322

the body-type, almost as thick: *Mrs. Valerie Dunstan Dermott, former wife of Kenya Mau Mau hero, Brian Dermott, G.M., seen dancing last night with Mr. Matthew Kamau, president of the Kenya National Amalgamation Party. Mr. Kamau arrived in London yesterday to attend a conference involving the forthcoming independence for Kenya. Mrs. Dermott's former husband, a Kenya farmer and white hunter, was twice awarded the George Medal for his work against the Mau Mau terrorists in the recent Emergency action in Mr. Kamau's country. Mrs. Dermott was awarded an uncontested divorce on the grounds of desertion in* 1958.

Katie let the paper fall, looking at the lovely, laughing, abandoned face of the woman Brian Dermott had called wife, at the smug possessiveness of the African with whom she danced. It was the kind of pictures they ran in the papers of newly-wed actors; of happy politicians and their fiancées. It was a picture of people publicly in love and dancing in their best for all the world to see.

Brian was back by now, a large, very dark drink in his hand. He was smiling brightly, all teeth and no eyes.

'See the social news from Britain? We've really gone multi-racial. I didn't mind so much when I saw those pictures of young Princess Alexandra with those sweating apes in Nigeria. Poor child, it's part of her job, and royalty have to be nice to everyone these days. But I do think that the female commoners are carrying fraternization a bit far, even for a family such as mine, which is taking the liberal view. I must say they make a pretty pair, Mrs. Valerie Dermott and Mister Bloody Kamau. I hope to Christ none of the boys saw this.'

'Boys?' Katie said stupidly. 'Boys?'

'*My* boys.' Brian jerked his head towards the campfire. 'My Wogs. They wouldn't understand their Bwana's Memsaab going out with a nigger. They don't understand that sort of equality yet. I'm trying to keep it from them. They can only handle so much *uhuru* at a time. They're not quite ready for it.' Now he was raising his glass with the nut-brown liquid in it.

'We'll drink a toast, shall we, to African self-determination, to *uhuru*, and to the Dermott contribution to One World in all its multi-racial glory! Here's to Mrs. Valerie Dermott and her nigger boy-friend, the next Prime Minister!' He drained the glass in a long rippling swallow. 'Do you suppose they'll call her Lady Kamau *na* Dermott, or will they just forget me in the honours? God, a horrid thought has struck. Do you suppose that her having been married to me will stand in the way of his political career? Could be jolly awkward, you know, in such a delicate time of racial emergence, taking up with the *bibi* of an ex-Mau Mau hunter. Frightfully awkward. "Have you met my wife—she was married to Brian Dermott, you know. Of course you remember Brian Dermott; he was decorated for cutting the head off your brother." '

'Stop it, Brian, stop it,' Katie said. 'This won't do you any good. Perhaps it's not what it looks like. Perhaps she——'

'Or maybe he won't have to marry her,' Brian ignored her. 'One doesn't necessarily have to go around marrying everything one sleeps with, does one? We have our case in point. Do you think I could force you to marry me, Mrs. Crane, to save my good name, seeing as we're all alone in the bush together? Suppose some bloody photographer snooped up and saw you sneaking out of my tent in the grey dawn, Mrs. Crane? Or even sitting here alone in the night, Mrs. Crane? You'd have to marry me, wouldn't you, Mrs. Crane?'

'Don't be a God-damned fool, Brian,' Katie Crane said sharply. 'Don't talk a lot of rot. I know you're hurt, but you don't have to——'

Brian reached out swiftly and covered her hand with his.

'Sorry, Katie darling. Truly. Didn't mean that at all. I guess—it's just that —I suppose I *am* hurt. She *was* my wife, you know. And seeing her in the arms of that ape, after she just left my bed a month ago. No wonder she didn't mind leaving. She was going back to her black lover. Of course it's all over Nairobi now. The sniggers in the bars . . .' He winced.

Katie reached out to touch him, but he moved away.

'*Uhuru*,' he said again. 'There's your *uhuru*, all wrapped up with a ribbon on it. This is how far we've come in seven years. In another six months' time it'll be all the rage here—the bigger and blacker your boy-friend, the more chic you'll be. Somehow you can believe it, even tolerate it, when it happens to somebody else, but when it hits you at home . . . In a way it's worse than when they chopped up the people you loved. Then they were only using knives. But she's actually enjoying it.' He got up and walked out to the chairs in front of the fire, and she could see him reach for the bottle again.

'I don't know what to say to help you, Brian,' she said, walking over and dropping into the chair beside him. 'All I can say is that I appreciate your feelings. It must hurt terribly to see her with *any* man—and for you, especially to see her with an African . . . But she isn't yours any longer and it's a new way of doing things, things are changing everywhere——' Her voice trailed off miserably.

'But you see,' Brian was talking almost to himself. 'I used to *kill* people like that. I got praised and decorated for killing people like that. People like that were savages, murderers, gangsters. They were vermin. The troops came and we hunted them like vermin in the hills. We did not dance in hotels with people like that. We did not let people like that *in* the hotels. We killed people like that. Sometimes with our hands. Any way we could, we killed people like that. We didn't dance with them. We didn't go to bed with them. We just killed them.'

He reached for the bottle again, drained it, and then shouted for Mwende. The usual bantering good humour was gone from his voice.

'*Lete whisky ingine upesi!*' he shouted, and hurled the empty bottle away. The old headboy took a frightened look at his master's face, brought the bottle and scuttled quickly off.

324

'Brian.' Kate started to say something, and stopped before the hurt in his eyes, the unbelieving hurt and the blind stupid anger.

'It would be better if he had killed her or raped her,' he said. 'That is understandable. This way she would not be touched. But she *likes* what she's doing; she probably *loves* what they have been doing and what they'll be doing again when they've finished dancing and have gone away to her flat or his room. She likes it, maybe she *loves* it,' his voice writhed. 'Or else what is she doing there in the arms of that baboon?'

'There's no use punishing yourself when you can't do anything about it,' Katie said. 'And there's no use getting drunk over something you can't help.' He drained his glass and reached for the fresh bottle. 'Getting drunk won't help.'

'Perhaps not,' he said, and leered at her. 'Perhaps I am only a drunkard who just wants an excuse to drink. Well, my girl, this is as good an excuse as any. I shall get drunk, I shall get blind drunk, and I don't want to talk any more. Go to bed, Katie. Go to bed and let me think about the good old days in the hills, when we taught them another kind of dance. Go to bed!' he suddenly shouted. 'The sight of white women nauseates me tonight!' He turned away and stared into the fire. 'The thought of any white woman, *all* white women, makes me sick!'

Katie shrugged. There was, she thought, not a thing she could do with or for Brian Dermott at the moment except leave him. She could go to the tent and watch him from the front there, in case he hurt himself or fell into the fire. The sooner he got drunk and passed out the better.

She dragged her camp chair out of the tent and pulled it into a little clearing where she could watch him. It was growing colder now, so she went into the tent and tugged the blankets from the bed and wrapped them about her. She dozed, finally, and when the grey cold wind woke her just at dawn, she saw that he was still sitting slumped in the chair before a few scattered coals of fire. She was tempted to go and cover him, but when she crept closer she saw that someone, Mwende or Muema or Kidogo, had already draped a blanket around his shoulders, and he was sleeping with his head sagged forward on his breast. Only an inch of whisky remained in the fresh bottle. Then she went back to her tent and crawled into the bed with her clothes still on, piling her blankets over her. Presently she slept and did not wake until the sun struck warmly through the tied-back flaps of her tent. She peeped out to see if Brian was still sitting in front of the fire, but he had gone. Katie Crane went back to her tent and yelled at her room-boy to bring her hot water for a bath before she faced the last of her safari days.

BRIAN WAS puffy-eyed and slightly greenish under the tan when he emerged, clean-shaven and neatly dressed, to meet her in the mess tent. He drank half a cup of black coffee and then called for Mwende to bring him a cold beer.

'I must apologize for last night, Katie,' he said, lighting a cigarette with trembling fingers. 'I'm afraid I tied on a very fine package for myself. It wasn't so much that nonsense in the paper. That was only old bitter ashes stirred up again, and in a most unsuspected fashion. I finally got the message that we're all finished, and Valerie delivered it personally. I wonder she didn't tell me when she was here. My apologies for everything, especially for the sour ending of the safari.'

Katie's smile was very cool.

'I quite understand, Brian,' she said. 'I suppose you must have felt dreadful, the thing hitting you suddenly like that. So unsuspected.'

He nodded, and carefully poured the beer on the ground. He made a face.

'That stuff's doing me no good. With your permission, I'll try the proper dog's hair. Mwende!'

'You *do* have to drive back to Nairobi,' Katie ventured as he drank his third gin and tonic while the boys went about the dreary business of breaking down the camp and stripping her home into its bare and ugly components.

His face really *was* green, Katie thought, and getting greener, and the gone-away look around his eyes . . .

'No, I'm fine,' he said again, stubbornly. 'It's just that I'm not used to so much booze in one sitting. In the old days we used to swim in the stuff, but I haven't been fighting it very hard lately. Out of practice, I guess. I think I'll just take a little walk and clear my——'

He pitched backwards out of the camp chair, his back arched, legs thrashing, and his face now gone the colour of mud. His eyes rolled backwards to disappear in his head, and strange strangled sounds came from his mouth. Foam flecked his lips, and now he was making mewing noises. Katie screamed. She screamed again and the scream brought both Kidogo and old Mwende running.

Kidogo spat something to Mwende, who seized a spoon and forced it into Brian's mouth, depressing the tongue, while Kidogo attempted to restrain the thrashing body. Then the powerful torso broke loose from the old man's arms, and racked forward in another hard convulsion. The eyes rolled, foam flew from his mouth, and his whole upper body hauled taut as the muscles contorted. Then nausea took him, and he vomited repeatedly with tremendous jerking heaves, as Katie, kneeling, held his forehead and the two old men clasped his body in its mighty writhing. Finally he stopped his convulsive jerking and fell on his back just outside the mess tent. His face was completely drained of colour, and he lay very still, seeming not to breathe, but moaning slightly.

Katie looked wildly at the headboy.

'What is it? What can we do?'

'No move. He have before. Very bad. We bring bed. Put him on bed here. Maybe he wake up. We put blanket.'

He barked rapid Wakamba at the porters who gathered round, and they went running off to fetch a camp cot and blanket. They lifted Brian onto the cot and the old man Mwende barked again. Another boy ran for the pillows in Katie's tent. Mwende placed them under Brian's hips. He looked up at Katie.

'All blood leave head,' he said. 'We do this before. Doctor want blood go back head. But no move. Last time like this. This worse.'

Katie was frantic. She was alone in the middle of East Africa, speaking small Swahili beyond 'thank you' and 'bring me', with a man who had just had some sort of desperate convulsion, and who, for all she knew, might not come out of it at all.

'Isn't there something more we can do?'

The old headboy shook his head.

'Bwana *kali* we do more. Leave alone. Here. You take drink. You no get sick too.' He poured half a tumbler of whisky into a glass and handed it to Katie. 'It good. *Mzuri.* You *kula*—drink.' Katie accepted it rather than argue, and took a small swig. It tasted horrible, and she set the glass down. She hauled up a chair, and sat, holding her fingers to Brian's pulse, feeling more helpless than she had ever felt in her entire life. Finally after what seemed ages—it had been less than half an hour—she saw his eyelids flicker. Then they opened, staring and sightless, and then slowly began to focus. They opened wider, and now they saw her. He grinned weakly.

'Hello,' he whispered. 'Must have cut out. Did it before. Out very long?'

She shook her head violently.

'How long?'

'Twenty minutes, half an hour. What do you want me to do? What can we do for you?'

'Wannabesickgain.' He made a violent effort to sit up, half-turning, but could only turn his head over the side of the cot. She held his head again as he vomited; violent, wrenching heaves that tore at his stomach muscles.

Mwende had thrust a napkin into her hand. She cleaned his mouth with it, then thrust out her hand for another napkin. She dipped it into the water pitcher and wiped his face. He lay back and closed his eyes. He seemed to sleep, then, but in a few minutes opened his eyes again. His face was very sick and pale.

'*Muema, Machoini,*' he said. '*Hambia kuja hapa.*'

The gunbearer and the lorry driver came and crouched by his side.

'Take Memsaab to Loitokitok *dukah* use telephone,' he said slowly in Swahili. 'Muema, take boys and fix airstrip. Machoini take Memsaab in *gari* to Loitokitok. Muema take boys in lorry fix airstrip. Mwende and Kidogo stay with me.'

He turned his head again, trying to find Katie's face.

'Driver will take you to village. Not far. Call telephone number Glenburnie

327

Farm. Number Nyeri two two. Ask find Doctor Locke. George Locke. Sister husband. Tell take plane fly strip here. Pilot know. Always check Game Department. Muema fix strip like always. Tell George hurry. I sleep now.' He closed his eyes. 'Sorry be nuisance.'

Katie looked desperately around. The headboy smiled at her.

'Bwana be all right. You go what he say. Other boys no understand telephone. You go driver. Machoini. Call *dokitari*. He come *upesi-ndege*.' He pointed to the sky and made an aeroplane noise. 'He come down field. Machoini show. You come back here. Muema wait field bring *dokitari*.' Mwende patted her roughly on the back. 'You no fright. All be okay *kabisa*.'

The images of the next two hours were blurred in Katie's mind. She recalled taking one last despairing look at Brian before she climbed into the Rover with the big driver, Machoini, and then there was the delusion of rough flying as the driver tore along the rutted roads, not feeling his way sensitively as Brian always drove, the man and the machine merging as a good rider handles a horse, but now hitting each rock and rut at full, flat-footed trot, rattling her teeth and jarring her spine. It was perhaps fifteen miles from the camp site to the little one-street town of Loitokitok, with its rival *dukahs* on each side of the clay road and the usual knots of curious ragged loiterers. She remembered one particularly repulsive-looking half-breed who leered at her with crossed eyes as she blundered through the loafers on the *dukah*'s porch. It was the first easily detectable mixed blood she had seen in Africa.

Aided by Machoini, who sputtered a firecracker Swahili, she made herself understood to the Hindu *dukah*-keeper that the Bwana *ya* Safari was dreadfully ill, and that she had to get through to the *dokitari*. There was the interminable hand-cranking of the primitive wall telephone while the trunk call was put through, then the waiting while the *dukah*-keeper tried to press a warm beer upon her, and finally the arm-waving Swahili wrangling into the phone and some more waiting until the *dukah*-keeper finally beckoned.

The connection was bad, full of cross-cutting Swahili, but there was the blessed relief of hearing the clipped, non-panicked English voice piercing through from the other end, while she alternately stammered and blurted symptoms and instructions. She was bathed in sweat when she had received the repeated assurance of the man who said he was Doctor Locke that he would be there within a couple of hours, just as soon as a charter aircraft could be arranged.

'Keep him quiet and if it seems likely he's going to have another fit, prowl around in his first-aid kit and look for the morphine syrettes,' the Doctor said. 'Jab him with one. It'll possibly relax him, and one can't hurt him. Tell the boy at the airstrip to be sure and run the motor-car down the field in the landing path when he sights the plane, and to see that all the pigholes are filled. It's no good coming down there and then tearing a wheel off the plane. And tell him to light a green brush fire in about an hour and a half's time. We should be heaving into sight about then. Got all that straight?'

Katie said she had all that straight, and lurched out through the curious mob to climb back in the Land Rover, which had chosen this time to have a flat tyre. The curious crowd of semi-tame Masai, Wakamba and Wachagga pressed round her, and the Sikhs and Hindi stared her appraisingly up and down. Her hair hung limply in sweaty wisps, and she was almost ready to weep when Machoini smiled at last and said they were ready to roll again.

They passed the pasture that was the primitive airstrip on the trip back, about halfway between the camp and the little town, and Katie wondered, panicky, how they would ever set a flying machine down on what appeared to be little better than another patch of high grass. But the men waved and smiled at her as they passed, and continued to chop at small thorn trees with their *pangas*, while others gathered fuel for the greenwood fire which would give wind direction to the little plane. Still others laboured with spades, filling holes, and she could see Muema driving the big truck up and down, up and down, through the grass, to make a discernible track which would serve as a runway. They appeared to know what they were doing; she felt better as she observed the casual air with which they did it. It seemed to be something they had done before.

Everything had an air of dream-like unreality now. She could not believe that she was barging around, left on her strictest own in the middle of wild Africa, with only a crew of half-savage natives, while her only bulwark against man and beast lay dying, for all she knew, in camp until some mysterious doctor dropped out of the skies to put things right.

Even more now Katie felt like laughing wildly. It was the first time, she felt, that she had ever come to close grips with what people were really like, naked and alone, where things happened with staccato rapidity, and crisis piled on crisis until the first crises seemed unimportant. It seemed a million years since she and Brian had made love: the terrifying enormity of her aloneness finally struck her. Once again the blacks had torn down and other blacks had built up; the men of Brian's safari group had acted as smoothly and as non-hysterically as a trained team of engineers and physicians. There had been no panic; no hysteria such as she felt and was feeling.

And now they were in camp, and she was running into the mess tent to drop on her knees beside Brian, who was breathing well, if still unconscious. Some of the vanished colour had seeped back into his face, and now old Mwende was handing her a hot cup of tea.

'Drink, Memsaab,' Mwende was saying, his long sad face concerned. 'Bwana okay much good. *Mzuri*. Doctor come now soon and everything okay you bet. Drink *chai*. You need take drink.' Mwende was patting her gently into a camp chair, and she wanted to fling herself on his white nightgown they called a *kanzu*, and sob. Instead she sat in her chair and sipped the scalding tea while she waited for Brian to wake or for the plane to come or for something else to happen over which she had no control, utterly no control, whatsoever.

Katie saw the plane first as a tiny silver fish in the sky; saw it before she heard it, then heard it throbbing louder as it prowled lower in the air, seeking the plume of smoke which marked the airstrip, the plume which she could not see. Then she watched it dart downward in a buzz, its motor roaring, swoop up and away, and straighten itself out for a landing approach. Then it disappeared from the sky, just as Brian began another series of hard convulsions, more violent than the first. It took half a dozen men to hold him this time, with Katie rummaging his tent, looking for the first-aid box, before she remembered that they always kept it in the Land Rover. It was a jumble of doses and bottles and small packets of instruments; by the time she had found the morphine she heard the rumble of the lorry and ran to meet it.

A lean blond man in tweeds jumped out of the cab and ambled towards her. 'Where is he?' he snapped at her. 'Has he had another fit? Have you given him anything?'

'There—in the mess tent!' Katie pointed, and trotted at his side. 'Yes. He just had his second one—worse than the first. I haven't given him anything—I was trying to find the morphine when I heard the lorry coming.'

'That's all right, so long as I know.' The doctor entered the mess tent and dropped on his knees by the cotside. He lifted one eyelid, and barked over his shoulder: '*Lete maji moto!*'

'*Maji iko Bwana,*' old Mwende said, holding out a jug of boiling water. The doctor rummaged in his kit and fished out a syringe which he sterilized and plunged into Brian's arm. He produced a stethoscope then and listened carefully to Brian's heart, keeping his fingers on the pulse of Brian's left wrist.

'He'll do for a bit,' the doctor said, rising. 'We'll just have a cup of tea and wait for him to come round a bit more. This must have been quite a shock for you, Miss—Mrs. Crane?'

'Mrs. Crane,' Katie said. 'I can't tell you how glad I am to see you. It's been pretty shattering. I was alone with him—except for the natives, of course.'

The doctor raised one mobile eyebrow in his long, sunburned face. His eyebrows and moustache were very blond, Katie noticed, and his hair, badly trimmed, stood up in a ridiculous tuft over one ear.

'I thought they mentioned something about a brother when I rang the office to lay on a plane,' he said.

'They did—there was. My brother went into Nairobi yesterday. We—we were going to stay a few days longer.'

'Oh.' The doctor's quirky eyebrow ran up his forehead again, like a lizard on a wall, Katie thought madly.

'You'd know of course that I'm Brian's brother-in-law, George Locke, in case things were too terribly confused. You got through to Brian's aunt's farm. I called Nairobi and they sent a plane to collect me. I expect Brian's mentioned me before this?'

'Yes.' Mwende came with the hot tea, and poured them each a cup. 'Yes,' she said. 'Quite a lot. He's talked to me quite a lot about his family. You are the one who told him not to drink—because he has had these things before.

330

You're "dear old George, who put me on the wagon for my own good".'
Katie almost clapped a hand to her mouth. 'Please excuse me. I didn't
mean——'

George Locke laughed unrestrainedly, loudly.

'That's quite all right. That's how Brian would refer to me, of course. He's
a fairly low opinion of people who want him to do things for his own good.
He *has* had these things before. And he *was* on the wagon for his own good.
I've told him that if he continues to drink that one of these things will kill
him—or worse, leave him mad or crippled or both. He suffers from a particular form of alcoholism which amounts to total poisoning of the nervous system,
and what he has just had is the physical and nervous equivalent of a violent
epileptic seizure, with consequent impact on his brain cells, his blood pressure, his heart muscles—a complete convulsion. Would you care to tell me
as much as you know about how he came to have it? Was he drinking very
much? Any particular thing that might have started him drinking?'

The doctor got out a pipe and loaded and lit it. He leaned back in his chair,
the long mobile horse-face calm and attentive. Katie felt a great sense of
relief and trust in his presence.

'We—he—he hasn't been drinking much since the first night he came back
from Nairobi when we were in the Northern Frontier. He had been back to
see—at least to be in town for—the hanging of that man Poole. He had stopped
off at his aunt's farm and I gather from what he told me that there was a
large family argument about—about his aunt's decision to divide the farm
among some African families.'

'Yes, you're right,' the doctor drawled. 'There was quite a flap. I'm afraid
I figured rather largely in it. Go on.'

'He was quite drunk when he came into camp—very late, or rather, very
early in the morning. He had driven all night and he was staggering when he
got out of the car. Not violent or anything like that; he was very apologetic
and quite funny. It was the first time I had seen him drink. He and I—I
might as well tell you that I am an alcoholic myself—were on the wagon
together during the first days I knew him.'

'Did he continue to drink heavily?'

'No. Not heavily. No more heavily than my brother, who was a very light
drinker. A beer in the morning, perhaps, a couple of gins and tonic before
lunch, a martini or so or a few whiskies in the evening. I wouldn't say that he
has been more than mildly exhilarated in a month. Certainly not tight. Never
drunk. Until yesterday—last night.'

The doctor's pipe had gone out. He made some show of relighting it and
puffing it into life before he asked her gently:

'And precisely what happened yesterday to touch this drinking session
off?'

Katie dropped her eyes.

'We—we quarrelled. Not quarrelled, exactly.' She raised her eyes to meet
the doctor's probing blue gaze. 'Perhaps it could be said that we were—that

331

we were about to be in love—and nothing came of it. Nor was anything likely to come of it. My brother knew about whatever there was between Brian and me. Paul went off into town, and left us alone to sort ourselves out.'

The doctor puffed steadily at his pipe.

'But there was no violent anger? No loud recriminations? No great—shall we say—*scenes*, that might have started him to drink heavily?'

'None. But something else happened that did. The lorry came back from town and brought the papers and mail. We were sitting around after supper looking over the papers when—let me see if I can find it.' Katie got up and went to the stack of magazines and papers piled neatly on one of the safari boxes. 'Perhaps he burned it last night . . . no, here it is.' She flipped open the paper and handed it to George Locke.

'*This.*'

'Ahhhh.' George Locke expelled his breath in a long, smoky sigh. He read the lines accompanying the photograph and shook his head. 'Of course. But of course.' He pulled gently at the little shelf of hair. 'Of course this would do it. Not only start him off drinking heavily, but the accompanying nervous and glandular turmoil. Poor chap. Poor, poor chap.'

He folded the paper and tossed it into a corner of the tent. He raised his voice once more to a professorial level.

'Each time Brian suffers one of these—these explosions, he destroys more brain cells. It is a complete blackout, primarily induced by the alcohol avoiding most of the organs which are designed to break down and destroy alcohol in the blood—avoiding those organs and rushing full-strength to attack the frontal brain lobes, here.' He tapped his forehead. 'There are millions of brain cells, but each time he has one of these attacks, more are destroyed. In marked recurrences, the path of such destructions is visible on the charting of an electro-encephalogram. Since the spasm—the convulsion— is so violent as to attack his brain, the nervous system, the blood, and the muscular organs, there is always danger of a permanent impairment, whether it is caused by a thrombosis or heart strain or what is just simply called the kind of stroke you get from high blood pressure. Sometimes if you are lucky you die without regaining consciousness. Sometimes you regain consciousness to find yourself permanently crippled, paralysed, or what is generally known as soft in the head. It is very unpleasant—especially when a man can be actually violently insane inside himself and outwardly normal. Nor does he ever see himself as insane or even peculiar. He feels himself to be perfectly normal and everyone else to be out of step. That is one of the major tragedies of this sort of attack.'

The doctor paused.

'Will he be—will he be—peculiar—when he comes out of this coma, or whatever it is?' Katie asked after a bit. 'Not—not twisted, as you said?'

'Physically, probably not. I won't know about the brain for a bit. The scars on that are harder to detect than the scars on the body.'

'What will you do with him, then? Hospitals, or what?'

'I don't know. I'd rather not say until I examine him a little more thoroughly later on.'

'Will you try to take Brian back to town—to the farm, or wherever you take him—today?'

'I think so. We'll see when he works off that calming jab I gave him. I'd like to get him somewhat closer to medical care than a tent. Formal medical care, I mean. Nurses and such. With a thing like this you can't tell how much nursing—or medication—he'll need. The last time he had one of these flip-flops we flew him out and into the nursing home in Nairobi. He was a holy terror. I've an idea the good sisters at Maia Carberry won't welcome the sight of him again. He went mad as a snake; nearly tore the place apart. Fortunately I was with him. Brian's got a true phobia about being shut up.'

'How about your pilot? In the confusion I had clean forgotten him.'

'So had I. Poor chap's standing by the plane. I wonder if we couldn't send a spot of lunch down to him? He doesn't want to leave the plane unless we post a proper guard over it. Native souvenir hunters, you know. If by any chance we have to spend the night, we can send a couple of boys to look after it, I suppose.'

'Surely.' Katie clapped her hands for Mwende again. 'You tell him about the lunch and sending it in the car, please, Doctor. I'm still not all that flexible in my Swahili.'

Mwende said something rapidly in return. George Locke looked surprised.

'They've already sent it,' he said. 'I didn't pay any attention to the car leaving. These seem to be very clued-up lads of Brian's. They seem to have handled a difficult morning very well, including that of the spoon to keep their boss from choking on his tongue. It quite often happens in seizures of this sort.'

Katie pushed back her soup and lit a cigarette. She looked over her shoulder at Brian, who seemed to be sleeping heavily but breathing evenly.

'They're wonderful, these black men,' she said. 'I had a small argument with Brian about them—and Africa—in general. My point was that if half the time had been spent teaching the fundamentals of ordinary civilized living to these people that was spent on training up a safari crew, there wouldn't be all these African problems and troubles. I know that's over-simplification, but it's still true basically.'

George Locke looked at her steadily, as Mwende took away his soup plate and set a platter of stew on the table in front of him.

'It's the kernel of what we're attempting—possibly too late—at the farm,' he said. 'The *hows* before the *whys*, so to speak.'

'I'd love to work with you,' Katie said wistfully. 'It's the first worthwhile thing I've run onto in a long time that seems completely free of claptrap and committees.'

'Why don't you?' George Locke said lightly. 'We can always use an extra pair of hands and a strong back at Glenburnie. Hello.' He got out of his chair and walked over to Brian. 'I think our patient's about to surface.' He pulled a chair away from the table and dragged it by Brian's cot. He took Brian's wrist again, and sat, quietly, holding it in his fingers. In a moment, Brian opened his eyes. He stared at George Locke for a minute or so before he smiled feebly.

'Hello, George,' he said in a weak voice. 'Come to pull me out of the soup again, eh?'

'That's right. How do you feel?'

'All right, I suppose. Weak, a little. Had another one of those things. I was talking to Valerie when I just cut out. What are you doing here in London, George? I thought you were in Africa. And where's Valerie?'

'She's all right,' George Locke said. 'Take it easy. Just take it easy.'

At that moment Muema the gunbearer came into the tent and walked over to say something to Katie. The movement attracted Brian's attention.

'I won't take it easy!' he shouted, sitting up straight. 'I'm going to kill that black son of a bitch there—and then I'm going to kill his white whore! I see her now! She's still with him!' He surged off the cot and leaped across George Locke towards Katie. His outstretched hands were clawed, reaching, and snarling noises came from his throat. George Locke held him around the waist, and Muema leaped to seize his thrashing legs.

'Call some of the other boys to hold him, while I give him another shot!' George Locke said. '*Hambia watu ingine kuja hapa!*' he snapped. Katie ran to the door, calling, and again the porters came to carry Brian back and hold him in the cot while the doctor fixed another syringe. In a minute or so, Brian had passed out again.

George Locke wiped his sweating forehead.

'Poor chap's having some rather gaudy hallucinations,' he said. 'His brain's still with that confounded newspaper picture. Hard to say how long these things'll last. Sometimes they flicker in and out for days. But he needs attention. Can't give it to him here. I expect Mathari's about the only place for it.'

He shook his head. 'As much as I don't like the idea. But we can't leave him in an ordinary nursing home, and I'm needed on the farm. I expect it'll have to be Mathari.'

'What's Mathari?' Katie asked, dreading the answer that she knew without being told.

'Hospital for the insane,' George Locke said bluntly. 'They have facilities for restraint until he comes round. There's no room for a case like this in the regular hospitals. He could be dangerous to himself if nobody else.'

Katie's eyes went wide with horror.

'You can't shut Brian Dermott up in an insane asylum!' She seized George Locke's arm, as if physically to restrain him. 'You can't! Of all the people in the world he's the last you can shut up in anything, even a hospital! You know how he is about things being shut up, even animals or birds! He'd find a way to kill himself!'

'Here, sit down, you're shaking all over,' George Locke said. 'I can't

334

handle two patients right at this moment. But we have to get him out of this bush and into some sort of civilization. I don't like the look of that sky. We can't be stuck here in the rains. The hospital wouldn't take him, unless I lied —not in this condition. So Mathari's the only answer. They're quite good there, I'm told.'

Katie banged the table.

'You can't put him in an African mental institution, no matter how good they are there, and you don't even know how good they are there! They may be awful there, if it's run like the rest of this God-damned country!' She was weeping now. 'Take him home! Take him home where he belongs! Start some of this damned human engineering at home, with your own people!'

George Locke snapped his fingers at the hovering Mwende.

'Brandy *moja kwa memsaab*,' he said. 'Here, drink this,' he said, pouring brandy into a teacup. 'Drink it *all*. There. That's better. Now, see here. We haven't anyone to nurse him at home. He may be ill a week, two weeks. His aunt's too old—everybody's got imperative work, too much work. He needs somebody with him every minute. He needs watching and tending like a child.'

'All right! I'll nurse him!' Katie snapped. 'Take me along to the farm! Take me and old Kidogo! Between us we'll look after him! Kidogo's looked after him all of his life, and I . . . I . . .' She put her face in her hands. Then she raised her streaked face and looked at George Locke. Her voice was calmer now. 'And if necessary I'll look after him the rest of mine.'

George Locke scratched his moustache. His eyebrow crawled upward.

'You might have a point. I know how he hates confinement. There's plenty of room at the farm, of course. It won't be any picnic—you'll probably have to do—rather distasteful things for him from time to time. What he needs is nursing . . . constant supervision until I can get his brain back to him, damaged or undamaged.'

'All right, supervision is what he'll get,' Katie said. 'And you'll be there on the farm. Brian said you were going to set up some sort of medical centre. There'll certainly be enough ordinary facilities to look after him—and you're a doctor. Brian said you were a good one. Here's one worthy African case you don't have to go bothering Doctor Schweitzer to find.'

George Locke coloured.

'All right,' he said. 'All right, Katie. We'll take him home.'

CHAPTER TWELVE

MATTHEW KAMAU yawned as he thumped down a thick mimeographed copy of the New Kenya Constitution, recently revived as a rather sneaky codicil to the Lancaster House political agreement of the early spring, and decided that he did not care very much for some portions of it, particularly the bits that dealt with the guarantee of all land titles. In his mind there was no such thing as a guaranteed title to African land, not if a white man held it. It had never been white man's land; from the beginning the Crown had been outside moral right to issue any land titles at all. That settled the New Kenya Constitution so far as Matthew Kamau was concerned. *Thump.*

Matthew Kamau had returned from his London conferences only two weeks ago, but it seemed to him he had been back in Nairobi a year, from all the problems that had landed on him. Matisia had accompanied him home, and there were certain problems that Matisia could solve once he had received the gentle hint that they wanted solution. But Matisia could not do it all. Matisia was very good at detail work, once you threw him an outline, and Kamau was careful not to question him too closely about the exact methods of accomplishment. There were certain tasks that had to be performed on lower levels which he felt better off not knowing about. For one thing, such knowledge distracted him. For another, his position demanded that he not be tied officially to these certain operations in case they backfired. His official position was that of a Messiah of his people, a sort of Caesar's wife, and he could not afford to risk soiling himself with the often crude practicalities which politics sometimes demanded. The leaping ululating crowd that met him at Embakasi airport when he and Matisia returned from London this time, screaming '*Uhuru! na Kamau!*' pleased him greatly. In his absence, *Kamau* had seemingly replaced *Kenyatta* when coupled with the freedom-shouting. And more than twenty thousand had turned up at the Stadium to hear him make his first speech after his return. Let the KANU and KADU boys squabble their heads off; his man Matisia would help them along in their nest-fouling quarrels.

He smiled at the idea. Quite a few of the nastinesses for which KANU blamed KADU had been the inspired work of Matisia. And certainly KADU's honest, shocked anger at KANU over other troubles had been the poisoned fruit of Matisia's organizational genius. The riot at Ngong with the Masai had been very cleverly seeded by this remarkably competent disciple, Abraham Matisia the Kamba; the free-for-all battles at Nyeri between the KADU and KANU partisans—which had momentarily proscribed political meetings in that area—had all been Matisia's work. Wrecked offices, again, and clever diversions to the right and left were portion to Matisia's fuelling of the licking flames of jealousy that threatened to destroy both KANU and KADU as united parties. Name-calling and accusations now had reached the point where steadier heads, like Doctor Kiano, and even Jomo Kenyatta from his exile, were pleading with the embattled politicians to stop kneeing each other in the groin for jealous position, and to unite in the common cause of One Kenya when, so soon, they would taste racial majority in the Legislative Council. And then—who knew—perhaps complete independence within the year? Not, by God, if they kept hamstringing each other, which suited Matthew Kamau just fine.

336

This time of talk for full independence was when, after the elections, he would send Matisia away for a long time, on some vague mission to some vague land where there were lots of pretty women. Then he, Kamau, would stride majestically to the fore to grease the troubled waters that Matisia had roiled. He and Stephen Ndegwa would be unbeatable at this water-calming —he, Kamau, the uncorruptible Messiah, the selfless Mahatma who bore the sacred torch of *uhuru*, of complete independence, and Ndwega, the white man's friend, the careful moderate. The white man would feel secure with Ndegwa, who had a decidedly swarmy way with the bwanas. And if the black man chafed at Ndegwa's creed of moderation and slow-paced progress, Kamau could always wave his own banner of *Independence Now!* and distract them from the fact that dear old Stephen in his plodding fashion was actually helping painlessly to separate the Crown from more and more of its crusted prerogatives.

He would be glad when Ndegwa returned to Kenya from America, although he gathered from press reports and correspondence that Ndegwa had not been idle. He had appeared unofficially but to great advantage in the caterwauling at the United Nations, when most of the African newcomers were at each other's throats, the Congo was making an ass of itself as usual and Khrushchev was creating more flatulently noisy commotion than one might expect even of Khrushchev. Dear old Stephen had sounded an excellent note of responsible dignity there, and certainly he had been the soul of dignity in a couple of his beautifully engineered strokes of publicity involving housing and educational prejudice against American Negroes.

It would not be very long now before the season of the white man's Christmas, and it would not be very long after the white man's Christmas that the first contests for the reserved seats—the primaries—would be held, with the common-roll elections coming in February. There had been no campaigning rush so far—the warring factions of KANU and KADU were doing all his work for him. At first the two established parties—or at the time, most nearly established, for they were both almost as new as his own Kaynap—had sneered at his coalition with Ndegwa as a shotgun marriage between splinter parties. Splinter parties, indeed! February would show them all whom they were calling a splinter party. A wrapped bundle of splinters made a faggot; perhaps Gichuru and Mboya had forgotten that. The Fascists never forgot it; the symbol of *fasces* was the bound sheaf. These political idiots here in Kenya were in fact splintering themselves with their eternal bickering and back-stabbing; he, Kamau, would be the man to bind them with the two circlets that distinguished the solid faggot from an awkward bouquet of stray sticks— a portable, useful weapon which, when set alight, could generate either benevolent heat and light or fiery destruction and fury. In that respect it resembled the atom bomb. That was *his* splinter party, and he would use it for good if allowed, but for war if necessary. It would serve for one as well as for the other.

Kamau got up and walked out onto the little balcony of his hotel suite.

He had taken on the suite again; the expense was considerable but it was justified in the end, he thought. There was really no such thing as a decent office to be had in the various dingy urine-smelling plaster buildings the Indians named after themselves, and he had not wanted to take rooms in the new Mitchell Cotts House, or the Stanvac or Shell Houses. He would erect his *own* building after the elections; he had already talked to the insurance companies in London and New York, and the plans had been drawn. KAMAU HOUSE would look very nice indeed when carved into granite or better, green marble, a convenient strolling distance from the Legislative Council. And, of course, with a bronze bust of himself prominent in the lobby.

Matthew Kamau stood then, a tall, lean figure framed in the french doors that gave on to the balcony, overlooking the city's rooftops. Nairobi had come on tremendously in the last five years. Even now in late afternoon he could see the Sikh *fundis* fly-crawling on their scaffoldings as new buildings shot up everywhere like mushrooms after rain; new mosques, new schools, new office buildings, new stores, new arcades—they said money was tight now and so it was. It should be. One of the reasons it was tight was that the Indians had sunk millions into building schemes, vast housing projects, just before the Lancaster House conference, and were now frightened copper-green that they would lose their non-liquefiable investment when Kenya went all black, as the conference had guaranteed. A stab in the back, the whites and Indians called it. Not so much a stab as a reshuffling of values.

Matthew Kamau smiled at the idea of any Indian losing any investment. He did not admire Indians; he considered them Pharisees, money-changers in the temples, and he particularly did not like Mr. Mukerjee, who was Mr. Ndegwa's law partner. He would, after things had settled down and he was as firmly emplaced in Kenya as his colleague Dr. Nyerere was settled in Tanganyika, use his personal shears to trim a few Wahindi tail-feathers, and he thought that he would begin the cropping with Mr. Mukerjee. The Indians had scavenged the African carcass long enough. The abolition of the practical monopoly they had on small commerce, the Indian ownership of *dukahs*, large and small, would be one of the first reforms he would undertake. A black man could run a store as well as a brown man, particularly when you considered that the customers were nearly all black.

Ndegwa. He wondered, exactly, what he would find to do with Ndegwa after *uhuru*. There would be no room for Ndegwa's Uncle Tomish approach to the white man after the transition. There were no living Uncle Toms in Ghana now. There was only Kwame Nkrumah, as he intended there to be only Matthew Kamau in Kenya. He was young—he would stay in power a long time before he considered the idea of a successor. Ndegwa was a problem. He would be harder to dismiss than Matisia. Ndegwa was a sturdy fellow; he was not a Matisia, who was useful only so long as there was a need for strong arms and expedient implementation—Matisia was a tool who could be thrown away once its edge was blunted or there was no longer anything for it to cut. Matisia would be easy enough to trip on his own appetites—he would steal too much, or there would always be a woman who would cloud his judgment.

Matisia and women. Kamau smiled at the memory of Matisia's rebuff by that Kenya woman they'd met in London, that beautiful Mrs. Dermott. Poor slavering Matisia had panted for her like a dog after a bitch in season, but had never, as Matisia so coarsely put it, managed to get up her stairs. Generally Matisia was successful with the white woman, but he had come a lovely cropper on this one. Well, he had more than made up for his failure with that vapid blonde Lady Something-Something. Matisia had confided that she had been insatiable. That was another trouble with Matisia. He *would* persist in confiding. He was like a small boy who must always boast of his conquests, must ever brag of his achievements.

Kamau once again picked up the advance copy of the Kenya Constitution he had obtained in London, which would soon create considerable commotion when it was announced in the press. He shuffled it absently. Of course it was not worth its own paper as a guarantee of land security, or any other sort of white security before the reigning law, once the independence was in and the Governor packed up and the country rested in his, Kamau's, strong hands. He would write his own Constitution, then, and write it any way it pleased him. But he particularly did not care much for the present broad hint that if any of the Royal conditions of internal security were breached, no reputable government would do business with a new Kenya.

That was not true, of course—in these strange days people always did business with other people if they wanted what you had to sell—but the intelligent thing was to knock aside as many stiff hurdles as possible *before* you became a self-governing nation with the eyes of the world pinned on you. Only a fool beat his women in public, if you could achieve the same corrective effect in private.

But now there was this new thing of the conscience-stricken government's tendency to lean more and more to land reform as a sop to the clamouring people, with government hoping to buy last-minute favour in the eyes of the simple Africans by opening up the White Highlands to more native agrarian consolidation schemes. The newest panacea was pending in the Legislative Council; they would spring it any day now, and noisily christen it in January or February—just about polling time.

Kamau picked up a sheaf of papers. What were they calling this bloody thing, anyhow? Central Advisory Board, Trust Land Board, Colonial Development Corporation, Land Bank, World Bank—wind, all wind. His mind parodied a later report: Concerning the scheme to settle underdeveloped or undeveloped land in the Scheduled Areas—'Scheduled Areas my foot, *White Highlands*', Kamau's mind snorted—it was determined by recent survey that out of three thousand six hundred registered farms (at present occupied by European farmers) only twenty-three are undeveloped and only seventy-eight underdeveloped. The three thousand six hundred farms total seven million acres. Undeveloped farms cover only twenty-four thousand acres and underdeveloped farms cover a hundred and ninety-three thousand acres. . . .

'Then,' Kamau spoke aloud, 'the report will say that practically all the land that's undeveloped would be impracticable to develop because of the poor soil or the lack of water or the shape of the terrain. It'll all be broken, rocky and arid.

'As for the underdeveloped land, that is suitable only for pasture and there isn't any water at all which is why the land is underdeveloped.

'And,' now Kamau's voice rose, 'the report will conclude that out of seven million acres only about forty thousand acres are unalienated, and out of those available unclaimed lands, only two *hundred* acres are suitable for cultivation, and only twenty-four *thousand* are suitable for grazing even if they had water which they haven't. End of report. End of bullshit.'

His fist thudded into his palm. The only true political issue in his country was *land*, and who owned it. And the only way to get that land, that lovely, loaming, creamy white man's land, was to *take* it—take it one way or the other, because the damned *mzungu* would never leave it so long as it was profitable.

So far the Crown had denied pleas for land guarantees and underwritten compensations if the privately held land were to be nationalized and re-parcelled by an African government, even though the Crown had underwritten the civil servants. The answer then was as simple as the fact that five fingers, when curled over a palm, made a fist.

If there was to be no compensation for confiscated lands, if there could be no guarantee of titles under a new government, then the thing to do was simply to scare the settlers into selling of their own accord. If the settlers could be frightened into selling cheaply, the purchase money could be pro-duced—from that same World Bank which had its people prowling round in Kenya at that very moment—to buy up the settlers' lands cheaply, for re-parcelling. Throw a scare into them and they would sell up, and sell cheaply to black buyers—black buyers with white and brown front-men who knew how to raise millions, if necessary, from other sources in other lands.

Matthew Kamau smiled again. His personal credit, abroad, was excellent —excellent with the huge insurance companies, excellent with the vast trade unions in America, and those trade unions were making almost as large business loans now as the insurance companies. The unions had become *that* rich since the last big war. There would be no trouble about the money— especially if you were buying frightened land, with the owners eager to get out and be gone because the good old lazy bwana days were over.

That was one of the fingers that completed the hand which, when clenched, made the fist. Doing it that way was much better than overt government confiscation, as that braying bearded ass Castro was doing in Cuba, and earning thereby world hatred and certainly international business apprehension. You couldn't expropriate a billion in sound financial foreign investment and hope that other countries would be trustfully eager to do business with you on the face of it. The same would apply to Kenya if you suddenly served notice on five or ten thousand farmers that they didn't own their acres any more; so sorry, please. It would frighten off the German and Japanese trade delegations which were snooping round at the very moment, sniffing for investments.

The big point, though, was in the thumb of this hand. That thumb made the rest of the hand functional, and that prime point was that the white settlers should *not* on any condition be allowed to appear as the benefactor of the poor, downtrodden native millions. There had been entirely too much talk already from some of the more 'liberal' white farms about incorporation of their own labourers into private schemes of socialized share-holding in the land. The big farm called Glenburnie, that huge holding up Naro Moru way, which owned other farms scattered all over Kenya, was one of these.

That old woman, the Widow Stuart, had got onto an idea which, if amplified, could cripple his own plans for a solid voting bloc of trustful, dependent Africans. It was not the place of the white settlers, at this late hour, to usurp the benefactor's position that the emerging black government was selling as its principal stock-in-trade. It *was* usurpation, pure and simple, this Great White Father business that he had read about of America of the olden days.

Even a thousand projects such as this old Stuart woman proposed could shake his future plans. She intended settling five hundred families on her Glenburnie estates, and eventually deeding over the land to them. Suppose there were to be a thousand such projects of that size? Christ, that was half a million *families*, or five million people if the families ran ten to the group! That was nearly the whole black population of Kenya!

Of course there weren't a thousand farms as large as old lady Stuart's, which could hand out ten acres to five hundred families just like that, *sawa-sawa bakshishi*, but the figures were still implicitly shocking. If just a few families gave out five hundred acres to fifty families, or five hundred acres to a hundred families at five acres each, there was a tremendous start towards this accursed middle class that Ndegwa and Kiano were always maundering about. Or if you computed it on even the smallest scale, two or three acres to a family, or even *one* acre to a family, to raise a money crop on, the family could show a cash return of two or three hundred pounds, perhaps, while living free off the bwanas. And living almost without personal responsibilities as well, while they gratified middle-class yearnings for bicycles and old motor-cars and fancy clothes and radios and beer.

And there was no doubt about this, either: Africa was not going to work out as the white idealists had so blithely painted it as little as six months ago. It was not going to be an experiment in Westernized democracy; Africa simply was not up to it. It would be, must be, *had* to be a One Party-One Man operation in the separate states, until some dim day when a loose sort of confederal merger could be worked out between strategically placed and sympathetically attuned nations. Perhaps some day there must be a Commonwealth or United States of Africa, but he doubted if his grandchildren would see that day. More likely it would be a sprawling, spidery Empire with one head—and Kamau wanted that head to be black; not white, and not, very especially, Red.

Matthew Kamau knew by now what sort of fuzzy impracticable ideas the Western world had about Africa—the exalted idea that a few years of education and Westernized indoctrination would transform the African into civilized Western people. He knew better; you only had to drive half an hour out of town to one of the reserves to see it clearly. You only had to fly two hours to be astounded at the Stone Agery of his people. No, they very much did *not* need a middle class, with selfish ideas and preoccupation with personal holdings. They needed to be united in a doughy mass, moulded into a kneadable whole under one strong hand. And Matisia was just the man to implement the moulding without boring him, Kamau, with the annoying details of how it was done.

Before he had left with Matisia for London on this last journey, Kamau had sent Matisia to plant some thoughtful perennial seeds up-country. They had already flowered beyond his best expectation. They would be fruiting soon.

The thoughtful seeds had been planted on a test seedbed—what was it called? Hardscrabble Farm, surely in a joke, by its owners, some old Kenya hands named Bruce . . . people he had arbitrarily selected as ideal for several purposes. His aim had been multiple with this farm which, by happy accident, was located close by and was sentimentally related to the big estate of Glenburnie. That was most fortunate. The large and small farms could now be used to work one against the other.

Hardscrabble had been his choice as an early proving ground because it was a smallholding; a one-man, hard-driving operation, a brilliant example of the white farmer's close dependence on his African common labour. It was typical of so many modest Kenya holdings which had only just managed to stay afloat—and which would certainly go under if the delicate balance of their operation was disturbed. This was the tailored example of the kind of white possession he wished to flush into the public domain—into *his* domain. In all the emerging countries, the mortgage-harassed smallholder had been the first to pack it up and flee—the first to let his fences go unmended, the first to fail to replenish his inventory, the first to smuggle his meagre savings abroad. If you could frighten the Donald Bruces of Kenya into defeat, you were gnawing strongly at the roots of the project. He smiled at the word *project*. Everyone talked about his projects these days. No other small farmer would buy the Bruce property—not after all the trouble that would be created on it, had already been created on it. And no bank would accept it as a stout risk for heavy refinance. It could be bought for its paper or less . . . or could merely be left idle until such fresh legislation was passed to take up 'idle' white land.

It had been necessary, and was becoming increasingly more necessary, to remind the black man that the bwana was not infallible; that the bwana was not always the stern but loving Papa who chastened and forgave, who solved all problems beyond the comprehension of the black man, so that the black man need only to run whimpering to lay his problems in his Bwana's lap. This was a tricky business in itself; his problem here was to tear down the bwana on *old* grounds without making the mass native too overweeningly uncontrollable in his fresh self-sufficiency. The path between old and new was delicately devious, involving witchcraft on the one hand and modern psychology on the other—its deft applications of the old fears and superstitions to achieve modern political results.

No, it would not do for the so-recent goatherd and spirit-worshipper to rise above himself into a delusion of sufficiency. To this end Hardscrabble Farm and the Bruce family combined to form perfection, as Abraham Matisia was the perfect implementer of this artistic effort.

Matthew Kamau had ordered Matisia to employ his old alumni from the prison pens to instigate a series of disturbances on the Bruce farm starting with the death of the old witch doctor—certain emotional disturbances and industrial 'accidents' which would throw the fear of God into Donald Bruce himself—which would eventually force Donald Bruce into discouragement and flight, the while satisfactorily evening old scores between the former Mau Mau and their real or symbolic enemies amongst the tame Kikuyu.

He had succeeded unbelievably well in his perversion of life on the Bruce farm.

The principal danger now was that this Kikuyu foreman of Bruce—he checked a notepad—this Njeroge, would be able to carry on successfully in his master's absence. This would do no good to his plans; it would not be at all helpful if a native substitute were allowed to stand erect in the Bwana's shoes and walk in the Bwana's footsteps. Njeroge was one of the old-fashioned bwana-loving Kikuyu, typical of the family-retainer type which had resisted forcible inclusion in Mau Mau. He was old, but still not too old to change his ways. He would now be forced to learn that he could not stand alone and himself play bwana. He would of necessity be humbled, and there was only one way to humble him. That was to bring him down to the level of people he feared and hated. He must be convinced that his salvation lay with these people—as so many similar bwana-loving Kikuyu, so many 'loyal Kikuyu', were now being painfully indoctrinated into the true brotherhood they had spurned when it was called Mau Mau. That was Matisia's field, as the disruption of the Bruce farm had been Matisia's field. The new black bwana, this fellow Njeroge, would be oathed whether he wanted it or no.

Matthew Kamau got up and poured himself a soft drink, and paced contentedly back and forth on the soft carpet of the suite. In all languages there was the simile about killing two birds with one stone. He was about to slay several birds with the sling of Matisia, using this headman Njeroge as the stone. He would follow one of the oldest Kikuyu proverbs here—*njama nderumaga imera igere*: 'A man does not insult two seasons' or, roughly, 'Pride goeth before a fall.'

It was true that some powerful catalytic agent had been and was necessary to drive out the weaker settlers from fear, as so many of the Belgians had fled the uprisings in the Congo, when the women were raped and the priests killed—to scourge out the more timid settlers and to goad the stronger, old-school settlers into wrathful reprisals.

But something else also was vital here as well—and that was the adjustment to proper perspective of a bigger picture, which centred on a much larger holding, the Glenburnie estate of Charlotte Stuart.

Kenya eyes were on the experiment at Glenburnie Farm—and so, shortly, would be the eyes of the world. It must be necessary now to convince three or four thousand people, the black men, women and children who comprised the membership of Charlotte Stuart's five hundred semi-squatter families, that it was not good *dawa* to strike out on their economic own, in meek collusion with the bwanas.

The *watu* who worked for Charlotte Stuart must be shaken to the roots; he knew how to shake them, at the same time that he was killing that other bird on the farm of Donald Bruce. Kamau would discourage private enterprise among his people once and for all, and at the same time he would pointedly settle savage disturbances while very likely goading the white man into censurable violence and blatant brutality which would enrage the world. But to settle a disturbance, you first had to create the disturbance—and to resolve a crisis one first needed a crisis to resolve. Matisia would provide the crisis. It was the thing he did best.

Symbolism was everything in dealing with these people—the centuries-graven symbolism that caused the burying alive of blood brothers, because the medicine was always stronger if you killed the thing you loved.

Now was a time for old symbolism. For proper symbolism one needed a proper oath. For a proper oath one needed a suitable candidate for the oath, and a symbol of the oath itself. The youngest son of Donald Bruce, a white young Kikuyu by adoption, might have served admirably as the flesh of the offering if Bruce had not been frightened into fleeing with his family. In the absence of the Bruce child, Kamau needed another child—not necessarily a *white* one—but a child who was all-important as a symbol to represent the birth of a new nation, just as a kid or lamb was sometimes more apt for offering than a mature goat or ram. A white *Kikuyu* child would have been very apt; but perhaps a Kikuyu *white* child would be even more appropriate to his purpose.

Christ died to save the world, so the missionary's book said, Matthew Kamau told himself. 'A little Child shall lead them.' A little child shall lead *us*, as well, and we will conform impeccably to what the white fathers taught me before they decided at my eighteenth year that I was not suited to be a priest—rejected me for the priesthood after they had torn down my gods and given me *their* God, only to snatch their God away because at eighteen I was

344

not suited to teach His ways! The missionaries, the blasted missionaries, you could hang them with their own Book, as Matthew Kamau had so often thought when he was a confused young man, bereft of two faiths, cast out from the priesthood he had aspired to, and exhorted by the good fathers to go forth and teach, but not to preach!

Well, he had taught, and he was preaching now. Perhaps he only had half-Gods—half of the old Ngai and half of the white man's Jehovah, but there was more than enough meat in the teachings of both for his purposes, and the garbled whole fitted his purpose in the new day. He prayed to both Gods alternately, and they both intruded heavily into his speeches, and oddly enough it was the white man's God who served the bloodiest purpose. It had been difficult to understand, at first, and at times it still was muddled in his head.

The native converts of the mission on which Kamau had been reared faithfully practised the Holy Sacraments, but they always found it difficult to understand that a sip of wine and a wafer comprised the symbolic blood and flesh of the dead Son if His killers had not bothered to eat the dead Son on the spot—if only to make the remembrance of the ceremonial eating more firmly founded in reason.

Everyone understood symbols, even the smallest child of aimless raising. How could you eat symbolic flesh and drink symbolic blood if the real flesh and the real blood had not been eaten and drunk? And in any case, why was it wrong to eat the man of today, out of respect—not from sheer animal hunger, as some of the Congo people still did, but to share his virtues of bravery and strength? For a fact, the white man's cannibalism, which they praised through the centuries, and the white man's tortures, which they exalted, were made to seem a vastly different thing from carving a chop off a brave warrior slain in battle and the staking out of an enemy on an ant-hill, or of giving him to the women to play with at their leisure. . . . And it really wasn't very different at all, if you studied on it.

As for the sacrifices in the Old Testament, they might have been taken bodily from the crafts of an old witch doctor, a wizened *mzee* in his monkey-hide cloak, with his cow-tails and oathing-stones and sacred gourds and *mbagé* beans and old bones and teeth and dried human genitalia and cowrie shells. The missionaries told that the ancient Israelites performed the same rites as the black man with their sacrifices.

What, then, Kamau had wondered, was so wicked about the witch doctor killing a goat, or even a man, under the sacred *mugumo* tree—sprinkling the blood around as he prayed to his Ngai on Kerinyagga? And if he ate a part of the goat, or a part of a man, was it not the same thing?

Matthew Kamau shook his head now as if to clear it of mists. His thoughts always became muddled when they travelled back to his youth as an acolyte, the devout and puzzled young student who aspired to the full cloth and who wound up as a trade unionist and politician.

One thing was clear: What he was about to do, what he was about to order Matisia to implement, was exactly the same as might be found in the White

345

Man's Bible, when God Himself ordered Abraham to slay his son. In this case, little Karioki Stuart, the fatherless son of all the tribe, whose parents were slain by the whites and who had been raised as a white boy, would return to his father and his father's father. He would bring good luck to the tribe, and propitiate Ngai. And Njeroge, who had strayed, would become an example to all good men who would see the errors of their ways and realize the might of God. And all the Kikuyu everywhere would be humbled and take notice that the way of the white man was evil, and must therefore be cast out and destroyed, as Njeroge himself would be destroyed if he did not eat the oath of Karioki, whose name meant 'restored to life'.

He had better talk to Matisia now, he thought, and intimate his latest instructions, speaking almost in parables. There was no need to spell things out to Matisia. It were better that Matisia serve as chosen instrument by intuition, almost by God's will.

He picked up the telephone and called a number. Matisia would be at home now. He was always at home at this time of the day, lusting after the flesh of that Belgian whore he had recently taken into his house. Soon, she too would have to go, but not before Matisia's work was done.

CHAPTER THIRTEEN

LISE MARTELIS hummed as she arranged the flowers—white and red carnations today, against some sprays of lily of the valley. She smiled at herself as she hummed; she was wearing toreador pants and a frilly apron tied round her, and she had just come from the big supermarket in Hurlingham, where she had purchased the makings of tonight's dinner. Once a *hausfrau*, always a *hausfrau*, she thought. How little it took to please a woman, really. A scrap of a house, a few sprigs of flowers, an apron; a stove and a fridge and a man. The black houseboy in his white *kanzu* and red fez shied out of her way; she had told Matisia to tell the boy to keep out from underfoot. He could make beds and sweep and clean and do the dishes later, but the kitchen was to be her domain.

'You sound almost like a married woman,' Matisia had laughed at her. 'Not like a——' She had clapped a hand over his mouth then.

'I do not want you to use that word again now that I am living in your house,' she said. 'Please, Matisia. It is not—it is not——'

'*Gentil, ce n'est pas poli.*' Matisia laughed. He was in an enormous good humour. 'You have used the phrase before. Very well, Madame. For all I care, you can call yourself La Duchesse de Matisia.'

This had been two weeks ago, after Matisia had returned from London.

346

He had come almost immediately from the aeroplane to the little Indian hotel where she still kept a room—from which, during the last month of his absence, she had almost been afraid to stir for fear of attracting police attention.

'Pack up,' Matisia had said, after he had briefly used her. 'We are leaving this flea market. I have taken a house in Hurlingham. Hurlingham is multi-racial—at least on the edges. Mukerjee has found me a house. It is coloured bright pink, and is constructed no more soundly than the average Indian atrocity. But it is new and clean and has two bathrooms—well, it has a bathroom and a half.' He slapped her affectionately on her behind as she got out of bed. 'You know, I've missed you. I thought of you often in London. I miss the dimples on your butt.'

She smiled hesitantly, pleased, as she put on her dressing-gown. 'And what did you really think of me in London? I thought you would be too busy to occupy yourself with thoughts of me.'

'What did I think of you in London? Why, for one thing, I thought that I preferred an honest whore to the kind of wishful whore I was in bed with at the time. Her name was Lady Bostwick-Hadley, and she was very blonde. But her underclothing was not quite clean, and when she became over-excited, she smelled. And she often became over-excited, though she was not very proficient at her work. Not so proficient as you, my little refugee from the Congo. Tell me, had you thought of going back there?'

Lise Martelis stopped in the act of drawing on a stocking and shuddered. 'It is more horrible than ever there now. It is impossible to say who is likely to kill you from one day to the next. I had thought that Kivu was safe —Kivu is becoming the worst of all with Lumumba's men in power there now that Mbotu has taken charge in Leopoldville. Have you had a chance to ask more about my papers?'

'They are still with Mukerjee. Don't worry about your papers; you can stay here as long as you want—rather, as long as I want. But I don't care to see you on the streets again—not even so discreetly as in the past. I prefer you to stay at home and pretend to be a housewife. I find I have grown senti-mentally attached to you, and I do not wish you to go any more with other men. I am a man of exceedingly jealous nature,' Matisia sneered elaborately.

'I will be delighted to stay at home and be a housewife. I was once a very good housewife,' Lise Martelis said, and bent to give him a darting kiss on his shining black shoulder. 'I will make you a very good housewife, chéri. Did you know I was an excellent cook?'

'Up to now I have had small experience with any of your talents apart from those you have demonstrated here on this bed.' Matisia sat up, and swung his legs to the floor. 'But if you cook as well as you'—he laughed aloud—'you must be a very good cook indeed.'

'What is so funny?'

'Nothing. I am always thinking how amusing life is. Me, a Kamba boy and former jailbird, no more than hours away from the last embraces of a titled

British lady, mere hours away from the respect of a Cabinet minister, about to move into an Indian house in the white neighbourhood in black Africa with a white Belgian whore who cannot live in the Congo any longer because of black politics. It is very droll, indeed. Come on, hurry with your packing. I want to get to our new *home*.'

＊

It was not a very grand home, Lise Martelis thought—not so grand surely as the big rambling bougainvillaea-strangled house on the river she had lived in outside Leo before the Lumumbas eliminated her protector just before *l'Indépendence* in July. But this was a pleasant little house of pink-plastered cinder block, set under flowering Cape chestnuts among glossy croton bushes. It was tucked well back from the road, so that passers-by could not see Matisia's green-and-white coupé when it was parked in front of the door. On a whim and in high good humour, Matisia had bought her several gifts, including a blue parakeet in a cage and a tiny puppy of unknown origin. He had named the parakeet Baudoin, and called the puppy Mac. He said he did not care whether it applied to Macmillan or Macleod—he merely enjoyed calling it Mac when he rubbed its nose harshly in the messes it made on the floor.

Matisia had brought home a radiogram-record player, and some sizeable stacks of popular records, mostly by French female singers and American Negresses. Lena Horne, Ella Fitzgerald and Genevieve were his favourites over all, although he dutifully listened to Harry Belafonte, also with a sneer.

Lise Martelis had not been bored in the little pink stucco house. She read the women's magazines and daily papers and some paperback books she bought in the New Stanley kiosk; she listened to the news on the radio and played the recordings. Occasionally she went for strolls down the leafy winding roads of Hurlingham, and now and again she took the bus into Nairobi to the moving pictures. Matisia was almost never home by day; he came late at night, and often left before she rose. She had learned some simple Swahili, but apart from an occasional order to Gitau the houseboy, she ignored the servant.

She had been cautioned by Matisia to stay out of sight when he came home with company, and she obeyed him. But she often heard the mutter of voices until she fell asleep, and on more than one occasion she heard him address another man as 'Matthew' or 'Kamau', and of course she knew who *that* was. She knew that Kamau and a man named Ndegwa, who was presently away, were the chief officers of the political organization in which Matisia held a very responsible unofficial position. Matisia mentioned them both derogatively, the more scornfully when he was drinking heavily.

And he seemed to be drinking more lately. He kept a full locked cupboard of drink, and occasionally, when he had sent the houseboy out to his quarters in the yard and there was nobody coming to talk business, he would sit up until dawn drinking and boasting vaguely about his doings—sit up until her repeated yawns finally caused him to curse her and drive her off to bed. They made love less frequently than at first; she credited that equally to hard work and the alcohol he was consuming.

Lise Martelis did not mind. She did not mind anything, very much. For many years—since she had fled Brussels for cause and had taken up with a series of varyingly affluent black men—she had consciously blurred her brain to the point where deep thoughts failed to torment her. It was enough that she was clean and well fed and comfortable and had some money hidden away; she could always earn a living with her body for a few years more, especially in dark countries, and one day, when Matisia tired of her enough to fix her some reasonable papers, she would move on to another country.

She was not too unhappy with Matisia, all things considered. Matisia was normal enough in his desires, although he made her do most of the bed work. And he seldom if ever struck her any more except as a kind of joke, as he jovially abused the puppy he called Mac. What Matisia liked to do chiefly now when he came home was to strip down to a *kikoi* and sit and drink and talk. He never talked *to* her exactly, but used her more as a sounding board, a presence, for his deep and beautiful voice. Sometimes he talked to her in French, but mostly he spoke in English, and the theme was nearly always the same: Great things were happening and would continue to happen in Kenya, and he, Abraham Matisia, was responsible.

'I work quietly and behind the scenes, *ma chérie*,' he said always. 'I am not the man who is applauded at the political rallies. I am not the man they maul with adoration when the aircraft comes in from London. But the people who do the applauding and aircraft-meeting are *my* people—they belong to me. Each day they belong to me more—how much more Kamau does not suspect; how much more Ndegwa does not know at all.'

Then he would chuckle and slap his knee and sometimes they would go off to bed. Once, when she had got up in the night and had gone to fetch him a drink, he pinched her on the thigh when she came back to bed and said:

'You are a very good girl, you know, as white women come. In a very few months' time I will be able to give you anything you want, because in a very few months' time I will have everything *I* want.'

The oddest assortment of people came to see her man Matisia. Quite often Indians, sometimes well-dressed natives, occasionally old Africans in tattered hand-me-downs or even blankets. They nearly always came furtively, and talked in mutters, and very often money passed between them. She knew that Matisia had several businesses, but he had one especially curious business she did not fully understand. It involved numbered slips of papers and seemed to be some sort of lottery. He received money for these pieces of papers, which he doled out to young, sharply dressed Kikuyu men from the town; loud-mouthed boys who wore bright feathers in their hat-bands and yellow shoes with a very high polish.

Matisia had himself identified this transaction to Lise one day when he

349

called her out of her room after one of his sharply dressed young men had departed.

'It's a pity you're white,' he said in his frequently fabricated tone of false joviality. 'What a pity. Else I could make you rich with one of these.' He dipped into his coat pocket and tossed Lise a piece of yellow cardboard with a number printed on it.

'What's this for?' she asked, turning the pasteboard in her fingers. 'It looks like a cloak-room or a car-park ticket.'

Matisia laughed. He stroked her fondly on the hip.

'You are right. That's exactly what it is. But if you were black and not very intelligent that would be worth a small farm somewhere in the South Kinangop. It's a lottery ticket and costs five bob. It gives you a chance on— let me see, number nine—the Partridge farm. Very nice mixed farm, too— pigs, sheep, pyrethrum, wheat, some cattle, and of course potatoes. All yours for five shillings.'

'I don't understand,' Lise said stupidly. 'How can this give me a farm?'

'It's a lottery ticket. When all the farms are taken from the white man, after freedom comes, the lucky ticket-holders will win those farms. Or so my boys tell their customers in the country. It is what the Americans call a racket.'

Lise was momentarily shocked.

'You mean to say that people actually believe that if they hold these tickets, they have a chance to win a white man's farm?'

'Of course. I don't see why you should be surprised; they raffled off everything in the Congo, in the cities, before last June the thirtieth. They sold one blonde Sabena hostess half a dozen times, for God's sake. They sold "*l'Indépendence*" boxes full of stones, and chances on every white house, motor-car and white woman in Leopoldville. I happened to be down there at the time, in the capacity of what the military calls an observer.' He took the raffle ticket back, and produced another paper.

'This is the valuable one, though. This costs from five hundred to a thousand shillings.'

Lise turned the long sheaf of clipped-together legal-looking papers over in her hand.

'This seems very orderly. It looks like some sort of deed. It even has a wax seal on it, and signatures. What is this?'

'It *is* a deed. It's a deed to the same farm. For one thousand shillings— which we will get from a syndicate of workers, if not from one man, the word has already been passed—this is the deed to the Partridge farm. It means that it will become the property of the new buyers as soon as *uhuru* comes. There are a great many farms in Kenya which have changed hands—as they once changed hands before, during the Mau Mau—without the proper owners knowing that the transaction has been made. I suppose,' Matisia puckered his lips and blew a kiss at the puppy Mac, 'it's every bit as legal as the way the present white owners got the farm in the first place.'

'But it can't be worth anything! Surely no one could be so stupid as to

350

believe that they can buy a white man's farm when the white man is still sitting on it!'

'My beautiful Belgian idiot, I have sold some farms three and four times already,' Matisia said. 'There will be a certain amount of baffled disappointment when the new government refuses to honour these title deeds, but as I shall be sitting high in government at that time, I shall see to it that all these small claims are paid back. Out of government tax funds, of course,' he added virtuously. 'We must not cheat the people.'

'But I do not understand how anyone could be so stupid,' Lise said. 'One might expect it in the Congo, where the niggers—oh, excuse me——' she clapped her hand to her mouth. 'I'm sorry, Matisia, I didn't mean——'

'It's quite all right. *Niggers* is what they are, and they are that stupid. I do not believe I will ever live long enough to explain to any white person just how brutishly innocent a bush coon can be. They are not basically, natively stupid, in their own world—it is just that—it is just that they are non-skilled in the application of a foreign intelligence; they are lost babes in the white man's wood. The *Mzungu* would be just as stupid in their domain, never fear. But the pitiful thing about these poor emerging idiots is that they *will* try to apply their own ancient standards to white innovations, and they will, unfortunately for themselves, believe anything at all that a fast-talking black man with shoes on promises them about the brave new world of tomorrow.'

Lise Martelis shook her head in a whore's disapproval of dishonesty.

'Are you not then ashamed to rob them of their poor little moneys? Does it not worry you, a black man, to—to steal from your black brothers?'

'Not a bloody bit,' Matisia said cheerfully. 'Someone will always be there to skin the yokel. The only difference is that I have organized the skinning. My Youth Wing—which I have observed you peeping at from a cracked bedroom door—merely enforces the sound premise that my business shall not be cut in upon by independent operators and the Youth Wings of the other parties. Considerable strife involving knives has already occurred over the invasion of what I believe the Americans call my "turf".' He snickered like a small boy.

'But this is stealing from poor people who believe in you, who think you will help them. I really do not understand. It is worse than what the white man does.'

'But we *are* helping them,' Matisia laughed. 'We are sophisticating them in the ways of the new world of white magic. See here, Lise: these stupid backwoods people have been fleeced of their pitiful surplus all their lives by their chieftains, their tribal elders, their witch doctors and by the white tax collectors, who give them nothing at all for their shillings. The tribute we exact is no more and no worse than they have always paid. It is even more benign—we do not kill them, as the chiefs did, or curse them, as the witch doctors do, for refusing to pay. But I will tell you something about our messiah, Mr. Kamau. He is worse than me; much worse than me.'

'This I do not understand, either. He is almost a holy man. You have said he does not drink or go with women, that he prays constantly, that he stays apart from the vicious battling that goes on among the other politicians.'

'Get me a drink.' Matisia's voice was harsh and angry now. He waited until Lise had returned with the whisky, then he said:

'I will tell you why he is worse man than me. He sends me always to wash his dirty drawers. He does not order; he merely suggests. And I, with these hands'—Matisia held up his clean pink palms—'with *these* hands I do the work that Kamau and Ndegwa need to gain control of the country when the voting starts—when the *uhuru* comes after the voting has started.' He took a deep gulp of his drink and then gestured for her to light him a cigarette. Lise sat silent, waiting for him to resume.

'You read the papers, I know. You read The *Standard* and The *Nation* and The *News*. Every day you see that things happen all over Kenya—a houseboy attacks an old woman on this *shamba*; there is a burning in Karen; a stock theft in Langata; a looting of a shop in Nyeri or a noisy bottle-throwing in Nakuru. You read of riots and strikes and demonstrations, of border incidents and road accidents, and inter-tribal troubles. You read of accusations in letters to the editors, you are always seeing some exposé or the other; some accusation of Odinga being in the pay of the Russians or of Mboya conspiring to keep Kenyatta in prison. Do you think all these things are accidents? Do you think Ngai sends them to keep the country in an uproar for his private amusement? The answer is *no*! They have a plan all right; a meaning, and I am the man who makes the meaning come true.

'But, my beautiful Belgian lady of leisure, I am not the man who starts the plan. I am only the poor simpleton who carries out the orders. I am the messenger who organizes the riots when the KANU or the KADU hold a speaking; my paid goon flings the first spear when the KANU is trying to sell their brand of *uhuru* to the Masai. When the time comes to vote, I will already have bought the votes. I, *me*, Matisia. I make the country run now—and some day I will run the country, as a confidential servant eventually commands his master.'

He finished his drink in a gulp, and handed her the glass.

'Again,' he said. 'I am angry at Kamau, that smirking plaster imitation of a saint, and anger makes me thirsty.'

'Why do you tell me all this?' Lise returned to hand him his drink.

'I tell you first because I am angry—and second because I am a little drunk, perhaps this is not my first drink today, and third because I have just done some more arranging that has turned out more perfectly than I had any reason to hope. Kamau is naturally very pleased—pleased with himself, rot him!—when it was my doing that marked the first step in the finish of the white man in this country except as a second-class citizen, a serf. I merely enjoy the pleasure of a pimp, which is not too gratifying—as you would certainly know.'

'I do not want to hear any more, Matisia,' Lise Martelis said. 'Please do

352

not tell me any more. I do not want to know; I am afraid.' She turned her head away.

'Nothing will hurt you so long as you remember you belong to me and take care to mind your manners,' Matisia said expansively. 'That is the first rule of pimping. But I will tell you just one thing more: *my* work has been responsible this day for driving a white man out of Kenya—a white man who would not have run from ten thousand Mau Mau ran quavering from me because of some things *I* did. And that bloody Kamau takes credit for everything, as always, although it was *my* hard work, with *my* men, that did the job!'

'I will go and make the supper now, Matisia,' Lise said, hastily rising from her chair. 'You rest here until I call you.'

Matisia reached out and snatched at the skirt of the dirndl frock she had put on as a change from the slacks she generally wore all day long in his absence. He drew her nearer, pulling at the skirt.

'Remember some day that I told you this: very shortly something will happen in this country which will give *me* the country more completely into my hands than Jomo Kenyatta ever hoped to conquer it with his Mau Mau. Kenyatta, the so-called father of his country, was never so far along as I— he never was, and never will be! Even if the old goat lives, which I imagine is exceedingly doubtful if the British are so foolish as to free him. Certainly Kamau and the rest of the political preachers can't afford the competition— and I—*I* will not permit it.'

'I go to make the supper now,' Lise said, and gently took her skirt hem from his grasp. As she stirred about the kitchen, she heard his chair creak as he went to pour another drink from the tabouret. Clearly something had upset him. This was not surprising; a man with so many businesses to occupy him must always tread the ragged edge of nerves.

CHAPTER FOURTEEN

NJEROGE SAT cross-legged on the floor in front of the hearth, on which a low fire flickered. The fire provided the only light in the room, and sent devilish shadows leaping madly on the walls. There was a hurricane lamp, of course, but that needed filling, and he had forgotten to fill it. The electric lights did not work; something had gone amiss with the generator, and even fat Kungo, who fancied himself a mechanic, had been unable to make it work. Kungo had pulled the generator to bits, but there was some sort of *thahu* on it that stubbornly refused to be lifted. It made little difference; the light machine drank petrol thirstily as a camel, and there was no money now to spend foolishly on petrol.

353

He had promised the Bwana he would stay on in the big house, and he wished he dared break his promise and go back to his comfortable cluster of huts on his own little *shamba*. Like so many other of the *watu*, he had often speculated with envy as to what it would be like to be a bwana and live in a fine big house. Now he was living in a fine big house like a bwana, and he didn't like it at all.

It was cold and lonely and draughty in a fine big house, and frightening, too. He could swear to that. He had tried first to persuade Murungwa, the old houseboy, to stay in his place, but Murungwa had refused. He had never lived in the house, but always in his own house at the end of the garden, Murungwa said, and he had no intention of leaving the comfort of his own snug hut to dwell in the big house with the Bwana's ghosts.

Njeroge had experienced no better luck with his wives. They had flatly refused to move in; it would mean leaving their own new tin-topped houses where they had all their treasured possessions arranged just so; they did not want to be away from their chickens and pigs; if they moved to the big house they could not frighten the birds from their wheat—on and on and on with a thousand female excuses until he had lost his temper and cuffed one soundly. He could not recall which he had struck. There was no use quarrelling with women; they were as simple in the head as the chickens they treasured. They would pursue a single worm of thought with beady-eyed intensity, like a hen, but they had no flexibility of intellect.

Njeroge liked to sleep where he ate. It was nearly a quarter-mile from the big house to the labour compound, and, as a light sleeper who roused often, he liked to eat frequently during the night. He supposed that he might have beaten his younger wife and forced her to come and stay in the Bwana's house to look after him, but quite frankly, it wasn't worth all the clucking and wing-waving that one received from an agitated, hen-minded wife. Even removing the young wife would argue favouritism and cause trouble. Things had not been the same in his little *shamba*, in any case, since his youngest daughter had hanged herself after the oathing. Women were terribly flighty. Two more daughters had run off to the towns, and shame hovered heavily over his household. There had been a coroner's inquest on his daughter's body, as well, and tongues had clacked. *Women.*

No, what with one thing and another, Njeroge found it easier to cook for himself here in the ashes of the Bwana's big fireplace. He had no cooking-stones, but the andirons served well enough, and his wants were simple. He boiled his *posho* in a pot he managed to wheedle from the *mpishi* before he locked up everything, and Njeroge spitted his meat on the poker. It was easier than traipsing back and forth for meals. He was too old for unnecessary commuting, and he worked from first dawn to black night seven days a week.

The trouble with the white man's house was that there was nothing really to *do* in it. A house should be a thing of closely related spaces—so much room for sleeping, so much for food preparation—if the weather forbade eating and cooking outside—so much room for children and goats and above all, the sense of pervading snugness, with the clouding smoke from the fire driving off the bugs and mellowing the atmosphere. There was also the companionship of actual contact with the flesh of your flesh. It was in all ways different in a white man's house, with its widely separated paddocks for nearly everything—you slept in one place, walked a league to eat in another, cooked in another, talked in another, relieved yourself in another.

The house reminded him now of a hut which had been abandoned because of untimely death within its walls. The structure was still the same, but there was no life inside. But the spirits remained—you could feel the spooky presence of the Bwana still, if only by his aching absence. And there was no use denying it: you did miss the Bwana's presence sorely.

That was a thing no *mzungu* would understand, Njeroge thought as he poked at his feebly flickering fire, waiting for the water to boil so that he might have tea. No white man would understand fully the strange components that went into the make-up of a bwana in the eyes of a black man. It was considerably more than colour of skin and texture of hair.

For instance, the thing of the guns. There were no guns here now. The Bwana had taken all his guns away because it was against the law to leave them in the house. Always Njeroge had thought of guns and the Bwana in the same mind; the gun was an extension of the Bwana as the trunk was an extension of the elephant. What would happen now if a leopard got among the pigs, or buffalo came down to trample the wheat? Could he sent a *mtoto* running to the Bwana to set things right with his gun? Or could he even come and get a gun himself? Of course not. For a start, he himself did not understand guns, even if they were here to be used. A Bwana was guns, as guns were a Bwana.

Aiiee, I am a useless old man, Njeroge thought as he watched his pot boil and bubble. I do not know how to use a gun, because no one ever taught me, and in any case, black men are not allowed to have guns in Kenya, unless they be members of the military or police or are *shenzi* bandits who steal the guns and run away to the hills. And I would not even know how to scratch myself any more with a spear, let alone throw one . . . it has been that long since I owned one. Truly an old man who had not been a warrior was useless. I was cheated of being a warrior by the coming of the white man at a time when I would have been a *njama* and blooded my spear against the Masai or the Kipsigis. I have worked in the fields like a woman, like an old scarecrow, most of my life, and I could not live long without the Bwana to defend me. In that respect I am no better than a woman. I am a man, but still I need a white *askari*.

And now the Bwana has gone, and there are the problems, always problems every day, and I have nothing but the Bwana's spook which haunts this house to come to for counsel. I had not realized until now how difficult it was to be a bwana. The tractor is useless now; they come to me when it is broken and ask me what to do and I cannot tell them. In the good old days— less than half a moon past—I would have gone to the Bwana and told *him*, as I told him so many times, that the tractor is sick, and so he would have healed it.

Now they come to me with questions and I do not know what to tell Kungo, if he cannot mend it, and must leave the extra toes and fingers of its anatomy lying around. I know that when you put the *petroli* in a tractor a fire is lit in its belly, causing it to growl and break wind and stumble along like an overfed horse, but I do not know what processes in its belly account for this behaviour any more than I know what happens to the food that I put in my mouth that makes it give me strength before I pass the waste and leave it on the ground. But the Bwana knew, and so did the Memsaab. Whether it was a bellyache in the tractor or a bellyache in a child, one or the other knew what to do about it.

What a sad house it is, Njeroge thought.

The white people were the motors of this empty house, and the children were the lights the motors made. Where are my children now, the little tow-heads, Angus and Ellen and Lois and Baby Jock? My own house is small, so it does not feel so vacant from the children that I have lost in one way or another, whether by illness or suicide or lately to the towns. But in this great house the noise of the silence is greater than the noise the children made as they racketed with their dogs—poor dogs. One dog gutted on the gatepost; the old collie bitch and her puppies shot by the Bwana as he left. The Bwana wept as he killed the old bitch and destroyed the puppies. He was right to kill them; he could not leave them. I have too much to do as it is, and in any case the leopards would have taken the puppies without someone to keep a sharp eye on them.

There were so many things to running a large *shamba* in the absence of the Bwana—so many things I never thought of, Njeroge said to himself. I remember well the time the Bwana took me high in the sky to mark the difference between the white man's plantations and the black man's *shambas*. High in the sky, sailing with the birds in the little aeroplane, it all looked so neat and pretty on the ground, like a picture. Here the Bwana had forced the land to perform at his command; there the Kikuyu had pleaded with his land but the land had not answered. You could see the land clearly marked in stripes and patches; the Bwana's land was rich and sparkling and bright with green crops and blue water; the native land was scraggly brown and tattered as an old pair of dirty pants. How easy then to envy the white man his bright patches of land; how easy to envy him and curse God for giving the *mzungu* better luck and better weather and the blessing of better crops than He allotted to the Kikuyu.

One does not see, riding high with the vultures, all the dirty, back-aching, sweated toil that goes into making the white man's land, Njeroge thought. One does not appreciate the labour of the ants when one sees only the ant-hill from a distance. I admit I was eaten with envy when I saw the beautiful land of the white man from the plane; I was ashamed then of the black man's land. Now I think I understand better. It is the same land. But it is necessary to stand close to the animal to see the ticks on its belly. The sleekest bull sometimes has the most ticks, and must be dipped or he will sicken and lose his sleekness.

Each day there are more problems here on the farm; everyone on the *shamba* has his own set of problems and there is only one of me to deal with all of them. Small wonder the Bwana used to curse with impatience when I came to him with the problems of the pigs and sheep and crops and fencings— small wonder his temper shortened when he was forced to deal with the men's drunkenness and the quarrels of the women. When the men drank and fought in the towns it was the Bwana who always had to go to the Bwana Police and put things right. When there was a dispute the Bwana settled it, even when he sometimes made two wrangling women strip themselves to the waist and flail at each other with staves. And the Bwana was very strong, so strong he did not often need to use his strength.

But now the *watu* pay no attention to me; they do not jump as they used to jump to the Bwana's commands. I am not young or strong enough to enforce my orders. I tell them to shut gates, and they leave gates open; I tell them to conserve water, and they laugh while they waste it; already they have begun to burn grass again instead of hoeing it, as the Bwana always commanded. And I see goats browsing openly now, whereas they were always kept secretly off the good fat land when the Bwana was here. I shout myself blue in the face and pound my fist and threaten them, as the Bwana used to, and they merely laugh at me. 'Go away, old man,' they say. 'Go away and gossip with the women.' They would not have said that in the good old days, not when the Bwana stood behind me. The man who defied me would have been off the land by nightfall; they all knew it, and so did not defy me or laugh at my orders, which were really the Bwana's orders.

Of course, the old man thought, it is just my imagination, but already the farm seems to look run-down and is growing seedier all the time. It is beginning to look, to look—his brain struggled for an apt simile—to look *exactly* like a *shamba* in the native reserve! The grass is uncut in the yards; the flowers are choked with weeds, the farm buildings are beginning to sag, and the stock roams aimlessly from one paddock to another without plan, for all my shoutings.

But the stock will not be important very long, not the way I am selling it off, following the Bwana's instructions. In my life I have never been a thief; now I feel like a thief. It is the only dishonest thing I have ever done, selling the sheep and cows in the dark of the moon for cash, with no proper pieces of paper to mark the sales—hiding the money like a thief under the Bwana's mattress until I take it to Nairobi to give to the Bwana Jenkins who wears the owl-eye glasses. I hope the Bwana Jenkins is sending the money to the Bwana Don and not spending it himself, but there is no way for me to know if the Bwana is receiving the money, and in any case I am only following his orders. I *wish* the Bwana would come home, he thought. Perhaps he will not be able to find work on the other side of the world, and will have to come home.

357

There is evil running loose in the hills, as bad or worse than it was during the time of the Mau Mau, and now we have no witch doctor, no Kinyanjui, to protect us with his magic—and no Bwana to protect us with his guns.

There is a thing that walks by night I do not care for, the old man thought, his brain fumbling for expression. There are too many secrets shared on this *shamba* now—secrets that I do not know about. It is the same as it was on other *shambas* during the Mau Mau, when some people dropped their eyes and closed their hearts to other people. I am outside this *shamba* now—in that one respect at least I am like the Bwana. I am no longer included among the *watu*—my own people. I am outcast. I am a bwana who is no Bwana.

One thing I do know, Njeroge thought grimly, one thing I swear to: they will not like it when they all become Bwanas. They will not know how to act or how to get the work done. They will have nobody to look after them and tell them what to do. People will come and bring them papers to fill out and they will not know what is on the papers or what is wanted of them. They will go about seeking leadership in anything so simple as firing a horse's tendon and they will find nobody to lead them. They will have nobody to borrow from, and no credit at the *dukah*. They will find that money does not grow on trees, and *posho* does not grow in the pot.

The thought of *posho* made him hungry. The old man took his pot off the fire, and set the *posho* aside to cool while he finished brewing his tea. He wished he had some *pombe* to drink, but he had forgotten to bring any from his own house and there was none of the Bwana's left. He considered walking down to his *shamba* in the dark, but decided against it. The dark outside was too populous with evil spirits for a man to walk abroad in it without company. There would be no spirits here in the house except the remembrance of the Bwana and the Memsaab and the children. The *mzungu* was not beset by evil spirits like the black man.

He poured his tea and was drinking it when a rap came on the door. Drat! the old man thought querulously. Something has gone wrong with the cattle or sheep again! Something is always going wrong at night on this *shamba*. Why does it never happen by the good light of day?

'Who is it?' he called irritably. 'What is wrong now?' His voice was very annoyed—exactly like a bwana's voice when his patience was strained.

'Kungo,' a familiar voice answered. Njeroge recognized it as belonging to the fat man who thought he was a mechanic. 'Open up. Your youngest wife is sick; she is asking for you.' The fat man hammered on the door.

'All right,' Njeroge grumbled, getting creakily to his feet. 'Wait a minute; don't knock the door down. I'm coming.'

He slid back the bolt and stepped out into the black of the night.

'Kungo, where are you?' he asked, still irritably. 'Why have you not brought a torch?'

He blinked in the dark, waiting for his eyes to adjust to the night.

'Kungo, where . . .' he was saying again, as there was a meaty crunch and all the lights went out in his head.

358

THE SUN poured golden through the window, and the light linen curtains stirred sweetly in the gentle morning breeze. There was a soft excitement to the air, creating a delusion of spring, although there was no spring in Africa. There had, however, been a little share of the short rains in the last two weeks, the black showers slashing violently for an hour or two in the morning, with the afternoons clearing overhead and yawning in the sun just before the swift nightfall sharply brought the cold again. There was some small fire still twinkling through the ashes on Katie Crane's hearth, but not enough to warm the night-chilled room. It was knifing cold in the Kenya hills of an early morning, and Katie snuggled deeper under the blankets when the boy came with the morning tea. In a minute she would get up and tackle the chill of the bathroom, before rushing to link up another of what seemed an endless chain of the most enthralling days she could remember. Well, better make the effort, old girl, she said to herself, and lunged from under her quilt to seize her woolliest robe. Mount Kenya stood boldly in her window; the birds were rioting in the garden, and the smell of wet grass and cedar forest and dew-plumped roses rushed through the broad double-shuttered window to greet her. She was, she thought, padding hunch-shouldered down the hall to the bathroom, hungry enough to eat a side of beef.

She sank shivering into the miraculously steaming water the boy had drawn; then rubbed herself pink with the towel and whistled as she dressed. Each morning she seemed to be feeling more chirrupy. If her hair were only in pigtails, as young Jill Dermott wore hers, she'd feel and almost even look about fourteen. Pants and sweater and jacket as usual; everybody in this house wore trousers except Aunt Charlotte and maybe Juma, who clung to the white billowing *kanzu* that flopped like a nightgown round his bare legs and feet. Everyone wore pants at Glenburnie because this was a working household, and there weren't any tea parties to demand frocks.

It was quite a thing to wake and kiss the dawn daily with smiling purpose, a thing of which she'd always read but never experienced—quite a different thing to surface with something more exciting to contemplate than lunch at the Colony. Safari had been exciting too, but that was a different kind of excitement. Safari was compounded of newness and strangeness and exotic animals and some delicious portion of contained fear. This now was solid, perpetuating excitement, as warm and satisfying as the breakfast she would soon be eating in the alcove by the big window with Mount Kenya thrusting its snowy head almost onto the tablecloth, and the scarlet hummingbirds skidding against the panes as they helicoptered from the trumpet-vine that roved outside the window.

She was up early; it was only six-thirty, and most of the folk didn't turn up for breakfast until seven. It would give her time for a stroll: across the broad green lawns, through the rock garden with its snickering artificial stream, and down to the blue dam. They called it a dam because it too was artificial, but it was big enough to permit ducks and geese on it, and fish in it; lily-pads on it, and great stands of flowering flags brave all round it. She loved this garden of Charlotte Stuart's—it was as if the old lady had picked up the best portion of a whole English county and had popped it into the cradle of the Kenya hills. Except in England you weren't apt to encounter frangipani trees and drunken excesses of bougainvillaea which clutched onto anything that would hold it off the ground.

She walked down the creaking, uneven broad stairs to the living-room and saw that somebody had already set the table and placed a silver bowl of yellow tulips on it, and somebody else had refurbished the fire in the big fire-place until it was breathing its oily aroma all over the room, making a rowdy, unconscionable amount of noise as it crackled in the morning quiet. The huge, two-level room was ablaze with morning sun, and the front door was flung open to let the newly laundered air romp joyously in. The flower-fixer had been busy indeed—roses on the piano, and a great bower of carnations banked on the dining-room table. Jill, she imagined, up with that boundless energy of youth that resented extra hours abed.

She strolled through the room, plucking a cigarette from a box on the coffee-table between the flanking great chairs, and walked down onto the crazy-flagged pathway that began at the foot of the veranda steps and twisted its flower-bordered way through the Cape chestnuts and eucalypti and for-bidding black cedars down to the little lake, where she could already hear the geese standing on tiptoe in the water to swear at each other.

She paused a moment, drinking a great gulp of the morning into her lungs, and ducked back when a fiery bolt of red gelding shot round the corner of the house and reared, neighing, as the girl on its back flung herself out of the saddle and threw the reins over its head. The big red horse was followed more sedately by a shaggy pony with a little black boy spraddled on its broad pie-bald back.

'Take the horses to the stables, Karioki!' the girl cried, and turned a cart-wheel on the lawn. Then she saw Katie for the first time, and her morning-wind-whipped face grew pinker.

'Yes, Miss Jill,' the little boy answered, and scooped up the reins of the roan gelding, towing the unwilling horse out of sight in the trees.

'Morning, Sister Kate,' the girl said, wiping her dewy hands on her trousers. 'I almost ran you down. Didn't see you at first. Excuse my cart-wheel. I just felt full of beans.'

'I must say, Sister Gillian,' Katie said with stilted primness, 'that is a most unseemly way for a young matron to act. I only hope your aunt didn't see you.'

'She'd cut a cartwheel herself if it wasn't for that gimpy leg,' the girl said. 'Wow! What a morning!'

She was a pretty girl of no particularly distinguishing features, her brown hair curly and trapped into pigtails, large brown eyes bright from the ride. She had a strong colour and the fine thin skin of some people who live at high altitudes, and seemed about to burst like a grape with the exuberant juices of her age. She was just twenty years old, and she had been married to Philip Dermott for a little more than a month.

She walked over and brushed her lips against Katie's cheek with the absently dutiful air of a child, and then calmly stole the cigarette from Katie's hand.

'Smoking before breakfast is dreadfully bad for you, everyone says,' Jill Dermott said. 'Personally, I love it.' She handed the cigarette back to Katie and said: 'Personally, I hope they have a horse for breakfast. I've always heard of people being able to eat one, and with my appetite I think I'd like to try it. You don't suppose I'm pregnant already and eating for two, do you?'

'Personally, I think that would be lovely,' Katie smiled, mocking her. 'But personally I think you're just young and full of beans, not baby.'

They walked slowly towards the lake, the girl beating gently at her jodhpured leg with her crop.

Katie looked at her with fond amusement.

'You know, sweetie, I didn't know they made the likes of you any more. I know you're a proper married lady, but I swear it seems downright sinful. You ought to be wearing bobby sox and leading the cheers at a high-school football game in some tank town in Iowa. It's a compliment, in a way,' she added.

'I can't help it if I'm the light-hearted type,' the girl said. 'Pip calls me Featherhead, and perhaps he's right. But I like being a girl and I like being married and I like it here on the farm and I like all the work I do with the Nigs and I love Auntie Char and I get along fine with Big Sister Nell and her droopy doctor. And I think that poor Brian's beautiful and I think you're divine, and I meant that last as a compliment, too, truly.'

'Well, now, I am flattered. Except I don't think you ought to qualify Brian with the *poor*. I think he's come on wonderfully. I expect he's come on so well I'll be packing up pretty soon and going back to the States.'

The dismay in Jill Dermott's face was honest.

'Oh, Katie, you *can't*! I thought that you and Brian—I thought that as soon as he got truly better you'd probably marry him and stay here at Glenburnie with us. I'm sure everybody else thinks so.'

Katie smiled at the girl.

'The only slight insect in that ointment is that nobody's asked me at all, at all,' she said. 'And I don't think it would be quite fair of me to add another permanent mouth to that table, big as it is. The table, not the mouth, smarty.'

'Oh, fiddle. Aunt Charlotte adores you, and we need any unpaid hired help we can scrounge around this—this bloody housing project! They told me that marriage wasn't going to be all fun and games, but darned if I knew they were going to yank me out of my bridal bed and put me to work straight away on a civic development for Wogs. Not that it isn't fun,' the girl added hurriedly. 'It's better than making a garden. You can watch it grow faster.'

361

'That's the truth. So you can.' Katie looked at her watch. 'Come on, youngster, it's breakfast-time. And don't bother asking me to race you to the house. You always win, and anyhow I'm too old for it.'

*

Breakfast at Glenburnie was very much an old-English buffet affair. The sideboard was congested with covered silver dishes heated by spirit lamps, each bearing such Old Country standbys as kippers and kedgeree; rashers of bacon and ham and beef, tropically jostled out of context by pitchers of fresh pineapple and orange juice, platters of peaches and bananas, and great yellow slabs of papaya. Aunt Charlotte made toast at the table, and old Juma stood by to take orders for preferences in eggs or hotcakes and to pass the marmalade and jams and black wild honey. To Katie Crane, breakfast had always been a society-shunning penitential ritual of juice and bitter black coffee, in some several recent years preceded by a vodka or two to ensure stability for the coffee. Here at Glenburnie breakfast was a robustious meal shared by convivial, healthy, hungry people who had slept soundly in the cold Kenya air and who were bursting with plans for the day.

The entire family now was either settled at the table or passing with gradually heaping plates before the sideboard. Charlotte Dermott was at the head of the table already; both Katie and Jill bent and kissed her as a ritual. At Glenburnie everyone seemed to kiss each other hello as abstractedly as you'd pat a dog. Katie rather liked it; it was an exact reverse of what she'd always thought of the reserved English at home.

Brian was placed on his aunt's right. He was very thin—he had lost weight shockingly for the full week during which neither Katie nor George Locke had slept very much, and then not at the same time. His mind had faltered aimlessly about in the lifting and settling fogs of intermixed reality and fantasy. It had been necessary to watch him every moment, as he wove his past into the present—his early days in the bush with Keg Dermott and the younger Kidogo; the violent days in the hills during the Mau Mau operations. Katie had become an expert diagnostician of the troubled wanderings of Brian's mind. She could tell when he was about to embark on another punitive expedition after the Mau Mau gangsters when Kidogo ceased being Kidogo and became either Dedan Kimathi, Jomo Kenyatta, or even more frequently, Matthew Kamau. Poor Kidogo; he had come on to the farm the following day in the lorry. He had moved a blanket into Brian's room and had slept soundly not at all, Katie judged, while he kept his Bwana clean and, most of the time, calm by his presence. It was only when the Bwana got a certain sly look in his eye and made elaborate preparations to throttle him that Kidogo called for aid from Katie or Dokitari Georgi.

In this recent bout of wrenching convulsions and soaring deliriums so vividly real as to sound almost convincing when the other Brian reported quietly that an army of Mau Mau gangsters had just marched through the wall and was encamped on the lawn by the dam, Brian's greatest problem

362

was that while his body appeared to rest, his brain would not relax with the rest of him. The brain burned brightly, like the pilot flame on a stove, and after five days, George Locke had said that unless they could put that incandescent brain to sleep, it was likely that Brian would die, and that dying might not be the worst of all the things that could happen to Brian. There was no good in using narcotics any more; Brian's physical rejection of opiates was startling. You could pump enough morphine to kill an average man into him, and the result was only a pleasant vista of a lovely lady who was confected entirely of cotton-floss candy with the exception of one leg, which was stoutly cork. Katie knew this lady existed from the time that Brian, outwardly serene and in seeming possession of his senses, had calmly lifted his Aunt's skirt from her knee and tapped her sore leg to see if it were artificial. He had bowed and thanked his aunt gratefully, and had gravely apologized for the mistake.

But he had a way of rising in the middle of the night and going on a long, roving trip to any place at all. Kidogo lay dozing athwart the door, and Katie or George Locke was generally in the room with the patient. But one night Katie had fallen asleep in her chair and Brian had risen stealthily to avoid Kidogo's body, and they had located him later stalking some elusive hostage of his disordered brain down at the edge of the little lake. After that Katie had got into bed *with* him in order to be more sensitive to his movements. This was during the time he mostly called her Valerie. George Locke generally appeared as Keg Dermott, and Kidogo could be anything at all that wore a black skin. What was most frightening was to see Brian actually being a little boy again, mentally tagging happily at the heels of a younger Kidogo and a George Locke who had been momentarily transmuted into Brian's father.

George Locke tried everything he knew to reclaim Brian from the mists, and finally relied again on the hallowed specific of the delirium tremens wards, the horrible-reeking paraldehyde. Katie and George Locke between them taunted Brian into downing half a glass of the vile stuff, and even then the truant brain was so separately alive that it needed more than half an hour for the double dose of the drug to slug him into a true unconsciousness. But when he went out this time he really went all the way out; he slept twenty hours and when he finally fought his way back to the rippled surface of reality, his brain and body swam into consciousness together. His weak 'H'lo, Katie,' was Brian Dermott again, and sanity had settled in his eyes.

He looked somewhat better now, Katie thought, dropping her hand lightly on his shoulder as she squeezed past to sit next him on the window seat. He had lost much of his deep tan, and he was very quiet—quiet and uncertainly tentative in his speech and motions. At first he was frightened to be left alone; he followed Katie about with single-minded purpose. Even when she went to the bathroom she would find him waiting impatiently in the next room, his eyes pinned to the doorway through which she had passed. When she did appear, he seemed to sigh and relax. So strange for Brian; he seemed beaten and timid and dependent on everyone.

363

He was not drinking, of course, and neither was anybody else in the house. Beyond the no-drinking nobody appeared to notice that anything had ever differed from the norm. After the first few days of rather feeble tottering about on undecided legs, Brian had fallen into the working routine of the farm, and Katie had dropped into it with him, staying at his side or disappearing occasionally, according to her best diagnosis of his mood.

There was so much to be done on Glenburnie that it was difficult not to keep busy at something. Aunt Charlotte went every morning to her *dukah*, and Katie loved helping her in the shop. She had always loved Jewish delicatessens and Italian and Spanish food stores in New York; she had spent happy hours in the Washington Market just window-shopping the game and fish and fruits and vegetables. The *dukah* was a combination of all those exotic bazaars, with a hardware store and a PX thrown in. Katie helped Aunt Charlotte sell everything, from used motor-car tyres (for cutting into sandals) to flyspecked peppermint creams to soft drinks to cheap surplus Army overcoats. She could not of course understand what the Kikuyu women said as they gossiped with the old lady, but sometimes Charlotte Stuart translated, and Katie was not at all astounded to discover that the yammer was much what one might hear at supermarket or beauty shop or any other common ground where women clustered at home.

Her relationship with the old lady was still undefined—had been undefined from the day the plane landed and George Locke had said bluntly: 'This is Kathleen Crane, Charlotte. She was a client of Brian's—she was with him when he got sick, she's come along to help out while he gets well.' The owner of Glenburnie had accepted Katie's presence as if young American women accompanied by desperately ill young men slid out of the sky every day. She had assigned Katie to one of the seemingly numberless guest rooms in the sprawling wings of the house, and had thereafter proceeded to treat her casually as an old member of the family. If she knew or assumed that there had been anything between Katie and Brian beyond client-hunter relationship, she never hinted it in her manner.

Apart from the conscious unreality of daily proof that she, Katie Crane, actually was living in Africa, on a working farm that nested in the middle of several thousand Africans who were no more than a leap from the Stone Age, Katie had never felt more comfortably at home than in the big shabby old house with its oddly assorted complement of people. She had felt accepted from the first—especially by Charlotte Stuart and the young wife of Philip Dermott. She was not quite so at ease with Nell, the sister, and put that down to a perfectly normal sisterly suspicion of her intentions towards Brian. But she struck it off very well with lanky Philip, a serious, hardworking crew-cropped young man who was away in the fields most of the day, and more than well with George Locke, whom she felt she knew closely as a result of their meeting in the bush when Brian had collapsed. But it was young Jill who jabbered artlessly with her, asking endless questions about New York and Florida and, of course, Hollywood.

They usually rode together for an hour in the cool afternoon, now, when Jill had come in from her work at the little schoolhouses she was helping Nell organize on various of the scattered farms which comprised the sprawling estate of Glenburnie. They rode slowly, Jill talking nineteen to the dozen, with little Karioki, the orphaned Kikuyu boy, following along behind them on his fat stolid piebald pony. Sometimes they dismounted for a stroll or to investigate some specimen of interest, an odd turret of rocks, or a clutter of old bones, or to shoot a few guinea-fowl or francolin with the little twenty-bore that Jill carried in a boot on her saddle. Then Karioki held the horses. It had gradually fallen into a pattern; at about five o'clock the child would appear at the front stoop with the saddled horses—Jill's dancy roan gelding and a more docile grey mare that Katie had adopted as a palfrey.

The early afternoons she usually spent with Brian, who was unconsciously accepting more and more of the farm's work. Brian was something approaching a genius with cantankerous machinery, and seemed never happier than when he was surrounded by the scattered viscera of a motor, greasy to the ears and humming tunelessly as he wheedled the refractory bits of metal into operative acquiescence again.

Most of Brian's safari crew had gone back to their homes in the various reserves, to see to their *shambas* and to be with their wives, but Muema the gunbearer and Kidogo had stayed on the farm with him. Muema's sound practical knowledge of tools created him immediate vice-president in the maintenance field, while Kidogo, who understood nothing of machinery, was insolently voluble in his advice to them both. Katie generally sat silently near by, asking a question now and again, sometimes lighting Brian a cigarette and pushing it between his lips. Brian seemed each day to be regaining more of his old strength and positive personality, but never, by so much as a word, had he mentioned his wife, the scalding picture in the paper, or his illness—not since he had finally emerged from his deliriums and had murmured again: 'Sorry to've been such a bloody nuisance, Katie. Thank you.' That was it, and that was all, and Katie was just as happy to leave it that way. She could not but think it unusual, though, that her continued presence on the farm should be so casually accepted. She would have to do something definite about that pretty soon, she thought every day—and kept putting off the decision for one more day.

CHAPTER SIXTEEN

WITHOUT FULLY realizing it, Brian had allowed himself to be absorbed into the routine of his aunt's huge experiment. He was not aware that he was working a formally full day, perhaps, for the diversity of his tasks kept the toil from assuming the aspect of chores. He found time to build a blind and bait a pair of leopards that had been pestering the sheep. For the first time, Katie sat up at night and waited for wild animals to come to a kill. Brian explained painstakingly here that he was not shooting for sport or trophy, but merely erasing a menace. Therefore it was quite legal and ethical to sit up with a torch and shoot the animal by night, if you did it on your own land and for a sound economic reason. She had sat silently with him in the blind and he had shot both male and female in the same evening, as they came successively to the kill and were blinded by the torch he flashed at the crunch of rending flesh. The killing lacked excitement and contained no emotion whatsoever. They picked up the dead leopards and gave them to Kidogo to skin, but it was as if they had collected a couple of paid-for pelts to sew into a coat.

The same lack of excitement applied to the thinning of a herd of buffalo that came down from one of the mountains to create havoc in the wheat. Brian bided patiently for a moonlit night, then took Katie and Kidogo along with him to wait for the buff to file down out of the hills. Brian shot methodically and coldly as the animals milled stupidly in the high grain, and when they went among the carcasses they counted a dozen or more dead and dying.

'This is farming, too,' Brian said. 'And it's the part I dislike most. I used to have to do a lot of this when I was in the Game Department. The worst of all was the elephants. Poor brutes, they're so huge they wreck everything they touch on a *shamba*, and sometimes I'd have to shoot fifteen or twenty out of one herd, generally at night and hoping mostly to kill the old cows who led the herds, or at least kill enough to scare hell out of the leaders. It was sickening to come back by daylight to collect the ivory, if any, and to see them all lying dead like lumps of mud. I hated that worst of all, but you can't buck progress, I suppose. For a while, after Aunt Charlotte's dream plantation really gets working, they'll need a full-time professional hunter to shoot the varmints out of the crops and flocks.'

'You admit now that it has a chance, then?' Katie asked him.

'Maybe,' Brian said grudgingly. 'Maybe. But she's not home yet, not by a long chalk. I am still waiting for some anti-progress reaction from the townies. I can't see the black saviours of the world letting dear old Auntie Char save it for them. Gives the world-saving business a bad name if it's a white person does it. We'll just have to wait and see. I know these people. Look what they did to poor old Don Bruce over at Hardscrabble.'

'Have you heard from them, since they left?'

'*I* haven't. Ken Jenkins—you remember him, the office-*wallah* in my firm —told me on the phone the other day that he'd had a letter from Scotland, somewhere around the Glenlivet area. Toumantoul, or some such name. Peggy's people are there. Don'll have to find something to do before long, if it's only leaf-raking. A wife and four kids consume a lot of oats.'

'Poor fellow. I suppose he'll come back one day?'

'I don't know. Maybe. Possibly.'

366

Brian grinned without mirth, showing his teeth wolfishly.

'Maybe you ought to buy that farm after all, Katie,' he said. 'We could have a barrel of fun for a while, convincing the political gentlemen that they'd chosen the wrong boy to bother.'

'The offer's still open,' Katie said. 'But *not* for the purpose you have in mind.'

'I was kidding, anyhow,' Brian laughed, too easily this time. 'I was just thinking of taking on Hardscrabble as a sporting proposition. It would be fascinating to see how many I could clobber before they collected *my* headskin.'

'I actually believe you're serious,' Katie said. 'I believe it and I don't like it. It frightens me.'

Brian laughed. It was not a happy sound.

'I'm quite serious. There will be lots of us feeling the same way pretty soon. Some have left—some more will leave. Some, like my friend Bruce, couldn't gamble with the lives of their wives and kids. But some of us won't run.' Brian scrubbed at his forehead.

'How can you make people understand what sort of folk we are here? We are not basically a . . . a *frightenable* people. Our potential for personal fear is very low, especially among the old stock. Aunt Charlotte'll do her best to get along with the Wogs, but in the final showdown, you'd find her poking a rifle out of a window and shooting until they killed her or burned her out. Most of them are like that, the old ones. It's their country. Some died trying to take it and tame it; most of the old survivors will die to keep it.'

'But your aunt, the thing's she's doing here——'

Brian shook his head. His voice was very sober.

'Too little and very much too late. Ten years ago, yes. Maybe even five years ago. But not now. The black gentlemen won't settle for anything but the lot now. The whole picture in Africa has changed. *Compromise* is a bad word in the African mouth.'

'Well, if you can't stay to live in peace and won't run, what exactly will you do?' Katie felt a fool for asking.

'Why . . .' Brian's voice was dreamy, 'why, Katie, we'll withdraw to a few well-chosen positions, like the old Boers used to *laager* their wagons, like your pioneers made circles of their wagon trains against your Red Indians. And we will kill Kikuyu. We will kill Kikuyu by day and by night. We will kill, very possibly, hundreds of thousands of Kikuyu.

'A great many of us have had a lot of recent practice killing Kikuyu,' Brian said, still in the same chillingly toneless voice. 'There is nothing a Kikuyu can do in the bush that we cannot do better. There is nothing a Kikuyu can do outside the bush that we cannot do better. A few score of us could wipe out the tribe, given enough arms and ammunition. We'll recolonize the bloody place if they leave us alone!'

'But that's nothing but barbarism, pure and simple. It's——'

'It's what the people who now propose to run the country were practising

367

six years ago—are practising right now, and will practise in the future. The only way to fight any sort of terrorism is to do it better. We only killed ten thousand of them in the recent do. We didn't burn villages or fire crops or kill many women or children. That's because we were hampered by the military. We only went after the gangs—and they were mostly male. Given a free hand, I rather imagine I could do for ten thousand all by myself, by the grace of God, luck and weather, if I didn't have a proper army to tell me what to do and not to do. And this time *we*'ll be the army—very small but very rugged.'

He laughed again, and the mirthless sound made Katie Crane's neck-hair prickle.

'This is stupid talk, Brian! Stop it!' Katie's voice stamped its foot. Now he smiled again, lazily and dreamily.

'Of course,' he said. 'Let's go get a couple of shotguns and collect some birds for dinner. Then I've got to go do something about that bloody thresh-ing centre's machinery. Better for everyone in the old days when they just trod the wheat out of the ear. Come on, we'll have a bit of sport first.'

The bleakness of mood apparently deserted him, and he whistled as he walked off to get the shotguns.

CHAPTER SEVENTEEN

A MONTH had passed since Brian's violent seizures and his return to Glen-burnie. He had cancelled a previous safari booking—'doctor's orders', he told Ken Jenkins on the phone—and he had found life on the farm not half bad. For one thing, he felt in absolutely tip-top shape again. He had gained weight and got himself sunburned anew. He had become infected to a degree by the enthusiasm for the endless work on the farm, and had more or less assumed the duties of chief technician on the engineering side. He and Muema had more than they could handle between them; he thought that he might send for Machoini, his bespectacled driver-mechanic, to come and help out at least until they got the whole mechanical *shauri* fairly well organ-ized. He had not himself realized just how untillable most of their fallow land had been. It would take years of driving effort and constant attention to make it flourish. It was not, suddenly, an ambitious development of five hundred small farms attached to one great one; it was literally one huge family complex, with each tiny piece dependent on the other.

It was all very fine, this early excitement, and it might even work so long as his Aunt Charlotte kept her health and young Philip continued cracking and the two girls, Nell and Jill, worked like nigger wenches from dawn to dusk. It was all very well while the enthusiasm held and the doctor's driving emphasis on common cures and sanitation was enforceable because the Nig had a new toy; while he thought he was getting something for nothing and so was tolerantly willing to amuse the white man in his latest folly. It was an interesting toy construction, and no doubt the Wog was childishly happy with seeing it grow. It was certainly novel, this massive combine of farms, and the Nig liked anything at all that momentarily gave him grandiose ideas of his own importance and close view of the dramatic mechanical problems of hill-moving and rock-blowing and bush-clearing. The Nig was enchanted with the flow of lorries and tractors, bulldozers and scoop-shovels, pile-drivers and cement-mixers and all the other clanking equipment that lumbered over the farm. It was very noisy; the Nig liked noise. Every day made a new *ngoma* of noise. The women were happy with their new market-place, with its stalls and booths and poured-concrete flooring. Aunt Charlotte was talking of getting permission to put up a big brewery with its licensed beer hall, such as the South Africans had for the gold-miners at Randfontein and the other large locations of native miners. There was considerably more activity here at Glenburnie right now than there was at Kahawa, where the big military base was daily growing from the raw ugly upturned clay.

Everything would be just dandy here at Glenburnie, Brian was forced to admit, until the excitement of completing the major chores was done, in perhaps another couple of months' time, and the Nigs settled down to dull routine on their own plots. Then the jamboree would be over; the hut-raising foolishness finished, and they would be each on his own with his private little kingdom of ten acres. Then was when you would see what the Wog was truly made of; then is when you could measure the worth of Aunt Charlotte's and George's highflown project.

It won't work, Brian's brain told him. It can't work. It won't work because it's never worked, and won't work when the Wog owns the country either, let alone when he's sharecropping it for somebody else. It isn't in the make-up of the black man to work any harder than he has to in order to drive his women to slave for him. What was it the man had said in the book: *The educated African will handle nothing dirtier than a fountain pen, lift nothing heavier than a pencil?* And also, *the prosperous African is the first to kick out his less prosperous brethren?* True words indeed.

His sister Nell and that sweet gawky young Jill were up to their ears in moonbeams about uplifting the African women—better education for the children, more emancipation for the young girls, cleanliness and home economics and God knows what-all. It wouldn't work—educate them and they're off to the towns even faster. Nobody who can push a pen wants to bend over to weed a yam-patch. The young wenches want lipstick and jitter-bug. They want to work in department stores and beauty shops and maybe factories for their own pay packets. They don't want to manicure a tea plant or wet-nurse a stalk of pyrethrum. How you gonna keep 'em down on the farm after they've seen *uhuru?* They ain't gonna be able to, Brian's brain

369

answered back. They'll take off in a cloud of the well-known owl dung and feathers.

Everybody's so bloody full of good works, Brian thought. They've even trapped Katie into it—which is not surprising. She is very heavy with love for her fellow man, including, I suppose, me. I expect I should be shocked at myself for not being equally full of love for my fellow man—and, I suppose, Katie. This little game they're all playing now: Katie staying on, and Aunt Char damned coy, and George so helpful and Jill matchmaking for all she's worth—Christ, I wonder how long before they start the kissing games on dull evenings.

The idea, I gather, is that I should marry Katie and settle down to a life of uplifting the noble Nig to a point where he is sufficiently humanized to kick me in the stomach from my own level, rather than sneaking up on me in the dark with a *panga*. If I admit I was wrong, and go to Aunt Charlotte and say see here, darling Auntie, I was a wicked boy and dead wrong; I mark the error of my ways and want to stay on always, fixing sick tractors and overseeing a flock of lazy niggers—if I say that she will greet me with open arms. Then Katie and I will marry and everybody will be happy. Except me. I will still want to be away in the bush. I am not for the farms. And I certainly am not for the people.

'You self-pitying son of a bitch,' he said aloud. 'You miserable, whining, Irish weakling. You professional little boy. You—*Bwana*. You *white man*!'

He dropped his face in his hands. He had been sitting under a lonely acacia on a tall hill, looking vaguely in the direction of The Mountain, which had misted over. He must have slept a little—chatter from a young voice woke him. It was Kidogo coming up the hill, and he was accompanied by the child, Karioki. The little boy carried a short bow, and a small quiver of arrows was slung on his back. In one hand he held the feather-ruffled body of a spurfowl. He lifted his victim high as he ran towards Brian.

'Look!' he shouted. 'See, Uncle Brian! Kidogo is teaching me to shoot with a bow, and I hit the bird fair and killed it dead!'

He came closer and held the dead partridge close for Brian to admire. It was the first time that the little boy had called him anything at all—the 'Uncle Brian' came as a shock, although he had become accustomed to hearing the child address his aunt as 'Aunt Charlotte'.

'That's a very nice one,' Brian said dutifully. 'He'll be very good to eat.'

'Oh, yes,' the little boy said. 'Kidogo has promised to build a fire later and we are going to grill it over the coals, exactly like he says you used to do when *you* were a little boy.'

Brian smiled honestly now.

'That's fine.' The old man had arrived and was squatting in front of Brian.

Kidogo's voice was indignant. 'Do you know, Bwana, that this child is almost ignorant? He has been taught nothing! He did not know how to shoot a bow until I taught him! He knows nothing of spears or knives or snares. He knows the *mzungu's* books very well—they send him to the book-school constantly. But he knows nothing of value as a man!'

Brian grinned, and took the bow from the boy's hand. He twanged it once, and handed it back.

'It is a good bow,' he said. 'Strong but not too strong. I am sure that Kidogo will teach you to use it well.'

'He is making me a spear now, too,' Karioki said. 'A small one. I tried to throw his spear but it was too heavy. Well,' he said, 'I have to run home now. I have to get the horses for Miss Jill and Miss Katie. We always ride at this time of day,' he said importantly. 'I am the syce.'

He ran off down the hill, the bird swinging from one hand, the bow counterbalancing in the other.

'He is a good little boy,' Kidogo said. 'It is a shame nobody has taught him anything of his own ways. Remember when we brought him home, Bwana?'

Brian grunted.

'I remember,' he said. 'Indeed, I do.'

'It is strange to think that if we had left him with his dead mother or knocked him on the head he would not be running happily downhill to get horses for the young Memsaabs,' Kidogo said. 'As I get older and stiffer in the joints I often think such thoughts as those—how things might be if other things had not happened. I have been thinking much lately.'

'What mostly have you been thinking, old man?' Brian got out a pack of cigarettes and shook a couple loose for himself and the old Ndrobo. 'I have been thinking some myself. I have been thinking much. I was thinking when you and the *mtoto* came up the hill. I was thinking that perhaps it was time that we went back to the bush. We've been here with the farmers long enough.'

Kidogo scratched the back of his neck. He looked older and scrawnier and greyer, Brian thought, more like an ancient black Chinaman than ever. He had not bothered lately to tweeze out the long white hairs which fell wriggling from his chin. The muscles of his chest had completely collapsed; his breastbone was as sharp as an axe-blade.

'Bwana?' Kidogo's voice was soft.

'*Eeeehhh.*'

'You will not be angry with me, Bwana? I have always spoken the truth to you.'

'*Hapana.* I won't be angry. What do you want to say?'

'I do not think that we ought to go back to the bush, Bwana. I do not think we should hunt all the time any more, Bwana. I think the time of hunting is past. I think we hunters will vanish—have vanished, like the Athi—with the exception of a very few. I am old, Bwana, and will die soon. Then there will be only you left and it is bad to be alone when you hunt. It is bad to do anything alone, but hunting alone is impossible. A man was not created to live alone. He was certainly not made to hunt alone.'

Brian said nothing. He would let the old man sweat this one. Kidogo too, he thought, with some bitterness. It's all a plot. Everybody's in the act.

'You know,' the old man said presently. 'You know that I will go wherever you go so long as I am able, Bwana.'

'I know it.'

'So I was thinking that perhaps it would be better if we did not go to the bush so much any more; that perhaps it would be better if you married and had some children so that I can still teach them before I am too old. I was thinking that it would be a shame for the Bwana's children to grow up as ignorant as this little boy Karioki, all because I am either dead or too old to teach them.'

'It would be a pity,' Brian drawled. 'So you're suggesting that I get married and have some children, eh?'

'That is right, Bwana. It is time you took another wife. Things were very disturbed when you married before. You are getting to be *mzee* like me now. Soon you will be too old to enjoy a woman.' The old Ndrobo cackled. 'I am joking, of course, Bwana. But you are not getting any younger. A man should enjoy his children; he should grow up with them when he is young, and not wait until he is old and too tired to teach them to hunt and fish and to know the animals and forests.'

'I agree,' Brian said. 'But I don't know any *mwanamuke* to marry. Also women are very expensive. I have no money to buy a wife.'

The old man laughed again.

'I know the Bwana has plenty of money. But if he didn't, the young Memsaab *Keti* has plenty of money, or she could not have afforded to buy the safari. All *merikani* women have much money, or they would not always be coming so far across the sea to hunt with the Bwana and me.'

'Point well taken,' Brian said in English. Then: 'But I do not know that the Memsaab Katie wants to marry me. Perhaps she has another husband. Perhaps she has had one husband and does not want another.'

'Now the Bwana is really joking. The Memsaab *Keti* weeps much when she thinks of the Bwana. She is sad because you do not marry her. I thought when you lay with her on safari, when she came to your tent, that you intended to take her for a wife. Did you not find her pleasing to lie with?'

'Mind your own bloody business, and never mind my love life,' Brian said. Then: 'Yes, she was pleasant enough. Tell me, *mzee*, is there any other reason you want to clip the hawk's wings, to pen the bull elephant in a *boma* of women and goats?'

Kidogo looked at Brian with almost pleading eyes.

'Do not joke me any more, Bwana. I am serious. I did not like it when you were sick again. I do not like it when you are sad and drink too much and get sick. If you go off again you will each time drink more, and you will get sicker, and then finally you will die or be crippled and useless to yourself, which is worse for a man like you than dying. If you die, Bwana, you will not know it the very moment you are dead. But you will leave many people

372

behind you who will be forever sad. I will be sad, and the Big Memsaab will be sad, and the Memsaab *Keti* and all the others. They will all be sad. It is not nice to make other people sad when you seek such an easy way out of the forest as merely to die, Bwana.'

'*Eeehhh*,' Brian said, for a lack of anything better. That time the old boy had touched a nerve. I hadn't precisely considered it that way, he thought. He nodded at Kidogo.

'Go ahead, *mzee*,' he said. 'I'm still listening.'

'The time of the big change has come, Bwana. In my life I have seen much change—change from when I was a little boy, change from when I was a young man and your father first came to the country, change when you were born and now, more than ever, big change. Very big change. All the *watu*, white and black, are changing. Soon there will be no big bush in Africa; soon there will be nothing but big *shambas* like this and more towns and always more people. I can remember easily when this was *all* big bush, Bwana. Almost in your lifetime. You see it now full of men and machines that snort like rhino and rumble their bellies like elephant, and do the work in a week that it would take a thousand men a year to do. There is nothing you can do about this change, Bwana, but to go along with it. I shall not live to see the resolution of it, but you will. And your children will. If you have any.'

Brian lit another cigarette. He blew a ring and punched a forefinger through it.

'I'm afraid you're so bloody right,' he said, more to himself than to Kidogo. 'Everything's changing but old *Dinosaurus Rex* Dermott, the incurable living fossil. Tell me, old man, what do you propose that I do about this change?' The fragments of smoke had ridden away on the afternoon breeze.

'Once when I was a wild young *shenzi* in the woods, before I met your father, I thought myself some day to be the greatest hunter in the world. I was afraid of nothing—single-handed I would kill an elephant with my spear. I was young enough to think that way at the time. Once I crept up on an old bull. The wind swirled and he caught my scent. He spun round and charged me, screaming horribly, with his trunk snaking out to snatch me. I threw my spear truly, but it only stuck for a moment into the top of his trunk before he shook it off. It was no more than the nip of a *tsetse* fly to him. My courage vanished, and I ran to one side, across the wind, and so escaped without honour. An old man had earlier heard my boasts, and now he also had heard of my narrow escape from death. So one day he took me into the forests, and we tracked a lone bull for a long time. We came up to the bull, and he was sleeping in the shade, rocking from side to side and snoring.

'The old man motioned to me to wait, and he crept very quietly behind the bull. The old man had a very sharp, very heavy *simi*, and one long slim spear. He plunged the spear into the ground and crept up to the elephant with only the sharp heavy sword. When he got up to the elephant's hind end, he swung the sword mightily against the elephant's leg, and hamstrung the elephant with the sword. The elephant cannot move about much on three legs, as

373

you well know. So the old man went back and got his spear, now leaving the *simi* plunged into the ground. The elephant was trumpeting with pain and anger, but being hamstrung he could not go away. So the old man watched his chance, and suddenly he darted in quartering from the rear and slipped his spear into the elephant's lungs, like a finger into fat. After a while the elephant bled to death, and then the old man took his knife and began to cut steaks off the dead elephant. I went back to tell the *watu* and we feasted for days, and everyone sang and danced and praised the old man for his wisdom.'

'I got the message, Bwana Aesop,' Brian grinned, when the old man had finished. 'There are more ways to kill a cat than choking it with butter.'

'Exactly,' Kidogo grinned. 'You cannot defeat what is coming by flying in its face or even running away from it, Bwana. It seems to me that the Big Memsaab, your aunt, has the same idea that the old man had when he taught me to kill elephants. There are many ways to kill elephant—with poisoned arrows, by a weighted spear hanging from a tree, by lying along a branch with a sharp spear and waiting for the elephant to pass, by making a snare of a circle with spikes that will trap it by one leg. But no man ever killed an elephant by running up to it and flinging a spear in its face. I think you should help your aunt to hamstring her elephant.'

'I would die if I stayed trapped here on this *shamba*, working like a *fundi* for all those farmers,' Brian said. 'I could not stand it.'

'You will certainly die if you do not,' the old man said sharply. 'A man can stand anything he has to stand. And you would be a fool as well. Only a fool fights battles he cannot win. You cannot win the battle of the new world by pretending that only you are right and the world is wrong. Times have changed, Bwana. I did not realize it so much until the last month, when I have watched your aunt making men out of monkeys. They are still monkeys, perhaps, but at least she is teaching them to climb the trees and throw down the nuts to other monkeys.'

'Maybe I liked it better when they threw the nuts at each other,' Brian murmured, considerably impressed by the old man's approach to Charlotte Stuart's farming project. 'You have other thoughts on the matter, *mzee*?'

'I have other thoughts. I always have spare thoughts in my quiver. Consider that the elephant, while the most intelligent of all animals, possibly does not know what he is doing when he eats so many dôm-palm fruits that he makes himself sick to his stomach. But he does know enough to move his bowels frequently, and so he passes the kernels of the dôm-palm fruit, and nearly always close by water. The kernels are trodden into the ground by the elephant himself. They grow into more palm trees, which bear more nuts, and so the elephant has created his own source of food in an endless cycle; first the nuts, then the passing of the nuts, then the tree, then more nuts, then the passing, then more trees. He not only has made a food supply, he has also created shade in which to stand while he fills his belly and makes more trees with the waste of his greed. And you notice that while the elephant knocks down most trees and strips them of bark, leaving them to die, he only bumps

374

the dôm-palm gently with his head, in order to shower down the nuts. This you have seen many times. How many dôm-palms have you seen an elephant wreck and kill?'

'True, true,' Brian said. 'Carry on, old man, I await your wisdom with eager hands and open head.'

'Better you awaited it with a receptive heart, as well,' Kidogo said sharply. 'The time has come to stop tearing down the forests and to plant some nuts, Bwana. The time has come to train the monkeys and teach them to be children. Then the time will come to teach the children to be men, as I was teaching that little boy to shoot a bow. That is all I have to say on the matter—except one thing.'

'Let fly,' Brian said. 'What is it?'

'You will be very angry with me for saying it. But I think the time has come for you to stop being a little boy, Bwana. I think the time has come for you to start learning to be a man. You have been a boy long enough; too long, Bwana, and you may strike me for insolence if you will.'

The old man stopped talking and bowed his head. Brian patted his shoulder.

'I would not strike you even for a lie. I will not strike you for telling the truth, even though it be a truth that hurts. I was thinking of similar things when you came with the little boy. But I say honestly, old man, I do not know if I have it in me to change.'

'You never know what is in you until you try a difficult task, Bwana. One time when you broke the back leg of the Land Rover so badly that its foot would not stay on, you pushed a stick under the long log that holds the two front feet, and so we came home on three feet and a stick. This is not usual. And remember too that when a leopard will not come to a bait, you do not give up all leopards and all trees and all baits. You try a different series of baits and trees until finally the leopard comes and you shoot him.'

Brian got up and stretched. He reached out a hand and drew the old man to his feet.

'Come on,' he said. 'Let's walk down to see the Bwana Dokitari. There are some things I want to talk to him about.'

'No,' the old man said. 'I have some small things to do at the big house. I am late; I must run now. Think well on what I have said, Bwana. The time has come to make up your mind. I hope you will decide now to be a man.'

Kidogo set out at a long ground-eating lope, showing no sign of the age of which he had just complained. He could run all day like that, Brian thought; run all day and all the night and maybe next day as well. Funny old man. Could it be that everyone is right but me? If Kidogo, one of the few true savages alive, can see things so clearly, is it possible that there is some chance of things working out here in Kenya for everyone, including black and white? Common sense says *no*, Brian's brain told him stubbornly, as he walked slowly towards the hospital site. The doctor wanted him to install a separate small electric plant which might some day come in handy for emergency operations at night if the big machine cut out. That's what I need, he thought sourly, an emergency dynamo for Brian Dermott, in case the big machine cuts out.

He looked from the crest of his hill, and he could see the raw red striping of newly defined roads. Vehicles crawled everywhere—trucks, half-tracks, tractors, 'dozers. Brian had hunted every inch of this land as a child when vast game herds had grazed over it. On the very hill on which he was standing, lions had tumbled in the sun. There was no game on the plains any more; nothing but bloody farms and bloody traffic, like the imported traffic he was seeing now. You might as well be living in a city. It was becoming more and more like this even on the fringes of the few unspoiled places which still held game. Ikoma in Tanganyika was one of Brian's favourite spots; native habitation there had spread in ten years from the Upper to the Lower Grummetti River, and square miles of land which had once cherished the enormous overflow from the migrations on the Serengeti now accommodated cattle and flocks of bleating goats. The God-damned white man, Brian thought; it's all his fault, with his bloody roads and bloody dams and bloody equipment. His bloody *progress*—progress for politics, progress for war, progress for greed, progress for unhappiness. *Uhuru* to progress. Bloody *uhuru*.

Well, Dermott, there you are, Brian thought, and heaved a sigh. It is time to face your facts finally. It is time to settle down and hope for the best. Build yourself a compromise, my lad, and make everybody happy except yourself. Go and have the old heart-to-hearter with Aunt Charlotte. Go and pop the fatal question to Katie. Go and fix the bloody dynamo for the bloody doctor. Detribalize yourself, boy, and throw away your spear. Pick up the plough. Tote dat bale. Television is just around the corner.

You would think I was sentencing myself to a life-term in jail, Brian thought with bitter amusement. Here is this lovely woman, this Katie of the silver hair and the great misted grey eyes; the kind Katie, the bruised-eyed, gentle, often funny-husky-voiced Katie who wants to love me and look after me and do something for all other people as well as herself. Here is this fine farm, which will be a third mine, if things work out, and no less mine if things *don't* work out. I have nothing to lose, at all, by the adoption of civilization. I must be a real clot to argue with myself about it.

Now he walked steadily towards the house. The doctor and his dynamo could damned well wait. Now was as good a time as any to have his chat with Charlotte Stuart, and for all his brooding sarcastic thought, he was a little bit relieved. It was a cinch he'd about had safaris and the old loose life that went with them. Safaris were generally getting sourer all the time, and he was weary of explaining natural history to American oil millionaires and their greedy-eyed wives. He might as well try explaining simple piston machinery to the future rulers of the world for a while. Perhaps some day they might be even able to distinguish between crankcase oil and Karo syrup.

KATIE CRANE clacked hard-heeled down the stairs, adjusting her feet to jodhpur boots, and spied Charlotte Stuart on the veranda. The little boy Karioki had already come to the front of the house, with the reins of Katie's grey mare and Jill's red gelding looped loosely over the pommel of his pony's saddle. Katie had siestaed; her face felt puffy and her lips dry. A gallop would do her good, she thought. She'd slept like a rock for an hour and a half.

'Where's Jill, Aunt Charlotte?' Katie asked the old lady, as she stepped out on the porch. 'I'm late, I'm afraid. Whooie! I slept like a log. I'm going to have to ease up on the Glenburnie lunches. I'm fair fit to lose me figger, as we used to say in County Cork.' She smiled.

'Jill's not riding today. She and Philip had to go off to Nyeri to see about something mysterious. Maybe we are having a baby—who knows? She said anyhow to tell you not to wait. Shall we send your self-appointed syce away and have a chat?'

Katie yawned.

' 'Scuse me. I don't think so. I've slept creases in my face. I think I'll go for a little ride anyhow. A brisk canter and some wind in my eyes—but I think today I'll ride that red thunderbolt of Jill's My old grey mare ain't what she used to be, in more ways than one. I'd rock myself to sleep again.'

'Hmmm. I suppose so.' The old lady scratched her chin. 'He's pretty lively, this red one, and a mouth on him like cast iron.'

'I can handle him. Come on, Karioki, take my horse back to the barn. I'll ride Miss Jill's.' She ran down the stairs. 'Here. I'll hold the red horse while you take Old Softshoe back to the barn.'

'Wait a minute, Karioki!' Charlotte Stuart cried. Then she said to Katie. 'I don't like the idea of you going off with just the little boy. Your horse might step in a pighole—anything. Better if somebody else went with you. Karioki, get one of the boys to run along behind you. The kitchen *mtoto*—anybody.'

'Old Kidogo is out behind the house,' Karioki said. 'Will he do? I don't know if he can ride a horse.'

'He won't have to ride a horse,' the old woman said. 'Go and fetch him. He'll do famously. He can run faster than either one of these plugs can gallop. All I want is somebody in the area, anyhow.'

'I don't mean to be a lot of trouble,' Katie said, climbing aboard the red horse, which danced nervously, circling, fighting its bit. 'Whoa! Easy there, boy, easy now.' She ran her hand along its neck, fingers creeping petting under the long red mane. 'Good boy. Easy.' The horse calmed, moving in a half-circle, neck bowed.

'Okay,' Katie said. 'You win. Send the bodyguard. I'm off. Tell my cavalry to follow the dust! Whoopee!' she yelled, and waved her hat as she dug her heels into the red horse's ribs. 'Let 'er rip!' The horse lunged into a gallop. He cleared a small hedge with daylight to spare as Katie urged him up and over.

377

'Jolly good pair of hands the gel's got,' Charlotte Stuart murmured. 'Does everything very well. Ah.' Karioki had come round the corner of the house again, with Kidogo jogging along behind him. Kidogo leaned on his spear at the foot of the steps and looked up at the old woman.

'Go along with the little boy and follow behind the Memsaab,' Charlotte Stuart said in Swahili. 'She is riding alone and I am afraid of the horse. He might shy at a snake or step into a hole and throw the Memsaab. Do not annoy her—just stay within reasonable distance of her.'

'*Ndio*, Memsaab,' Kidogo said, and saluted her with his spear. 'Come on, little boy. I can trot as fast as your pony can trot, maybe faster.' The old man set off in a swinging canter, with the fat little pony bouncing alongside. Charlotte Stuart smiled at the picture made by young and old Kenya; the old man loping along with his spear, the little boy posting smartly on his spotted pony.

CHAPTER NINETEEN

THEY HAD gone perhaps twenty minutes, and the sun was sliding steeply downward in the sky, when Brian Dermott walked up the steps and sat down at the top. He was hot and perspiring from his walk; his browning face was flushed and there was an eagerness in his eyes his aunt had not noticed since his illness.

'Where's Katie?' he asked, after he had settled himself on the top step, leaning back against the corner post of the railing and clasping one knee with his hands.

'Riding, as usual. Went off with the little lad. Jill's in town. I sent old Kidogo along as bodyguard. Katie's riding that red horse and I was afraid maybe he might throw her, or something.'

'Good show,' her nephew said. 'Bulldozers come and bulldozers go, but antbears and warthogs and honey badgers still make holes in the ground for horses to step in. I never understood why a horse goes so far out of his way to fall in holes and stumble. Basically I distrust all horses.'

'Me too, especially the ones I used to bet on occasionally at the Limuru meetings. Haven't been to a racing in donkey's years. Must do that again some time when the work's done. I hear that new course at Ngong is quite nice.'

'Haven't seen it myself,' Brian said. He leaned forward and his voice was urgent. 'Auntie, there's no use beating about the bush. Does your old offer still stand—the one where I'm allowed to settle down and be a jolly farmer with manure on my boots and hay in my hair?'

Charlotte Stuart raised an eyebrow, looking almost absurdly like her nephew.

'Of course it does. It's never been withdrawn. It would make me very happy if you did, you know that. What brings on this sudden change of weather in my fiddlefooted nephew's thinking?'

Brian clawed at his moustache and seemed embarrassed.

'Lots of things. Sort of a collection of things. I wouldn't want to come to you under any false flags, Auntie. I'm still pretty sure what you're trying won't work, and we'll all get thrown out sooner or later when the blacks come to power. But I admire your effort—and, well, I want to do any part in it to help you that I can. Maybe I can't do much, but at least I'm one more man around the place. Weak head—strong back. Useful-type nephew.'

'What about your safari business? What will you do about that?'

'Let it ride along as is for a while. Ken's good in the office, and there are plenty of other hunters who'll keep busy for the next year or so, at least as long as the game lasts. We've heaps of advance booking. I thought perhaps I might take a trip every now and then with one of the older customers—sort of a picnic safari. You know, when the smell of manure and clank of tractors get to be more than I can bear?' He grinned. 'You needn't worry, though. They'd only be the kind of trip I'd be able to take a wife along on.'

'Oh? And so ye're thinking of taking a wife now, is it? Whoever'd be after having ye?' Charlotte Stuart tried to keep the triumph out of her eyes.

'I was planning to ask our house-guest, Mrs. Crane, to marry me, if it met the approval of all, and I'm quite certain—being neither blind nor quite an idiot—that it does. The only people who haven't taken part in the match-making have been Katie and me. Don't play innocent with me in your bogus brogue, Charlotte Stuart.'

'I can think of nothing nicer than having the lass for another daughter,' Charlotte Stuart said. 'And I know full well she's mad for you. I don't understand why, but she is, in any case. I have only this to say: don't marry that good young woman only to run wild again and break her heart when you're bored, as bored you'll be bound to be. Unless you're certain in your heart you'll make her happy, leave her alone and go off to your safaris. We need you on the farm, but not badly enough for you to do us any undue favours with your presence. Is that plain enough?'

'It's plain enough. Now, suppose I tell you frankly that no miracle has occurred, as in the bad fiction and worse movies, to give me a sudden change of heart. What has happened is that I have been sitting on a high hill, with a long view, and what I see is certain ruin for me and everyone else unless some of us hold our noses and honestly try.

'I am not a young man, panting after an unkissed girl, Charlotte Stuart. Nor am I one of those passionate farmers who goes around crumbling clots of earth in his hand and nibbling at bits of grass. I am not a man to die for love nor one to kill myself on lost causes. But I do know when I can no longer live in the past, or in the future, as I'm certain my father did. Nor can I fly in the face of what is seemingly inevitable. I had a long talk with Kidogo today; he spoke hard sense at me; he spoke practical sense. I didn't like it, but I admit the sense of it. I guess I've just been slower than most in coming to grips with reality. Also,' Brian paused and smiled sheepishly. 'Also, he said it was about time I quit being a boy and took a shot at being a man.'

'I quite agree with him,' Charlotte Stuart said tartly. 'Past time, if you ask me.'

'I have reached the same conclusion,' her nephew said. 'I can only say this, Aunt Char: I will make the best effort I can of what I believe is a bad bargain in Kenya. I will work as hard as I can; I will bury my personal feelings as much as I can and try to make your experiment work with the best my mind and muscles afford.'

'Can't ask more than that,' Charlotte Stuart said. 'And what about Katie? What about marrying Katie? Do you love her enough to marry her, Brian? It's doing her no great favour if you don't, you know.' The old lady's voice went dry again. 'We don't want to stretch your self-sacrifice too far. And how about Valerie? D'ye still have that particular burr under your blanket?'

'Stop it, Aunt Char,' Brian said. 'I am trying to be as honest as I can. I don't know if I ever had the capacity for the great thing they call "love". Perhaps I did with Valerie and it got burnt out of me. In any case, Valerie's finished. I see no great reason why Katie would want to love me, want to marry me, except that I believe she does. I think that if we were to marry and settle down here to work with you it would make her tremendously happy. Perhaps that's the wrong word—tremendously—but certainly happier than if she goes back to the elaborate nothing she came from. She's told me as much. I think it would be only a matter of time before she was back on the grog again, too—and going back for Katie I think would be worse than going back for me, because I think I'd die faster.'

'You sound over-gloomy for a prospective bridegroom,' she said. 'But I can't say I don't admire your candour. And ye're well rid of Valerie. So?'

'This last blackout of mine in the bush has made me think a great deal, Auntie dear. It destroys—to be suddenly helpless and dependent—it suddenly destroys a considerable portion of old youthful arrogances and stubbornnesses and certainly unlimited self-sufficiencies. I don't want to be dependent on anyone—not physically, not as a casualty. Not as a helpless child.

'Old Kidogo said today that you can't hunt alone. Well, I don't think you can grow old alone—old and bitter and alone. I think you have to have something to love. I think my something to love is Katie. There is no living woman I want more to please, to take care of, to be with, and to make happy, if I can. Perhaps then I am in love, after my odd fashion.'

'You've not told her this? No, of course you haven't, if you've only just come to it yourself. I hope you'll tell her the same as you've told me, but leave out the last thing you said—leave out the "perhaps" and also the "in my fashion". You make me happy, Brian; I think it's in your power to make Katie happy, and if you make her happy, you'll make yourself happy. It's an odd thing that is understood only by women and some other dumb animals, and it's what Jill's generation would call corny. But it's true all the same. Now come and kiss me and then go and saddle that old grey horse and go and find your gel and tell her what you've told me.'

Brian bent to kiss his aunt's cheek as he went inside to the bar. Her cheek was wet; the old warhorse actually was crying. You know, Dermott, he said to himself, if you go on this way you'll soon have yourself believing it, and leading the choir of all the other hosannah-shouters. That'll be a bloody frosty Friday, he thought.

'I hope to hell she'll have me,' he said to his aunt. 'We've not paid much consideration to that.'

'She'll have you, all right,' the old lady said. 'But,' she called after him, 'one of the best ways to find out is to go and ask her before your deadly logic cools!'

CHAPTER TWENTY

THE TWO men crouched at the edge of the bush. They were dressed in faded khaki shorts and shirts, their garments patched white and very dirty. One man was short and heavy-chested, with very long arms. His name was Maina, but he was still called Nyani—'Baboon'—a name he did not like, from the old prison days at Hola, when so many of the detained Mau Mau took the names of animals or were called after familiar objects. His companion was called Kisu—'Knife,' although he had been named Kamia after his grandfather. He was called 'Knife' for his virtuosity with the heavy *simi* which, in his hand, became a sword or razor, depending on the need. Kisu was lean and ropy, with a long hollow-cheeked face that always looked mournful. He as well was a graduate of the prison camps. The men were about thirty years old. They waited now, squatting on their heels.

The bush led to the edge of a small pool, where the little river widened and riffled lightly over the shallowness of a sandbar. Along the edges of the bar were deeper pools, in which one could see trout hanging motionless in the shadowed water. Lichened rocks were strewn on the sloping banks that led to water, which was clear and cold and swift enough to be pure. Tiny button flowers pushed through the short clovery green at the water's edge. It was a place whose usual quiet was broken only by birdsong and an occasional monkey yell—cool and quiet and cut away by a thick hedge of tall trees from the broad fields on both sides.

The squat man, Nyani, squinted at the sky. The reddened sun was just beginning to slide behind the hills.

'They are late today,' he said. 'They usually come earlier than this to water the horses and cool themselves.'

'Hand me the bottle,' the other man, Kisu, said. 'It is chilly here in this shade as the sun sinks.' He unwrapped his arms from round his legs.

'Aha, hand me the bottle, my friend says. And who was it that told me not to bring it? Only the friend who now commands me to hand it to him. Oh, well. I am known for my generosity. Here.'

He produced a pint bottle of brown liquid and handed it to the other man. Kisu tipped it back and made a face as he swallowed.

'Here,' Nyani the Baboon said, reaching out for the bottle. 'Do not drink it all. I paid for it, not you.'

'This is powerful stuff,' Kisu said. 'I think they must distil it of lye, it burns so. But it warms the heart and puts courage in the stomach.'

Nyani the Baboon looked at him scornfully.

'Do you lack courage so much that you must find it in a bottle for a simple job like this?'

'I did not say I lacked courage. I was describing the quality of the *tembo*. It takes no courage to seize a little boy. We could have taken him easily any day in the last month. I am bored with waiting for the word.'

'Well, you won't be bored much longer. The word has come today, and our waiting is over. And if they are a little late it is all to the good. Most of the motor-cars and lorries will be leaving in the next hour. It will be simple enough to lose ourselves among the other lorries. Their tyre-tracks will hide ours. Who notices the extra wildebeest among the herd?'

'It is a good plan that they have thought up. Much easier to take him here than from the house. He always stays a good distance behind the memsaabs so they may talk freely. You know of course that the boy speaks English as well as any bwana?'

'Yes. He goes to the schools and lives in the big house as well.'

'On evenings past he has always come to water his horse after the memsaabs have dismounted and have occasionally gone into the bushes to urinate. He is a very good-mannered little boy—he would not embarrass the memsaabs by lingering near while they relieve themselves as women will, going together into the bush.'

'You are certain,' the man Kisu said after they had drunk again and tossed the bottle away. 'You are certain that the lorry-driver knows exactly what to do?'

'As certain as I am of the fact that his name is Karugu and that he is my younger brother. He has been a lorry-driver for a long time. He has worked on this farm since his release from the camp at Hola. He is hauling material for the building at the location of the doctor. Unless Ngai has willed otherwise he will dump his last load in five minutes' time, and will have engine trouble briefly at the point we decided on back there. He will pull out of the hauling line while he inspects his motor. He will wave any offers of help away. There are canvas tarpaulins and grain sacks in the back of the lorry. There are also people—the correct people—in the back of the lorry. They will jump down to help him with his motor. In a few moments the motor will be fixed.

382

The people will jump back in and the lorry will proceed. By that time it will be dark, or nearly dark. The lorry will drive away and it will be heavier by— by three passengers. One of the passengers will have his head in a sack, and a gag in his mouth.'

'Do you know what they will do with the boy?'

'I do not *care* what they will do with the boy. I only know what we will do to take the boy and give him to the other people. We are being paid for that. We are not being paid to worry about what happens to the boy after.'

'Suppose the memsaabs miss the boy and make an outcry? What then?'

'They will not miss him for ten minutes or more. They will not miss him until they get to the house and find he is not with them. Then they will either ride back to look for him or they will tell somebody in the house that he is missing or they will go first to the barn to see if he has beaten them home. All this will take time. In five minutes from the time we drag the boy off his little horse he will be in the lorry. In five minutes from the time he is in the lorry he will be off the farm. In ten minutes after he is off the farm he will be in another lorry. For God's sake, stop chewing at it. It's all very simple!'

'I am not chewing at it,' Kisu said. 'But I know that tonight is the night they want the boy—not last night or the night before or last week or the week before that; not tomorrow night or next week or next month. They must want him very badly for tonight, for we could have taken him easily at any time after we were commanded to seek work near the big house and to learn of his movements. I do not like this taking him by day.'

'It is the best way to take him,' Nyani said. 'He does not sleep in the native location with the others; he sleeps in the big house like a white *mtoto*. To take him from the big house by night would cause an uproar, if we could do it at all. We are very fortunate that he rides with the memsaabs every day. It has made it very easy for us. In any event the day is fast turning into night, and we cannot be followed.'

'Let me get this straight one more time, then,' Kisu said. 'I seize the bridle of his pony; you drag him from the saddle and knock him unconscious with a blow of your sandbag.'

'That is right. Just seize the horse, that is all I ask, and hold his head. Try to keep your head, as well, and do not get excited. I will handle the boy. He is only a child. It will be simple to haul him off the horse and tap him with *this*.' He swished a home-made cosh of sand-filled flour sack with a soggy thump into one palm. 'This *rungu* is a great invention. Quiet and effective and also it does not cut.'

'I like this better.' Kisu picked up the short two-edged stabbing sword and tested its edge with a thumb. 'A *kisu* is a man's best friend. It is more dependable than a gun, more trustworthy than a human friend, more faithful than a woman. It will kill a snake or cut firewood or kill an enemy with equal ease. And if it is sharp enough you can shave with it. Look.' He ran the blade slowly along his thin-haired calf—it left a neat swath behind as the hairs

383

curled over the blade. 'This is a very good *simi*. I had a smith make this for me specially out of a white man's steel. It is like a razor.'

'All right. Put it away now. I think I hear the sound of horses. Be very quiet and remember what I say. Seize the horse and do not think. All your brains are in your nickname.'

The men shrank farther back into the thick bush that rimmed the little pool. It was growing much darker in the heavy shade. Soon the sun would be down and night would fall.

CHAPTER TWENTY-ONE

THE BIG red gelding fought its bit, flirting blobs of froth, as Katie attempted to turn it off the track that led to the little dell where they always stopped by the pool. There was no point in stopping there tonight; there was no final chat, no last cigarette to share with Jill. Katie pulled on the right rein, but the horse danced and swung irritably towards the left, stretching its neck cantankerously and yawing violently.

'Oh, all right, my bone-headed friend,' Katie said. 'Be a creature of habit. We'll go and have your drink if you've got that pea-brain of yours set on it.'

She gave the horse its head, and it trotted towards the accustomed drinking ford. Katie had not enjoyed the ride very much. Most of the fun was doing it with Jill. The little boy Karioki on his pony was not much company; the short-legged little beast could not keep up, and then there was old Kidogo jogging along behind her to make her reproach herself for coming alone.

Feeling her hands lax on the reins, the red horse trotted eagerly towards the glade. It turned sharply left then around a jutting point of bush, and Katie, looking backwards, was no longer able to see Karioki or Kidogo. But she knew from the solid plod of the trotting pony's hooves that the little boy was following on, as usual. Her horse increased its pace as it neared the water, and waded out fetlock-deep into the stream. Katie let the reins go slack completely, and the red horse stretched its neck and pushed its nose down into the fast-rippling water. Contented burblings and snufflings came as it sucked the cool water past its teeth. Katie eased one foot out of the stirrup and raised her hip, shifting the angle of her body as she fumbled for a cigarette and stared backwards over her shoulder to determine whether Karioki and his pony were coming in to the water or going on back to the house.

A cool puff of swinging evening breeze struck her hot, dusty face at the same moment that the horse raised its head from the stream. Its eyes walled, its nostrils distended, it swung its head abruptly as an unfamiliar scent came on the changing wind. The horse reared, slewed violently and stepped frantically backwards. One hind hoof slid on a slippery rock, and the horse's body fought to maintain balance, sending Katie flying out of the saddle. She half-turned in the air and landed flat on her back, knocking the wind completely out of her and stunning her slightly as her head struck the bank. Amid a tremendous splashing, the red horse recovered its balance again, and thundered off in the direction of the barn.

Katie lay momentarily stunned and out of breath, her feet in the water and her head on land. She was still lying flat, gasping, when Karioki's pony trotted up to the water's edge. The little black boy flung himself off the pony and knelt by Katie Crane. His eyes were huge with terror, and he could only fumble at Katie's neck as he tried to raise her head.

The pony, free of rider, walked out into the water and began to drink.

'Memsaab, Memsaab!' the little boy cried in terror. 'Are you all right, Miss Katie? Can you speak? Do you hurt somewhere? I saw the red horse running with no rider, and I——'

He raised his head at a crackle of bush and saw two men rise from a low green covert and walk towards them. His face lightened with relief, and authority grew into his voice.

'Oh, good,' he said in Swahili. 'The Memsaab has fallen off the horse and perhaps hurt herself. Help me pull her farther out of the water, and let us see if she—one of you had best run to the house for help. Better, one of you take my pony and hurry, *upesi*! Can you ride?'

The big man with the long ape arms stared at the little boy, and then looked swiftly at his companion.

'She is unconscious; she has not seen us; it could not be better,' he said rapidly in Kikuyu. 'Quick, we take him now and we will be gone——'

'What are you say——' Karioki's voice rose shrilly in Kikuyu, and got no further as the big man struck him on the temple with the sand-filled flour-bag just at the moment that Katie Crane opened her eyes and shrieked in horror—just at the moment that Kidogo came running up from behind the point of bush. Karioki slumped and Nyani caught him.

The old man's eyes darted to the woman on the ground and flicked from Katie to the men and the unconscious boy; took in the solitary pony still drinking in midstream. Katie saw him coming and screamed again:

'Kidogo, help! Run for the Bwana! *Upesi! Bwana! Run! Lete Bwana upesi!*' She drew in her breath to scream again. The heavy man, Nyani, let the little boy's head drop and clapped a hand over Katie's mouth. The old man balanced his spear in his right hand and stepped close to the men.

'What has gone wrong here?' he snapped. 'Why are you holding the Memsaab so? What is wrong with the boy?' He shifted the spear to menace the two strange men. 'Who are y——' the word ended in a bubble. The man Kisu had stepped to one side as Nyani reached out with his free hand and seized the haft of Kidogo's spear, wresting it away from him. As the yank on the shaft pulled the old man off-balance, Kisu stepped in and swung the *simi* in a flashing arc that cut the old man's head nearly off his shoulders. Kidogo fell, blood pumping from the severed jugular, head hanging from the shred of neck while his body jerked and heaved.

Panic showed in Kisu's face as he looked at the bloody blade of the sword. He stared at the blade, then ecstasy slid into his face and his body leaped in a spastic jump. Suddenly he lunged and cut Kidogo's head completely free of his shoulders. Flecks of foam came to Kisu's lips; his body rippled from head to foot.

Wild indecision now convulsed the face of the man Nyani, who still had his hand clapped over Katie's mouth. The little boy Karioki was beginning to stir; the old man's headless body still crawled in its own blood; the woman's eyes were rolled backwards in her skull under his hand. She was choking—the heavy horny palm had closed her nostrils. Nyani did not know what to do—it had all come so suddenly. His assistant Kisu had gone blood-mad and was leaping in the old way the warriors danced before they ran in a long shouting line to kill—to——

'Kisu!' he shouted, and as he shouted the pony raised its head and smelt the blood and snorted in terror and dashed down the middle of the stream. 'Kisu!' He took his hand from Katie's mouth, doubled it into a fist, and brought it crashing down on her temple. Then he rose, found his sand-filled sack, which he had dropped in confusion, and stepped behind his convulsive companion to strike him on the back of the head. The man Kisu fell to the ground, momentarily freed of his fit.

Nyani the Baboon tried to collect his scattered wits. The horses were gone —soon people would be coming. They had the boy; the old man was dead, killed by that crazy Kisu who had gone mad with blood as so many of his ancestors had gone mad with blood. The lorry would be waiting; they had said to bring the boy tonight or *else*. What else was there?

They had the boy; the truck was waiting. The old man was dead; there was nothing to be done about that. If that damned Kisu had not lost his head and struck—the old man was *dead*. He could not bear witness if he was dead. What was there else, then? The woman. She was unconscious. But she would regain consciousness. He had not counted on the woman getting mixed up in this, any more than he had counted on a stupid old man rushing up waving a spear. *The woman*. What about the woman? They could be gone before she could summon help.

But wait a minute. The woman had been conscious. She had been conscious when the old man was killed. She had been conscious for quite a long time. It had been dark and it was darker now, but it had not been too dark for her to recognize his face. Not so much his face maybe but his long arms. Everyone knew Nyani of the long arms. If she told about the man with the long arms and he was missing from his hut they would come with the tracker dogs and—he would never be able to hide. And then there was the thing about getting the boy away, and soon.

It was a pity that this thing had become so fouled and blundered and botched. It was a pity because he had nothing against the old man, and nothing personal against this strange memsaab who was not even of the family on the farm. The little boy was stirring now. And the horses had had another thirty seconds to run. It was all a pity, but it could not be helped.

He went over to where the bloodstained *simi* lay and picked it up. Then he walked back over to where Kathleen Crane lay unconscious and tilted back her head. Tensing her neck muscles with his left hand, he cut her throat carefully, and then wiped the knife-blade on her blouse.

Then he walked over to the little boy. He took rope from round the waist of the still-unconscious Kisu and bound the little boy carefully, and then ripped off the blouse of the dead white woman to make a gag which he expertly stuffed into the little boy's mouth. The little boy was conscious now —his eyes were dumb with horror.

Then he stooped over his assistant, Kisu, and shook him. There was no response, so he took him by the shoulders and dragged him closer to the water. He scooped handfuls of water on Kisu's face until he opened his eyes. Nyani slapped him repeatedly until he muttered 'Stop!' and sat up.

'Where is my knife?' he asked dazedly. 'What—where——'

'Get up, fool,' Nyani said. 'Collect your wits. You have killed the old man. I have killed the white woman. We will hang if they catch us. We must take the boy and run, now. There is plenty of time still to meet my brother.'

Kisu scrambled to his feet and looked around him at the bodies. Then his eyes lit on his knife. He picked it up and slid it carefully into its scabbard.

'You killed the white woman,' he said dully. 'Why did you kill the memsaab?'

'I killed the memsaab because you killed the old man, fool,' Nyani said. 'She saw it all. She knew our faces. She could have identified us and testified against us. This way we are clean. We have only killed an old man who had not much time to live, and some strange white woman. They are nothing to us dead. Alive, they would hang us both. Come, take the little boy's feet and I will take his shoulders.'

'But you killed the white memsaab,' Kisu muttered foolishly again. 'I do not understand why you had to kill the white memsaab.'

'She is dead,' Nyani the Baboon said. 'White or black, she bleeds the same as you or me. Come, hurry with the boy. We must not be late and get my brother in trouble with his machine. We have only lost a minute or so of the time we might have spent if all had gone well.'

CHAPTER TWENTY-TWO

WHEN NJEROGE regained consciousness he was aware first of a throbbing head and second of his bound wrists and third that his old bones were aching on the hard floor of the back end of a pick-up truck. It was night; he could see the stars. There was a man in the back of the lorry with him; it was fat Kungo the mechanic. Njeroge rearranged his addled wits. It was Kungo who had called from outside the door. He had said that one of Njeroge's wives was sick. Then blackness had descended. From the feel of his head somebody had hit him very hard with a club. If Kungo had been there, then Kungo would know who had hit him with the club.

'Who hit me, Kungo? And why am I tied up?' The old man's voice was plaintive.

'I hit you,' Kungo said in a pleasant voice. 'And I tied you up. Other people helped me with this motor-car.'

'But why? And where are you taking me?'

'We are taking you to an oathing, old man. It is an oathing in your honour. It is designed to cure you of being a white man's nigger. Very important people are interested of curing you of this ill. You are to be made what they call an "example". It is a bigger oathing than the one your daughter attended. Many people will be there—from this *shamba* of which you think you are presently the Bwana, and from the big *shamba* Glenburnie. One of the principals in this oathing comes from Glenburnie.'

'What are you to do with all this?'

'I am the chief oath-administrator for the whole Nyeri area,' Kungo said. 'I have not changed. I was a Mau Mau before, and I did not get caught. I am a Mau Mau now. They may call it the Land Freedom Army and the GKM and other names, but it is still Mau Mau. We are still bound by the old oaths we took years ago in the forests. We are going to a place I know in the forest now. It is the place your daughter was taken for *her* oathing.'

'How can you know of that oathing?' The old man's voice was surprised. 'You were not there. *I* was there and did not see you.'

'I arranged it,' Kungo said. 'I arranged it as I arranged most of the things which have happened on your farm, Bwana Nigger. I arrange goats in gardens; I arrange the hacking of sheep: I arrange all sorts of little accidents. I would have arranged to take the youngest child of Bwana Bruce but the timing was not right. It is of no importance. We have another child—a black one.'

'What will you do with this child?'

'It is not so much what I will do as what you will do. You will eat him. It will cure you of your illness. You will eat him and you will be oath-bound as a result.'

'I will not take any oaths or be party to anything that is vile,' the old man said with a firm voice. 'This of the child is filthy. You people are no better than beasts. I have seen what you do—fornication with animals and the drinking of unspeakable things. I saw my daughter take part in such an oathing. She was a good girl; she hanged herself rather than live with such sin and shame.'

'You will take the oath, all right,' Kungo said. 'And if you do not the effect will be the same. You will be killed for not taking the oath, and the word will spread that this is what happens to the tame Africans of white men. You will be a sort of hero to the "loyal" Kikuyu—the dead father of your country.' Kungo spat. 'When we are finished the only "loyal" Kikuyu will be *dead* Kikuyu. The ones who live will eat the oath. This is no rattle-brained gangsterism like the old Mau Mau was. This is big business. It is a big snake with many heads. Its body lives in Nairobi, but its heads are in all the towns and on all the farms.'

Njeroge shook his head.

'I still do not understand. What do you hope to prove?'

'Only to re-establish the true faith. This is the Africans' country. The white man must go. And what is very important, *black* men with white hearts must change or die. You must eat the oath and become a Kikuyu again. The child is chosen for one reason only. He was the son of a Mau Mau leader who was slain. The child has been reared as a white man rears his children. The child's skin is black, but his heart is white. You will eat the child's heart and the child's brains. You will eat and you will swear. The child's soul will return to his fathers, his body will inhabit your body, and your brain will return to the old ways of thinking.'

'I am not all that important. And a little dead boy is only a little dead boy.' Kungo laughed.

'You think so, do you? Well, I will tell you something. Our master in Nairobi does not want you to succeed as a substitute for your precious Bwana Bruce. And most especially does he not want the big *shamba* Glenburnie to succeed in this great scheme they have been hatching to give the land to the workers—to convert the workers into slaves who can be corrupted to the *mzungu*'s uses. And when the word spreads through all Kikuyu about what will happen in these hills tonight, there will be no more nonsense of co-operating with the white man. Work will stop on Glenburnie. The *watu* will leave the *shamba* and return to the reserves. They will stop work and return to the reserves because it will be worth the life of a man—it will be worth the life of a man and his wife *and* his children—to co-operate more with such white schemes. This is the decision of our leaders in Nairobi. You and the child are prime examples for all of Kikuyu. It is a great honour, in a way.'

'I will not eat the oath; not if you kill me,' Njeroge said stubbornly. 'I do not care for this sort of honour.'

'Then we will kill you—rather unpleasantly,' Kungo said. 'Dead or alive, sworn or unsworn, you serve our purpose. Ah, the lorry is stopping. Wait. I will untie your legs. From here on you walk, but you will not run away.' He took the rope from the old man's legs and made a slip-noose in one end. He put the noose around Njeroge's neck and tightened it. 'It will do you no good to run,' Kungo said. 'I will be on the other end of this rope. And other men will walk behind us.'

'It is very dark to walk in the forest at night,' Njeroge said as he stretched his cramped limbs.

'I have a flashlight,' Kungo said. Then he shouted to the driver in the cab.

389

'Go back to Nyeri and pick up another load of people. There is time.' He twitched the rope round Njeroge's neck. 'Come on, old man. Come on, you other men.'

Njeroge watched the tail-light of the lorry blink as it went away.

'Will you have many people at the oathing?' he asked politely, as he walked ahead, stumbling in the dark.

'Some. Enough. Maybe a hundred. Perhaps fifty. It is hard to say.'

'I would not come willingly to an oathing at night no matter what,' Njeroge said. 'I do not like to walk around mountains at night. There are snakes and rhino and elephant here.'

'You would come to an oathing if somebody whispered that your firstborn son would be used in the next oathing if you failed to attend the one to which you are invited. You would come if an accident happened to your fattest wife. You would come, all right, and you would take the oath. It is after all an oath for your own good. It is an improvement over the old oaths in the days of the Mau Mau.'

'What would you have me swear, then, if I were to swear?' Njeroge asked. 'What do they demand?'

'The first part is the same as it used to be. You will hear it soon enough.'

'I would like to hear it now. Perhaps I might change my mind if you changed some aspects of the oath.'

Fat Kungo laughed.

'Only our leader in Nairobi has the power to change the oaths. This one goes as follows, I know it well, from long practice. I have earned many shillings off this oath:

> If I am ordered to bring my brother's head and I disobey the order, this oath will kill me.
> If I am ordered to bring the finger or the ear of my mother and I disobey the order, this oath will kill me.
> If I am ordered to bring the head, or hair, or fingernail of a European and I disobey, this oath will kill me.
> If I rise against Mau Mau authority, this oath will kill me.
> If I ever betray the whereabouts of arms or ammunition or the hiding-places of my brothers, this oath will kill me.
> If I disagree with the order of a superior and argue against it, this oath will kill me.
> If I co-operate in any way with the white man, this oath will kill me.
> If I am ordered to help free Jomo Kenyatta and do not, this oath will kill me.
> If I do not obey the teachings of Matthew Kamau and follow his orders blindly, this oath will kill me.

'There are some more oaths for the women, but they are sworn after they have been served sexually by the men. Their oath is that if they disobey our teachings in any way and sleep with a man, the man's body will kill them.'

'Who is this Matthew Kamau? I know of Jomo Kenyatta, of course, but I do not know of any particular Kamau.'

'Kamau? You must be very stupid not to have heard of him. He is our true leader. He is bigger than Kenyatta. He will rule the country soon. He is a very clever man, and a holy man. He is too clever for the white people who have tried to corrupt him with gifts of white women and property and motorcars.'

'He cannot be a holy man if he approves of blood oaths involving dead people and cannibalism, and of intercourse with animals, as I saw with my own eyes. I will not take his vows. I will not eat his oath. I am not a cannibal or a pervert or an animal. I am a man.'

Kungo twitched the rope again.

'Then you will shortly be a dead man; that is what I can promise you.'

'How will you kill me?' Njeroge's face was scornful, his voice almost disinterested.

'It is difficult to say. I should imagine that after we have broken your bones one by one, as one would break the bones of a goat, we will bury you alive. Yes, certainly. You are a plague, and all men like you constitute plagues for belonging to the bwanas. You are a curse on the land and we must return to the old ways and bury the curse—let it be washed away by pure water. I know just the spring for it. It is not far from where we are having the oathing ceremony.'

Njeroge braced his shoulders. His voice was shaky but dignified.

'Very well. Kill me. Bury me alive. I would rather be buried alive as a man than to live as an animal. And do not speak to me more, you dog and son of dogs, you hyena, you chameleon who bears evil tidings. Ngai will punish you. Your own filthy oath will kill you. That is all I have to say, dog.'

He strode on into the night, stumbling. The yellow light from Kungo's torch flickered out ahead of him. Soon the glow of fires showed redly in the sky. Soon he would meet his God, but he would greet him as a man who did not eat vile oaths by night. He was not afraid to meet his ancestors. They had all been good men, as he, Njeroge, was a good man. And good men did not eat vile oaths by night.

Njeroge spoke again. This time it was he who twitched the rope to hasten Kungo.

'Come, dog,' he said. 'Do not lag behind. It is unseemly, even for hyenas, to lag behind an old man.'

'Shut up and walk,' Kungo said. 'And that is enough talk of hyenas.'

'It is talk you will grow accustomed to,' Njeroge said. 'For it is as a hyena you shall surely live in all eternity.'

He strode on towards the firelight. He was an old man, and not afraid to die. He would not eat the oath.

WHEN HE heard the steady drumming of the red horse's hooves, Brian Dermott felt the old familiar twisting of his stomach muscles. He knew the horse would carry an empty saddle. He knew as well as if he were an hour older what he would find.

There was nothing he could do for or about Katie Crane. He knew that as soon as he saw the bodies—the headless Kidogo, the obscenely laughing red lips of wound on Katie Crane's neck. He only had to glance at the tracks for the story.

All the tales had been true, then. All of Don Bruce's fears for his children had been justified. It had all started again, but worse now—much worse than before. There was more thinking behind it; better organization. His aunt's plans for the farm were finished. He knew that as well as if it were next week or next month. The boy would be chopped up on some hillside in a few hours' time. There was no way to follow his trail. He would have been taken in a car. The Central Province of Kenya was large. The Aberdare was vast. The forests were black. There could be no tracking until morning. He did not care about the little boy, anyhow. It was a pity they had not followed the first inclination, those lost years ago, to knock the child on the head when they found it with his dead mother. If they had knocked it on the head Katie Crane would be alive now. Kidogo—old Kidogo—would be alive now.

He looked briefly again at the tousled silver-blonde hair, at the great grey eyes which were set and staring now. He could not bring himself to touch her. He did not want to see her again. He had no feeling of rage at the people who killed her. He only felt tremendously sorry.

'I'm sorry, Katie Crane,' he said aloud. 'I'm so dreadfully sorry. I only wish it might have been me.'

It was black dark now, with the first stars showing. He could not leave her alone in the dark. The hyenas . . . He would wait. He would have to wait. He slapped the grey horse on the rump and it trotted off towards home. When all three horses came in riderless they—Pip or George or somebody— would come looking. In the meantime he would stay here with Katie Crane, who had loved him, and with old Kidogo, who had also loved him, and who had been his father's friend.

But he could not leave her with her blouse torn off and her face—he would have to touch her. He took off his bush-jacket and arranged it over her upper body and her face. There was nothing to do about the old man's face or body.

He sat down then by Katie Crane and lifted her body in his arms, resting her covered head against his chest. He did not mind touching her now. He was still sitting in the same position when his brother-in-law found him half an hour later. George Locke had come in the Land Rover. Brian had been able to see its lights a long distance away, but he would not leave Katie Crane's body to call out and attract attention. If the Rover was looking for them it would find them eventually. It occurred to him that he had not touched a dead body for a very long time.

*

It was midnight and several of the necessary things had been done. The police had come, and the Provincial Commissioner, and the dreary afterbirth of death nearly cleaned away. The American consul-general had been called; Brian supposed the press had been informed. Certainly cables had been sent to Katie Crane's brother.

There was some talk of searching for the little boy Karioki, but it was half-hearted talk. Nothing much could be done about tracking in the middle of the night. The police were short-handed, as usual. They could not make a check of all the native labour lines in the dark. Everything would have to wait until morning. There was nothing to be done about sending Katie Crane's body home; there was no embalming facility here, and she were better buried swiftly. Autopsy was waived; the cause of death was more than evident. They put her in her bedroom until a casket could be made, and Brian laid what was left of old Kidogo in his own bed.

He felt completely emptied, now—and with it felt another, strange sense of freedom. He was free of the farm, free of all ties, free of love, free of life, free of obligation. He had lost the two things he came closest to loving in two strokes of a strange African's knife. There would never be any more Kidogo to weld him to the past, and there could never be any Katie to tempt him with the future.

He felt terribly sorry for Aunt Charlotte. Apart from her innocent responsi-bility in Katie's death—apart from her involvement with him—he felt terribly sad about Aunt Charlotte. For one thing there was nothing left for her in her dream of the farm. She would never be able to look at him again without thinking of all the troubles her own flesh, Brian Dermott, had brought upon her. He was finished on the farm, and in the life of his aunt, if only out of consideration for his aunt. No matter. There still remained George and Nell, Philip and Jill. Enough people for her old age.

Brian Dermott went to the strong room where the guns were kept, and collected a couple of rifles and his revolver. He went into the room where old Kidogo lay headless on the bed and got his tin safari box. It was already packed; it was always packed. He hoisted it up on one shoulder and went out a side entrance to where his Land Rover sat. Then he came back for his weapons. He could hear the family talking with the Bwana PC and the police, still. There was a rattle of glass as someone mixed a drink. Well, he was through with the drink. He was finished with everything. What he mostly did not want right now was to see anybody or say anything at all. He wanted only to go away—to get out. He did not know where or for how long, and did not care.

He started the Land Rover and drove quietly out of the yard. It was strange to be in the *gari* without old Kidogo. They had been welded so long as a

393

team in his mind—his car, his guns, himself and his man. Now it was only the car and the guns and himself. He would not think of Katie. He would not think of Katie with the lilting laugh, Katie with the tear-misted grey eyes, Katie with the occasional odd wry bluntness and self-teasing humour. Gentle Katie, loving Katie, *dead* Katie . . . poor dead Katie, who had loved the country so, and who wanted so dreadfully to love him so. And he had only been minutes away from telling her that she would be allowed to love him so. It would have been better for him if he had told her. He would never be able to tell her now.

It was strange that he had no inclination to drink. You would have thought that he might have been tempted to dive straight away into the bottle. He would never drink again. In some strange fashion he felt he owed it to Katie not to drink again. She had been such a very good chap about not drinking—she had looked after him when he was sick. From drinking. She hadn't nagged him. She had neither rebuked nor patronized him later. She had not despised him for being a weakling. She had merely loved him, or tried to. Poor Katie, who had tried to love him so.

He noticed with mild detached interest that the car had taken the north turning and was headed towards Nanyuki and Isiolo. That was good. He would go to his beloved north again. He could pick up the odd few necessities at the *dukah* at Isiolo or Garba Tulla or some place. He would go north and hunt elephant. He had one on his licence. It had been a long time since he had hunted elephant for himself. He might as well kill a fine elephant for himself. The way the Nigs were killing everything these days, he had better hurry and kill an elephant for himself. There was going to be an acute shortage of elephant soon, as there certainly seemed to be a growing shortage of good people.

Elephant? Why should he hunt elephant, to kill what he loved? It would be so much better if he hunted the people he hated, who would certainly be killing the elephant soon. He did not mean the men who had killed Katie. They were guilty of nothing more than being instruments. You might as well hunt the knife that killed as hunt the man who used it. He had no anger against the men. It was the well-intended people he hated; the politicians and the white weaklings in London—Jomo Kenyatta and the Colonial Office people and all the politicians everywhere. He hated Lumumba and Mboya and Iain Macleod and Prime Minister Macmillan and President Eisenhower and Nasser and—his capacity for hatred was unlimited. He hated nearly everybody who had changed the world away from his liking. He hated everybody who was going to have a hand in finishing the elephant.

No, it surely wasn't elephant that needed the hunting. Much more in point would be to drive north past Maralal to Lodwar, where old Jomo was still staked out by the government. He could hunt Jomo Kenyatta. He was on licence. He was after all the author of all this. When the last elephant died you could credit that to old Jomo, as well. It would be nice to take the old Burning Spear by his goat's beard and see if his neck held the same colour of blood that other animals lost. Poor old Jomo. He was past his prime and the young pups had come up in his wake—the smooth slick black bastards who wanted to run the country. It was such a nice country until they wrecked it with all these damned ideas about *uhuru* and freedom and self-determinism to poach everything. It was still a lovely country—what was it his aunt always said? Nothing wrong with it that couldn't be cured by killing all the politicians, black and white. If you killed the politicians you could maybe keep the game.

Brian Dermott was suddenly very sleepy. He pulled off to one side of the road and nosed his car into a bush. He would drive on when he woke in the morning. After all, he wasn't in any hurry. He wasn't going anywhere. That was something he shared with the country. The country wasn't going anywhere, either. Like the elephant. Very small future.

Dawn woke him with its cold breath. He did not know where he was for a moment. Then it all slid back into focus again—coldly, horribly into focus. That had not been a dream, then. For a moment he had hoped it was. Katie Crane was dead and so was Kidogo. It was all as real as his arm. He had been in a state of shock, he supposed, that merciful shock which blurs pain and blots sensation. That is how people stay sane, he thought. Shock. I suppose that's how a gutshot leopard feels. Shocked.

Well, the shock is gone and so is Katie Crane. All I am faced with is the idea of some endless days, endless years, living in a kind of vacuum, because everything I ever loved or wanted or needed has been taken away from me by those God-damned blacks. One way or the other the white man has been slave to those God-damned blacks. It's always the God-damned black who wins in the end. They killed Katie. They will kill the elephant and the rhino as well to make room for *uhuru*. The God-damned blacks.

My mistake was I didn't kill enough of them when it was legal. If the settlers had just had a free hand; if there weren't any United Nations; if the Americans hadn't pulled the rug out from under us in Egypt in '56 when we had Nasser on the run; if old Jomo hadn't been so clever that he came quietly when they arrested him; if they might have quietly shot Kenyatta, then——

A lot of time and life and trouble could have been saved if somebody had shot Hitler. A lot of time and trouble can be saved right now if somebody shoots Castro in Cuba. And as for that black son-of-a-bitch Kamau—Brian Dermott suddenly smiled a terrible smile. He *did* shoot animals for a living, didn't he? He had worked on animal control. He was really rather frighteningly good at his job: game control.

It is too late to shoot Jomo Kenyatta, Brian thought. But it is not too late to shoot Mr. Matthew Kamau. Mr. Kamau does not care what sort of eggs he crushes when he makes his omelet. Mr. Kamau and all the others like him do not care who gets killed in their rush to power. Mr. Kamau does not care whose wells he poisons, whose customs he perverts, whose lives he wrecks so long as he can have his *uhuru* and be a black king on a throne. Mr. Kamau thinks he is Jesus Christ; it would be interesting to discover whether he's immortal.

Of course, he thought as he drove, they hanged Peter Poole for killing that chap who stoned his dog. And I suppose they might hang the chap who kills the dog who has caused the death of this particular chap's life. The particular chap in question is me. Kamau has killed my life. He should be restrained from this sort of *amok*. In the public interest, of course.

I have nothing to lose. Perhaps now I can finally do the country a favour. Maybe they'll put up a monument to me some day—'Brian Dermott, Saviour of Kenya.' And in small print—'On such-and-such a date, Mr. Brian Dermott shot Mr. Matthew Kamau in the best interests of humanity. Mr. Dermott was hanged by an ungrateful government on such-and-such a date, but the nation prospered thereafter. Mr. Dermott made the shooting of politicians popular and it was not long before most of the members of the Legislative Council had been shot in various stages of undress by other selfless patriots. Several thousand elephant, rhino and worthwhile people survived.'

He grinned. He suddenly felt terribly light-headed and quite happy. He felt as if a load had lifted from his shoulders. He couldn't shoot *all* the Kikuyu —it would take too much time. Perhaps if you poisoned the water-holes? But right now he *could* dish Mr. Kamau with almost no trouble at all, and since he didn't have anything to live for it made no difference whether they hanged him or didn't hang him. It would be worth it just to see the expression on Mr. Kamau's face. Teach the son-of-a-bitch to go dancing with *my* wife. Teach the bastard to set his punks to killing *my* woman. Teach the sod to kill my elephants. Teach the bastard to stand aside when a white man passes. Off the footpath for you, chum. Teach all the other bastards to take it easy. We taught 'em once. Teach 'em again. Brian Dermott, patron saint of all the elephants. That's me.

Suddenly Brian Dermott began to roar with laughter. The whole thing seemed too utterly funny for words. He knew exactly where he'd shoot Kamau.

Brian Dermott could not seem to stop laughing. He hunched over his steering-wheel, and trod more heavily on the accelerator. He began to sing wildly: 'Get Me to the Church on Time', as he had sung it when he had driven in before to attend the hanging of Peter Poole. He glanced at his watch. If he really stomped on the pedal he would have plenty of time to go to the flat in Muthaiga and clean himself. He thought he would wear his hanging-suit again. It was hard to beat a decent blue for a solemn occasion. But he wouldn't want to be late. It would be a pity to keep Mr. Kamau waiting, so to speak, at the church.

BRIAN DERMOTT was not tired at all from the long drive from Isiolo to Nairobi. He had a wild sense of exultation—not a sensation akin to drunkenness, but more, he imagined, like having a really good skinful of marijuana. He revelled in the hot shower at the flat; he chose his necktie with care, and even selected a white, starched collar to go with the blue shirt and the blue suit and the sincere cravat and sober shoes. As always he gave minute attention to his nails. He did not take a drink.

There seemed nothing illogical to Brian Dermott about his plan to shoot Matthew Kamau. A man like Kamau needed killing. It was the Kamaus of the world who were responsible for all the troubles. That was what was happening to the elephants all over. Now Mr. Kamau would be trodden by an elephant of his own creation.

He looked at his watch. About lunch-time. A little early, yet, but he could sit and have a Coke at the Thorn Tree. It wouldn't make any difference if people came to commiserate with him. He just wanted to be there when Kamau arrived for lunch. He presumed that the foul-up on the farm was common knowledge to everyone by now, and that Mr. Kamau would have been out putting a flea in several ears all morning. Be nice if he came back to the hotel with one of his chums—that big Ndegwa or that slick 'Kamba, Matisia, who was his lieutenant. It had been a long time since he'd committed a really snappy right-and-left, Brian thought. A neat double in front of the Thorn Tree would make the oglers sit up, all right.

Good Christ, that reminded him. He hadn't fired his pistol in ages. He'd better have a look. He took out the gun, the blue-steeled Smith & Wesson thirty-eight, and unhinged the cylinder. Dust in the barrel, but clean. He shook the soft-nosed bullets out of the chambers and carefully reinserted each one in a different chamber. He swung the cylinder in with a click. The gun felt good in his hand, the cool checkered grip snug and well remembered. He supposed he might use a knife or a noose, and that was sort of *shenzi*. *Bure*. One didn't do that sort of thing at high noon in front of the best hotel in town, especially if one was wearing his best Sunday-go-to-meetin' blue. *Lèse majesté*, and all that sort of rot. There were some things a proper Sahib didn't do.

Well, that was about that. Brian shoved the gun back into its shoulder holster, and patted his coat over the bulge. It was as Kidogo had said—'like old times, Bwana. In the old days when we came to town you put on a necktie and a pistol.' Kidogo had asked that day if he were going to kill somebody when he had laid on the gun. My God! It was only just two months since they had hanged Peter Poole. Well, Kidogo, my old friend, if you asked me the same question today I would say a simple 'Yes', Brian said to himself. *Yes.* I am going to kill a black son-of-a-bitch of an African politician. In the interests of game conservation. At high noon in front of the Thorn Tree's Frenchified sidewalk café. *Pour encourager les autres.* These Wog politicians are always making great disturbances and producing demonstrations to create sympathy for themselves. Our Mr. Kamau never knew how much a sensation it was in his power to create.

Brian went down the stairs and climbed into his Land Rover. Are you quite sure you want to do this, Dermott? he asked himself as he slid into the traffic. There's no bounty on niggers, you know. You won't be able to sell the ivory. Yes, I am quite sure I want to do this, Dermott, he answered himself. I have nothing to lose but my neck. I am independently wealthy. I do not have to sell the ivory. Perhaps sentiment has changed. Maybe this is not the month for hanging white people for doing the odd Wog. Perhaps sentiment has changed in Whitehall in the last week. Perhaps Mr. Macmillan's winds of change have veered again as a result of his grousing trip to Scotland. Perhaps there is a fresh influence exerted by Paul Robeson on the conduct of American affairs. Whatever happened to Little Rock? Oh, a merry man am I, his brain sang, about to go and do something many people speak of wishfully but seldom ever accomplish. Banging down a politician. I mustn't wound him, he thought, I shouldn't like to have to follow him into the bush. Bugger might bite me.

This will make great headlines all over, he told himself again as he drove. I would imagine my safari trade will pick up considerably. This Kamau is as well known in America as Marilyn Monroe. What with poor Katie in today's papers and poor dear Mr. Kamau in tomorrow's, Kenya will be rather prominently discussed, I shouldn't wonder, for the next few weeks. Well, Auntie always wanted me to quit the safari business. I'm quitting at the top, with the clients clamouring for more. I'm quitting with the Number One trophy. I am shooting the original, woolly, curly-horned black galliwampus.

Maybe this will make me ultra chic. When the game's all gone, and there aren't any clients. Maybe I can book myself for a lecture tour on the strength of it all. Darkest Africa as I Knew It. How I Rid Myself of the White Man's Burden. Testimonials for Mr. Smith and Mr. Wesson. Wild Politicians I Have Shot. Go to Kenya and Blow Up with the Country.

Aha, here we are. We will just nip around old Lord Delamere—who would probably approve of me—and slip into one of those nice metred parking slots. Good old Lord Delamere. I'll bet that His Lordship doesn't know from his heavenly distance that I am possibly being quite constructively instrumental in his not being pulled down off his pigeon-spattered pedestal to make room for a Wog politico. Rest easy, My Lord. Be happy with the pigeons.

Brian Dermott walked around the corner, pausing to buy the *Nation* and the *News* and the *Standard*. The headlines told him blackly that all the world knew about Katie Crane at this moment. He'd just nip inside and ring up the leopard, in order to ensure that the beast was not in the tree. They were such nice carpets; he'd hate to mess up one of Mr. Block's pretty rugs. It wouldn't be elegant to shoot Mister Kamau in the suite. Not in front of the Bernard Buffet paintings.

A hush dropped on the drinking and eating crowd in the sidewalk café as

398

Brian Dermott walked through it and into the hotel. As he passed through the lobby, the receptionists stilled their chatter, and the boys in the lobby, the African porters and messengers, fell silent. Other people looked round at the silence in order to determine the cause. Looked, saw Brian, gasped, and quickly stared away.

Brian walked into the booth that housed the house phones and asked for Mr. Kamau. The operator said he did not think that Mr. Kamau was in his quarters, but he would ring anyway. Brian counted eight rings before he hung up. Mr. Kamau was not in. If Mr. Kamau was not in, he therefore was out, and he would return. If he returned, he would have to cross Hardinge Street or Delamere Avenue, and he would have to walk close to the little traffic island by the loading port in order to enter the front door of the hotel. There was a vacant chair—what a jolly fine idea this Thorn Tree open-air café was, especially on such a delicious bright day, with the breeze stirring lightly and the sun warm in the cloudless sky. It was so good to be alive. Katie would have liked being alive on a day like this. Brian would have liked having Katie alive on a day like this. So they could watch the elephants bathe together.

The waiter came hesitantly and Brian ordered coffee and a club sandwich. He was suddenly ravenously hungry, and he remembered that he had eaten nothing since lunch yesterday. No wonder he felt light-headed. Man's work demanded regular meals. No doubt about it, shooting on control wanted fuel for the engine.

He looked round him, lighting a cigarette. The tables were full of pretty, leggy girls and young men in shorts. Everyone was laughing and drinking tea or beer or Cokes. They were generally a handsome people, the Kenya people, he thought. Exercise and sport and fresh air does it. Like the Australians. Like Victor Mature. Even our Wogs are better-looking than the ones you see in the Congo and Uganda. Altogether first-class, tip-top, bung-ho, top-hole sort of types. White man's country, Kenya. That's what old Delamere called it. What a rough little cob he was. No nonsense about that one. Just like Gary Cooper. Yup.

The waiter had come with the coffee and sandwich. Brian produced money and paid the chit. He didn't want to stick the waiter with a check if there was going to be any confusion. Those poor chaps had to pay the cashier in advance for every order they served. That manager, Burrows, didn't trust anybody.

He noticed that several people were staring at him. One hand crept to his tie. It was securely knotted. He glanced at his shoes. He had remembered to put on matching socks. Perhaps it was because they were not used to seeing him in a blue suit on the morning following the murder of a client who had been a guest at his aunt's fabled farm. Perhaps they thought all white hunters should be drinking gin instead of drinking coffee and eating a sandwich just before they killed the country's leading politician. The sandwich was soggy. Too much mayonnaise. He'd have a word with Burrows about that some time. Soggy toast did nothing for a sandwich. Country was really going to pieces. Well, a Wog was a Wog, even in the kitchen.

He looked at his watch again. It was a good watch, and it said twelve-thirty. By this honest Rolex, Katie was alive this time yesterday, he thought, and hitched his shoulder holster around to where it rode more comfortably under his coat. His man should be along soon. Natives were creatures of habit, like animals. And certainly Mr. Kamau would show the flag in the Grill today—especially with all these headlines. He could not afford *not* to be on view.

Brian hitched his chair a little to his left, so that he could encompass a bit more of Delamere Avenue while still keeping his chief attention on Hardinge Street. That was one thing about hunting; whether it was leopard or man, bush-blind or a wire chair in the Thorn Tree, one mustn't ever allow one's attention to wander. He would just keep looking, and his man was almost certain to be along any moment now. And if he didn't arrive now there was always this afternoon and tomorrow and next week. Brian wasn't going anywhere. That was one of the nicer things about living in Kenya. You could afford to take your time.

CHAPTER TWENTY-FIVE

MATTHEW KAMAU arose and noticed with approval that the boy had brought both morning papers when he had come earlier with the tea. He would take them to the bathroom, as usual, before he rang down for his big breakfast. He chose the *East African Standard* for his first reading, and glanced idly at the headlines. What he saw destroyed any thoughts of going to the bathroom. He started to fling on his clothes, and changed his mind about using the telephone. It was early; Matisia was sure to be home.

He ground his teeth in frustration and anger as he read snatches of the story. Those bumbling fools!

No chauffeur-driven car today; he would take the little black Anglia he preferred for occasional anonymity. He kept it just round the corner in a covered alleyway. He did not need any witnesses to his visit to Matisia, and the big Cadillac always attracted attention. But he would ring from a public phone on the way out to Hurlingham.

Matthew Kamau drove with intent care as he headed the little Ford out towards the Hurlingham suburb. He did not drive much any more, and his motions were jerky. Also his legs were too long for the seat adjustment on the smaller car. His brain seethed. This kind of accident was the one thing he had not counted on. What was the bloody woman doing at Glenburnie farm anyhow? She had been a safari client; the paper said she was enormously rich and very social in America. That meant that the periodicals he lived by, that he had made his reputation from—the news magazines, the *New York Times*, the *Herald-Tribune*—all the big papers, would have reams on reams of stories, none of which would reflect credit on him or the country.

No one would pay any international attention to the disappearance of a small boy from an African farm; that sort of thing happened all the time. But just see the fuss they had made over the shooting of that newspaperman, that fellow Orde, in the Congo! And he was only a foreign correspondent, whose duties lay in expected danger. Fancy the flap when a Kenya killing involved the Social Register, Dun and Bradstreet, Palm Beach, a young and beautiful woman, white hunters, darkest Africa—my God! The press would be swarming round like vultures again. He set his face in a mask of impotent rage. Bloody, stupid fools! *Why* did they have to kill *her*, of all people? Better to have let the little boy go; they could always have collected him on another night. Fools!

Here was the petrol station. It would have a pay phone. He walked inside and dropped his pennies in the box. Matisia's voice answered sleepily.

'You know who this is,' Kamau said sharply. 'I must see you immediately. Get rid of that woman. Send her on an errand. It does not matter about the houseboy. We will speak English. Ten minutes. Good-bye.'

He drew his car into the driveway of Abraham Matisia's little stucco house and braked it to a bucking halt in front of the steps. He did not bother to close the car door as he leaped out, but mounted the steps in a series of angry bounds. He paid no attention to the Cape chestnuts or to the bougainvillaea —he did not notice that the lawn was neatly clipped and the frangipani still in flower.

'Matisia!' he called, in his deep voice, and hammered on the door. Matisia, in open-necked sports shirt and slacks, with sandals on his feet, met him.

'Come in, come in, Matthew,' Matisia said. 'I have sent the woman away. I have also sent the houseboy to the market. We are alone here. Do you want some coffee? It is still early——'

Kamau flung himself into a chair.

'No, I don't want any damned coffee. You have seen the papers!' He flapped a copy of the *Standard* angrily. 'Don't tell me you haven't seen the papers!'

'I have seen the papers. It is most regrettable. Those bloody apes'—he made a curving, negating gesture with his palm—'What can you do when you must use fools to run errands? Of course there was no way to know that the woman and the old man would be there . . .' he let his voice die. 'I cannot do everything myself. There had to be some synchronization between the other old man and the boy. That wants different people in different places.' He shrugged. 'I'm sorry, but it was one of those things, Matthew.'

Kamau looked at him balefully.

'One of those things! Do you know what this can cost us in America? In the world? This is not some nameless missionary that your gorillas cut the throat of! This is Kathleen Crane, whose other name is Drake! Your men cut the throat of half the money in Wall Street! They slit the throat of Palm Beach and the Racquet Club! Fools!'

'Fools indeed,' Matisia said smoothly. 'I will take steps to see that they will cut no more of the wrong throats. By nightfall I should imagine that their bodies will be found prominently in the reserve, with notes pinned to their own cut throats. It will be made to look the work of settlers. I thought that I would supervise this little chore myself.'

Kamau grunted.

'I think you can think of something a mite more original than that. I should suggest crucifixion or something more poetic—possibly soak them in petrol and set them alight in their own huts!'

Matisia paced, nervously, his hands locked behind his back.

'It is all very bad, I know. And the other event—that for which the boy and the old man were taken—was not so successful as I had planned. They used the boy, rightly enough, but the old man from the other farm did not swear. He refused. They had to kill him—and they also had to kill some others who refused. Also some few ran off into the bush. They will not talk, but they did not swear. My man came in the early morning to tell me. He was a man apart from the Glenburnie operation—he did not know about the killing of the white woman. I had just learned of that from the papers when you rang up. I'm afraid that we misfired here.'

Kamau smacked his fist into his palm.

'Misfired! *Misfired!* God Almighty! Bad luck, bad luck, bad luck! Well, what's done is done. I think we shall have to organize a few more episodes to upset the settlers. Things have been confused—the story of the woman could not have been on the news or safari broadcast last night. It is still early, and the people are just now reading the papers. Things would be in a state of disturbance and confusion with the police and the other confusions one has to make with unfortunate accidents. Let me see.'

'It is approaching midday,' Matisia said. 'Soon the Europeans will be gathering for their morning drinking at the Norfolk and the Stanley and on the farms. They will have had a chance to discuss the doings of last night— and the woman *was* a guest on the farm of this Dermott. Perhaps this Dermott, with his reputation as a drinker, and particularly as a wild one during the Emergency—you know he was twice decorated——'

'Yes, I know. I often go out socially with his woman when I am in London.' Kamau's voice was elaborately sarcastic. 'I also read the papers, especially when I am *in* them. Go on.'

'I was thinking that perhaps this Dermott could be put to some use. He is typical of the rougher element that worked in the pseudo-gangs and the KPR and in the irregular commandos during the Emergency. A bunch of cut-throats, all of them. And still dissatisfied—still angry about the old days. Perhaps . . .'

'It would be not too difficult, I suppose, for you to provide Mr. Dermott

402

and some of his friends with the names and descriptions of the men who were responsible for the death of the Crane woman and the old man—who, if I am correctly appraised, this Dermott held in even more esteem than he did the woman?'

Matisia grinned and lit a cigarette.

'It wouldn't be difficult at all. I keep my master list in my head. My oath-administrator for the area has not done so very well, either. He comes from the smaller farm, the farm from which we took the old man. It is unfortunate that Bruce, who owns the farm, is out of the country, as he is another of the Dermott stripe. But I should think that Dermott, after the first few drinks, would have small difficulty finding a few men who might be roused to extreme anger. Especially——'

'Especially if there were a few incidents in, say, Karen and the Kinangop, involving other white women. Not violence—fright. The usual letters and threatening gestures and perhaps an overturned car or two. The Crane woman was American and a tourist; her accidental death is not the same as if she were a Kenya woman. We could very easily make an accident look like the beginning of an epidemic. We would not need much to set off the younger settlers and some of the older hard cases who remember the easy days when you didn't even bother to report the death of a man you shot, so long as he was black.'

'I feel better now,' Matisia said. 'I was terribly upset over that business of yesterday. Maybe now we can turn it to our advantage. If so, all the better. She's only one more white woman. They have plenty to spare.'

Kamau got up.

'I am very displeased about the whole thing,' he said. 'Don't bungle this, Matisia. We want the death of the poor Mrs. Crane to be a regrettable accident for which the entire government, black and white, mourns. At the same time a certain amount of confusion could be started if the white toughs killed a few people—and if by some purpose an innocent meeting could be turned into a riot which would need quelling by white guns. We have not had a proper Sharpeville in Kenya. The time has come.'

Matthew Kamau turned to walk to the door.

'We only need one good riot to fix us a treat,' he said. 'Just one good juicy one. We will of necessity lose a lot of people. See if it cannot be arranged to lose a lot of deserving ones. And I would see if we could not deal as extensively as possible with the voting districts where KANU and KADU are stronger than we.' He grinned wolfishly.

Matisia put out a hand to stop his chief.

'Let me hear this completely straight, Matthew. You want the seeds of complete riot—of anarchy, even—but with all the blame to be put on the whites and the Indians and anybody else but us? You want it to be big enough and bad enough to be subject for troops? Troops from the Kahawa base, even? Machine-guns as well as tear-gas?'

'You grasp my meaning completely. I want the eyes of the world to turn sympathetically again to Kenya, where the white man is brutalizing the blacks. I want a fire to start that will make the Mau Mau look like a picnic. I want an anarchy, a state of siege—and I want a fire so hot that only I can put it out. And I want it before elections next year. I want it within a month, around the Christmas season—the sooner the better; I want it strong enough so that peaceful elections will come as a surprise, in February, and I will get credit for the surprise. I want the elections to be so peaceful that whatever potential threat I may have in check for after, involving the question of *uhuru*, will have the force of a sledgehammer in London. I want them to have a taste of what trouble can be if the government is *not* black and I am *not* at its head. Is that understood, once and for all?'

'Once and for all.' Matisia bobbed his head violently.

'No more mistakes, mind, or they'll be your last. Hear me?' Kamau pounded his fist into his palm.

'I hear you. Good-bye, Matthew. I will be in touch with you soon.'

'Wait until I call you. Don't ring me at the hotel. This is nothing I can help you with right now. And one thing more. I order you to get rid of that Belgian whore. We have enough complications. She can only cause more complication in the end.'

'That is unnecessary advice, Matthew. I realize it. I will tip her out shortly. I am sick of her, anyhow. A whore is only a whore, and there will be others who are younger and prettier. Don't worry about that.'

He followed Kamau to the door and watched him as he drove away.

'Sanctimonious bastard,' he muttered. 'All this trouble was his own idea. Serve him right if he slips some day. And when he does, I won't be there to catch him. But in the meantime——' He shrugged. His wrist-watch told him it was eleven-thirty. A gin and tonic wouldn't hurt him. He had a lot of work to do.

He was fixing his drink when he heard the bedroom door open, and Lise Martelis came out. He whirled and glared at her.

'I thought you had gone out!' he rasped at her. 'I don't like to be crept up on that way!'

Lise Martelis was wearing another of her dirndl dresses, and flat-heeled sandals. She held up a placating hand.

'Don't be cross with me, Matisia,' she said. 'I know you're upset. Is it something to do with what I read in the paper?'

'No, damn it, it's nothing to do with what you read in the paper! Why do you ask that! How would I have anything to do with what you read in the paper!'

'It's just that you seemed upset, and I knew Mr. Kamau was coming. That's why I came quietly in the back door. You were talking and——'

Matisia's hands shot out to her shoulders. He shook her until her hair flew back and forth, his fingers biting into the soft flesh of her upper arms.

'How long were you back? What did you hear?' He shook her again, then

404

released one shoulder and raised his right hand to strike her. 'Tell me, or by God, I'll——'

Her eyes went wide with fear, and one hand shot up to fend off the blow.

'I heard nothing, I tell you! Nothing! I saw his car was still here, so I came quietly round the back and let myself into the kitchen, and left my groceries there. Then I went into the bedroom to wait until I could hear his car leave. I know you don't like to be disturbed when you talk to Mr. Kamau, Matisia. I've done nothing wrong! Don't hurt me!'

Matisia dropped his hand and turned away.

'All right,' he said. 'That's all right. I guess I'm nervous—things like that happening—that in the paper. It makes us look very bad all over the world. As if we were only savages—— Forget it.' He drained his glass.

'I must go and change my clothes,' he said. 'I have much work to do.'

She stood with her arms at her sides, plumping face vacant.

'Will you be home for supper?' she asked.

'How the bloody hell do I know if I'll be home for supper?' he yelled furiously through the door. 'If I'm home, I'm home! If I'm not, I'm not!'

The bathroom door banged.

She went into her kitchen to put away the food. So he was planning to throw her out, was he, as he had told that Kamau there at the end? Get someone younger and better, eh? Sick of her already, eh? A whore is only a whore, eh?

Lise Martelis sniffled as she put her meat parcel into the refrigerator. She had become very fond of the little house. And besides, she had nowhere else to go.

CHAPTER TWENTY-SIX

MATTHEW KAMAU parked his car and walked back towards the hotel. He felt much better since talking to Matisia—much better. The man didn't panic, you could say that for him. Perhaps it was true that they could turn the whole sorry business into an advantage. The settlers were stupid—stupid and getting more nervous by the tick, if all he heard was true about secret organizations for defence and garden-party ladies attending a pistol-practice club. It shouldn't take very much to touch them off into a really explosive reaction against their dwindling days in Kenya—sufficient violence to get it read emotionally into the United Nations minutes. The thought of the implication of the big military base at Kahawa pleased him very much. There were two thousand five hundred crack troops at that base at Kahawa. If troops had to be called to quell a riot either way he couldn't lose. He didn't care if the troops rode down the whites or shot blindly into the blacks. Either way would

405

serve him well as long as it focused attention on England's last vestige of armed might east of Suez.

Matthew Kamau strode briskly along the pavement in Hardinge Street, pausing to look into shop windows. The short rains had evidently finished—there was much talk of serious drought. That pleased him, too. Any sort of natural catastrophe was useful in Kenya; it made the whites edgy, pressured the government, and drew world attention to the pathetic plight of the peoples. He could do with a bit of drought.

Well, now he was hungry. He'd go and have a spot of lunch, and then he would think seriously about Ndegwa. He supposed the time had come to call for a showdown with Stephen Ndegwa. It was just as well. A big confusion at this point, the shooting of the woman, later riots perhaps, martial law—would certainly convince Ndegwa that his old moderation was useless; that to talk moderation to Kenya settlers was useless. And to preach moderation to the black Africans who thirsted for *uhuru* was worse than useless. It was pitiful. He supposed he would call another general strike in aid of getting old Jomo loose. That was always good for some high feelings. No mistaking it, Kenyatta came in handy. You could always dust him off now and again to stir up the animals. So long as the Governor refused to let him out of open arrest in Lodwar the old man was useful, if a bit silly.

Matthew Kamau started across the zebra crossing and noted with approval that the white woman in the Volkswagen made a point of stopping while he strolled leisurely across the street towards the Thorn Tree. Two years ago a black man crossing Hardinge Street would have run for his life in front of white traffic. It was such a nice day; perhaps he would just eat a sandwich on the sidewalk today and watch the crowd.

He swerved slightly from the zebra crossing and headed for the entrance. He would have to buy more papers. He paused to allow a parking car to cut inside the island which protected the loading entrance, and as he waited, snapping his fingers, a man got up and walked towards him. The man was smiling, and looked familiar. He was dressed in a blue suit and he was someone Kamau had seen around Nairobi several times. That was the trouble with meeting so many people in politics; after a while everyone got to look alike.

He stood, smiling himself, bouncing lightly on toe and heel, a tall figure in a grey silk suit, waiting at the edge of the island. And now the man in the blue suit had headed towards him.

'Mr. Kamau,' the man was saying, smiling pleasantly, and Kamau smiled back. 'Yes,' he said. 'I am Matthew Kamau. You——'

'I don't believe we've had the pleasure of meeting,' the man said, still smiling, and Kamau felt suddenly that something was terribly wrong with the smile. 'We've not been properly introduced, but I believe you know my wife. Her name is Valerie Dermott.'

The man's left hand came out and rested lightly on Kamau's arm.

'Yes, I met——' Kamau started to say, and then his mouth dropped open, for the man had swiftly produced a blue revolver from a shoulder holster and had pressed it against Kamau's chest, pulling forcefully on his left arm. The motion was swift; the man's back was between Kamau and the throng on the sidewalk; they appeared to be talking as friends.

'I used to work on game control, Mr. Kamau, shooting vermin,' the smiling man said. 'I have come to prevent you from being a menace to other people's welfare. And that apart, I don't like the idea of your dancing with my wife,' the man continued levelly. The fingers viced deeper on Kamau's arm, and the pistol point dug into his flesh.

'Don't!' Kamau shouted, and flung up his free arm against the pistol. 'Don't, this is all a mistake——' His mouth was opening in the beginning of a scream when the man shot him in the chest, pushing him away at the same time he fired. Matthew Kamau fell staggering away and crumpled down to the pavement, clutching at his breast. He looked up with unbelieving eyes and said 'all a mistake . . .' as blood gushed chokingly from his mouth and his head sagged. He flopped over on his face and lay sprawled, his body jerking and his toes drumming gently against the pavement.

Brian Dermott looked briefly at the barrel of his pistol and holstered it in a smooth motion. He buttoned his coat, patted it in place, and was back at his table before the crowd could organize itself to do more than to gaze in horrified fascination. The people rushing out of the coffee shop at the crack of the pistol shot clearly heard Brian Dermott say in a quietly satisfied voice:

'Boy, another cup of coffee, please, while we wait for the police.' Brian Dermott lit a cigarette and gazed dispassionately at the quivering body of Matthew Kamau as it lay in a pool of blood, legs spraddled and arms outflung, on the pavement of Hardinge Street, just by the loading oasis of the best and newest hotel in town.

BOOK FIVE

VALERIE DERMOTT had just come downstairs in her robe and pyjamas for her morning juice and coffee when the telephone rang.

She coughed on the first cigarette of the day and reached for the instrument, which sounded unnecessarily raucous considering that she had no slight vestige of hangover. Her escort of the night before had departed after one weak whisky, and Valerie had gone off to bed with one of the duller contributions of a very uninspired season for mystery stories.

'Val?' It was Dawn Ethridge on the wire.

'It's not Madame Chiang Kai-shek.' Valerie produced a chuckle. 'Don't tell me you've another blind date for me. What's this one, a Chink?'

'Val, for Christ's sake, have you seen the papers?'

'No, Mrs. Thing is just bringing them with the coffee. Here she comes now—thank you, Mrs. Olcott—yes, I have them now, darling, what's upset you so?'

'Not upset *me*—upset *you*. For God's sake take a stiff gin or something and look at page one. Sit down while you look. I'm coming right over.'

'Wait a minute.' Valerie snatched the ink-smeary *Clarion* from the breakfast tray, and flipped back the first fold. There it was—all of it. One whole page of it.

'My God!' she gasped. 'My God!'

'Yes,' her friend's voice said on the other end of the line. 'My God!'

She stared unbelieving at the headline, at the huge picture of Matthew Kamau, at the smaller picture of Brian Dermott, at the picture of herself. She read the big type dumbly: it had to be true. Brian Dermott had shot and killed Matthew Kamau. And there again, unmistakably, was the garishly displayed picture of Valerie Dermott dancing with Matthew Kamau—the picture one of those vicious snoopers for the gossip page had snapped under the covering glare of someone else's legitimate flashbulbs.

The swift impression at first glance was that Brian had shot Kamau because of Valerie—and the older candid photo did not help to destroy that impression.

'My God!' she said again. 'I can't believe it!'

'*That's* what I said when I picked it up with my tea. Are you quite sure you're all right? I'll be there in half a jiff.' Dawn Ethridge rang off.

It was, Valerie was forced to admit even in a state of shock, still a striking picture of her and the dead man. It was obviously, very obviously, candid and unposed, but *what* a candid unpose. There she was, head thrown back, eyes half-closed in a movie star's leer, mouth parted in intimate laughter, white bosom flaunting, gazing low-lidded into the eyes of the handsome smiling Mr. Matthew Kamau, who was as black as his dinner coat. Her left hand rippled on the broadcloth of his shoulder, his left hand cupped her right hand tenderly. Her pelvis was thrown inward towards his hips; the other black hand cradled her hipbone possessively. He was looking down, smiling, in a most relaxed and very accustomed manner. Even the tilt of her head was a beckon, the invitation luridly strengthened by the lowered lids and the soft curve of her smiling mouth.

She stared desperately at the paper, dumbly memorizing the words of the story.

'Oh, God,' she said helplessly aloud. 'Oh, God, I didn't intend to do anything to hurt Brian again. It wasn't my fault. None of it has been my fault.'

Thoughts raced through her head. She could fly out to Kenya again, she supposed, but it wouldn't prove anything. Not at this stage it wouldn't prove anything. Divorced wives didn't prove anything by 'standing by' their husbands. Not with a bloody great picture in the papers of the wife dancing happily with the black man the husband had just shot. Not with her record of just having left Kenya for the second time. Her innocence of involvement had no bearing whatsoever on the fact that Brian had shot that Kamau man. She would just have to ride it out in London. If she went back to Kenya again she would be tacitly admitting that there *had* been something between her and Kamau. If that would help Brian it would be a different matter, but divorced husbands had no reference of righteous grievance.

Why had he shot him? Why, why? Whatever the reason, it wasn't her fault. It wasn't her fault if she couldn't stick Kenya, where everybody was always killing everybody else.

She thought as she ran blindly up the stairs to fall weeping on her bed that nearly none of the things you did that hurt people were ever really your fault. That was the trouble with the whole God-damned mess they called living. She wept until she heard the phone ringing. That, she supposed, would be the press. She had to face people some time. She might as well start facing people now, with her eyes unpuffed and chin up, as usual. She went into the bathroom to splash cold water on her pale face, and wondered what the ex-wives of prominent murderers wore to face the lip-licking London press. Probably the little black dress, but this time with not too much front showing.

It was a cute and comfy sort of cottage, Don Bruce supposed glumly—if you fancied huts. It was picturesque, true, under its canopy of Norwegian fir and the rowan-berry trees which sparkled like holly in a Christmas card. Its slanted peat-turf roof kept out the frequent rain and adequately contained the heat. It sometimes dribbled and in the rare dry would leak little waterfalls of dust, and was undoubtedly inhabited by rats.

It was a sweet little cottage, if you liked sweet little cottages, Don thought sourly as he parked the Land Rover in front of the door. It looked like Scotland. It looked as a gamekeeper's cottage in Scotland should look—hairy of board and silver-weathered to the Scottish countryside. It was a roof over one's head. It was shelter from the cold. It held fire and food and Peggy. That was all any house was, actually, when you came right down to it. A place of warmth and food and love. Pity there wasn't room in it for the kids, or for the furniture that they had shipped to England from Mombasa.

It was a fine cottage, really. They were lucky to have such a fine cottage. They were lucky to have any roof at all. They were lucky not to be in the spacious sprawling rooms of Hardscrabble Farm in Kenya. They were lucky not to be raking leaves on home relief or living off the bounty of Peggy's kin. They were lucky to be in Scotland, and Don Bruce was lucky to have found a good job so swiftly. Being a gamekeeper didn't pay much, except for the tips during the season, but with what Peggy made as a waitress in the Lodge, and with the rent-free house and the use of the motor-car thrown in, Don reckoned he should thank Ngai for the luck that had allowed them to settle so swiftly in a strange land. Don hated the cottage. He hated Scotland and he damned his good luck while being guiltily, consciously grateful for it. He put all that from his mind as he dismounted from the Rover and opened the door of the peat-roofed cottage he now called home near the Scots hamlet of Toumantoul.

Peggy Bruce, her round cheeks flaming from the heat of the blasting fire, plumped a plate of hot scones on the kitchen table and took the kettle off the hob. The door to the little crofter's cottage opened, and Don clumped in. He was wearing canvas gaiters and knickerbockers, a baggy tweed coat and a peaked tweed cap. His face was almost as red as Peggy's, but it was the raw wind-whipped red of the Scottish hills.

'Ah, ma braw bonnie laddie's back fra' the heels,' Peggy said, kissing him. 'Wi' his snitch as rosy as any meellionaire's fra' drinkin' the delectable dew o' the countryside. Do ye sit yeersel' doon, laddie, an' Ah'll fetch ye a mug o' tea.'

'*Jambo*,' Don Bruce said. 'And you can dispense with the low-comedy music-hall accent. Ah hae to speak it masel' wi' the sporrrts until I'm nigh to throwin' oop. *Shauri gani, Memsaab?*'

'*Mzuri kabisa*,' his wife said. 'It's no worse than muckin' the pigs back Home. We deal only in blooded gentry at the Lodge.'

Don tossed his cap in the corner. He walked over to the fireplace and spread his fingers in front of the blaze.

'I used to think that it was bitter on the Loita plains just before dawn—and possibly a touch colder at Maralal,' he said. 'But damn me if I ever saw anything like this Banffshire for continuing solid misery of wind and wet and chill. No wonder the Scotch are all drunks. You've got to stay potted to keep from freezing to death.'

'Now, now,' Peggy said, and went over to hug him in front of the fire. ' 'Tisn't as bad as all that. It was cold in Kenya, too. And we've been very lucky. Considering we only got here at the very end of the grouse season.'

'I suppose,' her husband said, and sat down at the table. 'My, these scones are good. I'm starved. A bracing day on the moors, et cetera. I wonder whatever Lady Chatterley *did* see in gamekeepers? They're a frowsty lot, it seems to me—seeing as I *am* one.'

'I think you're a lovely gamekeeper. And next season I shall be a lovely housekeeper over at Kilnadrochit. I've been promised. I shall minister to the inside appetites of the sports, whilst Honest Don the Gillie is leading them over hill and dale in search of Mr. Lagipus Scoticus, the most expensive bird in the world. I used to think safari cost money, but what these people spend to shoot eighteen ounces of feathers—wow!'

'The kids?' Don reached for another scone.

'Fine. Aunt Meg's being a double dear. It's really better for them. We do lead sort of irregular hours, you must admit. I never realized that being a waitress, even a fashionable sporting sort of waitress, cut up the day so. I must fly after the tea. I just skipped over to see my boy for a second.'

'I suppose. Well, the shooting's over shortly, and we can squeeze 'em all into this palatial manor-house of ours. I mean, four kids and two adults in two rooms isn't so terrible when you consider what a big living-room the kitchen makes. I've asked permission to tack on another couple of rooms, and the Laird allows all richt. I am becoming an excellent gamekeeper, I must say. Naught but praise for my way with the wee beasties.'

'It is sort of funny, when you come to think of it. Don Bruce playing nanny to old purple-faced gentlemen in knickers who come to shoot little birds. Does the urge to go on about elephant ever overcome you?'

Her husband grinned at her.

'Nay, lass. The wind up ma wee kiltie drives the thought of elephant from ma wee tiny mind. Also I am too concerned with things like braeberries and bearberries and sphagnum moss and strongyle worms and heather beetles and whortleberries and bog myrtle and white quartz and strongylosis and coccidiosis, not to mention crows, hawks, weasels, gulls, owls, foxes and ferrets. Not to mention poachers. Not to mention sex mania in the male grouse that wears out the cockbirds and ruins the clutches. I haven't worried about all these things yet, but I'm told I'll have to. I never knew before that a bloody Scots grouse was such a delicate critter.'

Peggy sat down at the table and poured herself a cup of tea.

'Seriously. I think we're dead lucky, my boy. Straight off the plane and bang into a job which at least keeps you out in the open and gives you some mountains and water to look at and some game to work with. How most wonderfully entirely fortunate we are, darling—if only because there's good schools for the kids and game and fish and fresh air.'

Her husband lit a cigarette. He looked upward at the peaked roof.

'I suppose it's better than leaf-raking, at that. Although you can't say we'll get ourselves rich off the wages . . .'

She rose and patted the top of his head.

'It'll get better. And when the kids are bigger, maybe things will have straightened themselves out, and we can go Home again.'

'That's twice you've used the word *Home*,' he said. 'I used to laugh at second-generation Kenyans referring to England as "Home". Now we live in England, if Scotland can be considered a part of it, and you speak of wild-and-woolly Africa as "Home". Sort of pathetic.'

'It isn't pathetic, really. We're here and we're intact. We've both got jobs of sorts, and there's more than enough money coming in so that we don't have to disturb our little hoard. I don't mind waiting table. It's rather fun, when you consider we were both brought up with a slew of Africans to fetch and carry for us. Now come on. Finish up your tea and drop me off at the Lodge. I think it's jolly fine we've the use of a Land Rover. Wee bit of reminder of Home. You go and have a few drinks at the pub and read the papers or something and then come back and make your supper. It's all ready.'

'Not cold grouse again? The stomach reels.'

'Yes, cold grouse again, from the master's deep-freeze. It's better than feeding them to his minks. Cold grouse and salmon—for God's sake, Don Bruce, do you know what that costs at the Savoy, and you're complaining?'

'All right. Count your blessings. Come on, old lady. I shall conduct thee to thy scullery.'

'I won't be a minute.' She bent and swiftly kissed him again. 'It's not really so very bad, Bwana. Think of the lovely free scenery and all the crows and hawks you get to shoot. It's really a kind of game control if you think of it that way—if you can see a weasel as a leopard and consider a hawk to be a marauding elephant.'

CHAPTER THREE

DON SAT in the local in Toumantoul, beetling over his pint and absently listening to the wireless. It was a good warm dark-panelled-and-pewter pub—friendly owner, friendly, common Scots regulars, the salt of the

415

earth, the Scots. They had been very friendly. Of course Peggy had her people here, and that helped, and you never went far wrong if your name happened to be Donald Colin Bruce in the European version of the White Highlands.

Everyone was very much interested in Kenya; they were more than interested when it became known that Don was a white hunter as well as a farmer, and that he had been active in the Mau Mau campaign. They were somewhat vague on Kenya tribes and African politics, but their interest in all game was keen, since the estates of Richmond and Gordon and Strathavon were all centred in the area, and the grouse and salmon were second only to whisky distilling as a local industry.

And the country was absolutely lovely after you got used to the weather. The scenery *did* make up for it—the heather misty purple on the craggy hillsides, the little burns laughing silver into the lochs and rivers and the rosy side of salmon turning to the hatch—the red-berried rowan trees and the tall deep-black firs. And if you twiddled a knob in your brain, the lovely green pastures stretching away, with their dots of cattle, brought you sharply back to the Masai country. The swans swimming in the lochs might even be spur-winged geese if you expanded the point sufficiently.

And it *was* outdoors. All his life Donald Bruce had lived outdoors. He did not think that he could have stood it if he had been forced to find work in some stuffy office, dealing with pieces of doleful paper which described intangible dull business transactions—a dry, musty life of prune-faced clerks and stale old-maid secretaries and deadly monotonous routine. Not Don Bruce, who had spent his life on and off the farm with animals. *Farm*: he closed his mind to the word. He did not want to think of what might be happening on Hardscrabble, his beloved, back-breaking, heart-breaking Hardscrabble that he had left after the oathing and the slaughter of his sheep had put the clincher on his decision not to risk his family further.

He never wanted to think of all the toil he had sunk into that greedily demanding property in the green Kenya hills, with its surrounding dark forests and menacing mountains and gleaming ribbons of chuckling water, so like these Scottish hills which had given the name Highlands to a long high ridge of savage Africa—so alike, even to the belt of heather on the high Aberdare. Only the people and animals and birds were different. The most dangerous beast in these Scottish hills was an occasional snorting Ayrshire bull; the most dangerous man a visiting sportsman whose overnight intake of whisky made him parlous with his shotgun as he fired down a line of butts or into the approaching beaters.

He did not want to think what was happening to the farm with old Njeroge in charge. Njeroge was a good man, but a Wog was a Wog, and they just didn't know how to take hold like a white man. Intentions were fine, but the implementation was weak. Evidently, though, the old man was having some fair success in his moonlight operation with the sheep. The first money had come in from Ken Jenkins in Brian Dermott's office—evidently Njeroge had slyly sold the sheep to some Indian or rich native and had faithfully delivered the money to Ken.

For some reason Don was stubbornly holding to the farm, even if it went to rack. He had enough money to meet the Land Bank interest payments for another year or so; he would ride it out and see what he would see. Maybe things *would* ease up after the elections—maybe things would straighten out and it would be possible to live decently or at least safely under a black government. Nineteen sixty-one would tell the story. Tanganyika seemed to be working out quite well under Nyerere, and there was talk of full independence in '61 for Tanganyika. That was when the crucial moment would come—not during the approach to *uhuru*, but when the country was literally handed over, and the Wog found himself in full control. That's when the stuff had hit the fan in the Congo; that's when the real gouge-and-grapple for power among those triply God-damned African politicians began. That was when the country had its fattest chance to plunge to perdition in a handbasket— that was when all the old scores would be paid, that was when all the old grudges and blood feuds would be settled and to hell with the innocent bystander.

Don sipped his beer and looked at the dartboard. It was a fine, old, well-pitted cork board. This was a good pub; it reminded him very much of the one at Kitale, a place of dart-throwing and wireless-listening and jokes and an occasional rude song and quiet draughts-playing and bread and cheese and hard-boiled eggs and 'Time, laddies, if ye please, we dinna want the constable upon us fra' misconstruin' the Queen's laws.' . . .

It was a fine country, Scotland, and there might be some way he could wangle a firmer hold on it. And it was *safe*. The climate was harsh, perchance, and the people bleakly rugged, but it was *safe*. He slept well o' nights, because he knew that his Angus and Ellen and Janet and Jockie were all snugged in with Peggy's Auntie Meg Ashcroft, after whom Peggy had been named. The other older Margaret was a seasoned stout widow, her own chicks grown and flown, and she seemed glad to fold the Bruce brood under her wing until such time as things settled a bit more. They had already entered young Angus in school, his first year, and Ellen would go next year. He'd just nip round after a while and have a bit of a romp with his kids. He and Peggy didn't see them much together, because she still worked at the Lodge on Sunday while the season lasted, but between them they managed a good couple of hours a day with the sprats. Count your blessings, Bruce.

'. . . in Nairobi, Kenya,' the radio was saying and the bulky barman was nudging him—'Stop yeer woolgatherin', Bruce ma lad, it's yeer ain land they're talking about the noo'—'throat cut and native servant murdered. Kathleen Crane, an American heiress, was found murdered on the large estate Glenburnie near Nyeri in the White Highlands of Kenya together with a native bearer. A small native child who accompanied them was kidnapped and has not been found. Meanwhile, in New York, Premier Khrushchev said today that . . .'

'Nosty bit o' worrk, that,' the barman said. 'D'ye ken the area?'

'Aye, I know the area,' Don Bruce said. 'Will there be more on the wireless? I *was* woolgathering . . .'

CHAPTER FOUR

THE PAPERS had been soaked with nothing else for several days. Sitting before the fire in the cottage after Peggy finished her chores at the Lodge, they talked of little else.

'The little boy was meant to be our Jock, of course,' Don said. 'When it wasn't possible to take our Jock they switched intention to that poor little black chap Brian and I brought home from the wars. I told you, Peggy—the day they fixed the sheep, after I'd got back from Charlotte Stuart's—I saw the little chap playing in the yard. Poor little blighter. And poor old Kidogo. No wonder Brian went up the spout and did for Mr. Bloody Kamau. And now I suppose they'll hang Brian as they hanged Peter Poole. Poor, poor bastard. God, we're well out of that mess.'

'I thank God you had the guts to make us leave, Don. I was all for staying on, remember. I'm just so terribly sorry about Brian. I suppose he and that poor girl were having something more than just a safari jolly-up. Else he wouldn't have taken her home. But I wonder why he picked on Kamau of all people?'

'I suppose if he'd had a chance at Jomo Kenyatta or Tom Mboya he'd have done either or both,' Don said. 'I imagine he just slammed the first representative Wog he saw. Remember how very hostile he was to Kamau and that other chap, Whatsisname—Ndegwa—that time we all got tiddled at the Stanley, the night they hanged Poole? Barged into them full tilt on in the lobby. I remember you gave him a tidy dressing-down about it.'

Peggy Bruce nodded.

'I wish I hadn't. Some things were chewing at him even then. Something must have bitten even more deeply, and to lose this Kathleen Crane and old Kidogo in one shot—no wonder.'

'I wonder if he was drunk when he did it? Knowing Brian, I'd bet he wasn't. He meant to kill Kamau, if I can make anything out of these bloody-awful papers, and he didn't give a damn about getting caught. Well, Charlotte Stuart told me that day I called on her that Ndegwa had hinted of something like this happening. I wonder . . .' Don paused, and drummed his fingers.

'You wonder what, sweetie?'

'I was just wondering about the farm—our farm. I wonder if anything else's happened there. God knows they were working us over hard enough

418

just before we left. There's been no word in the last week or so from Ken. It would be about time for Njeroge to send some more bootleg money. I think I'll shoot off a signal to Ken and ask him to run up and see how the farm's doing. And I wish . . . I wish——'

'Tell me what you wish.'

'I wish I was there. It seems so—so sort of cowardly to be sitting here all safe and snug with those bastards doing us in the eye. And poor bloody Brian. I just somehow can't make myself conceive of the idea of them stringing him up.'

'We don't know they'll hang him,' Peggy said.

'They hanged Poole, and all he killed was some cheeky houseboy. My chum has just dished the biggest Nig politico in Africa. They'll hang him, all right. Politics says they *have* to hang him, or they'll let the Whitehall side down. This is definitely not the year for killing coons in Kenya.'

Peggy got up and moved the coffee-pot closer to the coals. She stopped at her husband's side and put her hand on the rough thatch of carroty hair.

'See here, my boy,' she said. 'You *knew* something like this was coming. Perhaps you can damn me for female practicality, but so long as somebody had to collect it in this I'm glad it was the black child and not *my* baby. I'm glad it was the American woman and not *me*. I'm glad it was old Kidogo instead of old Njeroge. And I'm glad it's Brian they've got in jail instead of my man Bruce.'

Her husband reached up to catch her hand.

'I know. I know. I'm glad we left. It's just that I feel as if I'm shirking—hiding from my proper responsibilities at Home. Anyhow, I'm writing Ken. There's bound to be trouble all over and I'd like to know what the picture is on our *shamba*.'

'All right. But now let's go to bed. You've crows to shoot in the morning, my lad, and ferrets to trap. And I have to do something drastic about my dish-pan hands. Come on, gillie, off to bed we go.'

CHAPTER FIVE

EVIDENTLY THE letters had crossed. There was a letter in the post a week later, containing most of the surface details of the shooting of Kamau and the murder of Katie Crane. Towards the end a paragraph leaped from the letter.

'Listen to this,' Don said. 'Ken says: "On the same night that the poor Crane girl was chopped, your man Njeroge disappeared from Hardscrabble. The reason I know is I drove up to see how fared the farm, because old Njeroge had told me on his last trip in with the money that he was going to

419

make another sale soon and would have some more lolly for me to send you.

' "In all the noise about the knifing and, of course, poor Brian's dramatic dealing with the flower of our political flock, nothing much was mentioned about anything else. But it seems that your man Njeroge was taken from the farm the same night they hacked up Mrs. Crane and killed Kidogo and made off with the little boy. The suggestion was that they were both used in one of those filthy oathings.

' "This suggestion was made an eventual fact when one of your men, a sort of mechanic-handyman named Kungo——" '

'Kungo! Fat jolly Kungo!' Peggy breathed.

' "—named Kungo was found with his throat cut, and impaled on that now-famous spear-blade gate of yours. The note on him read: 'This is what will happen to all oath-givers in this area. This man led the oath-giving where the body of the boy Karioki from Glenburnie Farm was used against Njeroge the headman of this farm. Njeroge would not eat the oath so they killed him. Other bodies will be found on other fences soon.' And the intended suggestion was that his killing was the work of a white man. If *you* had still been here that might have been logical——"

'Not only logical, but a dead certainty,' Don interrupted himself;
' "—logical, but as you weren't, the PC thinks that it was a black job and that somebody just erased Brother Kungo as a safety measure. There have still been no discovered signs of any oathing, but that doesn't mean anything. It's a mortal cinch that your Njeroge and the little boy Karioki are both dead. They certainly weren't kidnapped for ransom, and by now they'd be settled anyhow if only as nuisances. The PC thinks that the kidnapping of Njeroge and the little boy from Glenburnie was a nasty plan to discourage black initiative on both properties—Njeroge on yours, and the whole bleedin' project at Glenburnie.

' "If this is the case, they certainly succeeded, because there's scarcely a Wog left on your property, and they have departed *en masse* from Charlotte Stuart's operation. It is difficult to get anyone to watch over your place, because if there ever *was* a magic ring round Hardscrabble, it surely no longer exists. The cops have moved in with a token force, but that's all that keeps the place together. If I were you I'd just let it slide back to the banks. . . .

' "Nobody I know has seen Brian since they tucked him away in the jail. I think that his brother-in-law has been or will be allowed to visit him with a lawyer, but who the lawyer is has not been announced as yet. It's not exactly a case which will cover the defence with glory. I've tried to see him, as manager of the firm, but so far no dice. I do know they've got a special guard more or less chained to Brian's wrist—I play golf with one of the prison officers— and that there's a very heavy police guard around the prison proper. They don't want to risk a lynch mob of a few thousand Kikuyu, I gather.

' "The town is very sinisterly quiet, and so are the reserves. The townies have left by thousands, and I believe a lot of the farm labour has departed for the ancestral acres on the reserves, as well. Everything is tense, but no real outbreaks of violence, and no massive demonstrations in favour of the dead Kamau. I thought by now they'd have a statue built to his memory. But they planted him quiet on the lone prairie, and flowers were omitted, please.

' "There's a lot of talk, of course, especially among the country people. Marie's mother is the same—she says this could never happen in South Africa. Wait until that one pops—zowie!

' "There's very little I can do for Brian or for you. Except there should be some instructions about the farm. Should what's left of your stock and equipment be sold by auction and the proceeds applied to your various debts, or what? We can't very well sell anything else on the sneak now. Write and let me know what I can do. Meanwhile, love to pretty Peggy and the kids, and consider yourself a very lucky boy to have got out with your neck—yours and Peggy's and the kids'. We're scared stiff at my place—the old girl sits up with a shotgun and damned near ventilated me the other night. Poor, poor Brian.

' "Ever thine,
Ken."

' "PS. . . . There have been a few cancellations in safari bookings since the big noise hit the papers. Evidently the rich millionaires don't feel that Kenya has the proper respect for rich millionaires any more. When they killed poor Mrs. Crane, they came close to putting money out of style. It's just as well; as tight as things are now, we'll soon be back to the barter system. I'm thinking of trading in my mother-in-law for anything at all." '

Don tossed the letter onto the table and walked over to a cupboard where a half-bottle of the country's still uncoloured high-proof whisky stood. He poured himself a neat dollop and tossed it off.

Then he looked round the homely cottage room—the peat fire in the fireplace which served as stove and heating system, the crudely adzed beams, the rough cobbled floor, the single table with its checkered cloth, the sink and the row of hooks on the walls and the pile of books and papers in a corner. Home, he thought bitterly. And fit for a bloody gillie, at that. Home, and lucky to have it. He thought then as swiftly of his own handcrafted house in Kenya, the lovingly fitted cedar beams, the great streaked cedar walls, the cunningly plaited cane, the vast fireplace, the shelves for his books, and Peggy sewing in a corner while he read up on his farm literature, whistling in another room. He thought of his yard with its circle of whitewashed stones and Peggy's flowers—and he thought of it that day it was overrun with goats, all the loveliness spoiled, all the planning wrecked.

He thought of his manicured acres, so painfully grappled from the bush. He thought of his drainage system and his windbreaks and his neatly fenced paddocks, his well-kept barns and his carefully prepared land that grew what he ordered almost when he ordered it. He thought of his native-labour housing settlement; of the new houses with the tin tops and the convenient wells. He thought of his butchered sheep, and he bit his pale lower lip until the blood ran. He clenched his fists and the breath whistled through his nostrils as he snorted like a buffalo. The freckles stood out like copper coins on his wind-burned fair Scots face.

'Old Njeroge,' he said slowly. 'Poor old chap. So they fixed him too. The cowbirds weren't content to leave their droppings. They came and pecked holes in the eggs and then flew into the elephant's ear. God damn it all to hell,' he said in a low voice.

'What are you talking about, cowbirds and elephants?' Peggy looked up. 'Have another drink and sit down, Don. You look dreadful. Your nose is pinched white and you've bitten clean through your lower lip. Here, take this handkerchief.'

Her husband ignored the handkerchief.

'Charlotte Stuart was right,' he said slowly. 'Njeroge was right, too. He told me a story about the cowbirds plotting to get rid of the elephants. It was the day after they oathed his daughter and she hanged herself. I never told you. But Charlotte Stuart was right. "One run, all run," she said. "Cut and run" were the words she used. I was wrong to run, dead wrong. *Look* at me!'

He flung wide the arms in the heavy cable-stitched sweater, and looked down at his knickerbockered legs, with the canvas gaiters still on.

'Look at me! A bloody flunky—a bloody gamekeeper on somebody else's land, in somebody else's country, while they tear up my own land, in my own country! Cowering in a bloody hut, my kids living on near-charity, my wife working as a waitress—look at us, hiding! Brian had the right idea, in any case. Kill the bastards and start at the top!'

Peggy sat quietly while he paced as best the narrow room would allow. Then she said in a low voice:

'What do you want to do? I'll do anything you say, Don.'

He whirled to face her.

'I'm going Home! I was wrong all along to leave! There's nothing for me here—not with my own country coming apart. It's not their bloody country —it's my country! If they want it they'll have to take it—and take it from the likes of me and the others that stuck! I'm going home, Peggy—Home!'

'All right,' she said quietly, getting up and putting both hands on his shoulders. 'If you want to go home, we'll go home. We'll find the money somehow.'

He shook off her hands, and went back to the sideboard for another drink. Something more than whisky now glinted in his bright brown eyes.

'No, my darling Peggy,' he said slowly. 'Not *we*. We left because of *we*. You're safe and the kids are fine and you owe it to the kids to keep them fine. It's no good us all going back—I'd go mad with worry and it wouldn't serve any proper purpose. No. You'll just have to stay with the kids. We'll give this hut up and you can move in with your aunt. I'll hunt again—all the bookings won't have dropped off. I'll make money—steal it or something and send enough for you and the kids to scrape by on.'

He smacked his palm on the wall.

'At least I'll be there! I'll live on the farm when I can and somehow,

somehow, I'll be able to'—he clashed his palms together—'A man named Harry Slater had a farm a long time ago in the hills. It was a very convenient farm for its purpose. Hardscrabble might be a very convenient farm for *its* purpose. That spear-gate has had a lot of practice lately.' He turned and spoke swiftly.

'I can't stand the thought of old Brian in jail. He'll go mad—he could never stand being cooped up. Maybe I won't be able to do anything for Brian, but at least I'll be there. Do you understand me, Peggy, at least I'll be *there*!'

Peggy spoke slowly, looking deeply into her husband's eyes.

'How about me? I'm your wife. I'm supposed to be with you. I'm not supposed to be *here*, with you *there*. I can leave the kids with Aunt Meg. They'll be all right.'

Don glared at her, reaching out to shake her shoulder.

'But can't you see, that's the nuts of the whole thing! You'd only be a hindrance to me now, Peggy! On my own I can make out fine. If I'm saddled with the worry of you, and worrying about you worrying about *me*, and you worrying about the kids, and me worrying about you worrying about the kids, I might as well cut my own throat and be done with it. You never went with me into the forests after the gangs, Peggy. Think of it that way now. If you're safe and sound the kids've always got you, and I can do whatever it is we have to do out there—we can at least consolidate the worries.'

'And just what is it you plan to do?' Peggy's voice was sharp.

'I don't know—but I do know the country and the people. We'll do something that won't depend on Mother England and the pimps in the Colonial Office and a lot of white bumboys for lousy black politicians. But it won't be the kind of thing that you can do if you are tied down by women and children!'

'I think I see what you mean,' she said quietly and dropped her eyes. 'In that case, go ahead, Don. I wouldn't want to go. Certainly I wouldn't want the children to go.'

'It's not as if it's forever,' Don Bruce said. 'It can't last forever. There'll be a showdown after elections and one way or another things'll work out. But not unless there are some strong people around to help them—to force them —to work out. They won't work out if everybody runs and hides!'

'All right, Don. Have it your way. We'll stay. Don't worry about us. And don't fret about us getting along—don't do anything foolish about getting money. I never told you, but I've quite a bit of money you don't know about.'

Her husband looked at her in surprise.

'How can you have? I thought I knew every farthing that came and went. How could you have any money?'

Peggy Bruce smiled a funny, sad small smile.

'I wasn't very honest with you, I'm afraid. I stole shamelessly from the household accounts in Kenya. You looked so—so desperate the time you had to sell your pitiful polo ponies—so I pinched a little here and a little there. I was hoping some day I'd have enough squirrelled away so that you could get your horses back and have a little fun. I just didn't tell you at the end, that's all—I thought the day might come when we could use a couple of hundred extra pounds we didn't know we had.'

Don Bruce knuckled his eyes savagely with his big chapped hands. He bit his lip and the blood flowed again.

'Oh, Peggy, Peggy,' he said, and reached out to hold her. Then he pushed her away and tipped up her chin, smiling down at her.

'I've a slight surprise for you, as well,' he said. 'I always had a lot more expensive guns than I ever needed. One day when we were in London I stopped off at Westley Richards and got rid of a couple of pairs of luxury doubles. I've a secret hoard of my own—enough to get me back to Kenya, anyhow. We'll be all right for money. I left more than enough guns with the police out there for my simple needs.'

'I imagine there's very little else to say, then,' Peggy said with false brightness. 'When do you plan to leave? Won't you have to give notice here? They've been very kind, you know. And we'll have to clear out of the cottage. I suppose I'll keep on working at the Lodge.'

'I don't expect they'll make any trouble about my leaving when I tell them why. The off-season's on us, and I'll possibly be back if they want me for next year. This thing in Kenya'll clear up pretty soon, I'm sure—one way or the other, a dead loss written off, or a decent agreement based on mutual fear. There are some letters I must write. I'll go in a day or so if they'll let me. I'm sure they will. It's rather like a war, you know.'

'Yes. I know.' Peggy's eyes swam and she blinked angrily.

'That's it,' Don Bruce said eagerly. 'Think of it as if I were only going off to a war that'll be over some day.'

Peggy came closer and pressed her head against his chest.

'Yes, darling,' she said. 'I'll try to think of it as if it were only a war.' Only then did she weep.

CHAPTER SIX

THE POLICE had come to Matisia's house just as he was about to leave for the country to see what could be done about plucking some of the more irritating burrs from Kamau's planning. His shocked surprise had been very believably apparent to the police inspector and his black constables. They had come, they said, only for help; did he know anything at all which might explain the shooting of Matthew Kamau by Brian Dermott? Had they clashed before? Were they old enemies? Did they even know each other at all?

'While my poor colleague and I were recently in London,' Matisia had told

424

the inspector, 'at a small dinner party given by an under-secretary in the Colonial Office, an unfortunate press photograph was taken without the permission of the principals. You may have seen it; it showed the wife of this man Dermott dancing with Matthew. It was all completely innocent. Certainly there was nothing to it—neither of us had met the lady before, and did not see her thereafter. But I believe—I was not here at the time—that the impact of the picture in Nairobi was considerable.'

'*Considerable* is a mild word for it,' the inspector had said. 'Shocking would be a better description. There's no white person in Kenya who didn't see that picture, or at least hear about it. The newspaper was a collector's item overnight.'

'It's my idea, then,' Matisia said, 'that this poor man Dermott must have gone slightly mad with rage when the American lady was killed on his aunt's farm. Somehow through association with the picture in the newspaper this man Dermott must have connected Kamau with the unfortunate killing of the American lady—killers are rarely logical. I had danced with Mrs. Dermott, myself, Inspector, as I also danced with our hostess and a titled lady who was present at the party. It is quite fortunate for me that no one snapped my photo while I danced with Mrs. Dermott, or I might very well be lying dead at this moment instead of poor Matthew.'

'You might very well, at that,' the policeman said. 'I suspected it was something of that sort. Well, I had no real idea that you would be able to help us. Merely a matter of routine. We may want you for further questioning. Don't leave Kenya without telling us.' The inspector leered. 'I know it may be an imposition. I know how much you chaps have to travel these days. I suppose it's deductible from your taxes.'

'What is to be done with the body?' Matisia asked.

'That's not my department. I suppose that unless somebody claims it it'll go to the public burial grounds. You don't by any chance want it, do you?'

'No,' Matisia said hastily, 'I certainly do not. I think the faster the burial and the less fuss made over the matter, the better. If I can be of any assistance in the future, let me know.'

'We'll let you know,' the inspector said. 'Come on, you chaps. Stir your stumps.'

He had gone down the porch stairs leaving Matisia pulling gently at his ear-lobe. Well, well—poor old Matthew. Here this morning and dead in the afternoon. He had hoist himself on his own petard, finally. So he was raising all manner of hell this morning, was he, about the necessity of creating some more noisy commotions in his divide-and-rule scheming? Dust off Kenyatta again; stir up the white men to a point where they'd massacre the natives for the edification and disapproval of the world? Create another Sharpeville; set the country ablaze—start such a huge fire that only Matthew Kamau could put it out—and on his terms? He wanted all that implemented by his trusty lieutenant, Abraham Matisia, did he?

Matisia chuckled. The chuckle grew into a peal, a roar of laughter. The irony of it all was too exquisite to be borne. Dear old Matthew, creator of symbols, the Messiah Matthew, the Leader Kamau—dead in the dust, done in accidentally by the hand of a man whose wrong was only fancied, tripped by an accident that had blundered into the crafty planning and plotting of Kamau. In a way Kamau had ordered the murder of Kathleen Crane: Kathleen Crane's boy-friend had killed Kamau and Valerie Dermott had triggered the whole thing.

Symbols, was it? By God, Matthew Kamau had built his own pyre for a burnt offering, and had then been turned by a wry trick of fate into acting as his own scapegoat. Matisia laughed until the tears ran down his cheeks. He must go and tell Lise—tell anybody at all about poor Matthew and the gorgeous irony of his untimely death in the street. The idea brought him up short and quenched his mirth.

What he would tell Lise would be to keep a still tongue in her head about anything she knew concerning his relationship with Matthew Kamau—keep that tongue unwagged or he would personally cut it out. He frowned as he thought of Lise. He did not really know how much she might have overheard of the conversation he had had with Kamau this morning. If she had heard any of the last it was very dangerous to him. Whore-like, she had confessed to nothing when he confronted her, but it was quite possible that she had heard enough to hang him.

Kamau had been right about some other things, if for a different reason. The men who had botched the kidnapping and the oathing ceremony must go immediately as well, as he had planned to remove them in the very near future on Kamau's orders of only this morning. He could accomplish that without leaving town; there were only half a dozen men to be eliminated and he could easily arrange that so that they would appear to have been killed by the white men in vengeance for the death of Kathleen Crane as Brian Dermott had killed Kamau. Poor Brian Dermott. He had certainly done Abraham Matisia a great service with his pistol this day.

But Lise. That was another kettle of conditions entirely. If Matthew had not been killed—or more, if Matthew had not come to him in a stupid rage this morning and shouted his instructions and ranted his displeasure over the fouled-up affair at Glenburnie—he might merely have slung Lise out on her well-padded rear and forgotten her. But with so much to gain, now, he couldn't take any chances on exactly how much she might have learned. It occurred to him also that he had got tipsy enough to talk too much on past occasions—much too much. It was a pity. He had grown really quite fond of the girl. She was comfortable; it would be a shame to lose her. He would have to give some thought to her disposal. It must happen in a way which could not possibly implicate him—possibly while he was away on a trip. Or better, even—when *she* was away on a trip. People did get drowned at Mombasa, and Lise might be pleased to take a short holiday there or at Malindi. That was the ticket. If something unpleasant happened to Lise Martelis in Malindi or Mombasa and Abraham Matisia were impeccably alibied in Nairobi or better, Cairo or Addis, nobody would make very much fuss over a Belgian whore who had sold her flesh to black men and who was in the country illegally anyway. People got lost so easily in Africa these days.

The idea now, Matisia, he said to himself, is to take it easy. Let the sleeping dogs lie, and wait for your friend Ndegwa to make his move. He is due back shortly; wherever he is he will know about Kamau pretty soon, within the hour, and he will come hotfooting back to Kenya to set things right and to establish himself firmly as Mr. Kaynap—Mister Kenya himself. I shall let him do that little thing—I want him built treetop-tall before I tear him down.

I will get rid of a few people up in the hills, and so will be clean on the deplorable business of the white woman and the old savage and the kidnapped child. I will regrettably have to close the mouth of my worshipping Lise pretty soon. It is a pity, but I can't risk having her talk, even from another country. She has been good for me and good *to* me—I shall make certain that she neither suffers nor is made to undergo indignities when she . . . er, passes on. And now here she was coming up the drive, looking very sweet in a red polka-dotted dress, he thought. Meanwhile, he would immediately remove those idiots who had botched the job at Glenburnie and Hardscrabble.

'Hello, Lise,' he said cheerfully. 'How pretty you look. I suppose you've already heard the sad news about Matthew Kamau?'

CHAPTER SEVEN

MATISIA HAD drunk too much again; he had boasted incessantly in the old vein, and then he had threatened her wildly and struck her, finally, as a fore-taste of what he said she would get if she opened her mouth about anything she had seen and heard. His hands on her arms had left marks; there was a purpling lump on her jaw where he had smacked her.

'Please, please,' she said. 'If you will only get my papers I will leave. Any sort of papers I will take. I will go to South Africa; I will go anywhere. Send me in the other direction. Send me to Cairo or Athens. There will be no trouble in Tangier if you will just get me any sort of papers. I would even take a chance in the Congo again—perhaps it would not be so bad in Katanga, where the whites are coming back and it seems to be civilized.'

'You are not going anywhere, pigeon,' Matisia said. 'You are staying here with me until I tire of you. I have grown accustomed to you.'

'But you told Kamau that you were already tired——' She clapped a hand to her mouth.

'Oh, so you *did* overhear us this morning, eh? You lied when you said you had just come back from shopping—you lied when you said you had heard nothing. How much did you hear? Tell me! How much?' He struck her heavily in the face. 'Tell me, or I will kill you now!'

'Nothing—nothing except at the last, when Kamau told you I must go, and you said that you had planned to kick me out—that you were going to get a better woman! Only that and nothing more, Matisia, I swear it!'

He raised his hand to strike her again, but his mood suddenly changed.

'Make me another drink,' he said. 'Perhaps I will get your papers arranged after all now. But if you open your mouth to anyone—anyone at all—I will twist your neck as certainly as I—rest assured I will kill you personally. I will not trouble to give you to the police to send back to the Congo or to Belgium or any place else. I will kill you myself, personally, as surely as my name is Matisia.'

He had smiled then as he took the drink from her, and kept smiling the same dreadful smile later when he took her to bed. He smiled when he placed his lean black fingers around her neck and let them linger in a long spiteful caress.

'Such a lovely white neck,' he said. 'What a shame to break it.'

Then he had used her brutally and had gone snoring off to deep sleep.

*

Lise Martelis rarely dwelt on her own history any more, except when occasionally Matisia, in a fit of perversity, had probed at her and lifted the scab of old memories. Men *were* perverse. She had never met one yet, black or white, who did not seek an answer to the question: how did you get in this business in the first place? It was as if they found extra pleasure in baring the anatomy of misfortune. The answer was generally so simple, but nobody was ever willing to accept the simplicity at face value. The history of nearly any whore was as simple as the history of a marriage. There was little difference between dull matrimony and dull prostitution; the edge of a knife, the roll of a die, the flip of a card, the turn of a corner spelled the difference between housewife and whore. The woman was nearly the same in both cases, the wife sometimes more whorish, the whore occasionally more wifely.

When she had first come under Matisia's eye, passed on as stateless people with the wrong papers and the wrong profession are generally passed along, he had asked her the same old question. She had told him the story that was old before they started chipping the basics of history on rocks: she was young, she came of stuffy, respectable bourgeois, she was innocent, she got herself pregnant by a young cousin, she was kicked out of the house by an outraged father, the baby died.

Matisia had struck at her once with a question: 'Did you really stab that man in Brussels?'

And she had answered, in all honesty. 'I do not think so. It was all so very confused.' It *was* all very confused—so many places and men and changes. They merged into one another, until she really could not have told a straight story about how she got into her business if someone had coached her, point

428

by point. From the time her father kicked her out and the baby was born, it seemed to have been just one bed after another, one man after another, one house, one city, one country, after another.

And Matisia had said once, scornfully: 'You act almost like a married woman.'

Of course she acted like a married woman. All women were married women basically, she thought. It was only the men who were unmarried. But you could not expect a man to realize that. A man lived in his head and his groin was secondary. A woman lived only in her ovaries, and her thoughts were all ovarian if she bothered to form thoughts at all. For a time she had been happy and secure in the little pink stucco house, and Matisia was no worse than any other man. She had thought to worry about the next step when she came to it, when she got better papers—— Cairo or Athens or Algiers.

But now Lise Martelis was frightened out of her wits. She knew that Matisia would never get her any papers, if he had ever had any intention of getting them. He suspected that she had overheard all of his conversation with Kamau. He himself had told her much more than he remembered, when he was drinking too much and feeling very expansive.

She shuddered when she thought of the killing of the American woman, her throat cut as casually as *that*. She had heard the talk of the arrangement of the kidnapping and knew the cause of the resultant killings; she had heard Kamau's loud angry instructions to Matisia just before Kamau had told Matisia to get rid of her. Matisia would get rid of her, all right—but not through papers, not via a ticket to Tangier or Cairo or Athens or Algiers.

She thought of going to the police, and could see no future to that, either. She knew the police: they would first ask her what she was doing in the country without correct papers, and then they would ask her why she had taken up with black men anyhow, and then they would refuse to listen to anything she had to say against Matisia because it would cause complications. What they would do, and she knew this as well as she knew her name was *not* Lise Martelis, would be to pack her onto an aircraft for Brussels, with a succinct cable to the police on the other end, and that would be the end of the Lise Martelis she had come to know better than she knew the other woman, Marthe Evert, the fugitive from a suspicion of murder, who had run stupidly to the Congo so long ago. They still had a guillotine in Belgium.

If they did not send her to Belgium they would send her back to the Congo, and judging from what got into the papers lately, she might as well stay on in Nairobi and let Matisia cut her throat. She had something to sell, and that was what she knew about Abraham Matisia and Matthew Kamau—something which had caused at least two direct murders and God knows how many indirect ones. She had something to sell and the idea was to sell it to the man who had the most to gain from it. That would be a black man, of course. She had learned that much as a black man's harlot. Black men passed white women from hand to hand, and there was no regaining white status once the black man's mark was on you.

429

The most logical black man was Stephen Ndegwa, this other member of the political team of Kamau, Ndegwa and Matisia. She knew that Matisia was frightened of Ndegwa—she knew also from Matisia's drunken boasting that he and Kamau had planned to squeeze out Ndegwa after draining him of his positive qualities. That was a curious thing to Lise Martelis, the way these black men always plotted and schemed against each other. She had never seen such jealousies, such bitter competitions, even among the worst whores in the worst bars she had ever worked in. These politicians were worse than homosexuals, always at each other's eyes. You could not pick up a newspaper without seeing some story of charge and counter-charge and cross and double-cross and bitter interchange of hatred among the men who called themselves nationalist leaders and who professed to have the welfare of their country at heart.

She was basically a kind and placid and admittedly not very intelligent woman, Lise Martelis thought, but she had been out here long enough for the suspicions and hatreds to rub off on her to where she was at least alert. You cannot touch pitch without—so if Ndegwa was like all the rest, he would be glad to have some whip to wave over Matisia. And there could be no stronger hold than the one she was prepared to offer Stephen Ndegwa when he returned to Kenya. That, Matisia had said, would be any moment now, since Kamau's death was being so importantly reported all over the world.

She looked round her at her little pink house, and saw that the boy had knocked some of the flowers askew in a vase. She swore under her breath at the clumsiness of all Africans as she rearranged the flowers. It was a nice little house; she had been quite happy in it. That was all she asked, to be happy and do her housework in a little house any place where it was peaceful. It was a shame that she was so often uprooted; some people had all the good luck, other people had all the bad. She was the bad-luck one from the day she had let that cousin put his hand up her frock. Maybe when this Mr. Ndegwa came back and she went to see him, her luck would change. They said it often happened with Africans, and she was overdue for change.

CHAPTER EIGHT

It all had such a curious dream-like quality, Brian thought, sitting with his head in his hands on the edge of the narrow hard cot in the dingy grey cracked-plaster, Lysol-smelling cell of Nairobi Prison. It had nothing whatsoever to do with him, all of the events which had landed him in this cage, with its seatless toilet bowl and one unpainted table and chair; its bars and its series of locked gates in this cheerless bare compound under the dusty eucalypti which was known as Nairobi Prison. The last time he had been near the prison was the night they had hanged Peter Poole; now he was not near it, he was *in* it. But he still felt as if he were outside looking in—outside the jail and outside himself as well.

All the events were perfectly clear; nothing was very fuzzy in his head. It was only dreamlike in the hindsight that none of it could have happened, and very soon the clouds would be dispelled and everything would slide back into focus. This was not a new thing to Brian Dermott. During the various actions of the Mau Mau period he had often experienced the same feelings. Once he was out of the bush, washed of blood and clean of killing and with a few drinks warm inside him, the doings of yesterday or of last night seemed completely impossible. The bright sun and cheery birdchirp of today wiped out the remembrance of last night's dripping black bush and vicious laced bamboo; bland daylight erased the bright spurts of gunfire and the savage yells of men as they fought and died.

It was similar now to then. Soon someone would come and take him out of this cage. One didn't put white men in cages except by accident. It just wasn't *done*. Bwanas did not live in cages. Bwanas put other people in cages. Bwanas lived free. It was only a matter of a short time before he would be living loose in the bush again. He hoped when the mistake was ironed out they wouldn't give him any more medals. He had enough medals.

The dreamlike texture of the last hours had begun with the discovery of Katie, dead, and Kidogo, dead. No one in his right mind would kill Katie; certainly nobody would want to kill old Kidogo. But one did not argue with cut throats. It was startlingly clear, as dreams so often were. They were both dead and there was no doubt about it. He remembered sitting with Katie until George had come. Then things fuzzed up a little, although he recalled driving a long time before the inspiration had come to him that now was the time to kill Kamau. The settling on Kamau as a man to kill had been a stroke of habit. They had always capitalized on habit when they were hunting the terrorists: always pin your aims on the ringleaders—men like China and Burma and Kimathi and Ndiritu—and the lesser fish would swim into the net. And so he had killed Kamau, who had become strongly fixed in his sub-conscious. He was not quite sure why Kamau had become fixed so strongly in his subconscious. Something from the past had dictated that Kamau must surely be responsible for the deaths of Katie Crane and old Kidogo.

So he had driven in—he remembered now, he had come in from the Northern Frontier where he had gone to think things out and to hunt elephant—and he had gone straight to where Kamau would be. Not exactly straight; he had stopped first at his flat to change his clothes because Brian greatly disliked the way some people lounged around town with their jacket loops full of bullets and their hats bedizened with snake-skin or leopard-skin bands, playing cinema white hunter for everyone to see. He believed in dressing the part, always, and so he had gone to bathe and shave and put on his city-going clothes before he had gone to the blind where Kamau would be sure to come.

He had known that Kamau would come as surely as he knew, as a hunter,

431

that there was a big bull elephant over the next hill, or that a leopard would return to a certain kill on a certain day. Animals as well as man were creatures of habit. You had only to trace the course of migrations, the concentrations of dung, the drinking and feeding habits, to know that. Even the most careful man, particularly when he was operating out of his element, was a slave to old ingrained habit. That enslavement had hanged more than one Mau Mau—it had implemented many an ambush. Somehow a man got used to evacuating his bowels at a certain time in a certain place, eating in a certain place, sleeping or even praying in a certain place. Even when he changed those places purposefully, he betrayed himself with the very unconscious rhythm by which he alternated, so that if you could watch him for a while you might easily plot his course of habit.

Brian had not been entirely sure he would shoot Kamau when he had walked up to him. If anything, he had hoped, as he had hoped once before when he had bumped into Kamau and Ndegwa in the lobby of the hotel, that Kamau would resent him and start something . . . start anything at all that would leave Brian free to demolish him. There was no doubt about it, Kamau had made a grab for the pistol. You didn't just stand there and let people take your pistol away from you. There was no way of knowing whether Kamau was armed or not when he walked up to him to tell him—to tell him what? Oh, of course, he remembered now. To tell him that he didn't want Kamau dancing with Valerie any more, even if she were only his ex-wife. No white man wanted his wife dancing with the Nigs, even if they were prominent politicians.

That's what all the fuss was about, of course. It was a common occurrence in Kenya, people being suddenly killed with guns or with other dangerous instruments in fights over women. You could generally count on a riot of one sort or another nearly every Saturday night.

It was all clear enough now. He had reproved Kamau for putting his hands on Valerie, his wife, and naturally he had his gun. Kamau had grabbed at the gun, and the gun had obviously gone off and blown a great hole in Kamau. That by God would teach Valerie to choose her company more carefully. It would teach her to keep clear of Wogs, once and for all. Then he had done— what? Oh, he had sat down again, and had ordered more coffee, and had told someone to send for the police, for these things were best cleared up immediately. It wouldn't be the first time he had been charged by a magistrate for involvement in a killing. Usually the fine was thirty bob and a laugh with the beak, and then everybody went and had a beer. There was probably some mistake somewhere, because he was still in prison, and nobody had come to retrieve him as yet. Shocking bad organization. Somebody'd get a rocket for sure.

He felt dirty and crumpled, after a night of sleeping in his clothes. His beard crawled and itched, and he felt as if there were bugs in the harsh grey-blanketed bed, even if there weren't. At least he couldn't find any *dudu*. Pretty soon if somebody didn't come he would rattle on the bars and demand his rights. That was the trouble with everything the government did—red tape and always changing shifts and one man handing over authority to another. He could understand them having booked him on a formality—but the formalities should have been cleared up by now, and he should be on his way back to the north. If it was bad now, it would be unthinkable when the Nigs took over.

Seeing Kamau's face when he plugged him was as good as a play. The Nig looked as if he were much too important to be shot at—as if he couldn't believe it, even when his life was rushing out of him, as the life had bubbled out of Katie Crane. He had seen the same expression on a Mau Mau gangster he had come suddenly upon in a turning in the bush. The man had looked positively amazed when Brian shot him. Well, *he* wasn't surprised that Mr. Kamau was a gone pigeon. That ·38 Police Special was deadly, and a soft-pointed bullet at close range made a dreadful mess. Kamau shouldn't have been so naughty as to try to take it away from him.

Naughty. What a word of understatement. Why had he thought *naughty*? Of course. 'Naughty' was what Don Bruce had said that day up the hill when he had shot the Mau Mau gangster as he was reaching for a *panga*, the morning after the ambush of the cattle raiders. 'Naughty,' old Don had said, and let him have it with a Patchett. *Bump-bump*. What a jolly sound they made at close range, those little riot guns. *Bump-bump*.

Apart from the lousy room service, Brian reckoned that the Kenya police-men had been remarkably swift, competent and courteous in their handling of him. He had barely finished his coffee, with the crowd still ringed goggling around him, when a police car roared up and a big rangy inspector who was unknown to him got out of it with a couple of *askaris*. He wished it had been his old policeman friend Terry Tolliver. The things he remembered about Terry Tolliver from the old days in the mountains when they were chasing Micks together . . . Terry would have thought the whole thing a huge joke. He'd have got the *askaris* to cart off the Nig, and then they would have gone somewhere quiet to have a drink and talk it over. But this tall inspector chap with the roan guardee moustaches seemed to think the whole thing very serious. He had demanded Brian's gun—which Brian gave him willingly enough; he didn't need it any more now, and he nearly always parked his weapons with the cops when he didn't require them immediately to hand—and then had snapped, of all things, handcuffs on him and hustled him off exactly as if he were a nigger, except he didn't drag at him.

There had been the usual mumbo-jumbo he'd seen in the moving pictures about 'I arrest you for the murder of So-and-so and must warn you that any-thing you say will be taken down in writing and used against you', or however the phrase went, and off they'd gone in the police car to the police station. He hoped somebody'd moved Kamau from where he lay in the street. He didn't look very appetizing to all those poor people trying to have their sandwiches and beer. Funny how much deader a man looked when he had clothes on than when he was nearly naked. Like wind-scattered rubble.

433

Brian watched a chameleon running up and down the dirty plaster wall and made shooting motions with his hands. The chameleon was the classic bearer of bad tidings for the Kikuyu. The sight of one was enough to call for the sacrifice of a goat. He giggled a little foolishly. He didn't have any goats to sacrifice, but he didn't exactly need one. He had already sacrificed his goat. And there were plenty more goats around to be sacrificed when he got out again.

It was boresome here in this cell, but many years of waiting in the forest, waiting motionless for beast and men, had taught Brian patience. Fidgeting never got a chap anywhere. He swung his legs up on the cot and stretched full length. Presently he went to sleep, and did not wake until he heard the warder's voice saying:

'Wake up, wake up, Mr. Dermott. There's someone here to see you.' And another voice saying: 'Are you all right, Brian? We must see about getting you out of here soon.'

Brian recognized that other voice. It was his faithful old brother-in-law again. Dear old George always seemed to be popping up to haul him out of the soup these days.

CHAPTER NINE

MR. REUBEN QUILLER, of the firm of Quiller and Moseby, Advocates, was a round little radish of a man with a bald head which had a dent in it. Patches of mousy hair stuck in tufts over his ears, and he had a long, sorrowful-looking walrus moustache. He dressed in a curious fashion, in exaggerated Edwardian clothes with four-button jackets and pipestem pants. He had merry blue eyes, one of which had a tendency to squint. He was about forty-five years old and had been a resident of Kenya since the war. He had a devilish reputation as a ladies' man, although there was said to be a Mrs. Quiller living undivorced somewhere in his European background, and he made frequent trips abroad to London and Rome and Berlin. Mr. Quiller had a large modern home with a swimming-pool in Muthaiga. He owned or was partner in at least five big farm-and-cattle holdings.

Mr. Quiller evidently found the practice of the law prosperous; he was much in court, and usually involved in trials of a criminal or other ill-tempered nature. He had a reputation for taking on hopeless cases, and a positive genius for flamboyant and unorthodox court-room performances in the defence of crimes of passion. A dazzling array of acquittals stood behind him, in some of the more flagrant affrays *d'amour* for which Kenya was noted, and he specialized in hung juries and bizarre approaches to surprise verdicts. He was very expensive, and the nature of his work usually demanded a heavy portion

434

of the fee to be paid in advance, because the defendants in the rare action which Mr. Quiller lost were not likely to concern themselves with the future payment of legal fees. They were much more likely to be dead, or at least incarcerated for a very long time.

After a hurried consultation with Charlotte Stuart and the rest of the family, George Locke had decided to take the problem of the defence of Brian Dermott to Mr. Quiller. Together George and Mr. Quiller had gone to visit Brian in jail, after he had been charged and remanded for trial. The visit had been unrewarding. Perhaps Brian was inwardly confused and disturbed, as George Locke knew in his heart and mind, but outwardly he was calm and in full possession of his faculties. He had been neither drunk nor to all accounts outwardly insane when he shot and killed Matthew Kamau. He had politely but adamantly refused to sign any statement, citing his constitutional rights to the arresting police. Police had collected a covey of bystanders from the onlookers in front of the hotel. All had sworn that they had seen Brian Dermott walk up to Matthew Kamau and say something to him. None could swear that they had seen Brian draw a gun; all had seen Brian take Kamau by the arm; all had heard the report of a gun going off, and all had watched Kamau fall. All had remained on scene while Brian Dermott resumed his seat and ordered another cup of coffee. All had heard him request that somebody call the police, and all had seen the police take the pistol from him.

There had been no choice for the magistrate before whom Brian had been arraigned after the arrest and the testimony of the witnesses had been taken. He had heard the witnesses and seen the gun. The recovered bullet would undoubtedly match the gun. Kamau was indisputably dead. The magistrate had committed the accused to trial by jury on a charge of murder in the first degree. And Brian Dermott had loudly refused the lawyer's first tentative suggestion of a plea of insanity.

'Let them hang me if they want!' he shouted. 'I'd do it all over again! But I will not spend the rest of my life in some booby-hatch! If I have to plead guilty, I'll plead guilty, but no insanity! That's final, George. I knew what I was doing and if I have to spell it out for the jury, I will.'

*

George Locke was talking now with Mr. Quiller, on their return from Nairobi Prison. They sat over coffee in Mr. Quiller's offices, which were large and airy and had a small porch running round the inner courtyard, in the old Malay States fashion, making a sort of catwalk along which messengers and clerks scurried. Mr. Quiller hauled savagely at his walrus moustache as he talked, a nervous mannerism which had the disconcerting effect of jerking his slightly cast eye downward in a monstrously exaggerated tic.

'I won't charge you anything at all for my advice, Doctor,' Reuben Quiller said to George Locke. 'And you won't like what I'm saying. But your brother-in-law hasn't a snowball's chance in hell for an acquittal. He shot this

435

elevated coon in full view of half of Nairobi. The only feeble prayer would be a plea of insanity—and from all I can observe, I doubt very much if that would work in this particular court of law.'

'But the man is *not* sound in mind, Mr. Quiller,' George Locke said. 'I've told you his medical history; the attacks he has had, his convulsions and seizures with the accompanying hallucinations and delusions. He has a long history of violent nervous aberration.'

Quiller shook his head, and clipped the end off a cigar with a gold penknife which depended from a heavily sealed watch-chain which crossed his round little belly. He lit the cigar with a kitchen match from an embossed green leather box on his desk-pad, and shook his head again.

'He has no *legal* history of nervous aberration. He has never been confined for nervous aberration. His illnesses have been in private nursing homes, and were not described as nervous disorders. And he's as outwardly sane as you and me. Perhaps he did his nut when the Crane woman was killed on your farm, and perhaps he was still off it when he shot down this Kamau. I should very much imagine that he was terribly upset when he killed Kamau. But it all shapes up legally as premeditated murder. It doesn't even relate to the Crane murder. It relates to a jealousy over an ex-wife. That makes it even worse. That shows clear premeditation.'

'But isn't there such a thing as temporary insanity?'

'Not unless you can prove that your man didn't know the difference between right and wrong at the time, and to the satisfaction of jury. He certainly shot him deliberately enough, and was certainly cool enough thereafter. Just his asking that the police be called—as a dozen witnesses have sworn in the preliminary hearing before the magistrate—is a damning admission that Dermott knew right from wrong.'

George Locke made an exasperated noise in his throat.

'Legally, perhaps, but psychologically it's a clear indication of his unsettled mind! A man like Brian Dermott, if he really set out to kill Kamau, would have killed him quietly and would have left no trace. Brian Dermott has spent his life killing without leaving evidence of it behind!'

Reuben Quiller hauled on his moustache again. He smiled tightly.

'I should not so testify if I were you when they get you in the box,' he said. 'It might just be rather additionally detrimental to the best interests of the accused.'

George Locke kneaded his temples with his knuckles.

'But isn't there something called irresistible impulse I have read about, where a man might know he's doing wrong but is powerless to fight against it?'

'There is. It's called a law of diminished responsibility, and is applicable in some American states. Unfortunately it does not apply in Kenya. Most of our law came here the long way round, via India, and has been adapted and modified according to need. Irresistible impulse is not a legal defence here. It is a modification only of the classic M'Naghten of 1843, when this chap

436

M'Naghten was acquitted by virtue of insanity of an attempt on the life of Sir Robert Peel.'

'But I read, or heard, somewhere——'

Quiller held up his hand.

'Whatever you read or heard, you will find that unless the accused is clearly not responsible at the time of the act, in the definition of the average person on the Clapham bus, he should hang. And that defined, quote, "is excused from criminal liability in the commission of the crime if at the time of the commission of the crime he is labouring under such a defect of reason as not to know the nature or quality of the act he was doing or not to know that the act was wrong". Unquote. And obviously your man was aware of what he was doing and whether it was right or wrong.'

'Is there nothing then—no possible excuse for Brian in the fact that his fiancée had just been murdered the day before, and his best and oldest African friend killed?'

Quiller wagged his head until his moustaches swayed like snakes.

'Absolutely none. The murder of Kathleen Crane and this man Kidogo have nothing to do with this case. Perhaps I could'—he smirked slightly—'perhaps I could sneak the murders in for the jury's benefit before the Attorney-General succumbed to apoplexy while shouting his objections, but the unsolved murders of Crane and Kidogo are not germane to the killing of Matthew Kamau by Brian Dermott. They do not relate.'

'Not even to show an upset state of mind?'

'Not legally. Not as an excuse or justification for the cold-blooded murder of an innocent man in broad daylight for reasons best known to the accused.' Quiller wagged his head again. 'No, sir. Not even if Dermott knew that Kamau *had* killed the Crane woman—not even if he had *seen* the killing and was unable to prevent it at the time.'

'But isn't there something called an unwritten law?'

'There is *not*. There are certain loose translations of laws according to communities and customs, but there is no legal right for the individual to exact personal vengeance for another crime. The right of punishment belongs only to the Crown. A man may kill to *prevent* a rape or robbery or theft at the time of commission of the act. He might possibly kill just after the fact, in an attempt to apprehend, and get away with it. But he cannot hunt down and shoot a man hours after a crime, even if he saw the man rape his wife or kill his mother or set fire to his house. Vengeance belongs only to the Law and to the Lord, and the Law has first terrestrial claim on it.'

George Locke slapped irritably at the top of his head.

'You're telling me then that there is absolutely no hope for my brother-in-law? That a man who was clearly out of his mind due to a personal tragedy— because of a succession of personal tragedies—must hang? That there is no defence?'

Mr. Quiller wrapped a moustache-end around one finger, and blew a thick greasy ring of cigar smoke.

437

'I didn't say that. There is always a contrived plea of insanity—of which the burden of proof is always on the defence. There is a plea of guilty, of throwing oneself on the mercy of the country. So far as I can see there is no possible legal justification of the homicide. I cannot even see how extreme immoral collusion with prosecuting counsel—and that has not been unknown in the past—could reduce the charge to second degree or a manslaughter. It is either first degree guilty, or first degree not guilty. If it is *not* guilty it is because the jury will choose to ignore the instructions of Milord Justice, or will find circumstances so extenuating that they will deliver a finding of not guilty in opposition to the explicit instructions of the court and the marshalled facts of evidence.'

'Supposing that you accept the case, which road would you follow?' George Locke asked. 'What would be our best chance?'

'A plea of guilty and throw ourselves on the mercy of the court—the jury. In other years it would undoubtedly work in favour of the defendant— sympathy angle for the killing, unsettled state of mind and nerves; actually it would amount to an unofficial plea of temporary insanity induced by shock. It might be sufficient to get Dermott off without the necessity of commitment to the insane asylum later. Or at least free him after a short incarceration at Mathari. But no matter how or what you plead at this time your brother-in-law won't get off.'

'What exactly do you mean by that?'

'I mean that you can't win a court case against an African today if you're a white man. Especially not against a dead African. Especially not a dead African of the magnitude of Matthew Kamau. I cite you the case of Peter Poole. He was obviously as much as or more mentally deranged than your brother-in-law, and had some reasonable excuse for shooting the African. If he had not signed that damning statement he might possibly have got off, but I doubt it. Even with motive, background, and the admissibly debatable question of self-defence against the man he killed, he was found guilty by an all-white jury. His appeal was denied, and his last-minute appeal for clemency refused. They hanged him high as Haman, because politically they *had* to hang him or risk a great big blow-up at a time that Kenya could not afford a great big blow-up. The Congo was in flames when they hanged him, but it *wasn't* afire when they convicted him. He was convicted because he was *white*, just as countless whites have gone scot-free in Africa only because of their skin colour in times past. You yourself know that Brian Dermott was decorated for killing Africans of Kamau's stripe no more than half a dozen years past. Now the Kamaus have inherited the earth. The situation is twice as tricky here now as it was a year ago, when poor Poole did for that native boy.'

Mr. Quiller had let his cigar go out. He went through the ritual with the kitchen matches again, and then continued:

'Brian Dermott picked a very poor time to go off his head. It is only months to our first free common-roll elections here; it is less than a year since they

438

signed the Lancaster House Constitution which gives Kenya to the African in as short a time as the African can force it by every noisy means in his unscrupulous power. The whole world's feelings today are against the white colonial and all he stands for.

'Jomo Kenyatta's still the hottest controversy they have, and London's frightened silly of a massive blow-up here. I'm frightened silly myself; I can't see why the killing of Kamau didn't touch off something horrible in the way of native uprisings and general murder and mayhem. I can only assume that somebody who is stronger than Kamau is holding the thing in check for a purpose.

'But this I know, and this I say. They avoided a big do last summer by hanging Peter Poole. If they don't try and hang Brian Dermott and get him out of the way before elections—before the elections lead to the final shouting and agitation for full freedom—they're in for the God-damnedest mess since the Russian Revolution! It'll make the Congo look like a hairpulling match between two rheumatic old women!'

Mr. Quiller gave a final emphatic tug to his moustache and sank back, puffing, into his chair. George Locke had sat quietly, his long face growing longer and longer. His voice was very soft when he spoke.

'I wouldn't be at all sure of that,' George Locke said. 'I wouldn't be too sure of that at all. But this gets us nowhere, really. My concern is for Brian Dermott; my regrets are for that poor girl and that poor old man and that poor little boy who are no longer alive on Glenburnie Farm. Brian's case can't be completely hopeless. We *must*—we *have* to save something.'

'Nothing's completely hopeless,' Mr. Quiller replied. 'Nothing's impossible. These black politicians might even stop cutting each others' throats one day and form a working government, with honesty and justice for all. Perhaps we won't live to see it, but—— Yes, there is just one hope for your brother-in-law. Just one.'

'Tell me,' George Locke said eagerly. 'Just tell me and we'll do it.'

'Get him a nigger lawyer,' Mr. Quiller said coarsely. 'Get him a coal-black nigger lawyer with tribal scars. Get him a witch doctor to testify to the devils in his soul. But first and foremost get him a nigger lawyer. All a good coon lawyer will have to do is pull on his wig and stand up, and the white jury will shout "Amen, Brother!" and set your boy free.'

'You're not serious,' George Locke said. 'You can't be serious.'

'I'm not—not very,' Mr. Quiller said. 'I'm not very serious because there's not a black lawyer in East Africa who would take a chance on wrecking himself politically—or getting himself done in on a dark night by taking on such a hopeless case as Brian Dermott.'

'It can't be that simple,' George Locke said. 'Certainly the aspects of justice go deeper than that.'

'Horseshit,' Mr. Quiller said even more coarsely. 'Pure, unadulterated horseshit. A black lawyer could have saved Peter Poole. A black lawyer would have saved the jury's face, which is all the jury ever wants; all the government ever wants. In all law face is paramount, but out here, where the basic issue is race, face is everything. I happen to know that there's one African barrister in this town right now who is still searching his conscience because he didn't help in the defence of Peter Poole. I also happen to know that the only reason he didn't appear at the defence's table was that several people told him quietly that they'd kill him if he did assist in the trial. He backed down. Poole was hanged.

'Look here, Locke.' Mr. Quiller's voice became hoarsely urgent as he slowly spaced his words. 'We do not deal in jurisprudence out here; we do not practise law today. We deal only in emotion, pure and simple, political, expedient, naked emotion. For hundreds of years it was the other way round, but the pendulum has swung and today the black man is scooping the pool. We want his friendship because we want to leech onto his country if only to keep its resources from the Russians. So we will hang a man here and there, and we will betray a whole nation of white colonials, and we will stamp and shout in the United Nations if only to cling to the black man's fickle affection. It's a waste of time—the bugger'll surely sell out to the highest bidder —but that's not important. The important thing is the view of practical realism, and the realistic picture is that today is the day of the Wog, and the white man is on the wane. A few more sacrifices won't make any difference to the perishing politicians, white *and* black!'

Mr. Quiller banged on his desk, and his inkwell jumped.

'With a reasonably peaceable approach to good riddance of its last important colonies, England will do anything at all to avert trouble now—and will see that its people are intimidated to a point where they will do anything to dodge trouble if it means pulling their paltry chestnuts out of the fire. They are sweating in England over this Kamau killing—they are sweating more even in America over the murder of Kamau than over the murder of that poor American girl. She wasn't political—she was only a bloody tourist and serve her damned well right, so to speak. But Kamau—he is black, first, and a leader of his downtrodden people, second, and he is black, third. Always the colour comes first.

'So I say if you want to save your precious brother-in-law from a rope, hire yourself a good lawyer who is as black as the deceased. Hire a respected man—hire a lawyer like Stephen Ndegwa to defend Brian Dermott, and Brian Dermott'll walk out a free man. All a chap like Ndegwa would have to do is show up in court, and the jury would start clamouring to go into conference. There are half a dozen legal ways to beat this case if the chief defence lawyer is black. There is no way to beat it at all if the defence is white.'

'You're surely joking when you mention Ndegwa,' George Locke said doubtfully. 'After all, he was Kamau's partner in Kaynap and——'

'You get the whole point,' Reuben Quiller said, standing up.

'I was certainly joking when I mentioned Ndegwa. Even if he wanted to represent Brian Dermott—even if he was grateful to him for killing Kamau, which I have no doubt he is—all that Stephen Ndegwa would sacrifice by defending Brian Dermott would be his personal political future, his Party, and very possibly his life. Yes, indeed, I was certainly joking when I mentioned Stephen Ndegwa.'

'Thank you,' George Locke said, holding out his hand. 'Ndegwa knows—is almost a friend of Charlotte Stuart. It wouldn't do any harm to have a word with him, in any case. He might have an idea we could use.'

'I tell you what I'll do,' Reuben Quiller said, showing George Locke to the door. 'If you get Stephen Ndegwa to appear for Brian Dermott, I will appear with him as assistant counsel. And I will not charge you a bloody cent.'

'I may just hold you to the bargain,' George Locke said as he walked down the catwalk to the stairs.

CHAPTER TEN

THE PLANE touched down at Khartoum in the early pre-dawn hours. Stephen Ndegwa awoke as the aircraft lurched to a halt. His mouth was sour and dry, and his eyes were scratchy from troubled, squirming semi-sleep. His ankles were swollen, even though he had kicked off his shoes and had used the foot-rest. His clothes were twisted on his body and his beard prickled and his shirt now was more soiled and stale and was creeping from his pants. Thank God nobody had got aboard to sit next to him when they had stopped in Rome. He did not believe he could have stood some homing missionary lady or a voluble Wahindi returning to his *sari*ed flock. Being all alone was bad enough. His dreams had been terrible.

He got up and walked across the tarmac to the offensively bright waiting-room in the airport. Khartoum hadn't changed in all the years he had stopped off there—and always in the caesarean hours of the morning. The same skinny, turbaned black servants, bandy-legged in sloppy diapers, the same sad men's room, the same bloody awful glaring lights, and the same bloody awfuller orange and lemon squashes in dirty glasses you got free—the same smelly half-cured skins and cracked crocodile bags and god-awful wood carvings and flyspecked ivory dingbats that also never seemed to vary. Ndegwa wondered as he wrinkled his nose over the lemonade if anyone ever bought anything from the curio shop. The inventory hadn't changed as long as he could remember.

He visited the men's room, and it seemed to him that the pervasive urine smell had richened with the years, if such a thing were possible, and then he walked out into the frowning grey dawn to sit in a chair by the barrier rail and watch the carrion kites swooping low, barely scraping the ground as they

441

skip-bombed in their search for refuse. The sight of the kites made him extra-queasy. They were just a touch too symbolic of his feelings at this moment. God, what a mess things would be in Kenya now, with all the human carrion kites sweeping and wheeling and squawking and competing for rotten bits in the filthy mess that Kamau had left by his death!

He lit a cigarette and slumped lower in the uncomfortable chair, resting his swollen feet on the low guard rail. It was fairly light now—the technicians were running back and forth in their dirty white shorts, and various vehicles were transfusing the long, ugly jet with whatever jets needed to subsist on. He hoped the weather would be all right over Nairobi—he did not fancy another delay at Entebbe or anything dreary like that.

Problems, problems, everywhere problems. Certainly America, which he had just left, was chewed ragged with insoluble problems. He had seen it in the faces of the too-many people—not just people of his own colour, but of all the people. They seemed to have lost faith. They seemed to have lost decision. They seemed to have lost arrogance—the old tough arrogance that had made them strong. They were irritable, impatient and confused. He wondered if being too rich too long had anything to do with it. They said they were having a depression, and there was much talk now of outflow of gold and balance-of-payment deficits and the kind of fretful whimpering you used to expect from the British as their colonies were shorn from them one by one. This young Kennedy was good as in, if only because he mirrored youth and confidence and pride.

It seemed odd though to hear the same British whining from the Americans —two cars in every garage and still they complained about a depression. Certainly there was unemployment, but there was no real gut-growling poverty. Poor people in America were better off than the richest Russians. He could not truly understand the Americans. They spoke vastly in the United Nations and they gave drunkenly of their wealth for everybody to misuse. They were undoubtedly noble in the mind if somewhat fuzzy in the aim. They wanted all the world to be rich and happy and to love them. Above all they wanted to be loved. All they accomplished was to look sillier by the tick.

They could not handle their own internal affairs. He had seen it and read it—he had spent much time in the ghetto of Harlem, and he had toured the depressed areas down south. He had watched the budding of massive riots which had not yet fully fruited, and had smelled the active fear of the white man against his own coloureds; seen the bitter hatred of the American Negro for the white American. I wonder what the hell they expect of us here, if they hate each other so in the stronghold of Democracy, he murmured to a passing kite, and flipped a cigarette butt at it. The bird stooped, voracious for the burning end, and Ndegwa could have sworn the kite scowled at him as the fiery coal repulsed its greedy beak.

Alackaday, he sighed—twenty million transplanted Africans who know nothing of their own Africa all ready to rise and strike down the white man in America—America the beautiful, America the bountiful, America the generous, America the frightened, America the stupid. . . . *And* that farcical United Nations, with old Khrushchev coming in and pounding with his shoes, and every inflated little black dictator from the squalling infant countries rising solemnly to clamour for a mature voice in the world's affairs when they could not even control their cousins at home in Mali or Togoland or Somalia. Two—no, really *three* sets of everything from the Congo—all screeching for recognition, and the whole dreary business sounding like a bad joke.

Joke? My God, Ndegwa thought. I sit here watching scavenger kites and I think *joke*, and I am going home to a horrid, tragic joke of my own. And I, or somebody like me, is going to have to start coping with it right this very moment.

They were calling the flight now, and Ndegwa got up and fished for his landing card to give to the guard. In a couple of hours' time, he thought walking towards the long-bellied jet, I have to face a harsh reality. The carrion kites are squabbling; I must be the lone eagle to drive them away. I must clean up some of the garbage and attempt some semblance of permanent sanitation. I am guilty of waiting too long; I have allowed these squabbling greedy politicians to rend and tear and peck at the eyes of the country, thinking that in the end I could profit from the confusion. That is my sin: I have played lion, lazy lion, to the jackals, and perhaps now I have waited too long.

I did not restrain Kamau and Matisia; I thought I'd let the others hang themselves while I made a name for myself in America, and now we have two accidents—you could not even call them assassinations—which have left the country a suppurating fester of scorn for all the hateful things they used to save for colonialism. And I am landed with it. It now belongs to me.

Who do I think I am, so early in the morning? He shook his head, settled into his seat, and fastened his lap-strap again. He closed his eyes as the jets murmured. He would try to steal a little more sleep. He could use all the sleep he could get, because the aircraft promised to be on time, and this was going to be a big day.

CHAPTER ELEVEN

THE BIG plane bumped to a standstill, and Stephen Nedgwa waited impatiently for the platform to be trundled up. That last minute of umbilical transference of the airborne body to the problems of the ground—*agghh*. He rubbed his itching whiskers again. They were beginning to grizzle, he had noticed in the lavatory, showing repulsively white against the mahogany hide with its sleep-pouched bloodshot eyes and the seamy bulldog lines of

443

jowl. His chalk-striped suit was a mass of horizontal wrinkles now, and his legs were unsteady as he went down the steps. The morning's blinding white sun struck him in the face, but the fresh breeze was brisk and invigorating after the air-conditioned body odour of the aircraft.

He squinted, eyeing the line of waving greeters from the top of the building, but saw no one he knew. Well, Mukerjee and Alibhai knew he was coming. One of them would surely be at the customs. One of them would certainly have brought the car. Perhaps Iris had come with them. He would be glad to see Iris, he supposed. It was strange how he so seldom thought of her. When he thought of Kenya he thought more often of his wives Mumbi and Wanjiro, on the reserve. Iris had never seemed like a wife. She seemed more like—more like the saucy modern round-limbed young things he had met in the Hotel Theresa in Harlem at some aimless function or other—the tawny-skinned young intellectual who had insisted on going to bed with him out of, he was quite sure, the sheerest curiosity about what a truly savage African was like in the normal male function.

I am becoming more and more like a white man every day, Stephen Ndegwa thought, leaving the sun and mounting the steps to Immigration, with its cool darkish waiting lounge. I am smitten with a consciousness of guilt when I return from a safari to the bosom of my family. I no longer accept the extra-marital favour with the casualness of the African. I have sinned, O Ngai; I have bedded with a woman not my wife—not even the wife of a circumcision brother.

He could see Vidhya Mukerjee now, waving at him. His partner in the firm of Ndegwa, Mukerjee and Alibhai had not changed, except that possibly Vidhya too was ageing. His skin was a little greener, his buck teeth more pronounced, his doe eyes larger and oilier. One thing was sure; he looked no poorer. Dear old Mukerjee, the man of many talents and enterprises—the man who would appear for you when you did not want to appear yourself; Mukerjee, the classic example of the man who could get it for you wholesale.

Mukerjee would fill him in on the details. By now he would have ferreted out most of the things that Ndegwa needed to know. By the time they reached his home in Eastleigh—the salmon-pink home he had bought from Vidhya Mukerjee—he would know nearly all he had to know about what had happened.

There was no fuss about passports; the Immigration *babu* addressed him by name. There was no fuss about customs; the inspector addressed him by name. There was no fuss about baggage; the porter addressed him by name. And now here was Vidhya Mukerjee, throwing wide his arms, shouting squeakingly, expansively how good it was to have him back in Kenya again! Then his face returning plop! to copper-greeny sombreness, as befitted a member of a mourning party. Mukerjee was, he noticed, wearing a black band on his beige pongee sleeve. Ndegwa jerked a head at the mourning stripe.

'The late Kamau or somebody more personal?' he asked.

444

'Our departed brother,' Mukerjee said, dipping his head. 'You must get one sewn on yourself, Stephen. But in the meantime, I have told reporters that we would meet in our office instead of here. I told them that you would not want to talk until you knew more of what has gone on here. I thought that is how you would want it.'

'That's fine. But what I really want,' Ndegwa said, 'is a shower and a shave and some fresh linen and a pressed suit and a very large gin and tonic. Then I will feel fit for everything, including reporters. Suppose we go to my house first, eh? I will say *jambo* to Iris, who I notice did *not* come to meet me. I faintly imagined she might.'

'I rang up and asked her,' Mukerjee said. 'But she said she would rather not. She has not stirred abroad much in the last two days. *Nobody* has stirred much abroad in the last two days. Well, come on. There's my car over there.' He pointed to a yellow Mercedes, twin in size and category to Ndegwa's white one. The chauffeur stood with open door.

'Where are the spontaneous crowds to bid me uproarious welcome?' Ndegwa stared around him. 'All I see is police—police and police cars and more police. Where are the howling mobs? I do not see any of the loyal *watu* with the garlands. I do not see any slogan-shouters or standard-bearers or even any unorganized, garden-variety *uhuru* screamers. I did not know whether to expect acclaim or a lynch mob, but I did expect *something*— somebody except police and porters and, of course, you.'

'I will explain in the car,' Mukerjee said, as they passed through several ranks of police, some of whom nodded, others of whom touched their caps as Ndegwa nodded back and strode briskly along to the waiting auto. They got in the car, and Ndegwa sank back with a sigh.

'It's good to be home again,' he said. 'Even under these conditions. You can breathe here. Now, start explaining.'

'I ordered no buses at all because the police disallow a mass congregation of Africans at the moment. No permits for speeches are being issued. Even small crowds of street loiterers are being dispersed. And government show-of-force parades have been held everywhere—in all the major towns and especially in the native locations. Half of Kahawa Base, it seems to me, has been turned out to demonstrate the mobility of its forces. And there has been much show by the King's African Rifles as well as the Kenya Police. Nairobi has been a very orderly city, believe me.'

'Spontaneous welcoming being discouraged then to such point that you were frightened of ordering several busloads of spontaneous welcomers, is that it? Militant democracy lies dormant because of a transportation shortage. Such are our times,' Ndegwa said. 'Well, jolly good show for the government. How have the people taken Matthew's murder?'

Mukerjee shook his head.

'Very quietly. Too quietly. I can only guess that nobody has dared organize any indignation as yet. I am certain that KADU and KANU do not wish to commit themselves until they see what *you* have in mind. It is pointless to

445

waste a political exploitation of violence until it aims somewhere. I have seen some foreign papers. There seems to be more indignation about poor Matthew in Russia than there does in Kenya. Certainly he is bigger news in England and America, in Europe and Asia—judging from Radio Moscow and Radio Peking—than he is here.'

Stephen Ndegwa looked out of the window at the herds of zebra and wildebeest grazing almost alongside the smooth surface of the broad highway, barred from the traffic only by the grassy shoulder.

'You know, Vidhya,' he said in surface wonder. 'You know it has only been ten years since they used to call the safari firms to shoot the zebra and wildebeest off the landing strips at the old airport in Eastleigh? Only ten years, Vidhya. And still we have them grazing almost atop this fantastic piece of roadway in a land which owned nearly no roads ten years ago. Perhaps the animals are not yet aware of the progress we have made and may still make, if we refrain from screaming *"uhuru now!"* long enough to lay some more roads and get some fences built to keep the zebra off the roads while still preserving the zebra. What were you saying about Kamau and the foreign radio and press?'

'I was saying that his assassination has been emphasized more abroad than here—that the people here seem to have taken it quite calmly.'

Stephen Ndegwa reached for the nickelled cigarette lighter in the back-seat dashboard and lit a cigarette.

'That is simple enough. It is merely a matter of communication. Nobody has told the people here to take it seriously yet. Nobody has hired the buses to herd them into mobs where they can be exhorted into taking it seriously. Nobody has stirred up the animals yet. Speaking of stirring up the animals, where is Abraham Matisia?'

'He is here, but not answering. I rang up just before coming to the airport and was told by the houseboy that he was not at home.'

Ndegwa nodded.

'I surmised I wouldn't find him. I imagine he'll be off to Cairo soon. He'll be happy for a while, I expect, with Peter Koinange and the rest of that splendid cultural group who send the correct broadcasts to the correct people on Radio Cairo's Swahili beam. It'll be interesting to see what tack the broadcasts'll take.'

'Speaking of tacks . . .' Mukerjee picked at his buck teeth with a thumbnail. 'Speaking of tacks, I suppose you realize fully that you are now the inheritor of Kamau's torch? You wear the master's mantle. There is nothing big left in Kaynap now but you. You hold everything that Kamau accomplished in your palm. You have only to speak at a few meetings, when the tension relaxes; you have only to endorse what he has achieved, and you own Kenya. The others will join you if you say. They won't like it, but they'll have to talk business. They'll talk business as Mboya had to talk business with Gichuru when Gichuru tucked Macleod in his pocket in London last spring. All of a sudden Mboya's People's Convention Party disappeared into the air—just as the Nairobi District African National Congress went away . . .'

'You are suggesting that I completely change my coat, then? You are suggesting that I put on Kamau's cape of violence and civic disobedience and tribal rivalry and white hatred and Kenyatta propaganda and land reform and—Mau Mau practice, if you like. You forget I am supposedly the progressive moderate—the Uncle Tom, the white man's nigger. You want me to set the world afire to warm my own political backside, in order to force freedom on these people twenty minutes after the elections, do you?'

Mukerjee hunched his shoulders.

'I did not choose those harsh words. They are your own words. I am always advocating practicality. This truly is a boiling pot, Stephen. The lid is on, and it will probably stay on until after election, tipping only slightly now and then to let off a little steam. But it will blow. It will certainly blow. And right now no one is ahead in the power scramble. Perhaps Kamau was . . .'

'You are espousing another Congo, then? You want stories every day like the stories that come out of Kivu and the Kasai and Katanga? You want the country run by bandit chiefs and murderers who mock decency and order and who could not control their own people from here to Thika? And you want me to declare myself the leader of that screaming mob by ratifying and perpetuating all of the rabble-rousing that Kamau stood for?'

'I did not say that. I did not say that at all. But rationalize your position; tell me, why did you join with Kamau if you disapprove so strongly of his methods?'

'Why did Mboya join with Gichuru and Koinange in London? Why did Touré flee to the Russians? Why did Haile Selassie run to the Reds? Expediency. Nothing but expediency. Why do they still shout for Kenyatta's release? They don't really want Kenyatta loose. Expediency. Nothing but black politics. I am not proud of it—perhaps I thought I would ride along and watch them founder one by one. I thought that perhaps cooler heads would prevail, and mine would be the coolest head of the lot. I was wrong. As you say, I have inherited Kamau's scarlet mantle. I suppose I will have to accept the filth he has left behind if I am to stay in politics and remain alive in competition with the other carrion crows. Tell me, what actually happened on that farm?' He shot the question.

Mukerjee shrugged for the third time, drawing his head almost level with his shoulders.

'The man who could tell you most accurately if he would, which he would not, is Abraham Matisia. He handled those things, as you know. There was an organized raid on the big farm—something to do with an oathing. This oathing was supposed to discourage the big agricultural project at Glenburnie. A small Kikuyu boy——'

'I read briefly about the small Kikuyu boy. Go on.'

'Evidently in the process of removing the small boy, some stupid accident happened and it was necessary for the kidnappers to kill the American woman

447

and the old man. There was another kidnapping, from another farm, a small one, which has only just been reported to the police. An old man named Njeroge-wa-Something disappeared on the same night as the little boy. He has not been found, either.'

'What makes him interesting enough to destroy?'

'Again, Matisia could probably tell you. This Njeroge was headman for the farm of a man named Donald Bruce, a settler with a large young family, and a man who had been active against the gangs during the Emergency. After a series of intimidations, I gather, Bruce gathered up his wife and children and ran off to England. The old man who was kidnapped was serving as Bruce's manager *pro tem* on the Bruce farm. It was called Hardscrabble, I believe.'

'How would you know all this if you have not talked to Matisia?'

'I know it because the physical presence of a man named Kungo wa Marenga was found impaled on a spike on the gate of Hardscrabble Farm this morning. His throat had been thoroughly cut. There was a note pinned on his jacket which said: "This is what will happen to all oath-givers in this area." It was printed in English. It said further: "This man led the oath-giving where the body of the boy Karioki from Glenburnie Farm was used against Njeroge the headman of this farm. Njeroge would not eat the oath so they killed him. Other bodies will be found on other fences soon." '

Stephen Ndegwa pressed his temples with his hands, shoving hard.

'This was not in the newspaper, certainly?'

'No. Not bloody likely. I have a few informers of my own,' Mukerjee said. 'Someone called the police and my man was one of the *askaris* who went along to investigate. He told me—also early this morning. I have been up since dawn.'

'You've had a busy morning,' Ndegwa said. He said then in Kikuyu to the driver, 'Stop at my house.'

'Do you want me to wait?' Mukerjee asked.

'I suppose so. Do you want to come in?'

'No. I'll wait in the car. Do not be too long. Remember we have the press conference.'

'I won't be long. Tell your boy to bring my bags in.'

Ndegwa got out and walked up the steps to the veranda of his salmon stucco house. It looked like most of Mukerjee's houses, boxy and ugly and scrolled and curlicued. But it had a flame tree in the yard and a boxwood hedge, and someone had been cutting the grass. The lawn-mower stood primly, lonely at the end of a broad swath. The borders by the house were a jumble of gladioli and purple fuchsia and dispirited dusty Michaelmas daisies. The door was locked; he hammered on it.

A pockmarked sullen houseboy in a soiled blue *kanzu* opened the door. This was a new boy. Every time he went away and came back there was a new houseboy. This one looked routinely stupid. Iris never seemed to be able to keep a servant long.

448

He strode past the boy, scaling his hat at a yellow cretonne-covered chair.
'I'm the Bwana here,' he said to the boy. '*Wapi memsaab?*'

'*Memsaab nataka lala sasa.*'

'I won't wake her, then,' Ndegwa said. 'Bring my bags to the spare room.
Help the driver with them.'

He walked back through the small living-room with its unevenly parqueted
floors and its shallow little alcove where he kept the fundamentals of a bar
when he was home. The Mombasa rose-design carpet was out of kilter on the
floor, which was smeared. There were flowers in the vases in the room, but
they needed changing. The unlit dining alcove looked cheerless with the
blinds drawn and, he saw, bolted from the inside. He made a face as he went
to the bathroom.

'Who is it?' came a voice from the bedroom, a voice muffled by the closed
door. Evidently his heels had clacked too harshly on the hardwood.

'It's Stephen,' he said. 'Back again. I didn't mean to wake you.'

'I'll be up in a moment,' the voice said. 'I must just have gone back to sleep
after the boy brought my tea. What time is it?'

'Just on ten. The plane was a little early. Take your time,' he said. 'I'm
going to have a shower and a shave. Then I have to dash. I'll be home for
lunch, and we can talk then.'

'All right,' she said, and the voice sounded relieved. 'Don't come in. I'm
covered in face-cream and I've got my hair in curlers.'

'All right,' he said, thinking it was just as well that he kept his clothes in
the spare room, and slept there more often than not. Iris was very peculiar
about being disturbed while she dressed. There were so many things that
upset Iris, including the thing for which he had married her.

Stephen Ndegwa looked round him in the purple-tiled bathroom, as he
stripped for his shower, and observed that nothing much had changed in the
last six weeks. The soiled flower-silk peignoir still drooped on the door, but
failed to completely cover the hose of the douche bag. Assorted pots of
creams and vials of liquid congested the window ledge and the shelves above
the hand-basin. There was still the same knobbly knitted cosy on the broken
toilet-seat—and the same streaked rust marks inside the bowl. Nor had the
shower changed. Inside its clammy plastic curtain its clogged head begrudged
an erratic dribble of water, and the temperature of the water shifted from
raging hot to icy cold, with little amelioration between. Even so, it was good
to cleanse himself of the aeroplane stench and exorcise the contamination of
stale clothing. After he had shaved his fingernails smelled better, and a solid
gum-bleeding tooth cleaning made a new man of him. His sombre eyes in
their heavy pouches had cleared somewhat.

He dressed himself in a fresh set of clothes, and paused briefly at his alcoved
sideboard to see if there were any gin; there was, Allah, a half-bottle, and so
he plodded to the kitchen to see if there might be any cold tonic in the fridge.
There was not; there was only a pot of what appeared to be face cream and
some other odd non-edibles he preferred not to investigate, but no tonic.

Stephen Ndegwa downed a neat belt out of the gin bottle on his way out, under the disapproving stare of the pockmarked new houseboy, and departed muttering that the boy should tell the Memsaab he'd be home to lunch at 12.30 and to send to the *dukah* for some more tonic and some more gin.

'You look twenty years younger,' his partner said as he climbed back in the car. 'And how did you find the beautiful Mrs. Ndegwa?'

'In the sack, as they say in America. She wasn't up yet,' Stephen Ndegwa snapped. 'Now tell me a few more things so I won't be entirely at sea when I take on the press. How was the arrest made on this man Dermott—tell me everything you know about this man Dermott. First, exactly how did it happen?'

'I was not there, but there seems to have been a hundred eye-witnesses; the names of several the police took down when they came to make the arrest. After all, Dermott shot Kamau at full noon in front of the Thorn Tree. You know what the pack is like at that hour.'

'How do you mean eye-witnesses? Did they see him actually draw the gun? Did he call out before he shot? Was there an altercation—a vocal or physical disagreement?' Ndegwa did not know why he asked, except that he was a lawyer who dealt instinctively in admissible evidence.

Mukerjee shook his head.

'Evidently not. The whole thing happened so swiftly. From all reports this Dermott was waiting quietly in a chair. He waited until he saw Kamau cross Hardinge Street, and then walked up to Matthew and shot him at the range of inches as they stood by the little unloading island. I gather there was no quarrel; he merely shot him. Obviously Kamau was not expecting it. After he shot him Dermott calmly walked back to his chair and ordered another cup of coffee in a loud voice, and suggested that someone call the police. One of the waiters ran for a manager; the manager called the police; Dermott surrendered his gun; the police took him away. I presume he was formally charged and booked and I know he is now in jail. I also know there is a heavy guard around the jail. Of course they feared—*fear*—a riot. But from the killing to the arrest to the disposal of the body it all seems to have gone off very smoothly.'

'Kamau died immediately?'

'Within seconds, I should say. They autopsied him yesterday. I was able to get a report. Death was caused almost instantaneously by a bullet which ploughed upward from the centre to the top of the heart, eventually shattering the lungs as well. It was a soft-point bullet and exploded on his spine. It made a ghastly mess of his back.'

'What disposition was made of his body?'

Mukerjee produced a rat's smirk, lifting his upper lip over his buck teeth.

'Standard operating procedure in such matters. Hallowed doctrine from Poona '02 that's been drummed into every District Officer and ADO in all the far-flung outbacks of the erstwhile Empire. Hurry-up-for-the-record autopsy and then get rid of the body unless there is a powerful claim. Kamau seemed to have no immediate family——'

'He was an orphan, I know that,' Ndegwa said.

'—and nobody else seemed terribly anxious to place him in the family plot. Certainly neither KANU nor KADU wanted immediate custody of an opposition martyr, and I don't imagine the British wanted to bury him in state.'

'What shocking cynicism,' Ndegwa muttered.

'In the absence of any desire to make a shrine of him, they took him some place far afield—I should imagine close by in the common burial ground—and bunged him into an unmarked grave. No firing of rifles—no blowing of bugles. That's my surmise, in any case. Maybe they just left him out for the hyenas.'

'And there's been no demonstration, no old lady friends or aggrieved creditors rending their garments and seeking to fling themselves wailing on his non-existent grave?'

'None that I know of. Perhaps in private. No public demonstrations, no public nothing.'

'Hmmmm.' Ndegwa rubbed his nose with the back of his hand. 'Do you know if Dermott signed a statement when he was being arraigned by the magistrate?'

'I'm not sure. What are you thinking of?'

'I'm thinking of Peter Poole, who signed a statement, poor bloody fool. The statement hanged him—well, the statement plus some political pressure and the exotic temper of the times. All right. Forget Dermott. What about this other killing?'

'All the details of that were handled in Nyeri. But she seems to have been first knocked unconscious and then killed immediately with a knife. Her throat was cut from ear to ear.'

'And the old man who was with her?'

'His head was cut completely off.'

'Removed from the scene?'

'No. That did not seem to be the object. It was found to one side of him. Dermott found the bodies. He was in turn discovered by his brother-in-law. They said that Dermott was sitting in a stupor, holding the woman's dead body in his arms. Shortly after the police came I'm told Dermott disappeared, and did not reappear until just before he killed Kamau.'

'Exactly how much agitation? By white and black, I mean?'

'Very strangely, none. Or almost none. Some odd knots of loafers. It was as if they were almost waiting for someone to tell them when and how to demonstrate. It has been a most peculiar city for two days, Stephen. Like the deadening lull before the storm. A sort of heaviness in the air. Everybody walking softly and talking quietly. And a great many people keeping to their homes. Oh—one thing. Very important to me.'

'What's that?'

451

'A great many town natives have gone back to the reserves. I'm told the same thing is happening on the farms. I sent Alibhai yesterday to check. *All* work has stopped on the Glenburnie project—I knew you would be interested in that. Most of the natives have gone back to the farms. There are only a handful left—houseboys, cooks, a few old retainers, the likes of that. Some few *mzees* who've never really lived any place else.'

'It worked then. Better than the bastard knew,' Ndegwa muttered.

'What?'

'Nothing. I suppose there's nobody left on the Bruce farm, especially since they found the late Whatsisname—Kungo—stuck on the spike with a note pinned to him, just like old times?' Ndegwa asked rhetorically, bitterly.

'I believe it was short-handed, anyhow, ever since Donald Bruce left with his family. I think at the moment the police have sent some people there. Certainly there will be some Kenya Police Reservists doing some farm-watching pretty soon, if not already.'

'Just like old times,' Ndegwa said again, even more bitterly. 'Just exactly like old times.'

'Not exactly,' Mukerjee said. 'In these old times you spoke of they began by murdering the chiefs who attempted to work with the white men. Then they began to murder the settlers and each other. Then everybody murdered everybody. Then the troops came and it became a war. You may remember. It only got officially terminated last year.'

'That's what I had in mind,' Ndegwa said. 'Tell me. Any signs yet of any-body actually *doing* anything with Kamau's death? Martyrdom? Living legend? That sort of thing? Or haven't they had time?'

'They really haven't had time. I think everyone's waiting to see which way you jump. And as we're now approaching the office, which way *will* you jump? The gentlemen of the press will be panting. There're two or three foreign correspondents in already. Shot in yesterday from the Congo. I presume more will be arriving as Dermott's trial approaches.'

Ndegwa reached for the door-handle as the car drew to a halt on Government Road, its shops and arcades seething with the pressing surge of Nairobi commerce.

'I shall speak in splendid platitudes for the moment. I will tell them where I've been and advocate unity of purpose for a new and better Kenya. I am not a Kikuyu *and* a lawyer for nothing. I speak well with two tongues, even in English. Will you stay on?'

'I don't think so. You'll do better without me. I'm an Asian, don't forget. I'd just confuse things by my presence. Do you want your car sent round?'

'Yes. Have that idiot chauffeur here about noon. I presume I still have the same chauffeur? Nobody's been kind enough to stick *him* on any gateposts?'

'I'm afraid not. Will I see you in the office after lunch?'

'No. I think we'll keep politics out of the office—our office. Perhaps the time has also come to move it out of hotel suites. I shouldn't fancy the management

452

would crave a repeat performance of our departed colleague. *Persona non grata. Non ars gratia artis.* Surely you've space in one of your buildings?'

'I've nothing but space in *most* of my buildings,' Mukerjee said sorrowfully. 'Since you left the capital has been rolling out in a tidal wave. Leases lapse and nobody renews. Credit is tighter all the time. Well, call me when you need me, and I will do something immediately about a new office for Kaynap —of which, I might say, Sahib, you are the undisputed head. Congratulations. I will put the office on the second or third floor, so it cannot be so easily wrecked by the opposition.'

'Save the sarcasm. It ill becomes an Indian. See you later.'

Ndegwa got out of the Mercedes and walked up the dark steps of the grey-dingy plaster building with the effluvia of intermingled urine and tangible despair which seemed deep-grained in most Indian-constructed plaster buildings in Nairobi.

CHAPTER TWELVE

IRIS WAS up and properly produced for public scrutiny when Stephen Ndegwa returned to his salmon-coloured house in Eastleigh. Seeing her anew was always a shock; he never quite remembered how pretty she was until he went away on a trip for a few weeks. Today she had taken her time with her face and hair, and she was wearing a white piqué frock with no shoulder straps. The hair was only vaguely kinky—it had been tortured by the hairdresser into a glossy wave. Her skin was the colour of cinnamon toast, and she had a dimple which, some people said, made her look like Lena Horne. Her teeth were very white and her lips only a little too thick, her nose only a little too flat. She might very well have been a Cuban, Stephen Ndegwa thought as he kissed her. Certainly her Negro blood comprised no more than a quarter, if that.

Stephen Ndegwa thought it was odd that Iris always made him feel a touch nervous. He couldn't imagine why; completely white people didn't make him feel nervous. Iris gave him the oddest sensation of intrusion, of non-belonging. Even when they went to bed together he felt as if some impossible favour had been granted him, which invariably made him clumsy and occasionally impotent. There was no—no sense of true *communion* with Iris. To this day he did not know exactly why he had married her, except that it seemed a good idea at the time and she had appeared to want it. She had been, after all, only a secretary in a large government office, although from her airs you might sometimes think that she was a film star or at least a television performer. He had met her at some large party or other in London, and she had immediately attached herself to him. He had found it easy to be flattered by

453

a small, tawny woman with large brown eyes and only a suspicion of kink in the coarse black hair she wore at shoulder length. It was more than easy to be charming to a honey-coloured girl with rather astounding breasts and legs which were only a trifle too skinny, a behind which was only a trifle too pronounced. He had told her she looked like a Somali queen, and she had loved it at the time.

Iris looked sensually hot, with her fleshy red lips and exaggerated swaying walk. Actually she was quite the other extreme of hot, or so Stephen Ndegwa had found. She was technically expert enough in her wifely duties, but Stephen Ndegwa always felt that he was bedded down with someone who was practising a recent dance step she had learned by correspondence and wished to perfect before she attempted it in public.

Somehow everything Iris did and said seemed to have been learned from frequent attendance at the cinema, and you kept expecting Harry Belafonte to walk into the scene with his shirt knotted around his bare belly. Iris was a sort of parody of the calypso girl she was trying so hard not to be. Her *as* were too broad, so that she pronounced 'that' as *thot*, and even when she talked she seemed to be practising before a mirror with someone else's mouth. Her words seemed to be shot from between her teeth, spaced like seeds popped from a water-melon.

Her moods varied from *femme fatale*, when she was heavily sultry, to old Lupe Velez film termagant, when she stormed, or to wide-eyed little girl, when she pouted prettily and even her tight-toed mincing walk resembled baby-talk. Stephen Ndegwa found it very difficult to keep in step with her moods, and even more difficult to talk to her for any length of time. Her attention wandered; her thoughts flitted lightly as a hummingbird from one topic to another.

Today the mood was not as yet determinate. Stephen Ndegwa was of no mind to sort it out until he had had at least two stiff gins.

'You look very pretty,' he said, after he had kissed her. 'Have you done something to your hair? Did you miss me?'

'I've changed it a little,' she said. 'This is supposed to be what they are wearing in London now. Or at least what they are wearing thot they have copied from the French. It is not very successful because the hairdressers here are all such fools. They seem to think they are doing you a favour when they make a botch of your hair. I told that girl, I told her——'

'Would you like a drink?' Stephen Ndegwa said. 'I need one. They were two very hard flights.'

'Well, perhops a very tiny one,' she said. 'But not much gin. Only a very little one. Gin makes me bilious.'

Stephen Ndegwa looked at the ice-bucket and found no ice. He poured about four fingers of gin into his own glass, and barely covered the bottom of hers. Gin did not make Iris bilious; it was more apt to make her drunk.

'Go and sit over there so I can look at you,' he said. 'You're looking very pretty.'

'You have already said thot,' she said, walking with her vamp's sway to the other room. Ndegwa noted idly the ridge of a sanitary belt under the tight piqué frock. Good, he thought. At least I have a reprieve from *that* for a few days. It's easier when I've been around a couple of days. She wants a bit of getting used to.

'Did I?' he smiled. 'I guess I only said it because I meant it. What have you been doing since I left?'

'The usual,' she said waspishly, crossing her knees and tugging unsuccessfully at the short tight frock. 'Nothing. There's nothing to do in Nairobi. It's bod enough when you're here. When you're away it's impossible. I won't stay here without you any more, Stephen. I won't!'

'You know it's almost impossible to take you along when I'm on these trips like the last one,' he said. 'One town after another. One hotel after another. One appointment after another. No time of my own. And it's very expensive.'

'Well, I don't see why I can't go with you, unless you're ashamed of me. Unless you're afraid I'd cromp your style. I suppose you meet all kinds of pretty women when you're off doing whatever it is you do.' This last with a nose-tilted sniff.

'Very few. Very, very few.' Stephen Ndegwa grinned at her. 'Most of them are the kind of women you find on committees. Painfully serious and usually very badly corseted. Lumps and bumps and bones. Very intense women with common-sense shoes and loud strident voices.'

'Do you ever meet any—any *coloured* girls—or is everybody you see *white*?' The words *coloured* and *white* came as an effort.

'Almost entirely white. Lady politicians and such. Very seldom interesting. Everybody's so painfully eager to learn about Africans now. They sort of scrub at you to see if the colour's fast. They seem rather surprised to discover that you talk English. Occasionally I'm tempted to growl and shout *boo!* at them.' He chuckled half-heartedly and saw that his wife was not amused.

He took another bite out of his drink and then said:

'I brought you something from America.'

Her eyes lit and pleasure wiped some of the petulance from her mouth.

'Oh, what?'

'I'll get it out of my bag for you when I unpack. Nothing very much. A handbag. Some perfume. A sweater set. Not very much, I'm afraid. I never know what to buy for you. What you'd like, I mean. It's very difficult. I never seem to have any time.'

'Oh.' Iris seemed disappointed. She expressed no desire to investigate the gifts. 'I suppose you're right. There's no place to go here to wear anything even if you'd brought me a mink coat.'

Stephen Ndegwa sighed. This was heavy going, as always.

'What *have* you been doing with yourself?' he asked her again.

'I told you, nothing. I read some and go to the pictures when there's anything worth seeing. I listen to the radio and play the gramophone and do crossword puzzles. There's nothing else to do. I've *been* to the Game Park,' she added, spitefully.

'What about this new boy?' Stephen Ndegwa tried another tack. 'When did we acquire him?'

'Last week. The other one was impossible. One of those *uhuru* spivs. Up half the night at meetings and a dead loss for any work the next day. Also I think he was stealing. I know he was rude. He called me *Memsaab* as if he was laughing at me. I hate these people, all of them. Stupid, dirty, ignorant——'

'Niggers?' Ndegwa asked softly, unable to resist.

'Yes, damn it, niggers! Shiftless, sneaking, thieving niggers! I hate them, Stephen! I hate them all! I hate the way they *don't* ever see you—they look through you and around you and every place but *at* you. You can't tell what they're thinking, but you always feel they're laughing at you for—for pretending you're white!'

'Well, sweetie, you *have* got just a tiny touch of the tar,' Ndegwa said. 'I'm rather somewhat more than average dark for an Italian myself . . .'

'You know what I mean!' Ndegwa could see the whites showing over the top of her eyes now. 'I don't care what colour I am, I'm not an Ofrican! I'm English! And because I'm English I'm frightened out of my wits! I never go anywhere because I'm afraid to go anywhere. I'm afraid of this new boy. I'm afraid I'll have my throat slit, like the houseboy did to thot Indian woman the other day. Like thot poor white woman the other day!'

And so now we approach it, Stephen Ndegwa thought. We will now get into the basic topic. This day is going to be one basic topic after another, I can see that. He got up and walked over to the bar.

'I think I'll have just another tiny spot before lunch,' he said, his back towards her, as he poured the same stout four fingers into his glass. 'How about you?'

'No, I don't want any more,' she snapped at him. 'And you always move or turn your back or change the subject when I say something you don't want to hear. I want you to listen to me, Stephen: I'm frightened. I'm serious—I think someone will kill me if I stay. If only for being married to you. Don't think I haven't heard what they say. I understand thot much Swahili.'

Drink in hand, Ndegwa turned to face her. By Jove, she really was upset. She was trembling, and her foot was kicking nervously back and forth, swinging like a pendulum suspended from her crossed knees. That was a sure sign she was upset.

'What do they say that you've heard in Swahili?'

'They laugh. They say there goes a brown *bibi* who actually thinks she's a memsaab. They say I look like a good piece of—of stuff.' She used the word *nyama*, which means both 'meat' and 'game'. 'They say they'll try some of thot, and they mean me, one of these days. And what's worse some say thot there goes the wife of Stephen Ndegwa, who thinks he is white, and who has brought back a half-white wife to try to prove that he's white.'

'Dear,' Ndegwa murmured. 'How very coarse of them. Anything else?'

'Don't laugh at me, Stephen.' Iris was near tears now. 'I'm quite serious. I think there's going to be bod trouble. I want to go bock to London. I don't belong here. I'm not Ofrican and I'm not white and I've no one to turn to, no place to run to, no place to hide!'

Oh God, Ndegwa thought, she *is* going to cry. He heaved himself out of the chair with a grunt and went over to his wife's chair. He sat on the arm and patted her shoulder.

'Please don't cry,' he said. 'Nothing will hurt you. Nothing will hurt me. This is just rather a peculiar time in the country. After the elections everything will be fine. I'm standing for the Legislative Council. We shall have independence soon, and with any sort of luck I'll sit high in the Cabinet.' Any old sop, he thought, throw the puppy a bone. 'I might even be Chief Minister.'

Now she opened her mouth and howled.

'Bot we still won't know anybody, and there still won't be anything to *do*!' she wailed, her shoulders shaking. 'I can't be an Ofrican woman in a *shuka* like those poor dumb creatures they—even you!' she flared suddenly—'even you are married to! The only white women I meet are political wives who look down their noses at me, who shake hands and then give their gloves to be washed instanter! The Indian women are worse—they aren't even people. They're just something walking inside a *sari*! I've seen enough of thot in Jamaica!'

Ndegwa took his handkerchief out of his breast-pocket and held it to her nose.

'Blow,' he said. 'You'll feel better in a moment. Here, I'll get you just another teensy drink. Do you a power of good. And I tell you what we'll do. To hell with having lunch here. You dry your eyes and dab a little powder on your nose and we'll just whip down to the Stanley and have lunch in the Grill. How'll that be?'

She blew and sniffled and blew again. Then she shook her head.

'I don't want to have lunch in the Stanley,' she said. 'I don't want to be stared at. And if you must know I'm afraid to go out with you. I don't want to be shot at and I don't want my throat cut. I want to go home to London. I want to live in Europe again where people are civilized—where there's people to talk to and things to *do*!' The last word was a wail.

Stephen Ndegwa patted her again.

'Come on, drink your drink,' he said. 'Maybe you're just having a little girl trouble or something and everything'll be brighter when——'

Iris raised her head and glared at him.

'I *am* having what you call a "little girl trouble", you great kind mon!' She was no longer weeping; she was noisily angry. 'I'm menstruating and it's out of schedule and it's always out of schedule and I want to tell you something else, Stephen Ndegwa; there's not another white woman in this God-damned country who's had a regular period in the last six months! What do you think of *thot*?'

Stephen Ndegwa shook his head.

'I'm sure I don't know,' he said. 'Wherever do you women learn these things about each other? I shouldn't think that——' He stopped. He had almost said: 'I shouldn't think that the white ladies would come running to you with their personal hygiene problems' and was quite glad he had bitten off the words.

'I know what you're thinking,' his wife said, red-eyed. 'There is not any colour bar in the beauty shops. Women under driers are the same pretty much the world over. I can understand English, too, even if I am brown-skinned and married to a block mon! They talk; women always talk—and I hate them for talking because they talk in front of me exoctly as if I weren't there, as if I were a—they talk as if I were a block servant with no ears and no feelings! I hate them, I hate them, I hate them!'

'If you only had some friends of your——' Ndegwa started fumbling to say, but his wife cut him off.

'And I hate these half-breed Seychelloise worse, because everyone thinks I am one, just because we're the same colour. And the Arab women hate you with their eyes over the *haiks*, and the block women look like they'd like to tear you to pieces, and the Indian women pull their *saris* over their faces when you poss, and even these cheap tarts that come out here to work in the hairdressers and dress shops look at you as if they were spitting and saying: "Who's thot nigger think she is, coming in here?"'

Iris collapsed into tears again.

Stephen Ndegwa did not know what to do so he got up and walked over to the window and looked stonily out at the flame tree. Poor girl, he thought, I suppose she *is* lost here in this shabby citadel of shabbier snobbery.

'What is it you really want to do? And stop crying, it only puffs your face and makes your eyes red,' he said sharply, turning back to his wife.

'I want to go on a long holiday at least to London for a while,' she said, looking at him directly and raising her chin. 'I want to go to the Continent or even bock to Jamaica. But I don't want to live here any longer.'

'But—we're married,' Stephen Ndegwa said lamely. 'My home and my work are here. We're married, you know. By a proper preacher.'

'I don't care any more,' Iris said. 'You don't care anything about me. You —you only married me because I was light-skinned and—and pretty. You married me as if I were a white woman—not just because I was a girl you liked. You are like all the block men everywhere—you do not want a woman as dark as you. You all want to marry white women and when you can't do thot you marry the next best thing. I do not want to be the next best thing to a white woman, Stephen.'

'Oh, the pleasures of the simple savage life,' Stephen Ndegwa murmured. 'Man, the master of his brutish wives. See here, then. You don't mean holiday, really. You actually mean you want to leave me permanently.'

'I love you, Stephen,' Iris said, 'but I do not think you care very much for me or any other woman. And I do not love you enough to live here in this

458

country where I am—I am not a simple nigger and there are no real coloured people and the white people won't have me except when they have to because it is politics. I am nothing in this country, and I am frightened of it now. Perhaps I am nothing in London but I am not a novelty in London and at least I am not frightened. I want to go, Stephen—as soon as I can. I want to go before somebody kills me just because I am nothing in this country.'

'For better, for worse,' Ndegwa said. 'Right. You have some money in your account, I know. I will give you a thousand pounds. That should get you back to London or even to Jamaica and keep you for six months at least. If you need more, write. Perhaps I can afford a small allowance. But remember, Iris, it is *you* who are leaving *me*. You have no claim on me for any whacking great alimony, if someone hears my name and puts a flea in your ear. You have no grounds for legal complaint. Remember that.'

'I will remember it. And you remember this too. It is generous of you to give me the money, but I would swim, I would walk, I would do anything to get out of this country of block apes and poor white trosh who think they are Bwanas! I hate the very word *Bwana*. Thank you for the money, Stephen. I am sorry I have not been a better wife, but it is impossible to be a good wife to a block mon in Kenya unless you shave your head and walk behind your husband!'

'You may very well be right,' Stephen Ndegwa said, as the houseboy, whose name Ndegwa did not know and did not particularly care to know, came into the room softly on his bare feet. He had changed from the coarse blue working *kanzu* of the morning into a clean white gown.

'*Chakula tayari*, Bwana,' he said.

'Lunch is ready, Stephen,' his wife said.

'I speak Swahili,' Stephen Ndegwa replied. 'And I do not think I have much stomach for lunch. Lunch is a white man's meal in any case. We Africans eat only at night. I think I shall go out to my *shamba* and see how the black folk are doing. Perhaps one of my wives may be constrained to give me a couple of yams and some *posho* at nightfall. When do you leave?'

'As soon as I can pock and book a ticket,' Iris said. 'Maybe tomorrow, if there's a plane.'

'There's always a plane,' Stephen Ndegwa said heavily. 'Sometimes I think it's a pity.'

He touched his fingertips with his lips.

'Ta,' he said, and went out the door, to find the chauffeur asleep in the back seat of the big white Mercedes.

'Wake up, *nugu*,' he said, reaching through the window to shake the man's shoulder. 'Drive me out to the reserve.'

TRUDGING BENT-HEADED up the long hill to his little *shamba* in the reserve, Stephen Ndegwa pondered the proposition of Iris, and concluded that he was relieved. No matter how things worked out for the future, Iris would never have fitted. In a way she had been placed in the same category as the white schoolteacher Jomo Kenyatta had married in his early days in London —suitable for the moment and the purpose thereof, but useless as a mate for a dedicated African politician. He mused wryly that it was quite all right for an African to marry white in a white man's land, but few African politicians dared marry even off-white as yet in their own country—not if they wanted to hold their restless people. Farewell, my light-brown fancy, said Stephen Ndegwa, as he opened the gate of the euphorbia-cactus *boma* which surrounded the huts of his Kikuyu wives.

They were both at home this time, talking in the shade of the big fig tree, and the sight soothed Stephen Ndegwa. This was the Kenya he would always love most, despite his white man's clothes and his big car. It was Kenya as God made it and very possibly intended it to remain. This was the true black man's Kenya.

The older woman, Mumbi, was holding forth on some topic with such vehemence that her hugely pierced earlobes flapped violently as she talked. The younger, plumper, prettier one, Wanjiro, was nodding in agreement. There were a couple of tin-cans of something that Ndegwa imagined was beer at their side, and now Mumbi was interrupting her tirade to take a deep swig out of one of the cans. It was beer all right; flecks of the thick gruel-like *pombe* clung to her lips. Both women sat squatting on their heels. They wore *shukas*, and as it was hot, they had allowed them to slip their moorings and both were unashamedly bare to the waist. Wanjiro was holding a fly-whisk made from the tail of a wildebeest, mounted into a carved wooden handle, and she automatically flirted it at the flies which came buzzing, attracted to the beer.

The ground of the compound, which held the two huts of his wives—one old-fashioned beehive, the other iron-roofed and oblong—and the granary and *thingira* or bachelor hut, was bare of grass and raked smooth. A few tail-switching spotted goats picked over the dungheap to the rear of the dwellings. More slept knee-folded in the cool shade, in good companionship with the two yellow big-eared *pie*-dogs. The banana patch seemed healthy—the broad leaves deeply glossy, and the bunches of fruit hanging thick and well developed. He noted with approval that one of the women had propped the trees well so that the burden of the fruit might not collapse the pulpy stalks.

There was a neat stack of firewood piled by each of his wives' huts, denoting commendable providence. A thin grey curl of smoke rose from the outdoor set of triple cooking-stones. Birds called lazily from the trees, and the hills lay blue and comforting in the distance. It was a good scene—a sight for sore city eyes, he thought. He shifted the parcels in his arms and called out:

'*Hodi.*'

'*Hituka,*' the senior wife answered in return, but looked womanishly annoyed, as if he had broken up a vastly more interesting discourse than he could possibly be expected to repair with any conversational tinkerings of his own.

At his approach both women swiftly adjusted their dress to cover their naked upper bodies. He squatted down on his heels beside them. One of the *pie*-dogs got up and walked lazily over to sniff at him, its heavy yellow tail curved so exaggeratedly backwards that its tip nearly reached the shoulders. A hen followed by a parade of chicks marched sedately round the corner of one hut, but emitted a frightened cackle and clucked angrily off with her brood when she saw the stranger. Stephen Ndegwa handed each woman a package.

'I have been far across the seas again,' he said. 'In the iron *ndege*. Here are some few little things I have brought you as presents.'

The faces of both women were impassive.

'*Eeehh,*' they said. They pushed the packages to one side with no show of curiosity.

'I only have a little time,' he said. 'But I wanted to see if you were all right. Are you all right? How are your children, Wanjiro?' he asked his younger wife.

'They are well. They are at the school. They are good children.'

'They are always at the school when I come,' Stephen Ndegwa said. 'The school must run all the hours of the day.'

'When they are not at the school they are with the sheep,' Mumbi, the older wife said. 'Wanjiro's children are very good children.'

Stephen Ndegwa produced cigarettes, and handed one to each wife. Then he gave flame to all three and they puffed for a moment.

'I did not know what to buy for you in the towns across the seas. So I bought beads, and a bracelet each, and some lengths of real merikani, made by the wa-Merikani themselves, and sold in a big *dukah* in a town called Nuyorki.'

'Nuyorki is as big as Nanyuki? The names sound alike.'

'It is a little larger,' Ndegwa said gravely. 'A little livelier, perhaps. In any case, if you are not pleased with the gifts you can exchange them at the *dukahs* here. I am sure they will be pleased to exchange them.'

'*Eeeeeh,*' both wives said.

'It has been a long time, nearly two moons, since you left on safari to Nuyorki,' the senior wife said. 'Are there women in this Nuyorki?'

'Many,' Stephen Ndegwa said, laughing to himself. 'But they have men of their own and they are nearly all *mzungu.*'

'Then you have been a long time without a woman,' the senior wife said. 'It is not good to go so long without a woman. Wanjiro, go into your hut to prepare yourself while I kill a goat to purify the *shamba* for the master after his long trip. Or perhaps,' the senior wife Mumbi looked at Ndegwa with

461

what he thought suspiciously to be a twinkle, 'perhaps they do not make a
sacrifice on the homecoming in Nuyorki before a man lies with his wife?'

'Oh, yes, yes,' Ndegwa said. 'They make sacrifices, all right. Of a different
nature. But do not kill the goat now, Mumbi. Nor have I time to go into the
hut with Wanjiro; I must be running along soon. I have just come to make
sure that you were well and had everything you needed.'

'Have you time for a drink of *pombe*?' Mumbi asked him.

'Thank you.'

'Go into the house and fetch a gourd of *pombe*, Wanjiro,' the older woman
said sharply to the junior wife. 'Hurry.'

'She is a good girl but constantly needs to be told things,' Mumbi said.
'These younger women are not so well trained as the women of my circumcision age. But even so they are better than the much younger ones who go to
the towns to work and play the whore. Will you take another wife some day?'

'God forbid,' Stephen Ndegwa said in English. '*Aca!* No!' he said, in
Kikuyu.

'We must begin to think soon of the circumcision of the son and daughter
of Wanjiro,' Mumbi said presently, as Wanjiro came backwards out of the
hut with a brimming canful of beer. 'They will need instruction. Two years
of instruction. Who is to provide it? The schools talk much against it. That
is wicked. It is not good for a girl to go uncircumcised after she becomes a
woman. No decent man would buy her.'

'We will speak about it some other time when I have thought of the matter
more,' he said, accepting the can of beer from his second wife. He drank
deeply. 'That is very good beer,' he said politely. 'Thank you.'

'Wanjiro made it,' Mumbi said. 'It was her time to make it. We make beer
turn and turn about.'

'*Eeeehh*,' Stephen Ndegwa said, and after a moment:

'What is the talk in the market? What are they saying at the *dukahs*? I
have been away. I do not know much of what is happening here in Kenya.'

Wanjiro shot a look at Mumbi. The older woman nodded.

'They say that now Kamau is dead you are king of Kenya.' Wanjiro
giggled. 'The other women are very envious of us. They say that soon you will
own all the goats and cattle and land in Kenya.'

Ndegwa's eyebrows shot up.

'They do, do they? And what else do they say?'

'They say that you were very shrewd. They say it would take a very
intelligent man to play the white man's game so long and so well that you
could finally make the white man kill off your rival for you while you were
safely away on safari in the iron *ndege*. The police cannot touch you, they say.'

'Well, damn my bloodshot eyes,' Stephen Ndegwa thought. 'What a very
clever fellow I am.'

He shrugged.

'*Eeehh*,' he said. Then, 'Do they say more?'

'Oh, yes,' Wanjiro said. 'Much more. They say that this time there will be

462

a big war between the white and the black *watu*. If the white man you hired to kill Kamau hangs, the other white men will start the war. If he does not hang, then *you* will tell the black men to start a war. They say that he will not hang and when it is announced over the wireless that he will not hang, all the black men will take *pangas* and *simis* and strike down the white man, as it was intended when the Mau Mau began but failed through error. This time they say you will make no error.'

'And they say that the reason there was no war when the Bwana Peter Poole was hanged was because you stopped it. You did not want to waste a war then—you wanted to wait until you had Kamau killed so that when all the fighting was over there would be no one to dispute you as king.' This was Mumbi, crowding in with her bit.

'And that is not all.' Now it was Wanjiro. 'They say that you will get rid of Jomo Kenyatta and Mboya and Gichuru and all the rest. Some even say that you will have the white men do it for you, as you used the white men to kill Kamau. The white men will do it for you and you will reward them handsomely with wives and cattle and land. They say this is bad, for if any of the white men are rewarded and are left, it will not be long before they have *you* killed and then they will own Kenya all over again. They say that the white man is using you as a tool instead of you using the white man as a tool.'

'But of course there are very many opinions,' Mumbi said. 'There are as many opinions as there are different colours in a flock of goats, but all the colours make the same bleating noise.'

'I would like another horn of beer, please,' Stephen Ndegwa said, holding out his tin-can. Wanjiro took it and went into her house again. Mumbi continued to talk.

'And there are some who say that Kamau is not dead at all, that this of the other day was nothing but a clever trick.'

'What kind of a clever trick?'

'I do not know. They did not say. But if he pretends to be dead and in reality is not dead then it must be a clever trick, *aca*? Else what would be the point of pretending to be dead?'

Stephen Ndegwa shook his head in bafflement.

'But suppose he is really dead?'

'Then it would not be a clever trick,' Mumbi answered. 'What is clever about pretending to be dead if you really *are* dead?'

I'll pass on that one, Stephen Ndegwa said to himself. The irrefutable logic of women. He accepted the beer that Wanjiro brought him.

'Does anybody agree on anything at all when you talk in the market?' he asked in a moment.

Mumbi looked at her colleague. Then they both nodded.

'*Eeehh*,' Mumbi said. 'They all agree that Kenya will not get *uhuru* unless all the white men are killed or driven away. Otherwise they agree that the white man is craftier and will manage to cheat the black man, as he has always cheated the black man in battles of wits. They all agree on that.'

'They are only waiting to be told when to begin the war, they say,' Wanjiro added. 'When, and in whose name,' she added as an afterthought. 'The last time they tried it they did it in the name of Jomo Kenyatta's circumcision year—*Kahyo*, the big knife, the *panga*. They say that the next name will be *Mambo leo*—"the year of beginning of modern practices". That was the name of the circumcision year of Kamau, they say.'

God Almighty, Stephen Ndegwa thought, what a clever one that would be. *Mambo leo* was 1930, and it's close enough to a logical circumcision year to fit the sloganeering to a *t*. I'll bet friend Matisia had that one planted a long time ago, not knowing how handy it might come in some day. 'The beginning of modern practices', eh? Damn my eyes again.

'People tell me that Kamau is actually dead,' he said. 'They saw the blood flow; they heard the shot; they saw him carried away with a hole in his chest and his back blown out. Are the *watu* sad because he is dead? Are they angry because he is dead?'

Now Wanjiro looked at Mumbi. The older woman shook her head.

'No. They are not angry nor are they sorry. They say one politician is like another; chop one down and another springs up, like weeds.'

'Suppose I tell you I had nothing to do with the killing of Kamau, and that I do not want a war? Would you believe me?'

'Oh, yes.' They spoke together but their voices were sceptical. 'We would believe anything you told us to believe because you would have a good reason for wanting us to say we believed it. Are you frightened of the police? Is that the reason you want us to say we believe you did not kill Kamau?'

'I could *not* have killed Kamau,' Ndegwa pointed out patiently. 'I was far away with the wa-Merikani, across the sea, when he was killed.'

'We know you did not actually kill him, but only paid the white man to kill him. Is that what you want us to believe?'

Oh, God help us all, Ndegwa said to himself.

'Look.' He spoke patiently. 'I did *not* kill him. I did *not* pay the white man to kill him. I did *not* want him to die. And I do *not* want any trouble because of his death. I do *not* want a war. I do *not* want more killing. Now, do you believe me when I say that?'

'If you say so, we will believe you. If that is what you want us to believe.' Ndegwa sighed.

'Very well. Good. Now see here: when there is much loose talk at Kiambu, will you remember to say that you have spoken to me, your husband, and that you have been taken into my confidence, and that all this talk of killing and wars is wrong—not true. Kamau's death was only an accident, as when a child is hit by a passing lorry on the big road.'

'We can remember,' Mumbi said. 'But why do you not have a big meeting and tell them yourself? They will believe you more than they will believe us. The men will believe you, at any rate.'

'But not the women?'

'Women do not believe men because men do not care whether women believe them or not. They do not take the trouble to tell the women anything for the women to believe. You only talk to us because you have been with the *mzungu* a long time, and have come to think like a white man.'

'But women believe women?' Ndegwa was surprised at this cool frankness. 'If a woman tells another woman something as a fact, other women will believe her?'

'Of course.' It was Wanjiro, and her voice was surprised. 'If it were not for other women, no woman would have anyone to help her—help her with the crops, help her with the goats, help her to have the children.'

'The only time a man helps a woman is when he puts the child inside her for his own pleasure,' Mumbi said, and again Ndegwa detected the glint in the elder wife's eye. 'Men only think of sleeping and drinking and fighting and putting children inside women.'

Ndegwa got out his cigarettes again and passed them around. He smoked for a second, and drew designs in the dust with his fingers. He made a strange jarring picture as he sat in his natty, well-pressed brown gabardine suit with its brown-and-white loafers, sitting on his heels amid *pie*-dogs and goats with his two wives—one shaven-skulled with the enormous lobe-flaps to accommodate earplugs as big as a bottle; the other younger, comelier, plumper, and with a fine fuzz of hair standing stiff and round like a man's crew-cut on her head. Both wore the *shuka* with nothing under it; both were barefoot, and both wore long spiral ankle-and-wrist and upper-arm bracelets of burnished coiled copper wire cutting into their flesh.

Suddenly Ndegwa wanted to laugh. It was all so God-damned ridiculous. Here he was sitting among the goats trying to get a line on the thinking of a race of people whose thoughts ran around like a chicken with its head cut off. Earlier he had been listening to a hybrid product of Africa and Europe which wanted to escape from Africa because it, the hybrid that was Iris, feared the African blood that pumped through its veins. Before that he had conducted a very high-level press conference, and in his most elegant parliamentary manner, including a fat slice of oratorical ham at the end. It was all so bloody silly. The aeroplane that took him to America to make speeches was ridiculous. The atomic bomb was ludicrous. The only reality was goats, and the women who tended the goats.

Stephen Ndegwa got up creakily from his crouching position on his heels. It was hot now; very hot at four o'clock and he wished he were going into his cool *thingira* for an hour's nap, as he had done the last time. But there were too many things for him to do.

'Do you remember, Wanjiro, that we talked a little bit about you appearing with me the next time I speak to a big crowd of people—that you would say a few words of what I tell you to the women? Do you remember?'

'I remember. You said that you would give me some white man's *pombe*—some *tembo*—so that I would not be frightened.'

'Well, keep it in mind. One day soon I may come and ask you to help me talk to the women, as women always talk better to women than men. You and Mumbi both. Perhaps you would not have to say anything, but only to sit on the platform with me so that the *watu* can see that I am a true Kikuyu who has wives.'

'Will your other woman—the one you keep in the village—sit on the platform with us as well?' Wanjiro's question was whetted to a fine edge.

'No, no, of course not,' Ndegwa said hastily. 'Certainly not. I do not own her any more. I sent her back to her parents.'

'Was she lazy and would not work, then? Or was she flighty and always running off with other men when you are on safari?' Wanjiro's voice now contained satisfaction. 'Will you get the bride-price back? I suppose her father will beat her and send her home again, though, because he will not want to return the bride-price.'

'No, she will not come back. She came from across the sea—I have sent her back across the sea. To London. And the bride-price was not very large. She was not worth very much as a woman.'

Stephen Ndegwa had reached the gateway to the euphorbia-thorn fence now.

'*Tigwoi Nawega*,' he said. 'I shall come to see you soon. Then we will slay the goat and I will resume my duties as a husband. I am sorry not to have seen the children; I almost forgot, there are presents for them as well in the packages. A knife of many blades for the boy, a thing of paint and powder and mirror, called *compacti* such as the white women use, for the girl. Good-bye,' he said, and started down the hill.

'*Eeehh*,' they said, and returned to their original position under the tree. Both women slipped their *shukas* into more comfortable positions, tucked in around the waist, and the younger wife went back into the house for more beer. Presently they would sleep, until the children came home and it was time to cook the single meal of the day. They would open the presents later. It was no good opening them now; they were not going any place to show off the new jewellery.

He spied his car, parked by the roadside. The chauffeur was asleep again. Stephen Ndegwa toyed with the idea of setting fire to his shirt, decided against it, and poked him in the ribs.

'Come on, Sleeping Beauty,' he said. 'Back to the office.'

He dozed briefly on the short ride back to Nairobi, and wakened in front of the office. He clumped up the stairs, wondering where to commence all the work he had piled up, reflecting that he had better get a couple of well-feed cases pretty soon if he intended to send Iris any money at all—and he did intend to send Iris enough to live on. The poor little thing had earned it, living with him. Or without him, as the case more aptly was.

The office force had gone home for the day. There was a message on his desk. The message said to ring Mrs. Charlotte Stuart at her home at Glenburnie Farm. He read the message over again, knowing very well what the old lady had on her mind. He would call her tomorrow. Tonight he would go to a hotel and take off his shoes and go to bed with a bottle and a book. He had had enough to do with women for one day, and he was bound to feel better tomorrow.

CHAPTER FOURTEEN

STEPHEN NDEGWA woke in his hotel room feeling tired, scratchy-eyed and dry-lipped again. As the years crept up on him, it seemed to him that each year it took longer to get over extended aeroplane trips. He had made it on momentum through yesterday very well—press conference, Iris, his other wives, the lot. Today he would see Charlotte Stuart, and he thought he would just ride up there and have a look round the farm; have a look, and see how far the old lady had progressed in her project before it had been interrupted by the carefully planned disruption which had killed Kathleen Crane and, he was convinced, certainly led to the elimination of his partner Matthew Kamau.

He thought he knew what she had on her mind; it certainly would do with the farm—she would want help in getting started again. He had offered help in the past. Now the old woman was calling the loan.

But first, he thought, so long as he was touching all bases, he had best have a word with Mr. Abraham Matisia, his late colleague's *alter ego*, and disabuse him of any extravagant ideas he might be entertaining about the running of a political party named KNAP. Kaynap was going to be his, Stephen Ndegwa's, own dear baby from now on, and there would be no more of the kind of irresponsible dynamite that Kamau advocated and Matisia implemented. They had done enough damage; he couldn't help that. But the time had come to put a permanent cap on Mr. Matisia's spear-blade.

He picked up the phone and called his office, wasting no words.

'This is Ndegwa. Get hold of Matisia,' he said. 'I want to see him in the office in an hour's time.'

He rang down for some breakfast and busied himself with a shower. The clothes didn't look too bad—perhaps he wouldn't have to go home after all. He could buy a fresh shirt, and the boy could buy him a razor and bring it up with the breakfast. He rang down to room service again, and added a razor to the order of coffee and papaya and soft-boiled eggs. Then he interrupted himself again and thought he would like to see what they had made of yesterday's interviews. So he rang down for the third time, wondering if they thought the man in 231 had completely lost his mind, dithering about like an old woman.

The shower and the shave improved his outlook, and he found he was hungry. He looked briefly at the papers; they had used the good pictures of

467

him—the open-necked healthy-looking one in the *Nation*, the tribal regalia one in the *Standard*. The *News* would be along later. He hoped the *News* would use the sincere one where he looked straight at you from the page.

NDEGWA ASSERTS LEADERSHIP, CALLS FOR MODERATION. That was all right. NDEGWA STRESSES UNITY, TAKES KNAP HELM—that was all right too. Body of both pieces substantially correct. The touchy stuff left out. If they were all right, he didn't have to worry about Bartlett's story in the later *News*. He looked at his watch. Just about time enough to beat Matisia to the office. Actually he would have preferred to speak to him in private, but he might as well have this one on the record. Kamau had held many moonlight conferences with Matisia. As head man of the party, Ndegwa wasn't having any.

Stephen Ndegwa was seated at his desk, reading the papers more closely, when the receptionist showed Matisia in, and closed the door after him.

'Sit down,' Ndegwa said, and neither got up nor offered his hand. 'We'll keep it short. And let's not bother with any unnecessary amenities.'

Matisia grinned at him insolently. Ndegwa rather imagined that he had chosen his clothing with an eye to insolence. Matisia was wearing a loud checked sports shirt with the tails out, a pair of bright blue slacks and plaited rawhide sandals over no socks.

'Pardon my lack of formality,' Matisia said, gesturing at his naked ankles. 'But the call sounded urgent, so I came in my gardening clothes. I didn't want to hold you up as I'm sure you must be very busy.' He grinned again.

'I just wanted to tell you that the time has come to stop all this hanky-panky you and Kamau have been up to for the past two years. Stop once and for all. Finish. *Kuisha*.'

'Would you care to be more explicit?' Matisia lit a cigarette and squirted the smoke indolently and insolently through his nostrils.

'Yes. I don't want you on my conscience any more. You and Kamau went too far, and it backfired in more ways than one. I blame myself for allowing it. I don't want to blame myself any more.'

'I'm quite sure I don't know what you're talking about,' Matisia said. 'If you're hinting I had anything to do with the demise of our beloved Leader you're off your rocker. I was safely thronged by witnesses in my own humble home. As for the other unfortunate circumstance, I am equally quite sure I don't know what you're talking about.'

Ndegwa punched a finger at him, leaning forward on the desk.

'The time for monkeyshines is over. You have played Machiavelli too often and too much, Matisia. Perhaps your little plots had their place in the overall scheme. I don't know. Maybe only God knows if all the riots and disturbances and strikes and civil disobediences hastened the business of independence. Perhaps they did. Well, now I want it stopped. We're within an ace of achieving what we sought, and I want it done decently.'

'As you well know,' Matisia said smoothly, 'I have no real position with Kaynap. Kamau made the speeches. You made the speeches. You both formed the policy. I just sort of helped round the house. I don't know why you'd be taking this tone with me.'

'All right,' Ndegwa growled. 'Play it innocent if you want. But I'm warning you off. Don't get any ideas about starting any more disturbances. Don't get any ideas about filling Kamau's shoes. And don't get any ideas about getting in my way. You'll get hurt. You'll get hurt badly. Is that plain enough?'

'It's crude enough, certainly,' Matisia said. 'You don't seem to have learned any tact from the Americans this trip. What makes you think, Mr. Ndegwa, that you can tell me anything at all? What makes you think you can warn me off, as you so charmingly put it? I don't work for you or with you. I am a good trade unionist, and I rather think I *will* fill Kamau's shoes—at least in the union. As to the future, I really couldn't say.'

'If you want my advice——'

'I don't,' Matisia replied sweetly.

'Have it, anyhow. Go away from Kenya. Go far away. Go to Cairo and play poison with Peter Koinange and that mob that run the radio. Go kidnap Lumumba's children. They go to school there. Go learn how to be an Arab rabble-rouser. They can still use your kind in Algeria, from the look of things. But get out of Kenya, Matisia. You and Kamau between you have come close enough to wrecking things for everybody here.'

'I have no intention of going anywhere, Ndegwa.' Matisia's voice had lost its silkiness. 'It's a free country—or will be, pretty soon. It will be a free country and I intend to stay here and cash in on that freedom. So far the meek have not inherited any considerable earths. Ask the Archbishop. Ask the good citizens of Tunisia. Ask Mr. Nasser.'

'Well, that's all I had to say. When the roof falls in on you don't say I didn't warn you.'

Matisia got up, and this time he shook his finger under Ndegwa's nose.

'I don't know just who the hell you think you are!' he said angrily. 'But if any roof falls in on me it'll fall in on you as well, Stephen Ndegwa! Everybody in this independence business is guilty of everything that's been done to shove it along! You and I and Kenyatta and Macleod and Macmillan and Mboya and Nkrumah—all the people everywhere on this continent—are in this business together. We're not empire-builders—we're house-wreckers! And until the house the British and the French and all the other bloody colonialists built is torn down there's no room in the picture for the likes of you, my fat imitation-white friend!'

Matisia spun round and went out of the door, slamming it behind him. For a moment Ndegwa sat and stared at his clenched hands. Then he relaxed his fingers and smiled sadly, nodding in agreement.

'The sick, sore trouble is that he's dead right,' he murmured. 'One topples, all fall down. We started out as wreckers when old Gandhi first invented civil disobedience on a large scale, and once a wrecker, always a wrecker. It's time we started to build and nobody seems to know how.'

He got up and walked out past the reception desk. A row of hopefully staring people sat on the long bench, waiting to see him. People were queued up in the dirty hall outside. Mostly they were badly clothed. All were black.

'I'm sorry,' he said to the waiting people. 'I can't see you today. I won't be back in the office until tomorrow morning.' He pushed through the pack of Africans that clogged the hallway, and went down to where his car waited. It would be good to drive out to see Charlotte Stuart at Glenburnie if only to blow some of the stink left by Matisia off him.

'What am I saying?' he rebuked himself. 'Does one skunk smell another?'

CHAPTER FIFTEEN

THE BURIAL of Kathleen Crane and old Kidogo on the hillside under the kaffirboom trees—the recognition that the abducted boy Karioki was certainly dead—had inflicted on Glenburnie farm only a raw wound that time would heal, as creepers would grow over the cairn of stones which marked their graves. Vines had crept over the other stones—over the other symbolic graves that held no bodies; Malcolm Stuart, whose complete body had not been recovered from the Mau Mau gangs; Ian Stuart, who had been shot down over Cologne in the war; Keg Dermott, who had been buried elsewhere. There were other stones, marking other graves—the body of Brian Dermott's mother Norah, and the battered corpse of young Mac Stuart who had been trampled by the wounded buffalo. Ivy had blanketed them all, and would soon cover the three new ones. The wounds of the living would heal as the ivy grew.

*

Charlotte Stuart looked at George Locke with dull eyes as he recounted the burden of his day's visit to Nairobi. They had not, painfully conscious of it in the avoidance, dwelt long on Brian Dermott apart from questions about his health and spirits.

'He seems all right,' George said. 'Physically he's all right. He's quite calm and rather—almost serene. That's what's most frightening to me. It's almost as if he had left his body there in the prison, as a . . . sort of official proxy spokesman in his absence. I'm not saying it well, but he talks almost as if it weren't him there at all. He speaks of himself objectively—almost in the third person.'

'Is he—is he sane?' Nell Locke asked her husband.

'If you mean the usual right-from-wrong definition of sanity, he's sane,' George Locke said. 'Legally he's certainly sane. But really, truly sane——' He shook his head. 'It's as if he were in a state of suspended animation. But

470

rational, yes. And to outward appearances—normal, certainly. It's just that he's like a normal somebody *else*, anyone else, except himself. And I wouldn't call it shock exactly.'

'What would you call it exactly?' Philip Dermott snapped at him.

George Locke made a helpless gesture with his hands.

'It's—it's as if he started out to go somewhere and had arrived finally but was terribly tired. Medically I don't know what you'd call it. It's as if he had completed a plan and now was satisfied to rest. Or die, even.'

'That'll be a desperately fine description, I'm sure, in a court of law,' Philip said. 'If you wanted to hang him, I mean. It's another way of describing premeditated murder.' Philip's voice was strained and irritable. He got up, and a holstered pistol swung low on his hip.

'Anybody want a drink?'

He looked belligerently around the room. The rest of the family shook their heads impatiently, turning back to George Locke.

'Well, I do,' Philip said, and walked over to the bar. He tossed off a measuring glass of neat whisky, and walked back to his seat before the fire

'Just exactly what are we going to do to get my brother out of jail, George?' he asked levelly, and George Locke noted that the blue eyes were no longer soft, that the long nose turned down severely over a thinner mouth. The short-chopped hair lent cruelty to his head.

'I don't know whether the lawyer was joking or not,' George Locke said. 'But he says that Brian's only chance to escape—to—to avoid . . .'

'*Hanging*,' Philip Dermott said crisply. '*Hanging* is the right word, George.'

'To avoid hanging, then, is for us to persuade some respected African lawyer to represent Brian. He gave a lot of reasons why.'

'Suppose you let us hear some of them,' Philip said curtly. 'As an alternative to a few things I have in mind.'

His aunt turned and looked at him, startled by his tone.

'Perhaps we ought to hear your alternatives first,' she said, reprovingly.

'Never mind, Aunt Charlotte,' the young man said. 'They'll keep. In any case they'll want some more arranging. Go on, George.'

*

The sadness that soaked the farm spread far beyond the immediate tragedy. The sadness lay physically on the farm itself, and was implicit in the lividly raw, upturned earth of the unfinished grading and digging—great ugly gaping wounds of red earth with clotted mounds like war-time graves heaped to one side of the open pits. The sadness was in the buildings without roofs—the unfinished houses of George Locke's medical centre, with its bare bones of naked beams and glassless windows staring like empty eye-sockets. The sadness lived in the clusters of empty native huts—in the machinery that stood silent and rustily accusing. It lay in the empty schoolhouse, in the shuttered general store which Charlotte Stuart had so enjoyed running—it keened from the silent market-place with its barren concrete floor.

471

The rattling clang and noisy bustle of construction had stopped. The cement mixers no longer growled and gargled; the greedy scoops of the earth-movers no longer gulped great gobbets of soil. The cranes no longer swung, the juggernaut blades of the bulldozers no longer snouted at the earth or tore angrily at the bush. The tractors no longer humped unevenly along like huge inchworms; the trucks no longer dumped their loads with deafening crashes; the pound of hammer and whine of saw and chunk of axe were gone, and gone with them was the roll of bass laughter and falsetto giggle from the noisy Africans who had filled the interstices of the mechanical clamour with their working chants.

All of the new tenant farmers were gone—disappeared overnight, their small belongings hurriedly jumbled in wicker hampers. Many of the older labourer-families had left as well. The fugitives from the farm had gone back to the reserves. All had faded into the anonymity of the African hut-villages and far-scattered *shambas*. They had been there, vociferously present, on a day. Overnight they were gone as surely as if swallowed by an earthquake or a flood. Only rubble was left for a few abandoned dogs to prowl and pick over.

A small percentage of the African population of Glenburnie had remained. These were the long-settled squatters who years ago had wrenched up their roots in the reserves; old family-retainer Africans who had been born on the farm and knew no other home. They stayed on fearfully, the old men and women and the younger children, but most of the young adults had packed up and departed with the others. Of the usual working force of five hundred natives no more than a hundred were left on Glenburnie, and a good half of that number was next to useless for anything but light work and specialized chores of house and barn.

The newly cleared fields lay unclothed and pleading in the short rains that now were beginning to fall briefly in the mornings. Some of the fields would have been ready for planting soon, but now they would only invite to their eager embrace the strangling arms of weeds. The rains pounded in the morning, small gracious rains, eager to work for the farmers, the cherished short rains for which the parched country had panted. The little rains turned the opened earth to dark-rouge muck, and stood pinkly like blood in shallow puddles on the hard-packed naked ground where the ambitious construction had vibrantly, briefly lived, and had as abruptly died.

There was truly now a massive *thahu* on Glenburnie Farm, as explicit a curse as ever came directly from Ngai from his seat atop Mount Kenya. Ngai was more than displeased—He was violently angry, and He had clearly demonstrated His displeasure. The new buildings were cursed—the un-planted fields were cursed—the entire farm and everything on it was cursed. The remaining Kikuyu families procured goats and fat rams and slaughtered them immediately, binding their houses round with rawhide to keep out the malevolent spirits, but the curse was there and would remain. The curse was far-reaching—it had carried to the Bruce farm, which had given its

472

headman Njeroge to the sacrifice that ate the small boy Karioki. The Bruce farm was now nearly deserted. The curse had extended through the Bwana Brian all the way to Nairobi, and had caused him to kill the Kikuyu leader Kamau, the greatest man in all Kikuyu. Ngai was so angry at His people that He had slain the leader of all the Kikuyu as a sign of His towering wrath, and the implementation of God's curse had come directly from Glenburnie. God in His hot anger had smitten mightily about Him—He had killed the strange white Memsaab; He had killed the godless old wild man; He had caused to be sacrificed the little child who was born Kikuyu and raised *mzungu* and He had finally sacrificed the man who some believed to represent Ngai's earthly presence—His Son, some people said, in hushed tones. He was so displeased with the people He had called His begotten Son back to His embrace.

The people who believed mostly strongly that God had slain His Son, through the hands of another, had been those who had been profoundly affected by Biblical teachings in the missions. They said that according to the white man's teaching, the slaying of Kamau was comparable to the slaying of the white man's Jesus Christ, which had been done mysteriously and for the sole purpose of establishing Christ forever in the hearts of men as a reminder of the wickedness of humanity. Kamau, then, had been slain at the express command of God, and his killing had been no more ignobly accomplished than the crucifixion of Christ. If Christ, as the Bible said, had died to save the world, then Kamau had died to save the Kikuyu people from white infection.

And Matthew Kamau would certainly return some day to lead his people again, even if he took the form of another man.

Again the seeds of cult, similar to the dormant cults of the Dini ya Masambwa and the Watu wa Mungu of a dozen years ago were deeply sown in the idle acres of Glenburnie farm. Abraham Matisia had lost little time in setting about his work, as the Kikuyu flocked to the forests to pray under the *mugumos* and to sacrifice their sheep and goats quietly away from the sight of the white man. Goats and sheep would have to do for the moment—they would suffice until the day of massive offering of more important flesh.

CHAPTER SIXTEEN

IT WAS early afternoon when Stephen Ndegwa arrived at Glenburnie Farm. He had spent the midday hours in the reserve, after dealing with Abraham Matisia, and had talked to just enough people to become more worried. Each man he had spoken to had seemed tensely eager, as if waiting for instructions. He had mentioned Kamau several times, and eyes had brightened

473

expectantly—almost as if the owner expected more than Ndegwa was volunteering. As if they expected a signal, a password, Stephen Ndegwa thought gloomily.

'Drive round the farm on some of these new roads,' he said to his driver. 'Anywhere at all, for about half an hour.'

The driver rambled helter-skelter over the farm, and Ndegwa was surprised at the immense amount of work which had been started, and which now lay sadly incomplete. In all truth the old girl had gone at it with a right good will, he thought—another month or so and she would have completed an unbelievably ambitious operation. No wonder my colleagues wanted it stopped, he thought. And they certainly stopped it. It looks like the original deserted city—almost bombed-out by the look of the buildings.

Somehow, he thought, looking at the stacked rough-cut lumber warping from the rains, the rubble heaps of blasted rocks, the uneven piles of brick and the disconsolate half-empty kegs and lonely sawhorses, somehow something that's killed before birth looks worse in death than when it's killed in its prime. This looks like an embryo torn from a dying animal, ripped living from its mother for the hyenas to wrangle over. And the new-cleared fields —the pitiful raw red earth that my people have clamoured for. It lies there gape-legged for insemination, and there is no one to give it seed. I wonder, Stephen Ndegwa thought bitterly as he drove, if this dreadful afterbirth of abortion is a blueprint for my country when it is free to determine its own way? The thought depressed him greatly.

'Drive to the big house now,' he said to the chauffeur.

'I am afraid of this place, Bwana,' the driver said. 'I do not want to stay alone in the car. This place has a curse on it.'

'Don't be a bloody fool, and for the last time, stop calling me Bwana,' Stephen Ndegwa said. 'Nothing will hurt you here. There's no curse on the farm—unless you count a pack of damned fools like you who make their own curses.'

'I will stay in sight of the house with the car,' the driver said. 'If anything tries to harm you, call out loudly and I will go for the police.'

'Oh, Jesus,' Stephen Ndegwa said. 'You can go off the farm to the big *dukah* if you like. Come back for me in about an hour. I want to be back in Nairobi before dark.'

'So do I,' the chauffeur said. 'So do I.'

*

The old lady looks done in, right enough, Stephen Ndegwa thought, mounting the steps. And I can't say as how I blame her. Poor old duck. Living out the last of her days in a shambles of a life's work.

He held out his hand to Charlotte Stuart who was awaiting him in her chair on the veranda.

'I won't say anything at all about how the little rains have helped your flowers,' Stephen Ndegwa said. 'No small talk at all. I'll just say that I am

474

deeply, deeply sorry for everything that's happened here, and not only for the tragedies of the poor woman and your nephew in his involvement with my late colleague. And my sorrow is not mostly for the dead people or your nephew. I have just ridden briefly over your farm. I have seen what you intended to do and what has happened to it as a result of all this dreadful business.'

'Thank you, Mr. Ndegwa,' Charlotte Stuart replied. 'I won't mince any words either. You offered me your help once. I am now reminding you of the offer. I don't want my nephew to hang. And I don't want to lose what we've begun here on Glenburnie. Somehow I think what we have begun here on Glenburnie is bigger than whether or not my nephew hangs—but I also think that one is a part of the other, and if we solve one thing we may solve another. Nor would I have to remind you of all people that neither my nephew nor my farm are in themselves important. It is merely what they represent that is important now.'

Stephen Ndegwa cleared his throat. Here it comes, he thought. Might as well jump in feet first and get it over with.

'What do you want me to do?'

'We have engaged the legal services of Mr. Reuben Quiller, of Quiller and Moseby. I am certain you know them.'

'I know them. I know Mr. Quiller very well. We have—ah—collided in interest on several occasions. Usually he has won. He is a very, very able man. Any advice he gives is the best.'

'Exactly.' Charlotte Stuart dipped her head. 'And he has advised us to ask you to represent my nephew.'.

Stephen Ndegwa's mouth gaped slightly. He had fully expected to be asked for help about getting her people back to work on the farm, and was prepared to give it. He even had hatched a plan which, he thought, might coincide neatly with his own interests—and, he amended his thoughts hastily, the interests of the country. He had thought perhaps she might want advice on the defence of Brian Dermott. But the last thing he had expected to be asked was for himself to defend the murderer of his late partner!

'Surely you must be joking, Mrs. Stuart,' Stephen Ndegwa said. 'Or perhaps I misunderstood you?' He ran a finger under his collar. It was hot here on the porch—even in the shade.

'You did not misunderstand me and I am not joking. I want you to defend Brian Dermott. Quiller tells George Locke—he's my nephew's brother-in-law—that the only hope of getting my Brian off is for an African counsellor to represent him. The reasons, I am quite sure, would be as apparent to you as to Quiller. They are certainly apparent to me—and we have to reach no further back than the trial and hanging of Peter Poole.'

Ndegwa gnawed at his underlip, and fumbled for a cigarette. He shook his head.

'I don't know what to say except that it is of course impossible. It is necessary to hang Brian Dermott for all the reasons you know very well, apart from the question of his guilt. Not to hang him would certainly put Kenya into a bloody uprising by the natives. He has, after all, killed their leader. And if Kenya creates a blood bath, it cannot help but spread to the neighbouring countries. In this case the African will accept nothing less than an eye for an eye. He can't afford to.'

'You believe that? You believe that we will just keep on killing and hanging, hanging and killing, to avoid wholesale slaughter?'

'I believe it,' Ndegwa said. 'I don't endorse it but I believe it. And I don't see any way out of it.'

Charlotte Stuart clapped her hands, and Juma's head popped through the door.

'I have been remiss in hospitality,' she said to Ndegwa. 'Would you like a drink?'

'I would love a drink. A gin and tonic, please.' He nodded to the servant and spoke to him in Swahili. Juma grinned dutifully and scuttled away. Both Ndegwa and Charlotte Stuart sat silently, smoking, until he had returned with the drinks. Charlotte Stuart raised her glass ironically.

'Welcome back to Kenya,' she said. 'I would like to hear about your trip to America—some other time. Now see here, Ndegwa. You know that the guilt or innocence of my nephew has nothing to do with whether he'll hang. Quiller was right in what he told George—you can't win a case in Kenya today against a black man, especially a dead one, in the temper of these times. That's wrong—as wrong as it was when a black man couldn't win a case against a white one. And platitude or not, you people are not going to be able to build a country by continually compounding old felonies. There's been enough tribalism—black and white. Too damned much, if you ask me.'

'I couldn't agree more, Memsaab. But let's put it this way. Selfishly. Somebody's going to have to lead my wretched people to the light, and it looks very much as if it will be me, in the regrettable absence of Kamau. And while I admit that two wrongs don't make a right, and that something more than Brian Dermott is on trial in this instance, what do you think is going to happen to *me* as a political leader if I should get emotionally carried away sufficiently to stand up in court in defence of your nephew?'

Stephen Ndegwa drew the hard edge of his hand across his throat and made an unpleasant grating noise with his tongue.

'If not physically, certainly politically, I will be finished—washed up, through, *kuisha*. If I thought I could show justification for the act—I might just possibly risk it. I might risk it for a single, sober reason: I believe that justice should be administered only in the courts of law, and that it should be administered equally by, for, and to all people of all colours. I would like the world to see, for once, that there is at least one African politician who does not merely see black—selfishly black. The eyes of the world are on us, and it would be good for the world to see a black man defending a white man at a time when the defence of a white man in an emerging black country is indefensible practically. But I dare not. I *dare not*, Charlotte Stuart.'

476

The old lady looked steadily at Ndegwa. She smiled slightly.

'You have just offered me the argument I was prepared to confront you with,' she said. 'And why dare you not, if such a thing could be in the best interests of this country of yours—ours?'

'I dare not, for the simple reason that my own people would never understand my motives. They do not want unbiased logic or justice yet. They are not interested in a larger picture. All of us have made the mistake of courting the mob—I am guilty of that as well—and we must continue to court the mob until such time as we have the mob with us. Then, bit by bit, we can risk disenchanting the mob for its own long-term good.' He sighed and took a sip of his drink.

'It's a pity, but there it is, Memsaab. You might say that I, as a moderate, am the best of a poor bunch.'

Charlotte Stuart smiled again, more generously this time.

'At least you assess yourself honestly,' she said. 'And I'm inclined to agree with you. But surely, Ndegwa, you're not going to carry on rabble-rousing just to stay in the driver's seat? You're certainly not going to follow in the hateful footsteps of that man Kamau?'

Now it was Stephen Ndegwa's turn to grin slightly. He raised his glass an inch in her direction.

'No, Memsaab, I'm not going to carry on in Matthew's hateful footsteps, as you so neatly define it. I am going to try to do my best to reach outside Kamau's pattern of preach and promise, pray and incite. I am going to try to spread a little hard-headed reason, like manure over a sickly crop, to see if I can make something healthy grow.'

'But I take it finally that you will have no part of defending Brian Dermott?' The old lady fixed him with her eyes.

'I will have no personal part of defending Brian Dermott. One reason is expediency, as I told you. But a tiny bit of morality has edged in here, as well. I'm not as good, not so flashy a lawyer as your Mr. Quiller. But I do recognize the cynical truth of what he says. I *could* save Brian Dermott by defending him in symbols—black man defending white man in terms of white man's tribal history. A switch, the Americans call it. I could clap on my wig and stand up and shout *Hallelujah!* and my bare presence in the court would suffice to take the curse of right or wrong off the jury's conscience, and Brian Dermott would walk out a free man.'

He paused, and cleared his throat.

'. . . a free man. What a wonderful connotation in the simple words *free man*. We have never been free men here, Memsaab. The mere presence of a white man in your courts has made us automatically guilty. We are not tried by a jury. We cannot as yet even *sit* on juries, because we are nobody's peers and a jury must be composed of peers. We are tried not even by a tribunal, but by a white judge with native elders who may hesitantly advise but may not decide innocence or guilt or pass sentence.

'I do not suddenly admire the idea of preserving the procedure and

477

becoming a one-man black tribunal to set free a white man merely because of the ancient conflict of colours. I have too much—perhaps *pride* is as good a word as any to describe my refusal to use myself cynically, as black men have gone cynically free in the past if a white man said a good word for *them*. If I believed that your nephew was justified in the killing of Kamau perhaps it would be a different matter. But I will *not* be a cheap black publicity stunt, and this is what it amounts to . . . a shoddy shyster trick to free a guilty man.'

'You mentioned tribal history,' Charlotte Stuart said. 'From what little I know of courts and the Kenya laws, when a black man is tried, his tribal background and tribal laws are taken into consideration. Is not that right?'

'To a point. Only to a point. They are taken in consideration by a tribunal of one judge and three assessors. The assessors come from the tribe of the accused. They are assistants but cannot rule. They may express opinion but they cannot influence the judge. Who is always white, but who is not bound to abide by the opinions of the elders.'

'But the verdict is arrived at according to English law?'

'No, indeed. Not always. In Kenya the English law has been amended by legislation to encompass what would be reasonable considering the race, and the tribal community. In Kikuyu country, to spit in a man's face might be a high compliment or a deadly offence, according to the background of the deed. There are cases here in law where men were freed for killing an oath-preparer. In England, for instance, words alone are never accorded to be sufficient provocation for violence, but in Kenya words might constitute spells, and so be defined as a direct attempt to take a man's life. You might even go free of murder on grounds of self-defence if it could be shown that a man were preparing to lay a curse on you. Apart from the African, homicide has been shown to be justifiable before a court of law when the accused killed a man for raising the veil of a Mohammedan woman. It's all according to the neighbourhood of the deed and the climate of the crime.'

'Then,' the old lady whetted her voice to a cutting edge, 'would you not be able to salve your conscience in terms of my nephew's tribal history in Kenya—especially if there were some concrete clue as to why he hunted out Kamau and killed him? Or if it could be proved that he was in a state of curse —of temporary *thahu*—due to something for which Kamau was responsible, would he not then have a defence? Is it fair to punish a man for exercising his tribal customs which are approved within the tribe?'

'It is not fair, to that last, but I must admonish distinguished counsel that a great many black men have swung for the sin of violating the white man's tribal law of "Thou shalt not kill" when the black man was killing according to his most anciently cherished and tribe-blessed beliefs, which is that killing an enemy is not only justifiable but highly commendable.'

'Point taken. So we will hang my nephew for doing what he received medals for doing half a dozen years ago, in order to satisfy politicians and keep down rebellions and ease the conscience of those—those baboons in Whitehall and in the United Nations and all the rest!' Charlotte Stuart spluttered the last of her words.

'Distinguished counsel is eminently correct. That is exactly what we will do, and we will *not* take into consideration your nephew's tribal background and history, germane as it may be to the issue.' Stephen Ndegwa's voice was flat. 'It is not practical now *not* to hang your nephew.'

Charlotte Stuart's shoulders slumped. Then she raised her chin.

'I have known that all the time, I suppose,' she said. 'But I thought it would do no harm to try.' The chin dropped again.

'I am afraid so. But I am afraid of something else, Charlotte Stuart. I am also afraid of *your* people—of the kind of people who make up the racial and tribal background of your nephew. I do not know what they will do if we carry blithely on with this playing everything the black man's way as the whites kneel down before the takeover. Perhaps some of the whites will not want to kneel—and perhaps we have as much or more to fear from a white rebellion as from a black uprising. In any case, the tragedy would be equal.'

The old woman held up both hands in dismayed negation.

'I have thought of it too often and I don't want to think of it!' she cried. 'I don't like to think that me and mine have been at the core of it! I accept the guilt, Ndegwa, for trying an experiment here in all honest sincerity. I thought—and you seemed to think so too, at the time—that we had a good chance here to make what you called a test case of some sort of feasible working agreement between the native and Europeans! It has seemingly gone all awry and it does not appear to be anyone's particular fault that I can lay hand to. We got caught up in it and here we are, with my poor wild nephew even more of a test case now than ever the farm was!'

Charlotte Stuart showed deep emotion now for the first time. Her eyes misted, and she blotted at them angrily with her handkerchief.

'I'm sorry,' she said in a moment. 'Forgive me. I didn't mean to play the weeping woman for you, Ndegwa. What we need is another drink. Juma!' she bellowed. '*Lete ginni ingine!*'

'What I mean to say,' she said in a few moments, in a quiet voice, 'is that what seemed to be a good idea wound up in disaster through what seems like a dreadful series of accidents—to that poor girl Katie Crane, which certainly is what made Brian shoot Kamau—and it was not meant to be anything but some sort of effort at a peaceful compromise. But the accidents were not just accidents. Certainly they happened as part of a planned evil by your own people! You cautioned me yourself, Ndegwa! You said there were people— politicians, and how I despise the word—who would try to stop me! Well, they stopped me, all right enough. The only thing they hadn't planned on was the Crane girl getting murdered and my nephew going daft enough to shoot one of the connivers!'

'We don't know that Kamau had anything to do with it, Mrs. Stuart,' Ndegwa said mildly. 'It could have been anyone in my party or in the others.

479

We are all guilty of incitement—of over-zealous rabble-rousing for selfish ends. But we do not know it was Kamau who ordered the kidnapping of the little boy. And we certainly do know that Kamau had not counted on getting himself killed as part of any scheme to stir up the animals.'

'His getting killed's the only bright spot in the whole—— No, I don't mean that,' Charlotte Stuart said. 'But whatever was schemed, it's all wrecked, in any case. It seems to me the land is rushing steadily backwards, and the people with it.'

Stephen Ndegwa clutched one knee with both hands and rocked back in his chair.

'That is another aspect of why I am here,' he said. 'I speak frankly, Mrs. Stuart—I am afraid of so many things. I know as well as we sit on your shady porch that all the old rumblings have started—are starting—and all because of the death of Matthew Kamau. All that's been needed is the right kind of martyr, and we are right back again with The Man in Red—remember?—and the madman, Elijah Masendi, who got out of Mathari asylum in nineteen forty-four or forty-five and started a cult in less than six months. And under the protective coloration of *uhuru* and the upcoming elections and a proper, God-sent martyr all laid on, heaven knows what'll happen unless something's done to try and shove things back in perspective.'

'But what, for God's sake?' Charlotte Stuart cried. 'I'm not telling you—you know that there's no such thing as "perspective" with your people! It won't make much difference who it is that starts what, if the whole country's ripe for explosion. The first man to drop the match in the powder keg——' She nodded her head. 'And I used to think that old Jomo Kenyatta was a menace to security, like the Governor keeps saying.'

Stephen Ndegwa also shook his head vigorously. He leaned forward now, and lowered his voice for effect.

'The simple people can only see one thing at a time,' he said. 'Fortunately the thing they see right now is me. I don't know how long they will keep focusing on Ndegwa, but I haven't a great deal of time to lose, or somebody else will slide into the spotlight and proclaim himself Kamau's successor.

'I propose to harangue the multitudes, Mrs. Stuart—to confront them in the name of peace and prosperity and co-operation, and above all, responsibility. I want to assume the leadership of the country, formally and on the record. I want some sort of positive start towards the elections and certainly, later, after we've formed a government, towards *uhuru*. I want to make a plea for what I've always stood for—moderation and slow steady steps to progress.

'I want to impress on them a need for co-operation with the whites, and I want to impress on them their need *of* the whites. I can think of no more dramatic way to do it than to lift the curse off Glenburnie Farm—to get your people to come back to work, and for you to press on with your project. *And* under my endorsement and approval for all the *watu* to see and hear. Matthew Kamau will doubtless spin in his grave, wherever they've put him, but I shall approve you and endorse you under his name, as well, even if I have to swear on my grandfather that he has visited me in a dream with the instructions!'

'Now,' Charlotte Stuart said. 'Speak slowly. I will be most interested to know just how you propose to lift a curse as big as the one that's smothering Glenburnie at this moment.'

'I would like to be able to lift the curse and to lay Kamau's ghost at the same time,' Ndegwa said. 'It can be done if it's approached in the right way. We are a simple people. We usually heed explicit example, which is why our witch doctors persist. If I can let just a little bit of sunshine into the darkness of the moment, if I can preach sweetness and light instead of superstition and darkness, if I can make hard work and common sense believable, we will lift your curse and lay Kamau's ghost in the same stroke.'

'You'll have to be a witch doctor yourself,' Charlotte Stuart muttered. 'It'll take a proper miracle.'

'I don't think so,' Ndegwa said. 'I think that if we have a big meeting here —and I can assure you that I can provide the transport—in full sunlight, and I can explain that you are not monsters and that what has happened was all accidental, not a curse or a sign from God or anything so dear to the sorcerer's heart, we will be halfway home to sanity.'

'And then?'

Stephen Ndegwa paused, and spoke hesitantly.

'This is not a promise. But in this instance, moderation is sanity, and sanity is strength. If they will accept me, they will not make an unholy issue out of a dead man. And if they do not make an issue out of Kamau, if they do not set him up as a saint, then perhaps the trial of your nephew will not become a burning election issue—will not become the bonfire on which the whole definition of *uhuru* is lit. Perhaps we will be able to proceed calmly to our elections and our eventual independence, and perhaps the political necessity to hang your nephew as a cynical sop to the black majority will not be so strong.'

'I really do not quite understand,' Charlotte Stuart said. 'First you said it was hopeless and now you are holding out some hope to save Brian's life? You think what happens here will have a bearing on whether my boy hangs or not?'

'I am not holding out much hope,' Ndegwa said grimly. 'Not much. But some. Better than none at all. At least if the curse is off the farm on my say-so, they will be following me. And you may be very sure that I shall not make any fiery election fodder out of your nephew. We can postpone the trial until afterwards—this I know can be arranged—and perhaps when we have our safe majority in the spring and have formed our government, then the people will have forgotten Kamau and will not thirst so for his killer's blood. They will have a new toy to play with. And perhaps the British government will not be so pantingly eager to quench that blood-thirst. It is a hope—a faint one, but a hope.'

'And how would you be after trying to get these people to trust me, and by trusting me, to trust you—or is it the other way round?' Charlotte Stuart attempted to keep the eagerness from her voice, but the slight lapse into brogue betrayed it.

'By calmness, as I said—and by my bland assumption of fatherhood over the flock. By letting them see me—see me here—by letting them see me with you, in friendship and co-operation. They will see me with my family, and they will see you with yours. We will talk—you and I—and my women, as well.'

'Your women? What women?'

He stabbed at Charlotte Stuart with his forefinger, and then closed his hand to smack it into the other palm.

'I propose to make an example, Charlotte Stuart! I propose to resettle my wives and children here on Glenburnie Farm, and to take a hand in running your project myself! I will be one of your foremen if you will—I will live a good portion of my time on Glenburnie Farm with my wives and children!'

'Where exactly do you propose to make your talk?'

'Here. Right from this porch. Where better? The curse is on the house. We will lift the curse from the house by speaking from the house. I will bring my wives and two children. We will speak here from the porch, to the people in this vast yard and garden of yours. God on The Mountain is looking over my shoulder as I speak—and I imagine that with a little ingenuity we can rig an adequate loudspeaker system from house to trees so that He can hear my voice. I will speak from the veranda with you and your family around me. You will speak, and my wives will speak—and perhaps your niece and nephew and the rest of the family will speak. Nothing long-winded. All very simple. How does that strike you?'

'Anything at all you say at this moment strikes me as wonderful. I won't know what to say, but perhaps you can tell me.'

'When we have finished talking we will go—I will walk through the crowd —to your doctor's new hospital site. One of my wives will go to the school-house, the other to the unfinished living locations. I trust your niece or your nephew's wife will go along to the other places with them. We will all do something very symbolic—the time-trusted political gesture. We will drive a nail or lift a plank or raise a ridge-pole or roof. We will return to the basics of solid Kikuyu goodwill—the communal effort to make a house for a bridal couple.'

'Surely you'll have difficulty arranging a permit for such a big political gathering?' the old lady said anxiously. 'I know there is a ban on any congregation at all at the moment. They've already read the riot act over the loud howlers the day Kamau was killed. It's still in effect, George Locke tells me.'

'I won't have any trouble with government, not when I tell them what this little picnic of ours is in aid of,' Ndegwa said. 'I want the usual number of police and a bit more, though. If all goes well we might have a fairly beery bunch of citizens on our hands. I had thought of asking some Masai and Wakambas to join the fun.'

'Are you sure it's wise having the Masai and the Wakamba here as well? You know how they are with Kikuyu?' Charlotte Stuart's voice held a note of anxiety.

'It's a gamble, Memsaab. But the Masai live in Kenya, too. So do the Wakamba. They'll have to start getting along with each other sooner or later. We'll make them leave the spears and the *rungus* in the cloakroom. And there is a very healthily positive thing about mixing the races. One group may very well serve as a check on the other. Racial pride, and all that. This is an effort on behalf of multi-racialism—we might as well shoot the works.' He shrugged. 'In for a penny.'

'I know I've nothing to lose,' Charlotte Stuart said. 'God bless you for a good man, Ndegwa.' She held out her hand. 'Good-bye and thank you. When do you want this jamboree to take place?'

'A week. Ten days. There is very much to be arranged. In the meantime I'll whistle up your lawyer in Nairobi. Perhaps it will be possible for Quiller and me to go and pay a call on your nephew together. If he'll see an African. Perhaps we can dig up a little extra in the way of sound defence for Quiller to work with. I'll try, anyhow. At least I'll have a word with Quiller.'

He was standing on the top steps, waiting for his car to come from a shady spot under the trees, when young Philip Dermott walked out of the living-room onto the porch.

'Aunt Charlotte, Jill says that——' He stopped as he saw Ndegwa standing on the steps. His eyes took in the big white Mercedes crawling forward in the drive.

Ndegwa turned to see a lean, bristle-haired, hard-jawed young man, with a downturned disapproving nose and a mouth that squeezed itself from softness into a thin pale line. The young man was wearing a short-sleeved khaki shirt and dirty blue jeans. A holstered pistol rode his hip. His eyes flicked coldly from Ndegwa to the approaching white automobile.

'I'm sorry. I didn't know you were busy,' he said to his aunt in a harsh flat voice, and turned to go back into the house. His aunt reached out and caught him by the pistol holster.

'Wait a minute, Philip,' she said. 'This is Mr. Ndegwa. He's come to help us with the farm and maybe with Brian as well. This is Brian's brother, Philip Dermott, Mr. Ndegwa,' she said. 'Mr. Ndegwa is a friend, Philip.'

Ndegwa turned, and started towards Philip Dermott with his hand outstretched. 'I'm glad to know you,' Ndegwa said. Philip looked coldly at the hand, and then spoke past Ndegwa to the trees.

'I thought the likes of him had already helped us *enough* with both the farm *and* Brian,' he said nastily. 'What's he come for this time, Aunt Charlotte? To take over the place and move in with his *maridadi* car?'

He looked straight into Ndegwa's eyes and then spun on his heel to walk slowly and insolently into the house.

'I'm sorry, Ndegwa,' Charlotte Stuart said.

'I understand,' Ndegwa said, heading down the steps again. 'I understand completely. Don't worry about it. Maybe we'll have that straightened out too in another week or so. I'll be in touch, Charlotte Stuart. Keep well. Good-bye.'

'Good-bye, Stephen Ndegwa,' the old lady said. She looked after the car until it had disappeared in its own dust. Then she thumped the floor violently with her stick.

'Philip Dermott!' she shouted. 'You come here, and God-damned *upesi sana*!'

CHAPTER SEVENTEEN

WORK AMONG the whites had swiftly trebled on Glenburnie Farm. Agriculture was necessarily forgotten for the moment; all white hands and as many blacks as could be dragooned turned to the vitally basic chores of milking and stock-feeding. Young Philip Dermott cursed and turned dairy cattle into fields of barley and wheat, and loosed the pigs among the potatoes. The cows must be milked, even if the milk had to go to the pigs as well. The stock must be fed; the mechanics of feeding them were too involved for the number of hands remaining on Glenburnie. Let the bastards founder themselves, Philip thought, it's better that our own cattle eat the wheat than leave it to mildew in the field. Let the bloody pigs have the potatoes and the milk—there's nobody about to chop the potato tops, and the milk will only sour.

Philip Dermott had buckled on a pistol just after his brother had found Katie Crane, and it was beginning to feel comfortably normal to him now. A week—God, it seemed a year—had passed since the dirty business on the farm and in Nairobi, and Philip felt exactly as he had felt as a half-grown youth during the Mau Mau years, when a gunstock drooped permanently from the crook of his arm and a pistol on his hip felt as natural as a handkerchief. When he rode around the farm now, on a day that began in the black pre-dawn and ended when he finished it somewhere around ten or eleven at night, he tucked a rifle under his leg in a saddle-boot.

He had always been a very quiet boy, and now Philip Dermott was almost entirely silent when he was in the house. His young wife looked at him with questioning, frightened eyes, as he barely spoke during the late uninspired supper and then took her off to bed. He latched the door from the inside, as they had locked doors during the Emergency. They had, in fact, taken to locking up the entire house again, and once Jill had wept when Philip had snapped at her for forgetting to draw a curtain.

He barked at Juma, who ran out his lower lip in a nearly perpetual pout. He was short with George, and barely spoke to his sister. He was polite as always to Charlotte Stuart, but in the last few days had been so seldom in the

484

house that he did not often see her. Jill and his sister Nell had pleaded to be allowed to do some of the heavier work on the farm, but in an entirely strange voice for the mild young Philip Dermott, he flatly forbade their straying out of earshot of the main house. There was enough work to do and more around the barns, with the cows.

'We've had enough women with cut throats to last us for the moment,' he had snapped.

Laughter fled entirely from Glenburnie. Meals were something to be finished in a hurry, and were eaten in silence. Weapons now leaned against chairs and tables: Philip had brusquely ordered it so, and was as unreasoning as a sergeant-major in seeing that the arms were personally accounted for at all times. In a week, he seemed to have matured and toughened tremendously. Even his soft voice had gained harsh authority.

Charlotte Stuart, in the same week's time, appeared to have aged ten years. Her eyes had sunk in; the muscles in her face sagged. Only young Jill kept the physical brightness of her limitless reservoir of youth, but some of the gaiety had left her eyes as she turned them to her husband's long-nosed lump-jawed face. The name of Katie Crane was no longer mentioned, except occasionally by accident, and then the hush that followed was like a blow in the face. There was no further reference to the cable they had received from Paul Drake. Katie Crane's brother had wired simply that his sister had loved Africa and would be happy to be buried there and that he had no intention of ever visiting the continent again. He had requested that any expenses incurred in her funeral be sent for payment to his secretary in the New York office, as he expected to be travelling in other portions of the American continent for quite some time.

George Locke and his wife were desperately trying to hold the place together, as Charlotte Stuart seemed markedly enfeebled and Philip Dermott had reduced his young wife to frequent tearful silences. Neither Philip nor Jill mentioned to the rest of the family that they were sure Jill was pregnant. They did not even discuss it themselves. There seemed to be no point in planning for a child at this time.

CHAPTER EIGHTEEN

IN HIS attempt to keep Glenburnie from falling apart, George Locke found himself walking more gingerly than at any time in his life. He had thought himself well integrated into the household; now he felt himself more of a stranger than when he had first come. He even felt that his wife held him in a small way responsible for the plight of the family, although she said nothing

485

of a recriminatory nature about his part in the experiment which had ended so tragically for all concerned. But if Nell Locke was hesitant about the I-told-you-sos, her brother Philip Dermott was not.

In the war, George Locke had seen men age overnight—had seen them suddenly become the finished characters for which they had been originally shaped. It was thus with Philip Dermott; he had always been the younger brother, always shaded by Brian and his sister. He had enjoyed no early remembrance of mother and father. He had straggled at the tail end of his Aunt Charlotte's litter, and he had mostly worshipped his big brother from afar. He had been little more than a child during the Mau Mau, and had come early to guns and killing. Then he had seemingly retreated into child-hood again, with so much bustle happening within the family—Brian married and then speedily a famous hunter; George Locke's own entry into the house and the change that marriage had wrought in the scarred face and heart of Philip's sister; finally, the bringing of Philip's own wife to the farm had been overshadowed by Brian's frightening illness and the presence of Katie Crane. The whole was wrenched apart and set by the upheaval on the farm, as Charlotte Stuart attempted to turn Glenburnie into a co-operative—on, George Locke was forced to admit, his own counsel and against the advice of Brian Dermott. The killings had finally firmed Philip Dermott into a pre-destined adult mould which bore small resemblance to the boy.

And now Philip Dermott was a man, George Locke was forced to admit. George Locke felt futile and weak—especially after Philip had lashed him with his tongue when he had ventured to suggest that maybe things weren't as bad as they seemed, that something might, albeit Micawberishly, turn up. Philip Dermott fixed him with a corrosive stare and spoke in a voice one might use in explaining the facts of life to a not-too-intelligent stranger.

'You see, George,' he used the name maddeningly, 'it has turned out that my brother was right. He was right all along. He knows Wogs—he didn't allow himself to be turned aside with all this come-to-Jesus that you and Aunt Charlotte hatched, and which I fell for. I blame me for not sticking with Brian.'

Even the way he paused to strike a match on the stone of the fireplace was disdainful; the way he flipped the match on the hearth without seeming to care whether it fell on the floor or not was insulting.

'He knew all along this pipe-dream wouldn't work. The night we had the row and he left the house about the last thing he said was something about Africans getting their signals mixed and killing innocent bystanders in their mad scramble for this *uhuru* nonsense. He had quite a bit to say about grati-tude and dependability and curses and selfishness and a lot of other things. He was dead right; they all ran off as soon as trouble came—and the trouble came out of the political Wogs who didn't even want to see their own people succeed for their own betterment.

'Poor Brian was dead right all along, and now he's in jail for his pains—he'll swing for his pains. The only thing he's been wrong about was the *way* he went about killing that bastard Kamau. I can only imagine that he was off his head—it would have been much more intelligent to waylay the son-of-a-bitch and cut his throat like Katie Crane's throat was cut. We gained very little when Brian shot that ape. We just lost Brian—momentarily, anyhow, and we could use a few Brians right now. Your sort will have to come later, George—after the armistice.'

He had slapped the gun on his hip and swung off, leaving George Locke rubbing slowly at his pale pinkish moustache. Through the doorway he heard Philip shout that he was driving into Nyeri. The other day it had been Naivasha, and the day before Nakuru. Each day he seemed to have one particular errand that kept him from his otherwise endless duties on the farm. And when he went off in the car he always took young Jill with him. He seemed very much disinclined to let her out of his sight, which George Locke thought to be entirely natural under the strained circumstances.

*

Charlotte Stuart spoke of little except Stephen Ndegwa's plans for the farm. She had set off a tearing fight with Philip after Ndegwa's departure, and they were speaking stiffly only as strangers now. She had outlined briefly Ndegwa's ideas for a mass political meeting on the farm. George Locke and his wife were enthusiastic; Jill looked warily at her young husband and said nothing. After several days of Philip's taciturnity, finally Charlotte Stuart addressed her nephew directly.

'You've said nothing, Philip. What is your opinion of this now that you've heard all the details?'

'Any thoughts I might have would be rude,' he said. 'If you want my opinion I'll tell you and risk the rudeness. I've faint hope that you'd listen to it.'

'Express it and we'll listen to it, right enough. Go on.'

'I think that what your precious Mr. Ndegwa is offering you now is nothing but a political trick to pull his own chestnuts out of the fire—to make credit for himself with government and the world outside. If it goes wrong and there's a big *kelele* he can blame it all on you and still be in with his own bloody flock. He's black and he's a politician and it seems to me we've had enough experience with black politicians for one family.'

'That's your final opinion then, is it?' his aunt said as if talking to an intrusive outsider.

'That's my final opinion.' His reply was as devoid of family warmth as his aunt's voice.

'And what do you choose to do—pack up and leave, or fight? And how will you fight, pray? Go and shoot Ndegwa in front of the Stanley and move in with your brother in his cell?' The old lady was angry, and her voice had risen.

'I'm not packing in. I'm definitely sending Jill to England, though.'

'Pip! You haven't said anything to me—you can't!' His wife entered the

487

conversation for the first time. She half-rose, and her face was very pale. 'I won't go off to England and leave you—I won't!'

'You will if I say so.' Philip Dermott did not look at her. He kept his eyes on Charlotte Stuart. 'We've mucked with Wogs long enough. I've said before I prefer my wife without a slit throat. I still mean it. Jill's going off to England as soon as I can get her packed and on the plane.'

'I won't go! I don't have to go! Do I have to go, Aunt Charlotte?' She turned pleading to the old lady.

'You're married to Philip,' his aunt said. She swung back to her nephew. Philip Dermott swivelled slowly round and looked at everyone in turn. His lip curled slightly as he rested his eyes briefly on his brother-in-law.

'You won't need me,' he said. 'One peacemaker in the house is plenty. George will look after things for you.'

'I'm not going! I will *not* go! I'm staying on here with Aunt Charlotte. I'm staying here—I'm staying at *home*!' She dropped her face in her hands and burst into a storm of tears. Her husband made no motion to comfort her. After a moment her tears stopped, but she kept her face in her hands.

'If you stay here you stay without me,' he said. 'Nor will I answer for you if you stay here. I'm telling you again, Jill—come with me to Nairobi tonight. You can go and visit your people until things straighten themselves out here.'

'I won't go unless Aunt Charlotte says so—unless she refuses to give me house room!' the girl said. 'I will not leave here and go off to England! I'm not running away! I don't want to run away! Please, may I stay, Aunt Charlotte?'

'I'll neither keep her nor throw her out,' Charlotte Stuart replied. 'It's my home here; she's welcome in it. With you or without you she's welcome in it. If she wants to stay on she stays on unless you physically carry her off the premises, and that I wouldn't advise, even for a Dermott.'

'All right, then.' Philip Dermott shrugged, again looking more and more like his brother. 'Please yourself, Jill. Go or stay. If you stay you can scrub me.'

Jill began to weep again, and this time she got up and left the room. Silence smothered them all. Finally Charlotte Stuart broke it.

'And what do you propose to do then, now that you've decided to break that poor girl's heart and shirk your responsibilities here?' Her voice struck him like a club.

'Be as rough as you like, Auntie. Here. Read this. I collected it in Nyeri today. It'll give you a rude idea.'

He handed her a cablegram. Charlotte Stuart fumbled for her spectacles and adjusted them. She read through the cable and looked at her nephew.

'Read it aloud,' he said. 'Wait. Jill!' he called. 'Come back. I want you to hear this, too!'

'It's signed "Bruce". I presume that's Don Bruce. It says: "Hold fort until I arrive SAA flight two one seven Tuesday meet if possible discuss plans best Bruce." '

She dropped the cable in her lap and looked up at her nephew.

'And this is supposed to mean what?'

Again Philip swept the room with his gaze.

'Don Bruce is coming home again,' he said. 'I rather imagine we'll set up shop in his house. Don found out he couldn't do your kind of business with the Wogs. Now he's coming home to do our kind of business with the Wogs. I'll be in easy hail, Auntie.'

His aunt leaned back in her chair and sighed. Her face seemed to crumple.

'It's what I was frightened most of,' she murmured almost to herself. 'It's what I most wanted to avoid. First Brian and now you. The whole thing over again. The whole terrible thing over again. All right, Philip.' She raised her eyes to his face. 'Take what guns you want and go.'

CHAPTER NINETEEN

LISE MARTELIS had waited afrightedly for several days for some sign that Matisia had plans for her disposal. She had expected it ever since the day he had threatened to cut her throat. So she was not at all surprised when Matisia had suggested casually one Friday that she was looking a mite peaked, that perhaps a little trip to the Coastal Strip might set her right. He was overworked, as well, and could use a change.

'I will be busy myself for a few days,' he had said. 'Why don't you take the plane down to Mombasa and dig in at the Nyali Beach for a week or so? I'll join you later, but I've several days' work up-country to do and I'd thought of closing this house and looking about for a bigger one. I expect to need larger entertainment facilities pretty soon. Does a little trip of a fortnight or so sound attractive?'

Lise Martelis had smiled and said that it sounded wonderful; it had been very poky sitting by herself so much lately with him away all the time.

'When do you want me to go?' she asked submissively.

'Any time you like,' he had said, all smiles and affability. 'Today? To-morrow? Whenever you like.'

'I think tomorrow then,' she said.

'That will be fine. Give us a kiss, now, I must be off. And what a stupid clot I am—I forgot money. Here.' He produced a wallet and peeled off twenty hundred-shilling notes from an enormous wad of notes. 'That should be plenty until I arrive. You won't have to pay the hotel bill at all. Now.' He kissed her hurriedly. 'I'm gone.'

Lise Martelis watched him go, and then went back to her bedroom to commence packing her few clothes. In a funny way, she would miss the little pink house, she mused, as she folded her underclothing carefully. When she had finished packing she looked carefully round to see if she had forgotten anything. When she was satisfied she went to the fridge and took out a jug of iced tea. She put a sprig of mint in the tea and had a long drink before she picked up the telephone and rang the office of Stephen Ndegwa.

*

Ndegwa had suggested meeting her at his own home—where, he said, they could talk freely, as his wife had gone off visiting to London and he was currently between houseboys. He had given her the address, and she felt very much at ease with the big, broad-faced, kindly-smiling man who relieved her of the bag with which she had tottered from the point where, at his suggestion, she had dismissed her taxi.

He had been comforting to see in his sports shirt, slacks, and loafers, and he had offered her a drink and lit her cigarette for her. Stephen Ndegwa seemed such a different man from either the violent, volatile Matisia or the imperious Kamau; she wished that she might have met Ndegwa first, instead of the others.

'And so you have come to me now,' he said. 'Why not before? And why would you trust me? Why not go directly to the police? You have told me more than enough to put Matisia behind bars on a murder complicity charge. You have told me enough to hang Kamau if this man Dermott had not already killed him.'

'I did not know where else to go,' she said simply. 'I know Matisia means to kill me now, or he would not suggest that I go to Mombasa. If he did not mean to kill me he would merely throw me out. But he is afraid the police would take me, because I have no papers, and then I would perhaps talk to the police if he only throws me out. So he will kill me now unless you help me to get away.'

'But why *me*?' Stephen Ndegwa persisted.

'Because Matisia and Kamau seemed to hate you so that I thought perhaps you might be a good man. Also they both seemed frightened of you. If you are a truly good man perhaps you would want to have some power over Matisia. If not now, for the future.'

'Hmmmm.' Stephen Ndegwa pulled at his chin. You could not say that whores always thought crookedly.

'Supposing I could guarantee you a safe exit and even perhaps some paper of entry to another country—would you be willing to sign a deposition of all this information? Swear to it under oath?'

'I would,' she said eagerly. 'I would. I would do anything just to leave. If I could get to South Africa—far away. I would even go under my real name. It is Marthe Evert. That way they might have no connection with me here. If I could go to Morocco or Algeria. Anywhere.'

'That could be fixed. Tell me one more thing: would you testify in a court of law to all the things you have told me about the connection of Kamau and

Matisia to the murder of the Crane woman and the old man and the abduction of the little boy—would you appear as a witness on my word and the word of the Governor that you would be allowed to leave here?' He smiled slightly. 'We could of course swear you then on your real name and allow you to resume your old and more accustomed name of Martelis for travel purposes. It might be less embarrassing all round.'

The woman dropped her hands in despair.

'There is nothing I *can* do but trust you. I have some money—some of my own as well as some Matisia gave me. But if you do not help me there is no one to whom I can turn except the police and I am afraid of any police unless there is someone to speak for me on a high level with them.'

Stephen Ndegwa rocked back in his chair and thought a minute.

'It would take some time to arrange your papers, there are people to see, and I have a tremendously busy day tomorrow. A day I cannot afford to miss. What will you do now—go to Mombasa? Certainly not back to the house?'

'I do not dare go to Mombasa, and I am afraid to go back to the house. He often comes back by surprise when he has said he will be away. And if I go to Mombasa—I might very well find him waiting for me in Mombasa. Or what is more likely someone whom he has sent.'

Stephen Ndegwa pulled at an ear-lobe and thought some more.

'I don't think it would be very intelligent, from a standpoint of security, to keep you here. I have an idea that our friend would speed up his intent to slit your throat if he thought you had talked to me. I think, Madame, that the best thing we can do with you is to sling you in jail.'

One protesting hand shot up to her face, but Stephen Ndegwa smiled to reassure her.

'No charges. No problems. Just a thing called protective custody. We often do it with witnesses for whose safety we fear. You will be quite comfortable for a night or so, until I can arrange something semi-official which will get you safely out of the country and also out of Matisia's reach. I'll ring up an inspector of police I know who'll tuck you away tidily as a favour to me.'

'This won't be held against me?' Suspicion came into her voice.

'Not at all. To the contrary, it'll be held in your favour. You see, I do not quite know how to use what you have told me. I will have to give it some heavy thought.'

'Tomorrow night is when Matisia is due back from the country,' the woman said. 'He made a particular point of telling me.'

'I shouldn't be at all surprised,' Ndegwa said, and then spoke into the phone. 'Hello, Inspector Barnes? It's Stephen Ndegwa here, David. I wonder if you could produce me a little personal favour, having to do with the health of the country. I want free board and lodging for a friend of mine, for her protection, for a couple of days. All right? Fine. I'll tell you some of the details when I bring her over. Twenty minutes. Thank you. Good-bye.'

He turned again to face Lise Martelis.

'We won't mention anything at all about Matisia and Kamau. You are merely a Belgian refugee from the Kivu, and you're frightened out of your wits. You want protection until some satisfactory means of transport can be arranged to get you out of town, and chance acquaintance sent you to me. That's all Barnes need know until I see what can be done for you. They won't ask you any questions. It's the best I can do.'

He went into another room to get a coat.

'I'll drive you myself. I've sent the chauffeur home. Come on, now where's your bag ?'

'I've never been in jail before,' the woman said suddenly. 'Is it very bad ?'

'Not so very bad,' Ndegwa said. 'The cot may be a little hard, but at least you can sleep soundly. People even grow accustomed to prison.'

'You know,' the woman said, and put her hand on his arm, 'you are very good to do this for me. If I can ever repay you——'

'Don't worry about repaying me. Just keep quiet and have a good night's sleep. You'll be a good deal safer there than in any church. Here we are.' He slid the car over to the curb. 'This is the inspector's house. He'll take over from here. Don't forget, I'll see you tomorrow.'

He got out and walked to meet a burly man who was coming down the drive.

'Nobody in or out of the cell except you or me or the turnkey, David,' he said, after shaking hands. 'She could be rather important to all our lives—whichever way the straw floats. I can't tell you any more than that right now. And thanks.'

'Good enough,' the man said. 'I'll plump her into one of the better suites. Where we put the rich cheque-bouncers and distinguished drunken sons of lords.'

Stephen Ndegwa watched them drive away in the police inspector's van. He waggled his jowls sadly as he climbed back into his own motor. *What* a choice, he thought. The chance of a lifetime to crush a serpent, and because of some strange mechanics involving a man named Brian Dermott, who is also in jail, and some unusual activities tomorrow on the farm of Brian Dermott's aunt, I must put strange whores in prison and hope to find bogus papers to smuggle her out of the country before what she knows desecrates the memory of a filthy saint named Matthew Kamau, and deposits all of us, black and white, innocent and guilty alike, completely in the soup. He was still shaking his head as he mounted the steps of his own house to go to bed —but not, he thought, to sleep.

CHAPTER TWENTY

THE BULGING buses began arriving at Glenburnie Farm as early as eight in the morning with their passengers hanging out of the windows and congealed tight-packed in the aisles. The motor-buses looked as unlikely as whales stranded in the broad green fields on the farm. There had been no rains for three or four days now—the puddles had dried, leaving harsh-ringed dimples in the hard-panned clay, but the fields had greened, and a slight pale fuzzing of grass was showing on the unplanted fields. The flowers had lilted with the recent wet. Charlotte Stuart's long gardens were Christmas-lit with their bright poppies and cannas, their geraniums and carnations and fuchsias, with one whole bed of yellow roses drooping dew-heavy, as large as taffeta cabbages, from the lissom stalks. The bougainvillaea writhed and crackled with life, and the Cape chestnuts and frangipanis boasted loudly against the sombre cedar and eucalyptus. Here and there the jacaranda wept violet against the fierce brave scarlet of the Nandi flame. The treetops were vibrant with birds, and the fingering arbors quivered with bees.

The sky was completely free of cloud now and The Mountain's snaggled fangs showed clear against the laundered blue of the Kenya sky. It was a day as close to European spring as Africa ever saw—the short rains had packed in, evidently, and there would be no more rainfall until March, when the long steady downpours were supposed to begin. The rains had stopped too soon— the country would be in for a faminous dry unless they resumed again, but with the way weather was these days you were jolly well grateful for anything you got that wasn't a screaming catastrophe.

Sitting on the veranda over her fourth coffee, Charlotte Stuart watched the people beginning to seep shyly into the green plate of garden. She was so excited she could scarcely bear it; the whole house trembled with excitement. It was like a day before a great wedding, she thought, and dismissed rudely the grey intrusive sliver of idea that it was frequently sunny on funeral days. She watched the people spilling like the children of the Old Lady who Lived in the Shoe from the buses which arrived on monotonous schedule, and reflected that Ndegwa had indeed already worked a marvel to get so many people to come at all. She did not know how he did it but she did not care. A thousand had arrived by ten o'clock, and from the look of the fattening ingress another four or five thousand would be aboard before the palaver started at noon.

It was Saturday. That might partially account for the crowd, and especially for the enormous number of women. She thought she had never before seen so many women in comparison to the men, not even on the big market days at Karatina and Kiambu and Njabini. The women were dressed in their best *shukas*, in violent hues of blue and green and orange. Many were dressed in white woman's clothes, but almost all seemed to be barefooted or sandal-shod. There were few proper shoes among the early group, Charlotte Stuart noted with relief. She had mentally written off the lawns and most of the flowers, but a flat bare African hoof would probably propound less damage to the turf than spike heels or great clumping brogans.

They had brought the *watoto*—the children. That was a good omen for a fair day, she thought, and additionally thanked God for the fair day. She imagined that no curse obtained properly anywhere by full daylight, especially in the mob safety which such numbers brought. The smiling day and promise of unlimited beer and beef and dancing would have been enough to fetch the African on any sunny Saturday, but the trick would be to see how many remained as the sun waned and night frowned. She would know, of course, after the speeches. They would certainly be able to chart the future from the crowd's reaction—and would be able to specify more when she saw how the *watu* tucked into the barbecued beef and the beer. Charlotte Stuart was constrained to smile slightly when she thought of the divers arrangements for the big *ngoma*. There was such a very little difference between the African and the Irish, really. They were both inflammably excitable, and both loved a market day and the promise of a merry jig and a walloping mass of free grog and tucker mixed in with the forensics. With the Irish it was the fiddles sent them off; with the Wog it was always the drums.

The lumping knots of natives had not yet approached closely to the big house. They hung back, squatting on their heels in clusters under the big chestnuts and eucalypti and cedars that shaded the little blue dam with its geese flotillaed on the breeze-wrinkled water. The visitors were not making much noise—rather their talk compacted into a steady, even buzz, almost like an enormous swarm of migrant bees. Only occasionally did a loud laugh boom or a shrill giggle knife the comforting hum.

Some few Masai, she noticed, had arrived, and were keeping well apart from the Kikuyu. The Masai had got themselves up fantastically for the occasion—the men at least glittered like painted toy soldiers in the sun. They were smeared in moist ochre with fresh blue-and-white clay criss-crossings and zigzags, and their hair had been so newly terraced in their fanciful bangs and clubs and bobs and roaches that you might almost have planted a flower successfully in the glistening clay of their coiffeurs. They wore their red-dyed togas as arrogantly as ever over their daubed nakedness, Charlotte Stuart noted, but they seemed strangely lonely without their lean, gleaming oval-pointed spears. In all her life in Kenya she had never seen Masai without spears before.

But the police had arrived, as well—light-reflecting black *askari* in khaki shorts and padded-shoulder blue sweaters. They had come with their white officers in Land Rovers and in lorries, and already were taking up strategic points around the farm. So far, she had seen no Wakamba, but they would undoubtedly arrive later since they had to come from a greater distance. There would be some seepage of Embu and Meru among the Kikuyu, and she was quite certain a scatter of Luo and Kavirondo from the Lake, a sprinkling of Kipsigi and Nandi from the high country to the west.

She was pleased to see that they had arrived in a festive mood. They were prepared to dance. There was a flutter of feather headdress and pinioned staff among the crowd, and she could hear a gentle tonking of ankle-rattles and the tinnier clang of beer cans which the more modern Kamba and Kikuyu tied to their legs to replace the old iron war-bells.

Charlotte Stuart had never attended the big political rallies which had become popular over the last couple of years, when as many as twenty thousand natives swarmed to the stadium to chant and to make the high ululating keening that the women produced in moments of great emotion by tapping their throats with the hard edges of their fingers. What was gathering in her yard—what was walking in long, steady lines, over the gentle swell of the surrounding green hills and through the shallow ravines, was probably going to comprise more Africans than she had viewed at one time since she had first seen Kenya as a young woman.

Jill came out on the porch now, and Charlotte Stuart smiled up at her. Poor child, she was frightfully upset still over Philip's leaving the farm, but was mightily trying to conceal it. From the look of her, Charlotte Stuart was almost certain that she was pregnant. There was something about the face, the eyes—but that of course might be just the result of fresh-tasted unhappiness and nightly sobbing on her pillow. Jill was dressed now in a simple yellow frock, and she had unravelled the pigtails from her curly brown hair and had done it simply in a knot on the back of her neck. She wore sandals, and her long bare legs were very brown. The yellow dress, Charlotte Stuart thought, went very well with her brown hair and eyes and that wonderful clear child's skin from which no amount of sunburn could sponge the baby flush. The poor gawky filly had worked feverishly in the last few days, for Philip's absence had created a vacuum, as well as a tremendous labour lack, on the farm.

'How are things going, me darlin'?' she asked Jill, who had dropped onto the top step on the veranda.

'All right, Aunt Char.' The girl gripped her brown knees with laced fingers and leaned back against the newel post of the banister. 'At least I think so. Did you hear us testing the loudspeaker system very early this morning?'

'I heard some rude voice at about six saying something like "Hurray, hurray, it's the first of May, outdoor lovin' begins today" over some infernal contraption before I'd even tasted me tea. God, it's noisier than the Bull of Bashan.'

'That was George,' the girl laughed. 'He's feeling very chirpy today. I believe he thinks Mr. Ndegwa's elaborate pow-wow is going to work, and things will be brighter around here. Maybe then Pip will come back——' Her voice and mouth drooped simultaneously.

'He'll come back, darlin'. Never you fear. He's a man, and he's a Dermott, and mayhap a mite mad, but he'll come back as soon as he's found there's no profit to be had in this cowboy-and-Red-Indian thing he's caught up in. But he's quite all right for food and shelter. George stopped off there on his way back from Nairobi, you know. He says they're settled in very well in Donald Bruces's house.'

'I know. George told me. But I did do right, didn't I, Aunt Charlotte, not to go panicking off to London, like—like Brian's Valerie and some of the others?'

'Of course you did right. There's nothing to be solved or gained from

495

running. It's here that's your home and it's here you'll stay. After today I think everything will come right again—at least here at Glenburnie. Ndegwa's a good man, black or not.'

'Except for his colour you wouldn't think he was a Wog at all,' the girl said. 'He doesn't talk like one. He's easy. He's—well, I would call him *Bwana* the same as I'd call Pip or George *Bwana*. He's one of us, more—not like a native at all.'

'What, child?' The old lady was watching the natives and spoke absently.

'Nothing. I must run now and help George. He's still trying to get the beer barrels situated around various spots without attracting too much attention from the police. *Is* it illegal to give the natives beer?'

'There seems to be some division of opinion on the matter. It appears to be quite legal enough to sell it to them. I see no reason why you can't give them a few petrol tins full in the interests of good fellowship. And politics. Is there lots?'

'Oceans of it. George has mounted a guard over it down at the grove where the medical centre started and over by the schoolhouse and at the threshing shed and it's scattered all over the housing development.'

'And the cattle?'

'They're paddocked in various spots close by the beer, poor things. Nell and I've been wrangling the steers all morning. That's why I changed to *this* after.' She plucked at her frock. 'I smelled like nothing human—all horse and cow and sweat. We've earmarked fifty for the first slaughter. I must say they're not the pick of the lot, Auntie.'

'Not meant to be the pick of the lot,' the old lady grunted. 'But that's all right. A hungry Kikuyu doesn't care about pedigree or looks. He'll carve off a haunch and eat it while it's still kicking. I'm worried about the slaughter, actually. I hope Ndegwa and his people have that operation pretty well in hand. Everything we're doing here today is sort of mildly illegal. Nobody's supposed to bring any *pangas* or *simis* to the talk-talk, and I don't know if the proper vets' seal is on the *ngombe*. But Ndegwa says that after the proper speechifying everybody's more or less on his own, and it no longer constitutes a permitted assembly, or something. In any case Nairobi seems to be gambling with him.'

'This must be costing you a fortune.'

'It's costing nothing at all. If we don't get some people back here to work for us, the farm's gone in any case. I consider these few hundred quids' worth of animals as a very much sounder investment than fertilizer.'

It had been quite a week, the old lady mused, watching the sun striking fire off the shaven greased skulls of the Kikuyu women, and causing the red ochre make-up of the clumps of Masai to glow warmly. Ndegwa was indeed a fabulous man. The organization alone of this business was staggering as a logistical problem. Where *did* all the people come from? The fields were fair blackening with them now.

She was still not quite sure what Ndegwa was up to. He seemed confident enough. Certainly his organization in the reserve was strong enough to have collared all these people. Certainly the government trusted him. It was the first permit which had been granted for a speaking since the slaying nearly two weeks ago. So the government was gambling as well—as she was gambling, as Ndegwa was gambling—and as they were all gambling with the life of poor Brian, locked and fretting in a cell. She shivered when she thought of her nephew. He had always chafed indoors—even fidgeted at the constraint of city living for very long. What he must be feeling in a jail. . . . Well, that kind of thinking would get her nowhere.

God willing, Charlotte Stuart thought, we can save my poor lost Brian's neck. She looked at her strap-watch. She had better get off the porch now and cherish her appearance for the star turn. It wouldn't do to let the assembled *watu* get bored with staring at her. She took one last look down the sweep of hill. If the speakers merely stood on the steps they would be raised more than high enough above the faces of the crowd. It was funny; when you couldn't get about much on your legs, you were likely to forget what a steep pull it was uphill from the little lake to the house.

CHAPTER TWENTY-ONE

THE SENIOR Superintendent of Police got out of his Land Rover to stretch his legs. He was a burly man, with a heavy-jowled smooth-shaven face. He wore three rows of ribbons from two wars on his starched khaki tunic. His name was O'Flaherty. He watched the throngs of natives spreading ant-like over the rolling green fields of Glenburnie Farm, trudging on the newly defined roads, spilling from the overloaded buses and lorries. He tucked a swagger-stick under his arm and lighted his pipe, puffing as he stared under bushy pepper-and-salt eyebrows at the Provincial Commissioner.

'Are you quite sure you blokes know what you're up to with this shenanigan?' he asked. 'Looks very much to me as if there'll be topping five thousand of the blighters. And more Masai than I like to see. I wouldn't want to have to sort this out with my feeble forces. 'Specially as we're not supposed to shoot anybody.'

'I really couldn't say,' the PC said. 'All I know is it's got the blessing o' Nairobi. Not that it won't be my neck if there's a balls-up. It's still my Province.'

'Well, I've got my chaps deployed as best I can. We've plenty of tear-gas and the batons. But I don't like it even a little bit. You can't frisk the lot for weapons. All those women could have *pangas* under the *shukas*.'

'We'll see what we will see,' the Bwana PC said. 'Meanwhile, I suggest

497

we stroll over to pay a call on Charlotte Stuart and importune the guid auld lass for a wee drappie o' gin.'

'I couldn't agree more,' replied Chief Superintendent O'Flaherty. 'Riot-prevention seems to become thirstier and thirstier work the older I get.'

CHAPTER TWENTY-TWO

STEPHEN NDEGWA sat in the front seat of the big Mercedes with his daughter Nduta placed between him and the driver. Eight-year-old Nduta was dressed in her school uniform of green middy blouse and skirt. The little boy, ten years old, was sitting in the back, wedged between his mother Wanjiro and his father's senior wife Mumbi. He was dressed in khaki shirt and shorts. Both children were barefoot.

They were good-looking kids, Stephen Ndegwa thought with pride—husky, both of them and seemingly quite intelligent. They stood somewhat in awe of their father, which was entirely natural. After all, they knew him very little. He must make a point of seeing more of them in the future. He *would* see more of them in the future, for he had a strong hunch he would make his ex-urban headquarters on Glenburnie Farm. He would ask some land of Charlotte Stuart, and settle his wives and children on it, as he had said half in jest. There would be time enough for the big tea or coffee plantation of his own when he got the country straightened out. His mind had changed considerably in the last few days. Progress was as progress did, and just now progress was spelled Glenburnie Farm. Progress could even be a thing called Brian Dermott.

He would thrust Brian Dermott out of his mind in a moment but first he had to think a little more about him. There was no doubt the young man had been off his head when he shot Kamau. There were all sorts of madnesses. Ndegwa could make an insanity plea stick—*if* he made the plea, and told what he knew. Apart from the applicability of pure law, he could get Dermott off merely by trying the dead man, Kamau, for complicity in the murder of at least four people—Kathleen Crane, the old man Kidogo, the other old man Njeroge from the other farm, and the little boy.

And he would not even have to plead insanity, with the chance of the poor young man being shut up in Mathari for a long time. He could as easily wangle an acquittal, and with perfect balm to his conscience as a lawyer. Nobody had seen Dermott draw the gun; the witnesses had said there had been a bit of scuffle; they had said that they had seen Dermott put his hand on Kamau's arm. According to law, Dermott—or any other citizen—had a right to detain and arrest a man who was known to be implicated in a murder

498

in order to prevent him from repeating the crime. Perhaps he had merely tried to detain Kamau, and in the scuffle the gun had gone off . . .

The whore's testimony would do it. It would also hang Matisia, for there would be an immediate acquittal of Dermott and a second murder trial, and this time Abraham Matisia would be in the dock as the defendant—Matisia and any of the other accomplices who might still be alive. The accomplices made little difference. Matisia would certainly be found guilty of arranging the murders, and Matisia would swing. Kamau was already dead, and justice would have been done. Brian Dermott, while still legally guilty of premeditated murder, would go free. Dermott had at least saved Kamau from hanging with his clean swift bullet.

Yes, the Belgian whore's testimony would do it, all right. It would do other things, besides. It would blow his party KNAP to bits, sky-high, and it would blow Stephen Ndegwa forever to pieces politically along with the party. It would split the country wide open—leave Kenya ripe and achingly vacant for the freshest wild-eyed opportunist to step in and take over. It would splatter the headlines of the world, and all the stinking corruption of Kenya politics would be smeared in the world's face. Kenya would suffer, all Africa would suffer—the cause of the black man everywhere would certainly be horribly damaged—and above all, he himself would be eternally removed from any slight consideration either as a leader or as a man.

But there wasn't going to be any huge, explosive trial which would wreck Kaynap and hang Matisia and blast Ndegwa. He would have the whore out of the country in a few days. A few days in a cell wouldn't hurt her, and he didn't want to let her disappear as a potential witness until he had rid himself of Matisia once and for all. God, he thought, what a filthy business. I'm thinking like any other blackmailer, and blackmailer is what I am. I will tell our honest Abraham Matisia that unless he goes far, far away and stays far, far away, we will politely hale him into court and hang him high—string him up on the testimony of his own white mistress.

It's best this way. The important thing is to weed out the Matisias and reseed a little faith in the white population that we won't murder them all in their beds next year when we come to power. It's best this way: there need be no trial of Kamau as an already executed murderer. We won't have to hang Matisia, and we won't have to blow up me and the party. There won't be any Operation Anvil on Kaynap and Ndegwa and everybody else in the political business. Even the whore will be happy, because a quiet word with Government House will fix her up as fine a set of good-bye papers as ever the dear girl dreamed of. Timbuctu or Tahiti, Tangier or Tokyo, we will speed this bit of Turkish delight away from the country and out of our lives. It's an odd way to save a country, but it's the best way I know at the moment. Matisia and Kamau and their big mouths. Kamau brought to book by his long tongue, and Matisia hoist by his long . . . Well. And me, always tarred with the same brush.

So. I have inspected my conscience and found it non-existent, Stephen

Ndegwa said to himself. I will pledge Brian Dermott's neck in order to save his dear old auntie's farm, and with it myself and the country. This thing has to go off well today. It must. It must, or we have no faint hope of ever accomplishing anything here in the way of progressive permanency. Strange that one old woman and an idea could have suddenly become as big and as important as a whole country. A voice jarred him. His junior wife Wanjiro was speaking now.

'What is it?' he said irritably.

'I did not know this country was so large and so full of big *shambas*,' she was saying. 'I have never been this far away from home before.'

'Do you like the looks of the country?'

'It is much richer than ours. But then it is the country of the white man.'

'It will be the country of all men soon,' Ndegwa said. 'And for you and Mumbi and the children and me, it will be our country immediately. As I told you. We are changing our *shamba* to the *shamba* of the Big Memsaab.'

'I don't know if I will like it,' Mumbi, the elder wife, said. 'Perhaps I am too old to change—to live among strangers.'

'You will not be living among strangers,' Ndegwa said. 'They are your own people. You will merely be living on better land—with better schools for the children and less work for all to do to live better. You will like it here. Also it is not so hot as where we live.'

'What will happen to our goats and sheep?' Mumbi asked. 'From the old *shamba*?'

'We will bring them with us when we come,' Ndegwa replied, making a mental note to have a word with Charlotte Stuart about the advisability of allowing a certain number of goats per family when the project got going— at least for a while. A shortage of goats, he was convinced, was a perpetual source of irritation and unease to the older women, and it was the older women they must lean on for a while.

'Do you remember what you both are to say?' he asked his wives.

'It is not difficult,' Mumbi replied. 'I am to say that I am your woman, and am to name my clan, and repeat the names of my dead sons. I am to say that I am coming to live on the land of the Memsaab Shalotu on this big *shamba*, and as your senior wife will try to work hard to bring pride and riches to the family and the clan and the country. Then I will shout *Uhuru na Ndegwa!* and sit down. Whereupon Wanjiro will stand up and speak.'

'Excellent,' Stephen Ndegwa said. 'And what will you say, Wanjiro?'

'I do not know if I can remember it all, I am very frightened, and do not forget that you promised to give me a drink of the white man's *tembo* just before I speak,' Wanjiro replied. 'First I will say the same thing that Mumbi has said, except I will say I am your *junior* wife, and then I will put my hands on the shoulders of my children and call them by name.

'Then, if I can remember, I will say that I am speaking directly to the women. I will say that we must be all one nation and help each other and we must live in peace with the women of the other tribes and races, with the

500

whites and the Wahindi. Do I *have* to say the Wahindi?' she asked her husband plaintively.

'Yes,' Stephen Ndegwa replied. 'You have to include the Wahindi.'

'All right. Then I will say we will have to live in friendship with all races and all tribes, and we must work hard and not think that we will all be rich and ride in motor-cars and do no work as soon as *uhuru* comes. I will say that we must forget violence and not nag at our men to do acts of violence, because the days of violence for the men are over and now the men must work as hard as the women in a common cause.'

'Bravo!' Ndegwa said in English. 'If that doesn't fetch a flock of trills from the ladies I shall be enormously surprised.'

'The men won't like that last part and the women won't believe it,' Wanjiro said.

'They will believe it when I help you raise our hut in one of the little *shambas*,' her husband said. 'Go on. What else?'

'I will tell the young women not to try too hard to copy the ways of the white *wanawake*—that they do not have to carry handbags and wear high-heeled shoes and go to Nairobi and the other towns all the time. I will tell the young women and all children that they must go to the schools and study hard and in that way they will learn how to do all the things that the *mzungu* does—but I will say that the only way to have the things that the *mzungu* has is to study hard and work hard and be not envious. And I will say that some-day, when everyone is educated and clever then everybody will be equal in God's eyes in Kenya, black and white, man and woman, Masai and Kikuyu, Nandi and Kamba, Indian and Arab, and we will all be rich and happy and blessed by the Great God Ngai, wherever He sits and from wherever He sends His blessings. Then I will shout *Uhuru na Ndegwa!* and sit down.'

'That is very fine,' Ndegwa said. 'When you have finished, I will give you a very large drink of the white man's liquor. And what do the children do when their mothers finish speaking, and when I finish speaking? Nduta? Migwe?'

'We say very loudly, *Uhuru na Baba!*'

'Magnificent,' Ndegwa laughed. 'Freedom and Papa! It's a splendid combination. Well, we are almost there. We will go straight to the big house, and you will see inside a Bwana's big house for the first time. Some day we will have a house like that to live in. You will like it very much.'

'Is it like a king's house?' the little girl Nduta asked him.

'It is bigger and better than a king's house,' her father answered gravely. 'And the best thing about it is you don't have to be born a king or queen to live in a house like that—not if you work hard. You can make your house just as fine as you are willing to work hard. There it is now—you can see it on the hill there.'

'Look at all the people,' Migwe the little boy said. 'I have never seen so many people. Have they all come to hear you talk?'

'That's right,' said Ndegwa. 'They *have* come to hear me talk and to hear

501

your mother talk and see what fine children we have. So you must sit very still on the Big Memsaab's front porch and not fidget while the people talk into the little round horn that makes the voice roll over the land like thunder.'

'Oh,' the little girl said. 'You mean a microphone! I have heard them in Nyeri when there were other talkings going on from police cars.'

'Excuse me,' Ndegwa murmured in English, and then, in Kikuyu, 'Here we are. Remember, Nduta, you will make a little curtsy as I showed you, when you meet the old white lady. And Migwe, you will shake hands with everyone. Do not be afraid. They are good people, and very kind. Also just before the speaking starts I will ask someone to give you a Coca-Cola, for a treat.'

The car stopped at the bottom of the steps. Ndegwa got out, and went round to the boot, from which he took a bulky, paper-wrapped parcel. George Locke came down the steps to greet him, and the men shook hands.

'My family, Doctor,' Ndegwa said. 'In order of precedence Mumbi, Wanjiro; and the children are Migwe and Nduta. What'll we do with them before the firing starts?'

'Charlotte said into the living-room and let the youngsters play with the leopard skins and look at the trophies,' Locke said.' Perhaps also you'd best send the car away. It's a mite gaudy for our stage effects.'

'I'd thought of that,' Ndegwa said.

'Take the car behind the house and wait until I call you, Kipro,' he said to the driver. 'You may sleep if you like. Try not to dream while leaning on the horn.' He turned back to George Locke, and jerked a thumb at the chauffeur. 'The black man's burden,' he said. 'When *uhuru* comes I shall rise up and strike him down like a dog.' He grinned. 'I can use a few powder-room facilities myself,' he said. 'I've got all my stage properties with me, and they want a bit of fixing.'

He herded his family ahead of them with shooing motions up the steps. He walked over to shake hands with Jill Dermott, and said in Swahili: 'Will you look after my family please, Memsaab? This is Mumbi, this Wanjiro, that Nduta, this Migwe. Memsaabu Jilli,' he said. 'She will take care of you for a little bit.'

'I don't suppose I could tempt you with a gin, could I?' George Locke said, as they stood in the cool of the vast living-dining-room. 'The *watu* are still coming. How in the name of God did you arrange this turn-out?'

Ndegwa walked over and looked through the broad door towards the yard. It was swarming, now, with people—the crowd encroaching closer and closer to the immediate yard. As many as possible had clung to the edges of the little lake, and only an oval hundred yards of green lawn and flowers was completely free of people. A line of stopped buses limned like camels against the skyline on a hilltop, and from it flowed a thick treacly mass of humanity, moving as slowly as a line of safari ants.

'I was successful beyond my fondest wishes,' Ndegwa said slowly. 'I just hope that my partner Mukerjee, the transport baron, can cope with the overflow. I am afraid, Doctor Locke, that I let slip the idea that the earthly representative of the late Matthew Kamau might have something roughly akin to the Ten Commandments to deliver from the Mount this day. If I ever need another name you can call me Moise Ndegwa, the Moses of Ol Kalou. Did you say gin?'

CHAPTER TWENTY-THREE

JILL DERMOTT and Charlotte Stuart were sitting in the living-room trying to talk to Mumbi and Wanjiro, who were plumped cross-legged on the floor in front of the fireplace. Both of the Kikuyu women were drinking beer, and the children were sucking Coke through straws. The younger wife, Wanjiro, was barefoot, but she was wearing a simple shocking-pink cotton dress cut more or less along the same lines of Jill Dermott's yellow frock. Her copper-wire bracelets squeezed her bare brown legs and forearms, and there was a heavy rope of twisted blue-and-red beads around her neck. Ordinary heavy junk-jewellery white woman's earrings hid the sewn-up ring marks in her ears. Her hair was unadorned, and there was only a suspicion of rouge on her cheeks, a mild hint of colour on her lips.

The elder wife, Mumbi, was resplendent. A beaded cap of blue, white and red beads, worked into intricate design, completely covered her shaved skull. Great four-inch hoops of strung beads hung from the tinily pierced tops of her ears, and the enormous stretched hole in the flaps contained canisters of bead-studded copper. Two long bead-worked leather flaps hung shoulder-touching below the canisters, which were the size of a soup tin. Close-hugged to her neck were fifty or sixty strands of varicoloured beads of assorted shapes and sizes, the whole mass comprising the thickness of a big man's forearm. In longer loops, stretching down over one bare breast and her half-covered chest, were strings of cowrie shells and heavy pendants which hung from large silver clasps affixed to the thick choker necklace. Her red *shuka* was knotted over the right shoulder, and a sash of larger cowries traced the same line that the cloak followed across her half-bare trunk. Coils of copper wire snaked round her arms from wrist to armpit, and her fingers were lumped with heavy metal rings into which other beads and brilliant bits of glass had been implanted. Her bare legs below the *shuka*'s short uneven hem bulged over the long tight coils of copper wire. She had dressed in the fashion of a rich elder's wife of sixty years ago, when all the wealth that could not walk by itself was worn on the senior wife's back. When she moved, she rattled like a collection of tambourines.

The women had seemed very shy at first, but loosened stays somewhat as the talk turned to crops and children. Charlotte Stuart spoke an inexact

Kikuyu to the older woman, and Jill prattled away in up-country Swahili to Wanjiro. The children roved slowly round the room, fingering this and that vase or ornament, and stroking the leopard skins which draped along the backs of chairs and divans.

A door opened, and Jill Dermott looked up.

'Golly!' she gasped. 'Look at Mr. Ndegwa!'

Stephen Ndegwa had spent the last half-hour well. He had dressed himself as the most senior of elders, in the ancient fashion, and appeared, if anything, more startlingly gorgeous than his wife.

A great crown, as big or bigger than a Guardsman's bearskin, of black-and-white, long-silky colobus monkey skin perched atop his head. Long waving plumes of ostrich feathers framed his face. Strings of multi-coloured beads bound his forehead, and a tight metal band permitted an amulet to fall between his eyes. From his upper lips downward, his face had been painted in red ochre, and stripings of blue paint showed between the bead coronets on his forehead. His cheeks had been painted in white lime sunbursts, joined across the bridge of his nose by a jagged lightning slash of white.

He was naked to the waist except for a grey monkey-skin cloak flung over one shoulder, but his neck and chest were almost covered in beads and fine iron chains with a *juju* pouch depending from one of the necklaces. His beads were variously made of mother-of-pearl buttons and of intricately carved ivory, and one necklace was formed entirely of metal discs as big as shillings, pierced and packed together to form a rope like stacked coins. Cowrie sashes fell diagonally across his chest in one direction, and a broad ribbon of what looked like closely linked chain-mail crossed the cowries from the other shoulder. Heavy bracelets of close-coiled wire constricted his biceps, wrists, and the ankles of his stout bare legs. He wore a ceremonial short *simi* in a scabbard of bead-studded scarlet leather that hung from a grossly beaded belt. Under the belt was a kirtle of leopard skin, so fashioned that the tail fell behind and dropped between his legs as if it belonged to him personally. Beneath the leopard skin, worn kilt-fashion, was the ordinary merikani *shuka* of scarlet cloth. Iron rattles were tied round his legs below the knee, and his left hand held a long spear with a black puffball of ostrich feathers capping the blade, as a sign of peace. In his right hand was a long polished staff of office, its pommel crowned by a carved elephant.

'Wow!' Jill gasped again. 'I don't believe it!'

'I don't believe it myself,' Ndegwa said, waddling under the weight of his ornaments, and making a clanking noise as he walked. 'I've got on everything but the kitchen stove, and I may have on at least part of that.' He turned slowly. 'Does this seem awfully corny, Miss Jill—Mrs. Dermott?'

'I don't think it's corny at all,' Jill said. 'I think it's wonderful. And I'm sure you've a proper speech to go with your gorgeous get-up.'

'I have. Just so you won't think I'm indecent when I start to strip off my finery, I've a pair of regulation Army shorts on under this *shuka*. Taking off the regalia is all part of the act.'

George Locke entered with the police superintendent and the Bwana PC. 'My word,' the Chief Superintendent said, 'my word, you *are* got up a treat, Ndegwa. What's all this in aid of, and what about that spear?'

'I admit the spear violates your ordinance about coming armed to a political meeting, Super,' Stephen Ndegwa said as he got up to shake hands. 'But it's only a property spear. Laying it aside is part of the mumbo-jumbo. Locke, have you got that spade handy by the microphone?'

'Yes, indeed. It'll be leaning against the newel post of the banister to your left. The microphone is also dangling from the ceiling alongside the jamb. I just tested it—scared the *shukas* off the visitors. It works just fine. The Bwana PC here was down by the dam, and he said I came across very loud and most shocking clear.'

'D'ye want me publicly in this thing, Ndegwa? H.E. wasn't quite sure of your plans when he rang me up,' the Bwana PC asked, accepting his pink gin from George Locke.

'I rather think not, sir,' Ndegwa said. 'I think the less Serikali the better. We deal today in auld lang syne and new lang syne, with special emphasis on earthy earth and honest toil. The less government and politics and the more God and hard work the better, I should say.'

'How many people would you reckon now, Superintendent?' Ndegwa turned to the policeman.

'Just on five, perhaps six thousand. The land's fair black with them. All seems peaceful and orderly enough so far. I've got my people spotted just to be on the safe side, but it looks to me as if this'll be a good one. Unless you rouse your rabble a little too noisily,' he said bitingly. 'It's been known to happen in the past when your late-lamented colleague started plucking at the harp-strings.'

'I won't rouse any rabble,' Ndegwa smiled. '*Uhuru na kazi*—freedom and hard work—are an effective check on each other. Well,' he said, looking round him at the other occupants of the room, 'I rather imagine we'd best get the show on the road, as the Yankees say.' He drained his glass. 'You go first, Memsaab, and seat yourself in your chair, stage centre, and the others know what chairs they're supposed to take. As soon as you're seated I'll bung through the door and fire the first salvo.'

CHAPTER TWENTY-FOUR

CHARLOTTE STUART walked through the door, limping slightly against her cane, wearing her usual matching sweater set and her oatmeal tweed skirt. Behind her came the two Kikuyu women with the two children, then Nell and George and finally Jill Dermott.

The bright sun struck her like a fist in the face, momentarily blinding her, as she stood facing her garden, but she heard a long soughing '*aaahhhh*', rising like a sudden strong wind in the wheat, as she gazed squinting out over the yard, holding to the chair-back with one hand. Then her eyes adjusted to the white glare, and she looked down and away into a sea of black faces. The faces glistened as sun-touched water glistens, and under the faces the sea of white shirts and orange and blue and green *shukas* shifted like the moving sea. An unconscious swaying stirred the crowd—packed to the dam and on both sides and beyond, blotting out the green of the lawn, obscuring the brightness of the flowers, extinguishing the shrubs. For the first time in her life Charlotte Stuart felt that she was truly looking at the country she lived in. The sea of black had rolled over and obscured all the puny trans-plantations of English culture the white man had brought from his tamer lands.

She walked slowly round in front of her chair, and sat down, automatically propping her lame leg on the hassock which someone had just as automati-cally placed in front of the chair. She plumped her stick to its position of parade rest against her chair, and raised her head to look straight out over the crowd, chin lifted and proud nose high.

'*Jambo, watu,*' she said, without realizing that she said it, and forgetting entirely that the microphone dangled a few feet from her mouth. She was unprepared for the backcast of the 'Hello', and as equally unprepared for the massive '*Jambo, Memsaab*' that roared back from five thousand or more throats. It sounded like thunder in the hills, rolling, dipping, rising. '*Jambo, Memsaab,*' the crowd said, from force of long habit, and inside the living-room door, Stephen Ndegwa smiled, squared his shoulders and, clad in the ancient ornate trappings of his people, prepared to step out into the brilliant sunshine to address his tribe from the private porch of a member of the red-stranger clan which had once taken the country from the people who would hear him now. Charlotte Stuart heard his bracelets clink as he raised both arms high.

'*Uhuru!*' she heard him say in his deep voice, and again she heard the back-cast as the one ripe word rolled over the crowd. You could almost see the word physically.

'*Uhuru!*' came back in a mighty voice from the crowd. '*Uhuru!*'

Charlotte Stuart heard the bracelets clink again as Ndegwa lowered his arms and the crowd fell silent. The cawing of a crow in a distant field came frighteningly loud on the light breeze. Clouds had suddenly massed white and fleecy in the sky.

Stephen Ndegwa had turned now to face Mount Kenya, and was asking Ngai's blessing on His chosen people, and on all the other people so gathered as well. He was asking God soberly for the gift of rain and fertility, that the crops and flocks might fatten, and the women bear healthy children to honour His name. He was asking God to forgive their present sins, and par-don their enemies, and to wash away all the mortal sins of the past. His voice

506

came musically into the air, but it was controlled and low-pitched. The swaying motion of the crowd was slow and barely perceptible, for Ndegwa's voice had not yet keyed itself to rhythmic emotion. Now he was beginning his harangue.

'I come to speak to you in the names of Gikuyu the first man, and Mumbi the first woman, and in the names of the nine daughters to whom God gave husbands, after Gikuyu prayed long under the *mugumo* fig that faces Kerinyagga. I speak to you in the names of all the clans that came from these holy marriages—I speak in one tongue for Agachiku, Mwesaga, Eithaga, Mandoti, Mathathi, Chiera, Ndemi, Iregi, Maina, Mwangi and Muriungu! I speak to you in the names of the kings who bred our brothers, the Wakamba, and the name of the God who sits on Kilimanjaro to watch over our brothers, the Masai. I speak to you in the names of our ancestors, in the names of the spirits who guard us in the night and direct us by day! I speak in the name of one God for one people!'

The crowd was moved, now, at the sonorous repetition of the clan names. It swayed more, and a long, shuddering '*Eeeeehhhh*' came from its lips.

'I speak to you in the names of all our heroic dead!' Ndegwa said. 'And I come to you dressed in the way of our ancestors, that you may recall more vividly the glory of our past!' His body swayed from head to toe, and Charlotte Stuart heard his iron rattles clanking. The body of the crowd followed him in his weaving. The crowd-head was swaying now as the head of a serpent sinuously weaves.

'The past was glorious, and it is well always to remember that we have been a mighty race, and that God has given us all that we can see from this side of The Mountain!' Now the sway of the crowd-head increased, and again a low roaring murmur of assent came surging.

'But we must not live always in the past! The future is upon us! Today is yesterday almost before it dawns! There is no man, no woman, no child among you who has not seen the *ndege*—the iron bird—fly over your heads and land among your *shambas* and on your grazing lands! The wireless brings voices from afar, to the most distant *dukah* in the north! They have been brought by the red stranger who came into our midst in my father's time! He lives among us—I speak at this moment from his lodge—and he wishes to be our friend and help us if we will only allow him!

'The time of the spear has passed! The time of battle is done! The time of sickness and famine and war is finished! The time has come now for work and brotherhood! I speak truly the words of Kamau wa Muthenge whom God has called to His side! Kamau has left me behind to do his bidding, while he sits on the right hand of His Father high on Kerinyagga, and He has come to visit me in a dream, with a message for all!' Stephen Ndegwa raised his hands high again. '*Uhuru na Kamau!*'

Now a mighty roar swelled and broke from the throats of the massed people, and the body of the crowd began to rock and sway.

'*Uhuru na Kamau!*' came roaring from the single mouth of the crowd.

507

Stephen Ndegwa dropped his arms again, and his voice lowered to a blandly confidential tone.

'The work of God is mysterious to man, but it is plain that He sent a sign of disapproval to His people when He called His chosen Son back to His side. Ngai has been angry with us, and has snatched away His Son as a sign of His displeasure! Whom the Lord loveth He chasteneth, and who shall question the doings of our Lord?

'I speak to you now, today, with the mouth of Kamau wa Muthenge, whom the white fathers called Matthew, after a brave *njama* of the white man's Christ! The words of Matthew Kamau, which have come to me as I prayed beneath the *mugumo*, are these: I am with you now and ever afterwards!' Charlotte Stuart's flesh crawled, because Stephen Ndegwa's voice was no longer his own, but a careful mimicry of his dead colleague's. (She did not know that Ndegwa had spent hours listening to a tape recording of several of Matthew Kamau's speeches, and that the words he spoke now were routine words for Kamau when he concluded past speeches.)

'I am with you now and always, as I have been in the past, as I will be in the future, in the sacred fight for our rights in our country. My heart will ring with joy when I know that you heed my words and embark on the sacred work of bringing unity to our beloved Kenya! I beseech you all to unite, to forget the past, to bury your petty differences, to forget your personal quarrels and lusts and greeds—to unite in one effort, as one man, as brothers, with all who love Kenya, no matter what their tribe or colour! Only in unity will your country live! Only in work and love and unity will you taste the fruits of *uhuru*! Man alone is nothing—united he makes his country and lives forever in the heart of God!

'I will never forsake my African people! The best shepherd is one who never abandons his flocks! You have suffered in the past! You have been routed—you have strayed! You have stampeded from the shepherd! I will never abandon you, although you have stampeded and strayed, and lions have fallen upon you in your isolation! There is no way to *uhuru* but unity! Unity can only come with work! No man can be your enemy if he will work with you in a common cause! Unite and you will triumph! Divide and the hyenas will gnaw your bones! The past is dead! I command you to bury the past, as the sheep is buried with the curse sewed into its belly, that the pure waters of the Sagana can wash away the curse! Let the dead past belong to the past! Bury the past in hard work and cling together as brothers in unity, and I shall never forsake you in a thousand moons!'

Ndegwa's voice had risen a trifle with each sentence. It had been a pretty good speech before when Jomo Kenyatta made it first, before Matthew Kamau cribbed it. Now Ndegwa finished the last line with a full-throated roar, and then leaped, his rattles clattering, to yell until the loudspeaker system rattled:

'*Uhuru na kazi!* Unity and faith! Freedom and work!'

The roar of the human beast that stretched ahead of him was deafening

508

and the bodies heaved as they answered him with cries of '*Uhuru na kazi!*
Freedom and work!'

'*Kenya moja!*' Ndegwa screamed. 'One Kenya!'

'One Kenya!' the crowd roared back. '*Kenya moja!*'

Now Stephen Ndegwa spread his arms and flattened his palms over the
heads of the crowd, and spoke sonorously in blessing.

'I bring you the words of Kamau wa Muthenge, of Matthew Kamau, as
I was commanded in a vision,' he said, in a deep level voice. 'Kamau is
watching from the sky to see that we do his bidding. And I shall be the first
to show the way.' He pointed at The Mountain, where clouds had gathered.
Small black clouds were jostling the white clouds. They would grow larger.
With luck there might even be a storm.

He ripped off his headdress, and dashed it to the floor, treading upon the
silken monkey fur and ostrich plumes that made the enormous cap.

'The headdress is for war!' he said. 'I tread it into the dust, as we crush
underfoot the chameleon who betrays us!'

He ripped the beads from his throat, and scattered them by handfuls to
the crowd.

'The jewellery is selfish wealth and vanity!' he cried. 'I cast it from me and
share it with the people!'

He tore off his amulets and the magic medicine bag, and threw them into
the air.

'I throw the sorcerer's tools away, that they may vanish in the mists!' he
screamed. 'The time of evil witchcraft is past!'

He tore the long glittering *simi* from its scabbard, flourished it before the
crowd, and then flung it with all his force into the step beside him. The sword
bit deeply into the soft wood, and stood quivering, and all the eyes turned to
see it quiver.

'The time for stupid superstition and foolish fears is past!' he cried. 'I kill
any curse that may have been laid upon the *shamba*! I command the curse to
die, to disappear from the land and be no more remembered in the hearts of
men!'

He cast aside his monkey-hide cloak, and ripped the waistcloth from
his body. He took the cloth and scrubbed vigorously at the paint on his
face.

'I wash away the painting of the past, when men sought to appear differently from their brothers, and painted their faces for war! I come to you now
with one face—I come with one tongue and one face and one faith, in the
name of Ngai!'

Again the crowd screamed, and the women began their trilling, ululating
with shrilly throbbing throats.

Ndegwa now stood naked except for a pair of khaki shorts and his war
rattles. He bent and swiftly unfastened the rattles, tossing them to his son
Migwe.

'I give my rattles of war to babies to play with so that they shall not weep when their parents tend their crops! War is for children to play at! War is not for men!'

He stood in his shorts, heavy-barrelled and bare-chested, his short hair grizzled and his face cleaned of most of its paint. He held his spear over his head, and shouted:

'The spear is useless to me now! I break it and throw it away forever!'

He bent and broke the spear across one knee, and tossed it aside. He reached over and seized the spade, flourishing it over his head.

'This is the weapon of today! This is the tool of the times! *Uhuru na kazi!* Freedom and work!'

He shifted the spade to his left hand and brandished, very slowly, the polished staff of office, with the elephant's head carved on its pummel.

'See the staff—see the elephant in his wisdom! I hold here the staff of office—the rod of justice. It will be as wise as the elephant, as strong as the arm of God, and all men will be equal before its judgment! I give you work and justice, unity and faith, freedom and peace, and above all, the love of our Lord God! *Uhuru!*'

'*Uhuru!*' the crowd screamed back, and a loud voice took up the shout. '*Uhuru! Uhuru na Ndegwa! Ndegwa na uhuru!* Uhuru na Ndegwa!' and was joined by the crowd in a rising roar: '*Uhuru na Ndegwa! Ndegwa na uhuru!*'

Stephen Ndegwa smiled inside, as he laid aside his spade and staff of office, and turned to Charlotte Stuart. He had planted his claques well in the crowd.

'Bravo,' Charlotte Stuart murmured.

'Jolly well played,' George Locke said. 'I think we've won the day,' and looked again at the leaping, bobbing crowd. 'I don't like the look of the weather, though. There's more rain in those clouds.'

'I think so too,' Ndegwa said. 'You will come on next, Mrs. Stuart, and after you, my wives. We'll hope to beat the rain. I wouldn't want a thunderstorm to break up the camp meeting. Not until the right moment, that is.'

Stephen Ndegwa was extending his hand to Charlotte Stuart when a series of explosions ripped the air apart. A voice roared through another loudspeaker, and the voice was harsh and clear. It spoke in Swahili:

'Ndegwa lies!' the voice shouted. 'He is a white man's tool! He paid the white men to kill Kamau, so that he could steal Kamau's place in your hearts! He will steal the land and give it to the white man! Ndegwa is a murderer! He killed Kamau with white hands, and he is in the pay of the white man! Ndegwa is a murderer and a thief! He will steal your lands and sell you into slavery!'

'The Swahili voice stopped, and the same words were repeated in Kikuyu from a different direction.

'I am the true voice of Kamau!' A new, Kikuyu-speaking voice screamed. 'I tell you Ndegwa lies! He paid the Englishman to kill me! The land on which you stand is accursed, and if you stay, a blight will fall upon your crops

510

and your cattle will miscarry their calves and your women will go barren and hyenas will eat your children: I am the true voice of Kamau! Heed me, or my Father will destroy you from his throne atop The Mountain!'

A fresh series of explosions rocked the air. Some of the massed people began to jostle and push and turn, attempting to run and striking out blindly when the attempt was barred by the thick press of bodies.

Then the voice came on again, and now it was in Masai.

'Masai! The Kikuyu will enslave you! The Kikuyu only want your lands and cattle! The Kikuyu will sell you as slaves and steal your lands and cattle! Do not trust Ndegwa! He is Kikuyu! He speaks in two tongues, and wears the white man's coat as well! He killed his friend, and he will destroy you!'

Then swiftly, in Wakamba:

'Kill the Masai! They only want more land for their cattle, and will bring more cattle to graze upon your land! Do not listen to Ndegwa! He is in the pay of the whites! He will take the Masai land for himself and send the Masai to squat upon your country! Death to Ndegwa! Death to the Masai!'

There was another chain of scattered explosions, and then the furies loosed. Less than half a minute had elapsed while the crowd stood, stunned at first, then baffled, then impotently panicked in an effort to get away. The clouds were building, fatter and higher, one came suddenly across the sun, and the day lost its glister.

The Swahili voice was back again: 'Kill Ndegwa! Kill the old white bitch! Destroy the farm! The curse is here! Kill the *mzungu* or the curse will kill you all! I am the true voice of Kamau! Down with the white man——' Now the voice ended as a splutter, as the police located the speaker in a lorry which had been converted into a mobile broadcasting unit and which had been set up behind a hedge.

The explosions, of the shockingly loud variety which may be obtained from thunderflashes or giant cannon crackers, left a thin acrid film of scent on the clean-washed air. The explosions had also brought the Senior Superintendent of Police and the Bwana Provincial Commissioner out of the dark cavern of the living-room. They stood, tense on the veranda, momentarily as confused as everyone else.

Ndegwa had stood stricken in his tracks as the voices boomed from the hidden sound-trucks, and Charlotte Stuart had listened with mouth agape at the multi-lingual messages that reverberated over her lawn. Jill and Nell and George had leaped from their chairs to stand horrified; the two children had run to clutch the legs of their mother—of the entire lot, the senior wife Mumbi seemed calmest.

Stephen Ndegwa suddenly found himself grunting over his fat belly as he stooped and attempted to wrench the *simi* from its deep bed in the planking of the steps. He grunted and strained, and when the blade of the short sword came free, he almost tumbled ridiculously on his plump backside. Then he reached up to the dangling microphone and began to scream pleas for order. All he could think of to say was 'Peace! Don't fight!'

The policeman unhooked the flap of his holster and loosened the pistol in its sheath. Then he took the mike away from Ndegwa, and barked dispersion orders to his men. The Provincial Commissioner produced a flat ·32-calibre automatic which he had taken to wearing in his breast pocket of late. Jill Dermott ran into the house and snatched a shotgun from its cradle by the bookcases; Charlotte Stuart merely picked up her stick. George Locke stood and gawked; his wife moved closer to his side. All motions were accomplished in something less than twenty seconds. Then the microphone fell sick in the middle of one of the policeman's orders, emitting a banshee wail until the Chief Superintendent shook it into submission.

Flapping banners miraculously appeared in the crowd. DOWN WITH NDEGWA! was scrawled in red across a bedsheet. NDEGWA MURDERER emblazoned another. NDEGWA WHITE MAN TOOL was another, and NDEGWA KILLER KAMAU still another.

Separated shouts arose in roaring, screeching chorus, in Kikuyu and Swahili.

'Kill Ndegwa! Kill the whites! Burn the house! Kill the Masai! Kill the Kamba!' sprouted like evil toadstools in the composted confusion, from almost geometrically spaced portions of the mob. Then in Masai, 'Kill the Kikuyu! Kill the cattle thieves!' and in Wakamba, 'Kill the Masai! Take back our grazing lands!' Then in Kipsigi and Luo and Kavirondo and Meru and Embu, 'Kill the *mzungu*! Kill the Masai! Kill the Kamba! *Kill! Kill!*'

The Chief Inspector of Police stood with his hand on the butt of his pistol. Ndegwa stood with his fat belly hanging over his khaki shorts, clutching his *simi*. Jill Dermott held her shotgun, and George Locke felt foolishly to see if he had his pipe in his pocket. Charlotte Stuart grasped her stout stick as a stave. Nell Dermott moved closer to her husband, and the children seized Wanjiro's legs with a firmer grip. Mumbi's old fingers roved over her finery, and the Bwana PC looked at his automatic and hid it behind him as a child would hide a toy.

There was no place for the people on the porch to go. A solid turbulent sea of flesh surrounded them, the surface of black faces wind-chopped by excitement. Red mouths showing white tombstones of teeth opened and howled in horrid cacophony. And still the mob was a mass—animals from another age embedded in the rock of their own immobility as individuals. The mob leaped and shouted as one man, and the people on the porch watched the surging, rolling ocean of black.

More thunderflashes went off, more screams soared high, and now the mob began to split like paramecia into knots of components. A woman fell, was trampled, and began to moan. A hand clutched a sleeve—the sleeve tore. Nails scratched a face—the scratcher felt blood and skin and howled, his victim felt his skin torn and the blood flow, and howled back. A man butted another man in the face with the top of his head. That man, nose gushing blood, fumbled for a hidden knife and stuck it into the first soft surface near him. A woman produced a *rungu* from her *shuka* and struck another woman over the head with it. A child tumbled from its nest in its mother's cloak and fell to the ground, was lost, and was trampled underfoot. Its thin wail was smothered by the calloused hoof which crushed its tiny head.

Fists flailed. *Pangas* came miraculously to view. Now black hands groped for stones around the driveway. More clubs were exhumed from more *shukas*. Common pocket-knives and two-edged *simis* leaped flashing into use. The screech of 'Kill the Kikuyu! Kill the Masai! Kill the white people! Kill the Kamba!' were fattened by spontaneous screams and roars of wrath from individuals, as they fought to separate themselves from each other. The explosions of thunderflashes punctuated the grunts of slugging men and the wails of trodden children and the screams of clawing, biting, kicking women.

Now the mysterious chemistry of the conducted mob began to conduct its own special polarization. The electrolysis of steered action prevailed over common pandemonium. The hysteria of the inspired madness was channelled.

The Masai were separating themselves from the Kikuyu, as were the Wakamba. The Masai had not come unprepared. They had hidden their long spears under logs and behind stones and in the rushes that fringed the little lake. Running like cheetahs, they went springing off on their long lithe legs, cloaks flapping behind to expose their nakedness, in search of their spears. They found their spears and speedily formed a phalanx. They had not been trained by the *laiboni* for nothing—they were not *morani*, veterans of sixty-mile battle marches and iron discipline for a dozen of years, for nothing. They formed the battle array they used against charging lion—or, in the old days, against the Kikuyu. The Masai, once they got their hands on their spears, began leaping high and screaming. Their flat-footed stiff-legged jumps took them three feet off the ground, while the senior *morani* blew their hawk's-leg whistles and formed the men into a fighting front. They lacked shields—but against the hated Kikuyu no shields were needed. The senior *moran* blew three blasts on his eagle-thigh-bone whistle and the Masai charged, spears couchant, into the milling pack.

The Wakamba had bunched away, as well—and now knobkerries and *rungus* and other versions of clubs appeared, as well as the long heavy *pangas*, the bush knives, and the short stabbing *simis*. The Wakamba were lucky on this God-sent day—there were both Masai *and* Kikuyu there for the killing. Someone retrieved the dancing drums, and some few of the dancers leaped and tumbled as the drummers beat a war rhythm on drums as big as hogsheads. The Wakamba liked close work—in this respect they resembled Gurkhas with their *kukris*—the Kambas screamed a war-cry and plunged, short, thickset and fierce, into the heart of the milling crowd.

A hundred native police and twenty white officers had been detailed to supervise the political meeting of Stephen Ndegwa. They were dispersed according to well-rubbed custom by Senior Superintendent O'Flaherty, who had broken up mobs in India and Burma and Malaya as well as in Africa. The classic divide-and-rule technique of mob-control police is to employ vehicles as the Cossacks used horses, and to use batons to crack the odd skull.

But these tactics are better adapted to city streets and culs-de-sac than to the rolling acres of a Kenya farm. Tear-gas is useful, as well, especially in city squares, and in the narrow streets where so many mob scenes have their genesis. Tear-gas is of little use in the open country air with a brisk noon breeze to blow it back into the faces of the users. And O'Flaherty's police carried no tommy-guns. Machine-guns had been forbidden by Nairobi as apt to lend an obtrusively uncooperative tone to a meeting of goodwill.

Policemen—especially native policemen—bleed profusely when you stick them, and curse when you kick their shins. O'Flaherty's men made a baton charge into the middle of the screeching, slugging, kicking, biting, cursing, keening, elbowing, club-swinging, *panga*-wielding, spear-poking, *simi*-jabbing, head-butting confusion, and were promptly slugged, bitten, kicked, cursed, elbowed, clubbed, *panga*ed, spear-poked, *simi*-jabbed, and head-butted, which unduly annoyed a force which was 98 per cent Wakamba professional gendarmerie, with a vast disdain for anything and anybody that opposed the dignity of their chosen profession of cophood.

There is a saying in Kenya that one may amputate the Wakamba from Machakos, but you cannot cut away Machakos from the Wakamba. Policemen or not, the Kamba's mental teeth are still filed, and his father has tasted human flesh. The Wakamba *askaris* promptly went into business for themselves, for were there not Masai to bash with their batons, and Kikuyu to smite?

One of the white police officers, about to shoot a raging Wakamba policeman with the whites of his eyes showing madly over the irises, suddenly changed his mind and smacked the man across the face with the flat of the Webley. Sanity came back to the *askari*'s face, together with the blood, and he halted and saluted smartly. 'Oh, sorry, sah,' he said, and bared his bloody gap-toothed mouth in a grin before he let out another screech and plunged back into the thick of the fight.

In the recapitulation several things happened.

Some mad mullah, undoubtedly fired by native *bangh* and a few shillings of incentive pay, led a charge halfway up the steps of the big house of Glenburnie farm. He was followed by a stone-flinging horde of assorted strangers who screamed 'Kill the *mzungu*!' as they flung their stones.

One of the stones struck Charlotte Stuart in the temple, opening a great gash and knocking her unconscious.

Another struck Wanjiro, the European-dressed wife of Stephen Ndegwa, also in the temple, opening a similar gash and dropping Wanjiro unconscious in a spreading shallow smear of blood.

The mad mullah who was leading the charge was also waving a large *panga* as he mounted the steps in great strides. The presence of the *panga* caused Chief Inspector O'Flaherty to draw his pistol and shoot the mad mullah twice through the chest as he mounted the last-but-three steps to the porch. The mad mullah fell backwards into the arms of his followers, most of whom were wearing the red, green and black of *uhuru*.

The followers spurned the dying mad mullah to one side and were debating a fresh rush on the steps when Jill Dermott fired both barrels of her shotgun accidentally and discouraged the charge conclusively, although one diehard member achieved sufficient altitude on the steps to be discommoded bloodily by a swipe across the face from Ndegwa's *simi*.

With their temporary basic blood-lust satisfied, the Wakamba police regrouped and set out steadily to chop the rioters into containable segments with their batons. The first to submit were the Masai, who had thoroughly blooded their half a hundred spears on at least a hundred strangers, and who were now losing interest. The Kamba *askaris* had also sectored off their own tribesmen. The Kikuyu seemed suddenly weary of cutting and kicking and biting at each other.

But some knots of men still battled, and some women still clawed and kicked and bit. The Police Superintendent who had first directed his men through the loudspeaker, was able to join them as the crowd split apart, and the police methodically clubbed the last wranglers into a cessation of hostility.

Stephen Ndegwa had pleaded unavailingly through the microphone for the people to heed him, and to disregard the other exhortations, but the people showed no attempt to regroup into any sort of an audience.

The gathering clouds had thickened and blackened, and there was a deep rumble of thunder in the direction of Mount Kenya. Suddenly a flash of lightning tore the sky, and was followed by a tremendous crash of thunder. Rain came driving down like spears, and the whole sky, which had been so cleanly blue, frowned blackly while the day, which had been so bright, took on the sombreness of twilight. The rain sloshed harder—the sky was split again and again by lightning and rent apart by thunder. Ngai from his seat on The Mountain was very angry indeed.

Charlotte Stuart opened her eyes to find George Locke bathing the wound on her forehead. They had taken her and the woman, Wanjiro, into the house and had stretched them down on divans. Neither would suffer much of a concussion, Locke decided, but both had better stay quiet for a bit. The wounds would need a few stitches, which would hurt. The children sat frightened, big-eyed on the floor in a corner with the older wife, Mumbi. Charlotte Stuart shut her eyes in a determined effort to close her brain to the sickening acceptance of failure.

Stephen Ndegwa stood in the yard with the Bwana PC and looked around him at the shambles. There were at least a dozen dead—possibly more would die. The wounded were sitting up now, some of them—bleeding or with lumping knots on their heads. There were at least a hundred wounded, most of them not seriously, but the Masai spears and the Kikuyu *pangas* and the Wakamba clubs had drawn extensive blood. The presence of the police and the sudden eruption of the storm had combined to prevent a full-scale massacre.

The man who had led the stoning charge was lying spraddled in death at the foot of the steps. Other dead men lay like tumbled heaps of laundry around the yard, whose flowers and shrubbery had been crushed and trodden flat in the riot. Shards of glass still streaked the veranda of the big house, where the showers of stones had broken windows.

The Masai elders had taken their younger hot-bloods in tow, and were now herding them towards the buses and eventually home. The Masai's make-up had run in the rain—their finery was sadly bedraggled. They looked almost sheepish as they straggled, stork-legged in their short red togas, through the little valley by the dam and up and across to the hill-top where the lorries were.

The Kikuyu and Wakamba, mostly dressed in shabby city clothes, looked less rumpled than the Masai, but equally as sheepish as they wandered off in wet and tattered groups. Some who had come in the buses and lorries refused to ride back in them, but made their way on foot towards the main road. Once Stephen Ndegwa had seen that his wife was not seriously damaged, he had gone to the buses and attempted to marshal the passengers. Most of the Sikh drivers had stayed on in the vehicles, and were still available to drive. But the buses that pulled away one by one were going back half-loaded to the cities and reserves. The crowd had dispersed like crows scattered from a cornfield.

The police had arrested some few of the rioters, and were preparing now to take the wounded into native dispensaries. They had managed to collar one of the men who had screamed repudiation of Stephen Ndegwa's words through mobile loudspeakers in automobiles. But he had slipped his captors when the wholesale fighting started, and had been swallowed by the crowd. The cars themselves would prove to have been taken from a rental service, and the crudely effective broadcasting apparatus installed by some native or Indian electrician.

The policeman, O'Flaherty, looked gloomily at the dead men on the lawn—gazed apathetically at the wounded who were either hobbling or being carried away.

'I suppose we'll book the survivors with disturbing the peace,' he said. 'But there's not a murder charge in the lot. You never know exactly who pokes whom in these shivarees. But I must say it was a gaudy mess while it lasted, Ndegwa. Quite clever—using those thunderflashes to imitate bombs and then coming at you with those other voices from the cars. Thank God for the rainstorm. If it hadn't been for that my chaps would still be trying to stop this thing.'

Stephen Ndegwa shrugged.

'Quite obviously the powers of evil are still at work. It's a pity. Rather completely wipes out my fine scheme to settle Kamau's ghost *and* repopulate Mrs. Stuart's farm project. This'll be in all the papers, obviously, and that *Baraza* will go mad with glee in Swahili. And, of course, Radio Cairo. I'm just going to have to do something drastic to root out the trouble-makers. It'll want a giant step now, I shouldn't wonder.'

'I wish you luck,' the policeman said. 'Come on, Nigel. Let's get the dead and dying bods off the premises. I shouldn't imagine you'd be issued any permits for any more speakings any time soon, Ndegwa. And I'm certain this area will be off limits for anybody at all to hold one. Good luck with your giant step. Good day.'

'Good day,' Stephen Ndegwa said, and walked, head down, back to the house. Juma was busy on the front porch with a broom, sweeping up the broken glass. Another servant was scrubbing blood off the steps and floor of the veranda.

Philip Dermott was in the living-room talking to George and Nell Locke and to his wife, Jill, when Ndegwa entered.

He looked at Ndegwa with a flat expressior. of dislike.

'I believe they mucked up your little pinic, Ndegwa,' he said. 'I had a suspicion they would. A couple of the boys and myself sneaked in the back way when all the pow-wowing was going on and you were doing your strip-tease. We didn't know whether a little extra artillery might be needed if your flock got too violent. If it's any comfort to you, nobody would have come any closer than the steps. *My* chaps had sub-machine-guns. They don't believe in baton charges.'

'Thank you for your consideration,' Ndegwa said. 'It was thoughtful of you to worry about us.'

'I wasn't really worrying about you so much as I was about my wife and family,' Philip Dermott said cheerfully. 'But your day's not over yet. Some of the boys want to meet you—over at Don Bruce's farm. It's a purely well-meant method of apprising you of something else you're going to have to deal with.'

Ndegwa looked at George Locke, who gazed down at the floor.

'What's all this about?' he asked sharply. 'Who are "the boys", and who's to say that I want to have anything to do with them?'

Philip Dermott laughed, a harsh bark, and slapped his holstered pistol.

'The boys,' he replied, 'are mostly friends of mine—farmers and such. You might even call them patriots. They're a sort of militia. And *they* say you want to have something to do with them. *This*'—he slapped the pistol again—'says you want to have something to do with them. And if you want to get really specific, *I* say you want to have quite a lot to do with us.'

Ndegwa looked at the young man levelly.

'I don't like your tone, and I don't care at all for threats. There's still a certain amount of law and order in Kenya.'

Philip Dermott laughed again. He passed his hand over the bristles of his crew-cut head.

'Like what I've just seen in my aunt's yard? Is that your Kenya law and order? Look, Ndegwa. Whether you walk or get yourself carried is immaterial to me. We're actually doing you a favour. All we want to do is outline our position, so that you will know yours. Now, will you come, or will we come and collect you some darkish night?'

Stephen Ndegwa turned to George Locke.

'I suppose I might as well go along with this young man. How is my wife?'

'She shouldn't be moved for a day or so. We've put her in a spare room.'

'Could you find space for my other wife and the children as well for a few days? Any one of the houses in the labour location would do nicely, if somebody would see that they got food.'

'I'll look after them, Mr. Ndegwa,' Jill Dermott said, and looked at her husband as if she had never seen him before. 'Will you be coming back here tonight, after you finish with—*him*?' She nodded at Philip Dermott.

'No. I shouldn't think so. There will be some things I must attend to in Nairobi—some other things.' He glanced at Philip Dermott. 'That's of course if I am permitted to return to town?'

'Oh, yes. This time we have every intention of returning you to Nairobi. It's only the next time—if that should become necessary—where the possibility of your returning to Nairobi might be in doubt. Come on, are you ready?'

'I'm ready. Tell Mrs. Stuart how very sorry I am that everything turned out so badly, Locke. Perhaps we can think of something else. But at the moment it all looks very dark to me. I'm afraid the project at Glenburnie is finished, and the farm with it, unless you can bring in some labour from the other tribes.'

He went over in the corner and spoke rapidly to his wife and children in Kikuyu.

'I must go away with this man for a while, then I must go to Nairobi. You will stay here. You will be well taken care of. The doctor and these good white women will give you what you need, and they will watch over Wanjiro as well. Good-bye.'

He turned to Philip Dermott.

'You will give me five minutes to change into some proper clothes, if you please,' and disappeared, a stocky, fat-bellied, but oddly dignified figure in his shorts and what remained of the paint with which he had smeared his face.

*

Stephen Ndegwa looked at the young man who sat beside him in the back seat of the big white Mercedes. He saw a face which might very well once have been called almost girlish in its gentleness, and which now seemed as cold and unmoving as granite, with its severe long nose and the hard bulges of muscles at the jaw-corners. He was dressed in the costume of the country —bush jacket, shorts, high calf desert boots and thick wool socks. For comfort, he had eased the holster of his long revolver around to where it lay against the inside of one thigh. This young Dermott was very tall and rather skinny, but he had a rawhide look about him. He said nothing, smoked and stared out of the window.

Stephen Ndegwa had no wish to talk. His brain was bitter with the disappointment of the morning's *shauri* on the farm—with the debacle which had occurred. There was no doubt in his mind as to who had seeded the riot. This business today had the smell of Matisia all through it.

Matisia. Only this morning he had been thinking that the thing to do with Matisia was threaten him with what the whore had told him, and Matisia would run away. Now he was not so sure that Matisia *would* run away. He had shown a very strong and firm hand with this work today. He had, in fact, stalked unmistakably out into the open to challenge Stephen Ndegwa. Perhaps merely sending Matisia away wasn't good enough. Perhaps—Ndegwa put the thought away. He was sick of the connivings that led always to riots and so often to blood. There were a dozen or more dead men on his conscience from this morning's work. It couldn't be allowed to continue—but the riot at Glenburnie had showed clearly that the way to leadership in Kenya was not the way of reason and moderation if such had ever been the case. Matisia and the others like him had ruined reason, as Macbeth had murdered sleep.

Now this business of the short-cropped young thug at his side.

'*Hapa. Sasa. Kushoto,*' the young thug had tapped the driver Kipro on the shoulder, and was directing him to turn. They approached a gate composed of many different tribal spears, and the sign said simply: CAMPI YA MZUNGU.

As the driver got out to open the gate, Philip Dermott said laconically: 'They keep finding all sorts of things hanging on this gate. Dogs, sheep—the other day a fat black gentleman with a cut throat. Name of Kungo. Used to work here. It's really quite a handy gate for that sort of thing.'

They rode along down a rutty rain-carved road which had run to shaggy weed on its borders, passing fields where crops had gone to seed. Fences were broken in several places, and native sheep could be seen grazing, intermingled with goats. The farm had an air of general disrepair and of sad desertion; it wore the unloved look which comes swiftly to untended land.

'Used to be quite a little show-place, as Glenburnie was a big show-place,' Philip Dermott was saying agreeably enough. 'But so many things happened to wreck it that poor Don Bruce had to leave. You probably heard something about it—for all I know, you organized it.'

'And so now Bruce has come back, has he? What brings him back into the fire, after he was well away from Kenya?'

'He'll tell you himself. He felt he was a rotten coward for shirking his responsibility and running off to hide in England. He's third-generation Kenya. He reckons he's as much right here as anybody else. Of course he didn't want to gamble with the lives of his wife and kids. But once they were safely away his conscience got the better of him and now he's back. I must say he's in an ugly mood. You'll find most of the boys in a rather surly state of mind. They haven't very much liked the way things are run in Kenya for some time.'

There didn't seem to be any answer to that, so Ndegwa fell silent until they arrived at the yard. The grass had grown knee-high, bearded in weeds, almost obscuring the neat pattern of whitewashed stones which had defined a circular drive. Flower-beds had either gone to seed or were running riotously loose in unchecked profusion. No fewer than a dozen Land Rovers were parked under the shade trees. Dogs were tied on long swivels suspended between trees. They were mostly Alsatian or Alsatian crosses. A few were Doberman pinschers. They immediately set up a furious barking. Some of them were huge, Ndegwa noted—that big slavering black chap would weigh over ten stone.

'Tracker dogs,' Philip said laconically. 'Don Bruce used to run a tracking school. These beasts haven't heard about multi-racialism yet. They don't like black people. It's the way they were taught. Step a little closer to that nearest bloke and you'll see what I mean.'

'This is quite close enough for me, thank you,' Ndegwa said, as the slavering Alsatian hurled himself the full length of his leash at him, straining up on his hind quarters, forefeet flailing the air, eyes slitted, lips writhed back over the two-inch fangs. Ndegwa shivered.

'Come on in,' Philip Dermott said. 'It's nearly cocktail time. Some of the boys have been known to jump the gun on legal drinking hours. I'm sure we'll be able to find a drink.'

They walked up to the porch, and Ndegwa noticed that the windows had been recently barred.

'Seems peculiar running into window-bars and locked doors in *this* house,' Philip Dermott said. 'Even during the Emergency this house was never locked. It had a tame witch doctor with a very potent spell that kept the place safe from harm. Somebody killed the witch doctor and the spell died with him. After that they had nothing but trouble here. Last bit was when they pinched Bruce's headman to make a main course in an oathing. Never found the body, or would you know that?'

A huge man—roughly red-haired, with brown eyes and a ridiculously small nose in his broad freckled face—opened the door. He looked coldly at Ndegwa.

'Come in,' he said. 'I see you got the mess all tidied up at Glenburnie. How's Aunt Charlotte's head where the rock clunked her?'

'She'll do,' Philip Dermott said. 'Her nephew-in-law's hovering over her with wet cloths, or something. This is Ndegwa, Don.'

'Come in the house,' he said, and looked without emotion at Ndegwa. 'What we have to show you won't take very long. There's only the steering committee here, and I'm nominated to do all the spieling for the group.'

It was quite dark inside the room, since there did not seem to be any electricity. Only a small fire leaped hesitantly in the hearth. It took a moment for Stephen Ndegwa's eyes to become accustomed to the gloom, and then he began to pick out the faces of men. He saw them sitting in chairs and on the floor, leaning against the fireplace or wall. The room smelled of men—of tobacco and woodsmoke and alcohol, of grease and gun-oil and old sweated clothing.

'One of you blokes light a couple of lamps,' Don Bruce said. 'It's as black

520

as sin in here. I want our guest to have a look at all of us—and after a bit I want one of you to show him around the armoury and the petrol dump and the radio shack. You want a drink, Ndegwa?'

'No, thank you,' Stephen Ndegwa said. 'I'd rather get on with whatever business it is you have in mind. State it, and let me go about my affairs.'

'You see around you,' Donald Bruce said, 'a classic collection of the kind of men that used to be regarded as sort of rough heroes before it became popular to sneer at them. They are called colonials—the dirty, stinking, black-man-abusing, country-plundering colonials that everybody spits on now in this new world of Macmillan and Macleod and the United Nations. We are mostly family men—and most of us were in the armed forces during the last big war. We are farmers and lawyers and policemen and shopkeepers and game wardens and doctors and engineers. But mostly we are farmers. We are interested in land—in *our* land. We are interested in our land because we made it and we intend to keep it.'

'All right, I get the point,' Ndegwa said. He could see the faces clearly now—they were the faces that one saw around the bar at the Norfolk or Stanley, the faces one saw laughing with pretty women over a drink at the Thorn Tree, the same faces one saw in up-country *dukahs* and the smaller pubs. They were mostly Irish and Scots faces, but with here and there a darker face of Italian or Greek. They were not all young—some were in their fifties. They owned mostly hard-cut, craggy features, with prominent cheekbones and lumpy frontals, with big chins and uneven noses and stick-out ears. They were the kind of faces which went with hands like the hands of Donald Bruce—big, square, chapped, barked-knuckled freckled hands. They were the kind of hands that went with ploughs and the spare parts of machinery, and always with guns. They were hands that drove aeroplanes and tractors and Land Rovers. They were hands that knew the feel of horses and women and children and dogs. They were Kenya hands, Ndegwa thought, and the faces were certainly Kenya faces, as the cords and khakis and boots were certainly Kenya clothes.

'I'm pleased you are getting the point.' Don Bruce was standing spread-legged with his back to the fire. 'I suppose you know that your people ran me off my land. I freely admit that it was a mistake for me to run, as it was a mistake for Charlotte Stuart to think that she could do business with your sort. Well, Ndegwa, we're past running now. We want you to know it.'

Donald Bruce passed his big hand over the rough red hair, and licked pale freckle-splotched lips. He spoke almost in embarrassment.

'I really don't know what came over the Kenya white man, Ndegwa. Perhaps we read too much—perhaps we were preached at too much. But we suddenly changed from a race of men to a nation of whiners and skulkers and appeasers. I really do not understand it. But all that's over, now—and some semblance of the old sanity's back.'

He pointed a finger at Ndegwa.

'We will kill you people, Ndegwa. We killed you before. Now we will kill you massively. For every one of us you kill, we will kill a thousand of you. We will kill your women and children and set fire to your crops. We will burn your houses and slaughter your goats and cattle. We will track you with dogs, and hang you, and starve you. We will work you in slave gangs, and kill you for complaining. And we will start at the top, Ndegwa, with you and Gichuru and Mboya and all the rest. You will be the first to go.'

Donald Bruce turned away and walked over to a table to pour himself a drink.

'In short, Ndegwa,' Donald Bruce said, 'we propose to resettle Kenya. If you political clowns in this country have your way, it'll all be back in bloody barbarism and tribal warfare in a year or so, or else you'll give it or sell it to the Communists and they'll treat you worse than ever we did. We propose to prevent that.'

'And just how do you propose to prevent our coming to independence?' Ndegwa was furious, but managed to keep his voice smooth. 'We have been promised—guaranteed certain things by England. The elections are coming in a couple of months' time. We have a guaranteed majority. We will have an African cabinet and almost immediately an African chief minister and in no time at all, *uhuru*. Pardon, Mr. Bruce, but I do not see *how* you can prevent Kenya from coming free?'

'It's really quite simple,' Bruce replied. 'Simple if you think of it in terms of dead people. Dead people can't use *uhuru*. The Russians and Chinese have been getting away with it for years. For one thing, we will demand our independence from England. We just won't be a bloody colony any more. We will run Kenya as the Belgians used to run the Congo, as the Germans ran Tanganyika.'

'It all sounds very ambitious,' Ndegwa said, and lit a cigarette. He was mildly pleased that his fingers were not shaking. 'I just think that you're running against the world. The world won't let you do what you propose.'

'Are you so certain? Are you really so certain? The world lets Castro do as he likes with Cuba. The world may just be so bloody sick of the noisy incompetent bickerings of you trained apes that they'll welcome a little order once more!'

'I think I have heard enough of this sort of aimless bluster,' Stephen Ndegwa said. 'I should like to go home, please. Unless you had something concrete to say? Something less juvenile?'

'I have this to say. On the day they hang Brian Dermott, we will hang you and all the rest like you! If necessary, we will hang the Governor as well! And we will make a systematic extermination of your people which will amount to more bloodshed than Lumumba ever caused against the Balubas!'

Donald Bruce stepped closer to Stephen Ndegwa.

'I have this to say, juvenile or not. For every accident, for every intimidation, for every crime of black against white, we will retaliate more heavily than we did in the beginning of the Mau Mau emergency. We will kill you as the Portuguese kill in Angola—by the village!

'I have *this* to say, Ndegwa. If after your automatic majority that Macleod handed you this spring comes into being next year—if after you are in a clear majority at Legislative Council—if you make one move towards expropriation of *our* land, we will kill you by the thousands and destroy *your* lands in less than a week.

'And if, at the end, the world or England does attempt to shoot us down, we will scorch our own earth as well as yours, and we will die killing you! If you would care to step into my office in a few minutes, I can show you some rather elaborate maps for water sources to be poisoned, for villages to be fired, for fields to be burned—for ground to be ruined.'

Ndegwa spread his fingers and looked at his nails.

'Is there anything I can do to avert this—this holocaust—you people have in mind?'

Donald Bruce nodded his head.

'Yes. There is indeed. You have seen today that preaching sense to your people *en masse* is impossible. The only thing I can suggest is that you get together with the rest of your political chums and tell them that there's going to be no more intimidations, no more planned riots, no more loud boasting about what's going to happen after *uhuru*—no more molesting of our women and no more talk about taking all the *mzungu*'s land and of driving him into the sea.

'And,' Donald Bruce prodded him on the chest, 'see if you can't scheme up a way not to hang Brian Dermott! I'm telling you, if Brian Dermott swings for shooting Matthew Kamau, it will be because we haven't blown up the jail and the Governor's mansion and all of you blokes beforehand! You had your symbol—we've got ours!

'You might say, Ndegwa, that the future of this country rests on whether or not Brian Dermott hangs for killing Kamau! You nationalists have enjoyed your reign of terror too long. It's time somebody else showed you what a real reign of terror can be like! If we kill enough of you, perhaps then our precious Macleod will set *us* free! Show us some sincerity by delivering us Brian Dermott, and we may decide to live in peace with you and let you have your *uhuru*!'

Don Bruce's face was pale, and he realized suddenly that he had been shouting. He lowered his voice with an effort, and said: 'The group you see here is typical of an organization which is spreading and will spread further, all over Kenya. It is an honest open force of men who love their country and their families, and who have been driven finally to the wall. I can only warn you, Ndegwa, don't do anything—and don't let your other political friends do anything that will set us off!'

He looked away, then, and said to Philip Dermott.

'I'm finished. Take Ndegwa to see our equipment, if he wants to. I don't want to say anything more to him. Or look at him, either.'

'I will take your word about your equipment,' Ndegwa said. 'I would prefer to go home now.'

The barbed hostility of the harsh-faced men in the room scratched at him like thorns as he walked slowly through the room and into the yard.

He got into the car amid a tremendous clamour of dogs and leaned back against the soft leather cushions.

'On the way back to Nairobi,' he said to the chauffeur, 'drive by my *shamba* in the reserve.'

He thought, resting against the soft cushions as the big car bumped down Donald Bruce's weedy, rutted-clay road, that it really was foolish to drive by his little farm at all. Foolish, because he knew as surely as he knew his name was Ndegwa that he would find the *shamba* burned flat and the goats and sheep driven away. Whether the men of Donald Bruce or the men of Abraham Matisia had burned his farm was beside the point. One way or the other, his farm would be burned and his earth scorched.

CHAPTER TWENTY-FIVE

STEPHEN NDEGWA sat brooding in the lounge of his town house. It had gone well past dusk, and the musty room was dark, but he did not feel like turning on the lights. He preferred not to look at the shabby emptiness of the room. Smelling the blackened stems of decayed flowers was bad enough. The boy had forgotten to throw out the flowers when he sacked him, and he had been too busy lately to fuss with any petty details of household.

Great God, but it was quiet. Iris had been away only ten days or so, and it seemed an eternity. Perhaps her affected stilted gabble was annoying, but it had filled the house with sound, and usually she had her record-player yammering away.

He lifted the glass in his hand without enthusiasm. He was drinking whisky and soda, and it tasted stale and brown. The room smelled of cigarette-ends and flat soda and despair. He had his shoes off and his feet tilted on another chair, but was not appreciating his usual enjoyment from having his toes freed. He lit another cigarette and sighed. In a moment he would have to make up his mind.

It was strange. Of all the people so tragically mixed up in this tremendous mess, he was conscious that the greatest sin was his—the biggest fault belonged to Stephen Ndegwa. I have been like the lazy parent who deliberately watches his children stray until one drowns and the other sets the house afire, he thought.

Matisia is an animal. I should have crushed him. Kamau was half-mad with power lust and warped religion. I should have curbed him. I should not have stood by, in my own hypocritical aloofness, and watched these dangerous children play with fire and venture much too near the water. I have thought all this before, and have pushed it from my head.

And now I am saddled with the lot; saddled with the whole, hopeless, miserable lot. Your fault, Ndegwa, he said to himself. You knew better—you always knew things would happen and you were willing to let them happen. You are worse than the rest, because you had some moral standards to start with and tossed them all away. You said that before, too, Ndegwa.

All right, Ndegwa, half of him argued back, you can't say that it was all your fault that an innocent American woman and a poor child and a couple of members of your own race got killed in the crush, any more than you can hold yourself responsible because Matisia takes up with Belgian whores and white hunters go mad and shoot Matthew Kamau. Can't you accuse yourself, Ndegwa? I suppose you really can, if the part is vital to the whole. Wiggle out of that one, boy.

But the time for sophistry is past, boy, and you have to make up your mind in favour of some practical course. Today was certainly a miserable failure as a compromise. You might have brought it off. You might just have brought it off—and then blackmailed friend Matisia out of your future plans with the whore's information. You might have steered the country so smoothly given an honest free hand, and with some of the hyenas removed, that you might have worked out a decent agreement with the white settlers for a peaceful, prosperous coexistence. Or would you? Something else—some other Matisia—would always bob up to cripple your well-intended plans. That's the trouble with making compromises with morality. Boy. And don't call me 'boy'. *Boy*. We still have the country wide open for riot and rapine and tragic confusion so long as we have Matisia and the people like him who see no other way to power but keeping the animals fed on hatred. We have the greedy ones and the selfish ones who only see that power in terms of hatred for the white and lust for the white man's things—his land and his cars and his life, even if that life means the white man's houses and his women.

And, God pity us, we have a majority of simple folk who must be led, and who will follow blindly, out of ignorance, if only the leaders scream loudly enough and prey upon hatreds and rivalries and old evil customs and personal greeds. The evil is only with the leaders who lie to and mislead the simple people—the evil is not in the poor people who fling the spears and throw the rocks and scream for blood.

God damn all politicians, including me, Stephen Ndegwa thought. If we do not mend our ways, all Africa will be permanently aflame, and it will be because of the plots and connivings and childish rivalries of a handful of vain, selfish men who fancy themselves chosen to lead the blind majority.

Well, he thought, I cannot bring back the dead, and I cannot repair what has been done in the name of *uhuru* and its implementation. I cannot rescind the Mau Mau—I cannot revive Kamau. But perhaps I can still pull a few chestnuts out of the fire. With luck. Without luck nobody can do any thing. I have lost one wife. Another lies bleeding. My *shamba* is burnt. But I can

525

still do a couple of things, perhaps, that might ease some of the strain and pave a pathway for a better class of people. Some day, some dim and distant day.

I can save this poor madman, Brian Dermott, from hanging to make political propaganda for the English in order to appease the blacks. I know I can save Brian Dermott, for to save Brian Dermott I only have to hang Abraham Matisia, and I can hang Matisia very simply. I have more than enough to hang Matisia, and possibly thereby to discourage some of the others from stampeding too rapidly in their efforts to inherit the mantle of Matthew Kamau.

For as I hang Matisia, I can lay the ghost of Kamau. I can show Matthew Kamau only as a blundering plotter of murder who died for his crimes against his own people. I can show him as a greedy man, an evil man, who was more than willing to murder his own in order to steal from his own, and eventually to enslave his own. I am a very good *orator*, Ndegwa said, if not to say good *man*. I can sell that point of view with the right sort of rostrum, and there is no better rostrum than a court-house with a monstrous murder trial and full press bench. The eyes of the world will be on that trial. It will be a bigger trial than the trial of Francis Powers in Moscow. It will be bigger because it will not only involve East and West, but black and white, and right and wrong, as well.

I can at least prevent by this one symbolic action a massive retaliation by all those white men with guns whom I saw today. They will certainly rise in armed force and create a river of blood and a forest of fire if Brian Dermott hangs. His death is not worth that many innocent deaths in vengeance for a poor thing. If I can save him I might well be able to save a country, he thought, and was slightly cheered.

Keeping those white settlers contained is important, so important to the welfare of Kenya right now, he thought. The troops at Kahawa, the native constabulary, the white police, can put down any native riots which might flare if Brian Dermott is not hanged.

But if the whites rise *en masse*, will England crush her own? Will the imported soldiery at Kahawa turn their guns on their own flesh, in a strange land which the white rebels built from black jungle? I do not know, but the neck of Brian Dermott, as a trophy of vengeance, is not worth the risk. The embattled settlers have won that round, even though they could not know how easy it will be for me to defend Brian Dermott. With what I know, I could get him off even if I were *white*.

No, Ndegwa thought, I am being much too cynical. I have always been much too cynical. That has been my chief weakness, because cynicism is laziness, and in my case laziness has proved to be weakness and loss of moral fibre.

So I will defend Brian Dermott, and send him free in body at least, basically because I believe that vengeance belongs to the Lord and that right and wrong should be decided not by screeching mobs or by wild young men with guns—but by due course of law and legislation. The only place to make justice available to all is in legislative council and in a duly ordered court of justice.

In that respect I am not a cynic. Perhaps if the whole world sees a black man stand up tall in court to defend a white man for killing the black defender's own black colleague, in a black country which is howling for freedom, then the world might halt a moment and re-evaluate some of the vileness and violence of its current headlong rush to destruction.

Perhaps, if that point is made, intrinsically good young men like Philip Dermott and Donald Bruce will go back to work, and good women like Charlotte Stuart will be allowed peaceably to open her lands to emerging peoples without being harassed and trammelled by people like Matthew Kamau and Abraham Matisia. And *me*. Always the *me*.

The world will surely be aware of this spectacle. Too much is at stake here for the world to avoid notice of it. Perhaps, in his pathetic way, Brian Dermott is the most important man in the world today.

Stephen Ndegwa got out of his chair and switched on the lights. He looked round him at the disarrayed stale room, and shrugged his shoulders.

'They say it takes a good man to know when he's licked, Ndegwa,' he said aloud. 'I expect if that's true, you're a very good man indeed. Because there's one thing true, when you hang Matisia and convict your dead Kamau as a common crook and murderer, your political party explodes sky-high and you blow even higher with it. As a popular African politician, you couldn't be elected to the office of garbage inspector—or, as I believe my American friends say, dog-catcher. However . . .'

He walked wearily over to the telephone, and dialled the same number of the night before, when the Belgian prostitute, Lise Martelis, had been in this room. It seemed a million years ago. He waited, tapping his foot, and then said:

'Hello, Inspector Barnes, please. Ndegwa here. See here, David, I want you to pick up a man named Abraham Matisia. That's right. Kamau's pal. I suppose mine too, if you say so. I want him booked on suspicion of murder. You have his address. Plenty. For complicity in the deaths of Kathleen Crane, American, and three people whose full names I don't have—that's right, Karioki Something, Njeroge Something, and Kidogo Something. I *know* you haven't found two of the bodies—but Crane and the other's enough to swing him . . .'

The phone hummed.

'Yes, of course I haven't forgotten her. For Christ's sake don't put them in the same cell by any chance. She'll appear against him in his own trial, and as a material witness in the trial of Brian Dermott. *Of* course. I'll make the charges, substantiated by the woman. She's an eyewitness to the plot. I'll be down in an hour or so. I'm *not* being mysterious. Shall we say it's just a personal interest in both cases? Thank you.'

Stephen Ndegwa replaced the phone and walked towards his bedroom. He rummaged about in the wardrobe and took out a black hat-box. He reached into the hat-box, and removed a crumpled, yellowish-white, long-curled legal wig.

He plopped the wig on his head, and walked over to the rather crinkly mirror. The wig sat askew, and although it was dingy and age-sallowed, it looked snowy against the deep brown of the pouched-eyed, heavy-jowled bulldog face.

'Milord, ladies and gentlemen of the jury . . .' he said, mockingly, and then ripped off the wig and tossed it onto the bed. Whether it was periwig of the Law or a Kikuyu elder's headdress, he mused, he still looked like a dissolute old black man. He would buy a new wig tomorrow. It had been quite some time since he had defended a case, but he remembered a fresh crisp wig always gave added confidence when you went against the grave man in the crimson robes, who sat beneath the royal arms, and the twelve serious faces which ranked gravely two-tiered in the long box, with your client's life balanced in their hands and hearts and heads.

It was going to be a very busy day. Among other things, he had to announce the abolition of the KNAP as a political party, and disavow his own candidature for any political office. And he must find time to go and have a chat with his new client Brian Dermott. Brian Dermott might be difficult, because of his hatred for Africans, but he was sure he could get Dermott off. Stephen Ndegwa was just as sure of that as he was sure that he was finished for all time as a politician. Perhaps he would practise agriculture on some of Charlotte Stuart's land in between petty larceny cases. That was, of course, if he got any more legal work at all after the country went black.

Stephen Ndegwa whistled a little tune as he went down the steps towards his white car. The stars were out; that thunder-shower at noon had cleared things considerably. His Kipsigi chauffeur was sleeping again, his head pillowed on the wheel. Ndegwa nudged him rudely, and the driver's chin fell on the horn, which let out a loud blast. The chauffeur's eyes popped open.

'Drive me to the Bwana Police,' Stephen said. 'And step on it.'

'Yes, Bwana,' the driver said, still half-asleep. 'The Bwana Police?'

'The Bwana Police is what I said. And for the last time,' Stephen Ndegwa replied, '*don't* call me Bwana.' Stephen Ndegwa settled down into the soft comfort of the leather cushions and closed his eyes. It had been, he thought, a very long day, and tonight he would sleep better than he had slept since he was a bare-assed boy running wild on the slopes of Ol Kalou.